The PENGUIN BOOK of
CANADIAN
SHORT
STORIES

ALSO BY JANE URQUHART

Fiction
A Map of Glass
The Stone Carvers
The Underpainter
Away
Changing Heaven
Storm Glass
The Whirlpool

Poetry
Some Other Garden
The Little Flowers of Madame de Montespan
I Am Walking in the Garden of His Imaginary Palace
False Shuffles

The PENGUIN BOOK of

CANADIAN
SHORT
STORIES

Selected and Introduced by JANE
URQUHART

PENGUIN
CANADA

PENGUIN CANADA

Published by the Penguin Group

Penguin Group (Canada), 90 Eglinton Avenue East, Suite 700, Toronto, Ontario, Canada M4P 2Y3
(a division of Pearson Canada Inc.)

Penguin Group (USA) Inc., 375 Hudson Street, New York, New York 10014, U.S.A.
Penguin Books Ltd, 80 Strand, London WC2R 0RL, England
Penguin Ireland, 25 St Stephen's Green, Dublin 2, Ireland (a division of Penguin Books Ltd)
Penguin Group (Australia), 250 Camberwell Road, Camberwell, Victoria 3124, Australia
(a division of Pearson Australia Group Pty Ltd)
Penguin Books India Pvt Ltd, 11 Community Centre, Panchsheel Park, New Delhi – 110 017, India
Penguin Group (NZ), 67 Apollo Drive, Rosedale, North Shore 0745, Auckland, New Zealand
(a division of Pearson New Zealand Ltd)
Penguin Books (South Africa) (Pty) Ltd, 24 Sturdee Avenue, Rosebank,
Johannesburg 2196, South Africa

Penguin Books Ltd, Registered Offices: 80 Strand, London WC2R 0RL, England

First published in a Viking Canada hardcover by Penguin Group (Canada),
a division of Pearson Canada Inc., 2007

Published in this edition, 2008

6 7 8 9 10 (RRD)

Introduction, author biographies, and selection copyright © Jane Urquhart, 2007

The copyright acknowledgments on pages 699–703 constitute an extension of this copyright page.

Manufactured in the U.S.A.

LIBRARY AND ARCHIVES CANADA CATALOGUING IN PUBLICATION

The Penguin Book of Canadian short stories / selected and introduced by Jane Urquhart.

Includes bibliographical references.
ISBN 978-0-14-305443-6 (pbk.)

1. Short stories, Canadian (English). 2. Canadian fiction (English)—21st century.
1. Nouvelles canadiennes-anglaises. 2. Roman canadien-anglais—21e siècle.
I. Urquhart, Jane, 1949– II. Title: Canadian short stories.

PS8319.P452 2008   C813'.0108   C2008-001430-5

Visit the Penguin Group (Canada) website at **www.penguin.ca**

Special and corporate bulk purchase rates available; please see **www.penguin.ca/corporatesales**
or call 1-800-810-3104, ext. 477 or 474

Dedicated to My Mother

❧

Marian Quinn Carter
(1911–2007)

Contents

Introduction

JANE URQUHART

TWO YEARS AGO, when I agreed to select the stories for the anthology you are now holding in your hands, I did so with a combination of curiosity and uncertainty. The curiosity was that of the canoeist (to use a Canadian metaphor) about to journey beyond the lakes and rivers she knew well and into unfamiliar waters bordered by beautiful and oddly shaped shores. The uncertainty stemmed from the nagging suspicion that perhaps I was not the person best suited to the task. This was because, both as a writer and a reader, I—along with many others—had paid more attention in recent years to the short story's fat, loud cousin, the novel. I had, of course, fallen eagerly on any Alice Munro story I could get my hands on, and had read and reread—with great pleasure—the stories of Mavis Gallant and Alistair MacLeod, major figures who I knew would necessarily be significant presences in any anthology of Canadian literature. But when it came to the younger and newer writers in Canada, it was most often their novels I had turned to, novels that were written in many cases after positive critical responses to collections of what I have now discovered are startlingly fresh and original stories. Perhaps the greatest gift given to me in my role as an anthologist was my discovery of these voices. To walk into the pre-novel fictional worlds of Dennis Bock, or Joseph Boyden, or Madeleine Thien is to find them at the beginning of their careers singing in a pure voice simply because they feel there is a need for music, a need for song.

But there were other gifts as well. The country in which I was born and raised spent a great deal of time and energy bemoaning its lack of identity. The one in which I am living my adult life celebrates the multiplicity of its identities. This can only be an improvement. Moreover, there is no firmly emplaced official history to speak of—as there would be in, say, the United States—underpinning differences or fluctuations of mood and atmosphere, and yet speak and write we do, and now we are being read and heard all over the world. Canada—with its lack of official history, lack of rigidly defined identity, and with the super-consciousness of its largely uninhabited wilderness north, its vast Arctic, and its settlers (for, unless we are Aboriginal, we are still, and maybe always will be, settlers) from across the globe—is simply the perfect geography for something as fluid as the imagination. We no longer ask, as Northrop Frye did, where is here, because we know now, at least in terms of literature, that here is anywhere and everywhere. The light that one hundred years ago travelled like that of a star from Britain's literary tradition to our shores has hit the bevelled edge of the looking glass. When the point of view is no longer singular but prismatic, the possibilities are both gorgeous and endless. After a year and a half of constant reading, this was the second gift that was given to me: the knowledge that in our writing across time and space we have all been trying not to define but simply to explore who we think we are, so that the stories of Charles G.D. Roberts and Ethel Wilson ride easily alongside those of David Bezmozgis and Nancy Lee. A singular act of revelation joins with another and then another and the question of where the voice is coming from is kept alive, beautiful because it can never be fully or accurately answered.

OVER THE COURSE OF THE LAST TWO YEARS I have read the introductions to dozens of anthologies. Some were nineteenth-century collections in which the Canadian stories were added as an appendix to a British compilation of American literary material. Not much later there appeared anthologies of stories concerning the adventures of lively young British men engaged in a variety of northern wilderness exploits. One stunning example of a nineteenth-century anthology was a collection of Canadian fiction told entirely from the point of view of a series of anonymous maple trees living on the edges of battlefields or near Huron villages. The twentieth century brought us anthologies assembled by preachers and politicians followed by anthologies selected by poets and professors.

The one thing that all the introductions had in common was the standard apologia. Sorry, sorry. Mea culpa, mea culpa. Because I would rather write about why certain stories are included in the collection, and how the anthology is structured, I will confine my own act of contrition to a couple of declarations. There is never enough space, I have learned, for all that we want in life, so stories left out of an anthology serve as a wonderful metaphor for unfulfilled desire. Secondly, as the last couple of decades in Canada have witnessed the publication of a staggering amount of fine literary work, stories from these decades have taken precedence in terms of numbers over those from the past. Concerning the Canadianness of the authors included in this volume, I would like to quote from Margaret Atwood's introduction to the 1997 *New Oxford Book of Canadian Short Stories,* in which, with great wit and wisdom, she tells us that "Some are born Canadian, some achieve Canadianness, and some have Canadianness thrust upon them." And, finally, I was able to make my own selections with an almost clear conscience because I knew that, as a poet friend of mine once so brilliantly and accurately said, "Time is the great anthologist." This is not an abdication of responsibility, this is a simple truth. Posterity has always been an unpredictable reader. No one knows which stories or novels will remain alive, or where one or two hundred years from now the pulse will continue to beat.

And yet, I must confess that my first acts of selection were based on the notion of continuance; I decided to begin my collection with stories that were impossible for me to forget, stories that haunted me. Some of these stories—Merna Summers's "The Blizzard," for instance, Sharon Butala's "Fever," Hugh Garner's "One Mile of Ice"—had been haunting me for a number of years. "The Road Past Altamont" by Gabrielle Roy had haunted me for so many decades and to such a degree that I decided to include it even though it was originally written in French. Others, written by newer authors, were more recent ghosts—Lisa Moore's "The Lonely Goatherd," Rohinton Mistry's "The Collectors"—and I quickly added them to the gathering.

After that I moved on to stories I was certain were *going* to haunt me. Alistair MacLeod refers to this habit of endurance on the part of certain narratives when, at the beginning of his long short story "Vision," he states:

> I don't remember when I first heard the story but I remember the first time I heard it and remembered it. By that I mean the first time it made an impression on me and more or less became *mine;* sort of went into me the way such things do, went into me in such a way that I knew it would not leave again but would remain there forever.

All the stories in this collection have gone into me in some way or another. I know that I either already have or will have them with me always, and that I have recalled or will recall them—either in reflective repose or during certain emotionally significant moments in my life—and that in this way they either have continued or will continue to provide both pleasure and comfort.

The pleasure, of course, comes from being in communion with a work of art. The comfort, however, is another thing altogether, and perhaps has its origins in the idea of the solitariness of the writer of short stories, a solitariness that is shared once the reader enters the work. In Frank O'Connor's wonderful 1963 study of the short story, *The Lonely Voice,* the Irish writer tells us that "There is in the short story at its most characteristic something we do not often find in the novel—an intense awareness of human loneliness." This loneliness does not preclude fantasy or even laugh-out-loud humour but, at its very best, rises up to meet the reader and affirm the singularity of human character. We recognize it, somehow; it tells us something we didn't know we knew.

Odd then, that another of my paths into the anthology would be connected to memoir, that open sharing of secrets and memories which, at least on the surface, seems to be an engagement with complete disclosure. Originally, in an attempt to open up and make more interesting the definition of the short story, I wanted to include memoirs in this collection. In the end, however, I realized that unless I was able to put together a volume of encyclopedic length, this was not going to be achievable. Besides, as I continued to read I came to understand that the Canadian short story is more than sufficiently interesting all on its own and—much like the country it springs from—continues to defy all efforts to define it. Still, the notion of memoir stuck with me and eventually met, I hope more or less successfully, another challenge I was faced with: that of how to order the dozens of stories I had chosen.

It occurred to me that the placement of stories in an anthology is just as important as the situating of works of art in an art museum where pictures are assembled for a purpose within a series of rooms or galleries. Often, in more formal museums, works are drawn together within a cultural context in order to examine the style of artists connected to a particular time period. More recently, however, even in such official spaces as the National Gallery in London or the Museum of Modern Art in New York, one now and then sees an exhibition of works linked by an idea or theme. (About a decade ago, for instance, I saw at the Louvre a show comprising Constable cloud studies, drawings for Tiepolo ceilings, flying machines, choirs of angels, stars, and flocks of birds called "Le Bruit des Nuages," whose common theme was the examination of the sky across the ages.) This notion of works brought together by thematic or, perhaps more accurately, atmospheric connections intrigued me, and I remembered this when I began my own groupings for this book. I would need something, I realized, to establish an atmosphere or tone for each of the five sections that were beginning to take shape, and I knew from my reading that there were five excerpts from memoirs that would beautifully communicate the atmosphere of the stories that might follow them, allowing one story to speak to another as well as to the reader.

I began with an excerpt from Alice Munro's semi-fictional family memoir, *The View from Castle Rock,* knowing that, in some way or another, all the stories that followed would make reference to that experience so many of us in this century, or so many of our ancestors in previous centuries, have or have had in common: the act of immigration. The rock would be what my own Irish family, five generations later, still refers to as "the old country"; the view would be that of "the new land," the country of arrival. It matters little that the view in the Munro piece is an illusion (the writer's ancestor mistakes the Isle of Fife for the continent of North America), just as it matters little whether the emigrant is departing from the harbour of Leith in 1818 or from an airport in Bombay in 1969. Even the last glimpse of the homeland is ambiguous and involves distorted perception:

It turns out that the cry to say farewell has been premature—a grey rim of land will remain in place for hours yet. Many will grow tired of looking at it—it is just land, like any other—but some will stay at the rail until the last rag of it fades, with the daylight.

The stories in this section concern those who stay at the rail and those who turn away in favour of the possibilities of a new life, those who hold onto the view of the homeland and those who are affected, generations later, by inherited memories of that homeland. Sometimes these stories are set entirely in the "old country," written by authors who have already or will eventually come to Canada (Claire Messud's "The Professor's History," for example, or Sam Selvon's "Gussy and the Boss"). Sometimes they are written by authors who were born in Canada, authors who have only a distant ancestral memory of a lost landscape (MacLeod's "Vision" or W.G. Valgardson's "The Cave").

For a more immediate and contemporary view of who we think we are, I turned to Michael Winter's "This All Happened," the (again) semi-fictional, diary-like observations of the daily life of a writer living in St. John's and occasionally "round the bay" in Newfoundland. In the company of his creative compatriots he experiences love, loss, absurdity, tenderness, and humour with a vivid intensity brought about partly by the youthfulness of the protagonist and partly by the knowledge that all that is happening is taking place in real time. The sharpness of observation in this piece seemed to me to be echoed not only by the realism of each of the stories that would follow it but also the sense I got from their skilful rendering that this really *had* happened, that in some way or another these stories are emotionally and physically true. We feel we have accompanied Roth in Michael Redhill's "Flesh Collectors" into the rabbi's study and the doctor's office, or that like the mother in Nancy Lee's "Dead Girls" we have lost contact with a beloved daughter. The awareness of shared rather than told experience is vibrantly alive in this section's stories; the reader believes that he or she has come to know the characters in an intimate way, like lovers or close friends.

"Lunch Conversation" (followed by "Aunts") from Michael Ondaatje's fictional autobiography *Running in the Family* sets the tone for the third section, one that includes stories in which family, tribal, or social anecdotes and situations, to a greater or lesser extent, play a role. To my way of thinking, Ondaatje's wonderfully chaotic lunch in Sri Lanka seemed to be drawn from the same well as Ethel Wilson's delightful account of a child's disruption of a Victorian meal in the company of Matthew Arnold, which in turn seemed to connect to Margaret Atwood's child's-eye view in "The Art of Cooking and Serving." The touch in these stories is no less profound for appearing to be lighter, for with the lightness comes the luminous clarity that can be the result of something as simple as the search for a gift (Carol Shields's "The Scarf") or a look at the apparently perfect life of a privileged woman (Bronwen Wallace's "An Easy Life").

An excerpt from Wayson Choy's memoir of Vancouver's Chinatown precedes the stories in the fourth section, drawing us into a realm of fantasy and illusion as experienced in a small Chinese theatre of the 1940s. Myth, disguise, music, magic, and a complete letting go of the ordinariness that determines daily life are at work here—another world, or an "other world island" as they might have said a century ago in my own old country. Here I believe it makes sense to connect Barbara Gowdy's floating child in "Presbyterian Sidewalk" with Stephen Leacock's transmogrifying train interior in "The Train to Mariposa," or Thomas King's "The Baby in the Airmail Box" with Leon Rooke's "Gypsy Art." This section entertains, shocks, elicits laughter or longing, allows us to live in the distant past or the future, and takes us out of ourselves in the same way that small Wayson was taken out of himself and into the gorgeous surroundings of bright costumes and mysterious sounds.

And finally, for all those stories written by living authors looking back toward our past, or by authors who were a part of that past, I chose an excerpt from *My Grandfather's House,* the memoir of the great diplomat and diarist Charles Ritchie, caught in the act of resurrecting—rebuilding almost—the rooms of his childhood: furniture huddling under dust covers, mysterious portraits and panel paintings, dressing tables and naked marble statues. A surprising number of these stories (Garner's "One Mile of Ice," Summers's "The Blizzard," Sinclair Ross's "The Painted Door") concern death brought about by winter weather of such extreme behaviour that it practically assumes the role of protagonist. Not so surprising, perhaps, when one considers the lack of central heating, of motorized vehicles, and of global warming, and even now, in the twenty-first century, we can easily touch the hand of someone who has lived that life.

A friend once said to me that we write about the past because, believing we are finished with it, we think we can see it whole. But are we really finished with it? And can we ever really see it whole? The weather may have changed, but the narratives of the past continue to haunt us in the same way that the first stories I chose have haunted me. Charles G.D. Roberts's European beast of burden in "Strayed" is carrying his past with him—fatally as it turns out—into an unfamiliar wilderness landscape, and in Gabrielle Roy's "The Road Past Altamont" the past becomes a small village glimpsed once and then never fully recovered. The past is locked inside Ernest Buckler's locket, in the poems of the "sweet singer" in Alice Munro's "Meneseteung," and in Mavis Gallant's marvellous "Voices Lost in Snow." Gallant uses *frôler,* the French word for brushing against or skimming, to describe "that winter's story" from the past that, she tells us, was "a hand brushing the edge of folded silk, a leaf escaping a spiderweb." Later, the image returns in reference to looking back to the past: "I brush in memory against the spiderweb" is one of the most evocative lines in Canadian fiction.

IN THE END, what joins all the stories in this anthology and allows them to live together under one roof is the fact that in some way or other they are connected to all that is miraculous, and miracles, as Frank O'Connor observes in *The Lonely Voice,* are no proper subject for treatment in extended form. By their very nature they are subjects for the writer of one-act plays or the short-story writer, never for the novelist.

But short stories such as these also bring us to a clearer understanding of this brief, beautiful thing called human life, of our need to see it mirrored in art, and of our desire to hold it up to the light. We want to freeze the moment of engagement, the "hand brushing the edge of folded silk," in order to keep the texture—the shine of the material, the darkness of the creases, the vanished hand itself—in our minds "until the last rag of it fades, with the daylight."

Part 1

THE VIEW FROM CASTLE ROCK

THE STORIES IN THIS OPENING SECTION *are concerned with arrival and departure, with the view of the new land as well as the texture of the rock, or old land, from which the new land is sighted and imagined. In Alice Munro's fictional family history "The View from Castle Rock" both the point of embarkation and eventual destination are, at one time or another, longed for, despised, idealized, misapprehended, dismissed, and worshipped. This is true of almost everything we desire as well as everything we choose to leave behind.*

Canada is an unusual country in that almost everyone who lives here carries in their psyche a personal attachment to an actual place and the emotional tug of an altered, abandoned, or stolen terrain. Early and even more recent European settlers had often fled poverty or wars, leaving behind the Old Country only to later recall it as a kind of lost, sacred land. Legends born in Scotland (Alice Munro and Alistair MacLeod) or Iceland (W.D. Valgardson), therefore, could surface on the pine-clad hills of Cape Breton or in the prairie landscape near Winnipeg; German wedding customs (Dennis Bock) could be re-enacted on the shores of a lake in northern Ontario. Yet there is always darkness and disorientation associated with haunting, and the geographical revenant is no exception: the ghost of a landscape or its culture can sometimes be as blood-chilling as the appearance of Hamlet's deceased father. The landscape of arrival, on the other hand, is haunted as well by the inescapable fact of an Aboriginal world changed beyond all recognition by the flood of Europeans moving steadily westward across the continent in the nineteenth and early twentieth centuries.

The Asians, Caribbeans, and Africans arriving in Canada more recently have brought their own ghosts of course, but unlike the original settlers their cultural makeup has been thrust up against a transplanted but fully emplaced European world with at best the possibility and at worst the actuality of racism trembling at its edges. The racial inequality in Sam Selvon's "Gussy and the Boss" plays out in Port of Spain but could just as easily have been set in Toronto, where in Austin Clark's "Four Stations in His Circle" a recent Barbadian immigrant longs for a house in one of the city's upscale white neighbourhoods. Added to this is the poignancy of an Asian father, far from his place of origin, cooking for his family in Vancouver (Madeleine Thien) and a Muslim community trying to come to an agreement about funeral rites in Protestant Toronto (M.G. Vassanji).

But as Canada becomes more aware of itself as a multicultural country it is the commonality of experience that ultimately intrigues us most, with our writers focusing on place—the one they find themselves in and the one from which they or their forebears came—and the way both worlds are transformed by the literary imagination. The old world does not disappear as quickly as you might think, whether we stay at the ship's rail and gaze back at it or turn toward the shores of arrival.

The View from Castle Rock

ALICE MUNRO

THE FIRST TIME Andrew was ever in Edinburgh he was ten years old. With his father and some other men he climbed a slippery black street. It was raining, the city smell of smoke filled the air, and the half-doors were open, showing the firelit insides of taverns which he hoped they might enter, because he was wet through. They did not, they were bound somewhere else. Earlier on the same afternoon they had been in some such place, but it was not much more than an alcove, a hole in the wall, with planks on which bottles and glasses were set and coins laid down. He had been continually getting squeezed out of that shelter into the street and into the puddle that caught the drip from the ledge over the entryway. To keep that from happening, he had butted in low down between the cloaks and sheepskins, wedged himself amongst the drinking men and under their arms.

He was surprised at the number of people his father seemed to know in the city of Edinburgh. You would think the people in the drinking place would be strangers to him, but it was evidently not so. Amongst the arguing and excited queer-sounding voices his father's voice rose the loudest. *America,* he said, and slapped his hand on the plank for attention, the very way he would do at home. Andrew had heard that word spoken in that same tone long before he knew it was a land across the ocean. It was spoken as a challenge and an irrefutable truth but sometimes—when his father was not there—it was spoken as a taunt or a joke. His older brothers might ask each other, "Are ye awa to America?" when one of them put on his plaid to go out and do some chore such as penning the sheep. Or, "Why don't ye be off to America?" when they had got into an argument, and one of them wanted to make the other out to be a fool.

The cadences of his father's voice, in the talk that succeeded that word, were so familiar, and Andrew's eyes so bleary with the smoke, that in no time he had fallen asleep on his feet. He wakened when several pushed together out of the place and his father with them. Some one of them said, "Is this your lad here or is it some tinker squeezed in to pick our pockets?" and his father laughed and took Andrew's hand and they began their climb. One man stumbled and another man knocked into him and swore. A couple of women swiped their baskets at the party with great scorn, and made some remarks in their unfamiliar speech, of which Andrew could only make out the words "daecent bodies" and "public footpaths."

Then his father and the friends stepped aside into a much broader street, which in fact was a courtyard, paved with large blocks of stone. His father turned and paid attention to Andrew at this point.

"Do you know where you are, lad? You're in the castle yard, and this is Edinburgh Castle that has stood for ten thousand years and will stand for ten thousand more. Terrible deeds were done here. These stones have run with blood. Do you know that?" He raised his head so that they all listened to what he was telling.

"It was King Jamie asked the young Douglases to have supper with him and when they were fair sitten down he says, oh, we won't bother with their supper, take them out in the yard and chop off their heads. And so they did. Here in the yard where we stand.

"But that King Jamie died a leper," he went on with a sigh, then a groan, making them all be still to consider this fate.

Then he shook his head.

"Ah, no, it wasn't him. It was King Robert the Bruce that died a leper. He died a king but he died a leper."

Andrew could see nothing but enormous stone walls, barred gates, a redcoat soldier marching up and down. His father did not give him much time, anyway, but shoved him ahead and through an archway, saying, "Watch your heads here, lads, they was wee little men in those days. Wee little men. So is Boney the Frenchman, there's a lot of fight in your wee little men."

They were climbing uneven stone steps, some as high as Andrew's knees—he had to crawl occasionally—inside what as far as he could make out was a roofless tower. His father called out, "Are ye all with me then, are ye all in for the climb?" and some straggling voices answered him. Andrew got the impression that there was not such a crowd following as there had been on the street.

They climbed far up in the roundabout stairway and at last came out on a bare rock, a shelf, from which the land fell steeply away. The rain had ceased for the present.

"Ah, there," said Andrew's father. "Now where's all the ones was tramping on our heels to get here?"

One of the men just reaching the top step said, "There's two-three of them took off to have a look at the Meg."

"Engines of war," said Andrew's father. "All they have eyes for is engines of war. Take care they don't go and blow themselves up."

"Haven't the heart for the stairs, more like," said another man who was panting. And the first one said cheerfully, "Scairt to get all the way up here, scairt they're bound to fall off."

A third man—and that was the lot—came staggering across the shelf as if he had in mind to do that very thing.

"Where is it then?" he hollered. "Are we up on Arthur's seat?"

"Ye are not," said Andrew's father. "Look beyond you."

The sun was out now, shining on the stone heap of houses and streets below them, and the churches whose spires did not reach to this height, and some little trees and fields, then a wide silvery stretch of water. And beyond that a pale green and greyish-blue land, part in sunlight and part in shadow, a land as light as mist, sucked into the sky.

"So did I not tell you?" Andrew's father said. "America. It is only a little bit of it, though, only the shore. There is where every man is sitting in the midst of his own properties, and even the beggars is riding around in carriages."

"Well the sea does not look so wide as I thought," said the man who had stopped staggering. "It does not look as if it would take you weeks to cross it."

"It is the effect of the height we're on," said the man who stood beside Andrew's father. "The height we're on is making the width of it the less."

"It's a fortunate day for the view," said Andrew's father. "Many a day you could climb up here and see nothing but the fog."

He turned and addressed Andrew.

"So there you are my lad and you have looked over at America," he said. "God grant you one day you will see it closer up and for yourself."

ANDREW HAS BEEN to the Castle one time since, with a group of the lads from Ettrick, who all wanted to see the great cannon, Mons Meg. But nothing seemed to be in the same place then and he could not find the route they had taken to climb up to the rock. He saw a couple of places blocked off with boards that could have been it. But he did not even try to peer through them—he had no wish to tell the others what he was looking for. Even when he was ten years old he had known that the men with his father were drunk. If he did not understand that his father was drunk—due to his father's sure-footedness and sense of purpose, his commanding behaviour—he did certainly understand that something was not as it should be. He knew he was not looking at America, though it was some years before he was well enough acquainted with maps to know that he had been looking at Fife.

Still, he did not know if those men met in the tavern had been mocking his father, or if it was his father playing one of his tricks on them.

OLD JAMES THE FATHER. Andrew. Walter. Their sister Mary. Andrew's wife Agnes, and Agnes and Andrew's son James, under two years old.

In the harbour of Leith, on the 4th of June, 1818, they set foot on board a ship for the first time in their lives.

Old James makes this fact known to the ship's officer who is checking off the names.

"The first time, serra, in all my long life. We are men of the Ettrick. It is a land-locked part of the world."

The officer says a word which is unintelligible to them but plain in meaning. Move along. He has run a line through their names. They move along or are pushed along, Young James riding on Mary's hip.

"What is this?" says Old James, regarding the crowd of people on deck. "Where are we to sleep? Where have all these rabble come from? Look at the faces on them, are they the blackamoors?"

"Black Highlanders, more like," says his son Walter. This is a joke, muttered so his father cannot hear—Highlanders being one of the sorts the old man despises.

"There are too many people," his father continues. "The ship will sink."

"No," says Walter, speaking up now. "Ships do not often sink because of too many people. That's what the fellow was there for, to count the people."

Barely on board the vessel and this seventeen-year-old whelp has taken on knowing airs, he has taken to contradicting his father. Fatigue, astonishment, and the weight of the greatcoat he is wearing prevent Old James from cuffing him.

All the business of life aboard ship has already been explained to the family. In fact it has been explained by the old man himself. He was the one who knew all about provisions, accommodations, and the kind of people you would find on board. All Scotsmen and all decent folk. No Highlanders, no Irish.

But now he cries out that it is like the swarm of bees in the carcass of the lion.

"An evil lot, an evil lot. Oh, that ever we left our native land!"

"We have not left yet," says Andrew. "We are still looking at Leith. We would do best to go below and find ourselves a place."

More lamentation. The bunks are narrow, bare planks with horsehair pallets both hard and prickly.

"Better than nothing," says Andrew.

"Oh, that it was ever put in my head to bring us here, onto this floating sepulchre."

Will nobody shut him up? thinks Agnes. This is the way he will go on and on, like a preacher or a lunatic, when the fit takes him. She cannot abide it. She is in more agony herself than he is ever likely to know.

"Well, are we going to settle here or are we not?" she says.

Some people have hung up their plaids or shawls to make a half-private space for their families. She goes ahead and takes off her outer wrappings to do the same.

The child is turning somersaults in her belly. Her face is hot as a coal and her legs throb and the swollen flesh in between them—the lips the child must soon part to get out—is a scalding sack of pain. Her mother would have known what to do about that, she would have known which leaves to mash to make a soothing poultice.

At the thought of her mother such misery overcomes her that she wants to kick somebody.

Andrew folds up his plaid to make a comfortable seat for his father. The old man seats himself, groaning, and puts his hands up to his face, so that his speaking has a hollow sound.

"I will see no more. I will not hearken to their screeching voices or their satanic tongues. I will not swallow a mouth of meat nor meal until I see the shores of America."

All the more for the rest of us, Agnes feels like saying.

Why does Andrew not speak plainly to his father, reminding him of whose idea it was, who was the one who harangued and borrowed and begged to get them just where they are now? Andrew will not do it, Walter will only joke, and as for Mary she can hardly get her voice out of her throat in her father's presence.

Agnes comes from a large Hawick family of weavers, who work in the mills now but worked for generations at home. And working there they learned all the arts of cutting each other down to size, of squabbling and surviving in close quarters. She is still surprised by the rigid manners, the deference and silences in her husband's family. She thought from the beginning that they were a queer sort of people and she thinks so still. They are as poor as her own folk, but they have such a great notion of themselves. And what have they got to back this up? The old man has been a wonder in the tavern for years, and their cousin is a raggedy lying poet who had to flit to Nithsdale when nobody would trust him to tend sheep in Ettrick. They were all brought up by three witchey-women of aunts who were so scared of men that they would run and hide in the sheep pen if anybody but their own family was coming along the road.

As if it wasn't the men that should be running from them.

Walter has come back from carrying their heavier possessions down to a lower depth of the ship.

"You never saw such a mountain of boxes and trunks and sacks of meal and potatoes," he says excitedly. "A person has to climb over them to get to the water pipe. Nobody can help but spill their water on the way back and the sacks will be wet through and the stuff will be rotted."

"They should not have brought all that," says Andrew. "Did they not undertake to feed us when we paid our way?"

"Aye," says the old man. "But will it be fit for us to eat?"

"So a good thing I brought my cakes," says Walter, who is still in the mood to make a joke of anything. He taps his foot on the snug metal box filled with oat cakes that his aunts gave him as a particular present because he was the youngest and they still thought of him as the motherless one.

"You'll see how merry you'll be if we're starving," says Agnes. Walter is a pest to her, almost as much as the old man. She knows there is probably no chance of them starving, because Andrew is looking impatient, but not anxious. It takes a good deal, of course, to make Andrew anxious. He is apparently not anxious about her, since he thought first to make a comfortable seat for his father.

MARY HAS TAKEN YOUNG JAMES back up to the deck. She could tell that he was alarmed down there in the half-dark. He does not have to whimper or complain— she knows his feelings by the way he digs his little knees into her.

The sails are furled tight. "Look up there, look up there," Mary says, and points to a sailor who is busy high up in the rigging. The boy on her hip makes his sound for bird. "Sailor-peep, sailor-peep," she says. She says the right word for *sailor* but his word for *bird*. She and he communicate in a half-and-half language—half her teaching and half his invention. She believes that he is one of the cleverest children ever born into the world. Being the eldest of her family, and the only girl, she has tended all of her brothers, and been proud of them all at one time, but she has never known a child like this. Nobody else has any idea of how original and independent and clever he is. Men have no interest in children so young, and Agnes his mother has no patience with him.

"Talk like folk," Agnes says to him, and if he doesn't, she may give him a clout. "What are you?" she says. "Are you a folk or an elfit?"

Mary fears Agnes's temper, but in a way she doesn't blame her. She thinks that women like Agnes—men's women, mother women—lead an appalling life. First with what the men do to them—even so good a man as Andrew—and then what the children do, coming out. She will never forget her own mother, who lay in bed out of her mind with a fever, not knowing any of them, till she died, three days after Walter was born. She had screamed at the black pot hanging over the fire, thinking it was full of devils.

Her brothers call Mary *Poor Mary*, and indeed the meagreness and timidity of many of the women in their family has caused that word to be attached to the names they were given at their christening—names that were themselves altered to something less substantial and graceful. Isabel became Poor Tibbie; Margaret, Poor Maggie; Jane, Poor Jennie. People in Ettrick said it was a fact that the looks and the height went to the men.

Mary is under five feet tall and has a little tight face with a lump of protruding chin, and a skin that is subject to fiery eruptions that take a long time to fade. When she is spoken to her mouth twitches as if the words were all mixed up with her spittle and her crooked little teeth, and the response she manages is a dribble of speech so faint and scrambled that it is hard for people not to think her dim-witted. She has great difficulty in looking anybody in the face—even the members of her own family. It is only when she gets the boy hitched on to the narrow shelf of her hip that she is capable of some coherent and decisive speech—and then it is mostly to him.

Somebody is saying something to her now. It is a person almost as small as herself—a little brown man, a sailor, with grey whiskers and not a tooth in his head. He is looking straight at her and then at Young James and back to her again—right in the middle of the pushing or loitering, bewildered or inquisitive crowd. At first she thinks it is a foreign language he is speaking, but then she makes out the word *cu*. She finds herself answering with the same word, and he laughs and waves his arms, pointing to somewhere farther back on the ship, then pointing at James and laughing again. Something she should take James to see. She has to say, "Aye. Aye," to stop him gabbling, and then to step off in that direction so that he won't be disappointed.

She wonders what part of the country or the world he could have come from, then realizes that this is the first time in her life that she has ever spoken to a stranger. And except for the difficulty of understanding what he was saying, she has managed it more easily than when having to speak to a neighbour in the Ettrick, or to her father.

She hears the bawling of the cow before she can see it. The press of people increases around her and James, forms a wall in front of her and squeezes her from behind. Then she hears the bawling in the sky and looking up sees the brown beast dangling in the air, all caged in ropes and kicking and roaring frantically. It is held by a hook on a crane, which now hauls it out of sight. People around her are hooting and clapping hands. Some child's voice cries out in the language she understands, wanting to know if the cow will be dropped into the sea. A man's voice tells him no, she will go along with them on the ship.

"Will they milk her then?"

"Aye. Keep still. They'll milk her," says the man reprovingly. And another man's voice climbs boisterously over his.

"They'll milk her till they take the hammer to her, and then ye'll have the blood pudding for yer dinner."

Now follow the hens swung through the air in crates, all squawking and fluttering in their confinement and pecking each other when they can, so that some feathers escape and float down through the air. And after them a pig trussed up like the cow, squealing with a human note in its distress and shitting wildly in midair, so that howls of both outrage and delight rise below, depending on whether they come from those who are hit or those who see others hit.

James is laughing too, he recognizes shite, and cries out his own word for it, which is *gruggin*.

Someday he may remember this. *I saw a cow and a pig fly through the air.* Then he may wonder if it was a dream. And nobody will be there—she will certainly not be there—to tell that it was not a dream, it happened on this ship. He will know that he was once on a ship because he will have been told that, but it's possible that he will never see a ship like this again in all his waking life. She has no idea where they will go when they reach the other shore, but imagines it will be some place inland, among the hills, some place like the Ettrick.

She does not think she will live long, wherever they go. She coughs in the summer as well as the winter and when she coughs her chest aches. She suffers from sties, and cramps in the stomach, and her bleeding comes rarely but may last a month when it does come. She hopes, though, that she will not die while James is still of a size to ride on her hip or still in need of her, which he will be for a while yet. She knows that the time will come when he will turn away as her brothers did, when he will become ashamed of the connection with her. That is what she tells herself will happen, but like anybody in love she cannot believe it.

ON A TRIP TO PEEBLES before they left home, Walter bought himself a book to write in, but for several days he has found too much to pay attention to, and too little space or quiet on the deck, even to open it. He has a vial of ink, as well, held in a leather pouch and strapped to his chest under his shirt. That was the trick used by their cousin, Jamie Hogg the poet, when he was out in the wilds of Nithsdale, watching the sheep. When a rhyme came on Jamie he would pull a wad of paper out of his breeks' pocket and uncork the ink which the heat of his heart had kept from freezing and write it all down, no matter where he was or in what weather.

Or so he said. And Walter had thought to put this method to the test. But it might have been an easier matter amongst sheep than amongst people. Also the wind can surely blow harder over the sea even than it could blow in Nithsdale. And it is essential of course for him to get out of the sight of his own family. Andrew might mock him mildly but Agnes would do it boldly, incensed as she could be by the thought of anybody doing anything she would not want to do. Mary, of course, would never say a word, but the boy on her hip that she idolized and spoiled would be all for grabbing and destroying both pen and paper. And there was no knowing what interference might come from their father.

Now after some investigating around the deck he has found a favourable spot. The cover of his book is hard, he has no need of a table. And the ink warmed on his chest flows as willingly as blood.

We came on board on the 4th day of June and lay the 5th, 6th, 7th, and 8th in the Leith roads getting the ship to our place where we could set sail which was on the 9th. We passed the corner of Fifeshire all well nothing occurring worth mentioning till this day the 13th in the morning when we were awakened by a cry, John O'Groats house. We could see it plain and had a fine sail across the Pentland Firth having both wind and tide in our favour and it was in no way dangerous as we had heard tell. Their was a child had died, the name of Ormiston and its body was thrown overboard sewed up in a piece of canvas with a large lump of coal at its feet ...

He pauses in his writing to think of the weighted sack falling down through the water. Darker and darker grows the water with the surface high overhead gleaming faintly like the night sky. Would the piece of coal do its job, would the sack fall straight down to the very bottom of the sea? Or would the current of the sea be strong enough to keep lifting it up and letting it fall, pushing it sideways, taking it as far as Greenland or south to the tropical waters full of rank weeds, the Sargasso Sea? Or some ferocious fish might come along and rip the sack and make a meal of the body before it had even left the upper waters and the region of light.

He has seen drawings of fish as big as horses, fish with horns as well, and scores of teeth each like a skinner's knife. Also some that are smooth and smiling, and wickedly teasing, having the breasts of women but not the other parts which the sight of the breasts conducts a man's thoughts to. All this in a book of stories and engravings that he got out of the Peebles Subscription Library.

These thoughts do not distress him. He always sets himself to think clearly and if possible to picture accurately the most disagreeable or shocking things, so as to reduce their power over him. As he pictures it now, the child is being eaten. Not swallowed whole as in the case of Jonah but chewed into bits as he himself would chew a tasty chunk from a boiled sheep. But there is the matter of a soul. The soul leaves the body at the moment of death. But from which part of the body does it leave, what has been its particular bodily location? The best guess seems to be that it emerges with the last breath, having been hidden somewhere in the chest around the place of the heart and the lungs. Though Walter has heard a joke they used to tell about an old fellow in the Ettrick, to the effect that he was so dirty that when he died his soul came out his arsehole, and was heard to do so, with a mighty explosion.

This is the sort of information that preachers might be expected to give you—not mentioning anything like an arsehole of course but explaining something of the soul's proper location and exit. But they shy away from it. Also they cannot explain—or he has never heard one explain—how the souls maintain themselves outside of bodies until the Day of Judgment and how on that day each one finds and recognizes the body that is its own and reunites with it, though it be not so much as a skeleton at that time. *Though it be dust.* There must be some who have studied enough to know how all this is accomplished. But there are also some—he has learned this recently—who have studied and read and thought till they have come to the conclusion that there are no souls at all. No one cares to speak about these people either, and indeed the thought of them is terrible. How can they live with the fear—indeed, the certainty—of Hell before them?

There was the man like that who came from by Berwick, Fat Davey he was called, because he was so fat the table had to be cut away so he could sit down to his meal. And when he died in Edinburgh, where he was some sort of scholar, the people stood in the street outside his house waiting to see if the Devil would come to claim him. A sermon had been preached on that in Ettrick, which claimed as far as Walter could understand it that the Devil did not go in for displays of that sort and only superstitious and vulgar and Popish sort of people would expect him to, but that his embrace was nevertheless far more horrible and the torments that accompanied it more subtle than any such minds could imagine.

ON THE THIRD DAY aboard ship Old James got up and started to walk around. Now he is walking all the time. He stops and speaks to anybody who seems ready to listen. He tells his name, and says that he comes from Ettrick, from the valley and forest of Ettrick, where the old Kings of Scotland used to hunt.

"And on the field at Flodden," he says, "after the battle of Flodden, they said you could walk up and down among the corpses and pick out the men from the Ettrick, because they were the tallest and the strongest and the finest-looking men on the ground. I have five sons and they are all good strong lads but only two of them are with me. One of my sons is in Nova Scotia, he is the one with my own name and the last I heard of him he was in a place called Economy, but we have not had any word of him since, and I do not know whether he is alive or dead. My eldest son went off to work in the Highlands, and the son that is next to the youngest took it into his head to go off there too, and I will never see either of them again. Five sons and by the mercy of God all grew to be men, but it was not the Lord's will that I should keep them with me. Their mother died after the last of them was born. She took a fever and she never got up from her bed after she bore him. A man's life is full of sorrow. I have a daughter as well, the oldest of them all, but she is nearly a dwarf. Her mother was chased by a ram when she was carrying her. I have three old sisters all the same, all dwarfs."

His voice rises over all the hubbub of shipboard life and his sons make tracks in some other direction in dread embarrassment, whenever they hear it.

On the afternoon of the 14th a wind came from the North and the ship began to shake as if every board that was in it would fly loose from every other. The buckets overflowed from the people that were sick and vomiting and there was the contents of them slipping all over the deck. All people were ordered below but many of them crumpled up against the rail and did not care if they were washed over. None of our family was sick however and now the wind has dropped and the sun has come out and those who did not care if they died in the filth a little while ago have got up and dragged themselves to be washed where the sailors are splashing buckets of water over the decks. The women are busy too washing and rinsing and wringing out all the foul clothing. It is the worst misery and the suddenest recovery I have seen ever in my life ...

A young girl ten or twelve years old stands watching Walter write. She is wearing a fancy dress and bonnet and has light-brown curly hair. Not so much a pretty face as a pert one.

"Are you from one of the cabins?" she says.

Walter says, "No. I am not."

"I knew you were not. There are only four of them and one is for my father and me and one is for the captain and one is for his mother and she never comes out and one is for the two ladies. You are not supposed to be on this part of the deck unless you are from one of the cabins."

"Well, I did not know that," Walter says, but does not bestir himself to move away.

"I have seen you before writing in your book."

"I haven't seen you."

"No. You were writing, so you didn't notice."

"Well," says Walter. "I'm finished with it now anyway."

"I haven't told anybody about you," she says carelessly, as if that was a matter of choice, and she might well change her mind.

AND ON THAT SAME DAY but an hour or so on, there comes a great cry from the port side that there is a last sight of Scotland. Walter and Andrew go over to see that, and Mary with Young James on her hip and many others. Old James and Agnes do not go—she because she objects now to moving herself anywhere, and he on account of perversity. His sons have urged him to go but he has said, "It is nothing to me. I have seen the last of the Ettrick so I have seen the last of Scotland already."

It turns out that the cry to say farewell has been premature—a grey rim of land will remain in place for hours yet. Many will grow tired of looking at it—it is just land, like any other—but some will stay at the rail until the last rag of it fades, with the daylight.

"You should go and say farewell to your native land and the last farewell to your mother and father for you will not be seeing them again," says Old James to Agnes. "And there is worse yet you will have to endure. Aye, but there is. You have the curse of Eve." He says this with the mealy relish of a preacher and Agnes calls him an old shite-bag under her breath, but she has hardly the energy even to scowl.

Old shite-bag. You and your native land.

WALTER WRITES at last a single sentence.

And this night in the year 1818 we lost sight of Scotland.

The words seem majestic to him. He is filled with a sense of grandeur, solemnity, and personal importance.

16th was a very windy day with the wind coming out of the S.W. the sea was running very high and the ship got her gib-boom broken on account of the violence of the wind. And this day our sister Agnes was taken into the cabin.

Sister, he has written, as if she were all the same to him as poor Mary, but that is hardly the case. Agnes is a tall well-built girl with thick dark hair and dark eyes. The flush on one of her cheeks slides into a splotch of pale brown as big as a handprint. It is a birthmark, which people say is a pity, because without it she would be handsome. Walter can hardly bear looking at it, but this is not because it is ugly. It is because he longs to touch it, to stroke it with the tips of his fingers. It looks not like ordinary skin but like the velvet on a deer. His feelings about her are so troubling that he can only speak unpleasantly to her if he speaks at all. And she pays him back with a good seasoning of contempt.

AGNES THINKS that she is in the water and the waves are heaving her up and slamming her down again. Every time the waves slap her down it is worse than the time before and she sinks farther and deeper, with the moment of relief passing before she can grab it, for the wave is already gathering its power to hit her again.

Then sometimes she knows she is in a bed, a strange bed and strangely soft, but it is all the worse for that because when she sinks down there is no resistance, no hard place where the pain has to stop. And here or on the water people keep rushing back and forth in front of her. They are all seen sideways and all transparent, talking very fast so she can't make them out, and maliciously taking no heed of her. She sees Andrew in the midst of them, and two or three of his brothers. Some of the girls she knows are there too—the friends she used to lark around with in Hawick. And they do not give a glance or a poor penny for the plight she is in now.

She shouts at them to take themselves off but not one of them pays any attention and she sees more of them coming right through the wall. She never knew before that she had so many enemies. They are grinding her and pretending they don't even know it. Their movement is grinding her to death.

Her mother bends over her and says in a drawling, cold, lackadaisical voice, "You are not trying, my girl. You must try harder." Her mother is all dressed up and talking fine, like some Edinburgh lady.

Evil stuff is poured into her mouth. She tries to spit it out, knowing it is poison.

I will just get up and get out of this, she thinks. She starts trying to pull herself loose from her body, as if it were a heap of rags all on fire.

A man's voice is heard, giving some order.

"Hold her," he says and she is split and stretched wide open to the world and the fire.

"Ah—ah—ahh," the man's voice says, panting as if he has been running in a race.

Then a cow that is so heavy, bawling heavy with milk, rears up and sits down on Agnes's stomach.

"Now. Now," says the man's voice, and he groans at the end of his strength as he tries to heave it off.

The fools. The fools, ever to have let it in.

She was not better till the 18th when she was delivered of a daughter. We having a surgeon on board nothing happened. Nothing occurred till the 22nd this was the roughest day we had till then experienced. The gib-boom was broken a second time. Nothing worth mentioning happened Agnes was mending in an ordinary way till the 29th we saw a great shoal of porpoises and the 30th (yesterday) was a very rough sea with the wind blowing from the west we went rather backwards than forwards …

"In the Ettrick there is what they call the highest house in Scotland," James says, "and the house that my grandfather lived in was a higher one than that. The name of the place is Phauhope, they call it Phaup, my grandfather was Will O'Phaup and fifty years ago you would have heard of him if you came from any place south of the Forth and north of the Debatable Lands."

Unless a person stops up his ears, what is to be done but listen? thinks Walter. There are people who curse to see the old man coming but there do seem to be others who are glad of any distraction.

He is telling about Will and his races, and the wagers on him, and other foolishness more than Walter can bear.

"And he married a woman named Bessie Scott and one of his sons was named Robert and that same Robert was my father. My father. And I am standing here in front of you."

"In but one leap Will could clear the river Ettrick, and the place is marked."

FOR THE FIRST TWO or three days Young James has refused to be unfastened from Mary's hip. He has been bold enough, but only if he can stay there. At night he has slept in her cloak, curled up beside her, and she has wakened aching along her left side because she lay stiffly all night not to disturb him. Then in the space of one morning he is down and running about and kicking at her if she tries to hoist him up.

Everything on the ship is calling out for his attention. Even at night he tries to climb over her and run away in the dark. So she gets up aching not only from her stiff position but from lack of sleep altogether. One night she drops off and the child gets loose but most fortunately stumbles against his father's body in his bid for escape. Henceforth Andrew insists that he be tied down every night. He howls of course, and Andrew shakes him and cuffs him and then he sobs himself to sleep. Mary lies by him softly explaining how this is necessary so that he should not fall off the ship into the ocean, but he regards her at these times as his enemy and if she puts a hand to stroke his face he tries to bite it with his baby teeth. Every night he goes to sleep in a rage, but in the morning when she unties him, still half-asleep and full of his infant sweetness, he clings to her drowsily and she is suffused with love.

The truth is that she loves even his howls and his rages and his kicks and his bites. She loves his dirty and his curdled smells as well as his fresh ones. As his drowsiness leaves him his clear blue eyes, looking into hers, fill with a marvellous intelligence and an imperious will, which seem to her to come straight from Heaven. (Though her religion has always taught her that self-will comes from the opposite direction.) She loved her brothers too when they were sweet and wild and had to be kept from falling into the burn, but surely not as passionately as she loves James.

Then one day he is gone. She is in the line for the wash water and she turns around and he is not beside her. She has just been speaking a few words to the woman ahead of her, answering a question about Agnes and the infant, she has just told its name—Isabel—and in that moment he has got away. When she was saying the name, Isabel, she felt a surprising longing to hold that new, exquisitely light bundle, and as she abandons her place in line and chases about for sight of James it seems to her that he must have felt her disloyalty and vanished to punish her.

Everything in an instant is overturned. The nature of the world is altered. She runs back and forth, crying out James's name. She runs up to strangers, to sailors who laugh at her as she begs them, "Have you seen a little boy, have you seen a little boy this high, he has blue eyes?"

"I seen a fifty or sixty of them like that in the last five minutes," a man says to her. A woman trying to be kind says that he will turn up, Mary should not worry herself, he will be playing with some of the other children. Some women even look about as if they would help her to search, but of course they cannot, they have their own responsibilities.

This is what Mary plainly sees, in those moments of anguish—that the world which has turned into a horror for her is still the same ordinary world for all these other people and will remain so even if James has truly vanished, even if he has crawled through the ship's railings—she has noticed, all over, the places where this could be possible—and is swallowed in the ocean.

The most brutal and unthinkable of all events, to her, could seem to most others like a sad but not extraordinary misadventure. It would not be unthinkable to them.

Or to God. For in fact when God makes some rare and remarkably beautiful human child, is He not particularly tempted to take His creature back, as if the world did not deserve it?

But she is praying to Him, all the time. At first she only called on the Lord's name. But as her search grows more specific and in some ways more bizarre—she is ducking under clotheslines that people have contrived for privacy, she thinks nothing of interrupting folk at any business, she flings up the lids of their boxes and looks in their bedclothes, not even hearing them when they curse her—her prayers also become more complicated and audacious. She seeks for something to offer, something that could be the price of James's being restored to her. But what does she have? Nothing of her own—not health or prospects or anybody's regard. There is no piece of luck or even a hope she can offer to give up. What she has is James.

And how can she offer James for James?

This is what is knocking around in her head.

But what about her love of James? Her extreme and perhaps idolatrous, perhaps wicked love of another creature. She will give up that, she will give it up gladly, if only he isn't gone, if only he can he found. If only he isn't dead.

SHE RECALLS all this, an hour or two after somebody has noticed the boy peeping out from under an empty bucket, listening to the hubbub. And she retracted her vow at once. She grabbed him in her arms and held him hard against her and took deep groaning breaths, while he struggled to get free.

Her understanding of God is shallow and unstable and the truth is that except in a time of terror such as she has just experienced, she does not really care. She has always felt that God or even the idea of Him was more distant from her than from other people. Also she does not fear His punishments after death as she should and she does not even know why. There is a stubborn indifference in her mind that nobody knows about. In fact, everybody may think that she clings secretly to religion because so little else is available to her. They are quite wrong, and now she has James back she gives no thanks but thinks what a fool she was and how she could not give up her love of him any more than stop her heart beating.

AFTER THAT, Andrew insists that James be tied not only by night but to the post of the bunk or to their own clothesline on the deck, by day. Mary wishes him to be tethered to her but Andrew says a boy like that would kick her to pieces. Andrew has trounced him for the trick he played, but the look in James's eyes says that his tricks are not finished.

THAT CLIMB IN EDINBURGH, that sighting across the water, was a thing Andrew did not even mention to his own brothers—America being already a sore enough matter. The oldest brother, Robert, went off to the Highlands as soon as he was grown, leaving home without a farewell on an evening when his father was at Tibbie Shiel's.

He made it plain that he was doing this in order not to have to join any expedition that their father might have in mind. Then the brother James perversely set out for America on his own, saying that at least if he did that, he could save himself hearing any more about it. And finally Will, younger than Andrew but always the most contrary and the most bitterly set against the father, Will too had run away, to join Robert. That left only Walt, who was still childish enough to be thinking of adventures—he had grown up bragging about how he was going to fight the French, so maybe now he thought he'd fight the Indians.

And then there was Andrew himself, who ever since that day on the rock has felt about his father a deep bewildered sense of responsibility, much like sorrow.

But then, Andrew feels a responsibility for everybody in his family. For his often ill-tempered young wife, whom he has again brought into a state of peril, for the brothers far away and the brother at his side, for his pitiable sister and his heedless child. This is his burden—it never occurs to him to call it love.

AGNES KEEPS ASKING for salt, till they begin to fear that she will fuss herself into a fever. The two women looking after her are cabin passengers, Edinburgh ladies, who took on the job out of charity.

"You be still now," they tell her. "You have no idea what a fortunate lassie you are that we had Mr. Suter on board."

They tell her that the baby was turned the wrong way inside her, and they were all afraid that Mr. Suter would have to cut her, and that might be the end of her. But he had managed to get it turned so that he could wrestle it out.

"I need salt for my milk," says Agnes, who is not going to let them put her in her place with their reproaches and Edinburgh speech. They are idiots anyway. She has to tell them how you must put a little salt in the baby's first milk, just place a few grains on your finger and squeeze a drop or two of milk onto it and let the child swallow that before you put it to the breast. Without this precaution there is a good chance that it will grow up half-witted.

"Is she even a Christian?" says the one of them to the other.

"I am as much as you," Agnes says. But to her own surprise and shame she starts to weep aloud, and the baby howls along with her, out of sympathy or out of hunger. And still she refuses to feed it.

Mr. Suter comes in to see how she is. He asks what all the grief is about, and they tell him the trouble.

"A newborn baby to get salt on its stomach—where did she get the idea?"

He says, "Give her the salt." And he stays to see her squeeze the milk on her salty finger, lay the finger to the infant's lips, and follow it with her nipple.

He asks her what the reason is and she tells him.

"And does it work every time?"

She tells him—a little surprised that he is as stupid as they are, though kinder—that it works without fail.

"So where you come from they all have their wits about them? And are all the girls strong and good-looking like you?"

She says that she would not know about that.

Sometimes visiting young men, educated and from the town, used to hang around her and her friends, complimenting them and trying to work up a conversation, and she always thought any girl was a fool who allowed it, even if the man was handsome. Mr. Suter is far from handsome—he is too thin, and his face is badly pocked, so that at first she took him for an old fellow. But he has a kind voice, and if he is teasing her a little there could be no harm in it. No man would have the nature left to deal with a woman after looking at them spread wide, their raw parts open to the air.

"Are you sore?" he says, and she believes there is a shadow on his damaged cheeks, a slight blush rising. She says that she is no worse than she has to be, and he nods, picks up her wrist, and bows over it, strongly pressing her pulse.

"Lively as a racehorse," he says, with his hands still above her, as if he did not know where to drop them next. Then he decides to push back her hair and press his fingers to her temples, as well as behind her ears.

She will recall this touch, this curious, gentle, tingling pressure, with an addled mixture of scorn and longing, for many years to come.

"Good," he says. "No touch of a fever."

He watches, for a moment, the child sucking.

"All's well with you now," he says, with a sigh. "You have a fine daughter and she can say all her life that she was born at sea."

ANDREW ARRIVES LATER and stands at the foot of the bed. He has never looked on her in such a bed as this (a regular bed even though bolted to the wall). He is red with shame in front of the ladies, who have brought in the basin to wash her.

"That's it, is it?" he says, with a nod—not a glance—at the bundle beside her.

She laughs in a vexed way and asks, what did he think it was? That is all it takes to knock him off his unsteady perch, puncture his pretense of being at ease. Now he stiffens up, even redder, doused with fire. It isn't just what she has said, it is the whole scene, the smell of the infant and milk and blood, most of all the basin, the cloths, the women standing by, with their proper looks that can seem to a man both admonishing and full of derision.

He can't think of another word to say, so she has to tell him, with rough mercy, to get on his way, there's work to do here.

Some of the girls used to say that when you finally gave in and lay down with a man—even granting he was not the man of your first choice—it gave you a helpless but calm and even sweet feeling. Agnes does not recall that she felt that with Andrew. All she felt was that he was an honest lad and the one that she needed in her circumstances, and that it would never occur to him to run off and leave her.

Vision

ALISTAIR MACLEOD

I DON'T REMEMBER when I first heard the story but I remember the first time that I heard it and remembered it. By that I mean the first time it made an impression on me and more or less became *mine;* sort of went into me the way such things do, went into me in such a way that I knew it would not leave again but would remain there forever. Something like when you cut your hand with a knife by accident, and even as you're trying to staunch the blood flowing out of the wound, you know the wound will never really heal totally and your hand will never look quite the same again. You can imagine the scar tissue that will form and be a different colour and texture from the rest of your skin. You know this even as you are trying to stop the blood and trying to squeeze the separated edges of skin together once more. Like trying to squeeze together the separated banks of a small and newly discovered river so that the stream will be subterranean once again. It is something like that, although you know in one case the future scar will be forever on the outside, while the memory will remain forever deep within.

Anyway, on this day we were about a mile and a half offshore but heading home on the last day of the lobster season. We could see the trucks of the New Brunswick buyers waiting for us on the wharf and because it was a sunny day, light reflected and glinted off the chrome trim and bumpers of the waiting trucks and off their gleaming rooftops as well. It was the last day of June and the time was early afternoon and I was seventeen.

My father was in good spirits because the season was over and we had done reasonably well and we were bringing in most of our gear intact. And there seemed no further need to rush.

The sea was almost calm, although there was a light breeze at our backs and we throttled down our engine because there really was no reason to hurry into the wharf for the last and final time. I was in the stern of the boat steadying the piled lobster traps that we had recently raised from the bottom of the sea. Some of them still gleamed with droplets of salt water and streamers of seaweed dangled from their laths. In the crates beside my feet the mottled blue-green lobsters moved and rustled quietly, snapping their tails as they slid over one another with that peculiar dry/wet sound of shell and claws over shell and claws. Their hammer claws had been pegged and fastened shut with rubber bands so they would not mutilate each other and so decrease their value.

"Put some of those in a sack for ourselves," said my father, turning his head back over his right shoulder as he spoke. He was standing ahead of me, facing the land and urinating over the side. His water fell into the sea and vanished into the rolling swell of the boat's slow passage.

"Put them in the back there," he said, "behind the bait bucket, and throw our oilers over them. They will want everything we've got, and what they won't see won't hurt them. Put in some markets too, not just canners."

I took a sack and began to pick some lobsters out of the crate, grasping them at the end of their body shells or by the ends of their tails and being careful not to get my fingers snapped. For even with their hammer claws banded shut there was still certain danger.

"How many do you want?" I asked.

"Oh," he said, turning with a smile and running his hand along the front of his trousers to make sure his fly was closed, "as many as you want. Use your own good judgement."

We did not often take home lobsters for ourselves because they were so expensive and we needed the money they would bring. And the buyers wanted them with a desperation almost bordering on frenzy. Perhaps even now as I bent over the crate, they were watching from the wharf with binoculars to see if any were being concealed. My father stood casually in front of me once more facing the land and shielding my movements with his body. The boat followed its set course, its keel cutting the blue-green water and turning it temporarily into white.

There was a time long ago when the lobsters were not thought to be so valuable. Probably because the markets of the larger world had not yet been discovered or were so far away. People then ate all they wanted of them and even used them for fertilizer on their fields. And those who did eat them did not consider them to be a delicacy. There is a quoted story from the time which states that in the schools you could always identify the children of the poor because they were the ones with lobster in their sandwiches. The well-to-do were able to afford bologna.

With the establishment of the New England market, things changed. Lobster factories were set up along the coast for the canning of the lobsters at a time before good land transportation and refrigeration became common. In May and June and into July the girls in white caps and smocks packed the lobster meat into burnished cans before they were steam sealed. And the men in the smack boats brought the catches to the rickety piers which were built on piles and jutted out into the sea.

My father's mother was one of the girls, and her job was taking the black vein out of the meat of the lobster's tail before the tail was coiled around the inside of the can. At home they ate the black vein along with the rest of the meat, but the supervisors at the factory said it was unsightly. My father's father was one of the young men standing ready in the smack boat, wearing his cap at a jaunty angle and uttering witty sayings and singing little songs in Gaelic to the girls who stood above him on the wharf. All of this was, of course, a long time ago and I am just trying to recreate the scene.

On the day of the remembered story, though, the sea was almost serene as I placed the lobsters in the sack and prepared to hide them behind the bait bucket and under our oilers in the stern of the boat. Before we secreted the sack, we leaned over the side and scooped up water in the bailing bucket and soaked the sack to insure the health and life of the lobsters kept within. The wet sack moved and cracked with the shape and sound of the lobsters and it reminded me vaguely of sacks of kittens which were being taken to be drowned. You could see the movement but not the individuals.

My father straightened from his last dip over the side and passed the dripping bucket carefully to me. He steadied himself with his left hand on the gunwale and then seated himself on the thwart and faced toward the north. I gave the lobsters another soaking and moved to place them behind the bait bucket. There was still some bait remaining but we would not have need of it any more so I threw it over the side. The pieces of blue-grey mackerel turned and revolved before I lost sight of them within the water. The day before yesterday we had taken these same mackerel out of the same sea. We used nets for the spring mackerel because they were blind and could not see to take a baited hook; but in the fall, when they returned, the scales had fallen from their eyes and they would lunge at almost anything thrown before them. Even bits of other mackerel ground up and mixed with salt. Mackerel are a windward fish and always swim against the wind. If the wind is off the land, they swim toward the shore and perhaps the waiting nets; but if the wind blows in the opposite direction, they face out to sea and go so far out some years that we miss them altogether.

I put the empty bait bucket in front of the sack of lobsters and placed an empty crate upside down and at an angle over them so that their movements would not be noticeable. And I casually threw our oilers over them as well.

Ahead of us on the land and to the north of the wharf with its waiting trucks was the mile-long sandy beach cut by the river that acted as an erratic boundary between the fishing grounds of ourselves and our neighbours, the MacAllesters. We had traditionally fished to the right of the river and they to the left, and apparently for many years it was constant in its estuary. But in recent years the river mouth, because of the force of storms and tides and the build-up of sand, had become undependable as a visual guide. The shifting was especially affected by the ravages of the winter storms, and some springs the river might empty almost a mile to the north or the south of its previous point of entry. This had caused a tension between ourselves and the MacAllesters because, although we traditionally went to the same grounds, the boundary was no longer fixed and we had fallen into accusations and counter-accusations; sometimes using the actual river when it suited our purpose, and when it did not, using an earlier and imaginary river which we could no longer see.

The MacAllesters' boat was going in ahead of us now and I waved to Kenneth MacAllester, who had become a rather lukewarm friend because of the tension between our families. He was the same age as I, and he waved back, although the other two men in the boat did not.

At an earlier time when Kenneth MacAllester and I were friends and in about grade six he told me a story while we were walking home from school in the spring. He told me that his grandmother was descended from a man in Scotland who possessed *Da Shealladh,* two sights or the second sight, and that by looking through a hole in a magical white stone he could see distant contemporary events as well as those of the future. Nearly all of his visions came true. His name was either Munro or MacKenzie and his first name was Kenneth and the eye he placed to the stone for his visions was *cam* or blind in the sense of ordinary sight. He was a favourite of the powerful man for whom he worked, but he and the man's wife were jealous and disliked each other. Once when the powerful man was in Paris there was a big party on his estate. In one version "the prophet" commented rather unwisely on the pater-nity of some of the children present. In another version the man's wife asked him mockingly if he could "see" her husband in Paris but he refused. However, she insisted. Putting the stone to his eye he told her that her husband was enjoying himself rather too much with ladies in Paris and had little thought of her. Enraged and embarrassed, she ordered him to be burned in a barrel of tar into which spikes had been driven from the outside. In one version the execution took place right away, but in another it did not take place until some days later. In the second version the man was returning home when he heard the news and saw the black smoke rising. He spurred his horse at utmost speed toward the point where he saw the billowing smoke and called out in an attempt to stop the burning and save his friend, but his horse died beneath him, and though he ran the rest of the way he arrived too late for any salvation.

Before the prophet died he hurled his white stone as far as he could out into the lake and told the lady that the family would come to an end years hence. And he told her that it would end when there was a deaf-and-dumb father who would outlive his four sons and then all their lands would pass into the hands of strangers. Generations later the deaf-and-dumb father was apparently a fine, good man who was helpless in the face of the prophecy he knew too much about and which he saw unfolding around him with the death of each of his four loved sons. Unable again to offer any salvation.

I thought it was a tremendous story at the time, and Kenneth picked up a white stone from the roadside and held it to his eye to see if "prophecy" would work for him.

"I guess I really wouldn't want it to work," he said with a laugh. "I wouldn't want to be blind," and he threw the stone away. At that time he planned on joining the Air Force and flying toward the sun and being able to see over the tops of mountains and across the sea.

When we got to his house we were still talking about the story and his mother cautioned us not to laugh at such things. She went and found a poem by Sir Walter Scott, which she read aloud to us. We did not pay much attention to it, but I remember the lines which referred to the father and his four doomed sons:

Thy sons rose around thee in light and in love
All a father could hope, all a friend could approve;
What 'vails it the tale of thy sorrows to tell?
In the springtime of youth and of promise they fell!

Now, as I said, the MacAllesters' boat was going in ahead of us, loaded down with its final catch and with its stern and washboard piled high with traps. We had no great wish to talk to the MacAllesters at the wharf and there were other boats ahead of us as well. They would unload their catches first and pile their traps upon the wharf and it would be some time before we would find a place to dock. My father cut our engine. There was no need to rush.

"Do you see Canna over there?" he asked, pointing to the north where he was facing. "Do you see the point of Canna?"

"Yes," I said, "I see it. There it is."

There was nothing very unusual about seeing the point of Canna. It was always visible except on the foggiest days or when there was rain or perhaps snow. It was twenty miles away by boat, and on the duller days it reached out low and blue like the foot of a giant's boot extended into the sea. On sunny days like this one it sparkled in a distant green. The clearings of the old farms were visible and above them the line of the encroaching trees, the spruce and fir of a darker green. Here and there the white houses stood out and even the grey and weather-beaten barns. It was called after the Hebridean island of Canna, "the green island" where most of its original settlers were born. It was the birthplace of my grandmother, who was one of the girls in the white smocks at the Canna lobster factory in that long-ago time.

"It was about this time of year," said my father, "that your Uncle Angus and I went by ourselves to visit our grandmother at the point of Canna. We were eleven at the time and had been asking our parents for weeks to let us go. They seemed reluctant to give us any answer and all they would say was 'We will see' or 'Wait and see.' We wanted to go on the smack boat when it was making its final run of the season. We wanted to go with the men on the smack who were buying lobsters and they would set us ashore at the wharf at Canna point and we would walk the mile to our grandmother's house. We had never gone there by ourselves before. We could hardly remember being there because if you went by land you had to travel by horse and buggy and it was a long way. First you had to go inland to the main road and drive about twenty miles and then come back down toward the shore. It was about twice as far by land as it was by sea and our parents went about once a year. Usually by themselves, as there was not enough room for others in the buggy. If we did not get to go on the smack, we were afraid that we would not get to go at all. 'Wait and see' was all they said."

It seemed strange to me, as my father spoke, to think of Canna as far away. By that time it took perhaps three-quarters of an hour by car, even though the final section of the road was often muddy and dangerous enough in the wet months of spring and fall and often blocked by snow in the winter. Still, it was not hard to get there if you really wanted to, and so the old letters from Canna which I discovered in the upstairs attic seemed quite strange and from another distant time. It seemed hard to believe that people only twenty miles away would write letters to one another and visit only once a year. But at that time the distance was hard to negotiate, and there were no telephones.

My father and his brother Angus were twins and they had been named after their grandfathers so their names were Angus and Alex. It was common for parents to name their first children after their own parents and it seemed that almost all of the men were called Angus or Alex. In the early years of the century the Syrian and Lebanese pedlars who walked the muddy country roads beneath their heavy back-packs sometimes called themselves Angus or Alex so that they would sound more familiar to their potential customers. The pedlars, like the Gaelic-speaking people in the houses which they visited, had very little English, so anything that aided communication was helpful. Sometimes they unfolded their bolts of cloth and displayed their shining needles before admirers who were unable to afford them, and sometimes, sensing the situation, they would leave the goods behind. Later, if money became available, the people would say, "Put aside what we owe Angus and Alex in the sugar bowl so that we can pay them when they come."

Sometimes the pedlars would carry letters from one community to the other, to and from the families of the different Anguses and Alexes strung out along the coast. Distinguishing the different families, although their names were much the same, and delivering letters which they could not read.

My father and his brother continued to pester their parents who continued to say "Wait and see," and then one day they went to visit their father's mother who lived in a house quite close to theirs. After they had finished the lunch she had given them, she offered to "read" their teacups and to tell them of the future events revealed in the tea leaves at the bottoms of their cups: "You are going on a journey," she said, peering into the cups as she turned them in her hands. "You are going to cross water. And to take food with you. You will meet a mysterious woman who has dark hair. She will be quite close to you. And …" she said, turning the cups in her hands to see the formation of the leaves better, "and … oh …. oh … oh."

"What?" they asked. "What?"

"Oh, that's enough for today," she said. "You had better be getting home or they will be worrying about you."

They ran home and burst into their parents' kitchen. "We are going on a trip to Canna," they said. "Grandma told us. She saw it in the tea leaves. She read it in our cups. We are going to take a lunch. We are going across the water. She said we were going."

The morning they left they were dressed in their best clothes and waiting at the wharf long before the smack was due, clutching their lunches in their hands. It was sunny when the boat left the wharf but as they proceeded along the coast it became cloudy and then it began to rain. The trip seemed long in the rain and the men told them to go into the boat's cabin where they would be dry and where they could eat their lunch. The first part of the trip seemed to be spoiled by rain.

It was raining heavily when the boat approached the wharf at Canna point. It was almost impossible to see the figures on the wharf or to distinguish them as they moved about in their heavy oil slickers. The lobster buyers were in a hurry, as were the wet men impatiently waiting for them in the rain.

"Do you know where you're going?" said the men in the smack to their young passengers.

"Yes," they said, although they were not quite sure because the rain obscured the landmarks that they thought they would remember.

"Here," said the men in the smack, handing them two men's oil slickers from the boat's cabin. "Wear these to help keep you dry. You can give them back to us sometime."

They climbed up the iron ladder toward the wharf's cap and the busy men reached their hands down to help and pull them up.

The men were busy and because of the rain no one on the wharf asked them where they were going, and they were too shy and too proud to ask. So they turned the cuffs of the oil slickers back over their wrists and began to walk up the muddy road from the wharf. They were still trying to keep their best clothes clean and pick their spots carefully, placing their good shoes where there were fully dry spots and avoiding the puddles and little rivulets which rolled the small stones along in their course. The oil slickers were so long that the bottoms of them dragged on the muddy road and sometimes they lifted them up in the way that older ladies might lift the hems of their skirts when stepping over a puddle or some other obstacle in the roadway. When they lifted them, the muddy bottoms rubbed against their good trousers so they let them fall again. Then their shoes were almost invisible and they could hear and feel the tails of the coats dragging behind them as they walked. They were wet and miserable inside the long coats, as well as indistinguishable to anyone who might see the small forms in the long coats walking along the road.

After they had walked for half a mile they were overtaken by an old man in a buggy who stopped and offered them a ride. He, too, was covered in an oil coat, and his cap was pulled down almost to his nose. When he stopped to pick them up, the steam rose from his horse as they clambered into the wagon beside him. He spoke to them in Gaelic and asked them their names and where they were from and where they were going.

"To see our grandmother," they said.

"Your grandmother?" he asked.

"Yes," they said. "Our grandmother."

"Oh," he said. "Your grandmother, are you sure?"

"Of course," they said, becoming a bit annoyed. For although they were more uncertain than they cared to admit, they did not want to appear so.

"Oh," he said, "all right then. Would you like some peppermints?" And he reached deeply into a pocket beneath his oil coat and brought out a brown paper bag full of peppermints. Even as he passed the bag to them, the raindrops pelted upon it and it became soggy and began to darken in deterioration.

"Oh," he said, "you may as well keep all of them. I got a whole lot more of them for the store. They just came in on the boat." He pointed to some metal containers in the back of the buggy.

"Are you going to spend the night with your grandmother?" he asked.

"Yes," they said.

"Oh," he answered, pulling on the reins and turning the horse into the laneway of a yard.

He drove them to the door of the house and helped them down from the buggy while his horse stomped its impatient hooves in the mud and tossed its head in the rain.

"Would you like me to go in with you?" he asked.

"No," they said, impatient for him to be gone and out of sight.

"All right," he said and spoke to his uneasy horse which began to trot down the laneway, the buggy wheels throwing hissing jets of mud and water behind them.

They hesitated for a while outside the doorway of the house, waiting for the man to go out of sight and feeling ridiculous for standing in the rain. But halfway down the lane he stopped and looked back. And then he stood up in the buggy and shouted to them and made a "go-forward" gesture with his hand toward the house. They opened the door then and went in because they felt embarrassed and did not want to admit that he had brought them to the wrong house.

When they went in, they found themselves in the middle of a combined porch and entranceway which was cluttered with an odd collection of household and farming utensils. Baking pans and jars and sealers and chamber pots and old milk pails and rakes and hoes and hayforks and bits of wire and lengths of chain. There was very little light, and in the gloom something started up from their feet and bounced against their legs and then into a collection of jars and pails, causing a crashing cacophony of sound. It was a half-grown lamb, and it bleated as it bounded toward the main door, dropping bits of manure behind it. In the same instant and in response to the sound, the main door opened and the lamb leaped through it and into the house.

Framed in the doorway was a tall old woman clad in layers of clothing, even though it was summer, and wearing wire-framed glasses. On either side of her were two black dogs. They were like collies, although they had no white markings. They growled softly but deep within their throats and the fur on the back of their necks rose and they raised their upper lips to reveal their gleaming teeth. They were poised on the tips of their paws and their eyes seemed to burn in the gloom. She lowered a hand to each of their heads but did not say anything. Everyone seemed to stare straight ahead. The boys would have run away but they were afraid that if they moved, the dogs would be upon them, so they stayed where they were as still as could be. The only sound was the tense growling of the dogs. *"Cò a th'ann?"* she said in Gaelic. "Who's there?"

The boys did not know what to say because all the possible answers seemed so complicated. They moved their feet uneasily, which caused the dogs to each take two steps forward as if they were part of some rehearsed choreography. *"Cò a th'ann?"* she said, repeating the question. "Who's there?"

"We're from Kintail," they said finally. "Our names are Alex and Angus. We're trying to find our grandmother's house. We came on the smack boat."

"Oh," she said. "How old are you?"

"Eleven," they said. "Both of us. We're twins."

"Oh," she said. "Both of you. I have relatives in Kintail. Come in."

They were still afraid, and the dogs remained poised, snarling softly, with their delicate, dangerous lips flickering above the whiteness of their teeth.

"All right," they said. "We'll come in, but just for a minute. We can't stay long."

Only then did she speak to the dogs. "Go and lie under the table and be quiet," she said. Immediately they relaxed and vanished behind her into the house.

"Did you know these dogs were twins?" she asked.

"No," they said. "We didn't."

"Well," she said. "They are."

Inside the house they sat on the first chairs that they could find and moved them as close to the door as possible. The room that they were in was a primitive kitchen and much of its floor was cluttered with objects not unlike the porch, except that the objects were smaller—knives and forks and spoons and the remains of broken cups and saucers. There was a half-completed partition between the kitchen and what might have been a living room or dining room. The upright studs of the partition were firmly in place and someone had nailed wainscotting on either side of them but it extended only halfway to the ceiling. It was difficult to tell if the partition had been left incomplete or if it was gradually being lowered. The space between the walls of the partition was filled with cats. They pulled themselves up by their paws and looked curiously at the visitors and then jumped back down into the space. From the space between the uncompleted walls the visitors could hear the mewing of newborn kittens. Other cats were everywhere. They were on the table, licking what dishes there were, and on the backs of the chairs and in and out of a cavern beneath an old couch. Sometimes they leaped over the half-completed partition and vanished into the next room. Sometimes they snarled at one another and feinted with their paws. In one corner a large tiger-striped tomcat was energetically breeding a small grey female flattened out beneath him. Other tentative males circled the breeding pair, growling deeply within their throats. The tiger cat would interrupt his movements from time to time to snarl at them and keep them at bay. The female's nose was pressed against the floor and her ears flattened down against her head. Sometimes he held the fur at the back of her neck within his teeth.

The two black dogs lay under the table and seemed oblivious to the cats. The lamb stood watchfully behind the stove. Everything in the house was extremely dirty—spilled milk and cat hair and unwashed and broken dishes. The old woman wore men's rubber boots upon her feet and her clothing seemed to consist of layers of petticoats and skirts and dresses and sweaters upon sweaters. All of it was very dirty and covered with stains of spilled tea and food remnants and spattered grease. Her hands seemed brown, and her fingernails were long, and there was a half inch of black grime under each of them. She raised her hands to touch her glasses and they noticed that the outside lenses were smeared and filthy as well. It was then that they realized that she was blind and that the glasses served no useful purpose. They became even more uncertain and frightened than they were before.

"Which one of you is Alex?" she asked, and he raised his hand as if answering a question at school before realizing that she could not see him.

"I am," he answered then, and she turned her face in his direction.

"I have a long association with that name," she said, and they were surprised at her use of a word like "association."

Because of the rain the day seemed to darken early and they could see the fading light through the grimy windows. They wondered for a moment why she did not light a lamp until they realized that there was none and that to her it made no difference.

"I will make you a lunch," she said. "Don't move."

She went to the partial partition and ripped the top board off with her strong brown hands and then she leaned it against the partition and stomped on it with her rubber-booted foot. It splintered and she repeated the action, feeling about the floor for the lengths of splintered wood. She gathered them up and went to the stove and, after removing the lids, began to feed them into the fire. She moved the kettle over the crackling flame.

She began to feel about the cupboards for food, brushing away the insistent cats which crowded about her hands. She found two biscuits in a tin and placed them on plates which she put into the cupboard so the cats would not devour them. She put her hand into a tea tin and took a handful of tea which she placed in the teapot and then she poured the hot water in as well. She found some milk in a dirty pitcher and, feeling for the cups, she splashed some of it into each.

Then she took the teapot and began to pour the tea. She turned her back to them but as she poured they could see her quickly dip her long brown finger with the half inch of grimy fingernail quickly into each cup. They realized she was doing it because she had no other way of knowing when the cups were full but their stomachs revolved and they feared they might throw up.

She brought them a cup of tea each and retrieved the biscuits from the cupboard and passed the plates to them. They sat holding the offerings on their laps while she faced them. Although they realized she could not see them, they still felt that she was watching them. They looked at the tea and the biscuits with the cat hair and did not know what to do. After a while they began to make slurping sounds with their lips.

"Well, we will have to be on our way," they said. Carefully they bent forward and placed the still-full teacups under their chairs and the biscuits in their pockets.

"Do you know where you are going?" she asked.

"Yes," they said with determination.

"Can you see your way in the dark?"

"Yes," they said again with equal determination.

"We will meet again?" she said, raising her voice to form a question.

"Yes," they said.

"Some are more loyal than others," she said. "Remember that."

They hurried down the laneway, surprised to find that it was not so dark outside as it seemed within the blind woman's house. When they got to the main road, they followed it in the direction that led away from the wharf and it seemed that in a short time they could make out the buildings of their original destination.

It was still raining as they entered the laneway to the buildings, and by this time it was indeed quite dark. The laneway ended at the door of the barn and the house was some yards farther. The barn door was open and they stepped inside for a moment to compose themselves. It was very quiet within the barn, for all of the animals were away in their summer pastures. They hesitated for a moment in the first stall and then they were aware of a rhythm of sound coming from the next area, the threshing floor. They opened the small connecting door and stepped inside and waited for their eyes to adjust to the gloom. And then in the farthest corner they noticed a lantern turned to its lowest and hanging on a nail. And beyond it they could make out the shape of a man. He was tall and wore rubber boots and bib overalls and had a tweed cap pulled down upon his head. He was facing the south wall of the barn but was sideways to them and presented a profile. He was rhythmically rocking from his heels to the balls of his feet and thrusting his hips back and forth and moaning and talking to himself in Gaelic. But it did not seem that he was talking to himself but to someone of the opposite sex who was not there. The front of his overalls was open and he had a hold of himself in his right hand which he moved to the rhythm of his rocking body.

They did not know what to do. They did not recognize the man, and they were terrified that he might turn and see them, and they were afraid that if they tried to make a retreat they might cause a sound which would betray their presence. At home they slept upstairs while their parents slept below in a private room ("to keep an eye on the fire," their parents said); and although they were becoming curious about sex, they did not know a great deal about it. They had seen the mating of animals, such as the cats earlier, but they had never seen a fully aroused grown man before, although they recognized some of the words he was moaning to himself and his imaginary partner. Suddenly, with a groan, he slumped forward as the grey jets of seed spurted onto the south wall of the barn and down to the dry and dusty hay before his feet. He placed his left arm against the wall and rested his forehead against it. They stepped back quietly through the little door and then out of the barn and then they walked rapidly but on their tiptoes through the rain toward the house.

When they entered the porch and the screen door slammed behind them, they heard a voice from within the kitchen. It was harsh and angry and seemed to be cursing, and then the door flew open and they were face to face with their grandmother. At first she did not recognize them in their long coats, and her face remained suspicious and angry, but then her expression changed and she came forward to hug them.

"Angus and Alex," she said. "What a surprise!" Looking over their shoulders, she said, "Are you alone? Did you come by yourselves?" And then, "Why didn't you tell us you were coming? We would have gone to meet you."

It had never entered their minds that their arrival would be such a surprise. They had been thinking of the trip with such intensity that in spite of the day's happenings they still somehow assumed that everyone knew they were coming.

"Well, come in, come in," she said, "and take those wet clothes off. How did you say you came again? And are you just arriving now?"

They told her they had come on the smack and of their walk and the ride with the man who had the peppermints and of their visit to the blind woman, but they omitted the part about the man in the barn. She listened intently as she moved about the kitchen, hanging up their coats and setting the teapot on the stove. She asked for a description of the man with the peppermints and they told her he said he owned a store, and then she asked them how the blind woman was. They told her of the tea she had served them which they had left and she said, "Poor soul!"

And then the screen door banged again and a heavy foot was heard in the porch, and in through the kitchen door walked the man they had seen in the barn.

"Your grandchildren are here to see you," she said with an icy edge to her voice. "They came on the smack from Kintail."

He stood blinking and swaying in the light, trying to focus his eyes upon them. They realized then that he was quite drunk and having difficulty comprehending. His eyes were red-rimmed and bloodshot and a white stubble speckled with black indicated that he had not shaved for a number of days. He swayed back and forth, looking at them carefully and trying to see who they really were. They could not help looking at the front of his overalls to see if there were flecks of semen, but he had been out in the rain and all of his clothing was splattered with moisture.

"Oh," he said, as if a veil had been lifted from his eyes. "Oh," he said. "I love you. I love you." And he came forward and hugged each of them and kissed them on the cheek. They could smell the sourness of his breath and feel the rasping scratch of his stubble on their faces.

"Well," he said, turning on his heel, "I am going upstairs to rest for a while. I have been out in the barn and have been busier than you might think. But I will be back down later." And then he kicked off his boots, steadying himself with one hand on a kitchen chair, and swayed upstairs.

The visitors were shocked that they had not recognized their grandfather. When he came to visit them perhaps once a year, he was always splendid and handsome in his blue serge suit, with a gold watch chain linked across the expansiveness of his vest, and with his pockets filled with peppermints. And when they visited in the company of their parents, he had always been gracious and clear-headed and well attired.

When they could no longer hear his footsteps, their grandmother again began to talk to them, asking them questions, inquiring of their parents and of their school work as she busied herself about the stove and began to set the table.

Later he came back downstairs and they all sat around the table. He had changed his clothes, and his face was covered with bleeding nicks because he had tried to shave. The meal was uncomfortable as he knocked over his water glass and dropped his food on his lap. The visitors were as exhausted as he was, and only their grandmother seemed in control. He went back upstairs as soon as the meal was finished, saying, "Tomorrow will be a better day," and their grandmother suggested that they go to bed soon after.

"We are all tired," she said. "He will be all right tomorrow. He tried to shave in honour of your coming. I will talk to him myself. We are glad that you have come."

They slept together under a mountain of quilts and in a room next to their grandparents'. Before they went to sleep they could hear them talking in Gaelic, and the next thing they remembered was waking in the morning. Their grandparents were standing near their bed and the sun was shining through the window. Each of their grandparents held a tray containing porridge and sugar and milk and tea and butter. They were both rather formally dressed and like the grandparents they thought they knew. The drunk moaning man in the barn was like a dream they wished they had not had.

When they got up to put on their clothes they discovered bits of the blind woman's biscuits still in their pockets, and when they went outside they threw them behind the barn.

They stayed a week at Canna and all during that time the sun shone and the days were golden. They went visiting with their grandfather in his buggy—visiting women in houses and sometimes standing in barns with men. One day they visited the store and had trouble identifying the man behind the counter with the one who had offered them the ride and the peppermints. He seemed equally surprised when he recognized them and said to their grandfather, "I'm sorry if I made a mistake."

During their week in Canna they noticed small differences in the way of doing things. The people of Canna tied their horses with ropes around their necks instead of with halters. They laid out their gardens in beds instead of in rows and they grew a particular type of strawberry whose fruit grew far from the original root. When they drew water from their wells they threw away the first dipperful and the water itself had a slightly different taste. They set their tables for breakfast before retiring for the night. They bowed or curtsied to the new moon, and in the Church of St. Columba the women sat on one side of the aisle and the men on the other.

The Church of St. Columba, said their grandfather, was called after the original chapel on the island of Canna. St. Columba of Colum Cille was a brilliant, dedicated missionary in Ireland and he possessed *Da Shealladh,* the second sight, and used a stone to "see" his visions. He was also a lover of beauty and very strong-willed. Once, continued their grandfather, he copied a religious manuscript without permission but believed the copy was rightfully his. The High King of Ireland who was asked to judge the dispute ruled against Colum Cille, saying, "To every cow its calf and to every book its copy." Later the High King of Ireland also executed a young man who had sought sanctuary under the protection of Colum Cille. Enraged at what he perceived as injustice and bad judgement, Colum Cille told the High King he would lead his relations and clansmen against him in battle. On the eve of the battle, as they prayed and fasted, the archangel Michael appeared to Colum Cille in a vision. The angel told him that God would answer his prayers and allow him to win the battle but that He was not pleased with him for praying for such a worldly request and that he should exile himself from Ireland and never see the country any more, or its people, or partake of its food and drink except on his outward journey. The forces of Colum Cille won the battle and inflicted losses of three thousand men, and perhaps he could have been the King of Ireland, but he obeyed the vision. Some said he left also to do penance for the three thousand lives he had cost. In a small boat and with a few followers who were his relatives, he crossed the sea to the small islands of Scotland and spent the last thirty-four years of his life establishing monasteries and chapels and travelling among the people. Working as a missionary, making predictions, seeing visions and changing forever that region of the world. Leaving Ireland, he said:

> *There is a grey eye*
> *Looking back on Ireland,*
> *That will never see again*
> *Her men or her women.*

> *Early and late my lamentation,*
> *Alas, the journey I am making;*
> *This will be my secret bye-name*
> *"Back turned on Ireland."*

"Did he ever go back?" they asked.

"Once," said their grandfather, "the poets of Ireland were in danger of being banned and he crossed the sea from Scotland to speak on their behalf. But when he came, he came blindfolded so that he could not see the country or its people."

"Did you know him?" they asked. "Did you ever see him?"

"That was a very long time ago," he laughed. "Over thirteen hundred years ago. But, yes, sometimes I know him and I think I see him as well. This church, as I said, is called after the chapel he established on Canna. That chapel is fallen a long time ago, too, and all of the people gone, and the well beside the chapel filled up with rocks and the Celtic crosses of their graveyards smashed down and used for the building of roads. But sometimes I imagine I still see them," he said, looking toward the ocean and across it as if he could see the "green island" and its people. "I see them going about their rituals: riding their horses on Michaelmas and carrying the bodies of their dead round toward the sun. And courting and getting married. Almost all of the people on Canna got married before they were twenty. They considered it unlucky to be either a single man or woman so there were very few single people among them. Perhaps they also found it difficult to wait," he added with a smile, "and that is why their population rose so rapidly. Anyway, all gone."

"You mean dead?" they asked.

"Well, some of them, yes," he said, "but I mean gone from there, scattered all over the world. But some of us are here. That is why this place is called Canna and we carry certain things within us. Sometimes there are things within us which we do not know or fully understand and sometimes it is hard to stamp out what you can't see. It is good that you are here for this while."

Toward the end of the week they learned that there was a government boat checking lighthouses along the coast. It would stop at the point of Canna and later, on its southern journey, also at Kintail. It was an excellent chance for them to get home, and it was decided that they should take it. The night before they left, their grandparents served them a splendid dinner with a white tablecloth and candles.

As they prepared to leave on the following morning, the rain began to fall. Their grandmother gave them some packages to deliver to their mother, and also a letter, and packed a lunch with lobster sandwiches for them. She hugged and kissed them as they were leaving and said, "Thank you for coming. It was good to have you here and it made us feel better about ourselves." She looked at her husband and he nodded.

They climbed into their grandfather's buggy as the rain fell upon them, and carefully placed their packages beneath the seat. On the road down to the wharf they passed the lane to the blind woman's house. She was near the roadway with the two black dogs. She was wearing her men's rubber boots and a large kerchief and a heavy rubber raincoat. When she heard the buggy approaching, she called out, *"Cò a th'ann? Cò a th'ann?* Who's there? Who's there?"

But their grandfather said nothing.

"Who's there?" she called. "Who's there? Who's there?"

The rain fell upon her streaked and empty glasses and down her face and along her coat and her strong protruding hands with their grimy fingernails.

"Don't say anything," said their grandfather under his breath. "I don't want her to know you're here."

As the horse approached, she continued to call, but none of them said anything. Above the regular hoofbeats of the horse her voice seemed to rise through the falling rain, causing a tension within all of them as they tried to pretend they could not hear her.

"Cò a th'ann?" she called. "Who's there? Who's there?"

They lowered their heads as if she could see them. But when they were exactly opposite her, their grandfather could not stand it any longer and suddenly reined in the horse.

"*Cò a th'ann?*" she called. "Who's there?"

"'*Se mi-fhìn,*" he answered quietly. "It's myself!"

She began to curse him in Gaelic and he became embarrassed.

"Do you understand what she's saying?" he said to them.

They were uncertain. "Some of it," they said.

"Here," he said, "hold the horse," and he passed the reins to them. He took the buggy whip out of its socket as he descended from the buggy, and they were uncertain about that, too, until they realized he was taking it to protect himself from the dogs who came snarling toward him, but kept their distance because of the whip. He began to talk to the blind woman in Gaelic and they both walked away from the buggy along the laneway to her house until they were out of earshot. The dogs lay down on the wet roadway and watched and listened carefully.

The visitors could not hear the conversation, only the rising and falling of the two voices through the descending rain. When their grandfather returned, he seemed upset and took the reins from them and spoke to the horse immediately.

"God help me," he said softly and almost to himself, "but I could not pass her by."

There was water running down his face and they thought for a moment he might be crying; but just as when they had looked for the semen on his overalls a week earlier they could not tell because of the rain.

The blind woman stood in the laneway facing them as they moved off along the road. It was one of those situations which almost automatically calls for waving but even as they began to raise their hands they remembered her blindness and realized it was no use. She stood as if watching them for a long time and then, perhaps when she could no longer hear the sound of the horse and buggy, she turned and walked with the two dogs back toward her house.

"Do you know her well?" they asked.

"Oh," said their grandfather, as if being called back from another time and place, "yes, I do know her quite well and since a long, long time."

Their grandfather waited with them on the wharf for the coming of the government boat, but it was late. When it finally arrived, the men said they would not be long checking the lighthouse and told them to go into the boat to wait. They said their good-byes then, and their grandfather turned his wet and impatient horse toward home.

Although the wait was not supposed to be long, it was longer than expected and it was afternoon before the boat left the protection of the wharf and ventured out into the ocean. The rain was still falling and a wind had come up and the sea was choppy. The wind was off the land, so they stood with their backs toward Canna and to the wind and the rain. When they were far enough out to sea to have perspective, one of the men said, "It looks like there is a fire back there." And when they looked back they could see the billowing smoke, somehow seeming ironic in the rain. It rose in the distance and was carried by the wind but it was difficult to see its source not only because of the smoke but also because of the driving rain. And because the perspective from the water was different from what it was on the land. The government men did not know any of the local people and they were behind schedule and already well out to sea, so there was no thought of turning back. They were mildly concerned, too, about the rising wind, and wanted to make as much headway as possible before conditions worsened.

It was that period of the day when the afternoon blends into evening before the boat reached the Kintail wharf. During the last miles the ocean had roughened and within the rocking boat the passengers had become green and seasick and vomited their lobster sandwiches over the side. Canna seemed very far away and the golden week seemed temporarily lost within the reality of the swaying boat and the pelting rain. When the boat docked, they ran to their house as quickly as they could. Their mother gave them soup and dry clothes and they went to bed earlier than usual.

They slept late the next day, and when they awoke and went downstairs it was still raining and blowing. And then the Syrian pedlars, Angus and Alex, knocked on the door. They put their heavy wet leather packs upon the kitchen floor and told the boys' mother that there had been a death in Canna. The Canna people were sending word but they had heard the news earlier in the day from another pedlar arriving from that direction and he had asked them to carry the message. The pedlars and the boys' parents talked for a while and the boys were told to "go outside and play" even though it was raining. They went out to the barn.

Almost immediately the boys' parents began to get ready for the journey. The ocean was by this time too rough for a boat, and they had already hauled their boat up at the end of the lobster season. They readied their horse and buggy, and later in the afternoon they were gone. They were away for five days, and when they returned they were drawn and tired.

Through bits and pieces of conversation, the boys learned that it was the blind woman's house that had burned and she within it.

Later, and they were not sure just when, they gathered other details and bits of information. She had been at the stove, it was thought, and her clothes had caught fire. The animals had burned with her. Most of their bones were found before the door to which they had gone to seek escape but she had been unable to open it for them or, it seemed, for herself.

Over the weeks the details blended in with their own experience. They imagined her strong hands pulling down the wainscotting of her own house and placing it in the fire, consuming her own house somehow from within as it was later to consume her. And they could see the fire going up the front of her layers of dirty clothing. Consuming the dirt which she herself had been unable to see. Rising up the front of her clothing, rising up above her shoulders toward her hair, the imaginary orange flames flickering and framing her face and being reflected in the staring lenses of her glasses.

And they imagined the animals, too. The savage faithful dogs which were twins snarling at the doorway with their fur in flames, and the lusty cats engaged in their growling copulation in the corner, somehow keeping on, driven by their own heat while the other heat surrounded them, and the bleating lamb with its wool on fire. And in the space between the walls the mewing unseen kittens, dying with their eyes still closed.

And sometimes they imagined her, too, in her porch or in her house or standing by the roadside in the rain. *Cò a th'ann?* they heard her call in their imagination and in their dreams. *Cò a th'ann? Cò a th'ann?* Who's there? Who's there? And one night they dreamed they heard themselves answer. *'Se mi-fhìn* they heard themselves say as with one voice. It is myself.

My father and his brother never again spent a week on the green hills of Canna. Perhaps their lives went by too fast or circumstances changed or there were reasons that they did not fully understand themselves.

And one Sunday six years later when they were in church the clergyman gave a rousing sermon on why young men should enlist in World War I. They were very enthusiastic about the idea and told their parents that they were going to Halifax to enlist although they were too young. Their parents were very upset and went to the clergyman in an attempt to convince him it was a mistake. The clergyman was their friend and came to their house and told them it was a general sermon for the day. "I didn't mean *you,*" he added, but his first success was better than his second.

They left the next day for Halifax, getting a ride to the nearest railroad station. They had never been on a train before and when they arrived, the city of Halifax was large and awesome. At the induction centre their age was easily overlooked but the medical examination was more serious. Although they were young and strong, the routine tests seemed strange and provoked a tension within them. They were unable to urinate in a bottle on request and were asked to wait a while and then try again. But sitting on two chairs wishing for urine did little good. They drank more and more water and waited and tried but it did not work. On their final attempt, they were discussing their problem in Gaelic while standing in a tiny cubicle with their legs spread apart and their trousers opened. Unexpectedly a voice from the next cubicle responded to them in Gaelic.

The voice belonged to a young man from Canna who had come to enlist as well but who did not have their problem. "Can we 'borrow' some of that?" they asked, looking at his full bottle of urine.

"Sure," he said, "no need to give it back," and he splashed some of his urine into each of their waiting bottles. All of them "passed" the test; and later in the alleyway behind the induction centre, standing in the steam of their own urine, they began to talk to the young man from Canna. His grandfather owned the store in Canna, he said, and was opposed to his coming to enlist.

"Do you know Alex?" they asked and mentioned their grandfather's formal name.

He seemed puzzled for a moment and then brightened. "Oh," he said, "*Mac an Amharuis,* sure, everyone knows him. He's my grandfather's friend."

And then, perhaps because they were far from home and more lonely and frightened than they cared to admit, they began to talk in Gaelic. They began with the subject of *Mac an Amharuis,* and the young man told them everything he knew. Surprised perhaps at his own knowledge and at having such attentive listeners. *Mac an Amharuis* translates as "Son of Uncertainty," which meant that he was illegitimate or uncertain as to who his father was. He was supposed to be tremendously talented and clever as a young man but also restless and reluctant to join the other young men of Canna in their fishing boats. Instead he saved his money and purchased a splendid stallion and travelled the country offering the stallion's services. He rode on the stallion's back with only a loose rope around its neck for guidance.

He was also thought to be handsome and to possess a "strong nature" or "too much nature," which meant that he was highly sexed. "Some say," said the young man, "that he sowed almost as much seed as the stallion and who knows who might be descended from him. If we only knew, eh?" he added with a laugh.

Then he became involved with a woman from Canna. She was thought to be "odd" by some because she was given to rages and uncertainty and sometimes she would scream and shout at him in public. At times he would bring back books and sometimes moonshine from wherever he went with the stallion. And sometimes they would read quietly together and talk and at other times they would curse and shout and become physically violent.

And then he became possessed of *Da Shealladh,* the second sight. It seemed he did not want it and some said it came about because of too much reading of the books or perhaps it was inherited from his unknown father. Once he "saw" a storm on the evening of a day which was so calm that no one would believe him. When it came in the evening the boats could not get back and all the men were drowned. And once when he was away with the stallion, he "saw" his mother's house burn down, and when he returned he found that it had happened on the very night he saw it, and his mother was burned to death.

It became a weight upon him and he could not stop the visions or do anything to interfere with the events. One day after he and the woman had had too much to drink they went to visit a well-known clergyman. He told the clergyman he wanted the visions to stop but it did not seem within his power. He and the woman were sitting on two chairs beside each other. The clergyman went for the Bible and prayed over it and then he came and flicked the pages of the Bible before their eyes. He told them the visions would stop but that they would have to give up one another because they were causing a scandal in the community. The woman became enraged and leaped at the clergyman and tried to scratch out his eyes with her long nails. She accused *Mac an Amharuis* of deceiving her and said that he was willing to exchange their stormy relationship for his lack of vision. She spat in his face and cursed him and stormed out the door. *Mac an Amharuis* rose to follow her but the clergyman put his arms around him and wrestled him to the floor. He was far gone in drink and within the clergyman's power.

They stopped appearing with one another and *Mac an Amharuis* stopped travelling with the stallion and bought himself a boat. He began to visit the woman's younger sister, who was patient and kind. The woman moved out of her parents' house and into an older house nearer the shore. Some thought she moved because she could not stand *Mac an Amharuis* visiting her sister, and others thought that it was planned to allow him to visit her at night without anyone seeing.

Within two months *Mac an Amharuis* and the woman's sister were married. At the wedding the woman cursed the clergyman until he warned her to be careful and told her to leave the building. She cursed her sister, too, and said, "You will never be able to give him what I can." And as she was going out the door, she said to *Mac an Amharuis* either "I will never forgive you" or "I will never forget you." Her voice was charged with emotion but her back was turned to them and the people were uncertain whether it was a curse or a cry.

The woman did not come near anyone for a long time and people saw her only from a distance, moving about the house and the dilapidated barn, caring for the few animals which her father had given her, and muffled in clothes as autumn turned to winter. At night people watched for a light in her window. Sometimes they saw it and sometimes they did not.

And then one day her father came to the house of his daughter and *Mac an Amharuis* and said that he had not seen a light for three nights and he was worried. The three of them went to the house but it was cold. There was no heat when they put their hands on the stove and the glass of the windowpanes was covered with frost. There was nobody in any of the rooms.

They went out into the barn and found her lying in a heap. Most of the top part of her body was still covered by layers of clothes, although the lower part was not. She was unconscious or in something like a frozen coma and her eyes were inflamed, with beads of pus at their corners. She had given birth to twin girls and one of them was dead but the other somehow still alive, lying on her breast amidst her layers of clothing. Her father and *Mac an Amharuis* and her sister carried the living into the house and started a fire in the stove, and sent for the nearest medical attention, which was some miles away. Later they also carried in the body of the dead baby and placed it in a lobster crate, which was all that they could find. When the doctor came, he said he could not be certain of the baby's exact time of birth but he felt that it would live. He said that the mother had lost a great deal of blood and he thought she might have lacerated her eyes during the birth with her long fingernails and that infection had set in, caused perhaps by the unsanitary conditions within the barn. He was not sure if she would live and, if she did, he feared her sight would never be restored.

Mac an Amharuis and his wife cared for the baby throughout the days that the woman was unconscious, and the baby thrived. The woman herself began to rally and the first time she heard the baby cry she reached out instinctively for it but could not find it in the dark. Gradually, as she recognized by sound the people around her, she began to curse them and accused them of having sex when she could not see them. As she grew stronger, she became more resentful of their presence and finally asked them to leave. She began to rise from her bed and walk with her hands before her, sometimes during the day and sometimes during the night because it made no difference to her. And once they saw her with a knife in her hand. They left her then, as she had requested them to do and perhaps because they were afraid. And because there seemed no other choice, they took the baby with them.

They continued to bring her food and to leave it at the door of her porch. Sometimes she cursed at them but at other times she was quieter. One day while they were talking she extended her hand with the long fingernails to the face of *Mac an Amharuis*. She ran the balls of her fingers and the palm of her hand from his hair down over his eyes and nose and his lips and his chin and down along the buttons of his shirt and below his belt to between his legs; and then her hand closed for an instant and she grasped what she had held before but would never see again.

Mac an Amharuis and his wife had no children of their own. It was thought that it caused a great sadness within her and perhaps a tension because, as people said, "It's sure as hell not *his* fault." Their childlessness was thought also to prey on him and to lead to periodic drinking binges, although he never mentioned it to anyone. For the most part, they were helpful and supportive of each other and no one knew what they talked about when they were alone and together in their bed at night.

This, I guess, is my retelling of the story told by the young man of Canna to my father and his brother at a time when they were all young and on the verge of war. All of the information that spilled out of him came because it was there to be released and he was revealing more than he realized to his attentive listeners. The story was told in Gaelic, and as the people say, "It is not the same in English," although the images are true.

When the war was over, the generous young man from Canna was dead; and my father's brother had lost his leg.

My father returned to Kintail and the life that he had left, the boat and the nets and the lobster traps. All of them in the cycle of the seasons. He married before World War II; and when he was asked to go again, he went with the other Highlanders from Cape Breton, leaving his wife pregnant, perhaps without realizing it.

On the beach at Normandy they were emptied into ten feet of water as the rockets and shells exploded around them. And in the mud they fell face-down, leaving the imprints of their faces temporarily in the soil, before clawing their way some few feet forward. At the command they rose, as would a wave trying to break farther forward on the shore. And then all of it seemed to happen at once. Before my father's eyes there rose a wall of orange flame and a billowing wave of black smoke. It rose before him even as he felt the power of the strong hand upon his left shoulder. The grip was so powerful that he felt the imprint of the fingers almost as a bruise; and even as he turned his searing eyes, he fell back into his own language. *"Cò a th'ann?"* he said. *"Cò a th'ann?* Who's there?" And in the instant before his blindness, he recognized the long brown fingers on his shoulder with their pointed fingernails caked in dirt, *"'Se mi-fhìn"* she said quietly. "It is myself."

All of the soldiers in front of my father were killed and in the spot where he stood there was a crater, but this was told to him because he was unable ever to see it for himself.

Later he was told that on the day of his blinding, his grandfather, the man known to some as *Mac an Amharuis,* died. *Mac an Amharuis* was a man of over a hundred years at the time of his death and his eyes had become covered with the cataracts of age. He did not recognize, either by sight or sound, any of the people around him, and much of his talk was of youth and sex and of the splendid young stallion with the loose rope around its neck. And much of it was of the green island of Canna which he had never literally seen and of the people riding their horses at Michaelmas and carrying the bodies of their dead round toward the sun. And of the strong-willed St. Columba determined to be ascetic with his "back turned on Ireland" and the region of his early love. And of walls of flame and billowing smoke.

When I began this story I was recounting the story which my father told to me as he faced the green hills of Canna on the last day of the lobster season a long time ago. But when I look on it now I realize that all of it did not come from him, exactly as I have told it, on that day. The part about seeing his grandfather in the barn and much of the story of the young man from Canna came instead from his twin brother who participated in most of the events. Perhaps because of the loss of his leg, my father's brother became one of those veterans from World War I who spent a lot of their time in the Legion Hall. When he spoke to me he had none of the embarrassment which my father sometimes showed when discussing certain subjects. Perhaps my father, by omitting certain parts of his story, was merely repeating the custom of his parents who did not reveal to him at once everything there was to be shown.

But perhaps the story also went into me because of other events which happened on that day. After my father had finished, we started our engine and went into the wharf. By the time we arrived, the MacAllesters had gone and many of the other men as well. We hoisted the lobsters to the wharf's cap and I looked at the weight that the scales showed.

Whether the buyers noticed the concealed lobsters behind the crate we were never to know, but they said nothing. We unloaded our traps on the wharf and then climbed up the iron ladder and talked casually to the buyers and received our money. We planned to come back later for the lobsters behind the crate.

There were still other fishermen about and most of them shared my father's good mood because they were glad that the season had ended and pleased to have the money which was their final payment. Someone offered us a ride in a truck to the Legion and we went.

The Legion Hall was filled with men, most of them fishermen, and the noise was loud and the conversation boisterous. Toward the back of the hall I noticed Kenneth MacAllester with a number of his relatives. Both of us were underage but it did not matter a great deal. If you looked as if you were old enough, no one asked any questions. My father's brother and a number of our own relatives were at a table in the middle. They waved to us and I moved toward them. Behind me, my father followed, touching my belt from time to time for guidance. Most of the men pulled in their feet as we approached so that my father would not stumble. The crutch my uncle used in place of his missing leg was propped up across a chair and he removed it as we approached and leaned it against the table so that he could offer the chair to my father. We sat down and my uncle gave me some money to go to the bar for beer. Coming back, I passed another table of MacAllesters. They were relatives of our neighbours and although I recognized them I did not know them very well. One of them said something as I passed but I did not hear what he said and it seemed best not to stop. The afternoon grew more boisterous and bottles and glasses began to shatter on the cement floor, And then there was a shower of droplets over our head.

"What's that?" said my father.

Two of the MacAllesters from the table I had passed were throwing quarts of beer to their relatives at the back of the hall. They were standing up like quarterbacks and spiralling the open quarts off the palms of their hands and I saw Kenneth reach up and catch one as if he were a wide receiver. The quarts, for the most part, stayed upright; but as they revolved and spun, their foaming contents sprinkled or drenched those seated beneath them.

"Those bastards," said my uncle.

The two of them came over to the table. They were about thirty, and strong and heavily muscled.

"Who are you talking to?" one of them said.

"Never mind," said my uncle. "Go and sit down."

"I asked you a question," he said. And then turning to me he added, "I asked you a question before, too. What's the matter, can't some of you hear? I just thought that some of you couldn't see."

There was a silence then that began to spread to the neighbouring tables and the conversations slowed and the men took their hands off their bottles and their glasses.

"I asked you your age," he said, still looking at me. "Are you the oldest or the youngest?"

"He's the only one," said the other man. "Since the war, his father is so blind he can't find his way into his wife's cunt to make any more."

I remember my uncle reaching for the bottom of his crutch, and he swung it like a baseball bat from his sitting position. And I remember the way he planted his one leg onto the floor even as he swung. And I remember the crutch exploding into the nose and mouth of the man and his blood splashing down upon us and then the overturning of tables and chairs and the crashing of broken glass. And I remember also two of the MacAllesters who were our neighbours reaching our table with amazing speed. Each of them went to a side of my father's chair, and they lifted it up with him still sitting upon it. And they carried him as carefully as if he were eggs or perhaps an object of religious veneration, and the men who were smashing their fists into one another's mouths moved out of their way when they saw them coming. They deposited him with great gentleness against the far wall where they felt no harm could come to him, bending their knees in unison as they lowered his chair to the floor. And then each of them placed a hand upon his shoulder as one might comfort a frightened child. And then one of them picked up a chair and smashed it over the head of my cousin, who had his brother by the throat.

Someone grabbed me and spun me around but I could see by his eyes that he was intent on someone across the hall and that I was merely in his way. And then I saw Kenneth coming toward me, as I half expected him to. It was like the bench-clearing brawls at the hockey games when the goalies seek each other out because they have the most in common.

I saw him coming with his eyes intent upon me and because I knew him well I believed that he would leap from a spot about three strides ahead of him and that the force of his momentum would carry us backward and I would be on the bottom with my head on the cement floor. It all took perhaps a fraction of a second, his leap and my bending and moving forward and sideways, either to go toward him or to get out of the way, and my shoulder grazing his hip as he was airborne with his hands stretched out before him and his body parallel to the floor. He came crashing down on top of the table, knocking it over and forward and beneath him to the cement.

He lay face-down and still for a moment and I thought he was unconscious, and then I saw the blood spreading from beneath his face and reddening the shards of different-coloured glass.

"Are you all right?" I said, placing my hand upon his shoulder.

"It's okay," he said. "It's just my eye."

He sat up then with his hands over his face and the blood streaming down between his fingers. I was aware of a pair of rubber boots beside us, and then a man's voice. "Stop," he shouted to the brawling hall. "For Christ's sake, stop, someone's been hurt."

In retrospect, and even then, it seemed like a strange thing to say because when one looked at the bloodied men it seemed that almost everyone had been hurt in some way, although not to the same degree. But given the circumstances, he said exactly the right thing, and everyone stopped and unclenched his fist and released his grip on his opponent's throat.

In the rush to the doctor and to the hospital, everyone's original plans went awry. No one thought of the lobsters we had hidden and saved for our end-of-the-season feast; and when we discovered them days later, it was with something like surprise. They were dead and had to be thrown back into the sea, perhaps to serve as food for the spring mackerel with the scales upon their eyes.

That night two cars of MacAllesters came to our house. They told us that Kenneth's eye was lost; and Mr. MacAllester, who was about my father's age, began to cry. The two young men who were throwing the beer held their caps in their hands, and their knuckles were still raw and bleeding. Both of them apologized to my father. "We didn't see it getting that out of hand," one of them said. My uncle came in from another room and said that he shouldn't have swung the crutch.

Mr. MacAllester said that if my father would agree, all of us should stop using the fickle river as the boundary between our fishing grounds and take our sightings instead from the two rocky promontories on either side of the beach. One family would fish off the beach one year and the other the next. My father agreed. "I can't see the boundary anyway," he said with a smile. It all seemed so simple in hindsight.

This has been the telling of a story about a story but like most stories it has spun off into others and relied on others and perhaps no story ever really stands alone. This began as the story of two children who long ago went to visit their grandparents but who, because of circumstances, did not recognize them when they saw them. As their grandparents did not see them. And this is a story related by a man who is a descendant of those people. The son of a father who never saw his son but knew him only through sound or by the running of his fingers across the features of his face.

As I write this, my own small daughter comes in from kindergarten. She is at the age where each day she asks a riddle and I am not supposed to know the answer.

Today's question is, "What has eyes but cannot see?" Under the circumstances, the question seems overwhelmingly profound. "I don't know," I say and I feel I really mean it.

"A potato," she shouts and flings herself into my arms, elated and impressed by her own cleverness and by my lack of understanding.

She is the great-great-granddaughter of the blind woman who died in flames and of the man called *Mac an Amharuis;* and both of us, in spite of our age and comprehension, are indeed the children of uncertainty.

Most of the major characters in this story are, as the man called *Mac an Amharuis* once said of others, "all gone" in the literal sense. There remains only Kenneth MacAllester, who works as a janitor for a soap company in Toronto. Unable ever to join the Air Force and fly toward the sun and see over the tops of mountains and across the ocean because of what happened to his eye on that afternoon so long ago. Now he has an artificial eye and, as he says, "Only a few people know the difference."

When we were boys we would try to catch the slippery spring mackerel in our hands and look into the blindness of their eyes, hoping to see our own reflections. And when the wet ropes of the lobster traps came out of the sea, we would pick out a single strand and then try to identify it some few feet farther on. It was difficult to do because of the twisting and turning of the different strands within the rope. Difficult ever to be certain in our judgements or to fully see or understand. Difficult then to see and understand the twisted strands within the rope. And forever difficult to see and understand the tangled twisted strands of love.

Gussy and the Boss

SAM SELVON

THE ORGANIZATION known as Industrial Corporation was taken over shortly after the war by a group of European businessmen with interests in the West Indies, and renamed the New Enterprises Company, with a financial backing of £50,000. The new owners had the buildings renovated where they stood on the southern outskirts of Port of Spain, a short distance from the railway station.

While the buildings were being painted and the old office furniture replaced, none of the employees knew that the company had changed hands. They commented that it was high time the dilapidated offices were given a complete overhauling and they tried out the new chairs and desks and came to words over who should have the mahogany table and this cabinet and that typewriter.

When the buildings had a new face and they were just settling down with renewed ambitions and resolutions to keep the rooms as tidy as possible, Mr. Jones, the boss, called a staff meeting one evening and told them.

He said he was sorry he couldn't tell them before—some arrangement with the new owners—but that Industrial Corporation was going out of business. He said he had been hoping that at least part of the staff would be able to remain, but he was sorry, the matter was entirely out of his hands, and they all had to go.

There were ten natives working in the offices at the time, and there was a middle-aged caretaker called Gussy. Gussy had one leg. A shark had bitten off the other in the Gulf of Paria while he was out fishing with some friends.

The ten employees—four girl typists and six clerks—had never thought of joining a trade union, partly because they felt that trade unions were for the poor struggling labourers and they were not of that class, and partly because the thought had never entered their heads that such a situation might arise. As it was, they could do nothing but make vain threats and grumble; one chap went to a newspaper and told the editor the whole story and asked him to do something about it. The editor promised and next day a reporter interviewed Mr. Jones, and the following morning a small news item appeared saying that Industrial Corporation had been taken over by a group of wealthy Europeans, and that there was no doubt that the colony would benefit as a result, because new industries would be opened.

After two weeks the ten workers had cleared out leaving only Mr. Jones and Gussy. Gussy gathered his courage and spoke to Mr. Jones.

He said: "Boss, you know how long I here with the business. I is a poor man, boss, and I have a ailing mother to support, and I sure I can't get a work no where else. Please chief, you can't talk to the new bosses and them, and put in a good word for this poor one-legged man, and ask them to keep me? I ain't have a big work, is just to stay in the back of the place and see that nobody interfere with anything. Make a try for me please, pusher, the Good Lord will reward you in due course, and I would appreciate it very much."

Mr. Jones heard Gussy mumble through this long speech and he promised to see what he could do, grateful that the caretaker had given him the opportunity to make peace in his own mind, thinking that Gussy's salvation would absolve him from responsibility for the sacking of the others.

A week later the new staff arrived. Gussy hid behind a door in the storeroom and peeped between a crack because he was afraid to face all the new people at once. His agitation increased greatly as he saw that they were all white people. Were they all bosses then? The women too?

Later in the morning, while he was sweeping out the storeroom as noiselessly as possible, one of the new employees came to him.

"You're Gussy, the caretaker?" he asked in a kind voice.

Gussy dropped the broom and shoved his crutch under his arm quickly, standing up like a soldier at attention.

"Yes boss, I is the caretaker."

"Mr. Blade would like a word with you. He is the new manager, as you probably know."

"What about, sir? My job is the caretaker job. My name is Gussy. I lives in Belmont. Age forty-five. No children. I lives with my mother. I gets pay every Friday …"

"I know all that," the young man smiled a little. "I am in charge of the staff we have here now. But Mr. Blade wants to see you. Just for a little chat, he likes to be personally acquainted with everyone who works for him."

Gussy's eyes opened wide and showed white. "So I still have the job, chief? You all not going to fire me?"

"Of course not! Come along, Mr. Blade is a busy man."

When he returned to his post at the back of the building a few minutes later Gussy was full of praise for the new boss, mumbling to himself because there was no one to talk with. When he went home in the evening he told his mother:

"You can't imagine! He is a nice man, he even nicer than Mr. Jones! He tell me is all right, that I could stay on the job as the caretaker, being as I was here so long already. When I tell you the man nice."

But as the days went by Gussy wasn't happy at his job anymore. He couldn't get accustomed to the idea that white people were working all around him. He treated every one as he treated Mr. Blade, stumping along as swiftly as he could to open the garage door or fill the water cooler or do whatever odd chore he was called upon to perform. In the old days he was in the habit of popping in and out of the outer office, sharing a word here and a joke there with the native workers. But now he kept strictly to the back of the building, turning out an hour earlier to clean out the offices before any of the staff arrived. True, they treated him friendly, but Gussy couldn't get rid of the idea that they were all bosses.

After a week of loneliness he ventured near to the office door and peeped inside to see how the white people were working.

The young man who had spoken to him the first day, Mr. Garry, saw him and called him inside.

Gussy stumped over to his desk with excuses.

"I was only looking to see if everything all right, boss, to see if anybody want anything, the weather hot, I could go and get some ice outside for you right now …"

Garry said: "It's all right, Gussy, and I don't mind you coming to the office now and then." He lowered his voice. "But you watch out for the boss's wife. Sometimes she drops in unexpectedly to see him, and it wouldn't do for her to see you out here, because ... well, because here is not the place you're supposed to be, you understand?"

"But sure boss, Mr. Garry, I won't come back here again, not at all at all unless you send for me, I promise you that boss, sure, sure ...

Whenever Mr. Blade drove up in his Buick Eight, Gussy was there with a rag to wipe the car.

"You know, Gussy," Mr. Blade told him one morning, "you manage to do more with that one leg of yours than many a normal man I know."

"Thank you very much respectfully and gratefully, boss sir, all the offices clean, the water cooler full up, all the ink pots full up, the storeroom pack away just as Mr. Garry want it ..."

One evening when he had opened the garage door for the boss and he was reversing out—with Gussy standing at the back and giving all sorts of superfluous directions with his crutch which Mr. Blade ignored—the boss looked out of the car window and said:

"By the way, Gussy, how much do you work for?"

"Ten dollars a week chief sir, respectfully, it not very much, with me minding my poor mother, but is enough, sir, I can even manage on less than that if you feel that it too much ..."

"I was thinking of giving you more, what with the rising cost of living. Let me see, today is Wednesday. Come to see me on Friday morning and we'll talk about it."

Mr. Blade drove off with Gussy's effusive thanks just warming up.

The next afternoon was hot, and Gussy was feeling drowsy as he sat on a soapbox in the storeroom. He felt a strong temptation to go and stand near the office door. The knowledge that he was soon going to earn a bigger salary gave him courage. He got up and went and positioned himself just outside the door.

He was just in time to hear Mr. Garry telling the others about how his plane was shot down during the war, and Gussy listened wide-eyed.

Gussy heard a step behind him and turned around. He didn't know it was the boss's wife, but it wouldn't have made any difference, he would have behaved the same way with any white person.

"Just looking in to see if the bosses and them want anything at all no offence madam indeed ..."

This time he dropped the crutch in his consternation.

The woman gave him a withering look and swept past the outer office.

Mr. Blade was sitting in his swivel chair, facing the sea. It was a hot afternoon and he had the window fully opened, but the wind that came in was heavy and lifeless, as if the heat had taken all the spirit out of it.

Mr. Blade was a kindly man newly arrived in the colony from England. He was also a weak man, and he knew it. Sometimes Blade was afraid of life because he was weak and couldn't make decisions or face up to facts and circumstances. The palms of his hands were always wet when he was excited or couldn't find the answer to a problem.

As he sat and watched the sea sparkle, he was thinking in a general sort of way about his life, and when his wife burst into the office he started.

"Oh hello, dear, didn't expect to see you today."

Whenever Blade looked at his wife he saw the symbol of his weakness. All his faults were magnified and concentrated on her face, which was like a mirror in which he looked and shrank.

"Herbert." She also had a most disquieting habit of getting to the point right away. "I thought you had dismissed all the natives who were here before we came?"

"Of course, dear. As you can see, we only have Europeans and one or two whites who were born in the island."

"I met a dirty one-legged man outside the office just as I was coming in—who's he?"

"Oh heavens, he's only the caretaker! Surely you didn't think he was on the staff?" Blade shifted his eyes and looked at an almanac on the wall above his wife's head.

"You'll have to get rid of him, you know."

When she finished speaking, he knew that those last words would stay long after she left, from the tone in which she spoke. All their conversations were like that—everything else forgotten but the few words she spoke in that tone. He had gotten into the habit of listening for it. She had a special way of summing up, of finalizing matters. He knew, from that moment—in a quick panic of fear which brought the sweat out on his palms—that the caretaker would have to go.

"Let's don't argue about it now, dear. I don't feel very well in this damned heat."

And the next morning Blade sat down in the swivel chair and he faced the sea again. He knew he was going to fire Gussy, but he tried to think that he wasn't. He wiped the palms of his hands with a white handkerchief. All his life it had been like that; he felt the old fear of uncertainty and instability which had driven him from England return, and he licked his lips nervously.

He swung the chair and looked at the almanac on the wall. He addressed it as if it were his wife.

"That's a silly attitude to adopt," he said to the almanac in a firm voice. "You can't do that sort of thing. On the contrary, it is a good prestige for the place that we have a coloured worker. I think we should have more—after all, they do the work just as well."

He sneered at the almanac, then looked for some other object in the room to represent Gussy. He fixed his eyes on the out-basket on his desk.

"The way how things are at present," he told the basket, "I'm afraid you'll have to go. We don't really need a caretaker any more, and we can always get a woman to come in and clean the offices. I personally didn't have anything to do with it, mind you, it was … er, the decision of the directors. I am sorry to lose you, Gussy, you are a hard, honest worker."

For a minute Blade wondered if there wasn't something he could do—post money secretly to the man every week, or maybe give him a tidy sum to tide him over for a few months.

The next minute he was laughing mirthlessly—once the handkerchief fell and he unconsciously rubbed his hands together and he heard the squelching sound made by the perspiration. And he talked and reasoned with all the objects in the room, as if they were companions, and some objects agreed and others didn't.

The pencil and the ink pot said it was all right, he was a fool to worry, why didn't he get Garry to do the dirty work, and the almanac told him to get it over with quickly for Christ's sake, but the window and the wall and the telephone said Gussy was a poor, harmless creature and he Blade was a spineless, unprincipled dog, who didn't know his own mind and wasn't fit to live.

With an impatient, indecisive gesture Blade jabbed the button on his desk. One of the girls opened the door.

"That caretaker we have—what is his name—Gusher or Gully or something like that"—the lie in his deliberate lapse of memory stabbed him—"send him in to see me, will you, please."

Gussy was waiting to be called. He had told Mr. Garry how the boss would be wanting to see him, and that was why he was keeping so near to the office, so they wouldn't have any trouble finding him.

Gussy didn't have any idea how much more money he was going to get, but whatever it was, first thing he was going to do was buy a bottle of polish and shine down the boss's car to surprise him. After that, anything could happen.

He stood in a corner, quietly calculating on his fingers how much he would have to pay if he wanted to put down three months' rent in advance.

"Oh, there you are, Gussy," the girl caught sight of him as she came out. "Mr. Blade wants to see you. You'd better go in right away."

"Thank you madam, I am right here, going in to see the boss right away, with all due respects, no delay at all."

Gussy shoved his crutch under his armpit and stumped as softly as he could to the boss's door.

The Professor's History

CLAIRE MESSUD

THE PROFESSOR wiped his forehead with his handkerchief, and then took off his glasses and wiped them too, fussing over their wire arms and squinting in the vast light. The train spat clouds of grit and steam as it hauled itself back into motion and off, towards the naked mountains.

Around him, there was no station to speak of, just an empty shack with no door, and a jarring French railroad sign pinned to the wall, its fancy blue letters neatly, but dustily, announcing CASSAIGNE.

The professor—a slight, weathered man in his mid-forties, with a small forehead and a Gallic profile, carefully attired in a cream linen suit with a crisp straw hat—was not a man to look absurd: even alone, at the side of the endless ladder of the track, in the middle of the scrubby foothills, he managed to retain some of his composure. When he saw, in the distance, a man swaddled in a burnous, he did not call out. As befit a Frenchman, and especially a Frenchman so long in Algeria, he waited. The Arab made his way, unhurried, towards him.

Their exchange was terse, conducted in a pidgin that allowed each the room of his own language—for the words that mattered most. The professor was headed to Necmaria, a village in the foothills of the Dahra, midway between Algiers and Oran. He needed food, a couple of mules and a guide. It would be possible, said the local man, but would involve waiting, and leaving at dawn, aiming to traverse the fifty or so kilometres in a single, exhausting day. The man would not go himself, but his brother, who possessed two mules, could perhaps lead the expedition. They would take the man's son, a boy of about fifteen: there was strength in numbers. Tomorrow was possible. Tomorrow it would be. The professor could sleep the night with the brother's family—theirs was a larger house, the provision more adequate for a foreigner.

The Arab did not ask, then, by the train tracks, why the professor wanted to go to Necmaria. He thought he knew. It was an uncomfortable history between them, Arab and Frenchman, better not made explicit. Both were aware that the only reason for a Frenchman to travel to Necmaria was to see the caves of Dahra. A history better left buried.

In fact, the professor was working on a book. A strange thing to do, in the mountains of North Africa, in the middle of a war, when metropolitan France teetered (the line was so close to Paris that the troops were sent to the front in taxis), and all Europe was confusion and fear. The professor should not, for so many reasons, have been pursuing these stories, ugly and old as they were. If anything, he knew it was a time to be looking forward, beyond the war. He was driven, though, by something he had read, a sentence in the letters of a colonel. Bent over yellowing pages in the city library, intent upon his research, he had unearthed the letters of St. Arnaud, and with them the promise, or threat, of historical discovery: an act, an immense act, had passed unrecorded. A glimmer in a dusty corner, it drew him back, and back, and then, eventually, out of the city library and out of the city itself. Silently, the professor had grown convinced that this history was relevant—or even, when the glimmer was at its most insistent, crucial—to the current conflict. He carried the leather-bound volume of letters with him at all times, like a prayer-book. But he knew enough not to discuss his work with anyone.

Mustafa, the local man's brother, was not as restrained as his sibling. That evening, as they sat down to supper by the quivering fire, beneath a candy-coloured mackerel dusk, Mustafa asked why. He was entitled: they were his mules, and he was to lead them. But the question brought, nonetheless, a silence in which only the bleating of goats and the sharp reports of the burning kindling gave answer.

"I have business with the *caid*," answered the professor at last. He mopped at his stew with grave concentration and chewed on his bread. The firelight was reflected in his glasses, and the other men could not see his eyes.

"What business would that be?" asked Mustafa, playing his fingers in his beard. "He is not—may Allah forgive me if I am mistaken—not a man of any importance to your government."

"I am not a government official," said the professor, suddenly weary. "I am a historian. I record history."

"The caves," said Ibrahim, Mustafa's nephew, only now understanding. "You wish to visit the caves of Dahra."

The professor would neither confirm nor deny it, and Mustafa and Ibrahim knew it was so.

"Will you want us to stay, while you do your business?" asked Mustafa. "Or will you not be coming back to Cassaigne?"

The professor looked up, seemingly surprised that the wash of night had closed in around them, carried on the waves of chill air. "I don't know," he said. "I will decide tomorrow."

The professor did not sleep well. He felt oppressed by the secret music of other people's slumber—these exhalations and whisperings somehow more alien for being Muslim—and the earthen floor of the house poked bony and cold into his spine. Although very tired, or perhaps because of it, he found his mind restless, his imagination conjuring scenarios he could not wish to contemplate. It occurred to him that he did not know what tribe his hosts belonged to; nor did he know how long they had been settled in Cassaigne or, indeed, been settled at all. He did not know what to expect of Necmaria; nor could he gauge the relationship between Mustafa's people and those of that village. And where might the allegiances of the people of Rabelais fall?

The professor, in following the account in the colonel's letter, proposed to move onwards from Necmaria to Rabelais, a distance of a further hundred kilometres. There were caves near Rabelais also, and although their name—the caves of Sbéhas—did not carry the same weight of dread as did that of Necmaria, it soon would, if the colonel had written truthfully, and if the professor was to convey that truth to the world. In both cases, Necmaria and Rabelais, the story of the caves was not only a tale of Europeans and the natives: there were tribal tales, too, of betrayal and unsavoury rewards. The professor did not know enough. As he sought to align his limbs to the ungenerous curve of the ground, as he drew his coarse blanket closer around him and inhaled its greasy stink, he recognized that he did not know the full meaning or consequences of his work, that he was a learned man who knew nothing outside the walls of the city library. For a long time he lay, cold and sweating in his papoose, eyes open to the blackness, watching without seeing and measuring the darkness.

THE JOURNEY WAS LONG. Wakened before dawn by the call of the village *muezzin,* the professor performed his ablutions separately from the Muslims and busied himself with his notebooks while they prayed. In the city, despite the subjects of his research, he was conscious of these rituals only as a charming Oriental flavour to his adopted land. He found it at once embarrassing and miraculous to be at their centre, among the men and their families and their prayers in a guttural language, as if he had stumbled upon a naked woman for the first time and could not define his response to her shimmering flesh.

The mules were loaded as the sun rose. The professor was to sit upon one, while the other bore his case and the supplies. He was surprised at the pace set by Mustafa and Ibrahim, who walked behind and flicked, intermittently, at the baggage mule with a switch. There was no sound but this, their steps and the ticking of insects. None of them spoke. The route they followed was along the foothills, the mountains rising always alongside them. The terrain, although unsteady and, for the professor—whose back ached already from the night before—uncomfortable, was not difficult. The mules were dogged and unfaltering in their progress, but Mustafa and Ibrahim seemed to find them too slow. They yelled at the blinking beasts, who merely flicked their ears and did not change their pace. In the course of the day, the troupe paused only for prayers and a hasty *casse-croute,* consumed in the paltry shade of a wild-limbed shrub.

Twilight hovered as they glimpsed the cluster of houses that was Necmaria. In the gloom, the red dirt walls of the habitation glowed like embers. The professor's eyes were heavy-lidded, his glasses, unwiped, so smeared with dust that he could barely see. But the proximity of rest, of the long-imagined destination, revived him, and he straightened his frame as best he could. He made an unspoken effort to reassert his European authority, remembering that he commanded the two Arabs and not they him, a fact which their progress had served to deny. But it was Mustafa who approached the first fire they came upon and asked for the *caid's* house; and Ibrahim who helped the professor, bent to the shape of his mule, to dismount.

In so small a village, the *caid's* house was not difficult to find. Two storeys high, it loomed over the others, its heavy wooden doors studded and bolted to the street, and the high slivers in the walls that were its windows unlit.

Mustafa and Ibrahim had called four times before they heard the bolts shifting angrily on the far side of the door. It opened just a little, revealing a boy younger than Ibrahim, unbearded, bearing a torch. Alarmed, he proceeded anyway with the formal greetings in a tremulous tone.

"We wish to see the *caid*," explained Mustafa. "This man has business with the *caid*."

The professor stepped forward, into the pool of light. He spoke in French, and the boy did not understand. He tried again, his Arabic slow and careful. "I am a historian. I am here to discuss history with the *caid*."

"The *caid* is not here," said the boy. "He is from home on a journey of some weeks. His steward, my father, is with him. You are welcome, but I can offer you little." He opened the door wide to the gloomy passage, at the end of which spread the courtyard, where a small fire was visible. "Come in."

Ibrahim handed the professor his case, and the two men from Cassaigne made as if to withdraw. The professor was suddenly uneasy: he had not expected to be in the hands of a child, and he feared both that the expedition would prove fruitless, and that he would not find a way back from Necmaria. The city seemed very far away, and his worth in this bare world slight. Elsewhere, he remembered, there was war.

Mustafa sensed his confusion, and for a moment drew close enough to touch him. "We will sleep by the first fire, on the edge of the village. If you need me, send the boy." Then they were gone.

"Who remains, in the absence of the *caid*?" asked the professor, as the youth slid the iron bolts between them and the street.

"I do." The boy coughed. "My name is Menouira." The cough was an ellipsis that the professor understood: now within the walls he could hear the sounds of living, the muffled ring of voices and occasional laughter. The women—the *caid's* wife, perhaps, and daughters; the boy's mother; the servant girls—were in residence, but the professor would not see them.

The courtyard was encircled by arcades, and a dead fountain squatted at its centre, a mosaic trough that shone dry beneath the stars. There were doorways in the cloistered corridors, but all were shut. The boy stoked the fire and crouched down beside it.

"This is a house with many rooms," he said, "but I fear you will have to sleep by the fire with me. The *caid*, in his wisdom, does not leave me the keys. I cannot open any of the doors."

Even Menouira's food, it transpired, came not from the house stores but from his cousins in the village. The women were locked in their quarters like penned sheep, with food and water and lamplight enough for the duration of the *caid*'s absence.

"But what if something should delay his return?" asked the professor, amazed, picking at his meagre half of Menouira's supper and thinking of Mustafa and Ibrahim, warm and plentifully fed, on the edge of the village. "Surely this is a dangerous way for the *caid* to leave his affairs?"

The boy's face registered nothing. "The *caid*, in his wisdom ...," he began again. There was a circle of laughter in the walls, as if the women had heard and made mock.

"What sort of man is the *caid*?" the professor asked.

"He is a very learned man. A wealthy man. A just man."

"Of what age?"

"His beard is white, but he is not so old."

"And did he build this house?"

"His grandfather built this house."

"And his grandfather also owned the land?"

"He was given the land," said the boy, "by your government. By the government of France. It is a line of *caids*, always on good terms with the French. The land belongs to him on all sides, as far as you can see on a bright day."

"And can you see to the cave—the cave of the Ouled Riah, in the Dahra?" asked the professor.

Menouira was suddenly wary. "You can see to the cave, although you cannot distinguish it from here," he said, and was quiet.

"Were the *caid*'s people in the cave?" persisted the Frenchman, knowing the answer was everything.

"No," said the boy, sullen now. "The Ouled Riah are not the *caid*'s people."

"And the people of Necmaria?" continued the professor.

"They are of the Ouled Riah, perhaps half of them."

"And yourself?"

"My mother's family, yes. But not my father. Nor I." The boy poked angrily at the flames with a stick, and turned his body sideways.

This was the story of the caves of Dahra, as the professor knew it: on 19 June 1845, around a thousand people—men, women and children—concealed themselves from the French troops in the cave, along with their animals and belongings.

It was a cave the Ouled Riah had used for generations, father to son: a resting place, a hiding place.

The times, a mere fifteen years since the end of the nation's occupation by the Turks, were uncertain; and the French were as jumpy as the tribes were hostile. The Maréchal Pelissier—a brutal, straightforward, awkward man—found that his men, on approaching the refuge, were fired upon by the Ouled Riah. And in his anger, Pelissier ordered that the entrance to their hideout be blocked by fire, and burning torches thrown inside.

The troops stood by in the moonlight, while the screams of the families and animals echoed in the caverns like the laughter of the *caid*'s womenfolk in the house walls, and the rocks burst in the heat. For a long time, they did nothing. At dawn, as the anguish abated, Pelissier deemed his military goal accomplished. The soldiers—not hastily—doused the conflagration and removed the debris from the mouth of the cave. Under Pelissier's orders, the men then helped the choking survivors to safety, a mere hundred or so, those who had lain closest to the ground and hoarded the air from the dying. Their skin was blackened with smoke, and their eyes were streaming, their wails of mourning trapped in their lungs for lack of oxygen. Battered and humbled, these survivors stayed in Necmaria, making their lives in the shadow of their deaths, bearing their children before the monument of their holocaust.

The caves harboured another story too: Pelissier and his men had been seeking the tribe of the Ouled Riah, to conquer and adopt them in the name of France. But they could not discover their encampment. Nor would they have, not knowing about the existence of the cave, which was as well hidden as that of the Forty Thieves. But Pelissier unearthed, in the form of the *khalifa* of another tribe, his open Sesame. Feuding with the Ouled Riah, this *khalifa* cleaved to the French. He clearly explained the location of the hiding place (this knowledge had been passed on, father to son, for generations); and when the troops still could not find it, the *khalifa* dispatched his attendants. These loyal men revealed the cave to Pelissier and his battalion, leading them to it from above so that they could approach undisclosed.

The *khalifa* was well rewarded for his pains: he was named *caid* of Necmaria, and given the land around the village as far as the eye could see, for his own benefit and that of his descendants. A stone's throw from the site of his treachery, the *caid* raised his family in prosperity and ease, in the warmth of the French embrace; he ruled, and his offspring ruled, over the tattered remnants of his enemies.

"Will you take me to the cave tomorrow?" asked the professor.

"If you wish." Menouira did not look at him: he was pacing the arcades in search of an extra blanket for the professor. As he handed it to him, he said: "You are the first Frenchman in my lifetime to want to visit the cave. You shouldn't have come. It is better left buried."

The women's laughter carilloned in the walls.

IN THE MORNING, Menouira and the professor breakfasted with Menouira's relatives in the village. Under the clear sky, the professor could see the land dropping away on the far side of the *caid*'s house, an immense, roseate plain dotted with trees, and sheep and goats, and the hillside nubbed by the early shoots of crops, patterns of green in the red earth. The glistening mirror of Oued Zerifa zigzagged its way across the land. The *caid*'s triumph was glorious.

Mustafa and Ibrahim found him there.

"What of your business?" asked Mustafa in a voice that seemed to the Frenchman no longer friendly, but sneering. "Will you go to the cave without the *caid*?"

"I intend to."

"It is perhaps better that the *caid* is absent," Mustafa continued. "These, my brothers, are the people to whom the tragedy belongs. It is their place." He smiled, and Menouira and the others smiled also, as if this were a happy fact. "And will you return to Cassaigne? We shall wait."

The professor hesitated. "I would like to go on tomorrow," he said. "I hoped to go on to Rabelais." He paused. "Will you take me there?"

The group fell silent.

"I have important business in Rabelais," he insisted. "If you will not take me, perhaps someone else?"

"It is two days' journey. Why did you not tell me before?" asked Mustafa. "We would need another mule. We would need food."

"This could be arranged," said another man. "If you so wish it."

"In Europe, there is a war," said the professor, as if this were an explanation. "I must get to Rabelais. It is important."

"We will take you," said Mustafa.

"I will rent you a mule," said Menouira's cousin.

"I can provide food," said another. And the deal was struck.

Menouira and the professor set off to the cave near noon. The entrance itself was invisible from Necmaria, hidden among a cluster of coppery boulders. The path Menouira took, along the ridge of the slight escarpment, snaked outwards in an "s" from the village, dipped only to the *oued*, which they crossed on stepping stones, and rose again to bring the pair to their destination from above, just as Pelissier had been brought. The descent to the mouth was awkward: twice the professor slid, the second time scraping his hands as he fell, knocking his glasses from his nose. Menouira retrieved them and attempted to brush the red earth from the professor's sullied suit, to no avail. The dirt clung in the creases of the fabric like streaks of dried blood.

The professor, in his research, had not been able to picture the cave. He had not realized that a small stream would trickle so carelessly into its mouth; nor that the overhanging rocks would reach so ominously downwards, their tentacles like pointing fingers; nor that the breadth of the coloured plain would lie, like an invitation and a promise, at his feet.

When they entered it, the cave was not what the professor had, till now, understood by the word: strictly speaking a riverbed, it was comprised of a single gallery through the rock, without branches or smaller tributaries, wavering only slightly in its downward course. The *oued*, once underground, became a floor of muck rather than a river. The walls sweated, dripped their moisture like irregular footfalls into the mud. As Menouira led the way, the professor realized that the cave did not open out into any chamber, and at times, his elbows, outstretched, measured its width. There were moments when the torch-smoke wavered upwards into the darkness without illuminating any ceiling, so high was the gallery; at other points, Menouira's arm would reach backwards to him, urging his body into a stoop, as the passage dwindled to less than a metre tall. Throughout, their little light cast fantastic shadows, as of contorted figures beckoning along the wet walls, made surprisingly pale and uneven by accretions of guano. Hollow recesses offered the only variation: some high, others at the level of the men's knees; some rounded, as if sanded by craftsmen, others jagged enough to cut.

The professor stopped, after a time, and watched Menouira's torch diminish in front of him. He turned a full circle, breathing deeply. He fought the pressure of his heart in the cave of his ribs, the force of history like a life around him. A thousand men, women and children, with their animals and belongings, peopled the space: hunched in crevices, pressed against the moist walls, their cheeks to the cold stone, their buttocks and arms and feet meeting in the subterranean night. The animals lowed, the young women nursed their infants, soothing them with rhythmic words, clucking at the children who clung to their legs, up to their ankles in mud. There was no place to lie, no square metre any of these ghosts could claim for their own, huddled against one another and their beasts, cramped and stinking, giving off a sour heat. He heard the still waiting; sensed the cramping of muscles, the wriggling, weary children; shuddered at the dim whine of the sick and injured. And then the smoke, filtering slowly, then more rapidly along the gallery, cloudy whorls spiralling up to the invisible ceiling and drifting slowly back downwards, great bowls of smoke wafting into the minute spaces between the living beings.

"Menouira," the professor called sharply, focusing again on the now-distant button of light, "*Ça suffit*. Enough."

On the walk back, too, Menouira led the way. The distance which had seemed so great was now a matter of a hundred metres, the surprised O of the sky widening with each step.

Nor far from the exit, the professor stumbled over something. He reached down and pulled up a long, narrow object, slimed with mud. Menouira held the torch beside him, and he did his best to wipe the thing clean, but he knew before he had exposed its ivory cast, before even it saw the light, that he held a bone.

"I believe," he said, handing it to Menouira for inspection, "that this is a human femur."

Menouira took the bone and turned it in his hand. Without a word, he raised his arm and hurled it back into the darkness, where they heard its dull clatter against the wall of the cave, and the sucking thud as it settled back into the *oued*.

Only when the afternoon breeze swept upon his face and dried his tears did the professor realize that he had been crying.

PROGRESS WITH THREE MULES proved slower than with two, and the professor's crossing to Rabelais came to seem interminable. Hour after hour, the animal beneath him jangled his limbs and assaulted his spine, kicking up dust until his suit was wholly pink.

Ibrahim no longer waved his switch at the mules: he kept his eyes to the ground which, as they climbed higher, grew more unyielding. Mustafa strode several paces ahead, eyeing the landscape warily, scanning the horizon and the hills for movement. When they stopped, the two men from Cassaigne did not smile and made no attempt to converse with the professor. They spoke quietly to each other, almost furtively, and they ate their meals with their bodies hunched over upon themselves.

The professor was made nervous, but did not show it. Self-control was, he knew, the source of authority. But sometimes, as they jolted forwards, his stomach would leap. He wondered if uncle and nephew planned to murder him in the mountain pass, to abandon his corpse to the hyenas, and to return, in haste and with their extra mule, to Cassaigne. The Oriental character, he knew from his research—and from his experience with Menouira in the cave—was alien to his own. The compassion, the civilized impulse, was not there. Menouira had walked the length of the sepulchre where his ancestors had been massacred, and felt nothing. The Ouled Riah could live without revulsion under the rule of the *caïd*. What, to such people, was the life of the professor? They did not see the necessity of his work: history, too, meant nothing to them.

When they stopped to camp for the night, by the edge of an *oued* between two crests, the professor withdrew from the fire, and unbuckled his case. He took from it, surreptitiously, the wallet that held his money, and stuffed it against his belly, beneath his shirt, tucked into the waistband of his trousers. In this way he felt protected, somewhat, from the danger he imagined he now saw in Mustafa's gaze, in the way his delicate fingers plucked at his beard.

In the night, the professor woke to see Mustafa still seated by the fire, watching him and smoking. Conjuring a flicker of menace in the Arab's eye, he felt for the wallet, his wealth resting, like his name, against him.

"Do you not sleep?" he asked, in Arabic.

"I will sleep tomorrow night," said Mustafa. "When we reach Rabelais."

The professor closed his eyes again, and dreamt of his own murder.

RABELAIS WAS A LARGER TOWN, and merited a French administrator, who welcomed his bedraggled compatriot with enthusiasm. He was a tall, square man with a round, lined face, and he clapped the professor on the back, causing small puffs of coloured dust to whisk about them. Ushering him into the tiled domain, he offered him a bed and a hot bath, and hospitality for as long as the professor cared to stay. He also offered a cigar, which the professor smoked luxuriantly, seated, filthy as he was, in a soft chair in the administrator's office.

Through the window, he could see Mustafa and Ibrahim watering their animals at the fountain in the cobbled square, waiting for his instructions. The professor was overcome by annoyance at the two men from Cassaigne whom he believed had cast such doubt on his mission. Their busied forms were reproachful, and he wanted them gone.

He excused himself from the administrator's office and, cigar in hand, called to Mustafa from the steps of the government building. The French flag snapped and billowed above his head. Pulling the wallet at last from his belt, he counted out half again as much as they had agreed, a thick wad of notes, and pronounced them free to go. He was not a man to feel absurd, and it did not occur to him that he looked odd, beneath the flag, his clothes grimy, his glasses slightly askew; nor that it was strange to grant freedom to two free men.

"I wish you a safe journey," he offered, magnanimous.

"Inch'allah," murmured uncle and nephew in unison.

"We wish you luck with your history," called Mustafa, as the two men turned towards the narrow Arab streets at the edge of the square. The professor could have sworn he caught a smile quivering, insolent, in the Arab's beard.

The administrator, although he had been a decade in Rabelais, had no knowledge of the caves of the Sbéhas. He had not visited them, and showed only a bemused interest.

"I think you are mistaken," he repeated several times. "The *enfumade*—a great tragedy—befell the Ouled Riah, near Necmaria. That is the cave you should visit. Not that there could be anything particular to see."

"I have been to Necmaria. I've just come from there. I want to see the caves of the Sbéhas. Was the then Colonel Saint-Arnaud not stationed near here in forty-five?"

"Perhaps," said the administrator. He offered his guest another glass of local wine, holding his ruby glass to the light. "You might think it was from home, no? The viticulture is improving so rapidly."

He, too, to the professor's irritation, saw little point in the expedition. "Even if there was such an incident, it is best forgotten, surely?" he asked with a smile, his lips disappearing among the lines of his face. "Who wants to remember? In France, there is a war on: morale is of the essence. Who could wish to know about such a disgrace? These things are accidents of war; and our attention must be on the accidents at hand. I hear they are sending our boys to the front in taxis. May God save Paris from the Boche! Persistent buggers. Uncivilized."

Washed and changed, the professor became again his unflappable, urbane self. He sat in the comfort of the administrator's drawing-room, his head against an anti-macassar crocheted by Monsieur's charming wife. He opened the Colonel's letters, a leatherbound volume that he had carried with him from the city, all that way, and in which he had marked the relevant pages. He read again the correspondence from Saint-Arnaud to his brother, dated 15 August, 1845:

> The same day, the 8th, I sent a reconnaissance to the grottos, or rather, caverns. We were met by gunfire, and I was so surprised that I respectfully saluted several shots, which is not my habit. The same evening, the 53rd came under enemy fire, one man wounded, measures well taken. The 9th, the beginnings of the work of siege: blocus, mines, grenades, summations, instances, entreaties that they should emerge and surrender. Answer: insults, blasphemies, shots fired. 10th, 11th, more of the same. So, on the 12th, I had all the exits hermetically sealed, and I made of the cave a vast cemetery. The earth will cover forever the corpses of these fanatics. Nobody went into the caves— no one … only I know that interred therein are 500 brigands who will no longer slit French throats. A confidential report told the commander-in-chief everything, simply, without terrible poetry and without descriptions.
>
> Brother, nobody is good by taste and nature as I am. From the 8th to the 12th I was sickened, but I have a clear conscience. I did my duty as a leader, and tomorrow I will begin again. But I have taken Africa in disgust—and am taken with disgust for Africa.

The professor closed the book and wiped his glasses. He had found no record anywhere of the confidential report, and no mention was made of the event in histories of the campaign. But the professor believed. He closed his eyes and smelt again the cave at Necmaria, the air of death, and he was certain that Saint-Arnaud had not lied to his brother. The secrecy had been his military triumph: the deaths, expedient, had furthered the battle, and the dead could not speak.

"Perhaps I could speak to the locals?" he suggested over supper, served at the administrator's oval dining table, brought by boat and train from France and carrying with it the heavy smell of French polish.

"Perhaps," said the administrator's wife, who spoke little and, when she did, waved her plump, pale hands like mittens in the air. "Perhaps the professor should consult our hermit."

The administrator emitted a jolly snort and slapped the professor's forearm on the table. "Naim will take you to the hermit. If you find nothing else, he, at least, will provide a subject for study."

"What sort of hermit is he?" asked the professor, gingerly retrieving his arm from the administrator's grasp.

"Up in the hills," said the wife, "we have a hermit. A count, no less, and a very extraordinary man. He has wandered the desert for—how long, *mon cher*?"

"Decades." The administrator gulped his wine. "He is, indeed, a man of God, ordained by ... I forget by whom. But our church doesn't seem to be a priority. He doesn't preach, or even venture very often into Rabelais. He seems to prefer the company of natives, although I don't believe he has any intention of converting them. He has been known to deliver the Muslim prayers for the dying when the need arises. A sideline as an *imam,* if you like."

"I like him," said the wife. "He's a gentle man, and has taken the time to listen to these miserable people. They trust him. Whereas with us"—she fluttered her hands, a glinting implement in each this time—"Who can say? I don't like to be here when my husband goes away, because their faces ... their eyes ... you do not know."

"They carry the history we have forgotten," said the professor. "Our beginnings here were brutal."

"They have no interest in history," said the administrator. "The past to them is like their soil in summer, scattered on the wind. At Necmaria, you know, the *caid* is descended not from the Ouled Riah, over whom he rules, but from their enemies. And they don't know it, or care. Like dust, it's gone."

"They know," countered the professor, with new understanding born simply of dislike of the administrator. "And they won't ever forget. They live in front of their defeat, and it is always with them. But they're different from us. They know what is necessary for survival."

"And they will use it when they can," said the wife, sombre now. "Don't think, *mon cher,* that they won't. They harbour it like a seed, and nurture it in secret. One day, we will all pay."

"This is why the stories must be told," said the professor, eager yet again to convey his vital purpose. "There is a war in Europe now. We must learn from the past before mistakes are made. Do you see? For the progress of France, here and at home, the truth must be known. Knowledge ..." he stammered, flushed from the wine and conviction, "knowledge is the only salvation. For the past and the future both."

"Noble sentiments indeed," said the administrator. "But I suspect you have only the experience of your library. Forgive me, but I speak as a former military man, and

I can assure you, the maps of old battles are of very little use in the field. Wits and courage are what's called for: the rest is a waste and a distraction."

The professor did not respond.

"Tell me, what good is it? What difference will it make, to tell your story, even if it is true?"

This time, the professor did not bother to try.

NAIM, THE ADMINISTRATOR'S STEWARD, took the professor up into the hills. They walked for two hours, Rabelais reduced behind them to a silent hive, its French quarter invisible in the lacy comb of native houses.

The hermit's encampment, though remote, had a clear view of the town. The clay of the one-room building was weathered and covered, in places, by creepers, and in front stretched an area of ground trampled flat and even as a floor. Outside the doorway waited a neat pile of firewood. There did not, at first, appear to be anyone at home, and Naim beat his staff against the ground and called out in Arabic.

Two figures emerged from along a path that ran behind the building: a surprising sight. In front walked the hermit, a towering, skeletally thin man with attenuated limbs that stretched, puppet-like, from the cuffs and hem of his gown. His skin was so browned by the sun and his coarse garments were so ragged that initially only his shock of silvered hair confirmed his European breeding. A closer inspection revealed his patrician profile and his pale blue eyes, and the rich timbre of his French voice when he spoke left no room for doubt.

Behind him loomed an immense black African, powerfully muscled and clad in equally ill-fitting clothes. He was introduced as Kofeh, the hermit's assistant of long standing. He did not stay to talk with them, but returned to his work, skinning the sheep a local tribe had donated for their food.

Naim and the hermit spoke for some time in Arabic, about Naim's relatives and the birth of his third child. The hermit conversed in Naim's language as readily as in French, and the two spoke to each other as friends, without any lingering reserve. The hermit asked after other families in Rabelais, but he did not mention the administrator until he turned and spoke in French to the professor.

"How is our good friend, the standard-bearer of French glory?" he asked. "Do you know, he does not allow Kofeh into his drawing-room, and so I can't visit him often. I am partial, however, to his wife; and when he is called to the city, I try to stop in on her. They have no children. She is very alone in that house."

"I can imagine," said the professor. "She appears to have a nervous disposition. But I found her most sympathetic—it was she who suggested I consult you. You've lived a long time among these people, and I thought you would know of their history."

"I know a little."

"I wish to write a book. In seventy years, no one has told the truth about our campaigns in this region."

"That may be."

"The cave at Necmaria, from which I have recently travelled … I believe it is not the only cross we have to bear. Here, too …"

"Yes, here, too."

"You know, then, about the *enfumade* of the Sbéhas?"

"It is spoken of. Those French who acknowledge it speak only of a handful of brigands. You won't find any Frenchman who can tell you the story. Saint-Arnaud covered his tracks well, and who would wish to expose them? The lesson they leave, next to Necmaria, is that of a job well done. Not an agreeable lesson, but a useful one: if you want to succeed, kill them all. Leave nobody alive who can speak. It is a lesson I fear that mankind—even European men—should not learn too well. Because none of us is civilized enough. Even, and perhaps especially, to the enlightened, extermination is not a lesson to be taught."

"There were no survivors then?"

"Maybe that is what is to be gleaned. There are always survivors."

"Where can I hear more?"

The hermit looked to Naim, who frowned.

"Will you not?" the hermit asked, his face coaxing, his eyebrows slightly raised.

Naim spoke without looking at the professor. "My grandfather was one of those in the cave who survived. He was only a small boy. You walked on the corpses as on piles of hay," he said. "The cave is an underground *oued,* on two levels. Only those in the upper chamber had any hope of survival. At both ends, the cave is entered through waterfalls: the French did not only smoke them in, they cemented the exits, and camped, two weeks almost, outside, so no rescue could be attempted. The dead gave off gases, purulent rot, poison. And the water which kept the few alive ran beneath their decomposing bodies. My grandfather thought that he, too, had died: his mind was deranged. When at last he saw the light again, he believed he was in heaven, and that the men who helped him through the curtain of water to the air were his brothers and cousins, the very ones who had lain, homes to feasting maggots, in the mud beneath his feet."

"How did they get to safety?" asked the professor, the memory of Necmaria vivid in his mind. "Did the troops relent?"

"It is said," said Naim, "that a *caid* from a neighbouring region prevailed, finally, upon the commander. That he was desperate to see again the most beautiful woman in the mountains, whom he had planned to marry. And that he was determined to have her, alive or dead. The commander, it seems, who showed no mercy to a thousand of his fellows, understood the love of a woman and permitted the opening of the cave."

"And the dead?"

"She was among them, but the *caid* did not take her away after all. Her face had pulled back upon itself, the skin and the eyes were gone. He knew her only by the length of her hair and the gold around her neck and fingers. He left her there, and all the others. The cave was their tomb."

Kofeh, at this point, returned from behind the house, bringing tea. The story was at an end.

"My heart is confused," said the hermit to the professor, "when I hear of our legacy. What is the purpose of such violence? And yet, how else would I be here?" He paused to drink. "Must we believe that this is the will of God? Or does our life's struggle pass unheeded in heaven? I have no answer."

"Do you see that I must tell this story?" asked the professor, believing that he had found at last a man of vision and justice.

"I see that this is your struggle," said the hermit. "It is with you, and with God."

BACK IN THE CITY, the professor compiled his notes. Weeks, and then months passed. The days in the mountains of Dahra stood out from his life like the plain in front of the mountains, hazed in the light, an unreachable promise. The library where he worked was still and dark, its high windows and thick walls a silent, stifling enclosure against the contradictions of the country. The call of the *muezzin* reached his ears only as a muffled wail, the keeper of ritual and the passage of time.

For the first time in his many years of study, the professor was uneasy about his work. Even were he to finish his book, who would read it? It was not clear that this was a time for truth: extermination was not a lesson that the people needed to learn. But what might be the consequences of silence?

Eventually, he forsook the library for the clamour of the port, where the men worked bare-chested, heaving and shouting as the ships were docked and unloaded. He wandered, too, in the maze of the kasbah, among the hot perfumes of spice and dung. Even the bustling, bourgeois arcades of his compatriots were preferable to the silence of the library. He neglected his students as well as his work: he sought in the city the truth of the mountains, the air of the caves catching him, here and there, in gusts.

He learned that his nephew—only a boy when he had seen him last—had been killed at the front, in a battle over a patch of wet ground north of Paris. He learned, too, not long after, that the hermit of Rabelais and his hulking disciple had been slain in their sleep, their throats slit in crimson grins that neither Kofeh's strength nor the hermit's gentle patience could close up again. The newspaper made much of the hermit's noble birth, and the end of his lineage, of the fact that an ancient castle in southwestern France would now pass into the hands of strangers. The professor could see only the small building, alone on the plateau in the Dahra, crumbling again to dust, its firewood standing unused in a neat pile; and the town of Rabelais far below, living on, oblivious.

Long before he had even planned his excursion, before these stories had begun to consume him, the professor had discovered, within the safety of the library itself, mementoes of his ancestors' conquest. Unable to confront this horror, he had chosen to ignore it: it had been as easy as shutting a drawer. But now, troubled, he returned to the library. There, carefully stored in a cupboard in the corner, was a large jar of tinted liquid, in which swam a swarm of pinkish shrimp-like creatures. These perfect curls, some still trailing strands of hair, no two quite alike, were the preserved ears of native rebels, claimed by the French as a warning and a marker in the early days of the colony. For seventy or more years they had floated in their brine, waiting, listening for something unheard. For them, the professor decided at last, if only to them, he would tell his story.

The details of events at the caves of Dahra and Sbéhas are to be found in L'Algérie et la Métropole *by E. F. Gautier, Payot & Co., Paris, 1920.*

The Wedding
DENNIS BOCK

WE ARE ALL SUBDUED from the night drive home from the lake, where we have been for the last day and a half, sorting out details with the police. I've had my tie in my pocket since the accident. I take it out and lay it on the wood mantel above the fireplace, beside the photograph I haven't seen in years.

Nobody has said anything since we got in the car three hours ago. The crickets are in full force outside, excited by the thin chemical smell of swimming pools and expensive artificial fertilizers. Silently, my mother carries my sister up to her bedroom, careful not to wake her. On the way home, I massaged Ruby's feet while she slept. I knew her new shoes had broken the skin, though she hadn't complained or said anything the whole time. Only the stove light in the kitchen is on. The refrigerator is humming softly, like a dirge. Outside in the back garden my father's watering the sunflowers, though they're already covered in night dew and fast asleep.

From the mantel I take down the photograph of a group of twenty-two girls. It's been hidden for years behind the giant redwood pine cones my aunt Marian brought when she came from California to visit, and the large dusty candles shaped like eagles. In the picture my grandmother sits in the front row cross-legged and smiling, showing off her dimples and good health. This is her seamstress class, 1927, back in the black-and-white days of uniforms and vocational schools. On the back names and ages are written with little slashes through the middle of the sevens, European style. "Seventeen" is scrawled beside Lottie, my grandmother's name.

I examine each face, imagine the course each life has taken since this photograph was made. I want to believe my grandmother's smiling because they've been let out early that day. And because they're excited. I let my imagination slide backwards. Only a few have ever had their photograph taken. The camera is still something exotic, in the same class as the zebra, which all of them have seen but never ridden. They've all looked at photographs in magazines, seen wedding photos, fashion prints, pictures of the war.

There are four girls out of the twenty-two who seem to be taking this picture business very seriously. Two sisters, Louise and Greta Schriebmann, who no one likes to associate with because of their suspiciously dark hair. Last year in history class we studied anti-Semitism in Europe, Germany particularly. We watched films of the liberation of Jews from the camps. The sisters are intense and determined, their eyebrows lowered slightly, teeth clenched. They're standing in the back row—only two rows—so you can't see below their waists. Maybe they're holding hands.

Erika is the third girl. The girl with the long pointy nose. I can see the whole length of her body because she's standing at one end of the group, to the photographer's right. She doesn't want to smile in case the principal of the school asks for a copy of the photograph, which he will undoubtedly do. Since 1921 these class photos have been displayed under glass in the lobby of the college. Erika was gravely impressed the first time she saw them and hopes to affect future generations of students in the same way.

The fourth girl looks more sad than stern. This is Silke, my grandmother's childhood friend. On the back of the photograph, drawn beside her name in a youthful flowing hand, there is a heart pierced by an arrow.

EIGHT MONTHS EARLIER, just back from church on a grey autumn morning, my father's parents come for a visit. I'm signing the box of donation envelopes that my Sunday school teacher has given me, feeling resentful that I have to spend my Sunday mornings at church listening to Bible stories and the holier-than-thou attitude of the other kids in my class. I tell my parents about a holy war going on down there in the church basement, divided into rooms by portable walls and decorated with cloth-and-construction-paper Marys and Jesuses, bright and smiling like little elves. But they don't believe me. Everyone is bent on making brownie points with their teacher in the hope that word will filter upwards to the ears of Pastor Roar, who will either make you an altar boy or not. This is the mark of the model young Lutheran. I have not made it yet, nor do I expect to.

My mother's just fixed tea. Dad's wearing his accordion. He plays in a tango band two nights a week. When he has his way, the group experiments with spiced-up German waltzes.

"You know this one, Peter?" he asks, turning to me and smiling. *"Muss i denn,'"* he says. "We sing it when someone's leaving. It's a farewell song. Even Elvis did it before he went away to the army." He sings me a verse, the accordion somewhere beneath his voice.

Now I must leave this place
And you, my sweet, must stay

Dad also has a trumpet, upright and untouched in the sunroom on its brass-coloured flowering base, glittering in the half-light of this dim Sunday morning.

Ruby leaves her dolls, looks out the window to the Dodge Dart pulling into the driveway. "Oma and Opa are here," she shouts, the only two German words she knows, though she doesn't know that these words are German. My father walks over to the big front window, his fingers silently playing the last notes of this goodbye song, and looks out to his parents coming up the driveway. He's wearing his grey felt hat, the one with the green-grey ostrich feather sticking out the side. He's had it for years, as long as I remember, and sometimes wears it around the house as a joke. He says it makes him feel like a mountain man, a true yodeller, he says, although he's never gone so far as to actually yodel. He goes to the door, opens it, and says loudly in German, "Just in time for the poppy-seed cake." Ruby's out the door by now and down the stairs, hanging on our grandfather's leg.

I move to meet them, not as excited as Ruby or my father, unhappy with Sundays in general, but glad they're here. My grandfather bows to me in a pretend gesture of formality, and I respond in like manner. Then I walk down the steps and kiss my grandmother on the cheek. In German she says what I always know she's going to say because she says the same thing every time they come to visit: *Mein kleiner olympischer Spieler. My little Olympian.* Then we speak English.

We walk back up the green veranda stairs and into the house, shutting out the cold air behind us. Today they've brought a bushel of apples. McIntosh are better near Kingston, they say, where my grandparents have lived since coming to this country ten years ago. They always bring us food when they visit, a slice of their harvest. Enormous pumpkins, bushels of peaches and plums. They tell us they pick their apples at a friend's orchard. I can imagine them at it, brisk and efficient, shinnying up ladders, oblivious to the threat of gravity. They are both fit and energetic people. They go on hikes and turn over their generous garden twice a year. When my grandmother isn't gardening, she's preserving their harvest. We have jars of straw-berry and rhubarb preserve in the basement, clearly labelled in red marker, along with vats of slowly fermenting, burping sauerkraut. When my grandfather isn't planting or picking, he repairs his friends' shoes. His workshop's in the back room where he used to spend twelve hours a day when he was working at it full-time. He is a cobbler by trade, a word that rings magically when I hear it.

Today they seem more energetic than normal. They have something to tell us. They didn't call ahead like they usually do. They know we sometimes go for a Sunday drive after church. They probably decided to come on the spur of the moment. I'm thinking this as we sit down at the kitchen table and watch my mother cut into one of her famous cakes. On Sundays we eat like the Europeans do: big late lunches with lots of desserts. They tell us what the drive was like, how the weather is in Kingston. They say hello for the friends my parents haven't seen since they lived there briefly, before I was born.

"Irene wishes you'd come for a visit soon," my grandmother says in her curving Silesian accent. "You don't know how she misses you." I've seen pictures of Irene. She's tall with red hair like my mother's, but somehow American-looking. I remem-ber her dressed in a green, tight-fitting sweater, those circles of big fake pearls wrapped around her neck and wrists. They used to waitress together at the Palm Diner when my mother first came to this country. She claims Irene taught her all the English she knows.

Sometimes my father grows reflective when my grandparents come to visit—an odd thing, I think, because, as far as I can tell, this is not his natural state. There are so many forgotten habits and memories they bring with them, it seems, along with their preserves or a surprise pair of shoes.

"They started tearing down the corner store," my grandmother says. The store with the old open-top freezer that used to fascinate me on weekend visits when I was four years old. She and I used to step inside on hot summer afternoons and hang our arms into the cool air that lay thickly at the bottom of the freezer like invisible mud. But my grandmother usually stays away from sentimental stories of when my sister and I were younger. She prefers to talk about practical things, as my parents mostly do, not dwelling on the past. *The past is passed,* they always say. Aside from my mother, the Bavarian, they are from Silesia, a part of Europe which they refer to as "Polish-occupied Germany." An area known for its industrious and hard-working people, it is an equivocal province, half German, half Polish. A part of the world that's been strangled by history. I have no doubts about how my father and grand-parents feel about the past.

But today they surprise us all. We've just finished our lunch, giant gherkins wrapped in veal, stabbed with toothpicks to keep from unrolling. My mother's already doing the dishes. She likes to get things out of the way so she won't have to deal with them later. Calmly, my grandfather picks his teeth with one of the tooth-picks he's salvaged from the pile left over from the meal. I'm doing the same. He makes little clicking noises as he sucks his tongue off his teeth. My grandmother's been holding their secret all through lunch, savouring it as she would a special dessert.

"Rudolph and I are going to get married again," she bursts out finally. This sets my father to thinking. I can tell by the eyebrows, cocked slightly at the edge of disbe-lief. *But you're already married, Mom.*

Instead he says, "Why not, I suppose," looking at the floral wallpaper between his mother and father. "You could start planning right away."

"Oh, we have," she says. All this very brightly. "You know how organized your father is."

Click goes my grandfather's tongue off his teeth, smiling.

Next summer, the day of their thirty-fifth anniversary, they want to remarry on water just like they did their first time around, but this time aboard a rented house-boat on Sturgeon Lake instead of somewhere in the south of Germany. My father's reaction is lukewarm because he thinks the inclination will pass, in the same way clackers and streaking did. He knows his parents better than that. They're strong, not needy of sentimental gestures like the giving and taking of flowers, or hand-holding. They're veterans of Olympia. Together they watched Jesse Owens win gold and saw Hitler rise from his seat and leave the stadium without shaking the athlete's hand. A second ceremony would be going backwards, like returning to a place you left long ago to find only ghosts, or nothing at all. Probably he thinks his parents need short-term plans to keep them occupied, to keep up their spirits. To keep the wolf from the door. Maybe this is why they're so busy with the gardening and the hiking. They need something to do. They're old, after all. This will be nothing more than another seed planted and left for the crows and squirrels to dig up. It's the planting that counts, and not the fact that the seed is thirty-five years old.

WE DRIVE TO BOBCAYGEON, the walleye capital of Ontario, on the edge of Sturgeon Lake where my grandparents have decided to hold their second wedding aboard *Sweet Dreams*. Dad says *Sweet Dreams* floats twenty, but there will only be fourteen of us. On the drive up through the Ontario heartland I think of my father's reaction to the news after the *rouladen* lunch eight months ago, the look on his face that said his parents had finally gone crazy. As we drive north on Highway 35, the radio strangely silent, my mother sits beside him in the passenger seat leafing through *Pattern & Design*, a magazine for people who make their own clothes from scratch, something my mother does. She locks herself away in the room she's named "My Room" and dreams up impossible suits and dresses. The only thing I can tell for sure is that her favourite colours are yellow and green. She scans the drawings for ideas—

lapels, sashes, colours, pleats—nervous and a bit impatient. She's already snapped at Ruby and me. Instead of our usual game of I Spy we sit unmoving, hoping for the awkwardness to pass.

I know what my father's thinking. He's thinking about the side of his parents he's never seen before, the part of them they've kept hidden from him like a jewellery box in a secret drawer. Their longing to travel in time, backwards, to a time before he was even born. My father is usually the cheerful one. Level-headed and constant is my mother. Perhaps she understands the problem too, but she's not telling. She flips the page, adjusts her green-and-yellow shoulder.

The low-rent office buildings and factories on the outskirts of Toronto gradually disappear. From the grey cement and shimmering asphalt emerge enormous rectangular blocks of farmland. The emptiness is broken by a straight line of trees in the distance. We pass a modest hut of plywood on the side of the road under which an old woman sits, selling vegetables. Ten minutes later a pick-up truck pulled onto the gravel shoulder with a hand-painted sign propped up against a wheel: Freshe Vegetables. The variation in spelling probably someone's idea of pizzazz to attract city people on their way to and from the cottage.

The feeling of industry is here, although the factories are long gone. Now it's the efficient use of soil. Giant house-like combines silently pick and spray in the distance. Inside one I imagine a scientist sitting at a flashing control panel, a baseball cap pulled back on his head. But as we drive farther north, the tree walls on the horizon become smaller and thinner, replaced eventually by brush and stone. More and more granite boulders lying around, in the middle of pastures, on the side of the road. The Canadian Shield begins to shoot upwards through the earth in the form of granite outcrops and scattered rubble. Lakes appear, small and secretive, dotted with islands.

We've left home early. It's still before noon. My father says we should be at the docks and aboard *Sweet Dreams* by two o'clock. We're already dressed for the wedding. Our mother made Ruby and me try everything on last night to make sure there were no last-minute problems. This, our dress rehearsal, was my mother's idea. Everything was perfect because everything was hers. Designed, cut and stitched especially for the occasion. I'm wearing my first real suit, a soft grey, complete with tie. Luckily a summer suit of light cotton, the pants shortened to the knee. It's hot and sticky out. Even the artificial wind through the open windows brings no relief. It feels like I'm wrapped in soggy toilet paper. My mother's told me I'll have to pull up my long black socks when we get there. Until then I can wear them bunched up around my ankles.

Ruby's wearing a pink knee-length dress with a white sash wrapped around the waist. The new dress is carefully rolled up to her hips so she can feel the breeze on her legs better. Her shoes sit beside her feet, shiny and white and stiff. She hasn't said anything, but from where I'm sitting I can see the brown dot on both of her white Achilles tendons where the new shoes have broken the skin. She doesn't want to bug our mother. We both know the tension in the air. For now, better just to sit.

Our parents are dressed the way all adults dress for weddings. They look serious, important, as if they're going to greet the president of a foreign country, or perhaps a returning Olympic gold medallist. Ruby and I are not used to seeing them like this. Our father never wears a tie, something he says he's thankful for. He says he's most comfortable with a pencil stuck behind his ear and dressed in his shop apron, which he wears when he works on the sailboat in the basement. He started it last fall, a small two-man racer which he hopes to finish by next year. It's taken him longer than he expected because he only has weekends to work on it. The whole house has smelled of fibreglass for six months. This is something I don't mind, but it troubles my mother. She says he builds boats like boys build model airplanes. Sometimes she says this with admiration, as a comment on his eternal youthfulness. Other times I'm not so sure. This could be something else that's bothering him: a weekend away from his sailboat, his strips of fibreglass, his moulds, his protective goggles. The clothes he's wearing smell of bleach and detergent instead of glue.

We arrive at Bobcaygeon and drive slowly through the little town, observing the 15 m.p.h. speed limit. On the sidewalks people are dressed in short sleeves and cut-off jeans or track shorts. The younger ones wear their sneakers without socks, most of them tanned from top to bottom. You can tell who lives in town. They aren't many among the paler, better-dressed tourists. The townies wear baseball caps, the laces of their shoes broken or missing, scornful of the summer fashions we bring from the south. There are people carrying two-fours of beer from the Brewers' Retail to their cars. It's beer-drinking weather. They know to open their trunks before they buy their beer so they won't have to struggle with keys while their hands are full. Slowly we drive past the parking lot, looking into the popped-open trunks like dentists examining a line of gaping mouths. There are a few Michigan and New York State licence plates. I imagine these belong to the people with narrow heads and large sagging bodies, their children dressed in striped shirts and khaki shorts with zipper pockets.

Our father knows where we're going. We've been here before. We drive over the lock with the white-and-red signs on both sides warning us not to fish from this point. Then turn left, corralled by a driftwood fence into the parking lot of the houseboat rental, the marina where we're to meet between green pine forests and the smooth black waters off the tip of the dock. The parking lot crunches under the weight of our slowing tires.

Everyone's already here, including my aunt from California. After the wedding she's coming to stay with us. She's been with my grandparents in Kingston since she arrived two days ago. She's wearing a modest dress, almost casual, as if her long journey exempts her from the less comfortable wedding costumes forced upon my parents. At her ankles are the braces she's worn on her legs since she was a girl. When she sees us pull into the parking lot, she hobbles over and sticks her head through my mother's open window and gives her a big kiss. Aunt Marian's a painter. We have some of her landscapes displayed on our walls at home. They show a desert of large purple cactuses and looming blue mountains. My father talks about Aunt Marian fondly, but with a sad look on his face, as if there were something about her that he just can't pin down.

Ruby fixes her dress, my socks come up. I help her put her shoes back on. I take some Kleenex from my breast pocket and quickly make temporary pads for the cuts on her feet. We've never seen or heard of most of the guests. They are all large, a bit tense, showing their teeth through festive smiles. Aunt Marian shows surprise at how much I've grown. This makes me feel obvious, adolescent. I'm intimidated by the grey area between childhood and adulthood. I can't remember much of when I was a boy and I can't see myself when I look into the future. I close my eyes and see my parents, sitting old and toothless in rocking chairs. I see colonies in space. I can even see the day when the planet's overrun by insects. But I can't imagine my part in all this.

There are people here whom I'm supposed to remember from the times we visited Kingston. I don't remember any of them. I try to disguise my perplexed look by facing the sun, by turning the question mark on my face into a squint. The woman who taught my mother English at the Palm Diner hugs me like a long-lost son. Those big pearls grinding into my bony chest. She stoops slightly, too tall to embrace me without embarrassing the both of us. She tells my mother I have an angel's complexion. Then my mother leads Ruby and me over to Pastor Hawking, who is pairing his fingers in the middle of the crowd, graciously nodding his head up and down. I've heard the name before. He's been a friend of my parents since they came here fifteen years ago. He looks younger than my father, but not by much. We share hugs and kisses all around. I watch the grey streaks run through the thick black hair of the pastor's wife as she fingers her own set of pearls. Pearls they are, like milky seeds, but not as proud as the looping circles cast around the neck of Irene, the Palm Diner waitress.

There are also three old women my grandmother's age. It looks like they've come together. Literally, a set. Sisters, maybe. They're standing at the edge of the crowd, dressed as if by the same designer. They have kind faces, pink and luminescent with age, their heavy bodies propped up on spindly legs. It's obvious that the one in the centre is wearing a wig which, under the bright sun, takes on the light blue tinge of new fishing line. There are more people here. Ruby and I are introduced to them all. We forget their names as soon as we hear them.

The dockhands are getting the houseboat ready for launching. My grandfather has told me with some pride that it's the biggest one on Sturgeon Lake. It's been reserved since last winter. We wait politely on the large wooden dock with white poles evenly spaced around its perimeter, from which hang orange life preservers. The rental office is behind us, beside the parking lot, where people sign receipts and day-long insurance policies. There are three other houseboats, secured by heavy ropes. The rest are already out on the water.

Sweet Dreams is mostly white. A small house-like cabin rises from its centre, a yellow-and-white-striped awning stretches from the stern to the back portion of the cabin. It will provide a bit of shade if the sun proves too much for us in our rich costumes. Up front are neatly arranged stacking chairs, forming an aisle that runs up the middle of the deck to a white altar perched at the tip of the bow. Honey bees buzz in dizzy circles, attracted by the bouquets of flowers placed in white porcelain vases. Everyone boards but my grandparents, who haven't arrived yet. They plan to meet us out in the middle of the lake, chauffeured in a polished mahogany cigar-boat—I've seen the brochure—with a tiny Ontario Union Jack sticking out its nose.

People are fishing out on the water, not far from where the houseboats are docked. Any serious fisherman knows you fish for walleye at dusk, or better yet after dark and under a full moon. As I watch them cast out their lines, I wonder whether my grandparents had known ahead of time that they were planning on being remarried in the middle of a full-blown walleye tournament, surrounded by professional anglers from all over the continent. Both my father and I knew this because we were here two years ago, just when the tournament began.

In the middle of the lake we are surrounded by boats of various sizes: dinghies, aluminium outboards, canoes, cruisers. We're still waiting for our grandparents to arrive. The shoreline is clearly visible from here, a clean continuous wall of pines broken only for a moment by a cabin or dock. We're milling about, waiting for things to get started. Everything is in place. All we have to do is sit down. The pastor is ready. After the ceremony we're staying on the houseboat for the reception. The food and drink are set up at the stern under the awning. There is also a squared-off area, possibly a dance floor. Who is going to dance?

Pulling up in a separate boat, where did they get that idea from? Just like their first wedding somewhere in Germany long before I was born. These are all rituals of the land, clumsily transferred to the sea. Limo to the floating church. The only difference is water slows movement, makes things lighter, more dream-like. Probably this is why our floating church is named *Sweet Dreams*.

Somebody's head turns and we all look towards a dock on the far side of the lake. My grandparents. One of the employees from the boat rental helps my grandmother into the boat first. When she gets both feet in safely she motions to the young man. He leans towards her and she kisses him on the cheek. As she does, I see an earring catch the sun like a hot pinpoint. Then he helps my grandfather get in. The pastor's head is still gently bobbing up and down, his smile eager and calm. A few minutes later they pull up alongside the houseboat and are taken aboard. After more kisses and handshakes, my grandparents meet one another at the tip of the bow, nervous as two virgins. The polished mahogany cigarboat with the Ontario Union Jack has returned to the dock at the far end of the lake. Sitting beside the boat, smoking a cigarette, is her pilot, the young man my grandmother kissed, his feet hanging over the edge of the dock, his head turned towards us.

My father has helped everyone to their seat. We are respectful and quiet, as if at a funeral. Silence drops over us and I listen to the lake noises come from all directions, the hum of motorboats, splashing, weak conversations that pass over the flat water like tired sparrows. A speedboat roars by in the distance. The pastor formally welcomes us and thanks the Lord for this beautiful day. I am sitting beside Ruby. Although we know this is a serious matter, we feel like laughing and jumping into the water.

"Dearly beloved," he says. "We are gathered here this afternoon to reaffirm the holy bond of matrimony between this man and this woman." The pastor's head nods more deeply now. He is like a plastic bird poised on the edge of a drinking glass, insatiable, monotonous. On the upswing he looks into the eyes of my grandparents. As he does this the houseboat begins to rock, slowly, once, twice, echoes of the speedboat that has passed by in the distance. Then the big wave comes. The boat jerks slightly, suddenly, and the three standing figures adjust their footing. I am looking at the inside of my eyelids the moment my grandmother disappears over the side. Bright red with white dots following the quick jump and curve of my eyeballs. Voices scream with the rush of bodies to the bow to look over the railing. Like a stone. Down, down my grandmother goes, fading into layers of darkness and shadow and finally and forever into memory.

WE SPEND THE REST OF THE DAY until nightfall looking for her, some of the men diving in again and again. They slide into the water and return in frantic lunges for air. Those who are young and strong enough. Suit jackets and dress shoes are scattered over the deck. In their shoes, the divers have placed their watches and rings for safekeeping. Those who are too young or too old stand silently and look on in disbelief. I notice with shameful pride that my father stays under the longest. I wonder what he sees in that black underwater forest.

My mother collects Ruby in her arms when the harbour patrol begins shuttling guests back to the marina. She goes easily, drained now and weak from the crying. My grandfather sits in a folding chair, waiting, as if for a train. Alone now, as I've never seen him before. The young man my grandmother kissed is still sitting on the dock, dangling his feet in the water. I can see he knows what happened. It isn't long before the whole lake knows. The authorities begin dragging the bottom in a matter of hours. It's twilight when my father surfaces for the last time and is pulled from the water, panting and blue, teeth chattering. By now most of the guests have been taken ashore. At the stern, early-evening bees gorge themselves on chicken salad and melon.

My parents decide it's better to stay in Bobcaygeon tonight instead of driving all the way home, even though we're unprepared. Between us there is not one toothbrush. Aunt Marian has already taken my grandfather back to Kingston.

We check into a motel with a yellow vacancy sign shaped like a boomerang, its centre directed upwards to the heavens. The motel is just on the edge of town, where the wind in the trees and the thin traffic through the dark drowns out the sound of crickets and bullfrogs. The last available room has only two beds, side by side. I lie beside my sister's small warm body, our parents an arm's length away, and listen to their slow, deep breathing. Crisp foreign sheets prevent sleep. It's years since I've slept in the same room with my mother, in the same bed as my sister. Another move backward in time. My father's teeth begin to chatter. I hear my mother's hand searching the dark to comfort him, her palm softly cover his crying mouth.

In my dream a silent fraternity of boats gathers in the area where the accident took place, a congregation of those who believe the scent of a drowning attracts prize fish. They risk the chance of pulling her up for the equal chance of bringing in a trophy. I go down to the dock where my grandmother kissed the young man and watch the procession of fishermen float guiltily into the twilight. They don't anchor. They consider the currents and follow my grandmother's slow drift. I know their luck is good, for I hear them pulling the big ones out and the weight of the fish hitting against the bottom of the boats.

At seven the next morning, the motel keeper comes to our door, rubbing his red puffy face. The sun is shining through the spotted window. We're waiting for someone to tell us what to do next. On the brown dresser between the two beds little boxes of cornflakes and a carton of orange juice sit, a still life of this abruptly rearranged morning. The man at the door tells my father there's someone on the phone in the office. They leave together. While my mother and Ruby wash up in the bathroom, I slip out and walk down to the docks, fifteen minutes along the highway. At the edge of the water I overhear a rumour that someone found an old lady last night on the east shore, tangled in the bulrushes. They say her hair was still neatly tied back, her jewellery shiny in the moonlight.

A WEAK LIGHT from the street lamp opposite the house enters through the big front window. The house is settling into itself for the night. It creaks as the heat of the day drains from its dusty rafters, its secret corners. I'm standing at the fireplace mantel. I remember this photograph from years ago, when I used to play in the attic during the day. It's faded since then, but my grandmother is wearing the same smile, as if she sees something waiting for her on the horizon, something in the future.

There are the two sisters, Louise and Greta, just as I remember them, looking into the camera, uncomfortable. Now I know why they're sneering, half defiant, half terrified. Out of view their hands search for one another, convinced of something terrible to come. And here is Erika, the skinny girl with the pointy nose, efficient and wary. Then Silke, the girl with the heart and arrow drawn beside her name in my grandmother's youthful flowing hand. She hasn't changed either, though so many other things have since this photograph was taken, back when the world was new and alive with light, before there was any need to look back and remember.

Last Rites

M.G. VASSANJI

"SHAMSHU MUKHI," she said, "how are you?"

I had just stepped out of the front doorway of the Don Mills mosque and onto the stoop, where she had been standing, waiting.

"Hale and hearty, and how is the world treating you, Yasmin," I replied jovially. The formal address *mukhi* always provokes an exaggerated, paternal sort of cheeriness in my manner that I can't quite curb and (as I've realized over the years) don't wish to either, because it is what people expect, draw comfort from. But no sooner had my glib response escaped my lips than I was reminded by her demeanour that lately the world had not been treating Yasmin Bharwani very kindly.

I asked her, more seriously: "And how is Karim—I understand he's in hospital?"

A pinprick of guilt began to nag. It was more than a week now since I heard that her husband, who had been a classmate of mine, had been admitted for something possibly serious. I had not seen Bharwani in years, our paths having diverged since we ended up in this city; still, I had meant to go and do my bit to cheer him up for old times' sake. Only, with this and that to attend to, at home and away, that good thought had simply sieved through the mind.

She nodded, paused a moment to look away, before turning back to reply, "He's at Sunnybrook. I've come to ask, can you give him chhanta? ..."

"Now, now, Yasmin, don't talk like that. It can't be serious—he's young yet, we all are." (That irrepressible bluster again—who was I kidding, since when has the Grim Reaper given a hoot about age?) "And what will your unbelieving husband Karim say to my giving him chhanta—he will scream murder."

Chhanta is the ceremony at which a person is granted forgiveness by his mukhi on behalf of the world and the Almighty. You join hands and supplicate once a month at new moon, and then finally at death's bed. I recall a sceptical Bharwani from our boyhood days arguing with hotheaded arrogance, "What have I done against the world that I should crave forgiveness all the time?" And some of us replying, "If nothing else, you might have stepped on an ant and killed it, ulu—even an angel commits at least seven sins daily, and what do you think, that you are better than an angel?" We called him "Communist" in those teen years, which nickname he rather relished, for it had intellectual connotations and set him apart from the rest of us, all destined for the heavenly embrace.

"Try, please," his wife now begged me. "He's dying … and there's another matter too…."

At this moment Farida joined me, and we invited Yasmin to come home and have supper with us, when she could also unburden her mind. We had anticipated a quiet Sunday evening together, but such sacrifices of privacy have been our pleasure, having brought meaning to our lives as we approach what are called our more mellow years. It is a traditional responsibility that I hold, as presider of a mosque, father to its community; nothing could seem safer for someone so conventional, indeed mediocre, as I, until Yasmin and Karim Bharwani put me through an ordeal from which I don't think I recovered.

Yasmin must be some five years younger than both my wife and I; she is petite and trim, fair complexioned, with short dark hair. She was dressed smartly that night, though perhaps a bit sternly. She had her own car, so we met in the lobby of our building and went up together. At first we discussed anything but the gloomy subject at hand, her husband's illness. Finally, over a swiftly put-together supper, an assortment of leftover and fresh, I said to Yasmin, who was waiting for just such a prompt, "Now tell us what's this other matter that you mentioned."

She looked anxiously at me and said all in a rush: "My husband wishes to be cremated when he dies."

I spluttered out a quite meaningless: "But why?" to which nevertheless she answered, "I don't know why, I don't understand his reasons—he has plenty of them and I don't understand them."

"But surely you've not given up hope yet," Farida said, "it's too soon to talk of …" Her voice trailed off. We watched Yasmin break down silently, large tears flowing down her cheeks. Farida went and sat beside her, poured her a glass of water. "Pray for him," she whispered. "We will, too."

"You must come and give him chhanta … now," the grieving woman answered, wiping away her tears.

The three of us drove to Sunnybrook Hospital, Farida going with Yasmin in the latter's car.

Trust Karim Bharwani to pose a conundrum such as this one. Always the oddball, always the one with the dissenting opinion: why this way and not the other? Because the world is so, eh chodu, we would laugh him off. There were times when we vilified him, mercilessly, and tried to ostracize him, when he had wounded our pietistic feelings with one of his poisoned utterings. But he was too much one of us, you might as well cast out a part of your body. Now here he was, saying cremate me, don't bury me. The trouble is, we don't cremate our dead, we bury them, according to the Book, the same way Cain first disposed of his brother Abel.

I wanted to say to him, as I saw him, Look, Bharwani, this is not the time for your smart, sceptical arguments. This is real, this is how you leave the world; at least this once, walk along with the rest of us.

He had been washed. His face was flushed, but creased, and he looked exhausted and frail. He had always had rather prominent eyes behind big black-framed glasses; now his eyeballs were sunken deep inside their sockets, where two tiny black pools of fire burned with fervid life. There was barely any flesh on the cheeks. He reminded me rather of a movie version of an extraterrestrial. He said, in answer to his wife's concerns, that he had been taken for a short walk; yes, he had eaten a bit of the awful food, to keep his strength; and today the pain was less. He would die for a curry; he attempted a laugh. He sounded hoarse and a little high-pitched. He had let an arm drop to the side of the bed; I picked it up, cold, and squeezed it. "Ey, Bharwani, how are you?"

"It's been a long time," he said, meaning presumably the time since we last met. He smiled at Farida, who had gone and sat at the foot of the bed. "Mukhi and Mukhiani," he said to the two of us, with an ever so slight mock in his tone, "so have you come to give me chhanta?"

I threw a look at Yasmin, who turned to him with large, liquid eyes. "Let them," she pleaded. "In case. It's our tradition."

He said nothing for a moment, apparently trying to control himself. Then, in measured tones: "Doesn't it matter what I believe in or desire for myself?"

She had no argument, only the desperate words of a beloved: "For my sake...."

He fell back exhausted, closed his eyes; opened them to stare at me. I saw my chance then, in that helpless look, and drove home my simple argument: "Karim, it can't hurt, whatever it is you believe in." With a laugh, I added: "Surely you don't believe you have nothing to ask forgiveness for?"

He grinned, at me, at his wife, and said, "You have a point there."

I proceeded with the ceremony, having brought the holy water. When we had finished, he joked, "I should go to heaven now."

"You *will* go to heaven," Yasmin said happily, "when the time comes. But it was only a formality now." She smiled and her look seemed to drench him in love. "And you'd not asked forgiveness from God in years."

"But I asked forgiveness from you, not from Him."

"Oh." But she was not bothered.

"But I am firm about the other thing, I tell you. I insist. These two people here are witnesses to my wish. I would like to be cremated when I die, not buried in that cold ground at Yonge and Sheppard called Immigrant's Corner."

"But why, Karim, why?" For the first time, her voice animated, passionate.

"Because I *want* it so."

"It's not right."

"What difference does it make? I'll be *dead*. Doesn't it matter to you how I want to be treated in death, what I believe in?"

She wiped away tears, looked straight at him and said, "All right. But I'll have the prayers said over you by Mukhisaheb. A proper service."

"All right, Shamshu can say his juju over my body—if they let him."

HE KNEW it would not be a simple matter fulfilling his last wish. And so for him I was a godsend, a witness to that wish who had known him in the past and was not unsympathetic, and who was also a mukhi, with connections. He also used the presence of me and my wife to extract grudging acquiescence from his own wife. There the matter stood when Farida and I took leave of the couple in the dingy, eerily quiet hospital room, our footsteps echoing hollowly down the long, white corridors. We both believed there was time still, for Bharwani and Yasmin to wrangle further on the issue, for his other close family members to be brought into the discussion, for him to be pressured into changing his mind. Cantankerous Bharwani, however, died suddenly the following day, bequeathing me such a predicament that it would seem as if I was caught inside a maze from which there was no exit.

Once a death reaches notice of the community organs, as somehow it does almost immediately, the funeral committee goes into high gear. Cemetery management is requested to prepare the next available site, the body is sent for ritual washing and embalming, the funeral date is set and announced; relatives in different cities in the world learn about the death within hours and arrange for services in their local mosques. This is the way it always is.

"What should I do," Yasmin said to me over the phone from the hospital. "They have taken over, and I don't know what to say to them...."

If I had said, Nothing, she would surely have been relieved. It is what I felt strongly inclined to say—Do nothing, let them take over; he's dead anyhow, it won't make any difference to him. But it does make a difference to us, the living, how we dispose of the dead.

Does that sound right?

"What do you think you should do?" I probed her gently.

"My conscience tells me to follow his wishes, you know I promised I would. But I don't know what's right. I don't want him to go to hell or some such place because of his arrogance. Is there a hell, Mukhisaheb? What exactly do we believe in?"

She had me there. I had learned as a child that hell was the name of the condition in which the human soul could not find final rest in the Universal Soul; in that case the body was simply useless and disposable baggage. I was also told of a Judgment Day, when the body would be raised, and of a heaven where you had a lot of fun, presumably with many pretty young women, and in contrast a hell where you went to burn for your sins while giant scorpions gnawed at your guts. I was inclined toward the more sublime approach to the hereafter—though who has returned from the world of the dead to describe conditions there? It seemed a safe bet simply to follow tradition, to go with the blessings and prayers of your people. But mere tradition was not enough for Karim Bharwani; he liked to make up his own mind. He had never played it safe. How were we going to send him off, and into what?

I didn't answer her question. "Your husband has put us into a real quandary, Yasmin," I said instead. "Give me some time to think. Perhaps we can delay the funeral by a day, let me try and arrange that."

"His family has already started arriving, for the funeral … it's a big family … two brothers and two sisters and cousins and aunts and uncles, and his mother. What am I going to say to them?"

"Say nothing for now."

"I don't know what I would have done without you, you truly are a godsend."

Isn't that what I was supposed to be? But I found myself confounded, I didn't know what to do, where my duty lay.

I called up Jamal and Nanji, two other classmates from way back, to talk about "Communist" Bharwani's death, and we reminisced some. It was the first death to strike our group from school, not counting a tragedy in grade eleven, when a friend was hit by a truck. They told me that Alidina, Kassam, Samji, and perhaps a few others would also be arriving, from out of town, for the funeral. Bharwani was lucky, so many of his former classmates would be present to pay him their respects. Would he appreciate that? We believed so.

HE WAS ALWAYS INTENSE, always controversial. Broad shouldered and not very tall, he had a habit of tilting his head leftward as he walked. He parted his thick black hair in the middle and, even more outrageous for the time (this was high school), wore suspenders to school. He spoke English with a twang that made people laugh, for its foreign imitation, until they heard what he was saying, which always seemed profound. He was our star debater and actor. One day he brought in a four-page indictment of God, obviously culled from books of literature, and presented the typescript to our hapless religion teacher, one Mr. Dinani, who broke into tears and called Bharwani "Lucifer," which thrilled him ever so much. Mr. Dinani lives in Scarborough now, an insurance salesman recently awarded a plaque by his company for record sales. I lost touch with Bharwani when he went to England for university. When I saw him years later in Toronto, he seemed distant and perhaps even a bit disdainful; I gathered that my vocation as a real estate agent and my role as community worker did not meet his standards of achievement.

That night there was the usual sympathy gathering of family and friends, after services in my mosque, where I met my former classmates, six in all. Yasmin sat in the midst of the large Bharwani clan, beside her mother-in-law, a severe-looking though diminutive woman with hennaed hair furiously and silently counting her beads. Mr. Dinani too was present, and in his familiar, overwrought manner, was already in tears. But my former friends and I gathered afterwards at Jamal's lavish house on Leslie Street and gave ourselves a great reunion party, at which we remembered old "Communist."

Alidina, a heart surgeon in Kingston, recalled how Bharwani used to read and edit his English compositions at school. Once a small guy, fondly nicknamed "Smidgin," Alidina was now simply broad and short, a recently divorced man turned out in an expensive suit. According to a rumour I'd heard, he had been accused by his wife, at a reconciliation hearing, of almost strangling her. His imitation of Bharwani's arrogant manner was predictably hilarious. Nanji gave us a story the rest of us had never heard before. Late one afternoon, after classes were long over, while he was walking along a corridor he had chanced upon Bharwani and the new chemistry teacher Mr. Sharma sitting together in a classroom at the teacher's table; Mr. Sharma was in tears and Bharwani was patting him on the hand to comfort him. What to make of that? Bharwani with a tender heart was not an image we were familiar with.

The stories wove on, recalled after many years, inevitably embellished; the evening wore on, a good portion of the people getting progressively drunk, sentimental, louder. At these moments I always find myself adrift in my soberness. I debated briefly with myself whether to let them in on Bharwani's last wish, but decided the moment was not quite the right one to request intelligent input from my friends. I left, taking my secret with me, though I could not help warning Jamal in somewhat mysterious fashion that I might need his legal advice on a serious matter. As I drove through Jamal's gate, the question of the funeral seemed ever more urgent. Time was short. Wouldn't it be better just to let things be, let the burial proceed? No one would be the wiser, but for Yasmin, Farida, and me.

Messages were waiting for me when I arrived home. In one, I had been confirmed to preside over the funeral ceremony, which according to another message had been postponed from the next day to the one following, as I had requested. There was a frantic appeal from Yasmin—Please call, any time.

"I met with my in-laws today, to discuss procedures for the funeral ceremony," she told me when I called.

"Did you tell them of Karim's wish?"

"I didn't know what to say. I was waiting for your advice."

"What do your children think?"

"I've told all three of them. The older ones want to meet with you."

We agreed that I should go to meet her and the children early the next morning at her house.

THE HOUSE IS IN AN AREA of north Toronto called Glencedar Park, a locale so devoid of coloured faces—except for the nannies pushing strollers—as to appear foreign to the likes of me. A cul-de-sac, with access to it limited by one-way streets, the neighbourhood might remind the cynical minded of a fortress. There are not many such neighbourhoods left. I have taken clients to inspect houses in Glencedar Park, who after a single drive through it have instructed me simply to hasten out to somewhere else. Having parked my car and come out on the sidewalk, I met the curious though not unfriendly eyes of a couple of heads of households in long coats, each with a briefcase in hand and a folded paper under an arm, striding off to catch the subway on Yonge Street. I told myself this is where Bharwani had come to seek refuge from his people.

"How do you like the area?" I asked Yasmin when she opened the door.

"Very much," she said. "We've had no problems. Some of the neighbours are rather nice. The others keep to themselves."

All three children were waiting for me in the living room. The oldest, Emil, was a broad, strapping young man, conspicuously crowned with a crop of thick black hair slicked and parted in the middle, which reminded me of his father in his youth. He was at university. The second, Zuleikha, with the slim and toned looks of her age, resembled neither parent; she was finishing high school. The third child, Iqbal, was nine and rather delicate looking. They stood up and I went and embraced each in turn. I reminded myself that this was their time of sorrow, they had lost a father, who to me was only Bharwani, from a shared past, calling upon which he had put me in a delicate spot.

I muttered some inanities in praise of their father, my arm around the shoulders of little Iqbal, beside whom I had sat down, when Emil, after a nod from his sister, went straight to the point. "Mukhisaheb," he said, "our mother has told us about Dad's desire to be cremated. We would like to know what you think."

"Your father expressed that wish to me and your mother. I believe the ultimate decision is the family's."

"I think cremation's the best way," Zuleikha spoke up, sounding frivolously like an ad, which wasn't her intent. She had evidently not had much sleep, and she had spent time crying. There was a mild look of defiance in the glare she then awarded me. I have come to believe, in the few years I've held communal office, that to the young people I am a little like a cop, whom they would like to come to for help but whom they also resent.

"I differ," Emil said stiffly. "But of course Dad's wishes matter."

"I don't want Dad to be burnt," broke the quivering voice of young Iqbal beside me, and I held him tight at the shoulders as he gave a sob. His mother, saying to him, "Come," took him from me and out of the room.

This is a close family, I observed to myself. I thought of my own son, who had left home soon after graduating from school and was now in Calgary, never quite having looked back; and of my daughter, the same age as Zuleikha, who had grown distant from Farida and me.

"The problem is," I told Emil and Zuleikha, "that cremating is not in our tradition—you know that. It might even be forbidden on theological grounds. The community will not allow it. And there are other family members—your father's mother, and his brothers and sisters. They will have something to say, too."

"But he was *our* father, we have the right to decide," the girl said emphatically.

"What can the community do?" asked her brother.

"They can refuse the final rites to the body," I told him.

"Does that matter?" asked Zuleikha. "It wouldn't have mattered to Daddy. He would have refused them anyway, if he could."

"Your mother wishes the final rites and prayers."

Their mother brought in fresh brewed coffee and a plate of cookies. "He'll be all right," she told me, with a smile, referring to Iqbal. "I'm trying to explain to him that his father lives on in spirit." She quickly averted her eyes, so expressive of the turmoil and grief beneath her surface. In a cream cardigan over a dark green dress, she reminded me of how young women used to dress back in Dar a long time ago, during the cooler hours of the day. She had been trained as a librarian, as I was aware, and now worked in government. Ever since her call to tell me that her husband had closed his eyes for the last time while in the midst of chatting with her and Iqbal, she seemed to have kept her emotion in check.

Emil said: "Mum, what would *you* like to do, regarding Dad?"

"It sounds silly, I know, but I only want to do what is right."

"What is right is what *he* wanted," her daughter insisted, and tossed another glare at me. I could imagine her as Daddy's favourite, always ready at his defence during conflicts.

"Let's all give it a few more hours," I told them. "The funeral is tomorrow. Meanwhile … if you wish, you could inquire about cremation procedures and costs…."

BY THAT EVENING the community leadership had caught wind of Bharwani's last wish, and I received a stream of phone calls, all intended to sound me out regarding rumours already in circulation. No, I was certain, I replied, that the family was not considering alternative funeral arrangements. The ceremony would take place tomorrow, as announced. And, yes, I had seen Karim in hospital, delivered chhanta to him, he had not been out of his mind, ranting ignorant things. Finally came the call from the very top, the chummy but very commanding voice of our Chairman. "What is there to these rumours, Shamshu—something about the deceased's wish to be cremated. Word is that he spoke to you before he died, and that you are close to his family." I explained to him what the situation was and told him that since I was a witness to that last wish of the dead man, I felt somewhat obligated by it. The last remark was wilfully ambiguous, and I waited for his response. "We understand your personal predicament, Shamshu," the Chairman answered impatiently, "but first and foremost you are a mukhi; not just a presider but a representative of God. You know what is right. Just because the deceased had deviated from the right path—that's what I hear, he had become a communist—does that mean it is not our duty to try and save him? And it seems to me that this is the perfect opportunity, when he has fallen back into our hands. You said he let you do chhanta; that means he had a semblance of faith still left in him. Then let's save him. Otherwise he dies without the prayers of his people to go with him."

His was the kind of pompous, authoritarian voice that prompts one to rebel. What did the man know of the right path except that it was the official path, I caught myself asking, echoing Bharwani perhaps.

"It's his wife's and children's desire to fulfill his wish," I said.

"Then obviously they are misled. You can convince them as to what is right, can't you? If not, I'll give them a call myself."

He didn't wait, though, for twenty minutes later, while I prevaricated and sounded out Farida on what to do, Yasmin called.

"Mukhisaheb, the Chairman himself called. There doesn't seem much choice now...." Her voice petered out.

All she wanted was to be told what was right. The Chairman had done that, but she wanted to hear it from me. At that moment I made up my mind.

"Listen, Yasmin," I told her. "You and the children should decide for yourself. I can't advise you what to do. But the funeral ceremony will happen tomorrow. It's up to you and your children whether you choose to bury or cremate their father."

She took a long moment before saying, "All right."

Emil called that evening, and we talked for a while. Then Zuleikha called and said, "Thank you, Mukhisaheb. I know my father was right to depend on you." She added, just before hanging up: "You know what? Some of my uncles have found out about this, and may try to stop us. But we are ready. The law is on our side, isn't it?"

"I believe so," I answered, having checked with my legal expert Jamal in the meantime.

"If your conscience wills it that way," was Farida's response to my decision. Bharwani's desire to be cremated had appalled her, actually; she saw it as mischievous and divisive. But she, if anyone, knew that my resolution had not been an easy one to arrive at; and we both were too aware that the final outcome tomorrow was far from certain, and repercussions in the days ahead would yet have to be faced.

LAID OUT BEFORE ME and my associate performing the funeral rites, Bharwani looked a meagre, helpless rendition of his old self in the funeral casket. In small groups selected members of the congregation came and knelt before him, on his other side, and went through the ritual in which the dead is forgiven of sins. Earlier on I had spotted Iqbal and gone to give him a comforting pat on the shoulder. I had developed a possessive, protective instinct for him. We stood together, and when I went to take my place for the ceremonies he came and sat down beside me on the carpet, watching people come and kneel before his dead father.

Yasmin was wearing a white shalwar kameez, a dupatta covering her head—a mode of dressing that was never traditionally ours but, ironically, has been recently acquired in Canada. Beside her sat her mother-in-law pulling at her beads frantically, her head lowered, and the sisters-in-law. Bharwani's two brothers and other male relations sat grimly in a large group directly in front of me, ready for battle; somewhat to the side and quite distinct from them sat Emil with a few young men. It took me a while to find Zuleikha, also sitting away from her family.

The ceremony over, I stood up, motioning for the casket to be left as it was, and made a short speech. I said that our brother Karim Bharwani had made his wish known at his death bed that he wanted to be cremated. Karim, who was a classmate of mine, was a deep-thinking and not frivolous man. I had been told that his wife and children wished to respect our dead brother's last wish. Whatever our own beliefs were, we should open our hearts and respect their decision.

I motioned to the funeral committee to pick up the coffin and begin the chant, so that the male family members and congregation could carry it away. The women of the family began to weep.

"We do not cremate our dead, it is a sin!" boomed a deep voice from the back of the hall. It was the Chairman.

For moments nothing moved, there came only the moaning, sobbing sounds of the women. I was the person officially in charge, and the weight of all stares was upon me. I nodded to Emil, whereupon he and two hefty friends stepped forward to lift the casket. They gathered at the front end, somewhat nervously awaiting reinforcements, when promptly the dead man's brothers and a third man came and took hold of the back. The coffin was raised—and there ensued a tug-of-war.

At first, equal forces applied from the front and the back, the coffin hung still. Then it lurched forward, where the greater strength of the younger men lay. But these boys relaxed their hold and a sudden pull came from behind, where two large women had now joined forces. A fair crowd had gathered and was pulling aggressively at the back, having sensed victory for that side, ready to hand it charge—but two or three of those at the very back tripped and fell, bringing their end of the coffin with them. Poor Bharwani, after being buffeted this way and that in his box, was brought to rest at a forty-five-degree angle.

There was stunned silence, and then the eerily thin quivering sound of a snicker that turned heads. It was Yasmin, caught in a hysterical fit. Tears streamed down her face as she laughed, Zuleikha holding on to her shoulders. The women around them had moved away in fear.

In disgust I turned to Bharwani's relations: "Is this what you wish for him, this circus? To what holy end?"

Shamefaced, they retreated from the coffin, which was brought back to rest on the floor. Then Jamal, Nanji, and the rest of the classmates at one end, and Emil and two pals in front, unescorted by anyone else, the coffin bearing Bharwani slowly made its way to the door, outside which two hearses awaited to carry the dead to either of the two arrangements which had been made for him.

Bharwani, you won, I muttered, as I closed the door of my car on Iqbal, who was accompanying me to the crematorium. There were four cars in the procession that left the mosque, far fewer than would normally have accompanied the cortège, and our escorting policemen sped us through the traffic in no time.

My new friend Iqbal was chatty in the car. "When a person dies, he leaves the body, isn't that so? So the body is just flesh, and even begins to smell and rot."

I nodded. "Yes. That's why we have to bury it or … cremate it, as soon as possible." Or leave it exposed for vultures to eat, I said to myself.

"My dad is alive somewhere, I know."

"I know that too."

Simple Recipes
MADELEINE THIEN

THERE IS A SIMPLE RECIPE for making rice. My father taught it to me when I was a child. Back then, I used to sit up on the kitchen counter watching him, how he sifted the grains in his hands, sure and quick, removing pieces of dirt or sand, tiny imperfections. He swirled his hands through the water and it turned cloudy. When he scrubbed the grains clean, the sound was as big as a field of insects. Over and over, my father rinsed the rice, drained the water, then filled the pot again.

The instructions are simple. Once the washing is done, you measure the water this way—by resting the tip of your index finger on the surface of the rice. The water should reach the bend of your first knuckle. My father did not need instructions or measuring cups. He closed his eyes and felt for the waterline.

Sometimes I still dream of my father, his bare feet flat against the floor, standing in the middle of the kitchen. He wears old buttoned shirts and faded sweatpants drawn at the waist. Surrounded by the gloss of the kitchen counters, the sharp angles of the stove, the fridge, the shiny sink, he looks out of place. This memory of him is so strong, sometimes it stuns me, the detail with which I can see it.

Every night before dinner, my father would perform this ritual—rinsing and draining, then setting the pot in the cooker. When I was older, he passed this task on to me but I never did it with the same care. I went through the motions, splashing the water around, jabbing my finger down to measure the water level. Some nights the rice was a mushy gruel. I worried that I could not do so simple a task right. "Sorry," I would say to the table, my voice soft and embarrassed. In answer, my father would keep eating, pushing the rice into his mouth as if he never expected anything different, as if he noticed no difference between what he did so well and I so poorly. He would eat every last mouthful, his chopsticks walking quickly across the plate. Then he would rise, whistling, and clear the table, every motion so clean and sure, I would be convinced by him that all was well in the world.

MY FATHER IS STANDING in the middle of the kitchen. In his right hand he holds a plastic bag filled with water. Caught inside the bag is a live fish.

The fish is barely breathing, though its mouth opens and closes. I reach up and touch it through the plastic bag, trailing my fingers along the gills, the soft, muscled body, pushing my finger overtop the eyeball. The fish looks straight at me, flopping sluggishly from side to side.

My father fills the kitchen sink. In one swift motion he overturns the bag and the fish comes sailing out with the water. It curls and jumps. We watch it closely, me on my tiptoes, chin propped up on the counter. The fish is the length of my arm from wrist to elbow. It floats in place, brushing up against the sides of the sink.

I keep watch over the fish while my father begins the preparations for dinner. The fish folds its body, trying to turn or swim, the water nudging overtop. Though I ripple tiny circles around it with my fingers, the fish stays still, bobbing side-to-side in the cold water.

FOR MANY HOURS at a time, it was just the two of us. While my mother worked and my older brother played outside, my father and I sat on the couch, flipping channels. He loved cooking shows. We watched *Wok with Yan,* my father passing judgement on Yan's methods. I was enthralled when Yan transformed orange peels into swans. My father sniffed. "I can do that," he said. "You don't have to be a genius to do that." He placed a sprig of green onion in water and showed me how it bloomed like a flower. "I know many tricks like this," he said. "Much more than Yan."

Still, my father made careful notes when Yan demonstrated Peking Duck. He chuckled heartily at Yan's punning. "Take a wok on the wild side!" Yan said, pointing his spatula at the camera.

"Ha ha!" my father laughed, his shoulders shaking. "*Wok* on the wild side!"

In the mornings, my father took me to school. At three o'clock, when we came home again, I would rattle off everything I learned that day. "The brachiosaurus," I informed him, "eats only soft vegetables."

My father nodded. "That is like me. Let me see your forehead." We stopped and faced each other in the road. "You have a high forehead," he said, leaning down to take a closer look. "All smart people do."

I walked proudly, stretching my legs to match his steps. I was overjoyed when my feet kept time with his, right, then left, then right, and we walked like a single unit. My father was the man of tricks, who sat for an hour mining a watermelon with a circular spoon, who carved the rind into a castle.

My father was born in Malaysia and he and my mother immigrated to Canada several years before I was born, first settling in Montreal, then finally in Vancouver. While I was born into the persistence of the Vancouver rain, my father was born in the wash of a monsoon country. When I was young, my parents tried to teach me their language but it never came easily to me. My father ran his thumb gently over my mouth, his face kind, as if trying to see what it was that made me different.

My brother was born in Malaysia but when he immigrated with my parents to Canada the language left him. Or he forgot it, or he refused it, which is also common, and this made my father angry. "How can a child forget a language?" he would ask my mother. "It is because the child is lazy. Because the child chooses not to remember." When he was twelve years old, my brother stayed away in the afternoons. He drummed the soccer ball up and down the back alley, returning home only at dinner time. During the day, my mother worked as a sales clerk at the Woodward's store downtown, in the building with the red revolving W on top.

In our house, the ceilings were yellowed with grease. Even the air was heavy with it. I remember that I loved the weight of it, the air that was dense with the smell of countless meals cooked in a tiny kitchen, all those good smells jostling for space.

THE FISH IN THE SINK is dying slowly. It has a glossy sheen to it, as if its skin is made of shining minerals. I want to prod it with both hands, its body tense against the pressure of my fingers. If I hold it tightly, I imagine I will be able to feel its fluttering heart. Instead, I lock eyes with the fish. *You're feeling verrrry sleepy,* I tell it. *You're getting verrrry tired.*

Beside me, my father chops green onions quickly. He uses a cleaver that he says is older than I am by many years. The blade of the knife rolls forward and backward, loops of green onion gathering in a pyramid beside my father's wrist. When he is done, he rolls his sleeve back from his right hand, reaches in through the water and pulls the plug.

The fish in the sink floats and we watch it in silence. The water level falls beneath its gills, beneath its belly. It drains and leaves the sink dry. The fish is lying on its side, mouth open and its body heaving. It leaps sideways and hits the sink. Then up again. It curls and snaps, lunging for its own tail. The fish sails into the air, dropping hard. It twitches violently.

My father reaches in with his bare hands. He lifts the fish out by the tail and lays it gently on the counter. While holding it steady with one hand, he hits the head with the flat of the cleaver. The fish falls still, and he begins to clean it.

IN MY APARTMENT, I keep the walls scrubbed clean. I open the windows and turn the fan on whenever I prepare a meal. My father bought me a rice cooker when I first moved into my own apartment, but I use it so rarely it stays in the back of the cupboard, the cord wrapped neatly around its belly. I have no longing for the meals themselves, but I miss the way we sat down together, our bodies leaning hungrily forward while my father, the magician, unveiled plate after plate. We laughed and ate, white steam fogging my mother's glasses until she had to take them off and lay them on the table. Eyes closed, she would eat, crunchy vegetables gripped in her chopsticks, the most vivid green.

MY BROTHER COMES into the kitchen and his body is covered with dirt. He leaves a thin trail of it behind as he walks. The soccer ball, muddy from outside, is encircled in one arm. Brushing past my father, his face is tense.

Beside me, my mother sprinkles garlic onto the fish. She lets me slide one hand underneath the fish's head, cradling it, then bending it backwards so that she can fill the fish's insides with ginger. Very carefully, I turn the fish over. It is firm and slippery, and beaded with tiny, sharp scales.

At the stove, my father picks up an old teapot. It is full of oil and he pours the oil into the wok. It falls in a thin ribbon. After a moment, when the oil begins crackling, he lifts the fish up and drops it down into the wok. He adds water and the smoke billows up. The sound of the fish frying is like tires on gravel, a sound so loud it drowns out all other noises. Then my father steps out from the smoke. "Spoon out the rice," he says as he lifts me down from the counter.

My brother comes back into the room, his hands muddy and his knees the colour of dusty brick. His soccer shorts flutter against the backs of his legs. Sitting down, he makes an angry face. My father ignores him.

Inside the cooker, the rice is flat like a pie. I push the spoon in, turning the rice over, and the steam shoots up in a hot mist and condenses on my skin. While my father moves his arms delicately over the stove, I begin dishing the rice out: first for my father, then my mother, then my brother, then myself. Behind me the fish is cooking quickly. In a crockery pot, my father steams cauliflower, stirring it round and round.

My brother kicks at a table leg.

"What's the matter?" my father asks.

He is quiet for a moment, then he says, "Why do we have to eat fish?"

"You don't like it?"

My brother crosses his arms against his chest. I see the dirt lining his arms, dark and hardened. I imagine chipping it off his body with a small spoon.

"I don't like the eyeball there. It looks sick."

My mother tuts. Her nametag is still clipped to her blouse. It says *Woodward's,* and then, *Sales Clerk.* "Enough," she says, hanging her purse on the back of the chair. "Go wash your hands and get ready for supper."

My brother glares, just for a moment. Then he begins picking at the dirt on his arms. I bring plates of rice to the table. The dirt flies off his skin, speckling the table-cloth. "Stop it," I say crossly.

"Stop it," he says, mimicking me.

"Hey!" My father hits his spoon against the counter. It *pings,* high-pitched. He points at my brother. "No fighting in this house."

My brother looks at the floor, mumbles something, and then shuffles away from the table. As he moves farther away, he begins to stamp his feet.

Shaking her head, my mother takes her jacket off. It slides from her shoulders. She says something to my father in the language I can't understand. He merely shrugs his shoulders. And then he replies, and I think his words are so familiar, as if they are words I should know, as if maybe I did know them once but then I forgot them. The language that they speak is full of soft vowels, words running together so that I can't make out the gaps where they pause for breath.

MY MOTHER TOLD ME once about guilt. Her own guilt she held in the palm of her hands, like an offering. But your guilt is different, she said. You do not need to hold on to it. Imagine this, she said, her hands running along my forehead, then up into my hair. Imagine, she said. Picture it, and what do you see?

A bruise on the skin, wide and black.

A bruise, she said. Concentrate on it. Right now, it's a bruise. But if you concentrate, you can shrink it, compress it to the size of a pinpoint. And then, if you want to, if you see it, you can blow it off your body like a speck of dirt.

She moved her hands along my forehead.

I tried to picture what she said. I pictured blowing it away like so much nothing, just these little pieces that didn't mean anything, this complicity that I could magically walk away from. She made me believe in the strength of my own thoughts, as if I could make appear what had never existed. Or turn it around. Flip it over so many times you just lose sight of it, you lose the tail end and the whole thing disappears into smoke.

MY FATHER PUSHES at the fish with the edge of his spoon. Underneath, the meat is white and the juice runs down along the side. He lifts a piece and lowers it carefully onto my plate.

Once more, his spoon breaks skin. Gingerly, my father lifts another piece and moves it towards my brother.

"I don't want it," my brother says.

My father's hand wavers. "Try it," he says, smiling. "Take a wok on the wild side."

"No."

My father sighs and places the piece on my mother's plate. We eat in silence, scraping our spoons across the dishes. My parents use chopsticks, lifting their bowls and motioning the food into their mouths. The smell of food fills the room.

Savouring each mouthful, my father eats slowly, head tuned to the flavours in his mouth. My mother takes her glasses off, the lenses fogged, and lays them on the table. She eats with her head bowed down, as if in prayer.

Lifting a stem of cauliflower to his lips, my brother sighs deeply. He chews, and then his face changes. I have a sudden picture of him drowning, his hair waving like grass. He coughs, spitting the mouthful back onto his plate. Another cough. He reaches for his throat, choking.

My father slams his chopsticks down on the table. In a single movement, he reaches across, grabbing my brother by the shoulder. "I have tried," he is saying. "I don't know what kind of son you are. To be so ungrateful." His other hand sweeps by me and bruises into my brother's face.

My mother flinches. My brother's face is red and his mouth is open. His eyes are wet.

Still coughing, he grabs a fork, tines aimed at my father, and then in an unthinking moment, he heaves it at him. It strikes my father in the chest and drops.

"I hate you! You're just an asshole, you're just a fucking asshole chink!" My brother holds his plate in his hands. He smashes it down and his food scatters across the table. He is coughing and spitting. "I wish you weren't my father! I wish you were dead."

My father's hand falls again. This time pounding downwards. I close my eyes. All I can hear is someone screaming. There is a loud voice. I stand awkwardly, my hands covering my eyes.

"Go to your room," my father says, his voice shaking.

And I think he is talking to me so I remove my hands.

But he is looking at my brother. And my brother is looking at him, his small chest heaving.

A FEW MINUTES LATER, my mother begins clearing the table, face weary as she scrapes the dishes one by one over the garbage.

I move away from my chair, past my mother, onto the carpet and up the stairs.

Outside my brother's bedroom, I crouch against the wall. When I step forward and look, I see my father holding the bamboo pole between his hands. The pole is smooth. The long grains, fine as hair, are pulled together, at intervals, jointed. My brother is lying on the floor, as if thrown down and dragged there. My father raises the pole into the air.

I want to cry out. I want to move into the room between them, but I can't.

It is like a tree falling, beginning to move, a slow arc through the air.

The bamboo drops silently. It rips the skin on my brother's back. I cannot hear any sound. A line of blood edges quickly across his body.

The pole rises and again comes down. I am afraid of bones breaking.

My father lifts his arms once more.

On the floor, my brother cries into the carpet, pawing at the ground. His knees folded into his chest, the crown of his head burrowing down. His back is hunched over and I can see his spine, little bumps on his skin.

The bamboo smashes into bone and the scene in my mind bursts into a million white pieces.

My mother picks me up off the floor, pulling me across the hall, into my bedroom, into bed. Everything is wet, the sheets, my hands, her body, my face, and she soothes me with words I cannot understand because all I can hear is screaming. She rubs her cool hands against my forehead. "Stop," she says. "Please stop," but I feel loose, deranged, as if everything in the known world is ending right here.

IN THE MORNING, I wake up to the sound of oil in the pan and the smell of French toast. I can hear my mother bustling around, putting dishes in the cupboards.

No one says anything when my brother doesn't come down for breakfast. My father piles French toast and syrup onto a plate and my mother pours a glass of milk. She takes everything upstairs to my brother's bedroom.

As always, I follow my father around the kitchen. I track his footprints, follow behind him and hide in the shadow of his body. Every so often, he reaches down and ruffles my hair with his hands. We cast a spell, I think. The way we move in circles, how he cooks without thinking because this is the task that comes to him effortlessly. He smiles down at me, but when he does this, it somehow breaks the spell. My father stands in place, hands dropping to his sides as if he has forgotten what he was doing mid-motion. On the walls, the paint is peeling and the floor, unswept in days, leaves little pieces of dirt stuck to our feet.

My persistence, I think, my unadulterated love, confuse him. With each passing day, he knows I will find it harder to ignore what I can't comprehend, that I will be unable to separate one part of him from another. The unconditional quality of my love for him will not last forever, just as my brother's did not. My father stands in the middle of the kitchen, unsure. Eventually, my mother comes downstairs again and puts her arms around him and holds him, whispering something to him, words that to me are meaningless and incomprehensible. But she offers them to him, sound after sound, in a language that was stolen from some other place, until he drops his head and remembers where he is.

Later on, I lean against the door frame upstairs and listen to the sound of a metal fork scraping against a dish. My mother is already there, her voice rising and falling. She is moving the fork across the plate, offering my brother pieces of French toast.

I move towards the bed, the carpet scratchy, until I can touch the wooden bed-frame with my hands. My mother is seated there, and I go to her, reaching my fingers out to the buttons on her cuff and twisting them over to catch the light.

"Are you eating?" I ask my brother.

He starts to cry. I look at him, his face half hidden in the blankets.

"Try and eat," my mother says softly.

He only cries harder but there isn't any sound. The pattern of sunlight on his blanket moves with his body. His hair is pasted down with sweat and his head moves forward and backward like an old man's.

At some point I know my father is standing at the entrance of the room but I cannot turn to look at him. I want to stay where I am, facing the wall. I'm afraid that if I turn around and go to him, I will be complicit, accepting a portion of guilt, no matter how small that piece. I do not know how to prevent this from happening again, though now I know, in the end, it will break us apart. This violence will turn all my love to shame and grief. So I stand there, not looking at him or my brother. Even my father, the magician, who can make something beautiful out of nothing, he just stands and watches.

A FACE CHANGES OVER TIME, it becomes clearer. In my father's face, I have seen everything pass. Anger that has stripped it of anything recognizable, so that it is only a face of bones and skin. And then, at other times, so much pain that it is unbearable, his face so full of grief it might dissolve. How to reconcile all that I know of him and still love him? For a long time, I thought it was not possible. When I was a child, I did not love my father because he was complicated, because he was human, because he needed me to. A child does not know yet how to love a person that way.

How simple it should be. Warm water running over, the feel of the grains between my hands, the sound of it like stones running along the pavement. My father would rinse the rice over and over, sifting it between his fingertips, searching for the impurities, pulling them out. A speck, barely visible, resting on the tip of his finger.

If there were some recourse, I would take it. A cupful of grains in my open hand, a smoothing out, finding the impurities, then removing them piece by piece. And then, to be satisfied with what remains.

Somewhere in my memory, a fish in the sink is dying slowly. My father and I watch as the water runs down.

Four Stations in His Circle
AUSTIN CLARKE

IMMIGRATION TRANSFORMED Jefferson Theophillis Belle; and after five years, made him deceitful, selfish, and very ambitious. It saddened his friend Brewster very much; but he had to confess that Jefferson was the most successful of them all. Still, Brewster pitied him. However, Jefferson had qualities which Brewster tried to emulate, even though JTB was not a likeable man. He was too ascetic, and pensive, and his friends hated him for it. But Jefferson had his mind on other things: a house and a piece of land around the house. "I must own a piece o' Canada!" Every morning going to work, as the Sherbourne bus entered Rosedale, he became tense. The houses in Rosedale were large and beautiful; and so far as he could guess they each had a fireplace ... *because, man, I couldn't purchase a house unless it got a fireplace ... that fire sparkling, and playing games on my face in the winter nights, crick-crack! ...* and sometimes, at night, Jefferson would go to Rosedale (once he went at three in the morning) to watch the house he had put his mind on. But this house was not for sale! *Gorblummuh! That don't deter me though! 'Cause one o' these mornings it must go up for sale, and I will be standing up right here, with the money in my hand.*

One Friday night in the Paramount Tavern on Spadina with Brewster, Jefferson had a great urge to see his property. He paid for the drinks; said he had to go to the men's room; slipped out through the back door; and nearly ran into a taxi driver hustling women and passengers. He raised his hand to call the taxicab. But he realized that he had already spent a foolish dollar on Brewster; so he changed his mind, and mentally deposited that dollar bill to the $10,000 he had in the bank; and he set out on foot. The wind was chilly. *Look how I nearly throw-'way that dollar 'pon foolishness! I am still a very strong man at forty. I could walk from Spadina to Rosedale, man.* And when he heard his own voice say how wise he was, he walked even faster. Anxiously, he grabbed his left back trousers pocket; "Oh!" he said, and a laugh came out. He didn't trust anybody; certainly not Brewster. He was very glad the money was in his pocket; and yet, for a second, he imagined that the money was actually stolen, and by Brewster. So he unpinned the two safety pins, undid the button, and took out the money, wrapped in a dirty black handkerchief. His experiences with money had made him uneasy. Any day he might need it for the down payment (although he could not have known what it would be); and if he wanted a house in Rosedale, he must be prepared.

He walked slowly now (there was money in his hand) and when he came under a light, he counted it. Nine hundred dollars. This money went to work with him; went to church with him; went into the washroom at work and at home with him; and when he went to bed, it was pinned to his pyjamas. "Nine! Right!" He had so much money now, he counted only in hundreds. He put the money back into his pocket; pinned it, twice; and buttoned it down. And before he moved on, he made a promise to change the handkerchief. *Five years! Five years I come to this country, with one pair o' shoes!*

Sometimes, in weaker moments, he would argue with himself to get some education too. Coming through the university grounds once, by chance, he saw a line of men and women crossing the lawn, with the lawn strewn with roses and flashbulbs and cheers and laughter, and a few tears to give significance to the roses and the bulbs; and he felt then, seeing the procession, the power of education and of the surrounding buildings. And he had shaken his head, and run away. The three hours following, he had spent forgetting and getting drunk in the Paramount. That was five years ago. Now, he did not have to run. He walked through the grounds jauntily this time, because he had nine hundred dollars, in cash, in his pocket. And as he came out, to enter Queen's Park, he saw two shadows; and the two shadows grew into two forms; and one form was raising the skirt above the thighs of the other form; and when they saw him coming, the man covered the girl's reputation with his jacket. They remained still, pretending they were shadows, until a passing car pointed its finger at the girl's back; and Jefferson saw UNIVERSITY OF TORONTO, written in white letters on the man's jacket she was wearing. *Goddamn, he's so broke through education, he can't afford a hotel room!*

Far along Bloor Street, the boasting water-van is littering Toronto and making some pedestrians wet; and a man holds half of his body through the driver's window, and says, "'Night!" and this greeting carries JTB into Rosedale, quiet as a reservation.

Five years of hard work have brought him here, tonight, in front of this huge mansion. *I going have to paint them windows green; and throw a coat o' black paint on the doors ... The screens in the windows will be green like in the West Indies ... I going pull up them flowers and put in roses, red ones; and build a paling, and build up my property value* … And he goes up on the lawn and tries to count the rooms in the four-storey house. *Imagine me in this house with four storeys! And not one blasted tenant or boarder!* But he cannot count all the rooms from the front, so he goes through the alleyway to look at the backyard, and the rooms in the back, and … (a car passes; and the man driving turns his head left, and sees a shadow; and he slows down, and the shadow becomes a form; he stops, says something on the radio in the car; parks the car; walks back; and waits) … and Jefferson comes humming back to the front lawn, and tries again to count, and four men pounce upon him and drag him along his lawn, with hands on his mouth and some in his guts, and drop him in the back seat of the cruiser. He can hear voices, talking at the same time, coming through the radio speaker. "Good!" a living voice says. "Take him to Division Two." And they did that.

Jefferson Theophillis Belle, of no fixed address, unknown, labourer unskilled, spent a very long time before he convinced them that he was not a "burglourer"; and in all that time, his head was spinning from the questions and from the blows: because "You were walking around this respectable district, this time of night, with all that money on your person, and you're not a *burglourer*? To buy a house, eh? That doesn't even have a FOR SALE sign up? Who are you kidding, mack? And they gave him one final kick of warning; and with his pride injured *(God blind you, cop! One o' these days I'm going to kill me a cop! So help me God!),* he woke up Brewster, to see what *he* thought. *They should still be kicking-in your behind!* Brewster said in his heart, as he rubbed the sleep out of his eyes. Without compassion, he dropped the telephone on Jefferson; and when he got back into bed, his blanket was rising and falling from the breath of his laughter and unkind wishes—*should have kicked-in your arse, boy!* Brewster couldn't wait for morning and the Paramount to talk about it.

After this, Jefferson decided to visit Rosedale in the daytime only. When paydays came, every cent went into his bank; and his balance climbed like a mountain; similarly, his hate for the Police. A week later he took out a summons against Brewster, who owed him twenty dollars from three years ago. He tried to get him arrested, but his lawyer advised otherwise; so Jefferson settled for a collection agency. The collection agency got the money back, but Jefferson gave it back to Brewster. This success convinced him further that business was more important than intellect; money more important still. He had seen Jews in the Spadina garment district; he had seen Polish immigrants in the Jewish market; he had seen their expensive automobiles going *north* after a beautiful day of swelling profits; and he said, *Me, too! Soon I going north, tambien!*

He stopped drinking at the Paramount. He stopped going to the Silver Dollar for funk, broads, rhythm, blues, and jazz. He didn't want to see any more black people. He spent more time in his room, alone. On weekends he watched television and drank beer; and rechecked his bank book, *because anybody could make a mistake, but be-Christ, they not making no mistake with my money!* His actions and his movements became tense, more ordered. His disposition became rawer; and once or twice he lost his temper with his supervisor at the post office (his part-time night job) and almost lost his job; but he lost only a slice of pride apologizing.

The hate that grew in his heart because the Police presumed he was a burglar, that he could be burglarizing the house of his dreams *(God blind you, Mister Policeman. I am a man too.)*, presuming that he, Jefferson Theophillis Belle, a black Barbadian, could only through crime possess nine hundred dollars in cash *(Double-blind you, Mister Ossifer! When I am working off my arse, where are ...?)*, was systematically eating away his heart and mind. In isolation he tried to find some solace. He would tell himself jokes, and laugh aloud at his own jokes. Still, something was missing. The boisterousness of the Paramount was gone. He no longer enjoyed Saturday mornings in the Negro barber shop on Dundas, where he and others, middle-aged and cronied, would sit waiting for the chair, laughing themselves into hiccups with jokes, with the barber, about women they knew when they were younger men. He went instead *north,* from Baldwin Street to the Italian barber on College. The hair-cuts there were worse, and more expensive; and time did not improve them.

He had almost walked away from his past when, on that bright Saturday morning—"Goddamn, baby!"—the Voice picked him out, sneaking out of the Italian barber's, brushing the hair out of his neck. He squirmed, because he recognized the voice. It came again, loud and vulgar. "I say, goddamn, baby!" Jefferson pretended he was just one of the European immigrants walking the street. And he walked on, hiding his head in invisible shame. The Voice had disappeared. He relaxed and breathed more easily. And suddenly he felt the hand on his neck, and "Goddammit! Baby, ain't you speaking to no niggers this morning, you sweet black motherfucker?" All the eyes in the foreign-language heads turned to listen. Then in a voice that the eyes couldn't hear, Brewster said, "Lend me a coupla bucks, baby. Races."

Jefferson Theophillis Belle made a mental note, right then, never again to speak to black people.

He found himself walking through the campus grounds again, spending long hours pondering the stern buildings; the library crammed with knowledge in print, and the building where he had seen the lines of penguins dressed in black and white, like graduate scholars. *Education is a funny thing, heh-heh-heh! And I had better get a piece o' that, too.* He argued himself into a piece of education; but he held fast to the piece of property too. He visited some institutions, and took away their prospectuses to study ... *These things make me out as if I don't know two and two is four, that the world round, that Columbus discover it in 1492, that that bastard sailed down in my islands and come back and called them* Indian, *hah-hah! ... If it was me make that mistake, my boss would fire my arse, tomorrow! I am an educated man, therefore.*

And he began to see himself in the diplomatic service.

He telephoned the university to see how he could become a diplomat; and after the initial silence of shock, the woman's voice advised him to read *all* the histories of the world. He borrowed a book, *The History of the World,* from the public library on College Street, and an *Atlas of the World,* and he turned on the television set instead.

Mr. Jefferson Theophillis Belle was written on each of the four envelopes that brought more prospectuses. He felt inferior that nothing was written behind his name. So he wrote on each envelope, behind his name: *BA, PhD, MA, MLitt, DLitt, Diploma in Diplomacy, Barbadian Ambassador to Canada.* And he laughed. Then he got a basin, a new one, lit a match, and burned everything. (The last to burn was the prospectus from the Department of History in the university.) He watched all the knowledge he might have had burn and consume; and he laughed. This was on a Sunday; and he went on the couch, drinking and watching television. After a while he fell back on the couch, quite suddenly, as if the string that regulated his life was cut. The half-empty bottle of warm beer was still in his hand; the landlady passing through after bingo at her church pushed the door to say "Night-night!" and saw him on the couch. She turned off the television; she put the large "Plan of the Grounds of Ryerson" over his face; she took the bottle from his hand, and drank it off. She put two others in her coat pockets, said "Bringing them back" to the two beers, and she left.

Monday came too early. He could feel pebbles of hangover in his eyes; and the raucous shouting of his landlady: "You really tied one on last night, Mr. Jefferson Belle. You really tied one ..." was like an enamel plate banged on stone against his temples. And then, suddenly, he came to a dead stop before his 1949 Pontiac. Somebody had scratched FACT YOU, MUCK in shaky inebriated grease on the frost of his windshield and trunk. *A thing like this couldn't happen up in Rosedale. It couldn't.* All that day, at his full-time paint factory job, and all that night at the post office, he was tense.

He soon discovered that his energy was being sapped from him. He wondered whether he should quit his night job; he had enough money now; but *no, man, the house in Rosedale, man!* He worked harder that night, and when he went home, he did twenty-three push-ups. And then it happened!

A FOR SALE sign appeared—on the house *beside* his house. This threw him into a fit, trying to decide whether to buy that house (it was empty, no furniture, and had thirteen rooms), when a letter came from home. He recognized his mother's hand-writing on the red-white-and-blue airmail envelope, and refused to open it. The tension came back. He took the letter to the light bulb, to see if he could read the news inside without opening it ... *Look, Jeff, boy! Opportunity does knock only one time in Rosedale* ... And that was it. He called the real estate agent, and arranged the purchase.

The tenseness left him. He could see himself cutting red luxuriant roses he had planted; waving his hand at a beautiful woman; calling her, and pinning a rose on her bosom; but the rose he held in his hand now was the real estate agent's number; and when he realized this, he tore it up. The paper petals fell without a noise. But he was now Jefferson Theophillis Belle, Esquire, Landowner and Property Owner, Public School Tax-payer (he had no children!) ... He would give his occupation in the voters list as "Engineer, retired" ... *The letter, though, Jeff! Stop this blasted dreaming 'bout house and land and see what the Old Queen have to say, and don't let more sorrow fall 'pon your head; and remember where you beginned from, 'cause a mother is a mother, boy, 'cause—*

Dear Jeff, when you left this island I ask God to help you. Now, I want you and God to help me. I know He help you, because somebody tell me so, and still you have not send me one blind cent. But God understand. You did not know I was laid up with a great sickness? I have a new doctor now, a Bajan, who studied medicines up in Canada, where you is. He told me you can help me, because they is a lot of money in Canada. I need a operation. I feel bad to ask you, though. But, I am, Your Mother.

(signed) *Mother.*
POSTSCRIPT: *House spots selling dirt-cheap now in Barbados. Think.*
Love, Mother.
Don't forget to read your Bible, Jefferson; it is God words, son.
Love, again, still, Mother.

Months later, in Rosedale, he would see the page burning; and the words would haunt him, in whispers; and he would tell himself that he should have torn up the letter only; and not the Bible too. But when he had put his hands to it that day, he had no idea that it was such a fragile book ... and he should have sent the money to his mother, sick then; dead, probably, now ... the page, the last page before the Bible cried out in the fire; and the line "Remember not the sins of my youth, nor my transgressions" ... but life in Rosedale flourished like a red rose.

An invitation card of gold embossed print was dropped through his letterbox. He did not notice the name on the envelope which he tore up and tossed away; but he read that Miss Emilie Elizabeth Heatherington was engaged to Mr. Asquith Breighington-Kelly; and they were having a party, at Number 46—next door.

This pleased Jefferson. The next day, he joined Theophillis to Belle with a hyphen. For three days, he sunned his suit to kill the evil fragrance of camphor balls. He dressed for the party, and waited behind his curtains made of newspapers to watch the first guests arriving. Everyone was in formal wear. They came in Jaguars, in Lincolns and Cadillacs. He took off his brown suit, lit his fireplace, and spent the evening sitting on an onion crate. Long after he had return-posted his invitation in the flames, in anger and disappointment, he could still hear the merriment next door. He wondered why nobody called him.

But the fire died, and he was awakened by cramp and a dream of his mother. He puttered around his house; and he drew some parallel lines on the walls of three rooms, as bookcases; and he drew books between the lines, until he could get some real books from the Book of the Month Club. Before going to bed, he decided to change his car. He must buy a new car, because *living in a district like this, and being the onliest man who does do work with his bare hands, and, and-and ... that oil company president next door, Godblindhim!* comes along, limping on the weight of his walking stick, and smells the freshness of the grass and water and roses, and looks up and smiles and says, "Evening! Have you heard when they're coming back?" Jefferson always pretended he didn't understand. Another time, the old oil man said, "You're a darn fine gardener. Best these people ever had; and better than those Italians, too!" He had said this on the afternoon of the party ... and thinking about the old man's words, Jefferson had to look at that invitation again, to see something very important on it. But he remembered he had burned both the envelope and the invitation. He vowed never again to burn anything. There were many invitations printed in the blood of ink, and many Bibles with *"Remember not the sins of my youth"* printed on every page.

He traded his Pontiac for a 1965 Jaguar, automatic. It was long, sleek, and black. After this, he dressed in a three-piece suit for work, with a black briefcase. In the briefcase were old shoes, work shirt, and overalls. He would change into these in the men's room of the East End Café, near East End Paints Ltd., where he worked as Janitor and Maintenance, General. He bought a formal morning suit *and* a tuxedo for evening formal occasions.

Some time after, the stick that walked out with the old oilman next door tapped and stopped and said, "When? Are *they* coming back?" Jefferson got mad, and told him, "Look, I own this, yuh! And the name is Jefferson Theophillis-Belle!" The man of oil stretched out his hand, grabbed JT-B's, and said, amiably, "I'm Bill!"

JEFFERSON HAS JUST COME HOME on this Friday afternoon, and is changing into his night-shift clothes (there was no danger of being caught at night) when the doorbell rings. It is his first caller. He looks at the half-eaten sandwich of peanut butter, and wonders what to do with it (the doorbell is ringing); and he can feel himself losing weight; and he wishes he had filled the prescription the doctor gave him for tension ... He stops before the mirror he had hung in his imagination on the wall in the hall, to see if peanut butter is between his teeth ... But it is only Bill's wife, who came to invite him, for the second time, to the party on Saturday—when the scandalous Voice from his past entered and shrieked, "God-*damn!* Ain't you one big sweet black motherfu—" and Jefferson rushed out of one room and whispered, "Christ, man! Not now! Somebody here!" But the Voice, thinking past is present, said, "Man, we was looking for you for a crap game, last Sar'day night, baby! Man, those fellas drink whiskey like water!"—and Bill's wife came in, smiled, and said, "You're busy, but don't forget, Satteedee." And she left. Jefferson jumped into a rage; but the Voice merely asked, "What I do?" And after looking through the first room, and the second, the Voice exclaimed, "But wait, Jeff! Where is the blasted furnitures, man?"

IN THE JAGUAR, speeding out of Rosedale, the Voice was silent. "You ask me what you do?" Jefferson said at last. "But it is more as if I should ask myself, what *I* do?" The Voice took a long pull on his cigarette, and said, "Baby, you made your bed. Now, goddamn, lie down in it!" And he slapped Jefferson goodbye, and said, "Let me off here. I want to get blind drunk tonight."

They were opposite the Paramount. Jefferson had forgotten the landmarks on this street; he had forgotten the smoke and vapour from the Southern-fried chicken wings fried in fat, in haste, by the Chinaman whose face never showed a change in emotion; and in forgetting all these, he had forgotten to have time, in Rosedale, to enjoy himself … A party of rich, educated people of Holt Renfrew tastes; he, always, ill at ease: "Now, Mr. Theophillis-Belle, as a P.Eng., structural, I ask you, what do you consider to be the structural aesthetics of our new City Hall?"

In less champagned-and-whiskied company his answer, which showed his ignorance—"*That?*"—might not have brought cheers. And the Jewish jokes and Polish jokes, and he, Structural and Jefferson and Engineer, dreading every moment, in case the jokes change into negro jokes; or walking beneath a crystal chandelier and praying he won't touch it, and break it, and have to offer (out of courtesy) to replace it (and finding that he had to!); and standing before the mirror on Bill's wall, and suddenly seeing that he was not, after all, the fairest reflection of them all; and running out through the door … Jefferson turned off the car lights, and sat thinking; and Brewster appeared from nowhere with a white woman on his arm, sauntering to the LADIES AND ESCORTS entrance.

Since he has been living in Rosedale, Jefferson has not taken a woman—nor black nor white nor blue—up his front steps.

He blew his horn. Brewster looked back. The woman looked too, and said, "Piss off!" He closed the car door. He started the car.

He drove beside the Paramount, hoping to see Brewster. But only a drunk came out; and when he saw Jefferson he raised his hand, and coughed and vomited on the gravel beside the LADIES AND ESCORTS … Well, he might turn west for Baldwin Street, to see his ex-landlady, to see if the house is still there, or if the city or Teperman Wreckers have … But he turned east, for the post office. That night, he forgot to notice the letters addressed to Rosedale; he spent his time thinking of formal parties. All of a sudden he had a very disturbing vision which destroyed his joy in formal suits: instead of being at Bill's party, dressed and formal as an undertaker, he saw himself in a funeral parlour, laid out, tidy and dead, prepared for burial, with his hands clasped on the visible cummerbund; and on the cummerbund, his gold ring and his pocket watch.

Jefferson wondered who would dress him for his coffin; would the person remember to include *both* formal suits (he was thinking evil of Brewster)? Who would get his life insurance on his death? And his life savings, $300 and descending because of the new Jaguar, and the formal suits and the new curtains, and the True-Form mattress he had ordered yesterday from Eaton's, because the canvas cot was leaving marks and pains in his back ... his hands trembling with the letters in them, for twenty-three minutes; and before he knew it, the supervisor was there. "Come with me!"

Ten minutes later, three hours before his shift should have ended, he still could not understand why he hadn't killed the supervisor; why he had stood like a fool, silent, without explaining that he was a man under doctor's prescriptions, for tension; and *why, goddammit! he hadn't flatten his arse with a right! or smash-in his false teeth, because I've been on this post office job more than four years, even before that bastard* ... But he was entering tranquility and Rosedale now, and the only person he saw on the road was a black man: *a black man, in my Rosedale, at this time?* And then he saw her, close as a leech, walking beside him.

His house was empty and quiet. Tired now, he undressed, and stood for a while, thinking of what to do. He put on his pyjamas. He got into his cot. He got out of his cot; and dressed himself in his evening formal tuxedo. It was two o'clock Saturday, *a.m.*! He walked up to the full-length mirror on the wall, and smiled at the reflection the wall and his imagination threw back; and he adjusted his hat in the wall; straightened his shoulders and started walking in and out of each of the thirteen rooms, smiling at women—black women, white women, blue women—and it was *such a good evening, Miss Jordan ... good evening, Bill, thanks ... lovely party ... Lady Hawgh-Hawgh, the name is Theophillis-Belle, engineer, structural and retired, haw-haw! ... oh, Mr. Stein! I can now purchase four thousand shares at five ... my solicitors will contact you, tomorrow, Monday ... haw-haw! of course, it's Sunday! ... and don't call me, I'll call thee, haw-haw! ... well you see, Lady Hawgh-Hawgh, I was having cocktails in the Russian Embassy, discussing the possibility of granting nuclear weapons to Barbados and other Caribbean territories, when—*Brewster entered.

Only later did JT-B notice the woman there. Brewster was saying, Jesus God! Jesus God! over and over. And the woman's mouth was open, in terror and pity. *Comrade, may I introduce my colleague, the African delegate from—*"What the hell you playing, boy? You don't know Brewster? I just pass you on the street!"—*and his charming wife, also from ... Africa?* Brewster had to laugh. "Look you, you foolish bitch!" he said. "Take this." The telegram fell in front of Jefferson. "Your landlady send that. She had to open it, 'cause she couldn't find you. It's your mother. She *dead, boy!*" ... *Thank you, thank you, comrade, for these tidings* ... and Jefferson Theophillis-Belle continued to walk up and down the hollow house (Brewster and the woman still staring), muttering greetings in whispers to his guests, and answering himself; and holding the telegram in his left hand, that hand resting militarily on the black cummerbund, as he bowed and walked, walked and bowed, bowed and walked ...

The Cave

W.D. VALGARDSON

I FIRST CAME UPON Sigga Anderson at her cousin's farm. I had knocked on the screen door and got no reply, so I went around to the back and there, wearing a wide-brimmed hat, a white dress and no shoes, she was picking raspberries. I must have made some slight sound, for she glanced up.

Her blond hair was curled to her shoulders. Her skin was damp and pink with the heat and her lips were red with the juice of the berries she had eaten. We stared at each other without saying anything, then she rose and held the white enamel bowl toward me. The berries were piled so high that some cascaded down and dropped to the ground.

"*Godan daginn,*" she said.

"*Godan daginn,*" I said.

"*Tala thu Islenzku?*"

"*Nay,*" I replied.

"That's too bad," she said, in the slightly ponderous way that Icelanders have of speaking English. "You are Valgardson. I recognize you from Einar's description."

"Is Einar home?"

"They've all gone to the beach."

"But not you."

"Would you have me roasted alive? I'm not used to the sun yet."

"And the mosquitoes?"

"They're devils."

She put the white basin into my hand and lifted up her dress for me to look. Her legs were spotted with angry-looking lumps. Iceland does not have mosquitoes, and Icelanders who come to Canada suffer terrible reactions when they are first stung.

"Has Einar any beer in the well?" I asked. She let down her dress. "It was a long ride on my bicycle."

She was, I discovered, twenty, single and quick-tempered. The last did not keep me from making daily trips to Einar's. Nor was I deterred by the fact she was Gunnar Thordarson's great-granddaughter.

We went walking in the hayfields together and along the edge of the poplar bush, picking wild roses and Indian paintbrush and wild lilies. We filled buckets with berries.

More and more often, though, our trips ended at one of Einar's haystacks. At mealtimes and in the evenings, there were good-natured comments around the table about the work it took to make a good stack and how, if the tops were thrown about, the hay would not survive the rain and snow.

Until then I had not even considered marriage. As a matter of fact, I had frequently bragged that I would not marry until I was thirty and well established. Since I still had three years to go, my relationship with Sigga caused some sly comments and smiles.

By late August, I no longer cared about looking foolish. Quite confidently, I asked her to marry me. I didn't go down on bended knee. It would have been quite impractical. We had just made love and were lying on top of one of Einar's precious haystacks. It is one of those special times I remember with painful clarity.

There were three small, fluffy clouds sliding slowly westward. There was no sound except for the occasional shifting in the hay. I was lying with one arm under my head, the other around Sigga.

If I remember the incident as clearly as I think I do, I said, "If you wanted, we could get married before school starts."

"No." She said it so quietly and agreeably that, at first, I took it for assent. When it finally registered that I had been refused, I rolled toward her to look into her pale green eyes.

"Sooner?"

"Not sooner. Not later."

I felt as though my heart had stopped. I would have been angry except that I was so taken aback. "But I love you," I protested.

"Yes," she agreed.

"And you love me?"

"Yes."

With that, my heart started to beat again. Or, at least, I became aware that it was still working.

"Then why in heaven's name …" I had been so sure of her reply that I had already rented a small log cabin behind the school. It had a kitchen, living room and two small bedrooms. There were red shutters on the windows and a natural stone chimney. It had taken all my persuasiveness to convince the owner, who lived in Winnipeg and used it for a summer cottage, to let me have it from September until the end of June. "I've rented Brynolver's cabin," I blurted out.

"Good. Living there with you will be nice."

"Then, for God's sake, let's get married."

She let her eyes slide away from mine. "No. I would like to live with you, but I won't marry."

"Are you crazy?"

It was not a good thing to say. I felt her stiffen. I had momentarily forgotten that her great-grandfather had been Gunnar Thordarson and that her father was Valdi Anderson.

There are times to be silent. I lay back and studied the pale blue sky. Normally, Sigga would have curled against my side but now, although she remained with her head on my arm, her body was stiff.

"Remember the roses," I said.

One day after she had fallen asleep, I slid down the haystack, ran to the side of the road, and using my shirt like a sack, filled it with the petals of wild roses. I returned, scattered them over her naked, golden body. When she awoke and sat up, rose petals filled her lap, clung to her hair. We made love again and the bruised petals engulfed us in their sweet scent.

"If I marry, my husband will want sons. I will have no sons."

Earlier, the thought that I had a rival had made my head ring with jealousy. Now, I suddenly wished it were that simple.

"I'm a high school teacher. If we live together, the board will have fits."

"I had promised myself to care for no one," she answered quietly. "Then you appeared with your one pant leg held in place with a bicycle clip."

"I had promised not to marry until I was thirty and then only to a widow with a good income."

"It was your beard and the shocked look in your eyes." She squeezed my hand.

"This is madness," I answered.

"If only it weren't," she answered and began to cry.

If this were a piece of fiction, all this description would be irrelevant detail. I would follow Poe's dictum and start closer to the climax. I would organize it toward one effect and ruthlessly eliminate everything else. But it is not fiction. What matters is not plot or theme but only that you understand. To ask, for example, "What is your motive?" of someone is to imply a simplicity about life that, except for the stupidest of people, is hopelessly inaccurate.

What was my motive in researching the lives of Sigga's great-grandfather and father? To prove that they were not crazy? To reassure Sigga that if she was to have a son, he would escape their fate? To reassure myself of the same thing? To defuse the innuendo and gossip that have persisted about this family for over seventy years? And more. Some of which I, myself, am still not clear about.

Life, unfortunately, is not as tractable as fiction. I cannot invent my characters or their lives. They already exist. I can only attempt to discover and understand.

I began by visiting people I knew. There was nothing formal about it, nothing, at first, even deliberate. I'd drop by for coffee and, after we were settled around the kitchen table, ask questions about Gunnar and Valdi.

It was unproductive. Not so much because everyone was deliberately evasive, but because each person had such small fragments of Gunnar and Valdi's lives. At times, I felt like I was collecting the parts of a shattered stained glass window, the pieces of which had been picked up by people over the years and tucked away in drawers or cupboards. Some had forgotten where they put them, others still knew where they were and, if I was lucky, would go get them to give to me. Some, because of the passage of time, had mixed them up with pieces of glass from other windows and gave me fragments that caused nothing but confusion. Some pieces were never picked up and were irretrievably lost.

If it was not for the fact that Sigga discovered and gave me a fish box full of Gunnar's diaries and letters, plus her father's correspondence, I would have given up. These records were not complete. However, to stick to my stained glass analogy, these records provided the lead in the window.

Because I'm a short story writer—W.D. Valgardson is hardly a name to conjure with, but here and there, people have read my stories—I'm very conscious that if this were fiction, I'd not begin like this, with a lot of explanation and excuse making. Instead, I'd go right to the heart of the story and I'd leave myself out of it, become an effaced narrator, or if I used the first person, it would not really be me, but a mask.

One of the first things you learn in telling a story is to condense time for dramatic effect, but how can I condense four generations? In a piece of fiction, I cast about for the right structure, the method of telling the story that will get me closest to the truth. This research and retelling in which I have been involved has nearly driven me to distraction because there is no structure except the one that life has imposed, and if there is any lesson about life, it escapes me. What I have finally resolved to do is to take the coward's way out—tell the story in a reasonably chronological fashion.

My beginning is arbitrary. I chose it because there is a major change in the lives of the main participants, but I could equally as well have begun elsewhere. In life there are no real beginnings or endings. There are so many moments where one can say, "That's where it started," and, in most cases, it is both true and false. Life is nothing if not untidy.

Gunnar and Runa

GUNNAR'S FAMILY owned a good-sized farm, Hagar,[1] but the volcanic eruptions of 1875 reduced it to half its size. Just before the eruption, Gunnar had married Helga Jonsdottir. The marriage, by all accounts, was an unhappy one. Both were quick-tempered and proud. They took offence easily and were slow to give up grudges. Helga's father was, in Icelandic terms, well-to-do, and one day, when Gunnar—his family nearly reduced to penury by the destruction of their land—refused Helga something she wanted, she said she would ask her father for it. Enraged, he slapped her. She picked up a knife and, if being six months pregnant had not made her awkward, would have killed him. Instead, she left him with a cut that ran from his eye to his jaw. Sometime during the next week, with the help of a farmhand, she returned to her father's house.

Gunnar followed her and tried to force her to return home with him. Her relatives stopped him. He began to drink heavily and, at every opportunity, to abuse his wife's family with scathing verses that he recited to anyone who would listen. Then, abruptly, after his wife gave birth, Gunnar's behaviour changed. He called on her—sober, repentant, his voice gentle—gave her silver equal to the price of a cow. He no longer tried to get his wife back, but from time to time, he visited Reykjavik to see his daughter and to leave *skyr*[2] and mutton. Because of what had occurred, he would not enter his in-laws' house. Instead, he and Helga walked with the child to the home of mutual friends. This went on for two years.

Then, abruptly, Gunnar sold his farm and notified his wife that he intended to give the child part of the money from the sale. He also told her he was emigrating to North America. Two days before he was to leave, he arrived at his in-laws' front door and asked his wife if he might spend some time alone with the child. It was unlikely, as he pointed out, that he would ever see her again.

His behaviour had been so exemplary that Helga agreed. Besides, Gunnar's ship was not due to arrive for another day. They were gone all afternoon, but Helga was not overly concerned. She expected that Gunnar was going from house to house saying goodbye to his friends. However, when supper time came and passed, she began to worry. She put on her coat and went to see if she could find them.

It was too late. Gunnar and Runa were already on their way to Denmark on a small freighter. His planning was meticulous and must have been started shortly after his daughter was born.

---

1. Icelandic word for meadow. Icelandic farms were all named. The tradition was so strong it was carried to Canada.
2. An Icelandic yogurt.

Gunnar and Runa in Winnipeg

GUNNAR AND RUNA arrived in Halifax on July 23, 1878. They travelled from there to Toronto, stayed in Toronto three months and arrived in Winnipeg on October 28. Egil Fjelsted was a child at the time. He went with his father to the CPR station to meet them. He was very young and did not actually remember their arrival, but afterward he heard about it so often that he said it was as if he remembered it.[3]

October was no time to be arriving in Winnipeg. Summer construction and farm work were over. Gunnar spoke hardly any English, so most nonlabouring jobs were closed to him. He and Runa boarded in the West End at the Fjelsteds' until Crooked Eye Oddleifson turned up.

Oddleifson was a barrel of a man, slope-shouldered, with big, shovel-like hands and one eye that turned in so much he appeared to be looking at his own nose. He hired Gunnar to help him with fishing. No one else would go. Oddleifson's camp was more isolated than most. He had a reputation for feeding his help poorly, working them hard and, if he could get away with it, not paying their wages. That Gunnar accepted the job indicated how desperate he was becoming.

He could not take Runa. Even if she could survive the hundred and fifty–mile trek in the cold, the camp was no place for a child. The two men would leave every day before dawn and stay on the ice until dark. Reluctantly, he agreed to leave her in Mrs. Fjelsted's care.

Gunnar and Oddleifson

THE WEATHER WAS BITTER. Ten degrees below zero during the day. Thirty below at night. Oddleifson had brought a horse and sleigh but used it only for supplies. To keep warm, they walked. Fort Garry, Gimli, Icelandic River, Mikley and, finally, all the way to the camp. They slept at stopping places along the way. Breakfast they got from the owners of the houses, but lunch and supper were bread and smoked fish they kept inside their jackets so it wouldn't freeze.

It must have been a frightening experience for a man like Gunnar, who, in Iceland, was used to staying close to his own farm. Day after day, he walked over endless miles of drifted snow. In his diary, he compares it to entering a white hell. Before they reached the camp, he became snow-blind, and Oddleifson had to tie a rope around his waist and attach it to the sleigh. Gunnar was forced to follow helplessly, sometimes walking, sometimes running, frequently falling, while, behind him, the known world retreated.

The camp was worse than he expected. It was one room carelessly kept. Life in a

---

3. Fjelsted, Egil. Died, Betel, Gimli, Manitoba, 1968.

fish camp was hard enough, but Oddleifson was dirty without need. What he could have done to make life more bearable, he did not do.

The two men did not get along well. Oddleifson had been described by others as insensitive, even brutal. Because of his eye, he had a strange way of turning his head to one side and hunching his shoulders. It earned him a second nickname of "the Bull."

Gunnar, besides being a farmer, had been a poet of some reputation. Moreover, he was well educated and sensitive. Having to live day in and day out with Oddleifson, with his gross habits and crude conversation, must have been difficult. How it would have worked out was never discovered, because three months after they began fishing together, Crooked Eye put an ice chisel through his foot. His uncleanliness did him in. The wound infected, and within a week, he died.

Now, do you see what is so maddening? It is as if everything is connected and yet nothing is connected. Do you know what I mean? If this were a piece of fiction, I could have foreshadowed, dramatized and then subtly not revealed what actually happened. You would have deduced that Gunnar, isolated, angered, actually killed Oddleifson. There would be an epiphany and you and I would share a secret understanding of men's hearts.

I can do no such thing. I can find no evidence that Gunnar stuck an ice chisel through Oddleifson's foot, rubbed it with horse shit and then waited for him to die.

Nor can I make anything of the fact Gunnar did not go for help. Given the distance and the weather, there was no point in trying to take Oddleifson in on the sleigh, even if he had permitted it. What Gunnar did do, once Oddleifson was dead, was haul his body onto the roof of the shed so that the animals could not get at it, then each day, as his work permitted, chiselled frozen ground until he had a grave.

At this point, Gunnar was faced with a choice. He could return to Winnipeg and a winter's unemployment or he could stay by himself in the camp. He had received no payment for his work and, if anything, was worse off than he had been before. He chose to stay.

Although he did not realize it, the pattern of his life was set.[4] He lived in the camp and fished fall and winter. July he spent with Runa at the Fjelsteds'. A number of times, as Runa grew older, he talked of having her come and live with him, but Mrs. Fjelsted would not hear of it.

During his second year in the camp, he decided something that, at the time, seemed of no significance, and yet it ultimately affected him more than anything else he had done. His problem and his attempt to solve it was this.

---

4. There was an attempt some years later by a cousin of Oddleifson's to claim the camp as an inheritance. However, he was in Iceland, and Lake Winnipeg was a great distance away. When Gunnar heard of the claim, he only replied, "Let him come and get it."

During the winter, he kept his perishable food on the roof. Once the spring thaw set in, however, he had no way of keeping food fresh.

He began to search the limestone cliffs along the lake for a cave. What he hoped to find was one deep enough that if it was packed with ice and snow, would keep food frozen through the warm months. He searched for days and was on the point of giving up when he found what he was looking for—but in a most extraordinary way.

Along with being a poet, he had always been something of a mystic. Perhaps that's why events took the turn they did. He became ill, suffered nightmares and existed, for a time, in that half-asleep, half-awake mixture of reality and fantasy that leaves one uncertain of one's own sanity, for in it the familiar world shifts and changes into a quicksand of images. Finally, the fever broke and he slept soundly. During this sleep, he had a dream, and in this dream, he claims he found the entrance to the cave. The cliff appeared before him in great detail, as though it were magnified. He scrutinized the cliff, checking and rechecking all the cracks, then stopped before a place where the rock was thick with moss. There seemed to be nothing of interest there, but then the moss darkened and the rocks slanted inward.

When he woke, he remembered the dream clearly. However, he was still weak with fever and did not go out for another three days. Each night, as if it had a life of its own, the dream returned. When, at last, he was well enough to go out, the first thing he did was row a boat along the lake shore to the spot where the dream had taken him. When he came to a section of rock of which he had dreamt, it was as he remembered it. In the dream, as he had reached out to pull away the moss, he had always awakened, but now there was no waking. He felt the moss thick and moist under his fingertips; felt it tear in a long sheet. Here was a fissure that was just big enough for him to enter by angling his shoulders sideways.

He first thought it only a crack, but then, it widened. The air was cold. He went back to the beach, found a long strip of birch bark, set it afire and, using it like a torch, explored the narrow cave. Five feet from the entrance, the floor was a solid slab of ice. Where there were cracks in the ceiling, icicles hung down like stalactites. He was so excited by his discovery that in his diary, he exclaims, "What a find! Now, I can keep food all year if I wish."[5]

During the next winter, his only visitors were freighters who came to load his fish. He did not mind. He had brought with him a small library, and although most of his money went for Runa's support, he bought philosophical books that dealt, in one way or the other, with the existence of reality.

None fascinated him more than the theory of Bjorn Bjornson,[6] who claimed the

---

5. July 6, 1879.
6. Bjornson, Bjorn, 1750–1797, *Souls Adrift*, Oslo, private printing, 57 pp.

soul never slept but inhabited bodies in two worlds and passed back and forth between them. What we call madness was not, according to this theorist, the inability to tell what was real and what was hallucination but a leakage of information from one existence to another.

There is very little description of Gunnar's appearance and no photograph. We know that toward the end of 1910 he grew a full beard. His grey hair he let grow until it reached his shoulders. He wore a beaded deerhide jacket, which he had bought from the Indians. That is known because Axel Arnason, the freighter, recorded this in a report to his sister in a letter.[7]

At first, the cave was no more than a convenience, a place to keep deer and moose meat and enough fish to supply his huskies during the spring and fall when he could not get on the water. It was only later that it became an obsession.

During the winter of 1914, Axel Arnason arrived to pick up fish. There was no one in the cabin. That, in itself, meant nothing. Gunnar could be on the lake or in the bush. Axel lit the fire and waited. No one came, and as he said in his deposition to the police,[8] after a time he became nervous. The sleigh was outside the door, but there was no sign of the dogs. There were no tracks in the snow and there had been a heavy snowfall a week before.

He went outside, kicked at a mound of snow and found a dead husky. Then another and another, all still chained to their ground pegs. In the lean-to, the horse had frozen to death standing up.

It took the police a month to get a man out to the camp. There was no rush. Gunnar was certainly dead, probably under the ice or frozen in a snowdrift. His belongings were collected and put in fish boxes and shipped to Runa.

Gunnar's Diary
—translated by Miss S. Stephanson

August 18, 1911
The cave is seventy-five feet long, ten feet high at its highest point and four feet across. Its general shape is that of a canoe with blunt ends.

August 19, 1911
I returned to the cave today. This time I took a better torch, which I fashioned from reeds and pitch. The walls are thick with the past. It is like memory frozen in stone. Animals and plants bleached white. I made some sketches.

---

7. Icelandic collection, University of Manitoba.
8. RCMP archives, Regina, Saskatchewan.

His diary, more and more, records the details of the cave. He made a grid of string so that floor, walls, roof, were divided into three-inch squares. Each segment he mapped. At the same time, his recording of weather, of nets, of fish, begins to fall off.

Gradually, intertwined with his studies, grew the thesis for his essay "The Seasons and the Blood." From his reading, he began to collect every example that would prove history is cyclical and that the future can be predicted from the past. In 1939, Runa discovered this essay, made a copy and offered it to a number of Scandinavian publishers; however, arriving as it did in the face of a rapidly advancing technological age whose justification for its excesses lay in the assumption that time is linear and all change leads to improvement, it was rejected.

September 20, 1911
Today, I smashed through the curtain of ice at the rear of the cave. My axe discovered a narrow slit in the rock that I could hardly squeeze through. What is there?

What was there, he discovered, was a series of caves, a labyrinthine honeycomb that underlay the entire area. The surface looked, from above, impervious, solid, real, but although it supported infinite trees, marshes and animals, its solidity was only illusion. It was a secret world discovered by dreams, a secret world that altered his whole concept of reality.

For a time, he was satisfied to do no more than recalculate his earlier findings, refining and rechecking his measurements of the antechamber. On sheets of brown wrapping paper, he sketched each fossil in detail. He began to keep track of the waxing and waning of the ice. He planned to order finely calibrated instruments so that he could measure the annual lengthening of the stalactites.

The new entrance became a torment, a question demanding an answer. In December 1911, he was determined to block this entrance with stone. A week later, he was equally determined to squeeze through with a torch and a rope. In March he had still not committed himself, but he recorded that he had had a series of nightmares, all to do with his vacillation. Finally, at the end of May, forced into idleness by a spring thaw, he gathered five hundred feet of string, a hundred feet of stout rope, a lantern, four pitons made from ring bolts and a hand axe. He also took a dozen matches, a pound of mixed raisins and two *hardfisk*.

He drove a piton into a crevice close to the entrance, fastened the string to it, then forced his way into a small cavern that led downward to a larger cavern, which he described as big as the biggest whale.

The diary for the next two years is missing, but a letter to his daughter dated January 1914 stated that he had explored numerous caves, each one unique and full of wonders. In one there was a pool, and from it, he caught blind fish. He added that he was afraid but that he could not stop. "As much as I have learned the secrets of the earth," he said, "I have learned more about myself."

On the table the day Axel the freighter discovered the empty cabin, the dead dogs and horse, was this cryptic note:

"To the farthest depth ... "

Runa

BY THE TIME Gunnar had disappeared, Runa was married and had a son called Valdi. For some years, Gunnar had not come to town. The only communication between him and Runa were his infrequent letters. The result was that when he disappeared he was little missed. The few times he had visited his daughter, he had spent most of his time in his room sitting at the window and smoking his pipe. Silence had become a habit with him. Over the years the Fjelsteds had become Runa's true family.

The boxes of Gunnar's belongings were stored in the attic of Runa's Sargeant Avenue house. There they would have stayed if it had not been for Valdi.

Valdi Anderson

RUNA'S SON BECAME a teacher and taught for a year at Hecla.

It was there that, for the first time, he heard the Fjelsteds were not his blood relatives. The shock was so great that, for a time, he refused to believe what he had been told. At last, on a weekend trip to Winnipeg, he confronted his mother, who reluctantly admitted that his grandfather had been Gunnar. When he pressed her, she refused to talk about it.

"Leave it," she cried. "You did not know him. I did not know him. What does it matter?"

"It matters."

"The Fjelsteds loved me."

"What was he like?"

"I don't know."

He was still young and filled with the anger that seethes within the young like unexplained fire. He began to shout.

"Are you ashamed of him?"

"No. It's not that."

"Then what?"

"He lived. He died. I hardly saw him."

"How did he die?"

"I don't know." Runa, who was unused to confrontation, began to wring her hands. Her own early sense of abandonment, her own fears, welled up like debris that had been hidden beneath the waters of a deep lake and suddenly stirred. "Nobody knows."

Like his maternal grandfather, Valdi was large. Like him, too, he could take offence easily and nurse a grudge.

His mother, desperate to stop the questions, thought of the boxes under the eaves. She offered him these in return for peace.

There were three wooden fish boxes filled with letters, books, drawings and diaries. Valdi impatiently pulled loose the lids, certain that what had been hidden would now be revealed.

"I can't read this," he said.

Everything was in Icelandic.

In spite of this defeat, he took the boxes with him. Perhaps he was afraid that his mother would burn the contents, then deny their existence. From time to time, he returned to the boxes, puzzling over the carefully executed drawings of trilobites, clam shells, a feathery leaf. The books and diaries were dry and brittle, the paper yellow, the letters as fragile as last fall's leaves.

Caught up in the rush of teaching and marriage, he was too busy to pay much attention to these relics, but still, they posed a question. It was not the kind of question that demanded an answer but the kind that nagged, the way the picture of a small, ragged child begging will nag at the conscience of the well fed.

Do you see what I mean about this task? God help me. What love will drive a man to do. There are too many characters. Everybody gets involved. Already we've got four generations. Gunnar—Runa—Valdi—Sigga. Why can I not just condense it, make it less messy? There is no unity of time or place. Aristotle, wherever you are, give God some good advice. Tell Him to get organized.

Here's Valdi so busy teaching classes, grading papers, screwing his pretty little wife from Akureyri, taking classes for his certificate, repairing the roof, that he sets aside these three bloody boxes and, now and again, late at night, looks them over, promising himself that when he gets time, he'll learn to read and write Icelandic and translate them. I keep wanting to shout "Action. Get on with it. To hell with the picnic. To hell with going to Gimli for *Islindingadagurinn.* Never mind that damn birthday party."

Five years passed. How's that for a transition? Bugger the details, the character development, go for the main point. Five years passed, and damned if he didn't start to take Icelandic lessons in 1944 when he got a job teaching in Winnipeg at Kelvin High School. Twice a week, he took lessons with Rev. V.J. Eylands, D.D.[9] At last— in spite of the protests of his wife, who wanted him to get rid of the papers—little by little, he began to translate.

---

9. Dr. Valdimar J. Eylands, an able preacher and writer. A leader in the Icelandic community.

The more he read, the more the idea of the cave took hold. He began to question every elderly person he came across who might know some part of his grandfather's story. Soon he began to seek these people out. He followed rumours. He wrote letters.

He began to dream about the cave. From the notes and diagrams, he knew it more intimately than his own house. Awake, he found it intruding upon his thoughts. When he was certain he had pinpointed the location of the cabin, he bought a boat.

On a weekend at the end of July, he drove to Pine Dock. The road began in pavement, changed to gravel and finally dwindled to one lane of mud. Beside a sagging dock, an old woman lived in an abandoned ice shed. He saw her face behind a dusty window, but she refused to answer his knock. A black goat was tethered to a tree stump. He slept in his car. Before dawn, he slid his boat into the dark water. He travelled slowly, staying close to the shore and keeping the map on his knee. The forest pressed to the very edge of the lake. When he reached his destination and shut off his motor, the silence amazed him.

He was rewarded with the remains of a log cabin. The roof had collapsed and rotted away, but the silvered walls were still standing. Grass grew thickly from the mud floor. Outside the walls, grass and moose maple filled what had been a clearing. He could, when he closed his eyes, see the ice-covered window, the frozen dogs, the snow drifting in ragged lines over the ground. He returned the next weekend with his wife and daughter. He cleared a twenty-foot circle around the cabin. The discovery of the rusted remains of the metal pegs that had held the dogs excited him.

He did not have to teach until September, so he returned to Winnipeg, bought enough supplies to last him a month and returned by himself. Because of the cold wind off the lake, he set up his tent inside the cabin walls. A day after he arrived, he began his search. For all the details in the diary about the cave itself, the precise location was never described.

The shoreline was in ruins. Great columns of limestone had been weathered from the cliffs. Trees grew in profusion. He was not discouraged. He knew that the entrance could not be far away. A half-mile in either direction was the outside limit. A greater distance would have made transporting supplies difficult.

Clambering over the rocks was strenuous. At first, he had to rest frequently. As the days passed, he grew stronger and was able to search for hours on end. He took three rolls of film. He also had collected all the information about the area that he could find. It did not surprise him that there was no mention of caves. Knowledge, he had discovered during his academic career, looked extensive only until a specific answer was sought.

In the middle of August, he found a number of false leads, caves that disappointed him by going only a short distance before stopping. On August 25, he found a cave he thought was the one for which he was looking. On August 26, measurements demonstrated that it was not the right cave. When he was ready to give up, he found, in his grandfather's dreams, the clue he needed.

He closed his eyes and constructed for himself the cliffs as he remembered them. When he returned to the cliffs, he realized his memory had been inaccurate. Rather than continue his earlier fruitless physical search, he sat just offshore in his boat and watched the cliffs until he was certain their image was printed on his mind. Twice more he had to return, but then he lay on the grass before the log cabin and slept. In his sleep, he saw the entire cliff in every detail. A purple shadow and the slant of some rocks told him what he needed to know.

On August 30, he used a crowbar to clear the entrance. The cave was not as long as it had been, but he knew immediately that he was in the right place. His grandfather's piton he found embedded in ice.

He played his light over the entrance to the deeper caves. The walls were all highlights and shadows. Ahead was darkness and the unknown. Overwhelmed by his fear of being lost in the maze that he knew stretched before him, he resolved to return home and burn his grandfather's materials.

The next morning, he changed his mind. Instead of starting south, he entered the cave. He took with him fifteen hundred feet of blue thread to unroll as he went. The time of his leaving is known, for he wrote it down to the minute: 6:15, August 31.

Six months later, his wife returned to Iceland with Sigga. There Sigga stayed until just before we met at Einar's farm and had our summer together.

Because of her refusal to marry me, because of who we were, because of the times, our relationship did not last. I searched, during this time we had together, God help me, I searched, trying to find answers so that she need have no fears, but I could not then and cannot now make any sense out of it. No epiphany. Not for me. Not for you.

Sigga left. One day I went to work. When I came back, she was gone. A year after, I heard that she was living in Iceland. I wrote again and again but never received a reply.

I married someone else. That didn't work out either. We're separated and waiting for a divorce. I doubt if being married to anyone would have worked out. Sigga was too much in my heart. That summer we had together, drenched in passion and colour, made everyone and everything seem pale by comparison. Still, as the years passed, even Sigga faded.

Then a week ago, a letter arrived. It was from a Ragnar Williamson. He is, he says, my son. Sigga, he informs me, is dead. Cancer.

His mother was pregnant when she left here. She returned to Iceland, bore him, raised him, never married, never told him who his father was. Now, with a great deal of effort, he has tracked me down.

He is coming to visit me. He wants, above all, to learn about his family.

Tapka

DAVID BEZMOZGIS

GOLDFINCH WAS FLAPPING CLOTHESLINES, a tenement delirious with striving. 6030 Bathurst: insomniac scheming Odessa. Cedarcroft: reeking borscht in the hallways. My parents, Baltic aristocrats, took an apartment at 715 Finch fronting a ravine and across from an elementary school—one respectable block away from the Russian swarm. We lived on the fifth floor, my cousin, aunt, and uncle directly below us on the fourth. Except for the Nahumovskys, a couple in their fifties, there were no other Russians in the building. For this privilege, my parents paid twenty extra dollars a month in rent.

In March of 1980, near the end of the school year but only three weeks after our arrival in Toronto, I was enrolled in Charles H. Best elementary. Each morning, with our house key hanging from a brown shoelace around my neck, I kissed my parents goodbye and, along with my cousin Jana, tramped across the ravine—I to the first grade, she to the second. At three o'clock, bearing the germs of a new vocabulary, we tramped back home. Together, we then waited until six for our parents to return from George Brown City College, where they were taking their obligatory classes in English.

In the evenings we assembled and compiled our linguistic bounty.

Hello, havaryew?

Red, yellow, green, blue.

May I please go to the washroom?

Seventeen, eighteen, nineteen, twenny.

Joining us most nights were the Nahumovskys. They attended the same English classes and travelled with my parents on the same bus. Rita Nahumovsky was a beautician, her face spackled with makeup, and Misha Nahumovsky was a tool and die maker. They came from Minsk and didn't know a soul in Canada. With abounding enthusiasm, they incorporated themselves into our family. My parents were glad to have them. Our life was tough, we had it hard—but the Nahumovskys had it harder. They were alone, they were older, they were stupefied by the demands of language. Being essentially helpless themselves, my parents found it gratifying to help the more helpless Nahumovskys.

After dinner, as we gathered on cheap stools around our table, my mother repeated the day's lessons for the benefit of the Nahumovskys and, to a slightly lesser degree, for the benefit of my father. My mother had always been a dedicated student and she extended this dedication to George Brown City College. My father and the

Nahumovskys came to rely on her detailed notes and her understanding of the curriculum. For as long as they could, they listened attentively and groped toward comprehension. When this became too frustrating, my father put on the kettle, Rita painted my mother's nails, and Misha told Soviet jokes.

In a first-grade classroom a teacher calls on her students and inquires after their nationality. "Sasha," she says. Sasha says, "Russian." "Very good," says the teacher. "Arnan," she says. Arnan says, "Armenian." "Very good," says the teacher. "Lubka," she says. Lubka says, "Ukrainian." "Very good," says the teacher. And then she asks Dima. Dima says, "Jewish." "What a shame," says the teacher, "so young and already a Jew."

THE NAHUMOVSKYS HAD NO CHILDREN, only a white Lhasa-apso named Tapka. The dog had lived with them for years before they emigrated and then travelled with them from Minsk to Vienna, from Vienna to Rome, and from Rome to Toronto. During our first month in the building, Tapka was in quarantine and I saw her only in photographs. Rita had dedicated an entire album to the dog, and to dampen the pangs of separation, she consulted the album daily. There were shots of Tapka in the Nahumovskys' old Minsk apartment, seated on the cushions of faux Louis XIV furniture; there was Tapka on the steps of a famous Viennese palace; Tapka at the Vatican; in front of the Coliseum; at the Sistine Chapel; and under the Leaning Tower of Pisa. My mother—despite having grown up with goats and chickens in her yard—didn't like animals and found it impossible to feign interest in Rita's dog. Shown a picture of Tapka, my mother wrinkled her nose and said "foo." My father also couldn't be bothered. With no English, no money, no job, and only a murky conception of what the future held, he wasn't equipped to admire Tapka on the Italian Riviera. Only I cared. Through the photographs I became attached to Tapka and projected upon her the ideal traits of the dog I did not have. Like Rita, I counted the days until Tapka's liberation.

The day Tapka was to be released from quarantine Rita prepared an elaborate dinner. My family was invited to celebrate the dog's arrival. While Rita cooked, Misha was banished from their apartment. For distraction, he seated himself at our table with a deck of cards. As my mother reviewed sentence construction, Misha played hand after hand of Durak with me.

—The woman loves this dog more than me. A taxi to the customs facility is going to cost us ten, maybe fifteen dollars. But what can I do? The dog is truly a sweet little dog.

When it came time to collect the dog, my mother went with Misha and Rita to act as their interpreter. With my nose to the window, I watched the taxi take them away. Every few minutes, I reapplied my nose to the window. Three hours later the taxi pulled into our parking lot and Rita emerged from the back seat cradling animated fur. She set the fur down on the pavement, where it assumed the shape of a dog. The length of its coat concealed its legs, and as it hovered around Rita's ankles, it appeared to have either a thousand tiny legs or none at all. My head ringing "Tapka, Tapka, Tapka," I raced into the hallway to meet the elevator.

That evening Misha toasted the dog:

—This last month, for the first time in years, I have enjoyed my wife's undivided attention. But I believe no man, not even one as perfect as me, can survive so much attention from his wife. So I say, with all my heart, thank God our Tapka is back home with us. Another day and I fear I may have requested a divorce.

Before he drank, Misha dipped his pinkie finger into his vodka glass and offered it to the dog. Obediently, Tapka gave Misha's finger a thorough licking. Duly impressed, my uncle declared her a good Russian dog. He also gave her a lick of his vodka. I gave her a piece of my chicken. Jana rolled her a pellet of bread. Misha taught us how to dangle food just out of Tapka's reach and thereby induce her to perform a charming little dance. Rita also produced "Clonchik," a red and yellow rag clown. She tossed Clonchik under the table, onto the couch, down the hallway, and into the kitchen; over and over Rita called, "Tapka get Clonchik," and, without fail, Tapka got Clonchik. Everyone delighted in Tapka's antics except for my mother, who sat stiffly in her chair, her feet slightly off the ground, as though preparing herself for a mild electric shock.

After the dinner, when we returned home, my mother announced that she would no longer set foot in the Nahumovskys' apartment. She liked Rita, she liked Misha, but she couldn't sympathize with their attachment to the dog. She understood that the attachment was a consequence of their lack of sophistication and also their child-lessness. They were simple people. Rita had never attended university. She could derive contentment from talking to a dog, brushing its coat, putting ribbons in its hair, and repeatedly throwing a rag clown across the apartment. And Misha, although very lively and a genius with his hands, was also not an intellectual. They were good people, but a dog ruled their lives.

Rita and Misha were sensitive to my mother's attitude toward Tapka. As a result, and to the detriment of her progress with English, Rita stopped visiting our apartment. Nightly, Misha would arrive alone while Rita attended to the dog. Tapka never set foot in our home. This meant that, in order to see her, I spent more and more time at the Nahumovskys'. Each evening, after I had finished my homework, I went to play with Tapka. My heart soared every time Rita opened the door and Tapka raced to greet me. The dog knew no hierarchy of affection. Her excitement was infectious. In Tapka's presence I resonated with doglike glee.

Because of my devotion to the dog and their lack of an alternative, Misha and Rita added their house key to the shoelace hanging around my neck. Every day, during our lunch break and again after school, Jana and I were charged with caring for Tapka. Our task was simple: put Tapka on her leash, walk her to the ravine, release her to chase Clonchik, and then bring her home.

Every day, sitting in my classroom, understanding little, effectively friendless, I counted down the minutes to lunchtime. When the bell rang I met Jana on the playground and we sprinted across the grass toward our building. In the hall, our approaching footsteps elicited panting and scratching. When I inserted the key into the lock I felt emanations of love through the door. And once the door was open, Tapka hurled herself at us, her entire body consumed with an ecstasy of wagging. Jana and I took turns embracing her, petting her, covertly vying for her favour. Free of Rita's scrutiny, we also satisfied certain anatomical curiosities. We examined Tapka's ears, her paws, her teeth, the roots of her fur, and her doggy genitals. We poked and prodded her, we threw her up in the air, rolled her over and over, and swung her by her front legs. I felt such overwhelming love for Tapka that sometimes when hugging her, I had to restrain myself from squeezing too hard and crushing her little bones.

IT WAS APRIL when we began to care for Tapka. Snow melted in the ravine; sometimes it rained. April became May. Grass absorbed the thaw, turned green; dandelions and wildflowers sprouted yellow and blue; birds and insects flew, crawled, and made their characteristic noises. Faithfully and reliably, Jana and I attended to Tapka. We walked her across the parking lot and down into the ravine. We threw Clonchik and said "Tapka get Clonchik." Tapka always got Clonchik. Everyone was proud of us. My mother and my aunt wiped tears from their eyes while talking about how responsible we were. Rita and Misha rewarded us with praise and chocolates. Jana was seven and I was six; much had been asked of us, but we had risen to the challenge.

Inspired by everyone's confidence, we grew confident. Whereas at first we made sure to walk thirty paces into the ravine before releasing Tapka, we gradually reduced that requirement to ten paces, then five paces, until finally we released her at the grassy border between the parking lot and ravine. We did this not out of laziness or recklessness but because we wanted proof of Tapka's love. That she came when we called was evidence of her love, that she didn't piss in the elevator was evidence of her love, that she offered up her belly for scratching was evidence of her love, all of this was evidence, but it wasn't proof. Proof could come only in one form. We had intuited an elemental truth: love needs no leash.

THAT FIRST SPRING, even though most of what was said around me remained a mystery, a thin rivulet of meaning trickled into my cerebral catch basin and collected into a little pool of knowledge. By the end of May I could sing the ABC song. Television taught me to say "What's up, Doc?" and "super-duper." The playground introduced me to "shithead," "mental case," and "gaylord," and I sought every opportunity to apply my new knowledge.

One afternoon, after spending nearly an hour in the ravine throwing Clonchik in a thousand different directions, Jana and I lolled in the sunlit pollen. I called her "shithead," "mental case," and "gaylord," and she responded by calling me "gaylord," "shithead," and "mental case."

—Shithead.

—Gaylord.

—Mental case.

—Tapka, get Clonchik.

—Shithead.

—Gaylord.

—Come, Tapka-lapka.

—Mental case.

We went on like this, over and over, until Jana threw the clown and said, "Shithead, get Clonchik." Initially I couldn't tell if she had said this on purpose or if it had merely been a blip in her rhythm. But when I looked at Jana, her smile was triumphant.

—Mental case, get Clonchik.

For the first time, as I watched Tapka bounding happily after Clonchik, the profanity sounded profane.

—Don't say that to the dog.

—Why not?

—It's not right.

—But she doesn't understand.

—You shouldn't say it.

—Don't be a baby. Come, shithead, come, my dear one.

Her tail wagging with accomplishment, Tapka dropped Clonchik at my feet.

—You see, she likes it.

I held Clonchik as Tapka pawed frantically at my shins.

—Call her shithead. Throw the clown.

—I'm not calling her shithead.

—What are you afraid of, shithead?

I aimed the clown at Jana's head and missed.

—Shithead, get Clonchik.

As the clown left my hand, Tapka, a white shining blur, oblivious to insult, was already cutting through the grass. I wanted to believe that I had intended the "shithead" exclusively for Jana, but I knew it wasn't true.

—I told you, gaylord, she doesn't care.

I couldn't help thinking, "Poor Tapka," and looked around for some sign of recrimination. The day, however, persisted in unimpeachable brilliance: sparrows winged overhead; bumblebees levitated above flowers; beside a lilac shrub, Tapka clamped down on Clonchik. I was amazed at the absence of consequences.

Jana said, "I'm going home."

As she started for home I saw that she was still holding Tapka's leash. It swung insouciantly from her hand. I called after her just as, once again, Tapka deposited Clonchik at my feet.

—I need the leash.

—Why?

—Don't be stupid. I need the leash.

—No you don't. She comes when we call her. Even shithead. She won't run away.

Jana turned her back on me and proceeded toward our building. I called her again but she refused to turn around. Her receding back was a blatant provocation. Guided more by anger than by logic, I decided that if Tapka was closer to Jana, then the onus of responsibility would become hers. I picked up the doll and threw it as far as I could into the parking lot.

—Tapka, get Clonchik.

Clonchik tumbled through the air. I had put everything in my six-year-old arm behind the throw, which still meant that the doll wasn't going very far. Its trajectory promised a drop no more than twenty feet from the edge of the ravine. Running, her head arched to the sky, Tapka tracked the flying clown. As the doll reached its apex it crossed paths with a sparrow. The bird veered off toward Finch Avenue and the clown plummeted to the asphalt. When the doll hit the ground, Tapka raced past it after the bird.

A thousand times we had thrown Clonchik and a thousand times Tapka had retrieved him. But who knows what passes for a thought in the mind of a dog? One moment a Clonchik is a Clonchik and the next moment a sparrow is a Clonchik.

I shouted at Jana to catch Tapka and then watched as the dog, her attention fixed on the sparrow, skirted past Jana and into traffic. From the slope of the ravine I couldn't see what had happened. I saw only that Jana had broken into a sprint and I heard the caterwauling of tires followed by a shrill fractured yip.

By the time I reached the street a line of cars was already stretched a block beyond Goldfinch. At the front of the line were a brown station wagon and a pale blue sedan blistered with rust. As I neared, I noted the chrome letters on the back of the sedan: D-U-S-T-E-R. In front of the sedan Jana kneeled in a tight semicircle with a pimply young man and an older woman wearing very large sunglasses. Tapka lay panting on her side at the centre of their circle. She stared at me, at Jana. Except for a hind leg twitching at the sky at an impossible angle, she looked much as she did when she rested on the rug at the Nahumovskys' apartment after a romp in the ravine.

Seeing her this way, barely mangled, I started to convince myself that things weren't as bad as I had feared and I edged forward to pet her. The woman in the sunglasses said something in a restrictive tone that I neither understood nor heeded. I placed my hand on Tapka's head and she responded by turning her face and allowing a trickle of blood to escape onto the asphalt. This was the first time I had ever seen dog blood and I was struck by the depth of its colour. I hadn't expected it to be red, although I also hadn't expected it to be not-red. Set against the grey asphalt and her white coat, Tapka's blood was the red I envisioned when I closed my eyes and thought: red.

I sat with Tapka until several dozen car horns demanded that we clear the way. The woman with the large sunglasses ran to her station wagon, returned with a blanket, and scooped Tapka off the street. The pimply young man stammered a few sentences of which I understood nothing except the word "sorry." Then we were in the back seat of the station wagon with Tapka in Jana's lap. The woman kept talking until she realized that we couldn't understand her at all. As we started to drive, Jana remembered something. I motioned for the woman to stop the car and scrambled out. Above the atonal chorus of car horns I heard:

—Mark, get Clonchik.

I ran and got Clonchik.

FOR TWO HOURS Jana and I sat in the reception area of a small veterinary clinic in an unfamiliar part of town. In another room, with a menagerie of various afflicted creatures, Tapka lay in traction, connected to a blinking machine by a series of tubes. Jana and I had been allowed to see her once but were rushed out when we both burst into tears. Tapka's doctor, a woman in a white coat and furry slippers resembling bear paws, tried to calm us down. Again, we could neither explain ourselves nor understand what she was saying. We managed only to establish that Tapka was not our dog. The doctor gave us colouring books, stickers, and access to the phone. Every fifteen minutes we called home. Between phone calls we absently flipped pages and sniffled for Tapka and for ourselves. We had no idea what would happen to Tapka, all we knew was that she wasn't dead. As for ourselves, we already felt punished and knew only that more punishment was to come.

—Why did you throw Clonchik?

—Why didn't you give me the leash?

—You could have held on to her collar.

—You shouldn't have called her shithead.

At six-thirty my mother picked up the phone. I could hear the agitation in her voice. The ten minutes she had spent at home not knowing where I was had taken their toll. For ten minutes she had been the mother of a dead child. I explained to her about the dog and felt a twinge of resentment when she said "So it's just the dog?" Behind her I heard other voices. It sounded as though everyone was speaking at once, pursuing personal agendas, translating the phone conversation from Russian to Russian until one anguished voice separated itself: "My God, what happened?" Rita.

After getting the address from the veterinarian my mother hung up and ordered another expensive taxi. Within a half hour my parents, my aunt, and Misha and Rita pulled up at the clinic. Jana and I waited for them on the sidewalk. As soon as the taxi doors opened we began to sob. Partly out of relief but mainly in the hope of eliciting sympathy. As I ran to my mother I caught sight of Rita's face. Her face made me regret that I also hadn't been hit by a car.

As we clung to our mothers, Rita descended upon us.

—Children, what oh what have you done?

She pinched compulsively at the loose skin of her neck, raising a cluster of pink marks.

While Misha methodically counted individual bills for the taxi driver, we swore on our lives that Tapka had simply gotten away from us. That we had minded her as always, but, inexplicably, she had seen a bird and bolted from the ravine and into the road. We had done everything in our power to catch her, but she had surprised us, eluded us, been too fast.

Rita considered our story.

—You are liars. Liars!

She uttered the words with such hatred that we again burst into sobs.

My father spoke in our defence.

—Rita Borisovna, how can you say this? They are children.

—They are liars. I know my Tapka. Tapka never chased birds. Tapka never ran from the ravine.

—Maybe today she did?

—Liars.

Having delivered her verdict, she had nothing more to say. She waited anxiously for Misha to finish paying the driver.

—Misha, enough already. Count it a hundred times, it will still be the same.

Inside the clinic there was no longer anyone at the reception desk. During our time there, Jana and I had watched a procession of dyspeptic cats and lethargic parakeets disappear into the back rooms for examination and diagnosis. One after another they had come and gone until, by the time of our parents' arrival, the waiting area was entirely empty and the clinic officially closed. The only people remaining were a night nurse and the doctor in the bear paw slippers who had stayed expressly for our sake.

Looking desperately around the room, Rita screamed: "Doctor! Doctor!" But when the doctor appeared she was incapable of making herself understood. Haltingly, with my mother's help, it was communicated to the doctor that Rita wanted to see her dog.

Pointing vigorously at herself, Rita asserted: "Tapka. Mine dog."

The doctor led Rita and Misha into the veterinary version of an intensive care ward. Tapka lay on her little bed, Clonchik resting directly beside her. At the sight of Rita and Misha, Tapka weakly wagged her tail. Little more than an hour had elapsed since I had seen her last, but somehow over the course of that time, Tapka had shrunk considerably. She had always been a small dog, but now she looked desiccated. Rita started to cry, grotesquely smearing her mascara. With trembling hands, and with sublime tenderness, she stroked Tapka's head.

—My God, my God, what has happened to you, my Tapkachka?

Through my mother, and with the aid of pen and paper, the doctor provided the answer. Tapka required two operations. One for her leg. Another to stop internal bleeding. An organ had been damaged. For now, a machine was helping her, but without the machine she would die. On the paper the doctor drew a picture of a scalpel, of a dog, of a leg, of an organ. She made an arrow pointing at the organ and drew a teardrop and coloured it in to represent "blood." She also wrote down a number preceded by a dollar sign. The number was 1,500.

At the sight of the number Rita let out a low animal moan and steadied herself against Tapka's little bed. My parents exchanged a glance. I looked at the floor. Misha said, "My dear God." The Nahumovskys and my parents each took in less than five hundred dollars a month. We had arrived in Canada with almost nothing, a few hundred dollars, but that had all but disappeared on furniture. There were no savings. Fifteen hundred dollars. The doctor could just as well have written a million.

In the middle of the intensive care ward, Rita slid down to the floor. Her head thrown back, she appealed to the fluorescent lights: "Nu, Tapkachka, what is going to become of us?"

I looked up from my feet and saw horror and bewilderment on the doctor's face. She tried to put a hand on Rita's shoulder but Rita violently shrugged it off.

My father attempted to intercede.

—Nu, Rita Borisovna, I understand that it is painful, but it is not the end of the world.

—And what do you know about it?

—I know that it must be hard, but soon you will see ... Even tomorrow we could go and help you find a new one.

My father looked to my mother for approval, to ensure that he had not promised too much.

—A new one? What do you mean a new one? I don't want a new one. Why don't you get yourself a new son? A new little liar? How about that? New. Everything we have now is new.

On the linoleum floor, Rita keened, rocking back and forth. She hiccuped, as though hyperventilating. Pausing for a moment, she looked up at my mother and told her to translate to the doctor. To tell her that she would not let Tapka die.

—I will sit here on this floor forever. And if the police come to drag me out I will bite them.

—Ritachka, this is crazy.

—Why is it crazy? My Tapka's life is worth more than fifteen hundred dollars. Because we don't have the money she should die here? It's not her fault.

Seeking rationality, my mother turned to Misha. Misha, who had said nothing all this time except "My dear God."

—Misha, do you want me to tell the doctor what Rita said?

Misha shrugged philosophically.

—Tell her or don't tell her, you see my wife has made up her mind. The doctor will figure it out soon enough.

—And you think this is reasonable?

—Sure. Why not? I'll sit on the floor too. The police can take us both to jail. Besides Tapka, what else do we have?

Misha sat on the floor beside his wife.

I watched as my mother struggled to explain to the doctor what was happening. With a mixture of words and gesticulations she got the point across. The doctor, after considering her options, sat down on the floor beside Rita and Misha. Once again she tried to put her hand on Rita's shoulder. This time, Rita, who was still rocking back and forth, allowed it. Misha rocked in time to his wife's rhythm. So did the doctor. The three of them sat in a line, swaying together like campers at a campfire. Nobody said anything. We looked at each other. I watched Rita, Misha, and the doctor swaying and swaying. I became mesmerized by the swaying. I wanted to know what would happen to Tapka; the swaying answered me.

The swaying said: Listen, shithead, Tapka will live. The doctor will perform the operation. Either money will be found or money will not be necessary.

I said to the swaying: This is very good. I love Tapka. I meant her no harm. I want to be forgiven.

The swaying replied: There is reality and then there is truth. The reality is that Tapka will live. But let's be honest, the truth is you killed Tapka. Look at Rita; look at Misha. You see, who are you kidding? You killed Tapka and you will never be forgiven.

A Long Migration
VINCENT LAM

MY GRANDFATHER was an orphan. Either he never knew the identity of his biological parents, or he was never willing to reveal this information. For the Chinese, heritage is of great importance, but adoption forms a new and legitimate lineage. Thus my name, Chen, as a grandson descended of an orphan, is from my grandfather's adoptive merchant family in the province of Guangdong. At sixteen years of age, my grandfather suddenly left Guangdong for Vietnam. He said there was a plot against him that had to do with jealousy over grades at school. My uncle Will said he was told that my grandfather had an affair with the schoolmaster's young wife. Others said that the schoolmaster warned my grandfather to leave, because the concubine of a local warlord had eyes for him.

The family matriarch in Vietnam sent my grandfather to Hong Kong for school. My grandmother said that this was because he was a difficult person whom the matriarch didn't want to deal with, but my grandfather said that he pleaded with her, begged for a higher education until she sent him to Hong Kong.

In Hong Kong my grandfather, my Yeh Yeh, finished high school. He became a partner in a shipping venture. Yeh Yeh met my grandmother, my Ma Ma. The Japanese invaded Hong Kong, and Yeh Yeh said that he was persuaded to marry my Ma Ma in order to save her from the occupation. Yeh Yeh had papers that would allow him to return to Vietnam. Ma Ma asserted that he took advantage of this situation at a time when her family's power was thin, to induce her to marry. Both agreed that he was promising though not wealthy, and that she was the princess daughter of her father's dying empire. Ma Ma contended that Yeh Yeh thought she still had money and married her for this. Yeh Yeh said that he married her because he loved her. Also, he said, it was a gesture of goodwill toward her older brother, who had helped Yeh Yeh enter business and who was worried for Ma Ma's safety in Hong Kong.

I was sorting through these histories during that last winter in Brisbane. I had first met my grandfather when he was spending the last of his money touring North America. He was both the heroic and tragic figure of many family stories—at once shameful, legendary, and safely exiled in Brisbane. Now that I was to be Yeh Yeh's companion in the period preceding his anticipated death, I was anxious to find out what was true and what were the exaggerations of memory.

The accounts always changed a little depending upon who told them, and my Yeh Yeh's versions could shift from morning to evening. Rarely did a new version of a story require the old one to be untrue. Instead, it was as if the new telling washed the story in a different colour, filling in gaps and loose ends so as to invert my previous understanding of the plot.

During those months, Yeh Yeh pissed blood every morning. Sometimes it would be just a pink-tinged trickle, but often there would be flecks of clotted blood like red sequins swirling in the toilet bowl. Yeh Yeh had me inspect the toilet daily to give my opinion. One day it was red like ink.

This was the break after my first year of medical school. My family expected that I would use my wealth of clinical knowledge first to care for grandfather, and second, to alert them when things neared an end. I would pronounce his impending death, and this would set in motion a flurry of rushed phone calls to travel agents. On jets from around the world, my relatives would hurry to Australia to be with grandfather as he died. I felt obliged to forecast correctly. It would be awkward if all of Yeh Yeh's children flew to his bedside only to find him recovering from some brief crisis and not dying. Then they would wait, their workplaces would hound them, and they would finally be obliged to depart with grandfather still alive. Alternately, if I called too late, my aunts and uncles would make a frenetic dash hoping to witness grandfather's last living moments, and only be able to attend Yeh Yeh's funeral.

IN MY LUGGAGE, which was packed in Toronto, my grandmother sent an oblong wooden box that contained a series of small brown bottles held in felt indentations. Each thumb-sized bottle was capped with a tight cork, and tied around with string. There were two straight rows of these healing extracts. A paper label in Chinese was pasted on each bottle, and the strings were different colours. Each morning, after his urination, grandfather dressed himself while his tea was steeping. Always suspenders on last. He lifted this box from a drawer, removed the next in the series of bottles, and drank its contents. Then he poured a mug of tea for himself, and one for me. Yeh Yeh never said anything about this box of medicines. He was good at talking but had difficulty speaking about what was most important. My grandmother, Yeh Yeh's first wife, had divorced him forty-three years ago and now lived in Toronto, the geographical other side of the world. Yeh Yeh put the empty bottle back in its slot, and the box back in the drawer. He was quiet for a while as he drank his tea. Every morning he told me to thank my grandmother for this gift, as if forgetting that he had told me to do so the day before.

SEEING THE TOILET BOWL dark with the red-ink urine, I said to my grandfather, "These things can happen. Let's see if it settles tomorrow. Drink lots of tea today." I wanted to sound knowledgeable about the issue of bloody pee.

The next morning, it was a happy rose-coloured stream with clots like coarse sand. I felt certain that I would forecast the end accurately. I gazed into it, looking deeply through the urine into the drain, asking the liquid what it foretold. I also peed into the toilet, and the red swirled up like an eddy. Alive for a moment. I flushed the toilet and it funnelled out almost clean, with a little bit of staining at the water line.

"You're very smart," said my grandfather. "It is better today."

Renal cell carcinoma. They had operated once. My Yeh Yeh had refused a second operation. Just as well, said Dr. Spiros, it would only prolong things.

My grandfather lived in a cottage at Glenn Hill Retirement Village. There was a long cinder-block building fronted by a watered lawn. This building was divided into individual units, all accessible from a walkway. These were called cottages. The residents of the cottages ate in the main dining room along with the residents of the dormitories. The main difference was that the cottage-dwellers were able to walk and dress themselves, while many of the dormitory residents were wheeled to meals. Yeh Yeh did not participate in conversation at Glenn Hill meals. If asked a direct question at the dinner table, he would pause, raise his head as if unsure that he had been addressed, and say with a sad wave of his hand, "No speakie Englis."

In Vietnam, Yeh Yeh had been the proprietor, headmaster, and star lecturer of the Percival Chen English Academy. Early in the morning, my uncle Will—who was finishing high school at that time—would find his father sleeping on the couch in the front room. Yeh Yeh would still be wearing his tuxedo from the previous night of drinking, gambling, and bedding prostitutes. My uncle would help his father upstairs into bed. Yeh Yeh would sleep in the morning, and look fresh again by afternoon to go to the school. He had no fixed teaching schedule, but would appear in classrooms intermittently. Star lectures. That's what the students paid for, to be in his school, to be taught by Percival Chen. Decades later, there were alumni reunions in California. Many credited my grandfather with teaching them both English and an attitude for success. At that time, the Americans were sending platoons and money into Vietnam. English was a language of opportunity. Yeh Yeh's fortune was made but never accumulated. It was quickly gambled, vigorously transformed into cognac, and enthusiastically given away in late night transactions. There was a plaque from the Saigon Rotary Club on the wall next to his mirror: *To Percival Chen—For Exemplary Generosity and Community Involvement.*

On the telephone to Canada, I asked my dad whether grandfather really had forgotten all his English, or whether he just pretended to have lost it. My father said that when they were children, they all thought their father was a master of this language. Yeh Yeh told me that he had always faked it, that at the British school in Hong Kong he had learned that the British display great confidence when they don't know something. Later, at his own school, when he couldn't spell something he was teaching, he simply avoided writing it down. He claimed that he never really spoke English properly, but had convinced people that he did. The hired teachers were Canadians, Brits, and Australians. These people corrected spelling mistakes for the students, so he didn't need to. I suspect my grandfather understood more English than he admitted, but that he could not take interest in conversations at Glenn Hill. *Aren't the potatoes salty today?* In his cottage, Yeh Yeh kept a bottle of Remy Martin XO cognac in the cupboard above the sink.

MY GRANDMOTHER claimed that grandfather had ruined her life by gambling and womanizing. She said that his behaviour led her to nag and fight him, and this created bitterness in her. It was this wound that had made her such an admittedly difficult woman, she said. Sometimes she explained this after yelling at me or another family member. My grandfather said my grandmother ruined his life, because early in their marriage her nagging and fighting compelled him to seek solace outside their home. For a Chinese man living in Saigon when Vietnam was still Indochine under the French, this meant mah-jong houses. They would bring hot dim sum late into the night, and smiling compliant women at any hour. There was nowhere else to go, he said. Yeh Yeh admitted that it was wrong of him to spend so much time and money in unfaithful ways. He recognized that this would anger any wife, but said that he sought these comforts initially because there was no peace at home. My father told me that although the school was lucrative, Yeh Yeh never had any money. The school fees went directly to loan sharks. Yeh Yeh bought a new Peugeot with push-button gears, but once the family had to sleep in the school for several months because they could not afford to rent a house.

IN BRISBANE, my grandfather had many friends. Enough of the Chinese in Vietnam had emigrated to Australia that he still had social standing in this new, hot, white country. We were often invited to dinner. One couple who took us out was younger than my grandfather, but older than my parents. Dr. Wong was a retired orthopaedic surgeon who had graduated from the Percival Chen English Academy before studying medicine in Glasgow. After retiring, Dr. Wong had become an Anglican minister. He and his wife, with Uncle Will's encouragement, were trying to convert my grandfather to Christianity before he died. Grandfather was a prime candidate. He was previously sinful and glamorous, now reduced to economic subsistence although still drinking XO cognac and gambling once a week (I had become the chauffeur for these outings, which my uncle was not to be told about). We were having a dinner of scallops, delicate oysters, and the lobsters without claws that they catch in Australia. My grandfather produced his flask and asked the waiter to fill a glass with ice. He poured cognac for himself and offered it around the table, but no one took any. The minister and his wife were teetotallers. Yeh Yeh poured some for me. We talked about Jesus.

My grandfather was receptive and interested, although during years of friendship with Dr. Wong he had politely and charismatically sidestepped the issue of faith. He questioned Dr. Wong about the parable of the sower. Yeh Yeh asked whether God would mind if he had sown seeds that lay ignored for a long time before sprouting. Dr. Wong said that it was all the same as long as there was faith at the time of judgment. I imagined my grandfather weighing the odds. Death was an awaiting certainty and beyond that the odds were unknown, but there was nothing to lose by laying a few bets on the Bible. What was in the past could be repented for, and the future was short.

They set a date for the baptism.

My grandfather didn't drink tea in restaurants, because he didn't want to fill his bladder and have to pee blood during dinner. He sipped cognac on ice. A great deal of food remained on the table when everyone stopped eating, mindful of their cholesterol and their diabetes. They counted on me to finish everything, which I tried to do.

AFTER MA MA DIVORCED YEH YEH, she married a man whose business was mostly in Taiwan. This was daring at that time, for a Chinese woman to divorce her husband and then remarry. It was in the newspapers. While reading in his garden one day, her new husband was assassinated. The bullet travelled expertly through the back of his neck and out his throat. He would not have suffered. He was thought to be a candidate for leading a Chinese secession movement. My father said this was a political ambition only imagined by others, and that his death was unfortunate because he had been kind to my grandmother. This had helped to calm her. She was still excitable, and that was the last point in her life when her beauty could, at least superficially, compensate for her temper and vindictiveness.

Yeh Yeh no longer had an excuse not to marry his mistress, and so he did. She became Second Wife. Second Wife did not get along with grandfather's new mistress, who became Third Wife—although they were never legally married. Both wives lived in the same household. Third Wife was docile, and tried to submit to the will of Second Wife, who nonetheless continued to be unhappy with the situation. Second Wife tried to kill herself with a gun, but managed only to shatter her arm, which then had to be amputated. With the shame of the disabled upon her, my grandfather bought her a house and sent her money periodically. No one has been able to tell me what happened to her after that. Third Wife was kind to Fourth Wife. Fourth Wife was sixteen years old when she married my then middle-aged grandfather. Fourth Wife was more cunning than Third Wife, and insisted on a legal marriage. Soon after this, the Viet Cong changed Saigon to Ho Chi Minh City, the Americans were suddenly gone, and those who had links to the capitalist economy were being imprisoned or shot. My grandfather convinced the High Commission that he was a British subject by virtue of his having once lived in Hong Kong. When he fled Vietnam, Fourth Wife went with him because she had marriage papers, while Third Wife remained in Ho Chi Minh City with her child.

ONE DAY, my grandfather woke, peed in the toilet, and then went back to bed. He did not dress. He told me that he didn't want to get up that day. He felt tired, and the thing in his side was growing.

"Come and feel it. See what you think," he said in Cantonese.

His left flank bulged as if a balloon was being inflated under the skin.

"*Mo toong,*" he said. There is no pain. He felt his side delicately, and pulled up his shirt so that I could see it. I pressed the tumour gently with the tips of my fingers. It was firm, hard like cold Plasticine. What did I think?

"*Ho choy mo toong,*" I said. It was fortunate that it wasn't painful.

"*Hai,*" he agreed.

Yeh Yeh explained that he always wore suspenders in these past few months. If he wore a belt, he pointed out, it would rub his side where the tumour was growing under the skin. His biggest fear was that the skin would split over the growing lump. He wore his pants slightly loose—held up by suspenders to avoid friction on this area. The thought of the cancer escaping from the confines of his body and making itself public in a wet, bloody way horrified him. He said he wouldn't be able to care for himself if the thing broke through. They would move him to the dormitories. Go look in the toilet, he told me.

I looked in the toilet. There was thick blood. It seemed to have a surface to it, clotting as if there was so much blood that it had become independent of the urine. Experimentally, I flushed and saw the thickness of it break up and swirl. It was not as viscous as it initially appeared, but this was a deep and serious tone of red.

"Yeh Yeh," I said. "We should go to the hospital."

"No hospital."

"But you look pale. You are weak. Dr. Spiros said this might happen, that you might lose blood and need a transfusion."

"No more hospital. Your grandfather dies here."

"Yes, but if we go to the hospital, they may be able to help you live longer. We'll come back here, and you won't have to go to the dormitories."

"Who needs hospitals? Besides, you're a doctor. You're here."

I was early in my training and wanted to pretend to be a doctor. I suggested that we call Dr. Spiros.

"Bring me my medicine," said grandfather. He wanted the box of little brown bottles. I went to get them. There were eight remaining. I pried the tight cork from a bottle, gave it to Yeh Yeh, and made him a cup of tea. In Toronto, I had gone with my grandmother to the herbalist on Dundas Street to buy these medicines. I had been surprised by her concern for Yeh Yeh's well-being, and her desire to purchase medicines. She had questioned the herbalist vigorously in purchasing these herbal concentrates, which were reputed to invigorate the kidneys. She had insisted that the medicines must be of the best quality—nothing fake, nothing second rate. Before buying them, she produced her trump card, telling the herbalist that I, her grandson, was a brilliant doctor and would smell each vial before she would buy them. The herbalist smiled obligingly, I sniffed them each in turn—their odour both bitter and heady—and told my grandmother that they smelled very strong. She was satisfied and paid for them.

Dr. Spiros was not in his office. His registrar was there, but said that he couldn't assess anything without seeing the patient. We should bring him to the emergency department, and if they wanted to involve urology, they would page them. Yeh Yeh refused to go. I called Dr. Wong, who came to the cottage and spoke to my grandfather. He felt the mass, and then told Yeh Yeh that as an orthopaedic surgeon he didn't have much expertise here. Yeh Yeh should see his specialist, he said. I realized that real physicians, when called upon in awkward family situations, try to pretend not to be doctors. Grandfather said he was ready to die. Dr. Wong said he could bring elders from the church for a bedside baptism. Yeh Yeh agreed.

The two of us strolled down the walkway in the bright warm afternoon of the Brisbane winter to Dr. Wong's car. He said to me, "You know he's going to die?"

"That's why I'm here."

"Nay ho gwai," he said, patting my shoulder. You are very obedient and well-behaved. A Chinese compliment.

That night, I asked grandfather if he knew who his real parents were. He told me it didn't matter, that one always has to move forward, otherwise the past holds too much pain.

AFTER TWO YEARS in Hong Kong, my grandfather and Fourth Wife moved to Australia. Toward the end of the Vietnam War, my aunts and uncles had been sent to different countries. The idea was that someone, somewhere, would land on their feet. Uncle Will went to Sydney, and later sponsored Yeh Yeh from Hong Kong. After several months, my aunt Alice told Uncle Will that if Yeh Yeh continued to live with them, she would leave. He was drinking and gambling heavily. Fourth Wife was younger than all of Yeh Yeh's children.

My uncle helped Yeh Yeh and Fourth Wife buy a house in Brisbane. Yeh Yeh told me he had never wanted to stay in Sydney. Too cold. Brisbane is tropical. Fourth Wife started a restaurant, and began an affair with the cook. She divorced my grandfather but continued to visit him weekly in the retirement home they found for him. That was twelve years before the cancer. He told me that it's understandable. A younger woman wants a younger man. Yeh Yeh relied on Fourth Wife to bring him cigarettes. While smoking these cigarettes, he spoke sadly about the early arguments, the poisoned misunderstandings he had with Ma Ma. At that time they were younger than I was now, he told me.

THE NEXT DAY, Yeh Yeh was too weak to stand. His forehead was pale and sweaty. The toilet bowl was thickly stained with blood. I had to lift him under his arms to get him to the washroom. He wouldn't eat. I called my aunt Alice and uncle Will to ask what I should do. Should I take him to the hospital? They asked me what they should do, should they fly from Sydney? Everyone else was in New York, Los Angeles, Toronto. With the time difference I didn't want to wake them. In the evening, against my grandfather's wishes, I called an ambulance. The spinning red siren lights turned on the wall of the cottage, making it look like it was in constant motion. They took him out, wrapped in an orange tube of blanket. I tried to be medical and tell the paramedics about his condition, but I couldn't remember any of the details.

Two days and eight units of transfused blood later, my grandfather was complaining to Dr. Spiros that he should be discharged. Dr. Wong had come to baptize him, and had brought fried noodles in white styrofoam boxes. The Wongs had a place on Stradbroke Island, and suggested that I go there for a rest. Grandfather was more stable now.

On Stradbroke, I stayed across from the headlands beach. In the morning I woke early to watch the humpback whales migrating north. As the sun streaked low across the water, their spouts were small torches in the grey shadowless tide. The light became full and round. I saw dolphins diving out of the crests of waves to hunt the fish that were driven into the cove. The sun lifted higher and burned through the day. From the pay phone at the side of the road, I called grandfather at the hospital. He was doing all right, he said. He had sent Dr. Wong to the cottage for the bottles of Chinese medicine. There were two bottles left, he said. I should stay at the beach and enjoy myself, and see whether they had fresh crab in the restaurants. Yeh Yeh advised me to have them sauté it in cognac, that's what he would do. He said that I should remember always to move forward, to not allow the past to become hurtful. He advised me that this was sometimes a difficult thing to do. Yeh Yeh reminded me to thank my grandmother for the medicines, when I would soon return home and speak with her.

The Amores

JANICE KULYK KEEFER

IN HER DREAM she is at a railway station, an old-fashioned place with a glassed roof and wrought-iron pillars, the kind she can just remember having known in Hungary. Only she isn't a little girl, but her present age, seventeen—which makes it all the stranger that she should be dressed in a child's tam, an embroidered woollen coat whose full skirt finishes high above her knees, and ankle socks with lace-up leather shoes. In one hand she is holding on to a small suitcase, much too small for the things she will need on such a long journey. For in her other hand she grasps, as firmly as she can, a ticket the size of a blackboard, bearing an endless list of the stops she will have to make before she arrives at a destination whose name she hasn't yet discovered. A conductor leans out from the train urging her to board before she makes the whole party late. She tries to explain that she can't leave until her mother has come to embrace her and say goodbye. Her mother is always late, so in this dream it does not occur to her to think that Marta might have forgotten, or worse—

decided not to come at all. Pigeons wheel under the metal rafters, making a noise like soft thunder as the conductor starts to shout at her, shouting and shouting. He reaches down to pluck at her arm; the train begins to push out just as she catches sight of her mother running, wearing only a slip and bedroom slippers, so frantic has been her haste to come to her. And then, somehow, Anyès has jumped aboard, slamming the compartment door so hard that the conductor, still reaching out towards her, tumbles down to the platform. Always, it is the scream of his whistle—furious, bereft—which wakes her as the train smokes away.

HIGH ON THE WALLS of Miss Vance's classroom lay an ample cornice, upon which lodged her pupils' monuments to their teacher's indestructible enthusiasm for her subject. A model of the Forum, columns manufactured from white-painted corrugated packing paper; *papier-mâché* replicas of shields and amphorae; plasticine reproductions of figurines and jewellery; and a copy, one foot high, of the statue of Caesar Augustus reproduced from page ninety-seven of *Living Latin*. Dust furred the replicas. The columns of the Forum had begun to crack under the Caesar's cross-eyed gaze and warning finger, but the effect of the whole remained inspiring from ground-level, especially to the superintendents who came on their yearly rounds to assess what contribution the study of dead languages made to the acquisition of knowledge and school spirit.

You can learn everything you need to know in life from Latin and the Bible, Miss Vance could have told the inspectors—did tell each crop of students whose lot it was to learn every week a new declension, conjugation, item of vocabulary. To this day, many of those students who have gone on to become doctors, accountants, social workers, even school principals could, if ordered with the rap of a pointer to a blackboard, reproduce *bellum, belli, bello; amo, amare, amavi, amatum,* spurred into unwonted accuracy by the presentiment of Miss Vance behind them, Miss Vance with her short grey hair—clipped, not cut; her spectacles restraining the overbright, overround eyes that seemed like fluorescent tennis balls glowing in darkened courts. She wore straight skirts and tailored cotton blouses over breasts both enormous and flattened. Mannish, they had called her; an apparition of white and grey, with lisle stockings and lace-up shoes supporting legs that bore her up like pale, tapered columns under the massive weight of some temple roof.

Julia Vance, Anyès had learned from the flyleaf of a volume of the *Aeneid*—Miss Vance's own copy, through which Agnes had been allowed to leaf while her fellow students were still gnashing their pens over *arma virumque cano.*

"To my daughter Julia, as a reward for proficiency in her studies, with the hope that she may learn from the immortal Mantuan the sublime value of selfless service. Edward Archibald Vance." Miss Vance had often told her students about her father, his ministry and the travels father and daughter had undertaken before the Reverend

Edward Archibald had expired—not lingeringly, self-indulgently, but in his customarily efficient way—from a heart attack after Sunday service, lunch with the Missionary Society and an afternoon spent reading *The Presbyterian Herald.* She had shown them slides of the Reverend Vance standing beside a Celtic cross somewhere in County Kerry, and next to Vergil's monument, the one erected in Mantua. He was a large man wearing a peculiarly rigid fedora and a dog collar which brought to mind the spikes bulldogs wear around their necks, such severity of starch did it betray.

"We didn't care a hoot for Mantua," Miss Vance had said, in her loud, eager, yet authoritative voice. "Or for Italy, if it comes to that." And she had left the image of her father—his hand outstretched to the verses engraved on Vergil's monument—imprinted on the screen while cautioning her students about the inevitable shock they would feel if they were ever unwise enough to try to travel to the land of Caesar and Cicero and Publilius Syrus. "The only ticket there," she'd bellowed, thumping a copy of *Living Latin,* "lies in these pages."

She had been looking at the entire class when she'd begun her peroration, but on pronouncing "pages" fixed her eyes on Agnes Sereny who was sitting with her small feet primly together, her hands clasped on the desktop, her eyes fixed on Miss Vance's in an expression that might have been fear or reverence or perhaps just the desire to produce whatever it was her teacher wished to see reflected there. Shining in Miss Vance's eyes was a mixture of encouragement, admonition, and something she would not name. Stern, solid, selfless was Miss Vance's life, as befitted the daughter of such a father, a daughter who had lost her mother and shouldered responsibility for her father's well-being at an age when most girls have stopped playing with dolls, and started to become them.

Yet in this, the fifty-third year of Miss Vance's life, the thirtieth year of her vocation, she had discovered herself capable of something she feared was love. Not the passionate obedience she had shown her father, but rather, a desire to possess, not the girl's affections, but her very nature. Had Miss Vance's knowledge of the Classics ever flooded those water-tight compartments into which she'd deposited the rules of grammar and the laws of style, she might have had second thoughts about the story of Pygmalion, or at least about Venus's role in the whole affair (Miss Vance could never remember the name of the marble woman come-to-life, but then you weren't supposed to—she was hardly the point of the story). As it was, she focused on the fact that Pygmalion had got everything he wanted—it was one of the rare myths that ended happily.

She had taken Agnes to heart from the very first class. Perhaps it was nothing more than that the girl's name and her appearance went so fittingly together. Agnes—Miss Vance pronounced it with a hard *g,* even though she knew the girl's mother said "Anyès," the way the French do, turning the very softness of the letter into an endearment. *Agnus;* the kind of hair that was not blonde but white, an impossibly pure shade that always looked as if it would melt should you touch it. A body not short (that implied a defect) but small, and skin fresh, full—as if it would spring back at your touch. Round, brown eyes; not deep, not dark, but light and clear. Sweetness, whiteness: "lamb," Miss Vance would have called her, had she ever descended to endearments. There were aspects of Agnes' life, however, which obliged Miss Vance to treat her not as a pet, but as a child. Her own.

One of these aspects was the girl's undoubted ability as a Latinist. Whereas her classmates, however brightly they began their five-year immersion into the Latin tongue, ended by balking at the endless examples and exceptions to be memorized before each class, Agnes seemed to need them the way you do ground under your feet in order to stand up. On her face would appear an expression of utter serenity when she was construing difficult phrases. She didn't find Caesar's accounts of the Gallic wars at all tedious; she positively glowed when they tackled Vergil in the senior grades, and she'd shown herself particularly adept at translating the few, rigorously selected passages of Ovid to which Miss Vance allowed her students access (Catullus and Petronius were, of course, so far beyond the pale they didn't exist, even up on the dusty, distant cornices of Miss Vance's classroom).

But this unusual aptitude for Latin in an age when all but the best schools had axed the subject from the curriculum was not the deciding factor in Miss Vance's adoption of Agnes. It was rather the necessity the teacher felt, faced with her pupil's background and environment, to be more than an academic instructor. In the first place, the girl was Hungarian. There were certain foreign races—the French, the German, even, precariously, the Italian—which Miss Vance could accommodate in her conception of society. Though of pure Scots-Irish stock, she did not hold with those who would not acknowledge the existence, never mind the virtues, of those who were not Anglo-Saxon as well as white and Protestant. But she drew the line at certain sure points. She warned her senior pupils against applying to University College, for example, because there were so many Jews who went there; an Oakdale student would be much better off at Trinity or Victoria. And when it came to ethnic groups who didn't possess recognizable alphabets, whose language even the most rigorous phonetics could not decode, Miss Vance proclaimed not defeat but disgust.

About the Serenys she had obtained all necessary information. Agnes and her parents had escaped from Hungary after the uprising—that gave proof of endeavour, fortitude, however distastefully dramatic to Miss Vance's eyes. The family had established itself in a split-level suburban home some ten minutes' walk from Oakdale School; this was all unexceptionable. But a few years before Agnes made the transition from junior to senior high school, Mr. Sereny, a pharmacist with his own shop downtown, had gone bankrupt and died in much too quick succession. The suburban house had been sold, Agnes and her mother moving to one of the new and crudely built apartment towers that were springing up at the extreme edge of the municipality, disfiguring a skyline which previously had only to deal with immature blue spruce and maple trees. The apartment tower smelled of boiled cabbage and suspicious spices, one of Miss Vance's junior colleagues had told her—he'd been there looking for accommodation soon after his appointment to the school and had wisely decided to lodge elsewhere. Not, however, in the low-rise, respectable apartment house in which Miss Vance lived—across from the plaza, it is true, but screened by a high wall of impenetrable shrubbery.

That shrubbery protected Miss Vance from more than the sight of leather-jacketed, cigarette-spouting loafers at the plaza variety store. It allowed her and the other tenants of Oakdale Manor immunity from the kinds of activity that went on in less reputable buildings than their own. For the same colleague who had rashly gone one Saturday morning to inquire about renting a bachelorette at Oakdale Towers had witnessed, right in the lobby, an embrace between a young, badly dressed, foreign-looking man and an older woman whose too-short skirt and whose hair—peroxide-platinum—gave her away as none other than Mrs. Sereny, whom the teacher had encountered only days before at a Home and School. Luckily, Agnes hadn't been anywhere near the lobby—hopefully, might not even have been in the building, since the most scandalous thing about the whole episode, as Miss Vance understood it, was that the couple were obviously coming down from the apartment where they had spent time—perhaps the night—together. There had been a certain something about the way they clung together in that most inhospitable lobby, with its hard, narrow benches drawn up in a travesty of intimacy around a fake rubber plant. But at this point Miss Vance had silenced her informant with a look that went like a pin through a finger.

The next afternoon she had talked to the girl while everyone else was belabouring a tricky passage assigned as an impromptu translation exercise. Agnes, for whom the passage was no more difficult than the riddles on bubblegum wrappers, sat at the long table at the back of the classroom, working on a *papier-mâché* model of an aqueduct. Miss Vance watched her silently tearing strips of newspaper, and then abruptly asked whether she'd decided to which universities she'd apply at the end of the year. Agnes had neatly piled the strips of newspaper, tightened the lid of the glue bottle and finally replied in her soft, unaccented, yet not-quite-Canadian voice that she'd never thought of going on to university. There wasn't the money for that; she had her mother to think of; she would get work as a salesgirl at one of the shops in the plaza, take a secretarial course at night and, with the two of them working, they could afford a larger apartment. Miss Vance had only smiled. Then the buzzer rang; obediently, Agnes went back to her seat and left the classroom with the others.

That evening Miss Vance had checked the syllabus of her *alma mater,* a small liberal arts college in New Brunswick which had the reputation of turning out excellent classical scholars. On page eighty-two of the syllabus she found, among a list of entrance scholarships, exactly what she wanted: the Charles Maltman Award for Classics, to be bestowed upon a student whose exceptional ability was matched only by his financial need. There were even provisions for the student's being given summer employment tutoring deserving high school children from the local town. Miss Vance had lain awake till nearly two, plotting a campaign that would remove Agnes forever from the stink of boiled cabbage and immortality in her mother's apartment.

THE SERENYS' APARTMENT smelled most often not of boiled cabbage, but of chicken paprikash, poppy-seed strudel, brandied plums. For Marta Sereny, having sold the suburban split-level to help pay her husband's debts, met the rent on the apartment at Oakdale Towers by acting as cook at the *Hungarian Village,* the plaza restaurant— over-large and funereally underlighted. Anyès and her mother invariably dined off leftovers which Marta took home in aluminum baking dishes and small styrofoam containers. The *Hungarian Village* was perpetually on the verge of folding, except that the owner, a Mrs. Lampman who lived in Rosedale, operated the whole affair as a tax write-off and was rather fond of Marta Sereny and that small, pale daughter of hers, who waitressed on weekends, reading whole books between customers.

Mrs. Lampman occasionally came to lunch at the *Hungarian Village;* over coffee and dessert she would listen to Marta's fears and hopes concerning her daughter. It wasn't healthy, all this fussing with a dead language. Surely she ought to be taking something more practical, like typing and shorthand—things that would give the girl a chance in life, a chance at meeting the right sort of men—doctors, lawyers, businessmen, pharmacists. Worst of all, *that* woman was trying to turn the girl against her own mother, though it would never work; Anyès always told her every- thing, they were that close and Marta had held two rosy fingers, pressed together, inches away from Mrs. Lampman's eyes.

Mrs. Lampman went on stirring too much sugar into her tepid coffee as she listened, thinking how old Marta looked. Her face was like a map that had been creased and opened far too many times; she looked tired in the same way as do small children who've been allowed to stay up far beyond their proper bedtime, and in whose heavy eyes you read a reproach to grownups who should have known better. Marta's features, too, were exaggerated like a child's—her lips soft, wide, crisscrossed with lines like the palm of a hand; the blue of her huge eyes pale as though the colour had been carelessly scribbled in. Yet it was a face that also seemed blurred, as if you were always seeing it through tears, which was curious, Mrs. Lampman reflected, since she could not once remember Marta having cried all the times she had recounted items from her personal history.

That her marriage had not been a happy one, for example. Marta would put one small hand against the rise of her breasts—she favoured plunging necklines—as if to gesture to, and yet conceal the cause of her marital woes. It was no wonder there was only the one child, Marta had sighed. Yet Anyès had always been so attached to her father, though God knew he never had time for her. The end he made hadn't seemed to interfere with her schoolwork, though; she was an A student, the kind who worked so hard she had to excel. But in Latin? Come to the New World and study Latin? And that teacher—she was so masterful, so demanding, she had the girl staying up half the night to do extra projects. Anyès worshipped her, just as she had her father. It wasn't good for a child to worship anyone like that, especially when she had her own mother to help her and teach her things you didn't learn at school.

Mrs. Lampman listened without nodding or shaking her head. She said that she'd heard of the teacher in question; she possessed a marvellous reputation, had been with the school for years, had helped form the character of hundreds of children from the best families. If this Miss Vance felt that Anyès had a future as a Latin scholar, that her talents would be wasted with bedpans or carbon paper, why not let things take their course? Without waiting for an answer, Mrs. Lampman had pushed away the cold, sugar-saturated coffee, risen from her chair and told Marta in parting that she'd mention her name to a Mrs. Jablonski who needed a caterer and waitress for a birthday party she was giving in two weeks' time.

"Bitch," Marta had hissed after Mrs. Lampman closed the door, but it wasn't clear whether she was speaking of Miss Vance or the owner of the restaurant. She went back to the kitchen and began packing up leftovers from that day's cooking. Tonight they closed early—it was her evening off and Zoltàn would be coming. They would all eat the remains of the veal birds and poppy seed torte, and then Anyès would do her homework while Marta and Zoltàn took the bus down to the subway station, and the subway downtown. There they would walk, arm in arm, staring into lighted jewellers' shops and the endless windows of department stores; or perhaps they would see a Hungarian film at the Hall, and then have a beer in the Blue Cellar Room. It didn't matter what they did, so long as they stayed out long enough for Anyès to have finished her homework, taken her bath and fallen fast asleep in her bed—the fold-out couch which had been moved to the spot farthest away from Marta's room. And then Marta and her lover, who had been at university in Hungary but now worked at the Budapest Bakery and studied law at night school, would unlock the apartment door and creep toward the bedroom with such reverent caution you would have thought there was a newborn asleep on the couch. Would lock themselves into the bedroom and make love so desperately that it would wake Anyès from dreams so full of loss and confusion she could barely keep herself from crying out.

BETWEEN THE TIME that Miss Vance had put into her pupil's hand a letter confirming that the Charles Maltman had been awarded to Agnes Sereny of Oakdale School, and the night that Anyès had finally confessed to her mother what the scholarship entailed—four years in a place far enough away that neither Marta nor Anyès would be able to afford telephone calls, never mind visits to each other—Anyès began to have a recurring dream. She would be at a railway station waiting to board a train which always tried to leave without her. Unable to fall asleep again, she would switch on the lamp at the edge of the fold-out couch, pick up a book and read, hoping that the very sound of the words would soothe her to sleep. *"Foelix qui potuit rerum cognoscere causas / Atque metus omnes et inexorabile fatum / Subjecit pedibus, strepitumque Acherontis avari. / Fortunatus et ille deos qui novit agrestes, / Panaque, Sylvanumque senem, nymphasque sorores ..."* But the more she read, the more distressed she would become, as if her very fluency were mocking her. She would put down her book, realizing that Pan, Sylvanus, and the sister-nymphs meant no more to her now than the plates she washed at her mother's restaurant. And then all the maxims and mottos she'd ever had to translate would pummel her: *Dum spiro spero*— while I breathe I hope—*Nemo timendo ad summmum pervenit locum*—No man by fearing reaches the top—*Quod incepimus conficiemus*—What we have begun we shall finish. And she had had a vision of all the mottos at the headings of all the chapters of all the Latin textbooks in the world forming the bars of a colossal cage so intricately twisted that she was caught inside with no room to move even a finger.

The knowledge that she could leave the cramped apartment which had begun to seem even smaller once her mother and Zoltàn had started quarrelling, and get onto an airplane to a beautiful place—Miss Vance had shown her slides of it—hit her like a fist in the face. What use—no, what good was Latin since it had nothing to do with anything that had ever marked her life? Or was that why she loved it so much, because it made a marble labyrinth in which to lose herself, she who hadn't the slightest desire to find her way out again?

The conjunction *cum,* the Present Infinitive Active and Passive Indirect Statement—they had nothing to do with the young men she had seen being shot in the streets of Budapest, the young men her father had told her she was too young to have seen or remembered, even in a nightmare. Nothing to do with the last time she had seen her father—bruising her shoulder against the locked bathroom door, calling her mother, the two of them breaking into the room to find Anton Sereny in his business suit, with his hat on, stretched out in a tub of water pink as the roses on the wallpaper. Or, worse than all of this, the last quarrel, the one they hadn't tried to shut her out from by closing the bedroom door, so that she had heard, buried under the comforter on the couch, Marta accusing Zoltàn of watching Anyès when he thought she wasn't looking, of wanting to put his hands on her, touch her, and she only a child, innocence itself—. The crash of his hand against her mother's face so that she wouldn't say any more, as if saying it, not thinking it, made it true. And her own silence, hot, smothered under the comforter, knowing that her mother was right and also that she was wrong—for Zoltàn had come an hour early that evening, knowing

Marta to be still at the restaurant, and had stood over her as she worked at the kitchen table (consonant stems of third declension—*corpora, corporum, corporibus*) and put his hands on her shoulders and she had let him; and had slid his hands which were large but finely shaped—she had studied them as often as she had her conjugations—light as leaves against her skin, under her sweater and over her breasts, and she had let him, having no language to ask, or refuse, or explain, even to herself, what she wanted to be happening....

The night after all the nights Zoltàn had not come, Anyès had woken out of this dream of a railway station to hear, not the cries of lovers, nor the black hum of heating machines and electric wires in the apartment walls, but a sound she had heard only twice before: the night that her father had decided they must try to escape from Hungary, and the night before she and her mother had moved out of their house into the apartment. The sound of her mother weeping: not pleading or resisting, but as if she were mourning her own fate; as if she knew already what such travel would cost her, and that she didn't have the means to pay.

Anyès had pulled a sweater over her nightdress and gone soundlessly to her mother's room. The door was ajar, lamplight haloing its edges. Anyès walked inside. Dressed only in her slip, her mother was sitting on the bed, whose covers she had not bothered to turn down. Beside her was a bottle of brandy, nearly empty, the stars on its label tarnished, forlorn. Marta had looked up at her daughter, rubbing the skin above her breasts as she did so, the satiny slip cutting into flesh which Anyès saw was too soft, too white, too full to be touched without hurting. Wordless, Marta held out her arms to her daughter, wrapped them round the girl's small and delicate shoulders, drawing her in as if Anyès were an infant to be put to the breast, fed and comforted; as if her daughter's tears were milk spurting from Marta's nipples, soaking them both. "Don't leave me. I have nothing, don't leave me, my darling Zoltàn—Anyès—Zoltàn."

Anyès gently loosened her mother's arms around her, laid her down and pulled the flimsy blankets over her. Then she twisted the cap back on to the brandy bottle, turned out the light and sat on the edge of the bed, holding her mother's hand until she heard the slow, shuddering breath of Marta, sleeping.

MISS VANCE had proposed the presentation. Agnes had an obligation, she stressed, to mark the occasion of her winning of the scholarship with a demonstration, not only of her own intellectual capacities but also of the intrinsic value of classics in the classroom. Agnes would speak during the last Latin class of the year on an author of her choice. The principal, the guidance counsellor, the student teachers would all be invited to hear an exposition on the principal merits of the author in question, and a few well-chosen words of confidence in and gratitude for all that the Latin tongue could bestow upon its conscientious students.

Agnes had chosen Ovid—against Miss Vance's wishes (she favoured Vergil, something from the *Eclogues,* perhaps). If it had to be Ovid, the *Baucis and Philemon* from *The Metamorphoses* would be the obvious choice, Miss Vance had decided. Agnes had agreed—at any rate, there was no further discussion, and so her teacher had permitted her to spend the last month of Latin class in the library, construing that one safe story from Ovidius Naso's libidinous pen.

The library was dimly lit. Mrs. Paulson, the school librarian, still had vivid memories of blackouts and rationing in her native England. Classical literature was shelved in a crepuscular corner which the school's architect had originally intended as a broom closet. And so Anyès felt for, rather than looked out, the volumes she needed for her exposition; and so she came upon the volume of Ovid that had somehow got squeezed behind the *Metamorphoses* and the *Tristia*—a different sort of book with soft leather covers and a crested bookplate inside the cover: *ex libris* J.L. Stanhope.

Mrs. Paulson could have explained to Agnes that the book had not got lost behind the other volumes, but had been placed there deliberately. The library had received quite a generous donation of books from the late Mr. Stanhope, who had owned the farmland which was now the suburb of Oakdale, and whose large stone house, visible from the library's window, had become a Christian Science Reading Room. Among the books had been some texts in precarious, if not actively pernicious taste. Mrs. Paulson had not conferred with Miss Vance, whom she quite violently disliked. She couldn't bear the thought of throwing out books with perfectly good bindings, so had simply hidden them away. After all, they were printed in a foreign language, and she doubted whether the vocabulary lists to be found in *Living Latin* would permit even the most resourceful student to make much of this poet's dalliance with Corinna, that poet's address to Lesbia.

Yet in this one case—Anyès Sereny's happening to have chanced upon that supple, leather-bound version of the *Amores*—Mrs. Paulson had gravely erred. For the text was a dual Latin-English version, and the translations were lively indeed, so lively that Anyès sat for the length of each Latin class with them, and even returned at the end of the school day to devour the poems, oblivious to the rush-hour traffic returning faithful husbands from city to suburb; to the sunset's garish reflection in the windows of the Christian Science Reading Room; to the fact that Miss Vance expected her to help with repairing plasticene models; and that her mother was waiting for her to deal with dirty dishes at the *Hungarian Village*.

The afternoon of the presentation for Miss Vance, Agnes Sereny had taken her place at the podium in front of her fellow students, all of whom had by now the same repugnance for anything Latin as they'd have for objects in a mortuary. Yet as she began to speak they couldn't help but listen—not to Agnes' account of Ovid's life, but to the excitement that beat wings through her words, carrying her into some higher, richer air. And when Agnes started to read what Miss Vance had announced as *Baucis and Philemon,* that tale of marital devotion and fidelity, they'd leaned forward in their absurdly child-sized desks as if following the flight of some exotic and endangered bird.

> In a summer season, siesta time
> I lay relaxed upon my couch.

> One shutter locked, the other ajar
> let in a sylvan half-light …

> And then, Corinna—her thin dress loosened,
> long hair falling past the pale neck—

> lovely as Semiramis entering her wedding bed,
> or Lais of the many lovers.

> I pulled away her dress: she fought to keep it
> though it didn't hide much,

> yet fought as one with no desire to win—
> her defeat, a self-betrayal.

> Unveiled, faultless, naked
> she stood before me.

> Such shoulders and arms inviting my eyes;
> Nipples firmly demanding attention—

Miss Vance, erect at her desk but gasping for breath as if something had been holding her underwater for so long she thought she'd surely drown: "I think you've gone as far as good taste will permit. Sit down!"

On the girl's face an expression no longer somnolent, submissive, as Miss Vance dismissed the class, requesting Agnes Sereny to stay behind. Yet when teacher and pupil were left alone with the array of peeling replicas overhead, Miss Vance would not look at Agnes. Instead, she removed her spectacles and began rubbing her eyes with the heels of her hands, pressing them like a second pair of eyelids into her face. Watching her, Anyès felt the same shock of perception she'd had in seeing her father for the last time—knowing that it was the last time, that there was suddenly an immeasurable distance between them.

Miss Vance at last looked up, unsteadily. Whatever she meant to say, the words came out as this:

"Once, only once, did I do something I knew was wrong. Some 'friends' at university dragged me off one afternoon to a movie. *Ecstasy* it was called, or some such poppycock. It was supposed to be very daring. There was a woman swimming in a lake … But all I could think of was the work I should have been doing in class, of what my father would think if he ever found out. I hated every minute of it. And I never did a thing like that again. Ever."

Anyès made no answer. As Miss Vance covered her eyes again the girl thought of her mother as she'd seen her that night—dishevelled, exposed. And knew, suddenly, that she was free of them both, that she could never again give them whatever they needed from her, and that they knew this, too. There was no call for any valediction. She picked up her papers, took the library copy of *The Amores* and walked from the classroom as if out of a dream—in a hurry, as though she had a train to catch.

The Collectors
ROHINTON MISTRY

I

When Dr. Burjor Mody was transferred from I Mysore to assume the principalship of the Bombay Veterinary College, he moved into Firozsha Baag with his wife and son Pesi. They occupied the vacant flat on the third floor of C Block, next to the Bulsara family.

Dr. Mody did not know it then, but he would be seeing a lot of Jehangir, the Bulsara boy; the boy who sat silent and brooding, every evening, watching the others at play and called *chaarikhao* by them—quite unfairly, since he never tattled or told tales—(Dr. Mody would call him, affectionately, the observer of C Block). And Dr. Mody did not know this, either, at the time of moving, that Jehangir Bulsara's visits at ten a.m. every Sunday would become a source of profound joy for himself. Or that just when he would think he had found someone to share his hobby with, someone to mitigate the perpetual disappointment about his son Pesi, he would lose his precious Spanish dancing-lady stamp and renounce Jehangir's friendship, both in quick succession. And then two years later, he himself would—but *that* is never knowable.

Soon after moving in, Dr. Burjor Mody became the pride of the Parsis in C Block. C Block, like the rest of Firozsha Baag, had a surfeit of low-paid bank clerks and bookkeepers, and the arrival of Dr. Mody permitted them to feel a little better about themselves. More importantly, in A Block lived a prominent priest, and B Block boasted a chartered accountant. Now C Block had a voice in Baag matters as important as the others did.

While C Block went about its routine business, confirming and authenticating the sturdiness of the object of their pride, the doctor's big-boned son Pesi established himself as leader of the rowdier elements among the Baag's ten-to-sixteen population. For Pesi, too, it was routine business; he was following a course he had mapped out for himself ever since the family began moving from city to city on the whims and megrims of his father's employer, the government.

To account for Pesi's success was the fact of his brutish strength. But he was also the practitioner of a number of minor talents which appealed to the crowd where he would be leader. The one no doubt complemented the other, the talents serving to dissemble the brutish qualifier of strength, and the brutish strength encouraging the crowd to perceive the appeal of his talents.

Hawking, for instance, was one of them. Pesi could summon up prodigious quantities of phlegm at will, accompanied by sounds such as the boys had seldom heard except in accomplished adults: deep, throaty, rasping, resonating rolls which culminated in a pthoo, with the impressive trophy landing in the dust at their feet, its size leaving them all slightly envious. Pesi could also break wind that sounded like questions, exclamations, fragments of the chromatic scale, and clarion calls, while the others sniffed and discussed the merits of pungency versus tonality. This ability earned him the appellation of Pesi *paadmaroo,* and he wore the sobriquet with pride.

Perhaps his single most important talent was his ability to improvise. The peculiarities of a locale were the raw material for his inventions. In Firozsha Baag, behind the three buildings, or blocks, as they were called, were spacious yards shared by all three blocks. These yards planted in Pesi's fecund mind the seed from which grew a new game: stoning-the-cats.

Till the arrival of the Mody family the yards were home for stray and happy felines, well fed on scraps and leftovers disgorged regularly as clockwork, after mealtimes, by the three blocks. The ground floors were the only ones who refrained. They voiced their protests in a periodic cycle of reasoning, pleading, and screaming of obscenities, because the garbage collected outside their windows where the cats took up permanent residency, miaowing, feasting and caterwauling day and night. If the cascade of food was more than the cats could devour, the remainder fell to the fortune of the rats. Finally, flies and insects buzzed and hovered over the dregs, little pools of pulses and curries fermenting and frothing, till the *kuchrawalli* came next morning and swept it all away.

The backyards of Firozsha Baag constituted its squalid underbelly. And this would be the scenario for stoning-the-cats, Pesi decided. But there was one hitch: the backyards were off limits to the boys. The only way in was through the *kuchrawalli's* little shack standing beyond A Block, where her huge ferocious dog, tied to the gate, kept the boys at bay. So Pesi decreed that the boys gather at the rear windows of their homes, preferably at a time of day when the adults were scarce, with the fathers away at work and the mothers not yet finished with their afternoon naps. Each boy brought a pile of small stones and took turns, chucking three stones each. The game could just as easily have been stoning-the-rats; but stoned rats quietly walked away to safety, whereas the yowls of cats provided primal satisfaction and verified direct hits: no yowl, no point.

The game added to Pesi's popularity—he called it a howling success. But the parents (except the ground floor) complained to Dr. Mody about his son instigating their children to torment poor dumb and helpless creatures. For a veterinarian's son to harass animals was shameful, they said.

As might be supposed, Pesi was the despair of his parents. Over the years Dr. Mody had become inured to the initial embarrassment in each new place they moved to. The routine was familiar: first, a spate of complaints from indignant parents claiming their sons *bugree nay dhoor thai gaya*—were corrupted to become useless as dust; next, the protestations giving way to sympathy when the neighbours saw that Pesi was the worm in the Modys' mango.

And so it was in Firozsha Baag. After the furor about stoning-the-cats had died down, the people of the Baag liked Dr. Mody more than ever. He earned their respect for the initiative he took in Baag matters, dealing with the management for things like broken lifts, leaking water tanks, crumbling plaster, and faulty wiring. It was at his urging that the massive iron gate, set in the stone wall which ran all around the buildings, compound and backyards, was repaired, and a watchman installed to stop beggars and riff-raff. (And although Dr. Mody would be dead by the time of the *Shiv Sena* riots, the tenants would remember him for the gate which would keep out the rampaging mobs.) When the Bombay Municipality tried to appropriate a section of Baag property for its road-widening scheme, Dr. Mody was in the forefront of the battle, winning a compromise whereby the Baag only lost half the proposed area. But the Baag's esteem did nothing to lighten the despair for Pesi that hung around the doctor.

At the birth of his son, Dr. Mody had deliberated long and hard about the naming. Peshotan, in the Persian epic, *Shah-Nameh,* was the brother of the great Asfandyar, and a noble general, lover of art and learning, and man of wise counsel. Dr. Mody had decided his son would play the violin, acquire the best from the cultures of East and West, thrill to the words of Tagore and Shakespeare, appreciate Mozart and Indian ragas; and one day, at the proper moment, he would introduce him to his dearest activity, stamp-collecting.

But the years passed in their own way. Fate denied fruition to all of Dr. Mody's plans; and when he talked about stamps, Pesi laughed and mocked his beloved hobby. This was the point at which, hurt and confused, he surrendered his son to whatever destiny was in store. A perpetual grief entered to occupy the void left behind after the aspirations for his son were evicted.

The weight of grief was heaviest around Dr. Mody when he returned from work in the evenings. As the car turned into the compound he usually saw Pesi before Pesi saw him, in scenes which made him despair, scenes in which his son was abusing someone, fighting, or making lewd gestures.

But Dr. Mody was careful not to make a public spectacle of his despair. While the car made its way sluggishly over the uneven flagstones of the compound, the boys would stand back and wave him through. With his droll comments and jovial countenance he was welcome to disrupt their play, unlike two other car-owners of Firozsha Baag: the priest in A Block and the chartered accountant in B who habitually berated, from inside their vehicles, the sons of bank clerks and bookkeepers for blocking the driveway with their games. Their well-worn curses had become so predictable and ineffective that sometimes the boys chanted gleefully, in unison with their nemeses: "Worse than *saala* animals!" or *"junglee* dogs-cats have more sense!" or "you *sataans* ever have any lesson-*paani* to do or not!"

There was one boy who always stayed apart from his peers—the Bulsara boy, from the family next door to the Modys. Jehangir sat on the stone steps every evening while the gentle land breezes, drying and cooling the sweaty skins of the boys at play, blew out to sea. He sat alone through the long dusk, a source of discomfiture to the others. They resented his melancholy, watching presence.

Dr. Mody noticed Jehangir, too, on the stone steps of C Block, the delicate boy with the build much too slight for his age. Next to a hulk like Pesi he was diminutive, but things other than size underlined his frail looks: he had slender hands, and forearms with fine downy hair. And while facial fuzz was incipient in most boys of his age (and Pesi was positively hirsute), Jehangir's chin and upper lip were smooth as a young woman's. But it pleased Dr. Mody to see him evening after evening. The quiet contemplation of the boy on the steps and the noise and activity of the others at play came together in the kind of balance that Dr. Mody was always looking for and was quick to appreciate.

Jehangir, in his turn, observed the burly Dr. Mody closely as he walked past him each evening. When he approached the steps after parking his car, Jehangir would say *"Sahibji"* in greeting, and smile wanly. He saw that despite Dr. Mody's constant jocularity there was something painfully empty about his eyes. He noticed the peculiar way he scratched the greyish-red patches of psoriasis on his elbows, both elbows simultaneously, by folding his arms across his chest. Sometimes Jehangir would arise from the stone steps and the two would go up together to the third floor. Dr. Mody asked him once, "You don't like playing with the other boys? You just sit and watch them?" The boy shook his head and blushed, and Dr. Mody did not bring up the matter after that.

Gradually, a friendship of sorts grew between the two. Jehangir touched a chord inside the doctor which had lain silent for much too long. Now affection for the boy developed and started to linger around the region hitherto occupied by grief bearing Pesi's name.

II

One evening, while Jehangir sat on the stone steps waiting for Dr. Mody's car to arrive, Pesi was organizing a game of naargolio. He divided the boys into two teams, then discovered he was one short. He beckoned to Jehangir, who said he did not want to play. Scowling, Pesi handed the ball to one of the others and walked over to him. He grabbed his collar with both hands, jerking him to his feet. *"Arré choosya!"* he yelled, "want a pasting?" and began dragging him by the collar to where the boys had piled up the seven flat stones for *naargolio*.

At that instant, Dr. Mody's car turned into the compound, and he spied his son in one of those scenes which could provoke despair. But today the despair was swept aside by rage when he saw that Pesi's victim was the gentle and quiet Jehangir Bulsara. He left the car in the middle of the compound with the motor running. Anger glinted in his eyes. He kicked over the pile of seven flat stones as he walked blindly towards Pesi who, having seen his father, had released Jehangir. He had been caught by his father often enough to know that it was best to stand and wait. Jehangir, meanwhile, tried to keep back the tears.

Dr. Mody stopped before his son and slapped him hard, once on each cheek, with the front and back of his right hand. He waited, as if debating whether that was enough, then put his arm around Jehangir and led him to the car.

He drove to his parking spot. By now, Jehangir had control of his tears, and they walked to the steps of C Block. The lift was out of order. They climbed the stairs to the third floor and knocked. He waited with Jehangir.

Jehangir's mother came to the door. *"Sahibji,* Dr. Mody," she said, a short, middle-aged woman, very prim, whose hair was always in a bun. Never without a *mathoobanoo,* she could do wonderful things with that square of fine white cloth which was tied and knotted to sit like a cap on her head, snugly packeting the bun. In the evenings, after the household chores were done, she removed the *mathoobanoo* and wore it in a more conventional manner, like a scarf.

"Sahibji," she said, then noticed her son's tear-stained face. *"Arré,* Jehangoo, what happened, who made you cry?" Her hand flew automatically to the *mathoobanoo,* tugging and adjusting it as she did whenever she was concerned or agitated.

To save the boy embarrassment, Dr. Mody intervened: "Go, wash your face while I talk to your mother." Jehangir went inside, and Dr. Mody told her briefly about what had happened. "Why does he not play with the other boys?" he asked finally.

"Dr. Mody, what to say. The boy never wants even to go out. *Khoedai salaamat raakhé,* wants to sit at home all the time and read story books. Even this little time in the evening he goes because I force him and tell him he will not grow tall without fresh air. Every week he brings new-new story books from school. First, school library would allow only one book per week. But he went to Father Gonzalves who is in charge of library and got special permission for two books. God knows why he gave it."

"But reading is good, Mrs. Bulsara."

"I know, I know, but a mania like this, all the time?"

"Some boys are outdoor types, some are indoor types. You shouldn't worry about Jehangir, he is a very good boy. Look at my Pesi, now there is a case for worry," he said, meaning to reassure her.

"No, no. You mustn't say that. Be patient, *Khoedai* is great," said Mrs. Bulsara, consoling him instead. Jehangir returned, his eyes slightly red but dry. While washing his face he had wet a lock of his hair which hung down over his forehead.

"Ah, here comes my indoor champion," smiled Dr. Mody, and patted Jehangir's shoulder, brushing back the lock of hair. Jehangir did not understand, but grinned anyway; the doctor's joviality was infectious. Dr. Mody turned again to the mother. "Send him to my house on Sunday at ten o'clock. We will have a little talk."

After Dr. Mody left, Jehangir's mother told him how lucky he was that someone as important and learned as Burjor Uncle was taking an interest in him. Privately, she hoped he would encourage the boy towards a more all-rounded approach to life and to the things other boys did. And when Sunday came she sent Jehangir off to Dr. Mody's promptly at ten.

Dr. Mody was taking his bath, and Mrs. Mody opened the door. She was a dour-faced woman, spare and lean—the opposite of her husband in appearance and disposition, yet retaining some quality from long ago which suggested that it had not always been so. Jehangir had never crossed her path save when she was exchanging civilities with his mother, while making purchases out by the stairs from the vegetablewalla or fruitwalla.

Not expecting Jehangir's visit, Mrs. Mody stood blocking the doorway and said: "Yes?" Meaning, what nuisance now?

"Burjor Uncle asked me to come at ten o'clock."

"Asked you to come at ten o'clock? What for?"

"He just said to come at ten o'clock."

Grudgingly, Mrs. Mody stepped aside. "Come in then. Sit down there." And she indicated the specific chair she wanted him to occupy, muttering something about a *baap* who had time for strangers' children but not for his own son.

Jehangir sat in what must have been the most uncomfortable chair in the room. This was his first time inside the Modys' flat, and he looked around with curiosity. But his gaze was quickly restricted to the area of the floor directly in front of him when he realized that he was the object of Mrs. Mody's watchfulness.

Minutes ticked by under her vigilant eye. Jehangir was grateful when Dr. Mody emerged from the bedroom. Being Sunday, he had eschewed his usual khaki half-pants for loose and comfortable white pyjamas. His *sudra* hung out over it, and he strode vigorously, feet encased in a huge pair of *sapaat*. He smiled at Jehangir, who happily noted the crow's-feet appearing at the corners of his eyes. He was ushered into Dr. Mody's room, and man and boy both seemed glad to escape the surveillance of the woman.

The chairs were more comfortable in Dr. Mody's room. They sat at his desk and Dr. Mody opened a drawer to take out a large book.

"This was the first stamp album I ever had," said Dr. Mody. "It was given to me by my Nusserwanji Uncle when I was your age. All the pages were empty." He began turning them. They were covered with stamps, each a feast of colour and design. He talked as he turned the pages, and Jehangir watched and listened, glancing at the stamps flying past, at Dr. Mody's face, then at the stamps again.

Dr. Mody spoke not in his usual booming, jovial tones but softly, in a low voice charged with inspiration. The stamps whizzed by, and his speech was gently underscored by the rustle of the heavily laden pages that seemed to turn of their own volition in the quiet room. (Jehangir would remember this peculiar rustle when one day, older, he'd stand alone in this very room, silenced now forever, and turn the pages of Nusserwanji Uncle's album.) Jehangir watched and listened. It was as though a mask had descended over Dr. Mody, a faraway look upon his face, and a shining in the eyes which heretofore Jehangir had only seen sad with despair or glinting with anger or just plain and empty, belying his constant drollery. Jehangir watched, and listened to the euphonious voice hinting at wondrous things and promises and dreams.

The album on the desk, able to produce such changes in Dr. Mody, now worked its magic through him upon the boy. Jehangir, watching and listening, fascinated, tried to read the names of the countries at the top of the pages as they sped by: Antigua … Australia … Belgium … Bhutan … Bulgaria … and on through to Malta and Mauritius … Romania and Russia … Togo and Tonga … and a final blur through which he caught Yugoslavia and Zanzibar.

"Can I see it again?" he asked, and Dr. Mody handed the album to him.

"So what do you think? Do you want to be a collector?"

Jehangir nodded eagerly and Dr. Mody laughed. "When Nusserwanji Uncle showed me his collection I felt just like that. I'll tell your mother what to buy for you to get you started. Bring it here next Sunday, same time."

And next Sunday Jehangir was ready at nine. But he waited by his door with a Stamp Album For Beginners and a packet of 100 Assorted Stamps—All Countries. Going too early would mean sitting under the baleful eyes of Mrs. Mody.

Ten o'clock struck and the clock's tenth bong was echoed by the Modys' doorchimes. Mrs. Mody was expecting him this time and did not block the doorway. Wordlessly, she beckoned him in. Burjor Uncle was ready, too, and came out almost immediately to rescue him from her arena.

"Let's see what you've got there," he said when they were in his room. They removed the cellophane wrapper, and while they worked Dr. Mody enjoyed himself as much as the boy. His deepest wish appeared to be coming true: he had at last found someone to share his hobby with. He could not have hoped for a finer neophyte than Jehangir. His young recruit was so quick to learn how to identify and sort stamps by countries, learn the different currencies, spot watermarks. Already he was skilfully folding and moistening the little hinges and mounting the stamps as neatly as the teacher.

When it was almost time to leave, Jehangir asked if he could examine again Nusserwanji Uncle's album, the one he had seen last Sunday. But Burjor Uncle led him instead to a cupboard in the corner of the room. "Since you enjoy looking at my stamps, let me show you what I have here." He unlocked its doors.

Each of the cupboard's four shelves was piled with biscuit tins and sweet tins: round, oval, rectangular, square. It puzzled Jehangir: all this bore the unmistakable stamp of the worthless hoardings of senility, and did not seem at all like Burjor Uncle. But Burjor Uncle reached out for a box at random and showed him inside. It was chock-full of stamps! Jehangir's mouth fell open. Then he gaped at the shelves, and Burjor Uncle laughed. "Yes, all these tins are full of stamps. And that big cardboard box at the bottom contains six new albums, all empty."

Jehangir quickly tried to assign a number in his mind to the stamps in the containers of Maghanlal Biscuitwalla and Lokmanji Mithaiwalla, to all of the stamps in the round tins and the oval tins, the square ones and the oblong ones. He failed.

Once again Dr. Mody laughed at the boy's wonderment. "A lot of stamps. And they took me a lot of years to collect. Of course, I am lucky I have many contacts in foreign countries. Because of my job, I meet the experts from abroad who are invited by the Indian Government. When I tell them about my hobby they send me stamps from their countries. But no time to sort them, so I pack them in boxes. One day, after I retire, I will spend all my time with my stamps." He paused, and shut the cupboard doors. "So what you have to do now is start making lots of friends, tell them about your hobby. If they also collect, you can exchange duplicates with them. If they don't, you can still ask them for all the envelopes they may be throwing away with stamps on them. You do something for them, they will do something for you. Your collection will grow depending on how smart you are."

He hesitated, and opened the cupboard again. Then he changed his mind and shut it—it wasn't yet time for the Spanish dancing-lady stamp.

III

On the pavement outside St. Xavier's Boys School, not far from the ornate iron gates, stood two variety stalls. They were the stalls of *Patla Babu* and *Jhaaria Babu*. Their real names were never known. Nor was known the exact source of the schoolboy inspiration that named them thus, many years ago, after their respective thinness and fatness.

Before the schoolboys arrived in the morning, the two would unpack their cases and set up the displays, beating the beggars to the choice positions. Occasionally, there were disputes if someone's space was violated. The beggars did not harbour great hopes for alms from schoolboys but they stood there, nonetheless, like mute lessons in realism and the harshness of life. Their patience was rewarded when they raided the dustbins after breaks and lunches.

At the end of the school day the pavement community packed up. The beggars shuffled off into the approaching dark, *Patla Babu* went home with his cases, and *Jhaaria Babu* slept near the school gate under a large tree to whose trunk he chained his boxes during the night.

The two sold a variety of nondescript objects and comestibles, uninteresting to any save the eyes and stomachs of schoolboys: *supari,* A-1 chewing gum (which, in a most ungumlike manner, would, after a while, dissolve in one's mouth), *jeeragoli,* marbles, tops, *aampapud* during the mango season, pens, Camel Ink, pencils, rulers, and stamps in little cellophane packets.

Patla Babu and *Jhaaria Babu* lost some of their goods regularly due to theft. This was inevitable when doing business outside a large school like St. Xavier's, with a population as varied as its was. The loss was an operating expense stoically accepted, like the success or failure of the monsoons, and they never complained to the school authorities or held it against the boys. Besides, business was good despite the losses: insignificant items like a packet of *jeeragoli* worth ten paise, or a marble of the kind that sold three for five paise. More often than not, the stealing went on for the excitement of it, out of bravado or on a dare. It was called "flicking" and was done without any malice towards *Patla* and *Jhaaria.*

Foremost among the flickers was a boy in Jehangir's class called Eric D'Souza. A tall, lanky fellow who had been suspended a couple of times, he had had to repeat the year on two occasions, and held out the promise of more repetitions. Eric also had the reputation of doing things inside his half-pants under cover of his desk. In a class of fifty boys it was easy to go unobserved by the teacher, and only his immediate neighbours could see the ecstasy on his face and the vigorous back and forth movement of his hand. When he grinned at them they looked away, pretending not to have noticed anything.

Jehangir sat far from Eric and knew of his habits only by hearsay. He was oblivious to Eric's eye which had been on him for quite a while. In fact, Eric found Jehangir's delicate hands and fingers, his smooth legs and thighs very desirable. In class he gazed for hours, longingly, at the girlish face, curly hair, long eyelashes.

Jehangir and Eric finally got acquainted one day when the class filed out for games period. Eric had been made to kneel down by the door for coming late and disturbing the class, and Jehangir found himself next to him as he stood in line. From his kneeling position Eric observed the smooth thighs emerging from the half-pants (half-pants was the school uniform requirement), winked at him and, unhindered by his underwear, inserted a pencil up the pant leg. He tickled Jehangir's genitals seductively with the eraser end, expertly, then withdrew it. Jehangir feigned a giggle, too shocked to say anything. The line started to move for the playground.

Shortly after this incident, Eric approached Jehangir during breaktime. He had heard that Jehangir was desperate to acquire stamps.

"*Arré* man, I can get you stamps, whatever kind you want," he said.

Jehangir stopped. He had been slightly confused ever since the pass with the pencil; Eric frightened him a little with his curious habits and forbidden knowledge. But it had not been easy to accumulate stamps. Sundays with Burjor Uncle continued to be as fascinating as the first. He wished he had new stamps to show—the stasis of his collection might be misinterpreted as lack of interest. He asked Eric: "Ya? You want to exchange?"

"No *yaar*, I don't collect. But I'll get them for you. As a favour, man."

"Ya? What kind do you have?"

"I don't have, man. Come on with me to *Patla* and *Jhaaria*, just show me which ones you want. I'll flick them for you."

Jehangir hesitated. Eric put his arm around him: "C'mon man, what you scared for, I'll flick. You just show me and go away." Jehangir pictured the stamps on display in cellophane wrappers: how well they would add to his collection. He imagined album pages bare no more but covered with exquisite stamps, each one mounted carefully and correctly, with a hinge, as Burjor Uncle had showed him to.

They went outside, Eric's arm still around him. Crowds of schoolboys were gathered around the two stalls. A multitude of groping, exploring hands handled the merchandise and browsed absorbedly, a multitude that was a prerequisite for flicking to begin. Jehangir showed Eric the individually wrapped stamps he wanted and moved away. In a few minutes Eric joined him triumphantly.

"Got them?"

"Ya ya. But come inside. He could be watching, man."

Jehangir was thrilled. Eric asked, "You want more or what?"

"Sure," said Jehangir.

"But not today. On Friday. If you do me a favour in visual period on Thursday."

Jehangir's pulse speeded slightly—visual period, with its darkened hall and projector, and the intimacy created by the teacher's policing abilities temporarily suspended. He remembered Eric's pencil. The cellophane-wrapped stamp packets rustled and crackled in his hand. And there was the promise of more. There had been nothing unpleasant about the pencil. In fact it had felt quite, well, exciting. He agreed to Eric's proposal.

On Thursday, the class lined up to go to the Visual Hall. Eric stood behind Jehangir to ensure their seats would be together.

When the room was dark he put his hand on Jehangir's thigh and began caressing it. He took Jehangir's hand and placed it on his crotch. It lay there inert. Impatient, he whispered, "Do it, man, c'mon!" But Jehangir's lacklustre stroking was highly unsatisfactory. Eric arrested the hand, reached inside his pants and said, "OK, hold it tight and rub it like this." He encircled Jehangir's hand with his to show him how. When Jehangir had attained the right pressure and speed he released his own hand to lean back and sigh contentedly. Shortly, Jehangir felt a warm stickiness fill his palm and fingers, and the hardness he held in his hand grew flaccid.

Eric shook off the hand. Jehangir wiped his palm with his hanky. Eric borrowed the hanky to wipe himself. "Want me to do it for you?" he asked. But Jehangir declined. He was thinking of his hanky. The odour was interesting, not unpleasant at all, but he would have to find some way of cleaning it before his mother found it.

The following day, Eric presented him with more stamps. Next Thursday's assignation was also fixed.

And on Sunday Jehangir went to see Dr. Mody at ten o'clock. The wife let him in, muttering something under her breath about being bothered by inconsiderate people on the one day that the family could be together.

Dr. Mody's delight at the new stamps fulfilled Jehangir's every expectation: "Wonderful, wonderful! Where did you get them all? No, no, forget it, don't tell me. You will think I'm trying to learn your tricks. I already have enough stamps to keep me busy in my retirement. Ha! ha!"

After the new stamps had been examined and sorted Dr. Mody said, "Today, as a reward for your enterprise, I'm going to show you a stamp you've never seen before." From the cupboard of biscuit and sweet tins he took a small satin-covered box of the type in which rings or bracelets are kept. He opened it and, without removing the stamp from inside, placed it on the desk.

The stamp said España Correos at the bottom and its denomination was noted in the top left corner: 3 PTAS. The face of the stamp featured a flamenco dancer in the most exquisite detail and colour. But it was something in the woman's countenance, a look, an ineffable sparkle he saw in her eyes, which so captivated Jehangir.

Wordlessly, he studied the stamp. Dr. Mody waited restlessly as the seconds ticked by. He kept fidgeting till the little satin-covered box was shut and back in his hands, then said, "So you like the Spanish dancing-lady. Everyone who sees it likes it. Even my wife who is not interested in stamp-collecting thought it was beautiful. When I retire I can spend more time with the Spanish dancing-lady. And all my other stamps." He relaxed once the stamp was locked again in the cupboard.

Jehangir left, carrying that vision of the Spanish dancer in his head. He tried to imagine the stamp inhabiting the pages of his album, to greet him every time he opened it, with the wonderful sparkle in her eyes. He shut the door behind him and immediately, as though to obliterate his covetous fantasy, loud voices rose inside the flat.

He heard Mrs. Mody's, shrill in argument, and the doctor's, beseeching her not to yell lest the neighbours would hear. Pesi's name was mentioned several times in the quarrel that ensued, and accusations of neglect, and something about the terrible affliction on a son of an unloving father. The voices followed Jehangir as he hurried past the inquiring eyes of his mother, till he reached the bedroom at the other end of the flat and shut the door.

When the school week started, Jehangir found himself looking forward to Thursday. His pulse was racing with excitement when visual period came. To save his hanky this time he kept some paper at hand.

Eric did not have to provide much guidance. Jehangir discovered he could control Eric's reactions with variations in speed, pressure, and grip. When it was over and Eric offered to do it to him, he did not refuse.

The weeks sped by and Jehangir's collection continued to grow, visual period by visual period. Eric's and his masturbatory partnership was whispered about in class, earning the pair the title of *moothya-maroo*. He accompanied Eric on the flicking forays, helping to swell the milling crowd and add to the browsing hands. Then he grew bolder, studied Eric's methods, and flicked a few stamps himself.

But this smooth course of stamp-collecting was about to end. *Patla Babu* and *Jhaaria Babu* broke their long tradition of silence and complained to the school. Unlike marbles and *supari*, it was not a question of a few paise a day. When Eric and Jehangir struck, their haul could be totalled in rupees reaching double digits; the loss was serious enough to make the *Babus* worry about their survival.

The school assigned the case to the head prefect to investigate. He was an ambitious boy, always snooping around, and was also a member of the school debating team and the Road Safety Patrol. Shortly after the complaint was made he marched into Jehangir's class one afternoon just after lunch break, before the teacher returned, and made what sounded very much like one of his debating speeches: "Two boys in this class have been stealing stamps from *Patla Babu* and *Jhaaria Babu* for the past several weeks. You may ask: who are those boys? No need for names. They know who they are and I know who they are, and I am asking them to return the stamps to me tomorrow. There will be no punishment if this is done. The *Babus* just want their stamps back. But if the missing stamps are not returned, the names will be reported to the principal and to the police. It is up to the two boys."

Jehangir tried hard to appear normal. He was racked with trepidation, and looked to the unperturbed Eric for guidance. But Eric ignored him. The head prefect left amidst mock applause from the class.

After school, Eric turned surly. Gone was the tender, cajoling manner he reserved for Jehangir, and he said nastily: "You better bring back all those fucking stamps tomorrow." Jehangir, of course, agreed. There was no trouble with the prefect or the school after the stamps were returned.

But Jehangir's collection shrank pitiably overnight. He slept badly the entire week, worried about explaining to Burjor Uncle the sudden disappearance of the bulk of his collection. His mother assumed the dark rings around his eyes were due to too much reading and not enough fresh air. The thought of stamps or of *Patla Babu* or *Jhaaria Babu* brought an emptiness to his stomach and a bitter taste to his mouth. A general sense of ill-being took possession of him.

He went to see Burjor Uncle on Sunday, leaving behind his stamp album. Mrs. Mody opened the door and turned away silently. She appeared to be in a black rage, which exacerbated Jehangir's own feelings of guilt and shame.

He explained to Burjor Uncle that he had not bothered to bring his album because he had acquired no new stamps since last Sunday, and also, he was not well and would not stay for long.

Dr. Mody was concerned about the boy, so nervous and uneasy; he put it down to his feeling unwell. They looked at some stamps Dr. Mody had received last week from his colleagues abroad. Then Jehangir said he'd better leave.

"But you *must* see the Spanish dancing-lady before you go. Maybe she will help you feel better. Ha! ha!" and Dr. Mody rose to go to the cupboard for the stamp. Its viewing at the end of each Sunday's session had acquired the significance of an esoteric ritual.

From the next room Mrs. Mody screeched: "Burjorji! Come here at once!" He made a wry face at Jehangir and hurried out.

In the next room, all the vehemence of Mrs. Mody's black rage of that morning poured out upon Dr. Mody: "It has reached the limit now! No time for your own son and Sunday after Sunday sitting with some stranger! What does he have that your own son does not? Are you a *baap* or what? No wonder Pesi has become this way! How can I blame the boy when his own *baap* takes no interest ..."

"Shh! The boy is in the next room! What do you want, that all the neighbours hear your screaming?"

"I don't care! Let them hear! You think they don't know already? You think you are … "

Mrs. Bulsara next door listened intently. Suddenly, she realized that Jehangir was in there. Listening from one's own house was one thing—hearing a quarrel from inside the quarrellers' house was another. It made feigning ignorance very difficult.

She rang the Modys' doorbell and waited, adjusting her *mathoobanoo*. Dr. Mody came to the door.

"Burjorji, forgive me for disturbing your stamping and collecting work with Jehangir. But I must take him away. Guests have arrived unexpectedly. Jehangir must go to the Irani, we need cold drinks."

"That's okay, he can come next Sunday." Then added, "He *must* come next Sunday," and noted with satisfaction the frustrated turning away of Mrs. Mody who waited out of sight of the doorway. "Jehangir! Your mother is calling."

Jehangir was relieved at being rescued from the turbulent waters of the Mody household. They left without further conversation, his mother tugging in embarrassment at the knots of her *mathoobanoo*.

As a result of this unfortunate outburst, a period of awkwardness between the women was unavoidable. Mrs. Mody, though far from garrulous, had never let her domestic sorrows and disappointments interfere with the civilities of neighbourly relations, which she respected and observed at all times. Now for the first time since the arrival of the Modys in Firozsha Baag these civilities experienced a hiatus.

When the *muchhiwalla* arrived next morning, instead of striking a joint deal with him as they usually did, Mrs. Mody waited till Mrs. Bulsara had finished. She stationed an eye at her peephole as he emphasized the freshness of his catch. "Look *bai*, it is *saféd paani*," he said, holding out the pomfret and squeezing it near the gills till white fluid oozed out. After Mrs. Bulsara had paid and gone, Mrs. Mody emerged, while the former took her turn at the peephole. And so it went for a few days till the awkwardness had run its course and things returned to normal.

But not so for Jehangir; on Sunday, he once again had to leave behind his sadly depleted album. To add to his uneasiness, Mrs. Mody invited him in with a greeting of "Come *bawa* come," and there was something malignant about her smile.

Dr. Mody sat at his desk, shoulders sagging, his hands dangling over the arms of the chair. The desk was bare—not a single stamp anywhere in sight, and the cupboard in the corner locked. The absence of his habitual, comfortable clutter made the room cold and cheerless. He was in low spirits; instead of the crow's-feet at the corners of his eyes were lines of distress and dejection.

"No album again?"

"No. Haven't got any new stamps yet," Jehangir smiled nervously.

Dr. Mody scratched the psoriasis on his elbows. He watched Jehangir carefully as he spoke. "Something very bad has happened to the Spanish dancing-lady stamp.

Look," and he displayed the satin-covered box minus its treasure. "It is missing."
Half-fearfully, he looked at Jehangir, afraid he would see what he did not want to.
But it was inevitable. His last sentence evoked the head prefect's thundering debating-
style speech of a few days ago, and the ugliness of the entire episode revisited
Jehangir's features—a final ignominious postscript to Dr. Mody's loss and disillusion.

Dr. Mody shut the box. The boy's reaction, his silence, the absence of his album,
confirmed his worst suspicions. More humiliatingly, it seemed his wife was right.
With great sadness he rose from his chair. "I have to leave now, something urgent at
the College." They parted without a word about next Sunday.

Jehangir never went back. He thought for a few days about the missing stamp and
wondered what could have happened to it. Burjor Uncle was too careful to have
misplaced it; besides, he never removed it from its special box. And the box was still
there. But he did not resent him for concluding he had stolen it. His guilt about
Patla Babu and *Jhaaria Babu,* about Eric and the stamps was so intense, and the
punishment deriving from it so inconsequential, almost non-existent, that he did not
mind this undeserved blame. In fact, it served to equilibrate his scales of justice.

His mother questioned him the first few Sundays he stayed home. Feeble excuses
about homework, and Burjor Uncle not having new stamps, and it being boring to
look at the same stuff every Sunday did not satisfy her. She finally attributed his
abnegation of stamps to sensitivity and a regard for the unfortunate state of the
Modys' domestic affairs. It pleased her that her son was capable of such concern. She
did not press him after that.

IV

Pesi was no longer to be seen in Firozsha Baag. His absence brought relief to most of
the parents at first, and then curiosity. Gradually, it became known that he had been
sent away to a boarding-school in Poona.

The boys of the Baag continued to play their games in the compound. For better
or worse, the spark was lacking that lent unpredictability to those languid coastal
evenings of Bombay; evenings which could so easily trap the unwary, adult or child,
within a circle of lassitude and depression in which time hung heavy and suffocating.

Jehangir no longer sat on the stone steps of C Block in the evenings. He found it
difficult to confront Dr. Mody day after day. Besides, the boys he used to watch at
play suspected some kind of connection between Pesi's being sent away to boarding-
school, Jehangir's former friendship with Dr. Mody, and the emerging of Dr. Mody's
constant sorrow and despair (which he had tried so hard to keep private all along and
had succeeded, but was now visible for all to see). And the boys resented Jehangir for
whatever his part was in it—they bore him open antagonism.

Dr. Mody was no more the jovial figure the boys had grown to love. When his car turned in to the compound in the evenings, he still waved, but no crow's-feet appeared at his eyes, no smile, no jokes.

Two years passed since the Mody family's arrival in Firozsha Baag.

In school, Jehangir was as isolated as in the Baag. Most of his effeminateness had, of late, transformed into vigorous signs of impending manhood. Eric D'Souza had been expelled for attempting to sodomize a junior boy. Jehangir had not been involved in this affair, but most of his classmates related it to the furtive activities of their callow days and the stamp-flicking. *Patla Babu* and *Jhaaria Babu* had disappeared from the pavement outside St. Xavier's. The Bombay police, in a misinterpretation of the nation's mandate: *garibi hatao*—eradicate poverty, conducted periodic round-ups of pavement dwellers, sweeping into their vans beggars and street-vendors, cripples and alcoholics, the homeless and the hungry, and dumped them somewhere outside the city limits; when the human detritus made its way back into the city, another clean-up was scheduled. *Patla* and *Jhaaria* were snared in one of these raids, and never found their way back. Eyewitnesses said their stalls were smashed up and *Patla Babu* received a *lathi* across his forehead for trying to salvage some of his inventory. They were not seen again.

Two years passed since Jehangir's visits to Dr. Mody had ceased.

It was getting close to the time for another transfer for Dr. Mody. When the inevitable orders were received, he went to Ahmedabad to make arrangements. Mrs. Mody was to join her husband after a few days. Pesi was still in boarding-school, and would stay there.

So when news arrived from Ahmedabad of Dr. Mody's death of heart failure, Mrs. Mody was alone in the flat. She went next door with the telegram and broke down.

The Bulsaras helped with all the arrangements. The body was brought to Bombay by car for a proper Parsi funeral. Pesi came from Poona for the funeral, then went back to boarding-school.

The events were talked about for days afterwards, the stories spreading first in C Block, then through A and B. Commiseration for Mrs. Mody was general. The ordeal of the body during the two-day car journey from Ahmedabad was particularly horrifying, and was discussed endlessly. Embalming was not allowed according to Parsi rituals, and the body in the trunk, although packed with ice, had started to smell horribly in the heat of the Deccan Plateau which the car had had to traverse. Some hinted that this torment suffered by Dr. Mody's earthly remains was the Almighty's punishment for neglecting his duties as a father and making Mrs. Mody so unhappy. Poor Dr. Mody, they said, who never went a day without a bath and talcum powder in life, to undergo this in death. Someone even had, on good authority, a count of the number of eau de cologne bottles used by Mrs. Mody and the three occupants of the car over the course of the journey—it was the only way they could draw breath, through cologne-watered handker-chiefs. And it was also said that ever after, these four could never tolerate eau de cologne—opening a bottle was like opening the car trunk with Dr. Mody's decomposing corpse.

A year after the funeral, Mrs. Mody was still living in Firozsha Baag. Time and grief had softened her looks, and she was no longer the harsh and dour-faced woman Jehangir had seen during his first Sunday visit. She had decided to make the flat her permanent home now, and the trustees of the Baag granted her request "in view of the unfortunate circumstances."

There were some protests about this, particularly from those whose sons or daughters had been postponing marriages and families till flats became available. But the majority, out of respect for Dr. Mody's memory, agreed with the trustees' deci-sion. Pesi continued to attend boarding-school.

One day, shortly after her application had been approved by the trustees, Mrs. Mody visited Mrs. Bulsara. They sat and talked of old times, when they had first moved in, and about how pleased Dr. Mody had been to live in a Parsi colony like Firozsha Baag after years of travelling, and then the disagreements she had had with her husband over Pesi and Pesi's future; tears came to her eyes, and also to Mrs. Bulsara's, who tugged at a corner of her *mathoobanoo* to reach it to her eyes and dry them. Mrs. Mody confessed how she had hated Jehangir's Sunday visits although he was such a fine boy, because she was worried about the way poor Burjorji was neglecting Pesi: "But he could not help it. That was the way he was. Sometimes he would wish *Khoedai* had given him a daughter instead of a son. Pesi disappointed him in everything, in all his plans, and ..." and here she burst into uncontrollable sobs.

Finally, after her tears subsided she asked, "Is Jehangir home?" He wasn't. "Would you ask him to come and see me this Sunday? At ten? Tell him I won't keep him long."

Jehangir was a bit apprehensive when his mother gave him the message. He couldn't imagine why Mrs. Mody would want to see him.

On Sunday, as he prepared to go next door, he was reminded of the Sundays with Dr. Mody, the kindly man who had befriended him, opened up a new world for him, and then repudiated him for something he had not done. He remembered the way he would scratch the greyish-red patches of psoriasis on his elbows. He could still picture the sorrow on his face as, with the utmost reluctance, he had made his deci-sion to end the friendship. Jehangir had not blamed Dr. Mody then, and he still did not; he knew how overwhelmingly the evidence had been against him, and how much that stamp had meant to Dr. Mody.

Mrs. Mody led him in by his arm: "Will you drink something?"

"No, thank you."

"Not feeling shy, are you? You always were shy." She asked him about his studies and what subjects he was taking in high school. She told him a little about Pesi, who was still in boarding-school and had twice repeated the same standard. She sighed. "I asked you to come today because there is something I wanted to give you. Something of Burjor Uncle's. I thought about it for many days. Pesi is not interested, and I don't know anything about it. Will you take his collection?"

"The album in his drawer?" asked Jehangir, a little surprised.

"Everything. The album, all the boxes, everything in the cupboard. I know you will use it well. Burjor would have done the same."

Jehangir was speechless. He had stopped collecting stamps, and they no longer held the fascination they once did. Nonetheless, he was familiar with the size of the collection, and the sheer magnitude of what he was now being offered had its effect. He remembered the awe with which he had looked inside the cupboard the first time its doors had been opened before him. So many sweet tins, cardboard boxes, biscuit tins …

"You will take it? As a favour to me, yes?" she asked a second time, and Jehangir nodded. "You have some time today? Whenever you like, just take it." He said he would ask his mother and come back.

There was a huge, old iron trunk which lay under Jehangir's bed. It was dented in several places and the lid would not shut properly. Undisturbed for years, it had rusted peacefully beneath the bed. His mother agreed that the rags it held could be thrown away and the stamps temporarily stored in it till Jehangir organized them into albums. He emptied the trunk, wiped it out, lined it with brown paper and went next door to bring back the stamps.

Several trips later, Dr. Mody's cupboard stood empty. Jehangir looked around the room in which he had once spent so many happy hours. The desk was in exactly the same position, and the two chairs. He turned to go, almost forgetting, and went back to the desk. Yes, there it was in the drawer, Dr. Mody's first album, given him by his Nusserwanji Uncle.

He started to turn the heavily laden pages. They rustled in a peculiar way—what was it about that sound? Then he remembered: that first Sunday, and he could almost hear Dr. Mody again, the soft inspired tones speaking of promises and dreams, quite different from his usual booming, jovial voice, and that faraway look in his eyes which had once glinted with rage when Pesi had tried to bully him …

Mrs. Mody came into the room. He shut the album, startled: "This is the last lot." He stopped to thank her but she interrupted: "No, no. What is the thank-you for? You are doing a favour to me by taking it, you are helping me to do what Burjor would like." She took his arm. "I wanted to tell you. From the collection one stamp is missing. With the picture of the dancing-lady."

"I know!" said Jehangir. "That's the one Burjor Uncle lost and thought that I ..."

Mrs. Mody squeezed his arm which she was still holding and he fell silent. She spoke softly, but without guilt: "He did not lose it. I destroyed it." Then her eyes went moist as she watched the disbelief on his face. She wanted to say more, to explain, but could not, and clung to his arm. Finally, her voice quavering pitiably, she managed to say, "Forgive an old lady," and patted his cheek. Jehangir left in silence, suddenly feeling very ashamed.

Over the next few days, he tried to impose some order on that greatly chaotic mass of stamps. He was hoping that sooner or later his interest in philately would be rekindled. But that did not happen; the task remained futile and dry and boring. The meaningless squares of paper refused to come to life as they used to for Dr. Mody in his room every Sunday at ten o'clock. Jehangir shut the trunk and pushed it back under his bed where it had lain untroubled for so many years.

From time to time his mother reminded him about the stamps: "Do something Jehangoo, do something with them." He said he would when he felt like it and had the time; he wasn't interested for now.

Then, after several months, he pulled out the trunk again from under his bed. Mrs. Bulsara watched eagerly from a distance, not daring to interrupt with any kind of advice or encouragement: her Jehangoo was at that difficult age, she knew, when boys automatically did the exact reverse of what their parents said.

But the night before, Jehangir's sleep had been disturbed by a faint and peculiar rustling sound seeming to come from inside the trunk. His reasons for dragging it out into daylight soon became apparent to Mrs. Bulsara.

The lid was thrown back to reveal clusters of cockroaches. They tried to scuttle to safety, and he killed a few with his slipper. His mother ran up now, adding a few blows of her own *chappal,* as the creatures began quickly to disperse. Some ran under the bed into hard-to-reach corners; others sought out the trunk's deeper recesses.

A cursory examination showed that besides cockroaches, the trunk was also infested with white ants. All the albums had been ravaged. Most of the stamps which had not been destroyed outright were damaged in one way or another. They bore haphazard perforations and brown stains of the type associated with insects and household pests.

Jehangir picked up an album at random and opened it. Almost immediately, the pages started to fall to pieces in his hands. He remembered what Dr. Mody used to say: "This is my retirement hobby. I will spend my retirement with my stamps." He allowed the tattered remains of Burjor Uncle's beloved pastime to drop back slowly into the trunk.

He crouched beside the dented, rusted metal, curious that he felt no loss or pain. Why, he wondered. If anything, there was a slight sense of relief. He let his hands stray through the contents, through worthless paper scraps, through shreds of the work of so many Sunday mornings, stopping now and then to regard with detachment the bizarre patterns created by the mandibles of the insects who had feasted night after night under his bed, while he slept.

With an almost imperceptible shrug, he arose and closed the lid. It was doubtful if anything of value remained in the trunk.

Part 2

THIS
ALL
HAPPENED

THERE IS A CERTAIN KIND OF STORY *in which the immediacy of the action engulfs us to such an extent that we believe we have actually witnessed or even participated in the drama. The narrative need not necessarily unfold in our own time, or even in our own place, but somehow we feel as though the characters have disturbed the air around us. The semi-fictional diary of Michael Winter's Gabriel, in its refusal to declare itself as memoir or fiction or diary while at the same time establishing our belief in the absolute reality of the events described in its pages, seems the perfect introduction to stories such as these, stories that defy the notion of fiction as a genre simply because as readers we inhabit them so completely.*

Whether we are in India watching a servant girl lose her imaginary view (Anita Rau Badami), at a summer party during the conception of a love affair (Isabel Huggan), a hospital in a prairie city (Sharon Butala), or inside the nightmares of a labourer in Newfoundland (Michael Crummey), there is the feeling of recognition, of familiarity, as if we ourselves are as intimate with the characters as they are with each other. The narrative not only subtly instructs us; it affirms something that, by the time we are finished reading, we believe we already knew—whether we did or not.

We believe in fact that this did all happen, that we have seen it happen, and that we have been affected by what we have seen. Our view of the world has been altered, darkened or enlarged; certain faiths have been strengthened, others have been shaken loose. The news these writers bring is not only that, at least narratively, these events did take place, but that something else, equally arresting and believable, is more than likely going to happen very soon.

This All Happened

MICHAEL WINTER

December

1 Today I polished shoes. I took my old leather coat and stitched the armpit. I soaked my feet in an enamel basin. I threaded new laces. I scoured the bathtub. I drew a sketch of the harbour. I bought the *Manchester Guardian*. I finished a novel. It takes just as long to read a novel as it did ten years ago. It still takes nine months to have a baby. If a woman walks away from you, it's with the same gait as if it happened in the eighteenth century.

I have stopped eating pasta. I will make pastry and bake a pie. I will ignore the clock. I will wash down the windowsills. I will study the town with binoculars. I will extract the precise quality of love that objects possess.

2 We are learning carols at Oliver's. Max's new baby asleep in Oliver's bedroom. Una sitting by the piano hugging a stuffed cheetah.

Me: I dont think this is what Maisie had in mind.

Oliver: I think Maisie can have her mind changed.

Think she won't mind?

Oliver: I think she'll look in and say this is something else.

Maisie arrives. She has a box of beer and the carol sheets. A studded leather belt that makes her tough. She's letting her hair grow. She had asked my opinion on this, quietly, and I'd said let it grow. Around the piano she has Daphne and Alex while she plays and they try harmony.

Me: How can you know the next note?

Maisie: It's all written down on the sheets. You dont have to guess.

I look around for Oliver's pregnant student. I've forgotten Oliver is circumspect.

Being shocked at how badly Alex sings. Knowing she has said she cant sing but never knowing it was that bad. She was reticent about singing and we were all, separately, encouraging her and finally she blurts out a random note and at least her ear understands it's outlandish or maybe she recognizes now the reaction of others to tone-deaf singers but she stops after three notes and retires to the couch.

Oliver leaves on Silent Night because he can't handle singing a song that possesses serious, sentimental conviction. He doesnt have the bone you need to shift the corniness aside, the irony and the slyness to allow the heart room to manoeuvre in the mood of a genuine song. He left to get a beer and I wonder if he is bereft of a clear bone of sincerity.

Then I see he's just gone because he can't handle Maisie back in his house and all of the above is false.

Max and Daphne are leaving with Eli, and Max admits to taking a half-carton of egg nog topped up with my Old Sam. He has it tucked in the tweed pocket of his overcoat. Sorry about this, Max says. Will make it up to you. He opens the mouth of the carton to show me the contents. This is while it's sticking out of the coat pocket. I love the fact that he thinks he can do this. I love the comfort.

3 Maisie says, After Christmas, I want to party hard. I want to go out with Max and Wilf and I want to have a good time.

What about work.

I've been working. After Christmas I'm going to devote myself to partying.

I meet Oliver in the bathroom at the Spur. He says, You just missed out. A guy was sharing a line of coke. Man, it burnt my nostrils. I couldnt tell the guy it had no effect because it was a freebie. But good coke, Gabe, doesnt burn at all. If it burns, you know it's full of Old Dutch.

Oliver, Maisie says, is a guy who plays both sides. She says this with admiration. He's a lawyer by day and a hound at night. He's up at seven every morning and out till four every night.

4 Two cats in a tree. In the taller branches a brilliant blue jay. With a seed propped in its thin black beak.

Beyond them a barge docked in the rain. A man operates welding gear. Acetylene torches under a blue tarpaulin, flashing in the fog.

The smell of brewery as I jog past Lydia's.

I watch a man operate a Taylor down at the dockyard. He is lifting a blue Ace container off the back of an eighteen-wheeler. He turns (his rear axle turns) and lays the container onto a stack three-high. I know the hoister is called a Taylor because I've called up Oceanex.

What is that loader called?

Theyre called hoisters or tailers, either one.

Which is better?

Depends how much you want to spend. I prefer tailers.

How much would one cost?

About $700,000 Canadian. What do you want to lift?

Oh, about the same thing youre lifting.

You get them through Materials Handling, Bernie Faloney, he's the man to talk to. He used to play for the Hamilton Ti-Cats. The hoisters are French-made and theyre good, except when they break down, theyre a you-know-what to get parts for.

And who makes tailers?

Taylor makes them.

Oh, it's Taylor.

The eighteen-wheelers wait in line, snorting exhaust, the Taylor operator does not hesitate. He spends less than five seconds at the side of the transport truck, his hydraulic front end (at least forty feet high) clamps onto the container—is it magnetic?—lifts, the rear wheels pivot, he swings towards the neat stack of blue containers awaiting an Oceanex vessel. He pivots the rear wheels, returns to the next truck. The previous truck now making a slow loop around the stacked containers.

5 I attend Boyd's trial. I sit with Lydia and we share a look. That beyond it all life is peculiar, we're healthy and blessed, and we are curious. We are not going to be mean to each other. Oliver Squires allows Boyd to confess to taking 114 items from eight houses in the neighbourhood. His neighbours are all present. Boyd says it wasnt personal. He just needed things now and again and he was tired of waiting in line to pay for things. He says he's sorry.

The judge sentences him to three years.

6 Alex says things tailored for me. The ideas seem to be performed or moulded to what she thinks I'd like to hear. It's flattering but annoying. Because I want her to be herself. Lydia never did that, unless she was talking to Craig Regular. Perhaps we do it to those we have crushes on. I hate seeing it in Lydia, because it implies the person she is talking to is out of her reach.

7 Alex says, Have you ever been to the synagogue? Come on, let's go.

It's Hanukkah. A wall of windows made from Stars of David.

Alex: You might be expected to wear a keepah—there's a box of them at the door.

Is that the same as a yarmulke?

Yes.

Does this one fit?

It's fine, Gabe.

In a cold room plaques of the Israeli Declaration of Independence, proclamations during the Yom Kippur War. In 1931 Hymen Feder donated three dollars. A Chagall print of Moses with the Torah.

Alex says all synagogues smell the same. A mixture of must and stale seeds. She says only five people attend Friday meetings. It's outport Judaism, she says.

How do you know so much about it?

I keep an interest in what goes on, Gabe.

We sit in the warm room at a table near the stage. There is to be a children's play. The play has a scientist refusing to go to the Hanukkah party. When her friends leave, she is killed during a chemical discovery. Moral: beware the works of man.

We are sitting with a doctor and his wife. They are both learning Hebrew. There are no vowels. Alex asks if shellfish can be kosher. No, the doctor says, because they are scavengers on the bottom.

He sticks out his hands and scrabbles his fingers over the tablecloth, the cloth gathers under his fingers until a glass topples. Scavengers, he says again.

8 Una and I watch Max filing pyrophyllite. He sits cross-legged and wears a surgical mask. The soapstone is from Manuels. He pulls down the mask and smiles. Newfoundland, he says, has the best stone in the world. He's doing this piece for Daphne, it's slightly abstract. Near his knees are wedges of cast-off stone. That's a tail of a humpback, Una says.

Max says, You can have the humpback.

When I say a new word, like pyrophyllite, I have a propensity to forget it.

Una's game when we're walking home: Why does underwear start with an H? Why?

Because they lie in a heap on the floor.

9 Maisie's favourite found poem is: thick fat back loose lean salt beef. We are walking up from the Ship. She opens a frail yellow umbrella. The poem was on a piece of shirt card in Vey's corner store for ten years. Now Vey's has been sold, renovated, and is for sale again as a house. There was a pot-bellied woodstove between the aisles.

Maisie says there's wonder in this life. I say, And bewilderment. Thank you, Gabe. That's the word.

10 Alex says, There's your Christmas present. I look behind me, Where. There, she says. In the near vision I see a tight filament of dental floss and a small box hanging from it. At eye level. You look in the box. The box has a glass front that's been sand-blasted except for an eye, which you can look through. At the back of the box is another eye. It is a photograph of my eye. Then she shows me bits of furniture she's made: wooden arms for a chair. Human arms. She's adding pearls and chunks of mirror. Alex has sculpted an ear that she carved by feeling her own ear. She carved from touch. Translating touch into vision.

Alex wants to build a corner camera. You stand at an intersection and the two barrels of the camera take a picture of both streets converging. The photographic paper is at a right angle and you mount the photo in the corner of a room to get the correct perspective. Of two streets meeting. I say, Does such a camera exist? Alex: No. I'm going to invent one.

She says she's bored with flat art.

We eat off plates made of fired clay.

Everything in Alex's house is art.

We bake squash stuffed with lemon and dates and mushrooms and garlic.

We drink the wine and I walk home in the clear, cold air. Sometimes you can see more in night air than you can in the day. Maybe it's the city lights.

11 Oliver talks of legal scandals. He's not the only lawyer to have left his wife for a paralegal student. He puts on his overcoat, a new coat for him. I say, Nice coat. He says that Maisie never liked it on him. That it's grubby. She's got something against secondhand clothes. It's okay if you have money. But for the poor, it marks you as poor.

I tell this to Maisie later. And I say, The coat is a bit grubby. Yes, she says. Fact is, it doesnt look good on him.

12 Max: When they were building the office tower, I didnt think it would ruin the view. At first, the scaffolding around the infrastructure blocked only a little bit of the Narrows. It wasnt offensive. I thought I could live with that. Seemed a narrow building. Then I found out that was only the elevator shaft. So we grew trees in the backyard and now there's nothing.

13 I watch Craig Regular walking out of a restaurant carrying an Obusforme for his back. Tinker Bumbo at his side.

Craig holds the door. He is holding the door open for Lydia.

I follow them. I havent allowed myself to think that they really are an item.

They enter the Mighty White laundromat.

I stroke Tinker, who wags, blind, but his nose knows me. I think of the dog that saved Ernest Chafe. Chafe, lost in a storm, tied his sled dog to his wrist. The dog sniffed his way back to camp.

Craig is pushing detergent along the lid of a public washing machine, coaxing it down the crack in the lid. Wiping his hand over the lid to get all the blue detergent down. His money's worth.

Now, he's trying on a new shirt. I can tell that Lydia has bought the shirt. She tells him to try it on. Does she want to see if it will fit?

They get in Lydia's car. I follow in mine. They drive into the Battery. To Craig's house beyond the yellow rail.

I sit in the car and watch them through Craig's kitchen window. It is a beautiful window that looks back over St. John's. His view is the reverse of my view.

There are two frozen salmon steaks hauled out to thaw. Their pink skin crystallizing to a hot white. Craig turns on a light and closes the curtains.

14 There is a warm wind blowing, a soft buttery moon. Max baked a brie with glazed crushed walnuts, a date on top. There is fresh-baked sourdough bread. We dip chunks into the melted brie and drink wine.

I ask Daphne what they did today.

Daphne: Max cooked a pheasant.

A pheasant?

Max: Daphne told me you can find pheasant in Sobeys and I imagined them hiding in behind the boxes of Cheerios, wild pheasant nesting in the rafters.

Pheasant is a good dish, Daphne says.

Max: I stuffed it with plums and quince and sewed it up.

He pronounces sewed like lewd.

Daphne: Then we sat down and ate it.

I WALK HOME from Max's, a wind bouncing off the southside hills. It's on nights like this that things happen. It was a sinister wind. And the moon with fast wisps of cloud over it. Max raised a glass to Eugene Cernan, the last man to walk on the moon. On this very night.

15 Maisie launches her novel at the Ship Inn. She has a beautiful line where a character fires up her zipper. That's what I like about Maisie: she chooses the right word. There's more going on in the story, but it's that word I remember.

Maisie's nervous at the Ship. She has no need to be nervous. The work is good.

16 I walk past Lydia's house. I look in through the front window. I see Craig passing two pills to Lydia's cupped hand. Then a glass of water. Tinker Bumbo stretched out on the couch. Craig holds the water in his right hand and Lydia takes the pills into her left hand. So there is a moment when their arms are crossed, in reception.

I remember Lydia asking, But what do you love about me? When I paused she said, Youre obsessed with my body. Yes, I said.

Youre obsessed with being in love, she said.

I am obsessed with being in love. I admit to this.

Lydia: You are weak alone.

I've never liked being alone, it's true.

17 When you describe an experience, what you are recounting is your memory of the act, not the act itself. Experiencing a moment is an inarticulate act. There are no words. It is in the sensory world. To recall it and to put words to it is to illustrate how one remembers the past, rather than actually experiencing the past. Keep this in mind as you read the words of others as they remember an incident.

18 Catholics rehearse their stories. They tell stories over and over. The same story, torquing it a little, realizing a certain detail is not working, adding stuff. I've heard the same two dozen stories out of Lydia about thirty times. And then there are the

daily stories. Events that happen that she recounts. She'll tell me, and then she'll call Daphne, and then her brother phones and she tells her brother. The thing I find interesting about this story-telling is that if you heard only one of these stories, you'd think she was telling it for the first time. The enthusiasm behind it. That's definitely a Catholic thing. Protestants tell a story once and it's over with. They feel self-conscious to tell the story again. They are aware of who has already heard the story. Protestants tell a story best the first time; Catholics, the last time.

This follows through into making up after arguments. Lydia wanted to list every point in the argument, make sure it was fleshed out, whereas I was happy enough to say, Okay, let's apologize and get on with it. It's as if there is some pleasure in recounting each moment of the fight, who said what when, and admitting to each wrong turn taken. Usually, of course, I had taken the wrong turns. I'm not sure if this is Catholic or not, but Lydia was convinced she knew my true motives, and I would be a bigger man if I could only admit to them. But by that time the entire fight would have evaporated into a mist with no detail or shape to me any more, and to admit to wrong-doing would be a lie. I admitted to nothing. I can be stubborn in this.

19 I watch ships coasting into harbour with bulk. Or are they empty. So slow. Ships seem arduous. Yet if you take your eye off one, it has instantly docked or left harbour again.

I bought a crate of tangerines. This is the only export I have seen from Morocco.

Helmut has come for Christmas. He says, We should put candles on the tree.

Five months of sailing has made him thinner and ropey. He is like a coil of rope. He has tremendous strength in his grip.

He makes candle holders out of copper wire. He places twenty-six candles on the tree. We turn off the lamps as he touches the candles with a match. The candles offer light from below. The tinsel lifts in the updraft. It's a soft, uplifting light.

I watch Helmut in the kitchen, sharpening a knife on the back of a plate.

He gives me a stainless-steel spatula made in Sweden. It's wrapped and looks exactly like a spatula.

20 Wilf says his father used to sniff out fat fires. There was a man at bingo when his house burned down. They couldnt find any evidence of arson. It was a new house, properly inspected. So they gave him the insurance.

A couple of months later the police got a letter from the man with a cheque for the full amount, plus interest, and a confession to arson. The man had just found out he had terminal cancer.

People were visiting him and saying what an honest man he'd been all his life. He couldnt live with the guilt. Or better, die with it. Even his wife didnt know.

This is what he did: He crumpled newspapers and shoved them under the couch cushions and chairs. He doused a couch with a forty-ouncer of gin. He lit the paper and went to bingo. If you want to commit arson, use alcohol. It leaves no residue.

The man had burned down his house so he could build a new one down by his daughter's place. He wanted to be close to his daughter and he knew he wouldnt be able to sell his house for what it was worth.

Because of the cancer, they didnt charge him.

One final note, Wilf says. If it was a fat fire, Dad had no compassion. He'd let photographers take pictures of the bodies.

21 I am drunk and sentimental. Can't believe what I've said to Lydia. I called and said let's get married for a year. It would help me, I could let you go more, knowing you were mine for a full year, and then we could renegotiate the terms.

And Lydia thought about it, then spoke about Oliver's voucher. You dont like it when I talk about the voucher, do you?

I think it would be disastrous, I say.

One bacchanalian night a year. You go home with someone and there are no questions or repercussions. It was meant as a fleeting proposition, but Lydia has latched onto it. There is a corner of her, a small pocket with a line of lint in it, and the lint agrees with this voucher idea.

But really the voucher is a ruse. She's attaching herself to Craig Regular. She has been hurt by me and is drifting to that smooth smart goofy guy. Who wouldnt.

22 I tell Max, There's nothing better than holding tight to the one person whose smell, whose taste, youve craved all day long.

Love is a savage thing, he says. Love is all to do with head, heart, and animal.

Daphne: You do the silliest things to make that one person laugh.

Max and Daphne are over for lunch. Max: I've been busier than a mink on a rabbit trail.

I ask Daphne what she did today and she says, and she's got this raspy voice, these sharp features, and a deep larynx like she's been shouting all night—she says she got up at noon and read Maisie's new book and then took Eli out Christmas shopping.

Max: I'm tired of buying things.

Me: So what do you think of the book?

Daphne: It's not my kind of thing.

Me: I dont persist in things that dont grab.

She laughs: I like that bit of you.

On several occasions she says, Oh no, Max, Gabriel wouldnt do that, because he no longer bothers with things he's not interested in.

23 I hear Max say: So are you and Craig seeing each other?

Lydia says nothing. Then she says, So how are things with Daphne? Is sex good?

Coming and going, Max says.

Lydia: Is it more coming or going?

24 I'm with Max, Maisie, Una, Daphne, and Wilf singing We Three Kings in front of the dark fire station. Three garage doors ascend and yellow headlights wink under the edge of the doors, then beam out. There are five silhouettes with arms crossed standing in front of the trucks, legs splayed, theyre wearing gaiters. We sing and the fire-engine lights flick on silently and strobe red. The men walk towards us in their gaiters. We see their faces. They are grinning. The kids stretch up tiptoe and break from the carollers. They see that the firemen have candy. We follow. That was wonderful, one fireman says. We were just collecting for one of the men who's in hospital.

They show us the thick chrome pole. And three men slide down, bending knees to absorb the landing, and peel away. The kids scream at this. Theyre allowed to jump onto running boards and look in at dashes and tremendous gear shifts.

25 Lydia calls me early on Christmas morning. To say Tinker Bumbo is dead.

Lydia: He started to cough up blood and I took him to the vet and the vet gave him an injection.

She's crying on the phone.

Are you alone?

Mom and Dad are here.

Do you want me to come down?

I WALK DOWN. The harbour is covered in new snow, and the morning light is pink on the snow. The water is bright. The shipyard is quiet.

Tinker Bumbo is lying on his cushion. He looks asleep. Except he's not noisy enough.

Lydia's father says, We should bury him.

Lydia: Out in the woods.

She calls Max and Daphne and they come by with Eli, and Maisie comes too and we drive out together to the barrens on the highway. Lydia's father has put Tinker Bumbo in a canvas sack and laid him on a plastic sled. We tow him, single file, into a group of spruce trees beside the mouth of a pond.

Under a big spruce we push away the moss. And Lydia and I pry out a big rock with a crowbar. The rock separates from the frost.

I lay his blue blanket in the hole. Then lay him gently on it. He's cuddled into his position. Lydia covers him in moss, and I trim a few boughs and lay them over him.

We cover Tinker with the crystallized soil. The sun is soft on the water. There'll be grouse here soon enough.

Lydia's father says Lydia and I should come back in the summer and paint the rock for Tinker.

26 Last night I walked to three different parties. At three in the morning I'm at Maisie's. I am on the couch with Alex Fleming. I have Alex's hand cupped in mine. We are drinking beer Maisie found in a cupboard. Tonight Alex is taking care of me. We are all wounded in ways that require temporary solace.

I say to her, I'm blowing this popsicle stand. This entire city. I'm leaving it. I'm gonna drive my trusty Jethro to Heart's Desire and never come back.

Alex asks if I need company.

I wouldnt be good company.

You'd be a useless article.

Precisely.

27 The snow comes when you arent looking. Snow as fresh as a new, sinister avocado leaf.

I'm in my bedroom with the space heater on blast. The Star of the Sea looks large. Alex, at midday, comes over for a cup of tea. She's wearing funky inner-city sneakers that look as fortified as skates. I'm still in my pajamas.

Alex: I can't stand people asking me what I'm up to.

Me: I've noticed people dont ask me that any more, because times are so hard. I have no job and I broke up with Lydia. I've given up on the novel. I'm drinking too much. They ask me where I'm at, that's all. They dont want to feel embarrassed.

When she leaves I go back to bed. I look at the city through binoculars. The Christmas lights make me forlorn. I look in the window where Oliver lives, but he's not in. But later, when I call about the Heart's Desire house, he says he was there. On his back on the floor, keyboard on his stomach. He says I can go out there any time I want.

I am focused on the last saltbox house in St. John's. Then down to Craig's house in the Battery. Every spring the neighbours paint the rocks in his backyard white.

28 I wake up with a clenched, sore jaw. I drive out to Heart's Desire because Christmas in town is driving me to fury. It's so cold. And I think of Bartlett's candle. So cold at the pole the flame could not melt the outside of the candle. Merely the wick and a narrow pool down the centre. I make a smoked-salmon pasta when the jannies come in. A barrel-chested fellow with a dress on, a crutch, and a large beige bra on over the dress. He's wearing a rubber Halloween mask and rubber boots and

trigger mitts. A woman dressed as a man wiggles her behind, where a silver bauble dangles. A third janny quietly sits himself down and lights up a smoke. He has a green towel over his face, and he parts the folds to smoke.

Me: You'll be wanting a drink of rum.

And the one with the crutch says, We'll settle for that.

I put out the rum and some glasses and mix one with Pepsi and another straight.

Me: Now how am I going to guess you?

The crutch says, with an ingressive voice, Oh, you'll never guess us.

There is a scratching at the door then, and a little dog wags in. It's Josh's dog.

Oh, now there's a clue.

The dog barks then wags at the crutch man. Oh, he's a nice dog.

I guess them but it's not Josh and his parents. It's Toby and his mother and father. They are sweltering under their garb. They say, Come out with us now.

How come you have Josh's dog?

Oh, the Harnums moved to Alberta.

I wrap a quilt around my waist. Toby's mother takes down a sheer curtain and I place the curtain over my head. I shove on a beanie and they say, Youre perfect. Grab your guitar and let's go down to the road.

We'll leave the dog in here.

WE WALK PAST Josh's house. The windows are boarded over. A For Sale sign below the mailbox. And then I notice a lot of the houses in Heart's are boarded over.

The guitar loses its tune in the cold. Toby raps on the screen door.

Any jannies in tonight?

And in we walk, banging our boots in the porch.

They take down a bottle of rum and some glasses and get the girls down to look at us, but the girls arent interested. They frown at us. And the missus holds under her arm a little cocker spaniel that barks. She doesnt tell the dog to stop, and she doesnt take it away. Just points it at us, barking.

I play I Can't Help It If I'm Still in Love with You, in falsetto. And they all sing along. The guitar has warmed up again.

But they can't guess us, and they look interrupted, so we leave, and Josh wants me to continue down the shore.

I say, I'm heading home. No one knows me.

Sure, look at the length of you. Who else could you be?

Well, they never twigged.

WHEN I GET BACK I remember Josh's dog. He spends the night, at the bottom of my bed. The only thing left of the Harnums.

29 I realize living in Heart's Desire is agony. When youre on your own, you can focus on your agony all day long. I decide to drive back to town and confront it. I shovel Lydia's front steps, salt her path. I make Egyptian lentil soup.

I've decided to attend Lydia's party.

She is making quiche and pear melba pies. There are casseroles of turkey soup. I've learned, from Lydia, to make pastry without touching it. Craig is arranging a bowl of marzipan apples. I notice he's put on weight and let his hair grow an inch. He has a softer look. His glasses are made of titanium, the hinge is one single wire bent and the temple pushed down through the coil.

Max, out of allegiance to me, says, Hey Craig, nice glasses. They come in men's?

Craig: No. But I hear you do.

Craig has zippers on his front pockets. A quiet man.

Wilf is in a corner chanting to himself: Got to get through. January. Got to get through. February.

Pause.

Got to get through. January. Got to get through.

Craig corners me to confess a feeling for Lydia. So I pretend Lydia means nothing to me. That I highly recommend her.

He says, The human being can't live too long with uncertainty. It prefers failure to uncertainty.

Lydia says then, There are so many fucking mediocre artists in this country.

Then, to me: I suppose youre writing that down.

Max says to me, I can't believe how polite youre being.

What, should I start throwing furniture?

Cause a scene, man. This is your moment to shine.

Wilf comes over to me and says, So Tinker's gone, hey?

Yes.

Max: He was a dog especially loved for doggy acts.

Wilf: He was a dog's dog.

Wilf has strong forearms. And a willingness to try on a woman's pillbox hat.

Boyd Coady's television is still in the living room.

30 I wake up alone and open the blinds to the city. The harbour is frozen shut. Iris and Helmut have flown to Miami to study a sailboat. I'm the kind of man who craves to be alone, but once alone, I crave company. It's as though I'd prefer to live in a tough situation than to live in a vacuum. I'm thinking that I have to learn to live alone, but what I really need to learn is how to live with someone else. Happiness seems impossible.

I sing the saddest songs I know, Hank Williams songs. I cook some eggs and brew a pot of tea. Tea is far better for a hangover. I can feel the corners of my mouth drooping in sadness, and I laugh at my sadness. I can examine and appreciate my own emotional torment. Luckily, I'm not a man prone to moroseness. If it were not for my buoyant constitution I would slit my wrists in the bathtub. I would.

I have been reading writers who say, essentially, that we'll be food for worms soon enough, so make sure that what you are living you love. And it's true there was too much anguish and ruin with Lydia. And Lydia seems a far sight happier with that asshole. He's not an asshole. He's such a great guy he must be an asshole. No one can be that perfect. I bet he has a hole in his heart. I bet Craig is emotionally cold. Assholism is relative. It proves the theory of relativity.

I gotta leave this place. I gotta start over. I've used up everything here. I have to let the city go fallow.

31 It's the last party of the year and every one I love is in Max's house. The women are dancing in the kitchen. Wilf says, When women dance with women I get happy. I have to force myself to keep my eyes off Lydia and Craig. I ask her before midnight and she says yes she may be a little in love with Craig. Can she be in love with a chunky man with a little scar at his lip? Do I mind seeing her with him? I ask, Are you doing an Oliver Squires? and she says, Gabe. I never thought of Craig until it was over with you.

She has been going to his house to watch rented, subtitled movies. She did not want to watch foreign movies with me. She claimed they were too hard to follow on a TV. But it's the man, not the film you watch, who makes the difference. She is willing to concentrate for Craig. Fair enough.

I stand by a window and realize that love is not constant. Though I love Max and Maisie very much. I would kill myself to save them. I would do the same for Una and Eli.

Maisie says if you take care of the moment then regret will not creep into your past.

But always there is, circling around us, a sense of unfulfilled grasping. A moment winks like a black locomotive, harnessed fire, sitting impatiently on its haunches, forever primed to lurch and devour. And I'm getting older. My feet hurt, a wrinkle in my earlobe. When you are out of love you become disappointed with the weight of your body. Baths are good.

I've decided to leave St. John's. I will head west and look for a desolate, foreign place. All that can happen to me here has happened.

The Lonely Goatherd

LISA MOORE

THE HOUSES DIG THEIR HEELS into the hill to stop from tumbling into the harbour. The clapboard faces are stained with last night's rain. Everything is squeezed together and sad. Carl loves Anita but lately he's been sleeping with other women. It's not idiosyncrasies he's been sleeping with, it's bones. Cheek bones, hip bones, knees. He sees inside apartments of St. John's he will never see again.

Two nights ago he was in an apartment over Gulliver's Taxi Stand. The girl's stereo speaker picked up radio messages of the dispatcher. At about four in the morning Carl heard the taxi driver say, Sure that's only your imagination, almost as if he were tangled in the bed sheets with them. Carl felt like a kid.

The sad thing is Anita's art. She is painting golf courses from the TV set. The old man she nurses watches golf, tapes it with his VCR. She takes Polaroid snapshots of the screen. She wants to capture in her paintings the glossy finish of the Polaroid, the snowy texture of the video, the play of light on the manicured lawns, and the slow motion time of the ball flying through the air. She says it's an analytical reduction she's after, always keeping herself distanced from the subject. They don't talk about their problem, but when he looks at her paintings he feels she is stripping him like an onion, layer by layer, her eyes watering.

Carl works at the Arts and Culture Centre, building sets. He makes an adequate living working chiefly with Styrofoam. This week he is building sets for a fairy tale amusement park. He shows his own sculpture once a year.

A sea of white Styrofoam beads covers the floor, clings to his pants, his bald head, and sticks to his hands like warts. Thumb-tacked on the wall are several eighteenth century fairy tale illustrations, before illustration got cute. Red Riding Hood in the gnarled forest, eyes wide, the wolf, saliva drooling from his fangs. Where Red Riding Hood's cape parts you glimpse a white vulnerable breast. Carl flicks his pocket knife into the illustration like a dart. Carl has been provided with an assistant from the Student Employment Office. The assistant studies day care management. Her name is Sarah. She is about ten years younger than Carl, and is now sweating in her paper suit over the giant chunk of Styrofoam from which the wolf will be carved.

ANITA FOUND OUT she was pregnant the same time she took the job nursing Mr. Crawhall. He sleeps most of the time she's there. This gives her an opportunity to paint. The house is on Circular Road, surrounded by trees which block the sound of traffic. Toward the end of the first week with Mr. Crawhall she entered the house and was assaulted by a loud consistent buzzing. She thought it was the buzzer by his bed, that Mr. Crawhall had died and his hand had fallen on the buzzer, but it was the egg timer on the stove. She has to serve him a three-and-a-half-minute egg every day. Her fingers shake a little on the silver teaspoon when she brings it near his mouth. It's different from feeding a baby, there's the question of Mr. Crawhall's dignity. Because of her condition the egg makes her nauseous. Once a hairline crack ran down the side of the egg and yolk seeped through it over the gold rimmed egg cup down to the saucer, threatening Mr. Crawhall's thin white bread. He said quite slowly, with his hands squeezed in the effort to speak, Oh, how have we managed to waste all that lovely yellow yolk?

Anita thinks of painting the egg as seen from under Mr. Crawhall's magnifying glass, but the jelly of it and the overt symbolism make her sick. She's planning an abortion. The baby isn't Carl's.

SARAH, THE ASSISTANT, is more of a hindrance than a help. Her professional opinion after six weeks in day care training is that Carl is making fairy tale props too realistic. The Momma Bear and Poppa Bear look like real bears. Strands of melted clear plastic hang from their teeth. She says they'll have a damaging psychological effect. She feels fairy tales are violent and sexist. She thinks we should ship loads of grain to India, she talks about McDonald's hamburger containers polluting the environment, American aggression in Nicaragua, and acid rain. Carl is building a cage for her out of two-by-fours and plastic sheeting so she can work with contact cement and the fumes will be contained within the cage. He gives her a gas mask, tightening the rubber strap around her fine hair. He puts her in the cage with one of the wolves. It's impossible to talk with a gas mask on. The rest of the afternoon the studio is quiet, except for the chain saw.

ANITA WATCHES *The Sound of Music* with Mr. Crawhall. He tells her to fast forward over the scene with Liesl and her boyfriend in the gazebo where she sings *I am sixteen going on seventeen, innocent as a lamb.* This scene bores Mr. Crawhall, so they watch it in fast forward. The dance number changes Liesl into a maddened butterfly batting the wings of her white skirt against the boy's head. She circles round and round him, flinging her arms this way and that, trapped in the amorphous white cloud. Her face in the close-up is contorted and pulled like plastic across the jiggling screen. When Anita presses "play," Julie Andrews sings, *These are a few of my favourite things.*

WHEN CARL GETS ROUND to asking Sarah to sleep with him he tells her he is bored sleeping with his wife. Sarah asks, Is she intelligent?

Carl says, Yes, of course, she's a very articulate woman.

Does her conversation bore you? asks Sarah.

No, I love her.

Then I don't see why she should bore you in bed.

Well, her conversation might bore me if she were the only woman I had a conversation with in seven years.

He says after a moment, Don't worry about Anita; she gets it whenever she wants it. She has no idea how I feel.

Although Sarah feigns moral indignation, Carl feels her going soft like butter. She blushes when he compliments her and enjoys the special attention she gets around the workshop.

MR. CRAWHALL'S HOUSE is designed to allow as much sunlight as possible. When he's asleep Anita watches a white chair with faint apricot flowers. The shadows of the leaves on the chair are in constant motion. At about seven in the evening it's almost as though the chair catches fire, a silent fire. It's the only moving thing in the stiff-backed room besides the two goldfish. They are kept in a clear glass bowl with no plants or coloured stones. A soft spoken friend speaks to Anita over the phone, You really have no choice, Anita. This will hurt Carl so much. It was a one-night stand.

The goldfish are identical. Anita calls one fish the option of keeping the baby and the other the abortion. She watches them swim around and makes a game of seeing how long she can tell which is which.

That night Anita says to Carl, about her new painting, If you spend enough time alone the pain of emptiness passes and you realize your own voice is the only company you need.

The image is entirely nonrepresentational, red and yellow dots only, but the canvas shimmers with anxiety.

Carl tries to remember what it is he loves about Anita. The smell of turpentine on her flannel painting smock, burnt match sticks and beer bottle caps between the bed sheets. The squeezed paint tubes in her leather box, curled in on themselves, the limbs of their shirts and jeans twisted together on the floor. The photographs in his sock drawer, in the beaten Tooton's envelope, of the night they walked to Signal Hill. It was summer and the sky was a skin of ticklish rain. Anita was drinking pop that turned the down of her upper lip and tongue orange. She tasted like summer, childhood. In the photographs the lights of the city at night burned coloured sizzles on the film. They made love on the grass, watching out for broken beer bottles, an aureole of amber glitter around their bodies.

ANITA SLEPT WITH a tourist named Hans. He was a German gymnast who had trained for the Olympics for eleven years and gave it up. Now he was driving a VW van across Canada. St. John's was his starting point. He was golden, muscular, but small. He walked with his hands loosely by his sides. He seemed to place his steps, walking on the balls of his feet as if he were stepping onto a mat in front of a large audience. He had been sitting alone at the Ship Inn drinking milk. It was as though the blondness of his hair alarmed almost anyone who might have joined him. Hans and Anita discussed what was scenic, the hospitable Newfoundlander, and Jiggs dinner, briefly. He had come from California, that was his first stop in North America. He had learned to speak English in a place called Pure Springs, a self-awareness camp with hot springs where they practised Gestalt and taught hyper-ventilation to relax. Hans talked about group therapy.

You are one of twenty-five for a month. You come to know each other very well and one day you step outside the room and the others decide on one word or a simple phrase that describes your essence. Sometimes it's very painful, but for the first time you see your true self. Everyone hugs and is supportive.

Anita asks, What was your word?

Cold fish.

Outside the Ship Inn a rusted sign pole stuck out from the brick wall. The sign itself had been removed. Hans climbed on the windowsill easily and, jumping, gripped the bar. He swung back and forth, then with his legs straight, toes pointed, lifted himself into a handstand. It was the moment while he was upside down that Anita realized she would sleep with him because he was passing through and because her faithfulness to Carl was a burden. When he swung down, Anita felt the pocket of warm night air he cut with his body.

Hans swept the seats of the VW van with a small hand brush before she got in. The van was spotless. There was a string bag full of fruit, none of it bruised. On the wall was a calendar from Pure Springs. The photograph for June was four pairs of naked feet, toes twisted, all caught in the same hammock net. Nestled between the hand-brake and the driver's seat was a glossy purple diary. Anita picked it up and opened it.

What's this?

Inside were poems written in German, diary entries, dried flowers, and coloured pencil drawings of mountain peaks.

My ex-fiancée made that for me.

Hans took out his shiny Swiss Army knife from the glove compartment and effortlessly cut the rind from a pineapple while he spoke. She was a gypsy. Long dark hair, black eyes, small like me, we wore each other's clothes. We hiked together in the mountains of Switzerland for two and three months at a time. We were together for ten years and were to be married. The invitations were sent. One hundred invita-tions. A week later she said she wanted to go to Africa. She met another fellow there, a German. The wedding was called off.

Hans held a quivering slice of pineapple out to Anita on the blade of the knife.

You must be very hurt, said Anita.

No, at Pure Springs they taught me to see myself as I really am. When I have finished my trip I will return there as a counsellor.

They sat in silence looking at the stars over Long Pond.

The fruit is very sour, remarked Hans. In the morning Anita could see the Arts and Culture Centre from where they had parked. She saw Carl get out of his car.

Hans dropped her off later at Mr. Crawhall's. When he left she could only imagine him in a hat with a little red feather, shorts with straps, and a walking stick; Julie Andrews's voice echoing off the Alps. *Such is the cry of the lonely goatherd la-he-o, la-he-o, dee-lo.*

It shocked her later to think her baby might be blond with eyes like an iceberg, if she had it.

CARL'S TROLL is hunched under the bridge, naked, its long green fingers hanging between its knees. Carl is placing glass eyeballs in the carved eye sockets. Sarah is standing on a wooden chair, perfectly still, her pressed lips full of pins. She's modelling the Red Riding Hood costume for the seamstress. She's identical in size to the five Styrofoam Red Riding Hoods standing in various positions around the warehouse. The roar of the chain saw subsides. Carl holds the glass eyeballs over his own eyes and tilts his head mechanically from one side to the other. He laughs and snorts, feigning a limp.

My dear, what firm milky breasts you have, all the better to ...

He pops the glass eyeball into his mouth, rolling it between his lips, which close over it like eyelids. Slowly he reaches for Sarah's throat and pulls the bow of her cloak so it falls off her shoulders onto the floor. Sarah squeals through tightly pressed lips.

For Christ's sake, Carl, she'll catch her death of cold, says the seamstress.

CARL AND SARAH have been using a glue that foams into a cement. It has been taken off the market because the fumes are highly toxic, but over the years Carl has grown accustomed to using it and he knows a guy who imports it from Italy. It's a two-part solution and becomes active when the two separate solutions are mixed. Sarah and Carl are the only ones in the workshop. She's pouring the solution and he's holding the bucket for her. She spills the solution over his hands and frantically tries to wipe it. The foam has an acid base, and in her effort their hands have become stuck together. Carl shouts obscenities between his teeth and drags her to the sink. It's difficult for him to get at the cold water tap. Sarah is crying hysterically and his other hand is stuck to the bucket. It takes him fifteen minutes to separate their hands. The seamstress hears the commotion from the kitchen down the hall and gets the first aid kit. She wraps their hands with burn ointment and gauze. Carl apologizes for cursing at Sarah and sends her home. He stays a long time in the empty warehouse, his burnt hands cradled between his knees.

On Fire

ISABEL HUGGAN

THEY OPEN THE FIRST BOTTLES OF BEER in the early afternoon, sitting by the water where two small children are paddling. The children (as well as a baby asleep in the cottage behind the cedar hedge) belong to Alex and Casey, who have invited David and Lily up to the lake to spend the last weekend of summer. Casey sits under a large navy-blue umbrella, while Lily lies near her on a towel, trying to brown her body with a mixture of tanning oils and lotions. But the late August sun hasn't much power and although she's been on the beach since morning her skin appears unchanged. Lily likes to go into the winter with a little additional colour, she says, or else she looks washed out by the new year (she and David have not yet begun their annual Christmas trips to Cozumel).

Casey, on the other hand, guards her paleness like a virtue and is the same shade of ivory all year round. A decade before skin cancer becomes a fashionable concern, Casey is making pronouncements about the sun being her enemy, about dangerous rays and who-knows-what-all; Lily is really getting fed up with these exaggerated claims and phobias.

Casey never used to be like this when they lived together—there was a casual ease to her then, a daring. But now she is so careful, measuring out time and food and experience in precise bits, everything weighed and measured. Lily thinks having three babies in less than six years has affected Casey's brain as well as her body for she has changed in some terrible and irrevocable way. She'd expected Casey to be a wonderful mother, possibly a little frazzled and disorganized but happy, definitely happy; instead, she has become tight-lipped and tidy. Even with all her attention to diet she has gained weight and she sits now in the blue shade of the big umbrella like an early Picasso, thickened and humourless. Worrying.

Lily finds herself annoyed by her old friend much of the time they are together (which is not often any more, maybe twice a year). She suspects that her irritation isn't only because of Casey's fretful ways, but probably has to do with her own deep frustration at being childless. She cannot prevent herself from believing that she'd be much better at motherhood than Casey is, that she'd be more relaxed, more joyfully maternal. Yes, and grateful. Casey seems not to have a shred of gratitude for these wonderful babies.

Lily turns over on her stomach and lets the sun do its business on her spine, the backs of her long legs, the soles of her feet. But what can you do, she thinks, trying to bend her thoughts in a more philosophical direction. This is just the way things are. Maybe it doesn't seem fair but who ever said life was fair?

David is further down the beach with Roger, the eldest child, who has come out of the water blue-lipped, rubbing at himself with a beach towel in a sad, little-old-man way. David is kneeling, trying to distract the small boy from his shivering by building something in the sand. Hearing his voice, Lily raises her head and watches—it is only David who is making the fort, piling up pails of sand, laughing and talking as he works. He uses a small red shovel to smooth the sides, to fashion the turrets and towers with crenellated edges. He has sent three-year-old Vicki in search of sticks and feathers—fevvers, he calls them—to decorate the top when they are done.

Roger is sitting to one side, idly arranging piles of stones. He has clearly lost interest but David is happily humming to himself and starting to dig a small trench down to the water's edge. His idea of being a father, thinks Lily as she closes her eyes against the scene, is to become a child again himself. Perhaps it is not such a bad thing that they do not yet have children. Perhaps they will never have children and that will be for the best, the laws of nature working to prevent them from becoming the awful parents they'd no doubt be. She probably wouldn't be a better mother than Casey is, not really. She'd just end up being David's mother too.

With that, she feels the prickle of self-pitying tears and blinks rapidly, burying her head in the sandy towel. She has ended up crying about one thing or another the last few visits with Alex and Casey and she can't let it happen again.

The four of them have been friends for a long time, she and Casey since their first week at university when they met in a line signing up for Journalism. "How come *you're* taking this bird course?" Casey had asked her, and Lily had been astounded and offended. She wasn't going to study journalism because it was meant to be an easy option: she'd already decided it would be her major. She wanted to write for a newspaper, she loved writing more than anything in the world: she'd been cultivating a fantasy of herself as a hotshot reporter since she was fourteen. But this wasn't the answer she gave to the short rude girl next to her in line.

"Because I'm a bird," she'd said, drawing herself up to full height, one foot curled around her other leg, her thin arms wrenched up and out like spindly wings, and her large, rather beakish nose thrust out in what she hoped was the supercilious demeanour of a stork or flamingo.

"Oh, thank you," Casey had sighed, her grey eyes round with delight. "I've been really worried there wasn't going to be anybody to *like* around this place. What's your name?"

They had become inseparable after that, sharing rooms and flats for the next four years until, the summer of their graduation, Casey had married Alex and had gone off with him to Pasadena where he'd been given a large and prestigious fellowship. Alex was a graduate student in astronomy when they met him; he'd turned up auditing the same music appreciation course they were taking, given by a dotty old professor who'd known Stravinsky's daughter and who played all his music at top volume in a small basement room in the chemistry building.

Those Thursday evening music classes had had such an unlikely air about them it had heightened the romantic sense of destiny surrounding Casey's falling in love. Alex didn't much appeal to Lily—she found him too moody and remote. She much preferred the sociable, gregarious boys with whom she worked on the student paper, with whom she could talk easily and crack jokes and be herself. Alex always made her feel awkward and apprehensive. But she found herself spellbound by the dazzling intensity of Casey's passion, felt herself drawn into their ardour. It had happened so swiftly; one night, after the old man had played *Rites of Spring*, Alex had declared himself and instantly Casey was his. Their love was radiant, magical, as mysterious and overwhelming as Stravinsky's strange music. Even after Lily met and married David, she still felt a lingering nostalgia for that time, that place—the stuffy little room, the eccentric professor, that richly complex, dissonant music. A lingering envy.

With David, love had taken more time. There had been a lengthy engagement while she worked for a small newspaper in the town where he was establishing his law practice, since they both wanted to make sure they were compatible before committing themselves. For Lily, it had been a period of disillusionment, discovering that the career she'd dreamed of did not satisfy her at all; she knew she ought not be bored and restless, but she was.

She thought it might have been different if she'd started on a big city daily—there'd be excitement there, a core of energy—but as it was she found daily reporting a monotonous chore and began to think more and more about raising a family. She threw out her pills and waited for the signs which would mean she could ask for maternity leave, knowing in her heart she would never return to the paper.

They've stayed in that town, David and Lily, renovating a large, turn-of-the-century house, room by room. Nearly two years ago Lily quit her job hoping, as her mother had suggested, that staying home and leading a less stressful life would allow her to get pregnant. But although she and David have followed all the suggested procedures, nothing has happened. They are considering putting their name in at the Children's Aid Society, since everyone says adoption is a surefire way to suddenly find yourself expecting, and Lily thinks she wouldn't mind having two babies at once. But the only babies available seem to be ones with problems or mixed parentage, and neither she nor David are entirely sure about shouldering that kind of burden. Still, sometimes it seems to her that anything, anything would be better than this waiting for something to happen.

She has a standard answer now whenever friends inquire how she's getting along. "I'm just a lady in waiting," she says, and gives a small self-mocking and apologetic chuckle. One night at a party David overhears her saying this and adds, "Brooding about breeding is more like it!" She laughs as loudly as everyone else at the time, but when he repeats the same thing later she looks at him sharply to see whether he is trying to wound her with his wordplay. But no, his big handsome face is flushed with good humour, he is simply enjoying the sound of language, the taste of it in his mouth. It is what makes him such a fine litigation lawyer and is why his practice is flourishing, why they can afford to have Lily stay home. She has been thinking of doing some freelance writing for magazines, maybe trying her hand at some fiction, but the house seems to take so much of her time. She is stripping the varnish off all the woodwork, doing the jobs that might be difficult or dangerous once a baby comes.

Alex has left the beach. He has gone up to the cottage to check on the sleeping baby and to bring down more beer. Casey has said she won't have any more, one is enough, but Lily is already looking forward to the bitter liquid sliding ice-cold down her throat. She hopes Alex won't take too long, and with that passing thought suddenly realizes she misses Alex when he is absent. She is at a loss to know why, for in all the years they've known each other she and he have seldom talked alone: she has known him through Casey and with David, but never directly.

To some extent she still sees him as he was a decade ago, slouching in his chair at the back of the music class, thin and sullen and burning with desire for Casey. He wasn't talkative then and seems to speak even less as time passes. He only teaches one course now at the university and the rest of his time is spent doing calculations. His work is solitary, enormous, bright with portent and infinite possibility.

But he never speaks of it, maybe because none of them will understand what he's talking about. He barely talks at all, is even more self-absorbed than he was as a student. And yet as she thinks of him now, Lily sees him as the silent centre of their circle, the still pivot around whom the other three turn, talking, talking. Perhaps, she thinks, spending so much time on her own has brought her to a new appreciation of Alex, a feeling of unspoken affinity and connection—for she has found, working on the house day after day, a pocket of quiet within herself, a need for solitude she'd never known was there.

Sometimes when David comes home in the evening, spilling over with the news of his day in court, wanting to share everything word by word, she wishes he would stop. He is too overwhelming, too verbose. She will often pick up a book, or busy herself with something to avoid these conversations. "Could we chat later, Davey? I'm just in the middle of this right now." Always nice about it, or at least she means to be.

David is singing something silly and hearty from Gilbert and Sullivan as he cheerfully digs the moat deeper on Roger's instruction. The little boy is charmed by the way the sides cave in as the water rises and he urges David to go faster, faster. Soon the walls of the fort give way to the water and David is laughing along with Roger at the ruins, not minding that all his work has been for naught. He seems to have a child's easy understanding of pleasure as an end in itself. Watching him place a small feather in Vicki's hair, Lily is moved by the exquisite gentleness of the gesture. Maybe he would be an excellent father after all, she thinks.

Alex reappears carrying three bottles of beer held against his chest and the baby slung on one shoulder. He calls out as he comes through the hedge, "Travis was awake, Case." Lily looks up from her towel to see a grimace pass across the other woman's face, but she can't tell whether it is from resignation or resentment.

"Oh Alex, you bugger, I'll bet you woke him. He should have been good for another hour."

Alex plumps the baby down on Casey's legs in a jolly way, as if his movements might forestall the anger he sees flashing from her eyes. In her pale face the round grey eyes have always been startling, but now they are quite haunting—she has a way of opening her lids very wide, as if to see through the endless dark tunnel of baby-bound fatigue, which makes them seem even rounder and more expressive.

There is a grim set to Casey's jaw as she turns her attention to Travis, a yellow-haired and pink-skinned baby rolling in fat. "Little pig," she says, but she says it fondly, tenderly, almost as if she were speaking to a lover. "Little pig," again, as she pulls up her shirt on one side to reveal a large, brownish-purple nipple which has begun to leak milk even before the baby attaches himself.

Lily is both attracted and slightly nauseated by the sight of the blue-veined and bruised-looking breast. She tries to imagine herself with that slurping infant pulling at her body, but she cannot. "God, Casey, you must feel so useful doing that," she says affectionately.

"That's what you always say, Lil," says Casey, tossing her head back and looking at her old friend as from a long distance. "You think I'm feeling utterly fulfilled, don't you? Well I'm here to tell you what I feel is *drained*. Don't sit there and create a fantasy about motherhood, I'm telling you."

Lily feels a surge of indignation at Casey's tone of maternal condescension—it seems to her this is increasingly Casey's manner—but all she says is: "Here then, drink some of my beer and replace your bodily fluids. I'm going to swim."

She walks to the water's edge where Vicki sits with her short chubby legs stretched out in front of her, whooping with glee every time a wave washes over her feet. Lying beside her is Alex, eyes closed, balancing a bottle of beer on his flat stomach. His dry skin is freckled and almost entirely hairless (unlike David's, whose entire body is covered in crisp, wiry dark hair). On his chest the nipples are small and bright pink, like two sugar rosebuds on a cake; looking down at him, Lily thinks what foolish and futile things men's nipples are, only for decoration. As she stands there, she is filled with a rushing desire to crouch down and taste their sweetness. Alex opens his eyes and looks up at her, one eyebrow arched quizzically. "Would you care to dance?" he says.

Lily has the unnerving idea that her forehead has opened up and Alex has seen the picture in her mind. She feels her face redden and so she scuffs the sand with her toe and does a comic turn.

"Can't dance. It's against my religion," she says, and runs into the lake. She is stricken by the intimacy that has passed between them—nothing remotely like this has ever happened before. Even little Vicki seems to be caught in the crackling web of electricity and has thrown herself upon her father's body, smothering him with kisses and upsetting his beer. Alex is smiling.

Lily runs out through the shallow water to where it is deep enough to swim. This late in the summer the bottom never really gets warm during the daylight hours and the coldness Lily feels around her ankles and knees is somehow thrilling. Her bones ache as she plunges down into the dark water, her racing pulse slowed by the murky silence around her. Swimming, she feels her long hair streaming out behind her, feels it falling like scarves around her shoulders as she rises to the surface. She has swum directly out into the lake and is unable to touch bottom; she does this every time she comes here. Being frightened and not succumbing to the fear always makes her feel powerful, in control of her life. Something left over from her childhood, she guesses, this moment of decision, this moment of knowing she *will not* drown. She never allows the welling panic in her chest to rise up and close her throat.

As she swims back to shore Lily squints to see more clearly but from this far away the people on the sand are only blurs and smudges. Like a Seurat painting, she thinks, small dots of colour, my universe broken into fragments of light. Casey, the children, Alex, even David no longer solid … just dots of colour, unconnected. Dots. (Her mother, sitting very close to her on the couch, both of them perspiring in the summer heat, that summer she had turned nine. Her mother, explaining the facts of life. "And the little egg from which you came is no bigger than the dot a pencil makes, like the period at the end of this page.") Dots. Tiny little dots within her body which somehow are not making themselves available to David's eager and dizzy-headed sperm. Her fault, her dots.

With a smooth crawl she slices through the water until her knees drag on the sand and then she rises and runs toward David, shaking her hair so that the spray flings out wildly and glistens all over his body and face.

"You should have come in," she says. "It was wonderful."

David wipes away the droplets of water from his eyes and looks up at her mildly. "But you were having such a nice time out there by yourself, Lil, I could see that. I didn't want to intrude."

She feels absurdly angry at his observing her so closely and knowing her so well. He's right, she would have felt encroached upon had he joined her—but this knowing of her is invasive, too. Is this how Casey feels about her baby sucking at her, she wonders. Is this part of marriage and motherhood inevitable, this sense of being known, being owned, being completely overtaken?

"Another beer," says Lily. "I need another beer. You want one?" He shakes his head and she walks up the beach without asking Alex and Casey who are sitting together, talking intently over Travis's head. There are four stone steps up through the hedge to the cottage which belongs to Alex's parents; they allow Alex and Casey to use it every August. It is at least sixty years old, a white clapboard structure with dark green trim around the windows and eaves and a wide screened-in porch which once looked out over the lake but now has its view blocked by the cedar windbreak. There is a sparse, dry lawn, and on either side of a flagstone path leading to the porch there is a round bed of straggly petunias made even more forlorn-looking by a rim of white-painted rocks. The yard is rich in aromas—cedar, and the honeysuckle and trumpetvine growing up over the porch, and the sweet grass which thrives in this sandy soil.

Inside the cottage there are strong, specific smells of mothballs and damp wood and years of spilt coffee on the old woodstove. The cottage has electricity (there is an ancient Kelvinator out of which Lily takes the beer) but this family of Alex's clings to old ways as much as possible when they are at the lake. As if going back in time can provide some kind of balance to their present lives, as if not flicking on a light switch can somehow transform them into people with "real" values.

Lily leans against the refrigerator to drink the first half of her beer, enjoying the coolness of the kitchen and the way its vine-covered windows convert sharp sunlight to dappled green shadows. There is something secretive and hidden about this little cottage she likes a lot; she feels as if she were still down in the cold dark water of the lake. Maybe Casey's right, she thinks. Maybe the sun *is* our enemy.

Later, in the early evening, the kitchen has become bright and warm. The four adults jostle each other within its confines, sharing the tasks of making supper and feeding the children. David is inventing a new spaghetti sauce concocted from various tins found in the cupboard; Casey is making salad and Alex is setting the table and supervising Roger and Vicki, who are eating hot dogs with ketchup. There is a steamy closeness which is not unpleasant, a grittiness which comes from sand underfoot and the sensation of still-damp bathing suits on the skin.

They will change into comfortable clothing once the children are down ("putting the children down" is Casey's phrase and strikes Lily as peculiarly sinister, suggestive of doing away with them). Lily has asked if she might give Travis his nightly bath in the sink and Casey has agreed, adding, "Just don't get moony, Lil."

It seems to Lily that with each visit the last year or so Casey has taken on more responsibility for her emotional well-being, monitoring her every shift and swell of feeling, constantly on the alert for any display of sentimentality or self-pity. As if she can't bear to see the reality of Lily's unrequited longing for babies. Lily keeps reminding herself that intervention is a kind of love, but she wishes Casey would simply let her be sad.

At this moment, she has pretended not to hear her, and has gone instead to open herself another beer—her fifth—while the tap is running for the baby's bath. She feels languid and happy, as if she were still in the lake. Travis is a remarkably placid baby, nearly nine months old and very bright-eyed. As she lathers his fat body with soap he squirms with pleasure and as she washes the folds along his thigh he squeals and splashes her. She is conscious of his small penis floating in the bubbles like a wrinkled little rosebud, and she is shy of touching it, afraid he will emit such a scream of delight the others will turn and say, "Lily, what are you up to with that child?"

Lily wonders if there is any difference between her enjoyment of Travis as she washes him and what a mother would feel. Are there levels of feeling which can be identified, labelled, and categorized? She lifts Travis out of the sink, amazed at the weight and heft of his shining body. "He's not a little pig, he's a Buddha," she says to the room at large. "A little pink Buddha."

Beside her, David is chopping onions for the sauce, and he slides his hip along the counter so that he is touching Lily as she is drying Travis. She feels surrounded by sensation—the baby's flesh, David's hip, the smell of onion, smoke, soap, beer—enveloped and enclosed. She looks at David, whose cheeks are streaming with tears, and at first she thinks that he is overcome by the sight of her holding the baby and then realizes it's the onions making him cry. Still, she feels interfered with, as if he is attempting to join her in whatever she is experiencing with small Travis. Why should she be so antagonistic, she wonders; it doesn't make sense. Yet both Casey and David set her teeth on edge with their caring.

The meal, when it is finally served after many lullabies to the children, is exactly like scores of others they have shared. The pasta is overcooked, David's sauce is highly original and almost inedible, and the salad is too sharp, tingling with lemon juice and garlic. There is a lot of bread and a lot of wine—two bottles of Hungarian red—and the local mild cheddar they always buy on the way up to the lake. Two oil lamps are burning on a shelf above the table and from outside night sounds drift in: a few final whippoorwills, crickets, frogs, and the occasional lap of a wave. Alex says that every seventh wave is larger than the previous six. He always says this and no one ever challenges him or asks if it is really true. Because he knows about the heavens, somehow they all assume he must know about the natural world as well. Even David, who loves to argue and ordinarily will not accept statements without question, gives Alex a kind of elevated station and never disputes the business of the waves.

Alex goes at the close of the meal to a cupboard and brings out a bottle of German dessert wine. "It should be cold, honey," says Casey, in a tight, careful way they all understand means that she wishes him not to open the bottle. Instead, he goes to the Kelvinator and takes out a metal tray of ice cubes, and as he drops a cube in each glass of white wine, he smiles at Casey. It is much the same way he plopped the baby on her lap earlier in the afternoon, deliberately merry, making a movement which in itself swerves around disaster.

Lily knows this oversweet wine will give her a headache but she is past caring. She wants to drink more, she feels reckless. Casey used to drink as much as the others, but the last few years she has been breastfeeding or pregnant much of the time and so there's always been a reason to avoid excess. Lily wonders if Alex drinks this much when he and Casey are alone together or if it is only when she and David are around.

For now they are sitting around a table as they have so often, the wine slowing them down and bringing them into tight focus: they belong in the same frame. Alex is smoking Camel cigarettes steadily and David is lighting and relighting his pipe with his usual earnest, jaunty dignity.

Casey, who once went through a pack a day, has become an ardent nonsmoker, but even her show of being affected by the smoke—clearing her throat, wiping her eyes—does not deter the men. Alex shoves a pack across the table toward Lily and although she has never felt at ease with Casey's disapproval, she takes a cigarette out and smokes it. The gesture feels strangely defiant and adolescent.

Casey has become the centre of attention. She is animated, her grey eyes luminous, her round face glowing like a pearl in the light from the lamps. She is heated, having had just enough wine to fuel the rage she is now loosing upon them. "I'd damn well rather do it myself than have to have my husband's signature," she says.

She is telling about her latest conversation with her doctor, the obstetrician-gynecologist who has brought her three babies into the world, who knows her, she says, inside-out. She speaks of him with the fierceness women reserve for their fathers and doctors, those men with too much power. This man—she calls him Mac, they've been friends for years—is denying her the right to have a tubal ligation without Alex's consent.

"Consent!" she says, her voice harsh, and higher than usual in its force. "Consent! It's *my* bloody body and it's mine to do with as *I* bloody please!"

Lily looks at her friend and thinks how beautiful she is; with the extra layer of milky fat covering her bones, her even features are still perfectly defined but riper, more sensual. The bright colour now in her cheeks and the way she holds her head high are somehow thrilling, make her seem nearly glamorous in her fury at Mac. Someone else entirely from that frowning blue woman on the beach. Lily has the wildly unsettling notion, all of a sudden, that neither of these Caseys bears any resemblance to the one she thinks of as her old friend. She doesn't really know who this woman is. Nor does Casey know Lily, neither of them are the same any more. They've changed beyond recall.

"Be fair," Alex says softly. "It isn't just Mac, you know, it's the hospital's policy. And he has to work there, he has to do the operation within their regulations."

"Oh Christ, Alex, don't stick up for him." Casey's voice cuts in like a scalpel before Alex is finished, scornful and dismissive. "Mac is part of the system, he's no better than that old fart whatsisname who runs the place. He goes along with it all, he's a pig at heart the same as the rest of them."

David sucks noisily on his pipe, leans back in his chair the way he likes to do before making some sort of legal pronouncement. Lily watches him and wonders what on earth he does in court without his pipe as a prop. He is very calm and his large body stretches out from the chair, his face ruddy from the wine and the earlier laughter. But she can tell from his tone that he is upset by Casey's agitation and is responding in the only way he knows—by dampening her vehemence with reason and composure.

"Now you see, Case," he is saying, "these fellas are in a real bind. They can get themselves in trouble if they go ahead with one of these sterilizations and then later the husband says he didn't know, or he only wants her if she's fertile, etcetera, etcetera. Believe me, this is fresh ground for the courts, and everyone's being careful, not just your Mac. There are lawsuits and nasty precedents in the offing if anybody makes a wrong move. They aren't asking for consent so much as your husband's acknowledgement."

"Bullshit, David," says Casey. "If Alex signs, then that's consent. Look, you only see it from your point of view, the law. See it from mine. I don't want any more babies. Me, the baby machine."

Alex, who has been hunching over his last glass of wine and smoking heavily, speaks directly to David now as if somehow he, in his legal role, has become the arbiter of this dispute. "Look, Dave, I told her I'd go and have it done, I don't care, it means nothing to me, I only want Case to be happy. It's easier for us anyway, snip-snip in the doctor's office and done. I've told her."

His face beneath his freckles is livid with emotion. When he drinks he never gets sweaty and red-faced the way David does, he seems to become even drier. How does he drink so much and stay so lean, Lily wonders. For that matter, how do I?

"Oh, Alex, can't you hear what I'm *saying*?" Casey speaks now in a tone of sorrowful exasperation, as if to a child. "I'm fighting this on the very issue you're talking about. You don't need my permission for your snip-snip, but I need *yours*. Can't you understand? It's about my subordinate role, it's about male domination, but it's not theoretical stuff, Alex, it's real. Goddamit, listen to me!"

Lily realizes she may be a little drunk because she feels as if she is in a play but she has forgotten her lines. She knows she is meant to be on Casey's side and yet her sympathies are shifting somewhere else. "Surely having babies is not subordinate," she says. "It's because it's the most important thing in the world that these men get so uptight about it. Face it, Casey, you're only thirty years old. Couldn't Mac be concerned that in a few years you might want to have a baby again?"

Casey turns on Lily with quick, icy disdain. "You're such a romantic, Lil."

Lily is hurt but self-righteous—it makes perfect sense to her that a husband should know what's going on, after all, it takes two, doesn't it? She takes the rebuff with a thin smile, and gets up, goes to the bedroom and takes from David's overnight bag the bottle of French brandy he had stuck in at the last minute. He'd bought it last week after winning a particularly long and difficult case. "Didn't we bring this to celebrate with?" she says to David as she comes back to the table.

"What in heaven's name are we celebrating?" Casey asks, raising her eyebrows and making her eyes very round.

"The complexities of our existence," says David, in his pompous lawyer's voice, taking on a comic role to divert attention from the hostility in the air, anger so intense it is almost tangible. He loosens the heavy cork stopper and pours a little of the caramel-coloured liquid into four plastic tumblers. "You have some too, Casey," he says. "It'll do young Travis good to get some Courvoisier with his milk tonight. Here." He passes round the glasses and lifts his high above them. "To our complexities."

Lily drinks hers at one swallow while the others are still sipping. She feels an urgent need to act, to prevent the conversation from slipping back to that perilous place they've just been. She leans forward and takes the bottle by the neck, pouring herself another two fingers.

"I feel like a swim again," she says, inspired.

"You talkin' suit or you talkin' skinny?" David asks, in a mock accent he often affects to make people laugh. He has a good-ol'-boy aspect himself that makes the accent seem appropriate, even engaging.

"Skinny, honey," Lily says, flirting back in a way she never does if they are alone. "Have I evah been anythin' but skinny?"

They all laugh, for it is one of David's longstanding jokes that her knees, elbows, and hipbones are lethal weapons in bed, all of them sharp enough to draw blood. Lily *does* seem a ludicrous name for someone so angular and so unlike a flower, she thinks.

(She has had, over the past few months, a battery of fertility tests, one of which was meant to discover whether her hormonal development was retarded, but the results are inconclusive; her boyish body is no indication. There have been other tests of her inner workings as well, which have so assaulted her sense of privacy she is still, weeks later, injured in her spirit. She had lain, strapped down on a metal table under the eye of a camera, and watched on a small monitor her uterus, a white pear-shaped object glowing and fluttering on the dark screen; and then, not the neat bullshorns of medical diagram but two winding bits of thread, two tendrils of a climbing vine.

Casey wants these same slender, slivery tubes of life cut, or cauterized, or plugged with plastic. Getting your tubes tied. A simple operation, nothing to it.)

"Listen, Lil, honestly, we can't go out on the beach naked. You know, we're not in the middle of nowhere." Casey is sober and sensible, and although she is laughing she is taking it upon herself to keep Lily and David in line.

"Goodness, chile," David says, "it's after midnight. There ain't gonna be no pryin' eyes down there this hour. Why don' you jest whip off them rags and come dippin' with me and my fren'?" He turns the full force of his charm upon her, a man who can disarm with his caution-to-the-wind lopsided smile—and Casey is suddenly and inexplicably taken with this jovial mood he offers. She abandons her stance and rises from the table, agreeing to swim skinny.

"But we'll take the oil lamps down with us," she says. "I don't want to leave them alight in the cottage with the kids asleep. And we have to be quiet, I mean it, David. No chortling!" She is going along with him but she is making rules—as always, Lily thinks. She always has to be the mother now.

Lily looks across the table at Alex, who is stubbing out a cigarette. His clear green eyes make her think of water, which is odd because his skin is so dry and patchy, his tangled blond hair like a small forest fire springing from his forehead. "You're coming too, aren't you?" she says, knowing his preference would be to stay quietly at the table alone. He responds by taking the lamps in his hands and holding them out as if he were leading a parade. Casey gathers the towels and they all enter the night, David and Lily giggling and shushing each other.

Out on the sand there are transparent layers of mist lying between them and the water, shreds and strands of gauze floating in the dark. Only the occasional star glitters, only a handful of distant cottage lights glimmer along the shore. The sole sounds are of crickets in the hedge, the small lapping of waves, and from down the lake someone's stereo playing music which is too urban for this setting—the sad, sophisticated undulations of a tenor sax. Alex places the lamps on the sand and Casey piles the towels beside them, glancing anxiously back at the dark cottage and her sleeping children.

Lily knows that by convention she must not look at the others while they undress but she is caught by the sight of her husband as he slips off his shorts and underwear, by the clownlike appearance of his penis hanging from its fur collar of black hair—like a false nose, like a fleshy handle. (David had done his tests first, since after all his was the easiest, involving only one hilarious morning in which he had to jump immediately in the car and drive to the medical labs with the precious vial of semen. He and his equipment had passed with flying colours.)

She cannot help it, she looks over to see what Casey looks like naked now, and is startled by the despondent heaviness of her hips and belly, the hanging breasts grotesque rather than voluptuous. Even in the resigned and ungainly way she removes her clothes Casey seems deliberately unsexy, as if she wants to be old and done with that business forever. Lily's own thin body by contrast seems a blessing, and she moves her hands along the ridges of her ribs and along her flat stomach with pride. Well, everything has its price, she thinks. Nothing new about that. She looks now to see Alex, who is pulling off his sweatshirt, standing behind Casey. He is even more of an ectomorph than she is, sinew and bone. She waits for him to take off his underpants, feeling ashamed of her prurience yet unable to turn away.

But he doesn't. He keeps his white briefs on and taking Casey's hand walks quickly into the lake, edgy and furtive. Lily wishes they were like the people she's read about in California, at Esalen and places like that, who would hold hands and chant mantras together as they entered the water, four bodies in one mind. She feels the need of ceremony and ritual to cleanse them of that conversation about Casey tying her tubes. A conversation that is already hooking itself into their lives.

The cool night air makes the lake seem warmer than it was earlier in the day as she slides beneath the surface, enjoying the silky texture of the water on her skin. She flips over on her back and with a gentle flutter kick steers herself out past the shore-line mist, looking up at the cloud-studded sky, the drifting stars. The life Alex has chosen for himself, the security of unobtainable galaxies.

She hears David's voice calling her softly. "Don't go out too far, Lil, there's an undertow." And she turns, with a firm and graceful breast stroke making her way back to where he stands, chest-deep. He is only a little taller than she is, a wall of a man against whom she now leans, letting her wet hair drape over his shoulder. She feels the jutting of his erect penis against her thigh and brings herself closer to him, excited.

"Help," she says. "There's an enemy submarine down there." She wraps her legs around his waist and burrows her face into his throat, playfully kissing and biting the flesh of his shoulder, and then biting again so sharply that he pushes her away.

"Hey, that hurts, Lil. Cut it out!"

"Sorry," she says, unrepentant, and swims off in a dreamy way back out to deep water. She can hear Alex and Casey murmuring—they are sitting in the shallows, splashing each other softly from time to time—but she cannot hear what they are saying. It seems to Lily specifically matrimonial, this splashing of each other. The saxophone's lonely melody slips over the water and winds itself around them. But what is the tune? She almost catches it once but lets it go, and is left with an image of neon-speckled puddles on city pavement, footsteps of a departing lover down the dark street.

The haze on the lake is lifting and the night is moonless but clear when David announces he is going back to the cottage. Lily knows she has hurt him in some irre-deemable way by swimming off when he wanted her; she swims back now to where he is and tries to smooth things over. "I'm coming too, Davey," she says and stands up, the nipples on her flat breasts like small thimbles in the chilly air. They dry each other and then wrap the towels around themselves, carrying their clothes and shoes. Lily takes one of the lamps and leaves the other for Casey and Alex who have begun to swim a little, still talking.

It is only Casey's voice which is audible, and there is something brittle about it, something accusatory and plaintive. Alex's voice comes and goes in monosyllabic scraps, whetting Lily's curiosity as she walks slowly back to the cottage. It reminds her of how she used to listen to them talking in the kitchen of the flat she and Casey had shared their last year at school. Alex would bring Casey back from his place late at night and she'd make him coffee and they'd sit together at the chrome and red Formica table, talking and smoking cigarettes until dawn. Lily would hear their blurred voices through her bedroom door, not yet in love herself but on the outer shell of it, knowing the sound of it from the outside in. In the morning she'd see their coffee cups and ashtrays, proof of a complicity in which she had no part.

She sets the lamp down inside the porch and gets dressed: she pulls on one of Alex's father's old cardigans which hangs on a nail by the door and holds it around herself to stop the sudden trembling that has overtaken her. Seeing her shudder, David pours her a full tumbler of brandy, which smells strangely like rotting fruit to Lily now, vile and evil. But she drinks it anyway, needing its warmth to give her strength, and curls up in a wicker chair to wait for the other two.

First to appear is Casey, clad in a towel with her clothes around her neck, not covering her large swinging breasts. They are full—she has gone past Travis's usual feeding-time—and they seem bursting with self-importance. She clutches her clothes and towels to her body and runs to the cottage, her ankles splaying out from side to side as if she has a tight skirt on. She rushes past David who is sitting with his pipe on the wooden steps, past Lily and into the bedroom where they hear her getting the baby from his bed. When she re-emerges, in a blue bathrobe with Travis at her breast, her face has a lovely serenity and she is perfectly beautiful again. She settles into a chair next to Lily and smiles, stroking the fine blond hair on her son's small head.

The music from down the beach has stopped and the night is completely silent. There is only the uneven flutter of one oil lamp and then coming through the hedge the other one, held high by Alex. In his other hand he carries his clothing and towel; he is shining wet and bare to the night except for his white underpants. The light from the lamp reveals him, Eros and Psyche in one body.

Alex sets the lamp down in the centre of a petunia bed and piles his clothes beside it. He bows toward the porch and speaks in the manner of a ringmaster, a showman. "Ta-daa!" he says, and then again louder. "Ta-daa!"

This is so unlike anything Alex has ever done the other three sit open-mouthed, waiting to hear what he will say next. He is announcing that he will now dance a farewell to summer and will they all please hold their applause until he is through.

David looks back over his shoulder at Lily and grins, shaking his head; Casey mutters to Travis, "Your daddy is drunk again, sweetheart." Lily is mesmerized, taut with expectation, wondering what he is going to do.

What he does is to leap over the lamp, making the flame waver and nearly go out, and then leap again, higher in the air, his arms straight out at his sides, his head held aloft and haughty. Clearly this is meant to be a spoof, a late-night amusement to send them to bed with a laugh. But there is also something very serious about his dancing, serious in the way he is demanding their attention. It reminds Lily of the way small boys play games as if their lives depend on it. Now he is jumping and pirouetting in a furious parody of ballet, now crouching and stamping in crazy imitation of African tribal dancing, but noiselessly. He snaps his fingers sharply every so often as if to keep in his mind some marking of the rhythms he must be hearing. The music of the spheres, Lily thinks and plans to offer that up next morning at breakfast. A good astronomer's joke.

As Alex dances the three others settle into themselves and begin to feel comfortable with the strangeness of his performance. His body is making shadows on the hedge, deformed and lacy shapes which stretch and shrink out of all proportion as he circles the lamp. His eyes are ablaze with excitement—he is obviously having the time of his life—and it occurs to Lily watching him that as long as there is a hedge between Alex and the outside world he feels safe and capable of liberating himself in their midst. With this dance he is taking them all with him into the most profound and private part of his soul, she thinks, and wonders if Casey knows this. She looks over at her old friend, awash in fondness for her after all the years they've shared, and sees that Casey has closed her eyes, has nestled herself closer to the sucking baby.

It seems to Lily watching Alex that his long bony fingers stream fire, that his yellow hair has caught fire too, and that there are tongues of flame licking the air around his face. Even his bare feet have a brightness, seem to be strung on wires of gold, threads of fire itself. He is an unexpected comet searing crazily through the August night, he is a puppet sprung free of its master. He is dancing faster and faster, he is becoming a firebird, he is burning up and disappearing into the ether.

But it is really only Alex, a thirty-five-year-old astronomer given to one moment of frenzy; thin, freckled Alex in his wet underwear dashing and prancing over the grass.

It is a dance of good-bye to more than summer but none of them know that at the time. Years later, after one of the marriages has ended in divorce and the two women have let their friendship dwindle into oblivion, Lily will find a postcard Casey sent to her after that last August weekend together. It has an old black-and-white photograph of Nijinsky dancing on the front and, on the back, only this: *Booze is bad for the heart.* Lily will be shaken when she realizes the truth of what she reads, and how much Casey had understood, even with her eyes closed.

Glowing with sweat, Alex twists himself into one last glorious leap and for a grand finale lands at David's feet, arms outstretched. "The end," he says, panting, out of breath. David claps his hands softly. "Bravo," he says. "You're a real star." His voice is warm and appreciative.

Alex goes up the steps and through the door, and stands looking at Casey holding Travis, who has fallen asleep against the blue bathrobe. Lily gets up from her chair and reaches out her hand, her fingers pointing toward his chest. She touches one of his nipples, recoiling immediately as if she's received a shock.

"You're on fire," she says, herself as breathless as if she had been dancing. She will say this again later to Alex, much later when they have finally become lovers, but this is the first time she says it.

The Flesh Collectors

MICHAEL REDHILL

BY FORTY-EIGHT, Roth had had his midlife crisis, four children, and three wives, the last of whom was still interested in sex, but not in having babies, and who had developed a serious allergy to latex. It was bad enough that they were still using condoms at their ages (although, granted, Sybil was eight years younger than he and could still, theoretically, reproduce), but his wife had ruled out having any part of her body removed for the purposes of pleasure, since she believed, like most Jews, that it was crucial to go to the grave whole, or else when the Messiah came you might be walking around for eternity lacking a crucial component. A missing appendix was forgivable, and certainly anything that had to be shed for life-saving reasons was as well, just as it was not a sin to drink water on Yom Kippur if you had to take medication. "Doctor's orders," you'd hear someone saying in the synagogue hallway, pushing some capsule to the back of their throat and drinking long and deep from the fountain between the bathrooms.

The pill was absolutely out as well for Sybil, not because it was forbidden, but rather because it was apt to make her behave like a drugged monkey. Roth had often argued that some discomfort in the service of a happy marriage was an obligation to a good husband or wife, but Sybil had turned this argument against him. This was why Roth was staring down the possibility that he would soon have to submit a tender part of himself to a surgeon's knife. Such an operation would leave him whole—it was more a sundering than a deletion—and so, in the sense intended by the ancients, his options were considerably less fraught than hers.

His GP, Arnold Gravesend, told him that vasectomies, in this day and age, were twenty-minute affairs and didn't even have to be done by scalpel. Still, the prospect of having this part of his body interfered with made Roth woozy. He'd been delaying for months now, and Sybil was withholding connubially and building a wifely case against him. "I don't feel like breaking out into a yeast infection every time, Nathan. We're not newlyweds anymore. If you care about our marriage, you'll do what you have to do."

In principle, Roth agreed. To his own thinking, condoms provided biblical loopholes for people who were otherwise happy to follow the laws. His rabbi, Stern of Beth Israel, said that condoms did not release their users from the burden of sin. It was still spilling semen in vain, said Rabbi Stern. The good Jewish couple knows when the woman is in season and takes advantage accordingly.

Roth had relaxed his own strictures as he'd got older. With Adele, his first wife, he didn't even sleep in the bed with her when she was in cycle (a holdover of custom from his orthodox upbringing, even though he considered himself conservative now), but after they'd divorced he decided to be more "humane," as the therapist had put it to him, back when there was a chance to save the marriage. There was no sense in treating the person you loved as an opportunity *not* to sin if it meant hurting their feelings for one week out of every four. This was excellent advice, and his second marriage, to a dark-eyed beauty named Lila he'd met at a bazaar, would have lasted for life if she hadn't died. "The Cancer," Lila's mother had called it, as if there had been only one cancer in the whole world and it struck her daughter. At the funeral, she'd keened over and over again, *Why did we name her for the night?* "Lila" was Hebrew for night, a time when Roth's soul was always calm.

Sybil was a North Toronto woman. Not exotic, and street- rather than book-smart, but for Roth, it was time to slow down anyway and to lead a simpler life. Everything but his sexual urges, which frequently troubled him, had come to a better balance. He'd blown his relationships with his first two children, from Adele, but the last two, with Lila, were still growing up and hadn't yet learned to view him as an old fool. (That he wasn't old, not really, was of no consequence to the first two, to whom he suspected he'd been old since he was thirty.) As time went on, Roth seemed to fill with more love for his own children than he'd ever thought he could feel, and there was still a chance to hold Lila's and his children in the goodness of this love. These two still lived with him, ten-year-old Mitchell and his younger sister Sarah. Roth was all they had of their mother. They treated Sybil like an intruder and took his side in everything.

"Are you going to your doctor?" Sybil had asked at breakfast.

"Are you sick, Daddy?"

He was going to reply to his son, but Sybil turned her moisturized face toward the child and said, "There is nothing wrong with your father that can't be fixed in ten minutes."

"Is this the snip-snip?"

His sister, her spoon dripping with milk coloured by her cereal, looked up with her eyes creased. "What's the snip-snip?" she asked.

"I'm perfectly healthy, you guys," Roth said. "There's nothing wrong with me. And we don't use words like 'snip-snip' at the kitchen table."

"I can't remember the real word," said the boy.

Sybil collected her and Roth's plates and laid them in the sink. She didn't do dishes. The girl did the dishes. Roth hated having a maid, especially one that didn't live with them. It seemed to strip the position of any residual dignity it may have had, by forcing her to show up every morning to sweep through the house, and return every evening to whatever cramped squalor she no doubt lived in. "Vasectomy," said Sybil. The word caused a metallic wave of energy to run down Roth's spine, as if every bone in his body had been rubbed with aluminum foil.

"What is *that*?" said Sarah with disgust.

"It means Daddy won't be able to make a baby anymore," he said.

"Why?"

Sybil ruffled the little girl's thin black hair. "Because step-mummy doesn't want any kids."

"Oh," said his daughter. He'd already told her and Mitchell how reproduction worked. Rabbi Stern said it was all right to be explicit with children, as long as they were aware that the mysteries of sex were more important than its mechanics. Always foreground the wonders of the great fabric of life, said Stern. Roth had sought his advice less and less in recent years. *I've had divorce and death*, he thought. *It sounds like God's already made up his vast mind about me.*

When he'd sat down to talk with the children, he did so without the aid of a book or pen and paper. He simply told them the raw facts. What happened in the man's body, in the woman's. How it actually worked, sex. And after. The baby, inside, growing. They were fascinated. This was when Lila was still alive. It was the four of them, inviolate. The children got used to the fact that their parents had touched in that way. It made them all magical.

Now they considered that their father did much the same thing with their step-mother. Mitchell had some sense that it was not just for making children, and the snip-snip confirmed this. Their father wanted to stop having children for good, but he still wanted to put his penis inside their stepmother's vagina. Something else must be going on, thought the boy, like a hidden level in a video game.

Roth and Sybil got the children ready for the bus and saw them off up at the corner. She linked her arm in his. "I'm sorry," she said.

"What for."

"This whole operation thing makes you uncomfortable, and I'm being pushy.

Forgive me. If you do it, you'll do it when you're ready, and from now on, I'll be *schtum*."

"*Schtum* and you have never been that close, Sybil. But thank you. I am going to do it, though. I will."

"I know you will," she said, and she squeezed his arm tight to her body. "Then you can have me at the drop of a hat, Mr. Roth."

HE HAD TO ADMIT, there was an imperishable upside to the whole thing, and that was the thought of the entire garden of Sybil's body, open at all hours. He'd always been able to admit to himself that where his relationships were concerned, lust had always been a factor. Even the dourest rabbis of history would have told you no man or woman marries for the mere sake of a likeness of mind or spirit. How else to make you "as numerous as the stars in the heavens"? Such a covenant could not be accomplished without giving men and women the benefit of appetites. Roth had never had it in short supply. For a man whose external life had been as dull as the need for money can make it (he operated a company called Storage Solutions), his true life, his inner life, was lush. With Adele it had perhaps been wasted a little: the impatience and artlessness of youth. But with Lila. They'd worn the hinges off each other. Unlike many of the women he'd known then, she didn't care for the strictest of the laws, and she wore jeans and T-shirts. She dressed for comfort. Seeing her walking around the house in the uniform of the pagan world inflamed Roth terribly. He thought it was pathetic that something as banal as blue-jeans could do this to him, but desire blossoms in forbidden soil. He imagined that the sight of the tip of a woman's nose would have a similar effect on his Moslem brethren. As long as husband and wife could be kind to each other, the prohibited was the seedbed of passion.

ROTH'S UNCERTAINTY about his options (he would never have used the word *bewilderment*) brought him to Beth Israel, to see Rabbi Stern. Roth had long since given up on making sense of the many laws that were to govern his life and his behaviour. These things had been drummed into him as a child, which was part of the reason he had strayed, although straying from orthodoxy to conservativism was a deviation on the order of dark rye to light. In any case, much of what he once thought he knew was now so much clutter in his mind. Stern had admonished him about his confusion many times: Roth was dangerously close to leading an unguided—and therefore impious—life.

Stern's study at the temple was cluttered and dark. Only a fish tank that took up one whole wall provided a useful light. Going into the rabbi's office was like descending into an underground exhibit, with its blue glow and its undulating creatures moving back and forth behind glass.

"Sybil wants me to have a vasectomy," said Roth once he'd sat down.

"You have a problem with this?"

"No, not really." The rabbi unwrapped a candy and left the silvery paper on the tabletop. He waited for Roth. "My problem is that I've had three wives. How do I know this is the last one? What if I need—?"

"What if you need your *sperm*?"

"Yes."

"Mmm," said Stern. "You love Sybil?"

"Yes."

"So? Have a vasectomy. You're almost fifty, Nathan; Sybil's almost forty. It's over for children."

Roth nodded. It wasn't really about loving Sybil, though. It was about the future, and what it might want from him. What if, one day, it wanted him to start over, not as a husband, but as a father? What if he blew it this time too, with Mitchell and Sarah? "What if I *want* more children, though?" he said.

The rabbi leaned forward. He regarded Roth as one would look into a cloudy puddle, to judge its depth. "What are you thinking, Nathan?"

"I want to save some of my sperm. In case."

"You can't do that."

"Why."

Stern lifted his large hands off the table and let them drop back down. The noise startled Roth; they made a sound like two mallets falling. "Either you commit the sin of Onan, or you commit adultery—and not just a garden variety adultery my friend—one you're *planning*. This is like the same difference between first- and second-degree murder."

"I thought it was a *mitzvah* to have children, Rabbi. To repopulate the land."

Stern extended a hand toward Roth as if it held an offering. "Here, Nathan. You go to some place that will freeze your sperm, and if that sperm is not used to make a baby, then you've spilled it in vain. *But—*" and here he held out the other hand "— let's say you *intend* to make a baby with that sperm. We already know it's not going anywhere near Sybil. Correct?"

"Yes."

"*So*, this sperm is intended for *another* woman. That's your premeditated sin, Roth. This is not good."

Roth stood up then, irritated enough to raise his voice. "Look—"

"—sit down," said the rabbi.

"Can't you just advise me as a man? Either I do this thing that makes me a bad person, or I go crazy. You tell me."

"Don't do it, Nathan," said Stern. "It's not for me to tell you to go flush your soul down the toilet so you can have your cake and eat it too." He stared at Roth a moment, blinking. "You know what I mean."

Sweat slicked Roth's back. What had he thought the man was going to tell him, anyway? He shook the rabbi's hand.

"You've made up your mind?"

"I don't know," said Roth.

IS THERE MUCH DIFFERENCE, Roth wondered, between a person who is interested in your money and one who is interested in your soul? Should you automatically assume that the second person is looking out for you? From his years of working in a retail environment, Roth was sure he knew a great many more fulfilled people among those who had placed their faith in business, rather than in God. Money had a reassuring finiteness to it; money didn't get ambiguous or allegorical on you. And although he understood, abstractly, that money *was* a metaphor, it was still true that if something cost ten dollars and you had ten dollars, you could have it. It didn't seem to work that way in the Kingdom of Heaven. The news from up there was that through hard work and application you could ruin your first marriage, but then you could have a second chance, and you could even have two more lovely children and do it right this time. But then you could lose it all over again. If you invested your soul at ten per cent compounded over fifty years, you could still have nothing in the end.

Roth knew that this kind of talk was just some bitter kind of Hebraic stand-up routine that looped through the mind of anyone who'd lost something or someone important to them. In went all the way back to the Tribes of Israel in the desert outside of Egypt, when God said, *Guess what? You're not slaves no more. Congratulations. Oh, by the way, did I mention the desert? Forty years only, without nothing to eat except crackers and scorpions? I thought maybe I didn't say the desert part.* No doubt that when they finally got there—the Land of Milk and Honey—half got diarrhea from the milk, and the other half went into anaphylactic shock from the honey. No, blind faith was a bad thing, and perhaps the elders were just elders, a little confused from centuries of trying to figure out the worth of an ox. Roth was smart to go it alone.

As it was, he'd already had the advice of the vasectomist. He'd made and actually kept an appointment some weeks earlier. He'd gone to the doctor's office, out in the east end, and kept his eyes down in the waiting room filled with other men. There was a receptionist whose hair was the only thing that showed over the countertop. The sound of unread pages being turned was the only noise in the place, except for the occasional invitation to someone to go see the doctor. Then they'd come out and huddle over the desk with the secretary, and most of them, at one point, would offer a nervous laugh, then take their coat and leave.

When it was his turn, Roth went in and sat in the doctor's private office. It had all the soothing ornaments a doctor's office is supposed to have: the signed documents, the wood panelling, the framed pictures with their backs turned like embarrassed party guests. The only thing out of place was the big plastic testicle on the doctor's desk. This he used to demonstrate the brief, painless procedure with the brief, only slightly uncomfortable recovery period. Roth tried to pay attention to the big nut with its removable layers and tubes, but all he could hear the doctor say, at least three times, was, "Then we make a very small incision here."

"I thought there was a method that didn't require an incision," said Roth.

"Well, some doctors use a puncture method that's more like making a little hole through which the vas deferens is extracted, but it's essentially the same thing, Mr. Roth. You have to get into the scrotum somehow, and from there it's a cruel cut no matter how you look at it." He'd taken the top layer off to show the blue vas deferens beneath, and now he pulled the vas apart in the middle. It split into two with a neat little *click*.

Roth nodded. "I see."

"Do you have any more questions?"

"Can it be reversed?"

The doctor sighed dramatically and looked away from Roth, tapping the denuded testicle with the tip of his pen. Roth saw now that the top of the plastic model was stippled with pen marks. "If you are concerned with reversal, Mr. Roth, you may want to think harder about your reasons for seeking vasectomy. Are you sure they're *your* reasons? The point of a vasectomy is to take the bullets out of the chambers, so to speak. If you think you're going to want to use live ammo again, then maybe this isn't for you."

"I just want to know what my options are."

"Some doctors undo it," he said curtly. "I don't. It's not *meant* to be undone." He brusquely reassembled the model, snapping the two ends of the vas deferens back together and covering it with the scrotal sac. "And it's not this easy, either," he said.

Back out at the reception, the woman gave him a nice smile and stood up.

"Will you be making an appointment, Mr. Roth?"

"Yes," he said quietly. She looked down behind her desk and removed two sheets of paper, which she spun toward him so that he could read them. She pointed out what he needed to know with the tip of a pencil.

"No anti-inflammatories for ten days before the procedure," she said, "so no Aspirin or Advil, you know. Tylenol is okay." He nodded dumbly. "Make sure there's someone here to pick you up afterwards, and remember to bring this form—" here she brought out the second sheet "—which is a consent form you have to sign saying you understand the risks and that we don't guarantee sterility."

"It's not guaranteed?"

"Well, it is," she said, "but by law we have to put that. And will you be paying for prep or would you like to prep yourself?"

"I'm sorry?" Roth said.

"Someone here can shave the area for you, at a nominal cost, or you can do it yourself."

His mouth was dry. "I'll do it myself."

"Very good," said the receptionist, folding his information and slipping it into an envelope. "Just make sure you don't do the whole operation by accident."

Roth laughed nervously.

IT SEEMED TO HIM that in all the years he'd been seeing doctors the luxury of a bedside manner was one rarely found. If you weren't really that sick, it was a quick scribble on a piece of paper and out you went, there were sicker people than you. But if you *were* truly ill, if there was no hope for you, it was worse. Dead customers are no good for any business. When Lila had taken ill, he'd been amazed at the clinical distance they encountered at their various stops on the road to her death. It had got so bad that Roth wanted to strangle some of them. *What would it cost for a little comfort?* But Lila kept herself in check. She wanted to save her strength.

Little bits of her went off regularly to be tested. Cell counts and biopsies. The children didn't understand why their mother was losing weight. She told them she was tired from the sickness and didn't need as much to eat as she did before, but Roth knew it was because they were taking her away, biopsy by biopsy. Stern had been cold comfort here as well.

"She'll go to her death half the woman she once was," he'd complained to the rabbi. "And you tell me it's still kosher with the *meshiach*?"

"God's not going to keep Lila out of the Promised Land because she had a few operations. It doesn't work that way."

"Then how *does* it work?"

Stern stood up then, his face dark with worry. "Nathan, you need to go and be with her and with your children and stop worrying about the next life. She needs you."

He was shaking. "Do I keep everything they take out of her, Rabbi? Does it all get buried with her?"

"The cancer isn't *her*. And it's nor the point, Nathan. It's a metaphor, this whole thing. You want to present yourself to God as an *entire* human being, not just a complete body. Think about it like that."

THIS WAS WHAT was in Roth's mind as he drove north through midtown to the clinic he'd found in the Yellow Pages. The clinic was beyond where he'd grown up, clear beyond all the Reform synagogues with their big lawns and *goyish*-looking stained-glass windows. It was in a strip of offices beside a tennis club, a non-descript building with a sign on the door that said simply, FDS Technologies.

There was no one in this waiting room, and the secretary sat at a desk, where it was easy to make eye contact.

"Mr. Roth," she said. He was right on time. She stood up and came around the desk to shake his hand. "Why don't I take your jacket and you can fill out a few forms. Then we'll go in."

He took the forms from her and sat. He couldn't imagine how he was going to provide a sample; there was nothing about the place that made it likely. The lady took the clipboard back from him after she saw him sign it.

"It's two hundred dollars the first year and seventy-five for every year afterwards. That's for one vial. It's half-price for every vial after that."

"How many vials do most people give?"

"Oh, that's a personal decision, Mr. Roth. Some people give two or three, and some even come back after that and give a few more. It's whatever you think you'll need, and whatever you're comfortable with."

The image of the back rooms behind her desk filled with men on return visits filled Roth with disgust. Did some people treat this as a hobby? This last-ditch, strip-mall, storage facility? At least the place he ran had pretty signage and he could look his customers in the eye. "I think I'll just be doing the one."

"All right then."

"It's in case of …" He hunted in his wallet for a credit card. "I probably won't ever need it."

"If you ever get to the point where you want us to dispose of the vial, we do that at no extra charge."

"Can somebody else use it?"

"I'm not sure what you mean, Mr. Roth."

"Maybe for medical research. Or for a couple who can't have one on their own."

"We can't pass along unwanted specimens, I'm sorry. You can have it back if you choose, but otherwise we destroy it."

This information sent Roth into a strange revery, this notion that he could have his own sperm back. He imagined himself, perhaps twenty years down the road, a vasectomized man about sixteen hundred dollars out-of-pocket, finally returning to FDS Technologies to reclaim his specimen, and then onward to one of the doctors in town who actually did reversals, where he'd have his tubes reconnected and his own sperm put back into his own testicles. How he'd laugh at the rabbi then. *Who's a sinner now, Stern?*

"Mr. Roth," the receptionist repeated. "If you'll come with me?"

He followed the woman down a hall of doorways. To the clinic's credit, they had not decorated the walls with pictures. What do you put on a wall in such a place? Everything could be taken the wrong way.

The woman was approaching a door with a blue plastic tag on it. She turned it around on its hook to its red side and opened the door with a key. "For your privacy, Mr. Roth, the lock on the other side of this door, once you turn it, locks the room from the inside. So you can relax knowing there is no way that anyone can enter."

She pushed the door open and they went inside. There was a single bed and a La-Z-Boy chair, in a space that looked like a very nice bachelor apartment. There was a bookshelf with a few books on it (no erotic masterpieces, noted Roth, seeing the names Deighton and King), and there were a couple of cabinets and a television hanging from a steel pole in the ceiling. The receptionist put a glass vial down on a desk beside the door.

"Now, this room is yours, Mr. Roth, for as long as you like. In that cabinet over there—" she pointed to the space below the television "—are some items you may feel you need, and many men do use them, so please feel free. Don't be embarrassed. This is the business we're in and the thing we really want is a good, healthy specimen to be put aside and kept for future use, so it's important to relax and let your body do what it knows how to do. That's the way you get your money's worth. Now, some men prefer to take a nap and take advantage of one of those wonderful things about their physiology, and just do what they need to do as soon as they wake up. This is why we ask you to come in when you've got at least five free hours—that way you can nap if you like."

Roth listened carefully, nodding as if someone were telling him how to operate a new and interesting machine. He felt curiously empty, as though he'd somehow signed away all his worldly possessions and he was the only thing that remained of his life. The receptionist was explaining that there were normal television channels and normal books, everything you might need to feel that you're on a little vacation. She held out her hand and Roth took it with a fixed smile.

"Most men laugh when I say good luck, but good luck." Roth broadened his smile. "To get to the last thing, the actual placement of the specimen, we really do recommend that you use one of the sterilized condoms that you'll find in the drawer beside the bed and only worry about getting the specimen into the bottle once you've got it. So don't get all knotted up over the mechanics of aiming or anything like that. All right, then?"

Roth was still holding the woman's hand. "All right," he said, and she went out and he turned the big silver lock to the left and stood alone in the quaint, anonymous room.

A HALF-HOUR LATER, Roth lay under the covers in the little bed, thinking maybe he'd drowse. He'd told Rachel, his manager, that he was not going to be available all afternoon owing to the fact that he was having minor day surgery, something to do with his dermatologist and some liquid nitrogen. Sybil never called him at work, so there was little worry that he'd later have to square anything with her. At the very

least, he wouldn't have to square the details, since Rachel hadn't asked for any, derma-
tological procedures being the kind of thing people were not so naturally curious
about.

He had spent the better part of twenty minutes utterly failing to accomplish
something he'd been doing successfully since before his bar mitzvah. The banal
fantasies he'd called to action lacked any erotic dimension, and he'd lain in the bed
feeling squalidly lonesome. His imaginings had segued within five minutes to a
fantasy in which he was in front of a Russian firing squad, his pants around his
ankles, and he would be shot if he did not bring himself to orgasm. This was an
involving fantasy, but it had no power to bring about the required reaction, so he'd
stopped altogether. So far his experience at FDS Technologies (*A public company*, he'd
noted on the form he had to fill out) had veered between horror and despair.

Beside the bed was an array of switches, and he experimented with them until one
dropped the room into darkness. Being less aware of where he was might help, he
thought, and he settled himself down into the bed again. In the jet darkness, he
couldn't see anything at all, but he was suddenly more aware of the workings of the
building: the air being shuttled from one space to the next, overhead lights somewhere near, coolly buzzing, and even conversation, distant and with a hollow bass-
line, maybe even in the restaurant three doors down from where he was.
Nevertheless, he closed his eyes and focused, and began to build himself an imaginary woman. She was wearing a one-piece red bathing suit and her legs were oiled
with lotion. The straps coming off her shoulders barely contained her breasts. She
was darkly tanned, and her hair was raven black. Roth had her slip the bathing suit
off, one shoulder at a time, peeling it over her chest and down her belly. She gracefully brought out one foot and then the other, gestures that he found stirring. Then
she stood there naked in front of him, her legs open a little, one fist on a cocked hip,
a sun-kissed Amazon.

She was beginning to work for him; Roth kept his eyes squeezed shut and moved
a hand into place. But the moment he made contact with himself, the Amazon's
breasts began to sag and the nut-brown nipples enlarged and became uneven. Her
hair went sandy blonde, and dark lines appeared below her navel, rivulets of flesh
that swam down toward her pubic hair. The long, thin legs thickened, and puckered flesh popped out on her thighs. Roth tracked his gaze up her body—the loved,
imperfect body—and reached Lila's sad face. She was smiling at him, the smile
meant to reassure him. She put her hands on his chest, spreading her fingers so that
his hair sprouted between them, a forest of grey in the interstices of her long brown
fingers. And she put her mouth to him, taking him in, enclosing and containing
him, and he died there. She could not contain him, he could not allow that,
although he had wished the best of him, the most vital parts of himself could have
done that for her.

He opened his eyes on the darkness again and fumbled for the light. The room blinked into existence around him, the sterile replica of a warm and homey space. What kind of sin was it that not only was he about to spill his seed in vain (with his luck), but that he appeared to want to commit the infidelity that Rabbi Stern had spoken of with his dead wife?

He pushed the covers back with his feet, shoving them off the bed. He was not tired enough to nap and had no faith, anyway, that he'd wake up in a state of physiological readiness, as the receptionist had so admiringly suggested.

Roth went into the bathroom and splashed some water on his face. He was surprised to see how red his cheeks were. Then he went back out and, without a pause in his step, he strode over to the cabinet under the hanging television. The items the receptionist had referred to were here, magazines printed on a paper stock much glossier than in any of the magazines he read. He dared not touch them, sharply aware of the duties they'd been pressed into by other clients of FDS Technologies. Despite their glossiness, he was not sure how easily such things wiped clean. On top of the magazines was the television converter; a thin strip of paper taped to the bottom of it said, simply, "Channel 55." Roth switched on the television and found it was tuned to Channel 11. Haltingly, he went up the dial, station by station, pausing on all the soap operas and the home shopping and the midday movies. He passed all the cable stations he and Sybil watched in the evenings and was surprised to see that their midday programming was just as interesting. They showed yet more of the dangerous car chases and explorations of distant ecologies that were their nighttime specialties.

When he got to 54 (a channel that specialized in foreign sports), Roth paused, his eyes feeling heavy and his breathing tight, then he switched to 55. There, a bright pink surface moved rhythmically to a musical score that might have been written for a bad spy film. He knew he was looking at a body, or bodies, and after a moment he made out that the largest object on the screen was the back of a woman's leg, which she herself was holding up (he could make out her forearm at the top of the screen, tucked under the back of her knee), and therefore, following down, the expected anatomies came into view.

The camera changed angle, and now it was clear what Roth was looking at. Neither performer wore anything, although the woman still had on a pair of socks. He stared at the image, under which he could make out the repetitive sounds of the man's effort and the woman's apparent pleasure, and felt his body respond. Now he could probably do it, as long as he was quick about it and didn't think too much and didn't take his eyes off the television. This was why the La-Z-Boy was positioned the way it was, about six feet from the cabinet, since you could tilt it back and be right in the eyeline of the television. But whereas Roth could count on the bedsheets having been changed, the chair was upholstered, and nothing could compel him to sit down on it. Instead, he gingerly lowered his pants, put the converter on the floor, took a deep breath, and the man on the television withdrew himself from his partner and spilled himself in vain all over her face.

"For Christ's sake!" shouted Roth, completing some kind of sin circuit, and he reached down violently for the remote as the woman on the screen began massaging the vainly spilled fluids into her chest and neck. "Lord, Lord," Roth groaned, pushing the buttons to switch the images off. He pressed the power button, but nothing happened. He whacked the device against his leg in fury, stumbling backwards and wrenching his pants up. But this somehow turned up the volume so that the murmured sounds of approval coming from the woman filled the room with a low, wet growling. Roth's arms and legs went cold and he was afraid he might black out. He went right up under the television and jumped up to hit the power switch on the console, and on his second try, the converter slipped from his hand and hit the floor and the batteries spilled out. At the same moment, the channel changed as well, and Roth was looking at a news report from the Middle East.

He let his shoulders drop and he exhaled, his heart still squeezing madly inside his chest. He would not do this; he knew it now. This last moment in his life when his body might have had some role in the future had passed. He got down on the floor and started to look for the batteries, then had to sit up on his haunches to collect his air again. The sound from the television was encompassing; he was sure they could hear it three doors down. Instead of a hyperventilating woman, it was now an American newscaster's voice filling the room.

Someone had blown up a bus in Haifa. Above Roth's head, yellow tape flapped in close-up at the perimeter of the scene. The newscaster's voice numbered the casualties and reported that the work of the police had just begun. The camera closed in on the cramped space of the disaster, the shattered form of the bus at its centre, bits of red steel pointing up nakedly. The police stood outside the tape while men in green and white uniforms wandered the site, their hands protected by surgical gloves. The voice swarmed the air around Roth with its urgency, identifying the men as orthodox Jews appointed as representatives of the community, there to gather anything that looked like human remains for the sake of religious burial. They were allowed access to such disasters to do holy duty, combing with their bodies bent double the dark little spaces where someone's hand might have come to rest, where a strip of flesh might be clinging to a shard of glass like a flag. All of this went into their bags, to be blessed and returned to the earth where, at some longed-for moment in the future, the Angel of Mercy would open the graves and gather the assembly of the chosen, recreating their shattered bodies from remains.

Roth watched the scene numbly, his hands limp at his sides, his ears pulsing with the sounds of the ruined street. And as the men continued their terrible work, moving slowly back and forth over the smoking street, he realized they were calling his name, they were saying, *Roth, Roth*, over and over. They believed he was there. He was the only survivor and they were calling for him. *Roth!* they were calling. Hearing his name spoken like that made a strange kind of sense to him, and it filled his head with brightness, it made him feel like he was carrying a charge.

"I'm here," he said quietly, standing and stepping back so they could see him. He raised his arms; the men were frantically searching for him now, shouting *Roth, can you hear us?* His face lit up with hope, it glistened, he could hear them, they must be close now. He called out to them: "Here I am! I'm here!"

But despite answering them, they continued to look. What if they did not find him? What if he perished here, despite their efforts, what if he died under this great weight and he never again saw the children who still loved him? He would never fix then what was wrong in his life; his love would never grow to gather in his other children, the ones he'd lost, or grow to tie Sybil to him more perfectly. He would never have the chance to accept that he would grow older now, his strength would wane; here he would die at an age people would say was too young, and he didn't want that—he *was* too young, he still had much of his old vitality, he could have been a father again at this age if he'd wanted! All of this would fade from him, and he from it if the men gave up, and he cried out in desperation now, "HERE I AM!" until finally the door behind him was forced open and a security guard stood in the verge with the woman from the reception and they called out to him over the din. But Roth could not hear them; his attention was fastened to the flesh collectors. He was waiting until one of them turned and finally saw him there and reached out a gloved hand to deliver him to safety.

Nadir
Gayla Reid

THIS WAS THE CHRISTMAS Nixon carpet-bombed Hanoi and I went up to the lake to be with Max.

WE ARE SITTING in the house, waiting for the parents.

All along the south side of the house big windows look out to the lake.

They will come in through the front door, on the north side. There are no windows at eye level on that side of the house, just a long clerestory row.

The house itself is one big room. Last summer Paul put the windows in and insulated the place. Installed a fireplace and some space heaters.

The pink insulation, under stapled plastic, is everywhere.

It's like living on a construction site, says Paul, boasting a bit.

It's very cosy, says Max.

Very cosy indeed, I say.

Rosemary gets up and goes to the window, then turns and watches the door.

Rosemary, Paul's wife, teaches art at the school in town. I think of how she claims she is going to carve her family history on the front door. Hers and Paul's.

What about her extramarital affairs, I wonder. A border, perhaps?

And what will she do about her brother?

We listen for the crunch of tires.

We do not talk much.

"In for another ball-freezer," says Max, looking out to the lake.

When I get back to the city, I tell myself, I'll write him a letter. A carefully worded letter.

"What do you bet she'll be wearing a coat of good Republican cloth," Max says.

He's referring to Rosemary's mother. He isn't speaking to the rest of us, not really. He just needs to say it out loud.

Because of the war, Rosemary has not been on speaking terms with her parents. She did, however, go to visit them once, right before she and Paul and Max came to Canada. She took her mother's credit cards and went shopping for the things they'd be needing: blankets, cutlery, stainless steel cookware with copper bottoms. After she'd finished, she left the wallet with its credit cards on a park bench.

For others to share, she said.

Paul's parents, like Rosemary's, support the war. But they keep in touch, sending presents for birthdays, American Thanksgiving, Christmas.

Max's father, who is in the Communist Party, the CPUSA, thinks Max should have gone to prison.

To be in Canada was to be ineffectual, Max's father said.

Nobody is interested in what my father, far away in Australia, thinks about the war.

THE PARENTS ARRIVE. They walk in and sit down by the fire.

The mother, all unknowing, heads straight for the chair her son used last. She has the same red hair as Chuck's, but hers is carefully dyed. It curls in towards her neck in a style that reminds me of June Allyson, the fifties film star.

I can see her sitting at a dressing table, looking in a winged mirror. On the dressing table there is a silver brush, comb and mirror set, an anniversary gift from her husband.

The father is more like Rosemary, small and wiry. A pat reversal of genes. No hanky-panky here, folks.

The father is the kind of man I've seen getting on to planes first, travelling first class; the confident, tight-jawed American businessman. He was in the Pacific during World War II. That makes him one of those Yanks my own father so heartily approves of. The Battle of the Coral Sea. But of course you'd be too young to know about that, my father always says.

Chuck's mother and father sit meekly in their chairs and they listen to the story of what happened.

They helped put the bombers into the air.

They betrayed their own son.

I'D COME UP BY TRAIN. It was dark when I got on in the city and dark again long before I got off. The train laboured through the canyon and out into sagebrush country, where snow lay like salt on the dry ground.

I swept off the train as theatrically as I could. Max liked to greet me by bending over me and leaning me way back, as in some forties movie. Max had studied theatre arts down in L.A., so this kind of carry-on came easily to him.

Paul was at the station, too.

Paul did the driving. It was twelve miles out to the lake. Over the bridge and up the hill and we were waved over by the Mounties. They were wearing their big caps with furry earmuffs.

One of the Mounties stuck his head in, cap and all, to see if he could get a whiff. We were clean.

"Doing a brisk trade in drunks," Paul said, after we'd pulled away. "Drunks coming home from their office parties."

"Wouldn't mind one of those hats," said Max. "Very Russian."

None of us drank much. Drinking was what our parents did—the cocktail generation. Drinkers were limited people, weighed down, made dim, confused and finally nasty by all that liquid sloshing around inside them. (Although I did have a bottle of Bristol Cream in my suitcase. For Max and me to share.)

Come summer Max would be back with me in our apartment. He was only up at the lake until break-up. He couldn't leave his political work any longer than that.

He'd be coming back. That's why I didn't move up to the lake. It was for such a short time, as Max said.

"There's something you should know," Max said, as we left the highway and began to lurch along the road to the lake.

"Chuck's turned up."

CHUCK KEESING. Name right out of a cigarette ad. Chuck, Rosemary's brother. Unlike Paul and Max, who had managed to keep their student deferments going for years, and who had come to Canada days before their pre-induction physicals, Chuck had been drafted. He'd gone AWOL, intending to desert.

His father, with his mother's full support, had phoned the base and told his captain where Chuck was.

Chuck had done time in the stockade.

Waiting to be shipped to Nam, at Fort Ord, Chuck had gone AWOL again. This time, he made sure his parents didn't know anything. He went underground.

But he wrote to his sister, Rosemary. Letters with no return address, signed with the name of their childhood dog. Rosemary didn't have to be told who Rex was, and anyway she recognized the handwriting.

Chuck was in San Francisco, in Denver, in L.A. In San Diego he met a woman, fell in love. Her family were Quakers. She and Chuck moved in together above her father's shoe store.

Through that family Chuck became involved in antiwar politics. He joined the Winter Patriots Organization.

Rosemary showed Max Chuck's letters about joining the Winter Patriots Organization and Max put his arms around her for an awfully long time. Anyone would think that Rosemary had joined the Winter Patriots herself.

It's a play on words, Max explained to me. Thomas Paine spoke of the soldiers who deserted at Valley Forge as "sunshine patriots."

Thomas Paine. Valley Forge.

Americans expected you to know everything.

Chuck had done a lot of things with the Winter Patriots Organization, or the WPO, as Max called it. The WPO had speak-outs where vets described the ghastly things that had happened in Vietnam, and the way their training got them into a head space to butcher.

Rosemary's letters from Chuck were full of this. For Max, especially, who was organizing against the war from outside the country, Chuck's letters became news from the front.

Chuck was an underground fighter in the belly of the beast, Max said.

"WHAT'S HE DOING UP HERE?" I asked.

We had to go extra slow because of the fresh snow. Nearly all the places on this smaller road were summer cottages, deserted now.

Chuck's cover had got blown somehow. There were agents in the WPO, everyone knew that. Sometimes a group had more agents than real members, Max said.

The Quakers helped him out. They got in touch with some peace people in Vancouver. Who drove down to Washington to pick Chuck up. An elderly couple, ever so straight, in a big Detroit gas guzzler. Chuck in the back seat. Gliding up to the border guard.

Where are you from, sir?

Canada.

All Canadian citizens?

Yes, sir.

How long have you been out of the country?

Just down for the day, sir.

Are you bringing anything back? Cigarettes? Tobacco? Alcohol?

No, sir.

And gliding on through.

Illegal still, but out of reach of the FBI.

Chuck had spent the night with that family. Next day they put him on the train.

"Chuck's not in good shape," Max warned, as we stamped up the stairs to the house. "Not what you'd expect."

CHUCK WAS A THIN, long, red-haired man. He sat by the fire, rubbing his hands up and down his thighs.

"Did you get the cinnamon sticks?" Rosemary asked Paul.

"They were all out," he said.

"What about the red wine?"

"I forgot."

"You forgot."

"Yep." Not at all repentant, either.

"So much for that," Rosemary said.

She went over to the bedroom corner, behind the makeshift curtain, and began, noisily, to wrap presents. The paper crackled.

PAUL SAT in the biggest chair by the fire, opposite Chuck.

With fastidious movements of fingers and thumbs, Paul began to roll a few numbers. These he arranged tidily on a small table at his side, much as he had earlier piled wood by the fireplace: ready for the night ahead.

Between Paul and Chuck was Che's blanket. As soon as Che saw Paul settling in, he came to the blanket. Round and round, three times. Then, plop; sigh.

"Such a deep doggy sigh," Paul said, interrupting his joint rolling to caress Che's black head. "Were you bored without me, my precious?" Che leaned his head into Paul's hand. "You and me, babe," Paul told him, in a confidential tone.

Chuck rocked uneasily in his chair.

The Chuck of the letters would have even now been chewing the fat with Max, dissecting Nixon's sordid behaviour.

This Chuck had nothing to say.

MAX MOVED AROUND THE ROOM, humming. Hummed his way over to the bedroom corner. Went behind the curtain.

"What's up, kiddo?" he asked. You could hear everything, the curtain made no difference.

"We were going to have a little mulled wine," replied Rosemary. "But now, it seems not."

"A little mulled wine goes a long way," I said, to nobody in particular.

"Rosa want a back rub?" Max asked.

"Rosa want," she said, in a tiny girl voice.

I knew right away.

ROSEMARY IS SMALL AND DELICATE. Although dark rather than fair, she looks like Mia Farrow: waif. When the movie *Rosemary's Baby* came out, Max said, Better not get pregnant, Rosa. Wouldn't want to have to worry about the patter of tiny hooves.

Rosemary does want to get pregnant. She has a short cycle and only one ovary (she had a cyst on the other and they had to take it out). But then you never know, perhaps it is Paul. Perhaps Paul has a low sperm count; he hasn't gone for tests.

Maybe, I think, Rosemary hopes that Max …

But Max is a total fusspot. Have you got your gong in? Oh yes, Max always has to know. He takes more interest in that thing than I do myself.

Perhaps that's just with me.

IF YOU WENT into the bathroom and switched off the light, you could look through the breaks in the plywood into the big room. (They hadn't got the insulation up in the bathroom yet.) Behind the bathroom door there was a stepladder. Once you got up on that you had a really good look. You could see right over the bedroom curtain.

Max and Paul and Rosemary went way back to the old days at UCLA. They'd come to Canada together, the three of them. Driving up the coast, they'd heard that Bobby Kennedy had been assassinated.

Max would go up to Rosemary and Paul, put an arm around each. I really love you guys, he'd say.

But he'd never had sex with Rosemary. Paul couldn't handle it, Max would explain. And add: Between you and me, sweetheart, my good buddy Paul is a bit of a Kingston Trio type. All buttoned up.

So what had changed?

Did Paul know? Surely, he must.

Sooner or later they'd notice how long I was taking. I hurried down the stepladder, flushed the toilet, and left the bathroom.

Paul looked over right away.

"Come and put a record on," he said to me.

He does know, I decided. He's craven, like me.

Paul fiddled with his little pile of joints. Finally he lit one, passed it to Chuck.

Who took a toke and shut his eyes. Eyes still shut, Chuck reached down beside his chair, brought up a bottle. Southern Comfort. He was drinking it straight, but only in tiny, abstemious sips.

Whenever Chuck made any kind of move, I noticed, he rocked himself afterwards, as if he needed to regain his equilibrium.

Chuck's a space case, I thought.

I played the Carly Simon, just released. Carly was standing in front of a bunch of London traffic.

"Looks like Piccadilly," I told Paul.

Max and Rosemary came out from behind the curtain. They stood in front of the fire, warming their bums.

Carly was wearing a dark red top. You could almost see her nipples. Carly's big sensual mouth. You're so vain, she sang. Was she referring to Mick Jagger or Warren Beatty?

Max said it was Beatty.

I knew precisely what Max would like to do with Carly. On the bathroom floor. Would Paul?

Next Max played the new Bette Midler. We're going to the chapel and we're gonna get married.

"Remember that, Paul?" Rosemary asked.

Rosemary and Paul were childhood sweethearts; they'd met at high school; they'd gone to the senior prom together.

"And we'll never be lonely any more," Rosemary said. "You know we really believed that. Sweet Jesus."

Paul poked at the fire.

"Of course, you were so much older then, you're younger than that now," Paul said. He said this in a mild kind of way that threatened disaster. Not now, but later. It was a line from somewhere. I knew I was supposed to know it.

"Time for the news, folks," Max announced. He switched on the TV and we watched the CBC.

"In the wake of the peace negotiations deadlock, the United States has launched a massive aerial bombardment of North Vietnam. The air offensive, which was first denied then later confirmed by the U.S., is reported to have started Sunday in the Haiphong area and represents the first U.S. military activity north of the twentieth parallel since last October."

Rosemary had begun to hand around mandarins, wrapped in their small pieces of green tissue.

She stopped at this point, with three mandarins still in her lap. Max and Paul were holding their mandarins in their hands, the green tissue still around them.

"In Paris, head of the Hanoi delegation to the Peace Talks, Le Duc Tho, has condemned the raids as 'barbarous.' Meanwhile, President Nixon has said that the bombing will continue until Hanoi agrees to the peace terms."

"That bastard," said Paul.

"That total, utter and complete bastard," said Max.

"Radio Hanoi reports that the bombing has caused the deaths of many hundreds of civilians and the destruction of thousands of dwellings. The U.S. command insists that it is attacking only military targets."

This roused Chuck. "Fuckin' assholes," he said. "Fucking bleeding assholes."

It was one of the two things I ever heard him say.

AFTER THE NEWS, we went to bed.

Max's bed was on the opposite side of the room to Paul and Rosemary's corner.

I lay on my side of the bed, as close to the edge as possible. Did Rosemary wait until Paul's snores were genuine? (A wife can tell.) Did she then creep over here, to this bed, to my spot? And lie here? Daring, generous, welcome.

Chuck was still up. You could hear him by the fire, rocking back and forth in his chair, coughing once in a while.

Then he made his way to the bathroom.

Coming out, he tripped over Che's bowls. That seemed to rip something open inside him.

"What the fuck are they doing there?" he yelled. "What are they *doing* there?"

He began to kick the dog dishes, noisy and vicious with his feet.

Rosemary came over, pulling on her dressing gown.

"Just Che's bowls," said Rosemary. "Just the dog food bowls, Chuck."

She was at his side. She was holding him.

Max had got up, too.

"Chuck. It's okay, Chuck. It's all right, honey, everything is all right. That's right, sweetie, come with me. We'll get you into your sleeping bag, okay?"

She was holding Chuck and she was looking over Chuck's shoulder. She was looking over at Max.

I could see her face.

CHRISTMAS EVE MORNING.

We sat in the pale lemon sun and we ate Rosemary's French toast. (Ground cinnamon and walnuts.)

Chuck was still in his sleeping bag, but he was awake. Rosemary took his coffee and French toast and put it on the floor beside him. "Floor service," she said. She poured the maple syrup over the toast. The syrup glistened in the sun.

Max put Van Morrison on the stereo: "Brown Eyed Girl." Max sang along: "Making love in the green grass behind the stadium with you."

Rosemary giggled. A complicit, bragging giggle.

So, I thought, it has been going on since summer.

I took another piece of French toast.

"When that first came out, you know, they wouldn't play it," Max said. "Too explicit. Can you imagine?"

Max was the one doing all the talking.

"Hey man, remember 'Gloria'?" Max asked. "The strip was really wailing, man." I knew what Max was up to. The summer it was all happening, he'd been there (he'd been there, man). In L.A.

"And her name is," Max went on. "And her name is, G-L-O-R-I-A." Spelling it out, the way Van does.

While Max was hanging out on the strip, where it was all happening, tight-ass Paul was at summer school in Indiana, managing to miss the whole thing.

"Who's the grooviest of us all?" I said, as nastily as I could.

"Time to go for the tree," said Paul, asserting himself. "Is Chuck going to come?" he asked Rosemary, as if Chuck himself wasn't right there, in the sleeping bag.

"Do you want to come, Chuck?" Rosemary asked. She went over to her brother's side, knelt down, spoke to him. "Come on, Chuck," she said. "It'll be fun. You'll enjoy it. You'll see."

OFF WE WENT, Paul leading the way, with his chainsaw. We walked up the hill where the power line ran. It had turned perishingly cold, the kind of cold that takes your breath away. February rather than December weather.

I put my scarf around my mouth and nose, pulled my cap way down.

As a boy back in Wisconsin, Paul had been an Eagle Scout. I hurried along, trying to keep up with him. If I walked in Paul's footsteps it made the going easier. But he had such a long stride I couldn't keep up.

I fell back to where Max was.

Unlike Paul, Max was not at his best outdoors. He tended to flail about. Right now he was making things difficult for himself, plunging off the track into deeper drifts of snow.

It could be a perfectly fine sunny day and Max would have trouble finding north, Paul said.

"My feet are turning to ice," I complained.

"Let's wait for Rosemary and Chuck," Max said.

Rosemary and Chuck were way behind, walking much more slowly.

When they finally caught up, I heard Rosemary saying, "… you made a woman with breasts and Mom was nervous Dad would see."

The snow was much drier up here than it was down by the lake. But it still held some moisture. Rosemary lay down in it.

"Come on, Chuck," she urged. "Let's make angels. It was you showed me how."

Slowly, Chuck knelt down in the snow. He stopped and appeared confused, as if unsure what was expected of him next. Then he turned around and managed to lie down. He stretched out his arms and began, tentatively, to move them up and down.

Chuck, putting his arms out in the snow, to please his sister.

On the last full day of his life.

CHRISTMAS MORNING.

I brought out the Bristol Cream for us all to share. We drank it while we exchanged gifts.

It was a grey day but too cold for snow. After breakfast, the men were going out to the lake. This was Paul's idea. It was something he'd done on Christmas mornings as a child. They'd drive out on the lake, carve a hole, and fish. To keep warm, they'd build a fire.

Max gave me a roach clip he'd made himself.

Paul gave Rosemary a watch. "Oh," she said, looking at it, holding it away from her. "A watch. From my very own husband."

Max poured what was left of the sherry into a flask I'd just given him. It was old, with somebody's initials on it. I had found it in a junk store and had been extremely pleased with it.

"Hope it doesn't taste funny in this thing," Max said, sniffing it.

Paul scooped up a pile of joints and patted them into the pocket of his jacket.

"Okay, kids, let's go," he said.

And they went.

ROSEMARY AND I COOKED. From where we were, in the kitchen corner, we could see the three of them. They were small and dark against the grey and white of the day.

I peeled potatoes, chopped carrots, washed Brussels sprouts.

Rosemary did something complicated with red cabbage.

I put the plum pudding on to steam. I'd made it two months before, down in the city, and had moistened it regularly with brandy. It will make a terrific flame, I thought.

Carly Simon sang that sometimes she wished, often she wished, her lover hadn't told her some of the secrets that he had.

"What am I going to do?" Rosemary said suddenly. "About Chuck."

"Do you think he needs to see someone?" I asked.

"What do you think," she said. It wasn't a question.

"Maybe he could go to the clinic," I said. There was a free clinic in the city, no questions asked.

"He might need something more than a trip to the clinic," she said.

"Maybe we could find him a doctor," I said. "Someone political."

Because, of course, it would all have to be under the table.

"It's a thought," Rosemary said.

"Maybe I could get something lined up when I get back," I said.

But Max was the one who knew everybody. If there was some lefty shrink in town who'd be willing to help Chuck, Max would know.

Boldly, I asked: "Have you talked to Max about Chuck?"

"A little," she said. She began to look embarrassed.

We were both quiet then.

She rubbed the dishcloth up and down the counter.

I REMEMBER looking out at the lake just after that. There were only two of them out there. I thought that they looked like figures in a Dutch landscape painting, and that one of them must have gone off behind the bushes to take a leak.

I didn't consider this last thought carefully, or I would have realized that when you're out in the middle of a frozen lake you don't go all the way back to the trees. Especially if you're a man.

Paul and Max both saw him go; they told us.

He'd been standing near the fire, they said, stamping his feet to keep warm. The boots he was wearing were the ones he'd had on when he left San Diego and they were fairly thin. Rosemary had made sure he had gloves and a hat (Paul's old things). But nobody had given a thought to his boots.

Paul and Max had even discussed his leaving. He was walking not towards the house but farther east.

"He's heading for Zandowski's landing," Paul had said. Not only was there a track from Zandowski's to Paul and Rosemary's, but Zandowski was home. The whole family was spending Christmas at the lake because Zandowski, like Paul, had got the place fully winterized last summer.

"He'll be okay," Max had said.

They came home without any fish.

ROSEMARY KEPT THE FOOD WARM in the oven until three in the afternoon. Then we picked at the turkey. The veggies grew cold on the counter.

Paul took the truck out and drove around with Max. After that, we all went out together. By the time we got back it had been dark for hours.

"I think we'd better call the R.C.M.P.," Paul said.

"How will Chuck feel?" Rosemary asked. "Having the pigs set on him."

We got the dope out of the house. We cleared everything out, including the water pipes and my new roach clip. Paul stowed it all in an old cottonwood up the road, well away from the property line.

We didn't say anything to them about Chuck's status. It was normal for a brother to be visiting a sister at Christmas. They set out at first light: Paul, Max, two or three neighbours, some people from town. The Mounties. About noon the call came through.

ROSEMARY PHONED Chuck's girlfriend back in San Diego. They were on the phone for a long time.

Up on the bluffs above the lake.

Slipped, fell.

Lying face down on the lake.

No, it would have been the cold.

A neighbour, yes.

In the ambulance it would have been.

Just feel sleepy and pass out.

Yes, I hope so, too.

SOMETHING HAD TO BE DONE about the parents.

"They have to know, hon," Paul said. "You have to talk to them sooner or later."

"They can stay at a motel," Rosemary said. "Enough is enough."

THE PARENTS ARE SUBDUED when they are at the house. They see the antiwar posters, the coffee table made from an old door, the beds on the floor, the junk store chairs with their Indian spreads. And say nothing.

But when Rosemary drives them back to the motel, they argue. The parents want to take Chuck's ashes back and put them in the family plot.

"Chuck locked up forever in a plot full of Republicans," she tells us. "He just couldn't bear it. I know."

I BECOME THE ONE who stands at the edge of the circle of grief: I feed the others. Turkey sandwiches, cheese and fruit. Steamed pudding, even. Food that lies neglected on plates and is thrown out after a decent amount of time has gone by.

In the drab, pretend chapel attached to the crematorium there is a service of sorts.

"The lord is my shepherd, my ass," says Rosemary, when it is, at last, over.

WE ARE LYING on Paul and Rosemary's bed. Paul, then Rosemary, then Max, then me.

We're toking up, passing the joint silently back and forth. I can feel the bed falling down and down, right through the earth, until it comes out on the other side of the world, in my own country.

There, it is warm. It is summer. A few weeks ago they'd brought home the last of our troops from Vietnam.

In my father's backyard, by the shed, the jacaranda is a leafy world.

You can forget all about the war and just go to the beach.

PAUL REACHES OUT and turns on the TV. He moves it round so we can watch the news from the bed.

"U.S. B52 bombers and fighter bombers resumed attacks in the Hanoi and Haiphong areas of North Vietnam Monday after a thirty-six-hour bombing halt for Christmas.

"The U.S. command in Saigon has reported that bombers have blasted the area with more than 1400 strikes. It was the heaviest raid of the war, they reported, heavier than the massive offensive of the previous week.

"According to Radio Hanoi, the attacks began at 9:30 p.m. local time. The radio report said, and I quote: 'The U.S. B52s came in large numbers and from a high night sky dropped carpets of bombs in the middle of Hanoi and immediate suburbs.'"

Rosemary gets up off the bed and goes to the kitchen cupboard where she is keeping Chuck's ashes.

She boils the kettle and steams the label off the package. The label has Chuck's name on it, then the names of the parents, with Paul and Rosemary's address. It is typed with an ancient typewriter, and each line is indented in the old-fashioned way.

Rosemary unwraps the box and, with a soup spoon, ladles the ashes out into four plastic baggies.

The ashes look yellowish, coarse and somewhat greasy (although I don't touch them). There are bits of bone mixed in.

She wraps these baggies in a silk scarf and puts them in her chest of drawers beside the bed.

"Are you sure you want to do this?" Paul asks.

"Quite sure," she replies.

"Put some more logs on the fire," she tells Max. "Lots more."

IT HAS WARMED UP enough to snow. Now it's coming down in a blizzard.

"The airport will be out of commission," Paul says. "They won't be able to leave from that postage stamp. It'll be closed for days."

He's right, too. Afternoon comes and still the blizzard continues.

"I'll drive them down to the city myself," Paul announces. "Take the four-wheel drive. They can get their flight from there, no sweat."

"Why don't you come too?" Paul says to me. "You want to get back, don't you?"

THE NEXT DAY I drive into town with Paul. Max follows, with Rosemary and Che.

Rosemary gives her mother the package. "He can go home with you now," she says, to her parents.

Her mother takes the ashes. Holds them against her breasts.

"He's quite legal now, Mom."

At lunchtime we stop at a roadside restaurant. It smells of gravy and butter tarts and is overwhelmingly stuffy.

Paul nudges my knee. "Come," he commands.

We go down the hallway and into the men's washroom to do a joint. (We have this theory: it is easier for a woman to plead mistake, causes less ruckus.)

Out the window I can see the back of the Dairy Queen opposite. It has a stack of yellow milk crates by the door. As I watch, a very young man comes out and puts down a saucer of milk for a black cat.

The dope is making me feel tired. Right now, what bed will they be using? Rosemary's or his?

I put my face against the cold, none-too-clean wall.

"Don't fade on me yet, babe," Paul says. He takes my face in his hands and he runs his fingers over my lips. "Many miles to go."

The early dark comes and we drive and we drive, down towards the city. The windshield wipers clear a small space, and the headlights pick up the white stuff, coming at us out of the dark then going swiftly back into the dark again.

When we get into the city and drop the parents off, we'll go back to my apartment.

I wonder what Paul will be like. Will he need coaxing, as Max often does?

Then this happens:

Country Joe and the Fish come on the radio.

Paul begins to sing along. "Come on mothers throughout the land," he sings. He looks over at me and I join in. "Pack your boys off to Vietnam. Come on fathers don't hesitate…. Be the first ones on your block to have your boy come home in a box."

After Country Joe is through on the radio, Paul flips it off.

But we continue to sing that song, Paul and I. And singing it we drive on, down into the cold, wet city. The parents, mute in the back seat.

Behind them, with the suitcases, the surrogate ashes of their son.

One Down

DIONNE BRAND

THERE'S A PICTURE of you at the Hi-Hat Club in Boston in 1955. There's a curl on the left side of your forehead, you have hanging earrings, pearls perhaps, and a black ribbon with a diamanté around your small neck. Your eyes. What to make of your eyes? They are bright, direct, slightly sad because of the way your head tilts to the left. You are smiling. There is a tall glass on the table in front of you. The woman next to you dressed in a dark evening dress is your sister Wanda. She too has pearl earrings, her clutch purse rests on the table, she seems younger. She too is smiling. The man to your left is her husband. He is handsome, his hair is a slick lye perm, a cigarette dangles between the index and middle finger of his right hand. Milton has a beautiful smile—a Nat King Cole smile. All three of you seem cool sitting at the Hi-Hat Club in Boston. There must be music there. Dexter Gordon's band is playing "Don't Worry About Me." Your dress, your dress is two-toned. Was it beige lace and brown taffeta? Your shoes must be stiletto. Your feet are tapping to Dexter Gordon.

The Hi-Hat is packed with suave ebony men and beautiful women. Perfumes thicken the air. A chic well-being pervades. The band is swinging and you feel like dancing. You've been sitting there half the night talking, catching up on the news from Halifax. Talking louder than the music sometimes or dropping your voice behind Carl Perkins's piano solo. You're remembering Gottingen Street and all the young women who would crowd into the beauty parlour on a Saturday, their chatter and laughter and you telling them, "Ladies, ladies, please. We are ladies here." That pretty tilt of your head and the smile which makes you look wistful even at the Hi-Hat Club in Boston in 1955, did you always look that way? Is it the memory of Vi's Studio of Beauty Culture on Gottingen Street that brings it on?

Dexter Gordon's "Rhythm Mad" takes you back to Halifax. That 1940s Dodge sedan of yours—a clunker. When you just bought it, it seemed a slick ride. You were proud of it, you being a woman of moderate means, a woman with a future and plans. That Dodge sedan was your prize, wasn't it? For all the hard work, all the building of yourself you'd done. "Such ambition in a small woman," they must have said at the Cornwallis Street Baptist Church and anywhere else you went. You didn't expect to be in New Glasgow but the Dodge began to give out. Several times you'd stopped, started the engine up again, finally just praying to make it to a garage.

It broke down in New Glasgow on a good day in November 1946. A Friday, light snow fell in the morning but the wind from the sea took it right out. A day with a blue sky, brisk wind. One of those days you loved, crisp, bright. A good day for driving to Sydney. Had to see a man about a new venture. Vi's would be branching out. There were ladies in Sydney who needed their hair done and had nowhere to go. The white beauty salons wouldn't have them. A good opportunity for an ambitious woman like you. And there were young women who could be taught how to do hair, to press and curl and give a permanent, there was a market in Sydney for your hair product line—so it was a good November day. A clean sweet day to drive there—maybe stay over until the Saturday and drive back in time to go to Sunday service at Cornwallis Street Baptist as usual. What Dexter Gordon's saxophone can do! Sweep you back to Cornwallis Street Baptist Church—imagine that.

When you first bought the Dodge, the interior smelled as rich as the life you had in mind. A smooth life. You would work your way through the obstacles. They were just a way of God testing you. But if you had faith and kept your head up, life would open up. It wasn't so bad, if you had faith in God and yourself. The little prejudices would not hold you back. Things weren't always said, mind you, but it was there all the time—the colour bar. But if you put your head down and mind how you went, things would sometimes turn out well. Like the 1940 Dodge sedan smelling new and full of promise. The interior was plaid, green and brown.

Remembering when you bought it—you planned to carry the supplies you ordered from Montréal and, later on, the products from Madame C. J. Walker's of New York. If you had to, you could drive the sedan all the way down to New York City to visit Madame C. J. Walker herself.

The Hi-Hat feels suddenly hot. The band is in the middle of "Rhythm Mad." From the table behind you there is loud laughter. All around you there is quick movement and fast talk. Leroy Vinnegar is on bass. He is doing impossible things with his fingers. The strings on his bass lead to every sinew in the room. Your smile is more wistful, your eyes are brighter, you can see the road into New Glasgow that crisp day. The bass thrums that tensile memory stark. If someone had told you it would turn out the way it did, you wouldn't have believed them. Even though on waking up every day you anticipated trouble, you still wouldn't have believed them. Why a day that started out so simply would end that way.

The Dodge gave a final sputter and you were happy perhaps because at least it wasn't far to the repair shop. You knew how to see the good part of any setback. Maybe it was a small problem and you could get it fixed and be on your way again. At least you weren't stranded on a deserted road between New Glasgow and Sydney. You wouldn't complain. The Dodge was a good car though you'd been overcharged for it. You took the car dealer, Phillip Kane was his name, you took him to court for overcharging you. After all, there was a Wartime Prices Order and whatever his prejudices he didn't have the right to do that. That man didn't know who he was fooling with, Jack said. Jack used to tease you, he did. Said you were too proud. Said you wouldn't pick a stray penny up from the street if you were dying.

That face of yours with its sweet smile, its demure eyes. That face doesn't tell the half of it. There was iron in you. The man at the garage in New Glasgow said it would take time, might take till the next day. He had to put in a new part. He was backed up as it was, he said. Tomorrow for sure. Well, what could you do? No other way to get to Sydney or to get back to Halifax, and besides, you didn't want to leave the Dodge there, that would mean coming back tomorrow anyway.

Jack would be worried so you must've called him at the barbershop to say you'd be staying over. "The King of Gottingen Street," they called him. An easy man with people, friends. Being one of eight children had taught him to get along, smooth things over. A man people seemed to give their trust or love to easily. That was what took you about him. A man with an upward look and faithful, too. He'd travel all the way to Montréal to court you when you were in training at the Field Beauty Cultural School. A dear man. You must've called him. That time of day on a Friday, Jack would be waiting for the onslaught. Men coming out of ships at the dockyard, men preparing for Friday night at the Brown Derby—a cut or a lye slick—men sitting with lye burning their hair straight, having moustaches pruned and tweaked. The talk would be all about music and uplift and where a man could find work in this town—and why after the war and after they served in the army, why was it the same as before they went to fight Hitler. Men from Preston and Tracadie and Truro working day labour would haul their tired legs into Jack's if not to get a cut and shave then just to hear talk, just to meet with other men like them. Knocking the dust off their shoes, willing their rough hands to turn soft on the back of some fine woman that Friday night. They came to Jack's to talk themselves up, to give themselves a bit of courage for the coming week. A shave and a cut would transform them from men with scarcely a penny in their pockets to jazz musicians and athletes—men who could use the raw power of being to make something. "Man, did you hear about that Benny Carter? Said he can hold a note, I tell you. Gon' get me a horn myself someday …" "Seen young Joe Louis fight. No better man …" Every morning that week in November most of them had stood in the early cold of the docks, stamping their feet warm, hitting the numbness out of their bodies, waiting to be picked for a day of lifting and throwing load or cutting fish. It had been a good week and they had extra in their pockets to get a shave, to slip into Jack's chair with a warm towel around their face.

Jack is not with you now, he is not in that photograph at the Hi-Hat Club on Columbus Avenue in Boston. Good as he was, a distance opened between you that Friday in November 1946 when the Dodge broke down. Not right away, but little by little. When you called he must've said, "Do you want me to come out there, baby?" You must've told him that you were fine, no sense in two of you being stranded here and losing business. "Might as well make the best of it," you said. You thought you'd make an evening of it. You knew some folk to stay with overnight. No sense trying a hotel, no sense putting yourself out. No telling the way you'd be treated. So you decided on a movie. You'd packed yourself something to eat for the trip to Sydney. That was supper, and then you would go to the seven o'clock at the Roseland Theatre. This could turn out to be pleasant, after all, you thought, leaving the Dodge at the garage. Tomorrow would be a busy day at Vi's Beauty Parlour. You would have your hands full.

Saturday's at Vi's was quite the social event, quite the time. Everyone, just everyone, would have to get their hair done on a Saturday at Vi's. On Sunday mornings Cornwallis Street Baptist would be a parade of your hair designs. Your hands would ache with washing and shampooing and pressing and curling. The pageboys the French rolls the sleek chignons. Each woman wanted to be unique and you were the artist. You offered tea. You gave your soothing hands to that head, which had had a rough week. You knew that Mrs. Clark's husband was stepping out on her, that Rhoda Murray's son was headed the wrong way, that Glory Spencer had lost her job up in Glace Bay, that all seven children of Mavis and John Deeks had the chicken pox, and that Sylvia Hamilton was planning to run off next Saturday to New York City to be a singer in a band. That was the dream life of all the young girls on Gottingen Street, and Sylvia was determined to live the life. You knew all that Agnes Gordon needed was a little encouragement, a little brightening up to make herself into somebody; that Millie Gains was at the end of her rope with Isaac being late all the time; and you could tell that young one of James and Lettie Howe was hiding a pregnancy under a big coat she wore even on warm days. You knew all this and you knew that people only wanted to strive, to be better than they were.

Secrets and desires you kept like jewels. You had an open fondness for people. That is why your eyes remained bright even in 1955 at the Hi-Hat. No matter what happened you could see the good in it, you could see a positive outcome. The women who came into Vi's admired you for that. You would give them a lift, a feeling of style and charm that their own lives often lacked. The contralto Portia White had her hair specially done at Vi's. That's how classy Vi's Beauty Parlour was.

At Vi's Black women became the ladies they were, leaning back in chairs under heat caps; your gentle hands held the ears down to get the straightening comb at the tightest curls. All week most of the women had been at day jobs doing housework or ironing. Their own hands ached, their feet were talking. They moaned blissfully when they sat down in that chair at Vi's. You worked the oils into their scalps and coaxed kinks onto paper rollers and brush rollers and curling irons. You were careful that the shortest hairs along the hairline were done and you warned customers not to go out uncovered in the rain or snow or stand in a stormy place or else you couldn't be blamed for hair "going back." You added nails and feet to your repertoire. You kept up with new pomades and straighteners and hair greases. You imported Madame C. J. Walker's line of hair care and cosmetics. Cleansing creams, bleaching creams, hand lotions, and hair oils. You lectured on skin care, posture, and beauty secrets.

At the Hi-Hat Club your hands are not visible. What must they look like? Small, capable, strong. Strangely muscular, one suspects. Your nails varnished deep red, the cuticle stripped clean. Your hands lying in your lap, their intelligence hidden. Anyone could see your character in those hands, their wise and sure movement through strands of hair, sorting the different textures, the lengths, and what had to be done. Your hands belie the innocence of your face. It is as if this part of you, your hands, were travelling ahead of the rest of you—their energy, the force and knowledge of them, smoothing a path ahead of everyone, ahead of yourself. Your face reflects wistfulness, something longed for, lost. As if you're saying, "Ah, well, that is the way of the world." Your face is childlike and loving. Whatever is lost there, one can't help but wish it back for you. If only one could. But it is in your hidden hands that we would find the deep resolve of your life.

The Roseland Theatre was just down from the repair shop on Provost. Olivia de Havilland was starring with Lew Ayres in *The Dark Mirror*. You looked at the hand-painted billboard. "To know her is to love her. To love her is to die," it said. Olivia de Havilland. Talk about style. She had a sultry grace you may have admired. A romantic thriller. Just what the evening needed. The Roseland was plush. Beautiful wall murals of roses, cherubs over the doorways, red velvet curtains. Entering the Roseland was entering a place of dreams. Anyone, after passing through the rose-covered door, could find their other best self on the screen. Anyone could live in the celluloid of New York parties and grand staircases, in grand mansions, in ball gowns and tuxedos, in the intrigue of German spies and twisted love, in crazy dance numbers and slapstick humour.

You were a little late, not much, but most people were seated. You gave the cashier a dollar, said, "One down, please." You didn't notice that she gave you a ticket for the balcony with the change. You walked to the house to find a seat. You were ready to become Olivia de Havilland in love with Lew Ayres. A girl was saying something behind you. The ticket taker. It took a minute to register, but she said, "You've got an upstairs ticket, you'll have to go upstairs." Well, you'd asked the cashier for downstairs. Opening your hand with the ticket and the change, you realized the cashier's mistake so you head back to the wicket. "I asked for one downstairs and you gave me one for the balcony. I'd like to exchange." The ticket seller looked impatient. She shook her head at you and half turned away. You repeated, you said in your most polite way, "Excuse me, I'd like one down, you gave me one for the balcony." You felt odd. You didn't want to misjudge. You didn't want to assume but something was creeping up the back of your neck. A recognition, which no matter how often it happened was a shock. And it happened often enough but it always crept up. When the ticket seller's mouth said, "I'm sorry, but I'm not permitted to sell downstairs tickets to you people," you heard each word separately. It was hard putting them together. The time it took seemed long. You saw the oval of her mouth and you saw the words drop. They were hard and brittle, and when you brought all of your will to listening, they added up to what the ticket seller had said. "I'm sorry, but I'm not permitted to sell downstairs tickets to you people."

You people. You turned your back on her. Her words falling behind you. You walked back into the theatre, those hands of yours clenched onto your purse and your will. Olivia de Havilland's face secret and gloomy loomed on the screen. You took your seat downstairs. You weren't going to let it go this time. Enough was enough. Such an innocent desire. A picture show! Why couldn't a person express one tiny innocent desire without having to watch out. You passed the other girl, she would testify to that. You passed her and took your seat in the house. Lew Ayres smoked a cigarette onscreen. If you were a smoker, you would join him. But you truly did not feel his ease walking across the screen. You felt a shattering, your chest quivered. You felt like crying.

It was then that Dexter Gordon's band slithered into "I Should Care." You sipped your drink. Your sister squeezed your arm. She and Milton had gotten married just a few years gone. You hadn't seen her for a year. It was good to be with her. You both loved this jazz. And Nova Scotia, for all the hurt.

The girl came down to where you were sitting. Her tone was belligerent. She said, "I told you to go upstairs." She tucked a bit of brown hair behind her left ear. She was younger than you. In Vi's Beauty Parlour, a girl as young as she would have called you Miss Viola or Miss Desmond, ma'am. You didn't know then her name was Prima. Prima Davis. You refused to move. You ignored her so she stomped off to get the manager. You sat. *The Dark Mirror* was unintelligible. You heard nothing. You sat. You waited.

You heard their footsteps coming down the aisle. The manager, Harry MacNeil, spoke to you as if you were a child. "You have been told to go upstairs. I demand that you do immediately." He spoke in a low hissing tone at first, not wanting to attract attention. You could not see his face fully in the shadowy flickering half-light of the Roseland. Trying to explain only made him hiss louder. He said something about the right to refuse admission to objectionable people. But you had been admitted, you protested, the girl refused to sell you a downstairs ticket, you explained, she gave you one for upstairs but you never sat upstairs, your eyes, you couldn't see well from there. No matter what you said, no reason could prevail. You spoke softly, thinking virtue and decorum would succeed. Harry MacNeil became angrier and angrier, louder and louder, till there was rustling in the theatre. The voice of Lew Ayres was drowned out by the sound of the patrons. The intrigue of *The Dark Mirror* riffed over the commotion of the manager stalking out of the theatre, threatening to return with the police. The policeman came so quickly. Shock. Shock is all that can be described here. Only later you would recount stoically: "The policeman grabbed my shoulders and the manager grabbed my legs, injuring my knee and hip. They carried me bodily from the theatre into the street ... I was driven to the police station. Within a few minutes the manager appeared and the chief of police. They left together and returned in an hour with a warrant for my arrest." That is how you left the Roseland that evening. Harmed.

There's a way that Dexter Gordon has with a saxophone. It is so languid yet so immediate. He plays with the right timbre of melancholy and cynicism. As he plays "I Should Care," you listen in another time, wishing you had just that touch back then at the Roseland Theatre. You were younger then. The wistfulness had not crept into your eyes. That was the start, no, the confirmation of it. All the plans—the chain of Vi's Beauty Palours, the young women graduating with diplomas. You loved jazz, you were going to manage a few bands, too. You had already helped a few musicians to patent their lyrics. You had fallen fully into jazz on those days in Montréal and New York. You had been a cigarette girl at Small's Paradise. Heard Dizzy and Bird, Benny Carter and Bud Powell, while you studied in the daytime how to fashion wigs, how to style hair. You were younger and thought that things could be done. Prejudice could be fought.

At the Hi-Hat Club, Dexter Gordon put another spin on that hope. "I Should Care." You did then. Still do. Right there, right there in that jail, the cell next to the male prisoners, it was easy to lose faith. How they could put a gentle-minded woman like you in jail and for what? For what? That question rattled around in you. But faith is a good thing, no matter how rough life feels, your faith brings you through. So you put your white gloves on, they had not taken your purse, you put your white gloves on and you sat straight up and wide awake all night long in that jail cell. The hours passed slowly. Determined to stay awake as a witness, you went over the events of your life that led you to this. It was nothing in particular but an accumulation of moments. If someone had told you yesterday or even seconds before; if they'd said, "Vi, look out now, one day you'll be arrested and thrown in jail for sitting in the white section of a movie theatre," it would not have been believable.

The matron came in now and then, she had a half-sympathetic look. All night the officers kept bringing in more arrested men, drunkards, hooligans. They were none too mannerly. The cell was dingy as crude places are. There was a bunk and blankets, but your resolve would not let you lie down. If they were determined to bring you low, to take every bit of decency from you, you would not let them. The Dodge was at the garage. What would happen to it tomorrow morning? Jack could not have heard. There was no chance to tell him. And the ladies tomorrow, they would be disappointed. There would be no laughing and talking about how Duke Ellington played at the Mutual Street Arena in Toronto just two days ago, or that Coleman Hawkins played the day you got arrested, and Robeson, can you believe Robeson sang at Eaton's. Refused to sing if it was segregated, he did! That Ruthie Johnson was just crazy for jazz and Duke Ellington and had gone out to Toronto a month ago and vowed to be in the front row. She'd sent news about jumping the jive at the Palais Royale. There would be no catching up on Rhoda Murray's son—truthfully, she should send that boy to his daddy in Toronto so he could teach him how to be a man. Oh, you wished all night that you were there for that conversation.

It must have been about two or three in the morning when it got difficult. There was snoring and cursing from the men's cell, it was all you could do to keep your eyes open and so you set your mind even harder. This was a mistake, a terrible mistake, and as soon as you had the chance you would explain to the higher authorities. After all, there was no law, there was no sign in the theatre. If there had been, you wouldn't even have gone in.

When day broke you took it with relief. You stood up, dusted and straightened your skirt, pulled your gloves close, and waited to be taken to court. There was light signalling morning but it was impossible to say whether it was a sunny morning or a dull one.

New Glasgow woke up to warm itself in front of wood stoves, to cold bodies poured into night-cold clothes. If the day was dry enough, washing could be hung out. It was Saturday. Downtown New Glasgow would soon be bustling. The Roseland Theatre was closed. By mid-morning the ushers would come in and sweep last night's cache of paper bags and soda bottles away, peel off the chewing gum from the bottom of seats and empty ashtrays. The grand proscenium stage, where jugglers and minstrels used to perform a decade or more ago, folded itself in red velvet curtain dropping from ceiling to floor. *The Dark Mirror* had been returned to its can in the projection room. The land of roses painted along the walls lay in mute dimness waiting for the matinee crowd of children. New Glasgow woke up and, after morning coffee and bacon, went on with its life. Some who had been at the Roseland Theatre last night remembered the commotion. They mentioned it again at breakfast. "What did she expect, after all," the talk went. "Such a shame spoiling a nice evening out. That Olivia de Havilland is so beautiful. I got her eyes, you know." "Why, if I wasn't sitting there, I wouldn't have believed it. Right next to me, she was. To my everlasting surprise."

You stood waiting for the matron. Not hungry, you told her when she offered you tea. You were anxious when they took you to the courthouse. No one would blame you for feeling weak in the stomach. If you'd have drunk the tea, you couldn't keep it down. Anyone would waver between incredulity and fear here. When the daylight seemed never to arrive you must've been ready to give out, to swear that you'd lost your mind; that you were still at the Roseland smothered in celluloid and roses, dreaming like everyone else in the Roseland Theatre.

The magistrate said, "Viola Desmond, you are charged with violating the provincial Theatres, Cinematographs, and Amusement Act. How do you plead?" It sounded funny to you. A nervousness made you want to laugh. Magistrate Roderick Geddes Mackay was looking at you with such utter seriousness, you knew he would not hear you out. Mr. MacNeil from the Roseland, he said, "Sir, she refused to remove herself, she did not pay the tax or the right price." Prima Davis and the ticket seller backed him up. They all said you bought an upstairs ticket paying only two cents tax and then seated yourself downstairs, big as you please. And a ticket for downstairs had a three-cent tax on it. Taxes! No one had said anything about taxes. The girl at the ticket booth had said. "I'm not permitted to sell downstairs tickets to you people." *You people!* That phrase burned itself back into your head but they all kept talking about taxes. You felt alone. There were other prisoners in the courtroom. One for drunkenness, one for assault, one for stealing. You had nothing in common with them except the word *prisoner.* Your small strong hands sweated in their white gloves even though the courtroom was cold. The matron stood close by in case you tried to bolt. You thought that you felt her sympathy, but none of your senses were working so you couldn't be sure. You gathered yourself up when you took the stand. "I am the accused," you said. "I offered to pay the difference in the price between the tickets. They would not accept it." You said more but that's not in the minutes of the record. And what more you said about Coloured people and all, and the way you were hauled out of the Roseland, causing you physical injury, none of it mattered. You were convicted and fined twenty-six dollars or one month in jail.

Those two days in New Glasgow cost more than money. You sleepwalked through the courthouse door, through the arrangements with the mechanic, and through the rest of the day. The Dodge sedan was still at the repair shop. It looked like a good friend waiting. The Dodge seemed to drive itself back to Halifax. You noticed your white gloves on the steering wheel. You'd forgotten to take them off or you really couldn't bring yourself to take them off. They protected you somehow. Your hands didn't tremble as you knew they would if you'd removed their small armour. You daydreamed that it had turned out differently. The car had never broken down. The car had broken down and you had gone to see a movie with Olivia de Havilland and Lew Ayres at the Roseland Theatre, whose walls depicted a land of colourful blooms. The evening had been wonderful and you'd come out of the theatre and gone home. It had turned out differently. There had been no incident at all. The car had made it all the way to Sydney, and New Glasgow had been left behind. You daydreamed all this, time all changed; life all ordinary.

They don't know about this yet on Gottingen Street. It's late Saturday afternoon by the time the Dodge sedan draws up to Vi's Beauty Parlour and Jack's Barbershop. Only then do you take your gloves off. It's not over, you told yourself, no matter the efforts of your body to run and hide. You didn't run off at the Roseland. You stood your ground. Now there was a conviction against your name after all you'd done to lift yourself up. Jack's way of looking at things was to ease yourself along, don't make too much fuss. That was the way of the world, he said. "Take it to the Lord," he'd say. And this time, though he was angry himself, he still said, "You've got to know how to handle things—you can't be too forward." He knew about the Roseland, he did. When he was a boy running errands and working in the drugstore in New Glasgow, he knew they didn't allow Coloureds downstairs. "Take it to the Lord." That was his motto and it had taken him far. It was the way Nova Scotia was, he said, it was the way of the world. You open your mouth for something like this and whatever little there was would dry up too. So this fuss you wanted to kick up didn't sit well with him.

Remembering this at the Hi-Hat Club in Boston, you smiled. "Hotheaded," he called you. You could smile now of course, but then thank heavens for the good women around you. Miss Pearleen Oliver who said, "Dear God, Viola, what did they do to you?" and took it from there to the Nova Scotia Association for the Advancement of Coloured People. Miss Carrie Best who wrote it up on the front page of her newspaper *The Clarion*. "Disgraceful," she called it. "Jim Crowism." Wanda always said that you were not a person who liked to lose something righteous. Some didn't agree with you taking it further, said you were "looking for trouble." Who could blame them? They wanted life to be gentle with them, they wanted to walk away, calm it down, act as if nothing happened. But life was rough, not gentle. Something happened every day to prove this.

It took a while. People came together giving money to open the case. After trying to sue the Roseland Theatre for assault, malicious prosecution, and false arrest and imprisonment, the lawyer decided to take the case to the Nova Scotia Supreme Court. It took months and bearing up to the pressure from Jack. It was not his fault, he was just a practical man. Growing up in Tracadie and New Glasgow had taught him some things he couldn't put aside. Shouldn't put aside, when you come to think of it now. Days at the beauty parlour were tense. You could feel Jack's disapproval from next door. At home, things between you came to silence. But you, well, you had faith. You didn't want to live all a bundle of nerves, watching where you sat and where you walked and all the rest. Jack would come around, you thought—people didn't have to just take it all the time, he'd see. Even if they ruled against you, in your heart you would know that you'd taken it as far as it could go.

It's 1955. Wanda and Milton are beside you. The evening is draining away at the Hi-Hat Club on Columbus. Their faces are angled towards the camera taking this picture. You are looking straight into the lens. Your head tilted. You took younger than your years. Is that how we look when we face history dead-on? Youthful and knowing, as if having dipped oneself into a clear stream? Dexter Gordon is on the last notes of "I Should Care." This whole evening you've been thinking about Gottingen Street and Halifax and the places you've wandered since; and it fits somehow into the intricate riffs and squeaks, the driven bass and tender piano. You lost of course. One judge, out of the four, did say that the Roseland tried to "enforce a Jim Crow rule by misuse of a public statute." You still lost. Well, then again … Just as this music is a loss and a forgiving.

The Friend
ELIZABETH HAY

SHE WAS THIRTY, a pale beautiful woman with long blond hair and high cheekbones, small eyes, sensuous mouth, an air of serenity and loftiness—superiority—and under that, nervousness, insecurity, disappointment. She was tired. There was the young child who woke several times a night. There was Danny who painted till two in the morning, then slid in beside her and coaxed her awake. There was her own passivity. She was always willing, even though she had to get up early, and always resentful, but never out loud. She complied. In conversation she was direct and Danny often took part, but in bed, apparently, she said nothing. She felt him slide against her, his hand between her legs, its motion the reverse of a woman wiping herself, back to front instead of front to back. She smelled paint—the air of the poorly ventilated attic where he worked—and felt his energetic weariness and responded with a weary energy of her own.

He didn't speak. He didn't call her by any name (during the day he called her Moe more often than Maureen). He reached across her and with practised efficiency found the Vaseline in the bedside drawer.

I MET HER ONE AFTERNOON on the sidewalk outside the neighbourhood grocery store. It was sunny and it must have been warm—a Saturday in early June. Our section of New York was poor and Italian, and we looked very different from the dark women around us. The friendship began with that shorthand—shortcut to each other—an understanding that goes without saying. I had a small child too.

A week later, at her invitation, I walked the three blocks to her house and knocked on the front door. She opened a side door and called my name. "Beth," she said, "this way." She was dressed in a loose and colourful quilted top and linen pants. She looked composed and bohemian and from another class.

Inside there was very little furniture: a sofa, a chest, a rug, Danny's paintings on the wall. He was there. A small man with Fred Astaire's face and an ingratiating smile. Once he started to talk, she splashed into the conversation, commenting on everything he said and making it convoluted out of what I supposed was a desire to be included. Only later did I realize how much she insisted on being the centre of attention, and how successfully she became the centre of mine.

We used to take our kids to the only playground within walking distance. It was part of a school yard that marked the border between our neighbourhood and the next. The pavement shimmered with broken glass, the kids were wild and unattended. We pushed our two on the swings and kept each other company. She said she would be so mad if Danny got AIDS, and I thought about her choice of words—"so mad"—struck by the understatement.

I learned about sex from her the way girls learn about sex from each other. In this case the information came not in whispered conversations behind a hedge, but more directly and personally than anything I might have imagined at the age of twelve. In those days the hedge was high and green and the soil below it dark, a setting at once private, natural, and fenced off. This time everything was in the open. I was the audience, the friend with stroller, the mild-mannered wide-eyed listener who learned that breastfeeding brought her to the point of orgasm, that childbirth had made her vagina sloppy and loose, that anal sex hurt so much she would sit on the toilet afterwards, bracing herself against the stabs of pain.

We were in the playground (that sour, overused, wrongly used, hardly playful patch of pavement) and she said she was sore and told me why. When I protested on her behalf she said, "But I might have wanted it. I don't know. I think I did want it in some way."

I CAN'T REMEMBER her hands, not here in this small cool room in another country and several years after the fact. I remember watching her do many things with her hands; yet I can't remember what they looked like. They must have been long, slender, pale unless tanned. But they don't come to mind the way a man's might and I suppose that's because she didn't touch me. Or is it because I became so adept at holding her at bay? I remember her lips, those dry thin Rock Hudson lips.

One evening we stood on the corner and she smiled her fleeting meaningful smiles, looking at me with what she called her northern eyes (they were blue and she cried easily) while her heartbreak of a husband put his arm around her. What will become of her, I wondered, even after I found out.

SHE WAS STANDING next to the stove and I saw her go up in flames: the open gas jets, the tininess of the room, the proximity of the children—standing on chairs by the stove—and her hair. It slid down her front and fell down her back. She was making pancakes that were obviously raw. She knew they were raw, predicted they would be, yet did nothing about it. Nor did I. I just poured on lots of syrup and said they were good.

I saw her go up in flames, or did I wish it?

IN THE BEGINNING we saw each other almost every day and couldn't believe how much the friendship had improved our lives. A close, easy intensity which lasted in that phase of its life for several months. My husband talked of moving—an apartment had come open in a building where we had friends—but I couldn't imagine moving away from Maureen.

It was a throwback to girlhood, the sort of miracle that occurs when you find a friend with whom you can talk about everything.

Maureen had grown up rich and poor. Her family was poor, but she was gifted enough to receive scholarships to private schools. It was the private school look she had fixed on me the first time we met, and the poor background she offered later. As a child she received nothing but praise, she said, from parents astonished by their good fortune: They had produced a beautiful and brilliant daughter while everything else went wrong: car accidents, sudden deaths, mental illness.

Danny's private school adjoined hers. They met when they were twelve and he never tried to hide his various obsessions. She could never say that she had never known.

In the spring her mother came to visit. The street was torn up for repairs, the weather prematurely hot, the air thick with dust. Maureen had spread a green cloth over the table and set a vase of cherry blossoms in the middle. I remember the shade of green and the lushness of the blossoms because the sight was so out of character: everything about Maureen was usually in scattered disarray.

Her mother was tall, and more attractive in photographs than in person. In photographs she was still, in person she darted about, high-strung, high-pitched, erratic. Her rapid murmur left the same impression: startling in its abnormality, yet apparently normal. After years of endless talking about the same thing she now made the sounds that people heard: they had stopped up their ears long ago.

She talked about Maureen. How precocious she had been as a child, reading by the age of four and by the age of five memorizing whole books.

"I remember her reading a page, and I told her to go and read it to Daddy. She said, 'With or without the paper?' Lots of children can read at five, even her sister was reading at five, but few have Maureen's stamina. She could read for hours, and adult books. I had to put Taylor Caldwell on the top shelf."

A photograph of the child was tacked to the wall in Danny's studio. She was seated in a chair wearing one of those very short summer dresses we used to wear that ended well above bare round knees. Her face was unforgettable. It was more than beautiful. It had a direct, knowing, almost luminous look produced by astonishingly clear eyes and fair, fair skin. Already she knew enough not to smile.

"That's her," said Danny. "There she is."

The beautiful kernel of the beautiful woman.

SHE HAD ALWAYS imagined bodies firmer than hers but not substantially different. She had always imagined Danny with a boy.

I met the lover without realizing it. It was late summer, we were at their house in the country, a shaded house beside a stream—cool, green, quiet—the physical manifestation of the serenity I once thought she possessed. A phrase in a movie review: her wealth so old it had a patina. Maureen's tension so polished it had a fine sheen.

All weekend I picked her long hairs off my daughter's sweater and off my own. I picked them off the sheet on the bed. I picked blackberries, which left hair-like scratches on my hands.

My hands felt like hers. I looked down at my stained fingers and they seemed longer. I felt the places where her hands had been, changing diapers, buttoning shirts, deep in tofu and tahini, closing in on frogs which she caught with gusto. Swimming, no matter how cold.

I washed my hands and lost that feeling of being in contact with many things. Yet the landscape continued—the scratches if not the smells, the sight of her hands and hair.

An old painter came to visit. He parked his station wagon next to the house and followed Danny into his studio in the barn. Maureen and I went off with the kids to pick berries. It was hot and humid. There would be rain in the night and again in the morning. We followed a path through the woods to a stream where the kids splashed about while Maureen and I dangled our feet over the bank. Her feet were long and slender, mine were wide and short. We sent ripples of water towards the kids.

She told me that Henry—the painter's name was Henry—was Danny's mentor, they had known each other for years and he was a terrible alcoholic. Then she leaned so close her shoulder touched mine. One night last summer Danny had come back from Henry's studio and confessed—confided—that he had let the old man blow him. Can you believe it? And she laughed—giddy—flushed—excited—and eager, it seemed, to impress me with her sexual openness and to console herself with the thought that she had impressed me. A warm breeze blew a strand of her hair into my face. I brushed it away and it came back—ticklish, intimate, warm and animal-like. I didn't find it unpleasant, not at the time.

We brought the berries back to the house, and late in the afternoon the two men emerged to sit with us on the verandah. Henry was whiskery, gallant, shy. Maureen talked a great deal and laughed even more. Before dark, Henry drove away.

She knew. It all came out the next spring and she pretended to be horrified, but she knew.

That night sounds woke me: Danny's low murmur, Maureen's uninhibited cries. I listened for a long time. It must have occurred to me then that the more gay he was, the more she was aroused.

I THOUGHT IT WAS someone come to visit. But the second time I realized it was ice falling. At midday, icicles fall from the eavestrough into the deep snow below.

And the floor which I keep sweeping for crumbs? There are no crumbs. The sound comes from the old linoleum itself. It crackles in the cold.

Often I wake at one or two in the morning, overheated from the hot water bottle, the three blankets, the open sleeping bag spread on top. In my dreams I take an exam over and over again.

In the morning I go down in the socks I've worn all night to turn up the heat and raise the thin bamboo blind through which everyone can see us anyway. I make coffee, then scald milk in a hand-beaten copper pot with a long handle. Quebec has an expression for beating up egg whites: *monter en neige*. Milk foams up and snow rises.

Under the old linoleum old newspapers advertise an "equipped one bedroom at Lorne near Albert" for $175. Beside the porch door the linoleum has broken away and you can read mildew, dust, grit, *Ottawa Citizen,* May 1, 1979. The floor is a pattern of squares inset with triangles and curlicues in wheat shades of immature to ripe. Upstairs the colours are similar but faded; and flowers, petals.

During the eclipse last month I saw Maureen when I saw the moon. I saw my thumb inch across her pale white face.

I have no regrets about this. But I have many thoughts.

WE PUSHED SWINGS in the playground while late afternoon light licked at the broken glass on the pavement. New York's dangers were all around us, as was Maureen's fake laugh. She pushed William high in the swing, then let out a little trill each time he came swooping back.

It was the time of Hedda Nussbaum. We cut out the stories in the newspaper and passed them back and forth—photographs of Hedda's beaten face, robust husband, abused and dead daughter. It had been going on for so long. Hedda had been beaten for thirteen years, the child was seven years old.

In the playground, light licked at the broken glass and then the light died and we headed home. Often we stopped for tea at Maureen's. Her house always had a loose and welcoming atmosphere which hid the sharp edge of need against which I rubbed.

She began to call before breakfast, dressing me with her voice, her worries, her anger, her malleability. Usually she was angry with Danny for staying up so late that he was useless all day, of no help in looking after William, while she continued to work to support them, to look after the little boy in the morning and evening, to have no time for herself. But when I expressed anger on her behalf she defended him …

Similarly with the stomach pains. An ulcer, she suggested, then made light of the possibility when I took it seriously.

She would ask, "Is this all? Is this going to be my contribution?" She was referring to her brilliant past and her sorry present: her pedestrian job, the poor neighbourhood, her high-maintenance husband when there were any number of men she could have married, any number she said. Motherhood gave her something to excel at. She did everything for her son—dressed him, fed him, directed every moment of play. "Is this all right, sweetie? Is this? What about this? Then, sweetie pie, what do you want?"

Sweetie pie wanted what he got. His mother all to himself for a passionately abusive hour, then peace, affection. During a tantrum she would hold him in her lap behind a closed door, then emerge half an hour later with a small smile. "That was a short one. You should see what they're like sometimes."

Even when Danny offered to look after him, even when he urged her to take a long walk, she refused. Walked, but briefly, back and forth on the same sidewalk, or up and down the same driveway. Then returned out of a sense of responsibility to the child. But the child was fine.

At two years he still nursed four or five times a night and her nipples were covered with scabs. "But the skin there heals so quickly," she said.

WE MOVED to the other side of the city and the full force of it hit me. I remember bending down under the sink of our new apartment, still swallowing a mouthful of peanut butter, to cram s.o.s pads into the hole—against the mouse, taste of it, peanut butter in the trap. Feel of it, dry and coarse under my fingers. Look of it, out of the corner of my eye a small dark slipper. Her hair always in her face, and the way I was ratting on her.

It got to the point where I knew the phone was going to ring before it rang. Instead of answering, I stood there counting. Thirty rings. Forty. Once I told her I thought she had called earlier, I was in the bathroom and the phone rang forever. Oh, she said, I'm sorry, I wasn't even paying attention. Then I saw the two of us: Maureen mesmerized by the act of picking up a phone and holding it for a time; and me, frantic with resentment at being swallowed whole.

"Why is she so exhausting?" I asked my husband. Then answered my own question. "She never stops talking and she always talks about the same thing."

But I wasn't satisfied with my answer. "She doesn't want solutions to her problems. That's what is so exhausting."

And yet that old wish—a real wish—to get along. I went to bed thinking about her, woke up thinking about her and something different, yet related, the two mixed together in a single emotion. I had taken my daughter to play with her friend Joyce, another girl was already there and they didn't want Annie to join them. I woke up thinking of my daughter's rejection, my own various rejections, and Maureen.

IT SEEMED INEVITABLE that he would leave her—clear that he was gay and therefore inevitable that he would leave her. He was an artist. To further his art he would pursue his sexuality. But I was wrong; he didn't leave her. And neither did I.

Every six months he had another gay attack and talked, thought, drew penises. Every six months she reacted predictably and never tired of her reactions, her persistence taking on huge, saintly proportions. As for me, I never initiated a visit or a call, but didn't make a break. As yielding as she was, and she seemed to be all give, Danny and I were even more so.

Tensions accumulated—the panic as she continued to call and I continued to come when called, though each visit became more abrasive, more insulting, as though staged to show who cared least: You haven't called me, you never call me, you think you can make up for your inattention with this visit but I'll show you that I don't care either: the only reason I'm here is so that my son can play with your daughter.

We walked along the river near her country place. William was on the good tricycle, my daughter on the one that didn't work. Maureen said, "I don't think children should be forced to share. Do you? I think kids should share when they want to share."

Her son would not give my daughter a turn the whole long two-hour walk beside the river—with me pointing out what? Honeysuckle. Yes, honeysuckle. Swathes of it among the rocks. And fishermen with strings of perch. I stared out over the river, unable to look at Maureen and not arguing; I couldn't find the words.

With each visit there was the memory of an earlier intimacy, and no interest in resurrecting it. Better than nothing. Better than too much. And so it continued, until it spun lower.

We were sitting on the mattress on the floor of Danny's studio in front of a wall-sized mirror. Around us were his small successful paintings and his huge failures. He insisted on painting big, she said, because he was so small. "I really think so. It's just machismo."

How clear-eyed she was.

I rested my back against the mirror, Maureen faced it. She glanced at me, then the mirror, and each time she looked in the mirror she smiled slightly. Her son was there. He wandered off and then it became clear that she was watching herself.

She told me she was pregnant again. It took two years to persuade Danny, "and now he's even more eager than I am," smiling at herself in the mirror.

DANNY GOT SICK. I suppose he had been sick for months, but I heard about it in the spring. Maureen called in tears. "The shoe has dropped," she said.

He was so sick that he had confessed to the doctors that he and Henry—old dissipated Henry whose cock had slipped into who knows what—had been screwing for the last five years. Maureen talked and wept for thirty minutes before I realized that she had no intention of leaving him, or he of leaving her. They would go on. The only change, and this wasn't certain, was that they wouldn't sleep together. They would go to their country place in June and stay all summer.

I felt cheated, set up, used. "Look, you should *do* something," I said. "Make some change."

She said, "I know. But I don't want to precipitate anything. Now isn't the time." She said it wasn't AIDS.

HER LIPS DRIED OUT like tangerine sections separated in the morning and left out all day. She nursed her children so long that her breasts turned into small apricots, and now I cannot hold an apricot in my hand and feel its soft loose skin, its soft non-weight, without thinking of small spent breasts—little dugs.

She caught hold of me, a silk scarf against an uneven wall, and clung.

TWO YEARS LATER I snuck away. In the weeks leading up to the move, I thought I might write to her afterwards, but in the days immediately before, I knew I would not. One night in late August when the weather was cool and the evenings still long, we finished packing at nine and pulled away in the dark.

We turned right on Broadway and rode the traffic in dark slow motion out of the city, north along the Hudson, and home.

In Canada I thought about old friends who were new friends because I hadn't seen them for such a long time. And newer friends who were old friends because I'd left them behind in the other place. And what I noticed was that I had no landscape in which to set them. They were portraits in my mind (not satisfying portraits either, because I couldn't remember parts of their bodies; their hands, for instance, wouldn't come to mind). They were emotion and episode divorced from time and place. Yet there was a time—the recent past, and a place—a big city across the border.

And here was I, where I had wanted to be for as long as I had been away from it—home—and it didn't register either. In other words, I discovered that I wasn't in a place. I was the place. I felt populated by old friends. They lived in my head amid my various broodings. Here they met again, going through the same motions and different ones. Here they coupled in ways that hadn't occurred really. And here was I, disloyal but faithful, occupied by people I didn't want to see and didn't want to lose.

September came and went, October came and went, winter didn't come. It rained in November, it rained again in December. In January a little snow fell, then more rain.

Winter came when I was asleep. One morning I looked out at frozen puddles dusted with snow. It was very cold. I stepped carefully into the street and this is what I saw. I saw the landscape of friendship. I saw Sunday at four in the afternoon. I saw childhood panic. People looked familiar to me, yet they didn't say hello. I saw two people I hadn't seen in fifteen years, one seated in a restaurant, the other skating by. I looked at them keenly, waiting for recognition to burst upon them, but it didn't.

Strangers claimed to recognize me. They said they had seen me before, some said precisely where. "It was at a conference two years ago." Or, "I saw you walk by every day with your husband last summer. You were walking quickly."

But last summer Ted and I had been somewhere else.

The connections were wistful, intangible, maddening. Memory tantalized before it finally failed. Yet as much as memory failed, those odd, unhinged conjunctures helped. Strange glimmerings and intense looks were better than nothing.

The last time I saw Maureen, she was wearing a black-and-white summer dress and her teeth were chattering. "Look at me," she said, her mouth barely able to form the words, her lower jaw shaking. "It's not that cold."

We were in the old neighbourhood. The street was dark and narrow with shops on either side, and many people. I was asking my usual questions, she was doing her best to answer them.

"Look," she said again, pointing to her lips which were shaking uncontrollably.

I nodded, drew my jacket tight, mentioned how much warmer it had been on the way to the café, my voice friendly enough but without the intonations of affection and interest, the rhythms of sympathy, the animation of friendship. In the subway we felt warm again. She waited for my train to come, trying to redeem and at the same time distance herself. I asked about Danny and she answered. She talked about his job, her job, how little time each of them had for themselves. She went on and on. Before she finished I asked about her children. Again she talked.

"I don't mean to brag," she said, helpless against the desire to brag, "but Victoria is so verbal."

Doing to her children and for herself what her mother had done to her and for herself.

"So verbal, so precocious. I don't say this to everyone," listing the words that Victoria already knew.

She still shivered occasionally. She must have known why I didn't call any more, aware of the reasons while inventing others in a self-defence that was both pathetic and dignified. She never asked what went wrong. Never begged for explanations (dignified even in her begging: her persistence as she continued to call and extend invitations).

We stood in the subway station—one in a black-and-white dress, the other in a warm jacket—one hurt and pale, the other triumphant in the indifference which had taken so long to acquire. We appeared to be friends. But a close observer would have seen how static we were, rooted in a determination not to have a scene, not to allow the other to cause hurt. Standing, waiting for my train to come in.

Fever

SHARON BUTALA

CECILIA HAD SLEPT WELL the first part of the night, but later she was dimly aware of a restlessness on Colin's part that kept pulling her up from the dreamless depths of her heavy sleep to a pale awareness of something being not right. She remembered feeling hot and must have thrown off all her covers, an act unusual for her since she was almost always too cold, and often resorted to a flannel nightgown even in summer. About two-thirty she came fully awake, shivering because she was uncovered, and in her gropings for blankets, found that Colin was hugging all the bedcovers tightly to himself.

She woke him, pushing against his shoulder, then touching his cheek and forehead with her palm, puzzled and then alarmed by the hotness of his skin and by the dry heat radiating from his body.

"I'm sick," he mumbled, with a mixture of fear and irritation in his voice that woke her further.

"What's the matter?" she asked.

"I'm sick," he repeated, a whisper this time, and gave a little moan, involuntarily it seemed, as though he had been stricken suddenly with pain.

She fumbled for the bedside lamp, its location forgotten from the evening before when they had checked in, exhausted from their long flight and the delay when they had changed planes in Winnipeg. The lamp on, she blinked, staring down at him, trying to tell if his pallor was real or just the consequence of poor light or her grogginess.

"I'll need a doctor," he said, his eyes closed, and he clenched his jaw as if against the chattering of his teeth, or pain.

Cecilia was confused, vague pictures passed through her mind, vanishing before she could catch them. She sat up in bed, put both hands over her face, and tried to make sense of things. They had arrived in Calgary, Colin was sick, he said he needed a doctor. She put her hands down and was disconcerted to find him staring at her with an expression that was—surely not—beseeching. But yes, that's what it was. He was beseeching her to do something, and his eyes were the eyes of someone in extremity such as she sometimes caught a glimpse of on the news on television, frighteningly dark, holding depths she had never guessed at before.

She wanted to close her eyes again, to sink back into sleep, to wake in the morning to find him well, or gone.

Colin grunted once, softly, and she got out of bed, went to the desk, and opened the phone book.

"It's my stomach," he said, and his voice was strained now and pitched too high. She looked back at him, saw he had raised his head off the pillow and that his black hair, always neatly trimmed and short, was pushed by his restlessness into spikes like a punker's. She wanted to laugh. "Call the desk," he said, straining to say it loudly enough for her to hear, then his head fell back on the pillow. But the way his head dropped like a stone as if he had fallen that suddenly into unconsciousness made her dial zero.

They drove the short distance to a hospital in an ambulance, down deserted, icy streets, the siren senselessly screeching. Almost at once Colin was taken from the emergency ward to a bed in a ward three flights up. It was a small room across from the nursing station, and it was equipped with valves, dials and tubes attached to the wall at the head of his bed that the other rooms Cecilia had glanced into as they went down the hall, didn't have. This, and his proximity to the nursing station, alarmed Cecilia. Or rather, these facts registered, she knew this meant he was seriously ill, and that she should be alarmed. But she found she felt no fear, or at least, she didn't think she did.

It was four a.m. Cecilia stood by his bed looking down on him while a nurse on the other side, for at least the third time since their arrival, took his blood pressure, counted his pulse, and listened to his chest.

Colin's eyelids flickered open. Closing them, he said to Cecilia, "You came." She wondered if he had forgotten that she had come with him to Calgary, that he wasn't alone on this business trip as he usually was, and if he thought, in his fever-distorted mind, that she had flown in to be with him when he was taken ill. She drew in a breath to explain, but the paper-like sheen of his eyelids, which looked now as though they had been sealed shut and not merely closed, silenced her. She looked to the nurse but the nurse seemed to be avoiding looking at her.

"He's not likely to be awake much," she said to Cecilia in a tentative tone, casting a glance at her that Cecilia couldn't interpret. "The doctor wants to talk to you." Cecilia went out into the hall where the doctor was leaning on the counter and sleepily making notes in a patient's chart. When he saw her, he stopped writing. Cecilia approached him slowly, and waited for him to speak.

"He's a very sick man," the doctor said to her, solemnly. For a second Cecilia thought she hadn't heard him correctly. When she didn't reply, he said, "I know it's a surprise, since he's so healthy and strong looking, but whatever is bothering him has hit him hard. We'll have to watch him closely." He said something further about vital signs and some medical jargon that she didn't listen to. She interrupted him.

"But what's wrong with him?"

"We have to wait till the lab opens in the morning to get the results of the tests and to do more," he said, "before we can pinpoint the problem, but we've got a nurse with him full time for now, and if we need to, we can have him in the O.R. in minutes." He seemed used to the bewildered silences of relatives, because he filled the pauses when she, her mind crowded with not so much questions as dark, empty spaces that refused to form themselves into words, could only look up at him in silence.

"I think you might as well go back to your hotel and get some sleep," he said, looking vaguely, with red-rimmed eyes, down the empty, polished corridor. "Mrs. Purdy will call you if he should get worse." He said good night and left her standing there, holding tightly onto the nursing station counter with one hand.

She looked in on Colin once more, the nurse was taking his blood pressure again, before she took a taxi back to the hotel. It was when she was in bed that she began to wonder if he would die. Her mind shied at the idea, it wasn't possible. And what could be the matter with him? The doctor had given her no clue, at least she didn't think he had. She wondered if she had done the right thing by coming back to the hotel, or if she should have stayed at the hospital. Did the nurses think badly of her because she had gone? This worried her for a while, but finally, she fell asleep.

When she woke it was only three hours later. Light was streaming in around the curtains and she could hear traffic in the street below. She was at once fully alert and knew she wouldn't be able to go back to sleep. Before her eyes had opened she thought of Colin, remembering what the doctor had said and how Colin seemed to have gone away even from behind his sealed eyelids, and she felt momentarily angry with him for deserting her and then for spoiling their trip.

She phoned the hospital and was told that he was not awake, that his condition was pretty much the same, and that the test results wouldn't be back from the lab for a while yet.

"I'll be there in an hour," she said, feeling the need to assure them of her interest, and then, because it seemed to be important to do the normal thing, she bathed, dressed, and went downstairs to the hotel restaurant to order breakfast even though she was neither hungry nor thirsty.

The restaurant was almost empty. While she waited for her coffee she noticed a tall, thin man who looked a little like Colin, although he was not so dark, sitting at a table near the window eating breakfast. He glanced up and caught her watching him. She lowered her eyes quickly, but when he passed her table on his way out of the room, he smiled briefly, wryly at her, indicating by this the oddness of them finding themselves the only two people in such a big restaurant. She observed that his eyes were blue, not brown like Colin's. She recalled then that he had checked in just ahead of them the night before.

She drank her coffee and her orange juice and ate a piece of toast politely, carefully, not tasting it, then went back to the hospital.

As she arrived two white-coated women were wheeling Colin, bed and all, out of his room and down the hall in the direction where the labs were. The empty room, with intravenous and oxygen tubes connected to nothing, and the silent dials on the wall, gave her such a peculiar feeling that she went into the TV room to wait for them to bring him back. When he returned he was still drifting in and out of consciousness. Nurses, aides and lab technicians hurried in and out of the room, speaking in loud voices to Colin and softly to her, as if she were the sick one. They took his pulse, his temperature and blood pressure and poked him with needles, then measured his blood into little glass vials. The doctor came alone and nodded good morning to her, then left. Later he came again, this time with two other doctors. In the hallway they murmured in soft voices to her, speculating about the cause of his illness, enumerating the results of tests, and commenting on what each one might mean.

"But will he be all right?" she asked. The doctors looked at their feet and mumbled some more, while she stood too close to them, lifting her head to hear better, trying to understand what they were saying, or rather, what they were not saying.

In the afternoon Colin spoke to her.

"This will be all right," he said, in a new, high-pitched voice. Although his eyes were directed to her, she had a feeling that he was actually looking at something beyond or behind her. "I am frightened." Having failed to show any sign of fear, he closed his eyes. It was such a contradictory, puzzling message that she discounted it entirely, blaming it on the drugs they were giving him for pain and to control his fever.

Not long after that she began to wonder if the doctors had been trying to tell her that Colin might die. But she could not believe that Colin's death was in the cards for either of them at this moment, and after a pause, she dismissed the thought.

By nine in the evening his illness had still not been identified. Talk had gone from appendicitis or food poisoning to a malfunctioning gall bladder to a kidney ailment or bowel dysfunction to every possible virus from influenza to AIDS. Cecilia went back to the hotel, hesitated for a second in the empty lobby, since she still didn't feel hungry, then went into the restaurant anyway.

There were a few more people scattered around at the tables now, talking quietly, drinks on their tables in front of them, or cups of coffee. The hostess seated Cecilia, then left her. As she was picking up the menu, she realized someone was speaking to her.

For the last few hours she had had a steady, quiet hum in her head that put a distance between her and the voices of other people. She tried to make it stop by shaking her head, by concentrating very hard on anyone speaking to her, and then by reciting to herself her own name, Colin's name, the names of their children and their street address at home. None of these had helped and eventually she had given in and allowed herself to be lulled into the hum.

She turned her head slowly in the direction of the voice, expecting to find that it wasn't she who was being addressed. But the man she had seen at breakfast was leaning toward her from the next table where he was sitting.

"Pardon?" Cecilia said.

"I said the hostess seems to think we should talk to each other, since she placed us so close together." Cecilia glanced around. It was true. In a room three-quarters empty, the hostess had placed them at adjacent tables. How had she not noticed him? "I believe I saw you check in with your husband," he remarked. "I suppose he's off doing business."

"Yes," she said, "I mean, no." It was hard to talk through the hum. "I'm sorry, I haven't had much sleep. He was taken ill last night. He's in the hospital."

"I thought there was something wrong," he said, and leaned toward her again. "You looked," he paused, "sort of in shock. I hope it's not too serious." She hesitated, not sure what to say. There was a warm intensity in his blue eyes that calmed her.

"Yes," she said. "It's very serious. He's unconscious most of the time. I left because," she felt herself frown, "I was too tired to do anything else. I wanted to get away," then was embarrassed at what she had said. She had a quick mental picture of Ingrid Bergman being torn away from the bedside of her dying husband by well-meaning friends—No! No, I don't want to leave! Let me stay!—and managed not to laugh.

He seemed to be absorbing her remark, mulling it over, and now he nodded briskly, a quick acceptance or agreement.

"Yes," he said. "You need to get a perspective."

"I guess that's it," she said, a little dubiously. He smiled at her quickly, impersonally. They didn't speak again for a while.

"Please don't think I'm being too forward," he said after several minutes had passed, "but I'd enjoy it if you'd have your dinner here, at my table. It's lonely, all this eating by yourself." Cecilia found herself standing, then awkwardly sitting in the chair he held out for her. Some part of her perhaps regretted this action she was taking, but she found no will to resist what seemed to be her inclination.

"It is lonely," she agreed, in a serious tone.

The waitress came and took their orders. If she was surprised to find them sitting together, she gave no sign.

"I don't want to intrude on your privacy," he said carefully, not looking at her, "but do you know anyone in Calgary? Are you alone in this?"

Cecilia told him how Colin was thinking of opening a branch of his sporting goods business in the city if it looked like it would be profitable, how they had talked about maybe moving West if things went well, how she had come with him because she'd never been west of Winnipeg before, and now this had happened. And no, she didn't know a soul in Calgary.

"I've told our children he's sick, but nothing else, and I told his sister not to come … yet."

"Then let me be your friend," he said. Cecilia was overcome with embarrassment. She took a sip from her glass of water. "I'm a representative for a chemical company," he said. "I make regular rounds through southern Alberta, among other things, selling chemicals to the dealers who sell them to farmers. I have a wife and three kids in Edmonton where our head office is."

He was touching his cutlery, moving his hands with precision and a certain amount of tension which she couldn't read, but when he finished speaking he lifted his head and smiled at her in a way that was almost embarrassed. "And I liked you as soon as I saw you standing in the lobby last night with that same puzzled look on your face while your husband checked you in."

"I saw you too," she said, finally, and noticed that the hum in her head had lessened and that the room was a pleasant temperature, not too cold as she usually found restaurants. She relaxed a little, then thought of Colin.

"If you're worried, phone the hospital again," he said. "There are pay phones in the lobby."

When he left her at the elevator, he paused, and leaning in the open door, kissed her gently, not quickly, on her mouth. Thinking about it later as she lay in bed, she told herself, I knew he was going to do it and I didn't back away or try to stop him. I wanted him to kiss me. And she felt a burning through her body, even in her arms and the palms of her hands, a burning that she recognized as sexual longing. She who had never been unfaithful, who had never dreamt of such a thing, and Colin so sick.

She passed another restless night and was at the hospital before eight. Several doctors were standing around Colin's bed gazing silently down on him while the head nurse stood by tensely. She noticed Cecilia in the doorway and spoke in an undertone to one of the doctors.

"Ah," he said, turning to Cecilia.

"I'll stop in at noon," the second doctor said. He and the third doctor walked out of the room past Cecilia and down the hall.

"I'm Dr. Jameson," the first doctor said to her. "Dr. Ransom asked me to have a look in."

Colin lay motionless on the bed, his eyes closed, an unnaturally red spot of colour high on each cheek. His lips too, were more vividly coloured than usual. Dr. Jameson took her arm and said, "Let's just sit down and talk this over." He guided her into a small office behind the nursing station, held a chair for her and sat down himself.

"Now," he said, "your husband is very sick. But you know that."

She said, "Have you found out what's wrong with him?" He didn't reply directly, but instead, not looking at her, began to list the different tests they had done and the result of each. He remarked on certain possibilities and dismissed them with a gesture or left them open. Cecilia tried to listen to him, but her mind wandered to Colin's strange colouring, to the fact the head nurse was a different one, and to wondering who Dr. Jameson was and what might be his field of specialty.

Gradually it dawned on her that Colin was worse, a good deal worse, and that was why Dr. Jameson had brought her into this room and why the nurses and aides at the station or passing down the hall had avoided looking at her as she followed him.

She tried to get a grip on this idea, to admit, to force it to penetrate the shield of her own bewildering indifference. She repeated to herself, Colin is desperately ill, but still no shiver of fear passed down her spine. Dr. Jameson stopped talking and went away. Cecilia went back to Colin's bedside.

At noon he opened his eyes and spoke to her.

"They are coming with flowers," he said. "They want to speak to us. Be ready."

"Yes, Colin," she replied, and bent to kiss him on his hot, dry forehead, but as her lips touched his skin, he turned his head fretfully away from her much as a cranky, feverish child might, and screwed up his face before he lapsed back into unconsciousness. Later he said, "It is very big and there is an echo like silver."

They were keeping the door to his room closed now and had hung a "No Visitors" sign on it. Nurses moved swiftly, silently in and out of the darkened room, staring down at Colin with pursed lips before they went away again.

"I don't understand it," Dr. Jameson muttered to Colin on one of his several brief visits.

At eleven that night the head nurse came, put her arm around Cecilia's shoulders and told her to go back to the hotel and try to sleep.

"I know you want to be here, but you don't want to collapse when he needs you. Is the rest of the family on its way?" Cecilia shook her head numbly, no.

"His parents are dead," she said, "and I don't want our children here. If he isn't better by morning, I'll tell his sister to come."

"Go back to the hotel," the nurse said in a kindly way, "if you are carrying this alone. I'll call you at once if I think you should be here."

Cecilia obeyed and took a taxi back to the hotel. Just as she entered the lobby the doors of the elevator opened and the man she had talked with the night before stepped out as if he had arranged to meet her.

"You look so tired," he said to her, without any preliminaries or surprise. "Come and have a drink with me before you go to bed."

"I don't think I could sleep anyway," she said. They went together into the bar across from the restaurant and Cecilia had a glass of scotch. She inhaled its fumes, finding them delicious, she let them rush into her brain.

"He's worse," she said. "He may not live through the night," but her own words carried no meaning, she frowned with the effort to feel them, but they seemed to be as on the other side of an impenetrable glass wall. Finally she abandoned the effort;

she was too tired. "I guess I shouldn't be here," she said, meaning that she should have stayed at Colin's bedside, not that she shouldn't be in the hotel bar with a strange man.

He was thoughtful for a second, then shook his head.

"No," he said. "There comes a moment ... If it's his fate ..."

She studied him. He had such bright eyes, so blue, and the intensity in them fascinated her. She remembered Colin's eyes the night he had gotten sick, as if, behind their transparent glistening surface, they opened into worlds she hadn't been to, hadn't known existed, didn't want to know about. He took her hand and held it tightly.

"Hold on," he said. "You're not alone. I'll stick with you." At that moment all she could feel was the pressure, almost too hard, and the warmth of his hand around hers. And then he put his other hand on the side of her face. She turned her head into his palm and breathed in the smell of his flesh, she opened her mouth and touched her tongue to his palm, tasting the faint salt taste. They sat that way for a moment, she with her eyes closed, until he loosened his hold on her hand, and slid his other hand down to her shoulder.

"Better?" he asked. Yes, she was better. Surprised, she opened her eyes. He was staring at her with a slight frown, his blue eyes burning with a steady light.

He walked with her to the elevator and this time, instead of letting her get on alone, he got on too, and pushed the button for his floor which came before hers. The elevator stopped, the doors opened, he got off and began to say good night to her in an oddly formal, unsmiling way, when she stepped off the elevator beside him. He stared at her, perplexed, not speaking. She touched his arm in a tentative, supplicating way, holding her eyes on his face.

He hesitated, then took his room key out of his pocket and led her down the hall.

His room was identical to hers except that it was less tidy and he had left a lamp burning. The desk was covered with papers he had evidently been working on, and his pyjamas lay across the foot of his bed. She closed her eyes again and after a pause, he kissed her.

At one moment, finding herself in a posture both undignified and profoundly arousing, she had felt a second's horror at what she was doing. For she had never consented to such behaviour—or even thought of it—before in her life. She was reminded of the ugly grappling of pornography, and for a second she was filled with distaste at where her body had taken her, as though she had wakened now, but only to the flesh, to the room, to the rug on the floor and the bed and the walls and the dusty TV set in the corner, and to his hands and mouth on her, and hers on him; she was filled with amazement.

And my husband sick, dying, she thought.

She told him what Colin had said, about the big room with the echo like silver.

"Maybe he really is somewhere else," the man said. "Maybe he's somewhere in a big place and it has an echo like silver. It sounds beautiful," he added. "It doesn't sound like you should be worried about him."

"I didn't like the sound of it," she replied. "So remote, so cold." She shivered, lying in his arms, and was glad of the warmth of his flesh against hers.

"We thought it might be his pancreas," Dr. Jameson said to her in the morning, "but now we've ruled that out, too." She had given him their family doctor's number so that Dr. Jameson could consult with him about Colin's medical history. She could have told him there was nothing: flu, colds, a broken bone in his foot.

At noon the head nurse who had been on duty when Colin was admitted came in and read the record of his vital signs and intake and output of fluids that lay on the stand by his bed.

"That's better," she murmured, then went out without saying anything more. Cecilia meditated on this till the nursing shifts changed at three and the new nursing team came in and clustered around Colin's bed. She was about to ask if he was improving when the new head nurse said to the others, "A slight improvement here." Cecilia could see no difference, except perhaps that the unnaturally bright colour in his cheeks had faded.

After they had gone, she stood beside his bed.

"Did you hear that, Colin?" she asked. "They say you're getting better." Colin's eyelids flickered and he looked at her with that same well of darkness behind his eyes.

"The blueness of things," he said, in a voice that might have been awestruck, had it not been so faint.

"The antibiotics are working," she said. There was no response. She wanted to reach down and shake him. She was his wife, she had been his wife for fifteen years. They had children. What right had he to ignore her in this way? The doctors and nurses whisking in and out of his room barely glanced at her, spoke to her only occasionally, waited politely for her to leave the room before they pulled the curtain around his bed to do some unspeakable thing to him. Was she of no account at all? But Colin had become a stranger, while the man she had gone to bed with the night before was not. She tried to summon some remorse for what she had done, or sympathy for Colin lying so ill and in pain, but all she could feel was anger.

At six the nurse who took his vital signs replied, when Cecilia asked her, that Colin's fever was still elevated, and she smiled at Cecilia in a commiserating way.

"A little change this afternoon," she said, "but now he's much the same."

Around seven Colin said loudly, in a clear voice, "Let me sleep," then, more quietly, "I'm tired and the music lulls me." Cecilia put her hand on his forehead. It was damply cool now, and beads of cool sweat sat on his upper lip. He didn't respond to her touch and after a moment, she took her hand away.

At nine she went back to the hotel. The man she had slept with wasn't in the lobby or the restaurant. She went directly to the bar, stopped in the doorway and peered from table to table through the smoky gloom. He was seated on a stool at the bar and when he glanced back and saw her standing in the doorway, he stood at once, put some money beside his half-full glass, and came immediately to where she waited for him. They went to the elevator, got on, and went up to his room.

This time their coupling was less dramatic, less violently experimental than it had been the night before. Lying beside him on his rumpled bed before she returned to her room, she said, "Today when I tried to talk to him, he said, 'the blueness of things.' What do you suppose he was dreaming about?"

"Or thinking," he said. "Or maybe he was somewhere else."

"Do you think he's trying to tell me something?" Cecilia asked. "No," she answered her own question, "I don't think he is. But what did he mean?"

"Maybe he'll be able to tell you when he wakes up," the man said. "You should write down what he says so you can ask him."

"If he wakes up," she heard herself say, and refused to amend or qualify what she had said.

"Do you love him?" he asked her. In the same unemotional voice she replied, "Yes, or I did when I married him and we've been married fifteen years, so if I don't love him anymore, I don't think it makes any difference."

"Tell me then ..." he said carefully, and paused. "Tell me. Do you ever wish that ..." He paused again. "Do you ever wish that he would die?"

"No," she said. "Why would I wish that?"

He shrugged, was perhaps a bit embarrassed. "To free you."

She started to ask him why he thought she wanted to be free, then realized where she was and what she had just done. She got off the bed and gathered her clothing.

"No," she said. "I don't wish that." When she had dressed she left the room without saying good night. He didn't say anything either, although she had glanced at him before she closed the door behind her and saw that he was watching her steadily across the shadowed room.

In the late morning Colin opened his eyes.

"You're here," he said to her and his expression seemed almost amused.

"Yes," she said softly and rose from her chair in the corner to stand by his bed.

"I feel like I've been on a long journey," Colin said, looking up at the ceiling, "and now I'm so tired."

His words, his tone of voice were so obviously normal that her stomach turned over. He closed his eyes slowly and seemed to fall asleep. Cecilia went to find a nurse to report this turn of events to and the nurse was so surprised that she came with Cecilia, setting down the tray she was carrying on a trolley as they passed it. She took Colin's blood pressure, his pulse, and then his temperature.

"I think there might be some difference," she said cautiously.

Colin didn't wake again or speak until Cecilia was preparing to leave for the hotel. His voice was very faint as he asked her about the children and the appointments he had missed. Then he began to shiver so violently that Cecilia rang his bell and got a nurse in at once. The nurse came in, took his temperature, went out of the room and returned with a thick white wool blanket. She covered Colin and in a few moments he had stopped shivering. Cecilia waited a little longer and when it seemed clear that this had passed, she went back to the hotel.

Her friend was waiting in the bar for her and when he saw her coming toward him, he stood quickly and reached in his pocket for money. She crossed the room and sat on the stool beside him.

"I'll have a scotch and ice," she said to the bartender.

"Bad day?" her friend asked, after a moment.

"Good day, I think," she replied, and told him that although Colin was still very weak and sick, he was sometimes awake now and lucid.

"Have they figured out what was the matter with him?" the man asked.

"A rare tropical disease picked up off a toilet seat?" she suggested, and began to laugh. She put her hand over her mouth and bent her head, while her torso convulsed with spasms of rolling laughter that she couldn't stop. She couldn't catch her breath, she couldn't see anything for the tears of laughter filling her eyes. Alarmed, she made a great effort and managed to stop. She took a few deep breaths, wiped her eyes, and blew her nose. A giggle burst out and she caught it and stifled it. Her friend sat beside her looking at her in a way that was concerned, yet faintly amused. He didn't touch her.

"Come on," he said, and Cecilia rose and followed him to the elevators. They went to his room and he began kissing her hungrily, pressing her body roughly against his, holding her so tightly she could barely breathe.

"What?" he said, into her hair, sensing some coolness in her that had been absent before. He began to fondle her with less ferocity and more tenderness. They made love again, and Cecilia dressed and went to her room immediately after.

She found that she couldn't sleep and sat up in bed watching a long, silly movie, then lay in the darkness with her eyes open till very late. She was later than usual going to breakfast, too, and the man she had been spending her nights with wasn't there, had probably already left on his day of driving out to the nearby towns.

Colin was propped up in a half-sitting position when she arrived at the hospital.

"I think I remember getting sick," he said to her, as if she had been in the room with him all along, "but I don't remember the hotel room and I can't remember the flight here at all." After a pause he said, "Calgary," as if to remind himself. His voice was still weak and his eyes kept closing, as if he was too exhausted to keep them open. She bent to kiss his lips, but he turned his head away so that she met his cool cheek.

Off and on during the day he woke to tell her something as if he were reconstructing, for his own instruction, as much of the past week as he could.

"I came here in an ambulance, right?" he said, looking out the window to the even blue of the winter sky.

"Yes," she said. "I had to convince the doctor who came to the hotel that ..."

"It must have been late," he said. She opened her mouth to reply, but he had already moved on. "One-thirty, I think. I think I remember those numbers in red on the clock."

It went on like that, a monologue. A soliloquy, she thought, and gave up trying to converse with him.

Dr Jameson came in, and after he had studied Colin's chart and examined him, he took Cecilia out into the hall.

"He seems to be mending," he told her. "His fever's down, he's fully conscious, no longer complaining of pain."

"But what was wrong with him?" Cecilia asked.

"If he keeps improving, I'd think you could take him home in two or three days."

"But what made him sick?" Cecilia asked again.

"A good question," he said, and turned his back on her to walk briskly away down the corridor.

That night when she returned to the hotel she slipped quickly past the entrance to the bar, and waited nervously till the elevator came. She thought she had caught a glimpse of her lover sitting in his usual place at the bar, but she went past so quickly, she couldn't be sure.

He was waiting for her at breakfast the next morning.

"Where were you last night?" he asked.

"Nowhere," she said, embarrassed. "I was tired."

He got up from his table, bringing his coffee cup, and sat down at hers.

"I missed you," he said, and she noticed again how very blue his eyes were, and his manner of fixing them on her so that she seemed to be the sole object in the room. "Meet me tonight."

"Colin's getting better," she said, suddenly, running her words into his. "He's conscious and clear-headed. I'll be able to take him home in a couple of days." He set his cup carefully into its saucer.

"To tell the truth," he said, "this is my last day in this district. I leave in the morning." She glanced quickly at him and noticed that the intensity in his eyes had faded, that he was not even looking at her.

"Your wife will be glad to see you," she said.

He gave her a wry look, then glanced at his watch and said, "I'd better get going if I want to finish up today." She said, "I'm late, too," although she wasn't particularly.

At the door they stopped and faced each other. Cecilia was stricken with embarrassment, muttered a short, "See you," and hurried to the elevator. She didn't think he had said anything. Just before the door shut, blocking her view, she saw him buttoning his overcoat and reaching for his briefcase which he had set on the floor by his feet. He wasn't looking at her. The elevator doors shut.

"We've moved him," a nurse said gaily to her as she neared the nursing station. She pointed to a door down the hall, almost at the end.

Colin was awake, his intravenous apparatus had been taken away, and this room had no gadgets attached to the walls. It looked like a bedroom.

"They've started me on clear fluids," he said, and his voice was stronger. "They're going to get me up this afternoon."

"Oh?" she said.

"But I can't sleep," he complained, like a child. "I try to sleep, but I just lie there."

"You slept for a week," she said, cheerfully. "Maybe you don't need to sleep anymore."

"Of course I need to sleep," he said irritably. "I wasn't asleep before. I was ..."

"What?" Cecilia broke in sharply. "What were you doing all week? What?" She went close to the bed, but didn't try to kiss him or touch him. He looked up at her, disconcerted, and she saw that the blackness had gone from his eyes leaving them a translucent, yellowish brown. He blinked several times.

"What are you talking about?" he asked, his peevishness returning.

"All week," she said, patient now, "you said things to me. You said you were somewhere. You said ..." His expression was growing puzzled, was there an edge of panic creeping into his voice?

"What do you mean?" He squirmed away from her, like a small child.

"You said you were somewhere big. You said there was an echo like silver. You said ..."

"Don't, Cecilia," he said, and the sound of her own name stopped her, brought the blood rushing to her cheeks. Colin looked away again to the rectangle of pale blue that was all he could see from his window, then turned his head slowly till he was looking at the wall at the foot of his bed.

"I've been sick," he said, and the distance returned to his voice and his eyes. "I've been sick," he repeated, while she waited. "It's hard ..." She leaned closer, his voice had grown so faint. "To come back." His eyes closed, and gradually his face smoothed.

How thin he had grown. Now his nose was prominent, even hawk-like, and his eyes seemed larger. She found herself wanting to put her hands on each side of his face, gently, to kiss his thin, fever-cracked lips, to lie sleeping beside him, pressed against the warmth of his sickness-wracked body. She stood quietly, looking down on him as he slept.

She wanted to tell him that she too had been gone, that she had been exploring, lost, in a wild, violent country, that she had narrowly escaped, that she had had to tear herself away, lest the swamps and bogs and blackness claim her forever.

She stood looking down at her sleeping husband. His eyelids twitched, his lips moved, he winced as if the pain had returned, and out of the corners of his eyes, a few tears came and crept slowly down his temples to disappear in his hair.

Heartburn
MICHAEL CRUMMEY

SANDY WILCOX is dreaming.

Prickle of sharp air in his lungs. His feet are numb with the cold and wet, the salt water soaking through his boots, his two pair of wool socks, the thick pads of the heels where they've been darned. The sparse horseshoe of two storey houses in North Harbour is splayed behind him, the white puzzle of the ice field stretches to the horizon. He is copying from one pan to another, each stepping stone of ice dipping below the freezing water as it takes his weight, surfacing again as he moves quickly onto the next.

He can hear voices all around him, the shouts of other boys on the ice pans, although there is no one else nearby that he can see and he has the peculiar sensation of being completely alone. He is moving away from the shoreline, the exhilaration of the first minutes on the ice giving way now to fatigue and panic, the size of the pans diminishing as he moves, each one sinking a little deeper than the last, his pants soaked through to the knee. He knows the ice won't hold his stationary weight, that if he stops he'll fall through. His lungs feel raw, as if they've been flayed by a knife, he can taste blood in his mouth. Before long he knows he will fall, exhausted, that he'll sink into black water, dragged down by the weight of his soaked clothing, and he runs awkwardly over the sloppy ice to save his life.

HE SURFACES IN DARKNESS. The initial relief of escaping the dream lasts only moments. His eyes are open but the black is close, impermeable, as snug as a blind-fold. His body is soaked in sweat, his head aching from dehydration and the heat of the earth this far underground and the lingering stink of blasting powder. They have been under more than forty-eight hours now, just the one headlamp between them still has juice and they use it only when necessary.

He is lying back against bare rock. It hurts to breathe and he feels as if he is slowly drowning, the remaining oxygen in the drift being wrung from the air like water from a towel. He can hear the other men breathing around him like the sound of animals snuffling outside a canvas tent. He tries desperately to recall their names and faces. There are five of them, but that's all he can bring to mind, the number, and it terrifies him to think they may have forgotten him in the same way.

By this point he recognizes that he is still dreaming, recognizes the dream, although there is no comfort in the recognition of these things, and he begins to will himself awake by shouting. If he screams loud enough it will carry up through the overburden of sleep and drag him back with it.

GEORGIE IS ASLEEP beside him.

He lies still, reaching a hand to brush against the warmth of her skin through the nightdress. The window is open and he can hear the sound of wind in the trees outside. It could be he is still dreaming. Even the peace of this domestic scene could go wrong suddenly, close in on him. His heart is racing and he breathes deeply to calm himself, taking in the cool air coming through the window. It's a good sign. He can never breathe properly in the dreams. After a few moments he lifts his legs carefully over the side of the bed so as not to disturb Georgie and gets up.

He pads quietly out of the room and downstairs. No sense trying to sleep for a while. It's a queer thing, sometimes he wakes himself four or five times, only to discover he has surfaced into another nightmare, as if he's trying to escape a building on an elevator and continually getting off at the wrong floor. He takes the milk from the refrigerator, pours a glass and carries it into the living room. He considers sitting in the recliner and decides against it; too comfortable, he might drift off again. Instead he sits in Georgie's knitting chair, the broken spring in the seat digging into his backside. He's been promising to fix it for years, but is glad now for the persistent node of discomfort that will help keep him awake, alert.

And then Georgie appears in the doorway to the hall, her arms folded across her chest, her feet bare. Her grey hair and her nightshirt are ghostly white in the glow of the streetlight outside. "Bad night?" she asks, gravel in her voice.

He shrugs, holds up the glass of milk as if he's about to offer a toast. "Heartburn," he says. He hasn't told her about the dreams and doesn't intend to. She'll think he's going off his head. "You go on to bed," he tells her. "I'll be up in a bit."

When she turns away, he stops her. "Georgie?"

Her hand is still on the frame of the doorway, her face looking at him over her shoulder.

"No, nothing," he says. "Never mind. I'll be up in a bit."

SHE SUPPOSES she might never have married Sandy if he hadn't gone through the ice that winter and drowned.

Her mother used to say he was destined for it, what with the way his eyebrows grew together like that, an unbroken hedge of thick blonde hair across his forehead. "No way his mother should let that boy out in a boat," she said. Georgie had never looked at him as anything other than shy Sandy Wilcox before she heard her mother speak of him that way. He was plain looking, no question, and the single eyebrow made him appear less intelligent than he deserved to be given credit for. The pity she felt for him was an ordinary, uncomplicated thing before she learned it was a portent of something more mysterious and severe.

She wondered if he could tell, if he had a knowing inside to match the external mark of his fate. It would be an awful thing, she thought, to grow up with that awareness lodged inside you like a tumour. If he did, he gave no indication, and Georgie took his reticence as a sign of stoicism, of uncommon courage in the face of looming, inevitable disaster. It made him seem tragic and beautiful in her eyes and at the time there was nothing more she needed to fall in love.

AS IT HAPPENED, she was along the shore when he went through the ice that year. March of 1952. None of the other boys could reach him, the pans not large enough to hold their weight. They had to run for his father and then launch a skiff into the slobby ice, half poling, half hauling toward the spot where he'd last been seen, the rescuers going through to their waists and hauling themselves up by the gunnell, using the oars to pole to more solid ice and going over the side to pull further along. It was fifteen or twenty minutes at least before they reached him and dragged the body out from under the ice like a dead seal. A cold crescent of water sprayed from his sleeves as he flopped over the side into the boat.

She followed the group carrying the body back to the house. Sandy's father, Ned, held Sandy under the armpits, the boy's face against his chest bleached white by the water, his lips as dark as bilberries. Ned had a walrus mustache and a red, pinched face that made him look permanently angry. "Look out now," he shouted whenever Jeb Walsh, who had one of Sandy's feet, stumbled on the rocky path. "Hold him *up*, would you," he said.

At the house, the entire procession trooped through the door and into the kitchen where Sandy was laid out on the table. Martha Wilcox had seen them heading up from the harbour and was already wailing when they came in. There were twelve or thirteen people crowded into the tiny room where Martha had been baking bread and the heat was overwhelming. Georgie had never seen a dead person before and she was afraid she might be sick to her stomach.

Ned Wilcox tried to hold his wife, but she pushed him off and leaned over her son, crying helplessly. "Now woman," Ned said, "there's no bloody help in that." She ignored him and went on weeping. She clutched at the boy's clothing and shook him and finally punched on his chest with her rough fists. "Martha!" Ned shouted.

"Jesus," he said. But Jeb Walsh held him back by the arm and he finally turned away from the spectacle of his keening wife striking their dead son.

No one else uttered a word. Georgie can remember the lonely sound of the woman's fists on Sandy's chest like someone beating a rug. And then Sandy convulsed on the table, spat up a mouthful of water and started into a fit of coughing. His mother put both her hands to her head and screamed. And Georgie fainted dead away on the floor.

"SHE SWOONED," is how Sandy likes to describe it. "Only time I've ever swept a woman off her feet."

"I was fifteen," Georgie says flatly. "And you scared the bejesus out of me. Some romance."

There was a time, Sandy remembers, when she went along with him. When she'd hold the back of her hand to her forehead, flutter her eyelids as if she was reliving that moment. "Handsome?" she'd say. "My God, you looked better laid out dead than you ever have alive." Laughter from the company assembled, friends up to the house for a drink, or sitting around the table at a Legion dance. He tries to remember when their easy way with it changed, but supposes it could have gone on for years before he noticed the difference.

Stan and Laura Caines get up to take a turn on the dance floor, Everett King heads to the bar for a round of drinks. Georgie watches after Everett, his peculiarly stiff walk a memento of the accident in the mine. "He's doing alright since losing Sylvia," she says. "I thought he'd shrivel up and die."

Sandy looks down into his glass. "I s'pose you'd do alright without me too," he says. "If you had to."

He's gotten so maudlin these days. Hardly sleeping at night, sitting up with old photo albums of the wedding, the children when they were youngsters. And this kind of foolishness. Now's a fine time, she thinks, to be getting sentimental, to fall in love with a wife. "You're not planning on running off with some young thing are you Sandy?"

He laughs. "You've seen my ankles," he says. "I won't be running anywhere anytime soon."

Everett comes back with his fists crowded with glasses. He sits them on the table-top and slides them like chess pieces to the circle of chairs. Sandy lifts his drink and swallows a good mouthful.

"Yes now laddy-buck," Georgie says to him. "You'll be up all night again if you keep at the whiskey like that."

Everett raises his glass to Sandy. "Nevermind the old battleaxe," he says. "We can't afford to waste the few hours left to us asleep anyways."

Sandy reaches into the pocket of his suit coat and pulls out a roll of Tums. "I came prepared," he says.

HE'S BEEN DREAMING about the child. The one they lost, their first.

In the dream the child is inside his body, not Georgie's. There is no change in him that he can tell, no outward sign, but he senses the baby's presence, how his flesh surrounds it. His lungs feel crowded and inefficient; he can barely catch his breath. And he can feel the baby's urge to be clear of him, its panic, as if it was buried underground already. He strips off his clothing and examines himself, looking for an escape route for the child. Ridiculous, it gives him the shivers to remember this part of the dream, searching his own body for an opening that doesn't exist.

And then the dream changes. The child changes in the dream, and suddenly there is a dead thing inside him. How did Georgie bear it? He wants it out of him; he never wants it to leave his body. In the dream he begins bawling helplessly, a grief unlike anything he's ever felt coming over him, his body shaking, convulsing. And it's the weeping that wakes him.

He's afraid that one of these nights he'll cry out in his sleep, that he'll sob loud enough to wake Georgie. He lies beside her stillness, snuffling as quietly as he can, wiping his eyes with the hairy backs of his hands. He wishes he'd been less gruff with her at the time, less *sensible* about the whole thing.

He came to the hospital as soon as word reached him underground and stood in the doorway to Georgie's room, feeling awkward in his work clothes, his face still black with rock dust. More than anything he was embarrassed by the whole affair, as if he'd unexpectedly fallen in front of a crowd of spectators. The best that could be done in such a situation, he felt, was to carry on as if nothing had happened. He walked over to his wife and held her hand while she cried quietly in her bed. "Now woman," he said. "There's no help in that. We'll have others."

She had fixed him then, as if she'd just recognized him for someone she disliked and might someday learn to despise. "We're not collecting a set of dishes," she said. "It was a *baby* Sandy."

It's a wonder, he thinks now, that Georgie stuck it out with him for so long.

GEORGIE CAN STILL RECALL the night she made up her mind to leave her husband.

She had gone to bed before Sandy and was nearly asleep when he made his way quietly up the stairs to the bedroom. He undressed in the darkness, not wanting to disturb her with the light, then settled in beside her, his hands moving firmly across her back. She rolled over and pushed her face into his chest, automatically reaching under her nightshirt to help him fumble off her underwear, then turning to lie beneath him. He kissed the side of her face once, twice, and then lay still.

It was after he fell asleep that she started, almost sat bolt upright in bed. In the darkness she couldn't picture his face. Her heart hammered against her chest. Seventeen years of marriage, three children, and she had suddenly forgotten what the man looked like.

The thought that he might sometimes forget her in the same way made her skin crawl. She thought of him moving over her in the darkness without uttering a sound, and it struck her then that she had never heard him say the word love in her presence. His father's son, after all. Practical to a fault, plain-spoken. Plain-looking too, though she couldn't bring the details together to see his face in her head just at that moment. She slipped out of bed, heading downstairs where she sat in his recliner until the first grey light of dawn lifted the room out of darkness. She considered how long things had been the way they were, how numb she had become, as if she had spent a decade submerged in frigid water. Made up her mind.

THE FOLLOWING NIGHT, Sandy started on midnights. She did up his lunch tin, made him a cup of tea, saw him through the door. Then she went upstairs to pack, allowing herself one suitcase for her things, one for the kids. She wrote Sandy a letter, telling him she would be staying with her mother in North Harbour, that he could come and take the car whenever he wanted it.

She woke the children at six a.m. Helen, who was almost twelve, helped her dress the two boys. "It's a surprise," was Georgie's answer to every question about why they were up so early, and why the suitcases were packed, and where they were going without Daddy. She sat them at the table with bowls of cereal and carried the suitcases out to the car. She looked up at the sky, the long surf of pink light at the horizon beyond the row of houses as bright as a fresh scar. At that moment there was a waver in her heart, a doubt. And that's when the Company siren began wailing.

AFTER THE LOCAL NEWS Georgie lifts herself up out of the knitting chair and sets two pairs of wool socks with newly darned heels on the seat. Sandy watches her as she walks into the kitchen for a last glass of water before bed. There's a slight limp in her step and he feels a momentary pang of guilt about the broken spring in her chair. He could fix the damn thing, but he's afraid Georgie will read into it, that she'll think he's getting soft in his old age. He isn't about to let on if he can help it.

"You coming?" Georgie asks from the foot of the stairs.

"You go ahead. I'll be up in a bit."

Sandy has taken to staying awake as long as he can these days, partly because the dreams have become more persistent, and partly because it's a chance to leaf through the family photos in the cabinet under the coffee table without Georgie knowing. He hadn't paid much attention when she spent hours painstakingly putting the albums together, and couldn't see the sense in it when she wrote names and dates on tiny scraps of paper and taped the captions below each picture. "If you're that bored," he had said. "I wish you'd put as much effort into making a bit of supper," he had told her. "Would you lift your head out of those goddamn pictures for two minutes?" he'd said.

There is one page in particular that he finds his way back to every time he sits with the stack of albums in his lap. Like an alcoholic lured by the gravitational pull of a bar, Sandy inches towards a photo of a tiny grave marked by a white wooden cross. *Andrew Samuel Wilcox* in Georgie's careful handwriting. At the time, Sandy saw no point in naming the child and agreed to it only at Georgie's furious insistence. But he can't imagine anything quite as distressing as the thought of looking at this photo now without a name in his head to connect to it. He's wanted to tell Georgie this for months, but has never found the words or the courage.

It sometimes seems to Sandy as if he's lived all his days on that ice field in his dream, running to save his life and not looking back. As if he's slipped through his sixty odd years without paying enough attention to the world to remember the order of the seasons. For reasons he doesn't understand, he is just now becoming acquainted with himself, and he spends hours with the pictures, trying to set their peculiarly layered chronology to memory. As if they might be able to return a life he long ago misplaced.

EVERETT KING IS OVER for his daily snort. Ever since his Sylvia passed on he's made a habit of dropping by around three in the afternoon for a whiskey or two. It breaks up the day, he says, makes the house feel that much less lonely.

Georgie keeps a close eye on them. Occasionally she's slipped and they've gone and gotten themselves drunk before supper and then the silly buggers get out of hand. Reminiscing. Going back underground. Reliving the accident. Everett's leg was badly mangled by the rock fall and he spent the three days slipping in and out of consciousness. For his part, Sandy claims to have spent the whole time praying to see his three darling children again, to lie one more time in the arms of his wife. "Drunken old fool," is what Georgie thinks when he gets on like that. He has never said a word to that effect when he's sober.

"Georgie," Everett says, "you were a saint to my Sylvia. You were a rock, you were." There's a tell-tale quiver in his voice. "She always said she'd have gone right off her head if you hadn't been there with her."

"Now Ev," she says sternly, "don't you go getting teary here this afternoon. I won't have it, you hear me? And that's your last drink for today, I can tell you that. You too," she says to her husband as she gets up to start supper in the kitchen.

"Saint Georgina!" Sandy toasts, his almost empty glass in the air, and Everett offers a hearty "Hear, hear."

"Oh fuck off, the both of you," Georgie mutters.

It comes out angrier than she means it. And it's mostly guilt, she knows. Guilt about the fact that she *was* a rock through the whole ordeal. She spent her time comforting and encouraging the families of the other men underground with her husband. She fed and cared for her kids, for Sylvia's and for Laura Caines's four boys on top of that. She's ashamed to admit to herself that, more than anything, she was angry with Sandy. The thought never once crossed her mind that he might die, that she might lose him for good. There were moments when she was convinced this latest catastrophe was simply an elaborate attempt to hold onto her. As if he had planned it to happen just as she was about to leave him.

It wasn't until he arrived home safe and sound that she felt any pity for him at all. There were weeks of him waking from the same nightmare of being lost underground, crying out in the darkness. She'd *shush* him gently and hold him for hours afterwards, rocking him in her arms. It seemed impossible to her then, the thought of him waking up alone in this house, without her or the children. And almost despite herself, the pity worked at whatever was left of her love for him, the way ashes are stirred to build a new fire. It was a slow spotty fire by and large, the dirty bit of smoulder you get from burning green wood, more smoke and irritation than warmth. But enough finally to keep her where she was, and where she is now: mixing weaker and weaker drinks for an old man in the afternoon; clipping his thick yellow toenails once a month; allowing him the pleasure of an occasional waltz at the Legion. She'd made up her mind to stop being unhappy a long time ago.

"Georgie," her husband calls from the living room. "Any chance of one more little one for Ev before he heads home?"

HE DREAMS OF HIS PANIC beneath the ice when he was a boy, his exhausted body pressed to the cold weight of it above him; blur of blue-green light on his face like the colour cast by stained glass, an opaque barricade between himself and his life.

Then there is the heat of the kitchen and the sound of a woman crying, his body being roughly shaken; the thumping on his chest, as if someone was knocking at a door to wake a sleeper in a distant part of the house.

When Georgie finally manages to shake him awake his face is wet with tears.

"Sandy," she's saying, "Sandy, wake up."

He looks at the face leaning over his own as if it's the face of a stranger, a person he knew years ago and can't quite place. "What a Christly racket you were making," Georgie says, wiping the tears from his cheeks with the palm of her hand. His expression is silent and imploring, edged with equal parts desperation and embarrassment, like the face of a man who has been paralyzed by a stroke. The dream hasn't begun to leave him yet and the features of the room and the woman beside him have a slightly other-worldly feel, the grey of dawn nuzzling the windows, the edges of things softened by the dim light.

"What was it," his wife asks him. "What were you dreaming about?"

He shakes his head, the tears coming again, his body wracked with sobs. His lungs feel water-logged, useless. There's a burning sensation in his chest, it hurts simply to breathe. He buries his face in Georgie's chest and holds onto the warmth of her body. Prays he will never wake up.

Ring Around October

ADRIENNE POY

OF COURSE it only happens when we're on our way to the cottage, so I can't say that it has a *recurrent frequency* (my sister is a psychiatrist) or anything like that. I'll be sitting there rolling and unrolling the window in the back seat for the dog so he doesn't get *a*) a cold in his eyes or *b*) claustrophobia, and maybe I'll lean my forehead against the window and there it is bang, bang! It's always fall, you see, when this happens. With little folded-up dead brown leaves that you could never float in puddles on the sidewalk because they're full of pinholes. There were always leaves like that on Willow Street, bobbing around the gutters and whooshing up with every passing car.

We always sat on the porch, Gumby and I; after the supper dishes were done, and watched the leaves flying around. And Gumby would say that Willow Street had more trees on it than any other street in Larchwood, and I would agree. I'm glad Gumby was my grandmother because anyone else would have put her into one of those most-unforgettable-character things and they'd never have really caught Gumby's flavour. People used to say (especially Mrs. Estley across the street) that Gumby and I looked alike. Which was to say that neither of us looked like anything. Both of us had pale brown everything, including freckles. My best friend at college, Sally Jane, used to tell me that I fitted into every surrounding. Like a kind of human chameleon. Elsie, she used to say, as she brushed out her long, long, blond hair, you're so bloody lucky you only look as good as your surroundings; you'll never offend anyone. To this day the best picture I have of myself was taken on our honeymoon; me beside a giant purple rhododendron in Stanley Park, Vancouver. I guess you could say that my idea of happiness is to feel like I looked beside that bush. I didn't just fit; I belonged.

I never knew anything else besides the house, library and garden on Willow Street, Larchwood, until I was nineteen. My sister, who is fourteen years older than me, kept descending on us in successive Junes and demanding that I come with her on a bicycle trip through Provence, or on a tour of Scandinavian ("they're the cleanest people in the world, Elsie") mental hospitals. But Gumby would always say that Elsie could get her best view of rape, murder and romance three blocks from our very doorstep, so what was the point of travelling three thousand miles for it? And I would spend my summer clipping the croquet field that ran all around our house. That fall, for the first time in years, George Ernest Estley was home. He was six years older than me, and he had gone to agricultural college to learn all about soil cultures. And he did that, more or less, for a few years, and then here he was for the fall. George drank.

I guess the fall that he came home for good, he had been in my life for at least ten years. In it, but not of it, as they say. I lived on the third floor of our house and because Willow Street curved, I got a full side view of their house. I remember watching when he was still in high school. He wore running shoes all the time and baggy, dirty white pants and he went out with a girl called Waverley Wiggins who had brown hair like mine, but on her it looked like a Breck ad. Sometimes on Sundays she would come to dinner, wearing her beautiful white cloche her mother brought her from New York, with huge pink poppies all over it; she was also the first girl in town to wear her silk stockings rolled and make it respectable. She was clever; she had written *The Development of Larchwood's Natural Resources* for the Kiwanis Club Essay Contest and had won. It was the year of our centennial, so a great big fuss was made. I talked about her all the time to Gumby, and to myself; where I'd seen her, what she was wearing, what mark she would get in the Conservatory exams all the Larchwood pupils were taking. And I hated her. I hated her when I saw George Ernest come home at eleven and I knew that the Viscount movie house closed at ten-thirty and that it took fifteen minutes (full speed down Larch Avenue) to get to her house from downtown and fifteen minutes to get from her house to Willow Street; and I would hate her when he came home at one thirty-five a.m. and sat in his car smoking three or four cigarettes in a row before taking off his shoes and tiptoeing into the house. And maybe the next day, he would look up from washing the car and I would look up from replacing the croquet wickets, and he would shout, "Hi, Elsie-chick, how's your Gramma?" He used to come over and chat to Gumby when she weeded the front flower border; his conversation to me was limited to asking me how my bicycle chain was holding out. Or whether I wanted him to paint my pogo stick. I sat on a blue campstool and looked at him and thought that he couldn't be farther away if he were sitting on the top of Mount Everest. After he left, I would sit looking at the imprint his running shoes had made in the grass.

When he started to go to college, he came home at Christmas and announced that he no longer believed in God and wouldn't go to church. As his mother had just become president of the Mothers' Union, as well as the afternoon WA, this was more than embarrassing. I wasn't shocked; I hadn't believed in God since I was seven, the year after I stopped believing in Santa Claus. I just wondered that it took George Ernest so long to reach a conclusion I considered to be foregone. He now smoked openly. Every Friday and Saturday night when he was home, he *went drinking* with his high-school friends who now worked in the soap factory. It was generally acknowledged that he had *gone bad*. Waverley Wiggins had gone to the States to a big women's college where her mother had gone. They had only gone out once since then. And that time, he tore the right sleeve off her dress and actually bit her arm. Then he yelled horrible things at her (everybody on the street woke up) and dragged her out of the car and pounded on her front door, holding her by her bitten arm and calling to her father to come and get his whore of a daughter. And after that little display, the whole town was disappointed that she hadn't been raped and Jack-the-Rippered. But Mrs. Wiggins anxiously assured everyone that horrible George Estley was just mean drunk, as usual. So then, of course, no decent girl could possibly go to the corner with George without earning all kinds of unwarranted fame. And so George went out with Rita Carlos who had emigrated with her brother from New York and who didn't stand a fighting chance against good old George when he had a mickey in him, and with Olga Wasniewski who didn't know what the word *fight* meant, in more than one way.

Olga worked at the Pinelands Hotel and Grill and had spent most of her life in logging camps near Seattle. She came and helped us spring-clean two years in a row and I remember her tenderly because she told me she thought I would have a real nice little body one of these days. George used to smuggle her into the house when his parents were away at the Lake. She wasn't pretty, though; I was glad she wasn't pretty.

Then he failed, and off he went, hitchhiking. Gumby got postcards about every four months, telling her that the Danube was muddy, the Alhambra beautiful and the Parthenon overrated. Then we heard nothing.

In my Senior Matriculation year, he just walked into the house one day and swung Gumby around, told her she was still the spiciest Unitarian he'd ever seen and asked her if she could still make that Apple Betty. Then he looked at me. It was one of those wonderful onstage moments when I would have loved to walk toward him with both arms raised forward to shoulder level, à la Katharine Cornell, head tilted to one side, voice low and trembling, and said, "Welcome home, George."

He said, "Hiya, old Elsie. You haven't changed a bit." And I said, "Neither have you, George."

I was lying and I hoped he was too. He looked thin and brown and old. Even when he smiled he looked tired. When I looked at him, I wanted to cry. He looked so old, so old.

Let's say Larchwood didn't welcome George back with open arms. In fact, I was the only young person George Ernest Estley talked to. He drank with the soap-factory crew, he talked to Gumby, he saw Olga Wasniewski, who no longer had the sideline as waitress at the Pinelands, and he drank alone. Gumby said that he should be put to work or his brains would settle into his hind end, but I think she was as good to him as anyone in his life ever was. And I guess he paid attention to me as an extension of Gumby. Sometimes he would come over and just sit and watch while I did my crossword puzzles in the evening. One night he watched while I went through two and then he said, "Elsie, why are you so practical?"

I looked up at him. He held an open bottle of beer by one hand and with the other he pushed his heavy horn-rim glasses high up on his forehead. I said, "Because I'm not beautiful."

"Well, Elsie," he said, after a moment's pause to enjoy my obviously unpained admission of fact, "that's God's truth. But of all the unbeautiful people I know, you shine the most. You do."

I sat there, in all my eighteen-year-old unbeauty and thought, you handsome dissipated bastard, thanks a mill for less than nothing. But I said, "You sure know how to sweet-talk the ladies, don't you, Georgie?"

He looked at me quizzically and said, "For God's sake, you're the first female over the age of fifteen I've told the truth to, except your grandmother, and you think it's sweet talk. What's the matter, can't you tell honesty when you see it?"

"Maybe not." But I mentally added that I could certainly tell George Ernest Estley when I saw him.

We glared at each other. Then George leaned over and tugged my nose out and down. "Come on, heap big Elsie, let's be friends till the white hope of the Algonquins turns purple."

Other times our conversations made sense. We competed with each other and with Gumby in our reading and I attribute my present middle-aged (almost) fits of morbidity to the fact of my having been forced to read Schopenhauer before I ever knew what the word *will* meant. Gumby and George and I would bat ideas around an open fire; I think it might have been the only time when George didn't drink steadily.

Then at Thanksgiving time, the Senior Matriculating class gave an evening of recitations and music. I asked George to come because I wanted him to hear me reciting Keats's Eve of St. Agnes; after all, I had to take some chances. Gumby made me a new dress of bright pink (my eyes blink just to remember it) lace over more taffeta, with pink silk stockings to match. George came all right, but the only thing that kept him from reeling into row H in the auditorium of Larchwood Memorial Collegiate Institute was Olga Wasniewski. She waved and threw a kiss to me; she knew half the people in the hall and winked and smiled at them all. George fell asleep on her shoulder and snored through *Michael: A Pastoral Poem* and a choral version of Psalm 139 for four male voices. By the time the program reached *In Memoriam: Selections,* George and Olga had been led out by Mr. Watson, the school janitor. The next day, George appeared and told me that he hadn't come to apologize, but to be thanked for leaving before he ruined my recitation. I guess I was silly, and Gumby would have been ashamed of me, but I sat on the edge of the porch watching Mr. Estley light a bonfire of leaves and cried. Like faucets. George looked into my face, which must have looked like a freckled dishrag, put his hand on my shoulder and said, "Just remember, Elsie, that I am probably the worst person you'll ever know. As long as you live."

I just kept crying like a Greek widow, thinking of all the things I could tell him, if only I had had the courage and if only I didn't know that he would only smile his thin hardly-a-smile-at-all and shake his head. So I kept crying. And then George said, slowly, "Elsie, would you like to go for a ride to Winchen's to get an Eskimo Pie?"

"In your car?" I hiccuped.

"Yes, unless you'd rather go on your pogo stick."

We drove to the opposite end of town to get our Eskimo Pies. Across the street in the Esther Larchwood Memorial Park, the Orange Lodge Band was playing *My Hero* and the *Washington Post March*.

"George," I said, trying to sound elaborately casual, "George, are you still in love with Waverley Wiggins?"

He pushed his glasses up on his forehead.

"Elsie, from one old drunk to one little girl, never ask questions to which there are no answers. You only confuse people. And that's not kind, is it?"

He sat in the twilight looking at me. I glanced at him and then looked out the window. Whenever I looked too long at him, I got the funny sensation that I wasn't really seeing him, but only remembering him. As though his sitting there on the other side of the car, or the room, or the hall was only a result of my saying "George, George, George" over and over again.

He turned his head away and placed his forehead against the window. He rubbed it up and down, up and down.

"What would you like me to say, Elsie? You have your choice of the Giant yellow equivocation or the Jumbo pure-white lie. Any preference? None? Oh hell, you're no fun."

"You'd never listen anyway. I know you."

"Do you, Elsie?"

"Yes."

He shook his head. He started the Stutz and we roared back to Willow Street in silence.

"How do you know me, Elsie?" He was staring through the windshield as though he were still driving.

"I know you, George, because I've watched you all my life. From across the street. That's how."

He got out of the car and opened my door for me. I stepped out of the car and felt the autumn wind, sharp as a reproach.

"Sleep the sleep of the just and innocent, Elsie. It's such a limited privilege. Make the most of it."

I turned and walked up the path that leads to our back door. Gumby always maintained that front doors should only be used for funerals and weddings. I started making coffee in the kitchen. I went upstairs to put my coat away and to get my Latin Authors homework. He was sitting at the kitchen table when I came back.

"If you know me, then you know I'm a coward, don't you?"

I put the cups on the table, and the cream and the sugar. "I don't know what you want me to say, George."

"Nothing at all. Just wondering if you'd noticed *all* my gem-like qualities. From across the street."

We drank our coffee silently. George leaned over the table and said "Let's sing." So we sang *Whispering Hope* and *Pack Up Your Troubles in Your Old Kit Bag.*

"What'll we do now, Elsie? The world's not frightened away yet."

"We're going for a walk."

"Out there? It's cold out there."

"I'll get my coat."

We walked around the house over the croquet field, round and round. We passed the elm tree fourteen times before I lost count. And George talked. Not that he told me anything I didn't know, but it was strange somehow to hear him tell it. I was dizzy at the time, thinking how he was confiding in me. Actually, I guess I was a kind of microphone through which he was speaking to an empty hall. It was too bad; we both needed an audience and we just had each other.

"Elsie, I'm going away again. I just can't stay here."

"Where will you go?"

"Out into the night, naked in a wet mackintosh. Without a little girl to guide me in circles."

"What will you do?"

"What I do best, Elsie. Lie and cheat. And leave. Ah, back to the simple life."

He stopped suddenly under the elm tree which we were passing for the tenth mile and said,

"I talk too much, Elsie. Tell me about you. What's ever happened to you?"

"Well, mostly pogo sticks and Eskimo Pies, I guess, George. Maybe a couple of bonfires here and there."

"Is that all?"

"Yes." I lied. I never felt badly about lying to George. He needed it. It was the only thing you could do for him. Like using lullabies to keep puppies from barking.

"Well, that's good. You're a lucky little girl. A lucky little girl. Don't ever let life grind you down, Elsie. Kiss and don't mean it; hit and do. The secret to life's success. Remember?"

"Yes, George."

"To make sure you do." And he bent over and put his lips to my forehead just above my right eyebrow. Smooth and cold as part of the night. I remember thinking that the bark of elm trees was the roughest thing I'd ever leaned a frozen hand on. And feeling like running water with sun on it. No wonder it makes me feel old to think about it.

And standing there like that, George said very quietly, "Well, Elsie." And then, "Say that you know everything I've told you, Elsie."

Even as I wondered where I would get the voice, I heard myself saying, "I know everything you've told me, George." And his arms folded around me. I was sure that when I opened my eyes the stars would be gone and the tree and everything but us. Everything would be gone that wasn't rocking gently, lightly. Rocking warm past cold Willow Street on an October night.

I only saw him once after that. I don't know what I expected; maybe that he would declare suddenly-discovered love for me, or that he would ask me to carry his umbrella. It's been thirty years and Willow Street and Larchwood have passed silently out of my life, along with news of George Ernest Estley. Gumby used to say that pain was like having your tonsils out: maybe nobody could tell to look at you, but it had happened just the same. One October day, George Ernest hopped on the 1.52 for Toronto and the whole town said a collective good riddance. With him went my chance to be a tiger-trainer, or a spy, or even beautiful. He just didn't ask me. To be anything, I mean.

And the Children Shall Rise

CAROLINE ADDERSON

HE WATCHES HER small thin fingers, quick like animals, scrabbling, as they crouch together on the side of the road.

"Help me," she says.

He obeys, running his hand along the curb base until he strikes a pebble.

"Here." He smiles.

She takes the pebble and puts it in its place, her only acknowledgement acceptance, although he waits for a word.

"Give me that one." She points to a rock nearby. He needs two hands to lift it. He is only four.

"More little ones," she says.

Soon the circle of stones is closed. He places his palm in the centre, but she grabs his wrist and yanks him away. She leans forward, hair brushing the ground, then spits where his hand was. From her blouse pocket she takes a matchbox and holds it out to him. She shakes it; the sound is not matches.

"What's in there?" he asks.

Carefully, solemnly, she opens the little drawer.

"Caterpillars," he says.

She nods.

"Caterpillars! Caterpillars! Where did you find them?"

"Watch," she says.

She takes a caterpillar from the box and puts it in the centre of the circle, on the dark mark of her saliva. A beautiful thing, it is peacock and starred and fringed with fine hairs. It crawls away. With her finger she guides it back to the centre. He reaches out to play too, but she stops his hand again. Then, quickly, so quickly he sees only the fleeting blur of her arm, the arc of a movement, she slams the rock down.

He stares at her. After a moment she turns her face, squinting as if the sun is in her eyes, and lifts the rock. In the circle of stones is a jellied mass, green and yellow, glistening.

"Is it dead?" he asks.

"Yes. Do you want to do it?"

"No."

"Then you pick one."

He selects a caterpillar, then watches the stone crush it.

"What are you doing, Carol?"

They look up. His mother is standing over them.

"Nothing," Carol says.

"It's not nothing," says his mother. "You're killing things." She crouches too. "Look, poor caterpillars. How do you think they feel?"

"Dead," says the boy.

"How do you think they feel?" she asks Carol.

"How do you think I feel?" Carol replies.

He watches his friend walk away down the road. She has long black hair past her waist and a step that is smooth and careless. Barefoot, she moves as if she has her whole life to get to where she is going. She stops and bends, scratches her ankle, then walks on with her arms out from her sides like wings.

"It's not that I don't like Carol Bell," his mother says later.

"I like Carol Bell," he says.

"I like her too. But she's seven, you know."

"I'm four," he says.

"I know. That's what I'm saying, Philip. You are four and she is seven."

"You are a hundred," he says.

She laughs and kisses him. "I'm sorry there aren't other children your age here. Do you miss your friends?"

"I miss Daddy."

"Yes," she says. "Sometimes I do too, though I shouldn't."

They have left his father behind and come to this little house in this summer town, where the roads are always dusty and no one wears shoes. His mother is painting again now.

"I like Carol Bell," he says.

"Yes, she has beautiful hair."

HE IS PLAYING on the swings with Carol Bell. She swings high, then leans back so her hair sweeps the grass. He tries to do the same, but falls backward with a thump.

She peers down at him. "Do you want a push?"

"No."

Carol Bell has pushed him before, slammed her hands against his back and sent him to dizzy, terrifying heights. He called for her to stop, pleaded for her to stop, and when she finally did, she ran away. He does not want her to run away now.

"Let's sit sideways then," she says.

He gets up and they straddle the swings, facing each other. Carol sways back and forth, gazing up at the sky. Her eyes are dark and deep-set, ringed with a faint blueness like smoke. Without looking at him, she glides forward and knocks her swing against his.

"Don't," he says.

She knocks him again.

"Please don't."

Then she smiles, just slightly, turning up the corners of her mouth and making her lips look smooth like fruit skin. She smashes into his swing with such force that between his legs there is only a sharp, singing pain. His face crumples. He is going to cry.

"I'm hungry," she says quickly. "Go get us something to eat." She takes his arm and shakes it. "Get something to eat."

By the time he is in the kitchen, his hand between his legs, he no longer needs to cry. He comes back with carrot sticks in one hand, his mother holding the other. "She'll only give us carrots," he tells Carol.

She plucks one from his fist.

"Don't you get breakfast, Carol?" his mother asks.

"Yes."

"What did you have for breakfast this morning?"

"Pancakes with blueberries and strawberries. And coffee," Carol says.

"Coffee?"

"Yes. I always drink coffee. I like it."

"Do you want to have lunch here?" his mother asks.

"Yes." Carol takes another carrot stick.

At lunch his mother asks after Carol's mother. Carol says that her mother is dead.

"What?" his mother exclaims. Then she frowns. "You're not telling the truth. I met your mother. And just the other day I saw her drive by."

"It wasn't my mother."

"Yes, it was. She waved to me."

"Anyway," says Carol Bell, "my brother is always screaming because of it."

The boy stares at her with his mouth hanging open, showing his half-chewed sandwich.

"Carol," says his mother, "I don't think you're telling the truth."

"I am," she says. "He sounds like this." She throws back her head and screams.

The boy looks at his mother unhappily.

"Well, we hope that your brother will be all right," she says. Then, slyly, "Here's a cup of coffee for you. What do you take in it, Carol?"

"Nothing. I drink it black."

And she does. She drinks it down black as if it were chocolate. His mother puts her hand over her mouth. She knows better than to test Carol Bell, or the boy's father, or anyone.

THERE IS JUST THE BOY and his mother living together in the small house, warm and close.

"Two buns in a basket," she tells him, beginning their game.

"Two bugs in a rug," he says.

"Two birds in a nest."

"Two pigs in a pen."

They fall down laughing and snorting like pigs. There is a love in this laughter that clings like burrs. But the boy wets his bed at night and sometimes cries for no reason.

In the evening when he bathes she sits on the edge of the tub and sings all the songs he asks for—"Froggie Went A' Courting," "Little White Duck," "Suzanna's A Funny Old Man." She takes up the wash cloth but he always wriggles from her embrace.

"Dirty thing," she teases.

When he is in bed, she reads to him, not more than three, four, stories, then he must brush her hair the hundred strokes. He falls asleep before forty.

"One. Some people lie," she tells him as he draws the brush through her hair. It is shoulder-length and greying.

"I don't lie," he says.

"Two. Of course not. You would never lie. Ouch. Daddy lied."

"No."

"Three. Yes, and sometimes Carol Bell lies. I want you to know that. Four."

"Okay."

"And don't play with Carol Bell except in our yard. Five. All right, Philip?"

THEY ARE ALMOST IN THE YARD, just at the end of the driveway, on the road. They have collected sticks, handfuls of dried leaves and grass, bits of paper, and put it all in the circle of stones. Carol takes out the matchbox and shakes it. The sound is matches.

At first there is just smoke, a brown veil that catches on his face, makes his eyes tear. He remembers what his mother told him: smoke follows a liar. He gets up and stands behind Carol. She arranges and rearranges the debris, blows on it, mumbles quietly in sing-song. The pile ignites in a sudden burst of flame. She pulls her hand away and he sees that her finger is burnt. He wonders if she will cry and leans around to look at her face.

"You got hurt," he tells her.

"What?"

"You got burnt."

"No, I didn't," she says.

"You did. Look."

"I didn't."

She pulls a stick out of the little fire and waves it around in the air. The flaming end makes a glowing baton. The boy, seeing the circles and figure-eights she is drawing, laughs.

"Watch," she says.

She takes the end of her hair and touches the fire stick to it. He hears the sizzle, smells the stench. "That's awful," he says. She laughs.

Other days they build other fires, in the yard now, under the willow where they are hidden by the curtain of leaves, next to the swing set, on the walk. His mother catches them when the fire spreads to a dry patch on the lawn. She rushes out of the house with a doormat and beats the fire into the ground, but a star-shaped singe remains, a reminder. The mat is ruined. The boy stands by with his finger in his mouth. Carol Bell is gone.

THEIR CITY HOUSE was large with windows even in the ceiling, a fireplace, a spiral stair. His father is an artist too. Sometimes the boy was allowed to play in his father's studio. The paintings were huge, almost the size of the studio wall, bright as balloons and puzzling. In some smaller paintings the boy could recognize a subject, usually a person, but only because his mother pointed it out to him, saying, "Look. Who do you think she is?" and never answering when he said, "I don't know."

Now in this new town, this small house, his mother works all day. She paints him as he plays and later he laughs at the border of gold she always draws around his body. She bought him a bamboo cage and two finches, then painted the birds preening a plumage that was not theirs at all, too vivid, shocking. When she does not paint, she cooks and bakes, changes his sour wet sheets in the dark, kisses him. She throws down her brushes.

"I have hardly worked in four years. Now I have all the time I need. So what's wrong with me?" She says this aloud but, the boy knows, not to him.

HE SITS ON THE FRONT STEP with Carol Bell. She stretches her thin legs in the sun. Her feet are astonishingly dirty, the soles black, toenails encrusted. He has never seen her wearing shoes. While she speaks, he fidgets nervously. She says that everyone in her family has a disease; her sister was sent to where they put crazy people.

"Where do they put crazy people?" he asks.

"Far away. Another country, I think. They tie her to a chair."

Her mother coughs ceaselessly. "Sometimes blood comes out, sometimes green stuff, sometimes spiders."

He cringes. "Spiders!"

The boy does not know what to say about these horrors, so he says nothing. Then she gets up and walks to the middle of the lawn. She raises her arms in the air and lifts one leg so she is posed in a crude arabesque. The sun is on her back. He watches and waits for her next movement.

She does not stir for such a long time that he is just about to call to her. Suddenly her arms stretch wide and her hair comes alive, fanning and spreading into a wheel. He watches her, open-mouthed, watches and is dizzied. Minutes before she frightened him; now she mystifies, turns and turns, a bit of paper trapped in a wind eddy, and he is sure that she will rise up from the lawn and spin away. Seeing her prepare for flight, he kicks off his sandals and runs onto the lawn.

The moment he joins her, she stops. Embarrassed, he goes back to the step and struggles to rebuckle his sandals. Carol Bell, meanwhile, begins walking along the edge of the flower bed. From the corner of his eye, he sees her crouching. When he finally looks up, though, she has disappeared.

"Gone home," he says unhappily.

He shuffles over to the flower bed to see if she has left a print of her bare feet. He sees instead that Carol Bell has pulled the heads off all the flowers.

"Did Carol Bell do this?" his mother asks.

"No," he answers.

"No? Who did it then? Philip, who did it?"

"Me," he tells her.

"You? Oh, Philip, don't say that. I know it's not true." He looks at her and notices a streak of blue paint across her cheek. "Did Carol do it?"

"No. Me."

She sighs and takes his hand. "Now what am I supposed to do with you? Listen, Philip, if I catch Carol Bell at this sort of thing again, I'll go to her mother."

"Her mother has a disease," he says.

"Nonsense. Carol Bell tells stories. Carol Bell lies."

He says, "I like Carol Bell."

She covers the paint streak on her face with her hand, as if it pains her.

THE BOY BRINGS a tumbler of water from the house and takes it to Carol Bell who sits at the end of the driveway. He is conscious of his mother standing in the front window watching, the way she used to watch his father. Carol grips a stick between her knees and works at fraying the end, but her fingernails are too bitten down; finally she uses her teeth.

They have made a volcano, swept the dust off the road to shape a hill, then pushed a finger down through the top. Carol carefully pours water into the hole. Then she stirs with the frayed stick, adds more water to make a thin batter. "Paint," she tells him. He claps his hands in glee.

She bites her lip, showing small teeth, and her face twists with the strain of concentration. She begins painting in mud on the driveway.

"Do a boat!" he says, but she is not listening.

Soon her strokes steady. With each line he tries to guess her picture and hopes it will be a boat. He thinks that she, seven years old, must be a fine artist and capable of drawing a fine boat. Then his face falls. She is not drawing but writing. He cannot read.

He sits in silent disappointment. She appears to be writing a painfully long word. Bored, he looks up and waves to his mother at the window. She disappears and a moment later is walking down the driveway toward them, arms crossed, frowning. Carol continues writing.

In one motion his mother swoops down, tears the stick out of Carol Bell's hand and hoists her up by the arm. She shouts, "You wash that! Do you hear me? Wash it and never do it again!"

"What does it say?" asks the boy.

"Another thing. I'm going to talk to your mother. I'm tired of your pranks."

Carol Bell stands stiffly and allows herself to be shaken. He has never seen the girl frightened before. Now she stares at his mother with wide eyes. His mother's expression softens and reddens to a fluster.

"I have to tell your mother."

Carol's face stretches into a grimace. He thinks she will cry, but she just stands there with her terrible twisted face, then jerks her arm free. He watches her walk slowly down the road, rubbing her arm.

"Get the hose, please, Philip."

"What does it say?"

"Nothing."

HE IS BRUSHING HER HAIR. A finch died that afternoon and they are both saddened though he could not accept her comfort. They forget to count his strokes. She tells him that the bird was good and will certainly go to heaven. He asks her if Carol Bell will go to heaven.

"Oh, Philip. I feel sorry for the girl, poor pretty thing. That lovely hair, those filthy feet. But with her lying, her mischief, she's a bad influence on you. I should have talked to Mrs. Bell and not gone back on my word. But the look on her face! How could I?"

"Will you go to heaven?" he asks.

She turns to him. "What do you think?"

He is not sure, so he shrugs. Then he says, "If Daddy goes with you."

She breathes deeply, making a noise like wind to clear away his blame.

CAROL BELL IS GONE for several days and the boy misses her. He lingers at the front of the house, on the lawn where she once did her dance, down at the end of the driveway where they had their circle of stones. When at last he resigns himself to her absence, she appears, beckoning to him from behind the hedge. He goes to her delighted, stays the morning, but when he comes into the house for lunch, he is distraught.

He has trouble with his meal. He keeps his right hand under the table.

His mother laughs. "Is it a game?"

"What?"

"Eating like that. Are you playing a game?"

"Yes," he says and looks away. When he looks back, she is frowning.

"What's wrong, Philip?"

He begins to cry.

"Give me your hand. Oh, Philip!"

Carol Bell has carved a little figure across the back of his hand. It is not deep, and it did not hurt too much. He likes it, in fact: a strange mark, like a flower or a star, coloured rust with his dried blood.

"Come with me," she says, "We're going over there."

"No!" he cries.

"We must show Carol's mother what Carol did."

"I'm scared," he says.

So his mother goes alone, is only gone a few minutes. When she returns she forbids him to play with Carol Bell.

"CAROL BELL is on the swings!"

"What?" She comes and looks out the window. "You stay here. I'll go and talk to her."

This is the very next day. He can just see her form through the trees. Last night he dreamed of Carol Bell walking away with her arms out from her sides like wings. She spun once around and took to the air. He believed he would never see her again.

"Carol Bell is on the swings!" He follows his mother out the door.

His mother says, "Carol, what happened?"

"Nothing," Carol answers.

"What happened to your hair?"

"Nothing."

"Who cut your hair?"

"Nobody."

Carol's hair is hacked raggedly, shorter on one side than the other. She swings slowly and smiles at them.

"Did you cut your hair or did your mother cut your hair?"

"No one cut my hair."

"But it's gone!" cries the boy.

His mother takes him by the hand and leads him into the house again. She sits down on the sofa and stares at the floor.

"Did I make a mistake?" she asks. "Did I do the wrong thing? What would anyone do?" Then she looks at him, "Did you know?"

He does not have any answers for her. She holds out her arms and he comes to her, falls forward and touches her cheek. Then he takes her soft skin between his fingers, takes it and twists, pinches with all his strength. She cries out in pain, pushes him away and slaps his face. They look at each other, stunned, stunned by the hate there. Finally he comes again into the circle of her arms and they weep.

Dead Girls

NANCY LEE

YOU ARE ADDICTED to television news. The speculation, the body bags, the hopeful high school photos; dead girls, everywhere. The police have arrested a man in a suburb of your city—a retired dentist, a small bungalow, a large backyard. A mass grave discovered by a dog named Queenie, who followed a tennis ball through the snow and retrieved for her owner a browning scapula. The first of an undetermined number of female skeletons. Just off the patio, behind the picnic table, a manicured lawn, a soft-spoken man. So far, the victims are all prostitutes, bodies for hire, disposable girls. Between four and midnight, you watch five hours of local coverage. You switch from channel to channel at peak times, five and six, ten and eleven. You keep the volume high. When your husband comes in to ask if you want dinner, you watch his lips move, demand that he speak up.

YOU HAVE NO TOLERANCE for whispering, for delicate sounds. The soft swish of the broom as you drag it across the kitchen floor makes your teeth hurt. You look down at the small pile you've made: two popcorn kernels, a broken matchstick, an old twist tie; you and your husband leave so little behind. You dig the broom under the lip of the stove, force it between the refrigerator and counter, wish for something that isn't yours. A hair clip.

THE AGENT has told your husband it is difficult to make a sale when you refuse to leave the house during showings. She is forced to whisper, which, she has explained to your husband, makes her seem less than honest. She has also said that you unnerve the browsers with your awkward stares and constant pacing. You try to sit still while the agent is there. You are an exhibit, you tell yourself, a rare and pitiable specimen perched at the counter, sipping your tea. You do not smile, but focus intently on your cup, best they see you in your natural environment. The agent is huddled close to a young couple with twin toddlers; you hear yourself described as a "motivated seller." You hear the mother say, "It's much nicer than the photo." The toddlers, a girl and boy, pull on their mother's cuffs and pant legs, stuff their free hands into their mouths, sway toward you as if you are some curious animal. You bare your teeth at them. The girl moves behind her mother's thigh, the boy smiles, a thick, saliva-lipped smile. The mother looks over her shoulder at you; you stare back. You want to tell her that your family is broke and your husband is eager to sell the house you raised your child in, but if it were up to you, you would fight her for it.

YOUR HUSBAND'S WHISPERING is the worst. The sound of his pencil as he hunches over ledger books at the kitchen table, pressing so hard the silhouettes of his numbers carry through several pages. You hear every *scratch scratch* in every column; it drowns out the late night news. During a commercial break, you tear a stack of papers out from under his hands, the hospital invoices, the loan applications, the amortization forms, throw them in the air, cruel and ecstatic, scream at him, "This is a family, not a bank. You can't keep withdrawing!" He rests his forehead in his palms, then stands, places his pencil neatly in the seam of his book, and walks away from you, goes upstairs to bed. You stare at the papers on the kitchen floor, consider for a moment finding a glue stick and arranging the documents into a fiscal wall mural, something to horrify prospective buyers. Instead, you leave the paper scattered like debris and take your husband's seat at the table. You read his account of each transaction: name, expense, credit, debit. Your small family's history in numbers, balance falling from positive to negative in staggering increments. You study the back of each page, the relief of your husband's entries raised up like Braille. Every thought, every feeling he has had, focused into that tiny point of graphite. You run your fingertips over the contours of lines and loops, forward and backward, try to decode his closed, quiet language.

THE LENDING OFFICER at the bank had understood completely. A small man with dyed black hair in a neat crew cut. A crisp white short-sleeved shirt, a plain blue tie. As soon as he heard the words recovery centre, detox program, he approved your second mortgage. He showed you a pin and a small photo in his wallet of him holding a gaily iced supermarket cake. He told you in a hushed voice that he, too, was in recovery, then nodded as if you were conspirators. These things take time, he said. What he meant was, these things take money.

YOU HAVE STOPPED measuring her distance in days and weeks, you are on to months and years. You last saw her a year and a half ago in the bright light of the glass-walled treatment centre. Her last phone call was seven months ago, while you were waiting for the ten o'clock news. When you lifted the receiver to your ear, all you heard was a girl crying. It made you cry. Then you heard, "Mommy, Mommy," and you couldn't speak, could only press the cool receiver hard against your face. "Please Mommy, I'm sick." You knew that "sick" could mean a lot of things. There was a click. Your husband had run upstairs to the bedroom phone. His voice was gentle and focused. "Clare? Where are you?" And your daughter spoke again, sounding suddenly grown-up and pulled together, "Outside the art gallery." You wanted to tell her then about selling the house, but you didn't want to upset her, to tip her away from you. Your husband spoke, "Do you want us to pick you up, or meet you at the hospital?" And Clare started to cry again, her voice hiccupy and childlike, "Pick me up, Daddy." You and your husband drove to the art gallery with a blanket and winter coat even though it was July. You spent two hours waiting on the art gallery steps. Your husband walked to a Starbucks and brought back iced coffees. He didn't speak, except to comment on how warm the summer evening was. You could barely hear him over the scraping of skateboards below you. A group of skate kids were doing tricks around the lit fountain. You listened to their boards grating over the carved stone rim, the slaps of their palms as they passed one another, their jeering voices. You wondered where their parents were. Your husband walked down the small concrete steps to where the kids gathered, lighting cigarettes. He had a quiet talk with their slouched bodies, lifted a photo out of his coat pocket. They all shrugged and shook their heads, their hair swaying in front of their eyes like fine beaded curtains.

WHEN YOU GOT HOME that night the front door was broken open. Small things were missing: money from your dresser, the spare-change jar, your husband's electronic organizer, the portable television from the kitchen.

THE BODY COUNT is at twenty-three. A female broadcaster, whose hair has turned from dark auburn to medium blond in the days you've been watching, announces that skeletons have been found in sets of twos, threes, and fours, an elaborate corpse orgy, orchestrated by the accused. Hip against hip, skull upon skull, fingers entwined, a morbid collage. She warns that the following scenes may be difficult to watch, that parents should ask their children to leave the room. A live camera pans through a backyard with cedar fencing, past a white plastic patio set and a painted picnic table to a huge rectangular dirt pit, its muddy sides reinforced with wood planks; small orange flags dot its surface. To you it looks like the beginnings of an in-ground swimming pool. The camera moves in closer. Protruding here and there beside the orange flags, pale slivers and rounds, the bones of the unexhumed. Drowning hands. Then there are the victim photos—police record mug shots, thin, angry girls. The parents of a recently identified victim weep openly on the screen. The mother is dark-skinned, maybe Malaysian or Filipino; the father wears a baseball cap. They bow their heads, hold up a photo of their daughter at her high school graduation and repeat over and over that she wasn't a prostitute, that the police have confused the facts, that she was a good girl. Her face is homely beneath the tasselled cap, a smatter of acne across her brown forehead; she is a little on the plump side; her lipstick is pink, not scarlet. This is how they want their daughter remembered, they say, as they push the photograph towards the camera. You wonder if you would do it differently.

YOU AND YOUR HUSBAND have not had sex in over a year. You have thrown out your birth control pills, lubricants, anticipating you will never have sex again. It is as if the two of you have been accomplices in an unspeakable crime and can no longer return to the backroom of its conception. You move around your house like cautious guests, clothing wrapped tightly, eyes averted. Signs of affection have been reduced to domestic favours, someone has made breakfast for two, someone has put the bathmats in the wash. Each regards the other's suffering as something foreign and solitary; this awareness dilutes everything between you, reduces your connection to a thin wet strand, a tenuous liquid thread. If there were times you considered consolation in lovemaking, they were brief: a moment when he rested his hand on your hip, the second it took for you to brush an eyelash from his cheek. Until you remembered the act itself, the furious press of bodies, the hushed, plaintive cries. And its results: the frantic upstream swim, the penetration of nucleus and with it, the reckless joining of genetic material, the shrouded crapshoot of chromosomes. So much easier to believe that it all went wrong back then, in that hidden and automatic chemistry. Better there than under your roof, in your care. Nature versus nurture—where is it that life begins?

THE DAY YOUR HOUSE IS SOLD, the news breaks that the accused kept a record of his victims: first name, eye colour, left-handed or right-handed, bra size. The newscaster, an older man with a slouchy face and gelled hair, tells you that police hope this inventory will speed up the identification of Jane Doe skeletons. The document was leaked to the media early that morning by an unknown source; the police retaliated immediately by acquiring a court order barring the press from releasing what the police have been referring to as "the ledger." You are sitting at the kitchen table with your husband and the real estate agent; she is opening a bottle of expensive champagne and telling your husband a joke about a man and an alligator. The television in the other room is turned up so you can hear the news. Several newspapers and television stations have lawyers in court seeking permission to broadcast the ledger's contents, citing that it is the public's right to know. The agent fills three glasses and raises a toast. "To new beginnings." You carry your glass to the counter and pour your champagne down the sink.

WHEN YOU WERE A CHILD, your parents got divorced and the nightmare you had was this one: on a regular, sunny day, you walked home from school, the same route, the same trees, the same tire swing in the neighbour's yard. But when you reached your house, strangers lived there. An immigrant family, dirty and unkempt, filled the front doorway, stuffed together like old coats in a dark closet. When you asked them about your parents, they all screamed gibberish and flapped their arms wildly. The children, dwarflike, hidden in the shadowed archways of their parents' legs, hissed and spat at you. The smell from inside the house was like burnt milk. The door slammed shut. You stood on the steps and cried.

UNLIKE YOUR PARENTS, you and your husband are not getting divorced. You have decided, and suspect he has too, that it is far better punishment to stay together.

YOU HAVE SIFTED THROUGH memories and household items often, looked for signs of it all beginning. You have scrutinized photos of Clare, searched for a marker, a hint in the openness of her eyes, the set of her mouth, that she was changing, preparing to fall away from you. You study them with a magnifying glass, but there is nothing, just your bright smiling daughter perched on the edge of a swimming pool. You have kept report cards, receipts from piano lessons, Brownie badges, macaroni art, but these offer no indications, these are not clues. You cannot reconcile these artefacts of Clare's childhood with the memory of finding her, at fourteen, in the garage with a boy, her panties clutched in a fist behind her back, and the smell in that hot, dusty space, the musk of your own daughter's body. Or with the sadness that slipped over her like a veil, dulled her into a quiet melancholy, that made her difficult to talk to, almost impossible to rouse out of bed in the morning. You cannot pinpoint the event that pushed her from childhood to adulthood. A heartbreak, a seduction? Was it an older boy? A group of girls? Was it the lure of the liquor you left unlocked in the dining room cabinet, the liquor you found, a few months later, to be nothing but coloured water? How long, you had asked your husband in front of embarrassed guests, how long do you think it took her to drink all that? You are ashamed to admit it, but you have even looked at your husband and wondered about sexual abuse. You are looking for an answer that will relieve your own culpability, something that will prove you, if not innocent, then at least misled.

YOU HAVE REFUSED to pack up Clare's room. Each day you stand outside the closed door and hope the inertia of everything in there—clothes, books, stuffed animals, dust—will stop the planet from turning. What keeps you from going in is the silence, the unbearable absence of sound in that room. So, while wandering through a mall one day, you decide to buy a stereo, something to keep you company while you gather Clare's things. You choose a small portable one, with a five-disc CD changer. You try to select five CDs that Clare would like, but you don't know what Clare likes, so you buy numbers one to five from the Weekly Top Ten rack. You charge it all to your credit card. When you get home, your husband is in the drive-way in gloves and a toque, washing his car in the freezing cold. He offers to wash yours. "What's that for?" he asks, points to the large box in your arms. "Clare's room." He starts to say something low and serious but his voice is drowned by the spray of the hose dangling limp in his hand. You turn and walk away. Inside the house, you climb the stairs, balance the box against your chest. You turn the door-knob with two fingers, push the door open with your foot. You lean down, lowering the box to the ground, and what you see when you look up forces you to sit on the floor. The room is empty. He has made it there before you. Furniture, toys, clothes, all stripped away; even the curtains are gone. You try to remember pop star posters, school certificates, an endangered species calendar, the photos and stickers on her vanity mirror. When you open your eyes, there is only the dirty peach of the walls. You wrap your arms around the cardboard box. The corners pinch against your fore-arms and wrist, pushing you away, but this only makes you hold on tighter. You start to cry. Your husband appears in the doorway. "I thought it would be easier," he says. Before he can move to you, you shake your head, shout at him that he is not what you want. When you look up again, he is gone. You wipe your face with your hand. You kneel on the floor and begin to tear the box open, strips of cardboard and staples coming away in your hands. You set the stereo in the centre of the room, load in the CDs. You flip through the instruction manual, press some small metal buttons, set the machine for continuous play and turn the volume up high. You make sure the door will lock when you close it. You leave Clare's room, and slam the door behind you.

DAYS AFTER the real estate papers are signed, the telephone rings. You have decided to stop saying hello. Instead, you lift the receiver and wait for the other person to start talking. Your husband's barely audible tones. A suggestion of going out for dinner smattered with *are you there's?* You are distracted by the muffled bass of the music coming from Clare's room, a surrogate heartbeat. You hear yourself agreeing to meet at a Japanese restaurant at six o'clock; you know he wants to talk about the new apartment, the move; you will have to tape the news. You put down the phone and immediately it rings again. You forget yourself and say "Hello," as the receiver touches your ear. You hear whispering, amplified, close to the phone, a woman and a man. "Hello," you say again, your voice dashing down an empty corridor. A muffled conversation on the other end and the sound of someone smothering the mouthpiece. "Clare!" you shout into the phone. A tumbling sound; someone grappling with the receiver. A sudden tinkling, like small bells. A man's voice, "Sorry, uh …" Then you hear it, clear in the background, the throaty ring of your own child's laugh. The man's voice again, snickering, "Hey, wrong number." There is a click and you are disconnected.

THERE ARE CERTAIN CHANNELS open to you when your child has been arrested more than once, been hospitalized more than once. A government-run courtesy that is not wasted on parents whose children are mere underage drinkers or weekend runaways; a level of service reserved only for those like you, who have spent time in a holding cell, once cupping a handful of your daughter's vomit as she wretched and shook in front of you, once cradling a maxi-pad between her legs after what she and police called a "bad date." You pull the business card out of your wallet and call a constable who calls your phone company. Within minutes you have the address of a telephone booth downtown.

THE PHOTO YOU CARRY is a recent one, a Polaroid you took in front of the police station two years ago. Clare's face, drawn and dark, a bluish shadow around her left eye. She is slouched against the cement wall of the building, her body like thin cord beneath the denim jacket, her left shoulder jutted up in defiance, the right side of her body turned into the wall as if she is about to recede into it. You waited on the sidewalk while the picture surfaced; Clare smoked a cigarette. A social worker in the waiting area had lent you the camera. "Take a photo of her now," she said. "You'll find her faster next time. Faster than with that, anyway." She pointed to the photo you were holding, Clare's eighth-grade school photo. Clare in a bright red cardigan with a white t-shirt underneath. Her smiling face, still round with baby fat, touched lightly with the powder blush, mascara, and lip gloss you had helped her with in the morning. Around her neck, a thin gold chain with a single pearl pendant, the gift you had given her for her elementary school graduation. This was the Clare you were searching for. And though physicians and nurses and therapists had told you that it was best to approach the process without expectations, you clung stubbornly, secretly, to the hope that this Clare would return. On the sidewalk, you showed the Polaroid to your daughter, asked her, "Is this really you?" Clare held the photo in her dirty hands, squinted through cigarette smoke, shrugged and handed it back to you. The white bottom of the Polaroid was smudged with her thumbprint, a dark trail of swirls and circles that seemed to lead nowhere.

THE PHONE BOOTH is at an intersection on a busy nightclub strip. Though it's February, and barely dusk, working girls in miniskirts stroll the curb, clutching their fake furs around them. They hover, then move quickly toward the cars that slow down. Some of them troll the sidewalk, sashaying backwards as they proposition the men who are walking. When a man seems interested, a girl opens her coat, gives him a preview. From a distance, you study these girls, their narrow, youthful bodies, their confident postures, their carefully styled hair. You are relieved that most of them look healthy, strong, that they smile and joke with one another. You watch how they keep their legs rod straight, as if executing a gymnastics bow as they lean down into the open windows of cars; you notice that some of them don't bother with underwear. You approach the girls one by one, careful to not interrupt their transactions. You tell them, "I'm looking for my daughter," and show them the Polaroid. Some of them shake their heads without looking at the photo, some of them hold the photo and stare at it sadly. A dark girl in a purple stretch-velvet dress squeezes your hand, her long pink nails denting your skin, "I hope you find her." An older woman in a full-length fur coat pulls a pen and tattered notepad from her pocket. "Give me your name and number, I'll phone you if I see her." You write down your name, Clare's name, and your phone number. You see that other pages of the pad are filled with numbers. To stay warm, you settle in at a diner on the corner, the Lotus Café, a place you have visited before. As it gets dark, you keep an eye on the phone booth, and the girls doing business. You watch many of them leave and return. You wonder where they take the men. Do they kneel behind dumpsters? Stay in the cars and drive to a secluded parking lot? You want to remind them to be safe, to carry mace and maybe a knife, to keep the car doors unlocked and their seatbelts off, to have another girl memorize the licence plate. Make sure you count the money first and never, never go with more than one man. These are things your daughter taught you.

YOU HAVE OFTEN told Clare she was a difficult birth. You say it with pride, touching her hair, her hand, a shared trauma, a permanent bond. Thirty-two hours of labour and in the end, they gave you drugs, dragged her out with forceps. You had resisted the medication for hours, pleaded with the nurses, told the obstetrician you didn't mind going through pain for your child. The obstetrician laughed and said,

"You'll have plenty of time for that later." What you remember most clearly about the birth are the wet, slippery sounds: her mucousy slide from your body, the delicate slurps as they suctioned her nose and mouth, her first gargling cry, your husband's sobs behind his mask, and, when she was brought to you, the tiny, almost imperceptible sound her mouth made as it opened and closed.

"IF YOU'RE STAYING much longer, you'll have to order again." The waitress is collecting the plate from the Denver sandwich you finished hours ago. As she fills your coffee cup, you stare at her face; she is maybe ten years older than you. Her name tag says "Emily"; the cheerful energy of the name and the tired pallor of the woman seem horribly mismatched. On her lapel she wears a large novelty button, a portrait-studio photo of three kids and a teddy bear. "Are those your children?" you ask, pointing to the button. Emily looks down at her lapel as if to double-check. "Oh, no," she chuckles and shakes her head, "grandchildren." You nod and look at your watch, eight forty-five. You decide to go home.

THE NIGHT IS DARK, but the streetlights are beacons. The strip is jammed with cars, a slow parade of men with their windows rolled down and their stereos turned up. The working girls compete fiercely: some go topless beneath their open coats, some hike up their skirts to flash their merchandise. Outside the nightclub across the street, a line-up has formed. You examine the pairings. Men who are too old, too bald, too fat, too ugly, with beautiful girls at their side. Girls with steady smiles and dead eyes. Over the clicking of your heels on the pavement, you hear their stray laughter, their young offerings. You imagine these girls with their heads thrown back, their mouths open wide, the lengths of their necks callow and exposed. You know if you approached the men, accused them, berated them, they would laugh and shake their heads, wave you off with their ringed fingers. And the girls, the girls would cower, cling to those men, stare at you with guarded eyes. Not one of them would come with you to your car, not one of them would accept your offer of a hot meal, not one of them would let you take them home.

BEFORE RUNNING AWAY from the last treatment centre, Clare told you she would never live with you again. You were sitting across from each other on white rattan chairs in a solarium, surrounded by glass and ficus trees. Clare had just finished a session with her therapist. She explained her need for space and independence. You felt a small stab in your chest as if someone had slid a safety pin through your heart. Clare asked if you were okay. You said yes. You didn't tell her that it seemed unfair; you had been fighting to get her back for so long and now that she was here, safe in this place, surrounded by doctors and counsellors, you were being forced to let her go again. You didn't demand the years you were owed, the fairy-tale months of living together as mother and daughter. Instead, you laughed, nodded, tried to seem light-hearted, understanding. You remembered feeling that small sharp pain before, but couldn't recall when. Days later, the police in your living room, your daughter once again missing, the moment occurred to you. Her first day of kindergarten. You had expected her to cry when you got her to school, to cling to your dress and beg you to stay. Instead, the moment she saw the playground, the dome-shaped monkey bars, the wooden fort, the swings, she dropped your hand. She ran across the grass toward the other children, strangers, as if she couldn't join them fast enough. You stood still, not knowing if you should continue forward, not ready to retreat. Halfway there, she halted and turned to face you. You smiled. She was scared, the yards of grass between you, an immense distance to her small eyes. She would run back to you, or wait for you to catch up. But instead, she waved and shouted, "You can go now!" Clare bounded away from you, her arms outstretched toward the swings, her ponytail fluttering back at you like a dismissing hand.

YOU SIT IN YOUR CAR and listen to the radio news. A female broadcaster announces that a bomb has exploded in an embassy overseas; all twenty-nine bodies in the mass grave have finally been identified, all families have been contacted; the controversial ledger will be published in the next morning's paper. You rest your face against the steering wheel, feel the cold plastic against your forehead. This is real, you tell yourself, this is real. You sit back in your seat and close your eyes. The broadcaster is interviewing former neighbours of the accused. An elderly woman with an American drawl remembers that he posted a "no junk mail" sign on his mailbox. An older man, a retired welder, recalls him as friendly. "He seemed like a nice guy. He always said hello." A young mother of three, who declares over and over, Thank God my children weren't hurt, thank God my children weren't hurt, remembers that the dentist waxed his car an inordinate number of times. "Twice a week. I kept asking myself, why does he need it so shiny? I thought it had something to do with teeth."

IT IS THE SHUFFLE and clink against the car that startles you. Someone squeezing by. You look up and catch the backs of a man and girl walking. The girl, in a white leather coat that almost covers her short white skirt, takes long strides on high, chunky heels; the man, thin and older in a tight-fitting suit, follows quickly behind, looking around himself as he goes. You turn off the engine and get out of the car. You follow them down a short side road, then into the alley. They stop near the middle, against the back of a tall red-brick building. The alley itself is dark, but an emergency light farther down casts them in silhouette. There is an urgent smell of rotten fish and fresh urine; you press your palm over your mouth and nose. The girl says something, her voice too quiet for you to hear. The man shakes his head and the girl shrugs, turns away. The man says, "Hey," and grabs her arm. She yanks her arm away and holds out her hand. The man shakes his head again, pulls his wallet from his pocket. The girl counts the money, then slides the folded bills down into her shoe. She crouches in front of him, the pale of her hands reflecting some misdirected light. There is a quiet, rhythmic sound like soft panting, the musical jingle of thin metal bracelets. She is on her knees, her face buried in his open trousers while the man's head lolls back and forth. Her hair is twisted and gripped in his fingers, her legs, bent and stiff beneath her. You hold out your hand and trace the curve of her back in the distance. Sink into the awful hush, the muted groans and whispers, the tiny wet sounds, the dripping of water, the electrical buzz of the emergency light. You stroke the air in front of you, then look down at the ground, at the puddles of urine and wet garbage, the discarded condoms and needles. You will yourself to breathe, to take everything in. You force yourself to watch. When they finish, the girl stands, turns her head to the side, coughs. They both move away from you. The man walks to the back of the alley slowly, his hand dragging along the brick wall. The girl trots past him, veers left at the end of the alley, raises her arm to steady herself, her bracelets ringing like chimes as she turns the corner.

YOUR HOUSE IS SILENT. In the upstairs hallway, you see that Clare's door has been broken open, the door frame split and cracked to raw wood. The carpet littered with thin, ragged splinters, pieces of the stereo, stray buttons and dials, shards of black plastic casing, twists of metal and wire. Mechanical entrails. Your first thought is that somehow this is Clare's doing. Then you notice the hammer. This is your husband turning inside out.

YOUR BEDROOM IS DARK, but your hands find your husband in his usual sleeping position, fetal, turned away from your side of the bed. Your hands press into his shoulders, his chest, massage the muscles in his arms. You ignore his tired murmurs and *where were you's* as you climb onto the mattress, onto his body. You pin his shoulders with your palms, push yourself into him as hard as you can, rub your breasts over his chest; open your mouth wide as you kiss him. He is dazed, alarmed, arms at his side as you stare at him. You grab his right hand by the wrist and push it between your legs. He hesitates, keeps his hands still. You clench your thighs around his wrist, reach into his pyjama bottoms; you are coaxing him, begging him to become someone else. You drag your nails across his scrotum. He shivers and reaches up for your breast, squeezes it hard between his thumb and palm; you hear yourself moan. He grips your shoulder and turns you onto your back. He mounts you, pulls your panties down your thighs and enters you in raw, burning strokes. You slide your hands under his t-shirt and dig into his back; he whimpers. "I want to hurt you," you tell him as you dig your nails into his buttocks, "I want it to hurt." He whimpers again. He forces himself into you harder and harder, his hip bones spreading you, splitting you open. You feel a blunt pain through your stomach, the bed sliding, scraping against the hardwood floor. You cry out. Your husband stops, his whole body frozen above you, his eyes frightened wide, unblinking in long seconds of shame and ecstasy. He shudders. His body goes slack and for an instant you feel his full weight. You reach your hand to his face, to touch the sweat that has seeped from his skin, but he inhales sharply and moves off you. You turn your head and stare at him. His flushed skin, his startled eyes, his mouth open as he breathes. You want desperately for him to say something. You tell him about the news on the radio. He nods, wipes his face with the sheet, gazes up at the ceiling. His eyes start to close and you are afraid that he will fall asleep, leave you alone with a quiet house. You tell him everything then, slowly, deliberately. You begin with the phone call and the diner, the Denver sandwich and the waitress named Emily. You tell him about the alley, the smell, the needles. The girl, her arms, her knees, the man, her hair in his hands, her buried face. The wet sounds, the jingle of her bracelets. You tell him that she looked thin, but not too thin, not sick, not hurt. You stop. Your husband's face is tense and pale. For a moment it looks as if he is having trouble breathing, his chest strangely immobile, his jaw tight. You touch his arm and his face crumbles, he falls against you, cries into your breast, loud, heaving sobs, his chest shaking. You stroke and kiss the top of his head, rub your palm across his back, soothe him with your voice.

WHILE YOUR HUSBAND is in the bathroom, you open the bedroom window, let the cold city air fill the room. You listen to the sounds of traffic and sirens, rain on the pavement, someone's radio. You lie down on the bed, naked, hungry and tired, let the city wash over you, your body all gooseflesh, the insides of your thighs bruised and aching, a hot and empty soreness between your legs.

Ray

GUY VANDERHAEGHE

IT WAS RAY'S WIFE who was responsible for planting in him the notion that something had been askew in his childhood, wrong in his upbringing. He didn't want to believe this was true and Pam's persistence in claiming it was led to their first fight as a married couple.

"What about the train and the cards and all that?" she said. "You can't seriously suggest there was anything the least normal about that." He wasn't sure what his young wife meant. He had told Pam the anecdote intending to amuse her, but she had taken it all wrong.

Ray's story concerned the year he was ten. It was 1961 and his father was building a rec room in the basement. Just then rec rooms were all the rage, everybody on the block had one, or was building one, and his father didn't want to be left behind. That was the kind of man Ray's father was, always worried that somebody was stealing a march on him. Every night he came home from the mine where he was a shift captain underground, ate his supper hurriedly, without a hint of relish or appreciation, and then plunged downstairs into the basement to continue with his improvements. Only many years later did it strike Ray that his father had seen scarcely more than a few minutes of sun all that autumn. If he wasn't deep beneath the earth ripping out potash, he was down in his basement playing handyman in the artificial glare of a naked light bulb.

Most evenings Ray crept down the stairs after his dad and put himself quietly in an out of the way corner to watch him renovate, an awkward boy with embarrassingly heavy thighs, plump behind, and a mild, trusting face that led his teachers to smile at his infrequent, small misdemeanours and always think the best of him. Ray resembled his mother but it was his father he admired. In particular he admired the way his father looked, strong, lean, and rangy like the cowboys on his favourite television shows. Like those cowboys, his father seldom spoke and was inclined to stare away questions rather than answer them. Ray didn't ever ask him much, although by nature he was a curious boy. He would have liked to have been let in on the secrets of construction, to have understood how his father commanded and directed water and electricity to do his bidding, but he knew better than to make himself a bother and risk getting sent upstairs. Usually his father neglected to notice that Ray was even in the room with him, although once or twice in the course of an evening he would summon him to perform some simple task, to hold the end of a tape measure, to pass nails, to sweep sawdust. These rare occasions justified Ray's announcing to the kids on his street: "Me and my dad are building a rec room. We want to get it done by Christmas, for the parties. It's an awful lot of work."

Ray was agog with excitement over the anticipated Christmas parties. His family had not been in this particular town long, had never been in any town long because the nature of his father's profession kept them moving. An ore body played out, the bottom dropped out of a metal market, his father wrangled with a foreman, and the family pulled up stakes and moved on. For young Ray, the building of a rec room promised changes, the introduction of gaiety and permanence in their lives.

In the past Ray had heard his mother speak of a time when she and his father had "entertained." Whenever she talked about this his father stared at her, unblinking, until she stopped. If there ever had been such a time it went back far beyond Ray's recollection, back perhaps to when his brother Kenny was still alive. Ray understood, without resentment, that he was some sort of replacement for this dead brother. When he was six he overheard his mother say to a neighbour lady, "We just had to have another baby as soon as possible. It's the only way Ted could have got over it." And then she added, as an afterthought, "I felt the same way, of course." It always gave Ray a queer, unsettled feeling to think that he, too, might die one day and his place be usurped by a shadowy, unimaginable brother waiting patiently for his chance, in the wings.

BY THE END OF OCTOBER work on the rec room neared completion. Unlike anyone else who renovated, Ray's father had refused to invite the neighbour men over to drink beer and help. He said most of them couldn't be trusted to do the simplest job properly. He knew that much from watching them operate at the mine. Let them waste the company's time, not his.

Ted Matthews was a perfectionist, it was the word his wife relied on to describe him to strangers. The walls of imitation walnut panelling lining the recreation room were seamlessly fitted. There was tile laid on the cement floor and carpeting on top of the tile so that the cold wouldn't rise up in the winter and numb the soles of your feet like it did in so many other houses where people didn't care to do things right. At the end of the long, narrow room his father installed a wet bar and a second-hand fridge to keep beer and soft drinks cold. The refrigerator was the only item second hand. The chesterfield, the half-dozen wicker chairs, the pole lamp bought at the Saan Store mightn't be of the highest quality but they were new and not the junk and cast-offs which other people tried to pass off as furniture, stuff you looked twice at before you sat down on.

The only thing left to be done was run track for the railway. The railway was the crowning touch to the rec room, a bit of ingenious engineering that would allow Ray's father to speed drinks directly to his guests without ever having to step from behind the bar. It ran the length of the room, supported on brackets screwed into the wall panelling.

"What'll they think of that?" Ted kept demanding of his wife and son.

Ray was convinced his dad had to be just about the smartest dad in the world to come up with such a plan. Yet there was something about the railway he didn't completely understand. Several years before, Ray had been rooting around in his parents' closet and he had discovered track, a selection of railway cars, and a wonderful black locomotive packed away in a cardboard box. But when his father found him playing with it, Ray got the worst licking of his life, with an extension cord. His mother, trying to explain why to him later, said that because the train set had been Kenny's favourite toy his father couldn't bear the thought of it getting broken. "He wants to keep it just as your brother left it," she said. "That's why it must never be played with." Ray had accepted that, the way he accepted everything concerning his father. But now he was bewildered. What had changed, making it all right to use the train set?

The approach of the Christmas party not only got Ray excited, it got his mother all a-flutter too. Packing one-gallon ice-cream containers with homemade Nuts 'N Bolts to be frozen for the party one afternoon, she began to happily reminisce about his brother. "Kenny was such a people person," she said. "Your brother just loved people. When we entertained I used to put him to bed early but there was no way of keeping him there. Out he'd come in his pyjamas and start passing around the peanuts or whatever to the guests. He was so polite and cute. Everybody loved to see him playing the little host. He was definitely a people person, your brother Kenny."

The last week of November arrived and Ray's mother asked his father for a guest list. He said he was thinking on it. During the first week of December she warned him that it was getting late, he'd better make up his mind soon. He said he'd make up his mind when he was good and goddamn ready to make it up and not before. Anyway it was a christly hoax, Christmas and the whole chiselling season.

"Now why do you say things like that?" Ray's mother asked. "Don't you remember how you used to enjoy Christmas? The parties we used to have?"

"Shut up about the parties we used to have!" his father cried.

One evening in mid-December his parents had a fight at the supper table. Ray's mother said, "If you don't want to have a party just say so. If that's the case I won't bother knocking myself out getting all the stuff ready for something that isn't going to happen, the food, the decorations, the rest of it." Ray had never seen her look as she did then, wild, barely in control of herself.

His father didn't trouble to answer her. He just stared at her across the table.

"Don't you give me that look of yours," she said. "Give me an answer. Are we having the party? Yes or no?"

"No," he said. "We aren't."

"And why not?" she cried. "After all these years, why not? What would be wrong with a party? What harm would there be in it?"

"It wouldn't be right," his father said. "That's all."

Then his mother did something Ray would never have dreamed she would do. She got up from the table and put on her coat and scarf, leaving the scattered dirty dishes, the leftover pork roast just as they were.

"Where do you think you're going?" his father demanded.

"Out. To a movie," she said.

"Well you aren't taking the car," he said. "It's blizzarding out there and I've got no intention of paying for a tow truck to pull you out when you get yourself stuck."

"I'll walk," she said, slamming the door behind her.

His father sat without twitching a muscle and Ray did likewise. Neither looked at the other. Then his father slowly pushed back his chair from the table, stood, and walked out of the kitchen. Ray heard feet on the stairs and knew that his father was going down to the rec room.

Ray wasn't sure how to behave. Nothing like this had ever happened before. The unusual sight of food abandoned on the table frightened him, as did the sound of the wind, suddenly loud in the quiet kitchen. He got up and tiptoed after his father.

Ray found his dad sitting on one of the wicker Saan Store chairs. His father lifted his eyes from the floor and arrested Ray in the doorway with his gaze, held him there for several seconds, then nodded permission to enter. Ray ducked into the room and scurried to a chair across from his father.

"I guess you and me are bachelor boys for the night," his father said.

"I guess," said Ray.

"I don't forget how it used to be. I don't forget as easy as all that," said his father. "Piss on parties and piss on people who have to have them."

"Yeah," agreed Ray.

His father lit a cigarette, flourished the dead match at him. "There's ashtrays behind the bar," he said to Ray. "Be a good boy and fetch me one."

No sooner had Ray gained the bar than his father came up with a better idea. "Hey," he called, "ship it down on the train. And while you're at it, put a rye and Coke on the freight." He paused to glance at his wristwatch. "Put a rye and Coke on the 7:17 and we'll baptize the son of a bitch. We'll make a wet run."

Ray could scarcely credit the honour being done him, his rare good fortune. He wedged the ashtray securely in a coal car, balanced the tumbler of whisky on a flat car, and sent the train swaying cautiously down the line. When his father offloaded the freight, Engineer Ray backed up the train to the station at the bar. A dime lay on the flat car which had borne the whisky. His father saluted him with glass lifted high. "A lesson for later life," he shouted from down the room. "Always tip the bartender and you'll get what you want, when you want it. Remember that, Ray. Now mix me a vodka and orange juice, plenty of ice."

To be privileged to run his brother's train and serve his father was all Ray could ask for. Because Ted Matthews sat in the farthest corner of the room, isolated in the light of the pole lamp, it appeared, by a trick of perspective, that the train had to traverse a great distance to reach him. For an hour the locomotive crossed and recrossed this daunting span without mishap or incident, exchanging drinks for pocket change and empty glasses.

With four or five belts in him, Ted grew increasingly talkative and noisy, addressing Ray in an unusually loud voice. "You're all right, Ray," he said. "You may look like your mother but you think like me. So you can't be all bad, you goddamn little fifty-per-center, can you? I still had something left over after making Kenny, didn't I?"

"Sure," said Ray, laughing at the funny things his father said. He was settling the next drink, vodka and tomato juice, on the train with great care. His father hadn't requested the same drink twice.

"You've got a good heart, Ray," his father said. He attempted to pluck the Bloody Mary from the train before it came to a full stop and slopped a little of it on his wrist. "But you're not all that likeable. If I had one bit of advice to give you, it's this—work on your personality. Being good doesn't take you very far in this world."

Ray nervously bobbed his head.

"And always look both ways, twice, before crossing the road, and up, once, in case anything's falling out of the sky."

Ray laughed at this but his father sternly said, "Be serious. I'm giving you serious advice here."

So Ray composed a serious face and listened closely to all the advice his father started to expound. He must never marry a woman who dyed her hair and he must make sure to keep insurance policies in a safety deposit box. If he ever needed a lawyer, hire a Jew. Last of all, avoid leukaemia. "That was your brother's biggest mistake," he said. "He caught leukaemia and it killed him, the dumb little fuck."

Having emptied himself of advice, his father relapsed into his customary stony silence. When Ray persisted in trying to talk to him, his father curtly ordered him to scare up some cards. Drunk as he was, he cleaned Ray out of his tips. When Ray had no more money to play, that was the finish of blackjack. "Money talks and bullshit walks," was all his father would say. Ray was disappointed—not over the money—but because losing the money brought an end to this momentous evening. His father abruptly got to his feet, stumbled up the stairs, and fell into bed drunk.

The next day his mother cleared the supper dishes and did not go out to a movie as Ray hoped she would. His father offered him no more advice. The railway disappeared mysteriously from the rec room, although the screw holes were there in the wall for Ray, a doubting Thomas, to touch with his fingers.

YEARS LATER, Ray was convinced that the best explanation of himself he could ever give his new wife was hidden in the events of that evening. Yet when he attempted to relate the story he could not find the words to express how rich, how moving that strange memory was for him. Losing his nerve, he offered a trivial version which he struggled to make hilarious. A small boy milked his father for pocket money by running drinks to him on a preposterous toy train and then got his comeuppance by losing it all in a card game.

Pam's harsh reaction to his story surprised him. She didn't find it funny at all. The word she used was "sick."

"What's sick about it?" Ray wanted to know.

"For starters, what man in his right mind would insist that his kid play bartender and make him a witness to such a sickening spectacle? And what about winning all your money back and keeping it? That sounds to me like a pretty cruel thing to do to a ten year old."

Ray disputed all this, which was unusual. He seldom disputed anything Pam said. He hated disagreements.

"If you ask me, Ray," Pam said, "your father has never treated you very well."

"Why do you say that?"

"You're not a very good reader of human nature, are you?" snapped Pam.

Ray supposed he wasn't. People were always seeing subtly shaded motives where he only saw black and white. Maybe when it came to judging people he suffered from something akin to colour blindness. Living in the university-student residence he had been everybody's favourite mark, continually beset by practical jokers, borrowers and plagiarists begging for a peek at his assignments. He was always taken in.

Nevertheless, he instinctively avoided any of those subjects (philosophy, psychology, sociology) which purported to grapple with the puzzle of human behaviour. A modest talent with numbers saw him safely through the College of Commerce, although the compulsory first-year English course was a close shave, throwing him utterly at sea whenever the complicated motives and actions of bizarre characters were confidently probed and analyzed. Ray never forgot one of the questions on his first English quiz. The professor wanted to know why it was significant that the rescue boat in *Lord of the Flies* was a warship. Ray couldn't detect any significance unless it was that the navy was the logical branch of the armed forces to effect a rescue at sea, rather than, say, the army. So that was what he had answered. But that wasn't right. No, the significance lay in the irony of the boys being saved by a warship, symbol of the murderous impulses responsible for crashing them on the island in the first place, and of the murderous impulses which destroyed their idyllic paradise. Of course, once it was all explained, Ray grasped the professor's point. And all along he thought Mr. Golding only wanted him to feel sorry for poor Piggy.

Although stubbornly defending his father against Pam's charges, an irritating speck of uneasiness was introduced. He could not deny he had been wrong about this or that person before. Yet when Pam drew unflattering comparisons between his and *her* father, Ray couldn't help feeling it was unfair, like comparing apples with oranges. One was khaki work clothes. The other, white shirt and tie. A prosperous businessman could pet, indulge, and dote upon a beloved daughter. Boys needed a different preparation for the world. Maybe his father kept the money won in the card game not out of any meanness, but to teach Ray a useful lesson about the world. That was all.

If criticism of his father had come from anyone but Pam, it's likely Ray would have shrugged it off. But he genuinely admired his wife (perhaps even more than he did his father) and found it difficult to dismiss any of her opinions. Ray was convinced of her superiority to him in every respect.

It was this capacity for admiration that had brought Ray and his wife together in the first place. The daughter of the Ford-Mercury dealer, and mayor of a town of 800, meant Pam was small-town royalty, raised with the conviction that she was special. And it could not be denied that she was a reasonably attractive, reasonably intelligent young lady. Unlike other girls in town, Pam's hair was permed regularly at the beauty parlour, her dresses purchased in the city instead of from the catalogue, and she drove her own car, a 1965 Ford LTD convertible. The car alone would have made her somebody special.

In such a tiny parish, with its limited pool of talent, she passed for extraordinary. Pam was the perennial female lead in her Drama Society's productions, she sang the solos in the Glee Club, and played clarinet in the school band. Three times she was crowned Snow Queen at the Winter Carnival and it would have been four if there hadn't been a stupid rule against freshies competing. Her senior year she was unanimously chosen class valedictorian, as she knew she would be. Pam Ferguson was the planet around which her satellites gratefully arranged their orbits.

University had come as a dreadful shock to her. Suddenly she found herself demoted to ordinary. The professors did not listen respectfully to her opinions in class the way her high-school teachers had, and the boys favoured her with perfunctory attentions. In residence, on her floor alone, there were two girls better dressed than she was. At the end of two months, Pam was so desperately unhappy that she seriously considered returning home to let her father arrange a job for her in the local bank.

Then an acquaintance took her to a house party. Within an hour of arriving, the acquaintance was picked up by an engineering student and disappeared, leaving Pam to fend for herself. As she ranged through rooms plugged with strangers, looking for a familiar face, Pam bumped into a shy-looking boy with a gentle voice. This was Ray and he swiftly put Pam at ease by appreciating her the way she was used to being appreciated. In no time at all she confided to Ray her father's foolish insistence that all her Best Actress trophies be lined up on the mantel for the whole world to see. It was so embarrassing! He was also treated to a blow by blow account of her troubles editing the high-school year book. The evening flew by for both of them.

There was nothing much attractive about Ray. His rear end was still too big, his thighs too plump, and his face too innocent to be appealing to any woman under the age of forty. But his fervent devotion outweighed these handicaps and gave Pam a new lease on life. She found it possible to continue. They dated through all four years of university, although several times Pam broke it off. On each of these occasions Ray begged her to take him back and she consented—without Ray she felt common, plain, neglected. A month after they graduated Ray landed a job as a government accountant and she agreed to marry him.

Pam harboured ill will against her father-in-law from the start. The size of the cheque he presented as a wedding gift struck her as insulting. Added to that there was the annoyance of Ray having to repay a student loan.

"Why is it that your father didn't help you through university?" she asked Ray one day.

"Why?" Ray said. "Because he hasn't any money. He's just a working stiff."

"But I thought you mentioned he bought his R.V. while you were going to school."

"I guess he did," said Ray.

"It's nice he had his priorities straight," said Pam.

Ray began to wonder if there mightn't be something to what Pam said. He became less eager to phone his parents long distance when Pam called attention to the fact that it was Ray who always called, never his dad. Other sore spots developed. When Ray got a promotion after three years of work with the government he looked forward to impressing his father with the news. The old man interrupted him in mid-sentence and commenced his own story about how an expensive piece of machinery had been wrecked by the carelessness of a young miner. "The young ones are no damn good," he concluded. "I'm sure it's the same in your business." Ray would never have stopped to think that he, too, qualified as a "young one" if Pam hadn't pointed it out to him.

These insights of his wife's sometimes made him sad, but Ray was not a man inclined to dwell on the gloomy side of life; he consoled himself with his good fortune in having a woman like Pam to love. It was true that life was not always a bed of roses with Pam, she sometimes caught the blues and Ray had to do his cheerful best to raise her sinking spirits or keep her from turning sour. When she complained that her anthropology degree made her unemployable, condemned her to housewifery, Ray suggested perhaps she would like to return to school. When she charged six years of marriage with causing her to gain forty pounds, Ray assured her that she was every bit as beautiful and desirable as she had ever been.

"Can't you see how upsetting it is to me?" she would scream at him. "I'm not beautiful. I'm fat. You only say I'm beautiful so you won't have to talk about my problems with me. You're just like your father, Ray. You don't care about anybody but yourself. You'd tell me anything in the hope it would shut me up. You're selfish and uncaring—just like him."

It had been hard for Ray to accept Pam's view of his father but now that he did, he felt no hatred for him. Instead, he felt an odd shame, like the man who discovers he has been invited to a party because there was no way of *not* inviting him. As much for his father's sake as his own, Ray began to avoid him.

Shortly after Ray and Pam celebrated their seventh wedding anniversary, steering clear of his father became easier. His parents, two old gypsies, moved again, to

Pine Point in the Northwest Territories. The distance between them, a distance compounded by bad roads and the horrors of winter driving, gave Ray a plausible excuse for paying fewer visits. This was a satisfactory solution for a time, then Ray began to be plagued by mysterious premonitions of a disaster about to befall his father. As a small boy, he had known children whose fathers or brothers had been killed in mine accidents, and the possibility that one day the mine would slay or maim his father had always been there. Now it came forward and took possession of him. He imagined electrocutions, catastrophic explosions, cave-ins, entanglements with machinery. Whenever the imagined scenes became too real, too horrific, he would phone Pine Point. If he got his mother, he would speak. If his father answered, he simply hung up, comforted to know he was all right. Pam began to question him about the phone bill. "Five calls to Pine Point in two weeks? Why Ray?"

Two years after his parents moved north, the news Ray had been dreading broke. It didn't matter that his father wasn't killed in an accident at the mine but had drowned in a boating mishap, Ray couldn't shake the guilty feeling that somehow his dark reveries had dragged his poor father down through fathoms of icy water to his death.

PAM REMINDED RAY that life goes on and waits for no man. That he was responsible for managing his loss. But every time Ray made a step in that direction he suffered cruel setbacks. The worst was his mother's treachery. He encouraged her to move south after the funeral but she refused. The beauty of the north was in her blood, she said, Pine Point was home, she was perfectly happy where she was and knew her own mind, thank you very much. Not long after the first anniversary of his father's drowning Ray discovered what had really got into his mother's blood—a mechanic at the mine. In a tremulously defiant voice, she told Ray over the telephone that she and this man were getting married. Ray was not a person to be rude and cutting to anyone, let alone his own mother. But he was shocked and hurt by what she was doing—for his father's sake.

According to Pam he was acting like a child. "If you ask me," she said, "you ought to be glad your mother is getting married. At least she has someone to look after her and save you the worry. Besides, everyone deserves a chance at happiness."

Ray demanded to know what that was supposed to mean.

"Oh, nothing. Except that you never really saw how it was with your parents. You know, your mother was never happy with him."

"What do you know about it?" said Ray, using a peevish tone of voice Pam seldom heard.

"I know habit is only habit. It isn't love."

RAY CREDITED TWO THINGS—Pam and the grind of his professional life—with keeping him in balance. He was thankful for both. For nine years he had worked in government service, slowly and steadily riding a wave of modest promotions. There was no man better suited to the task he was called upon to perform than Ray; his unflinching doggedness and diligence were bywords in the office. The most recalcitrant accounting foul-ups were turned over to him to solve, tough nuts that never yielded to a single blow but only the most persistent knocking and rapping. He worked calmly and methodically on all problems, often remaining at his desk long after he had cheerfully waved his colleagues out the door. He did not begrudge the extra hours in the least, except for the inconvenience they caused his wife. To make up for this, Ray was always ready with small gifts, flowers, and dinners out in expensive restaurants.

It was at Ray's prompting that Pam renewed an old interest from high-school days and joined an amateur theatre group. To Ray's delight, his wife came to life, seemed happier than ever before. She enjoyed her new circle of friends and even shed twenty-five pounds so that she could get a crack at better parts. As she said to Ray, "It's difficult to play Blanche DuBois tipping the scales at one-sixty."

What particularly gladdened Ray's heart was the revelation that his wife could really act. Of course, he didn't rely on his taste to come to this conclusion, Ray realized that he didn't know beans about good acting. But from the way she was treated at cast parties, or at the readings sometimes held in the living room of their home, he could see that everyone respected Pam, even deferred to her. She was on her way to becoming a star in the small world of local theatre. Now it seemed she was out more evenings than he was himself, always at rehearsals, attending productions of the local professional company, or taking part in something curiously called workshops. Her happiness was proclaimed by a more flamboyant style of dress and the variety of accents in which she spoke to him, English, Irish, even German. When she said she was on her way to becoming a new person, Ray could well believe it. Sometimes he didn't know her himself.

Then she got her break, the artistic director of the city's one professional company offered her a role. It was a small part, the nurse in *Equus,* but for the first time in her life Pam would be paid to act. *Equus* played for two weeks, and during the course of the run, Ray attended four performances. He joked to the other accountants that if he went to all fourteen, he still wouldn't know what the play was supposed to be about, he was that dense.

At the end of those two weeks, Pam left him. Ray came home late from work and found a fat envelope resting on the kitchen table with his name on it. The long letter inside explained that it had nothing to do with him and everything to do with her. The last two months of auditions, rehearsals, and the show itself had been a process of awakening from an interminable, dreary sleep. At last she knew what she must do with her life. She must act.

What was important for Ray to understand was that this was nobody's fault. Their marriage had been doomed from the beginning because it had linked two incompatible natures, the practical and the artistic. Only the suppression and denial of her true, artistic nature had permitted the marriage to survive. She did not blame Ray that this relationship had nurtured him while she withered like a plant denied light and water, nothing was to be gained from finger pointing. But now they must go their separate ways. The cruellest thing he could do would be to try to dissuade her from "following her bliss." There was more in the letter, dealing with the practical matters that were supposed to be his specialty. Pam had withdrawn half of the money held in their joint account and suggested that the house be sold as soon as possible so the proceeds could be divided. She could not see him but he must promise to take care of himself.

RAY TOOK THIS BADLY but also, as was his habit, very quietly. In private he sometimes grew frantic, turning this way and that in his mind, seeking a way out, but his gaze always came to rest on a blank wall. When he studied a column of figures or read a newspaper or made himself a meal in the tiny bachelor apartment he rented after the house was sold, the wall was there, forcing its blankness upon him. Ray's face grew haggard and grey from twisting his neck in a futile effort to see beyond and behind the wall, to wherever Pam had gone. In time, this failure turned his stare apathetic and rubbed the innocence out of his face.

Nobody knew his wife had left him. If he had a friend, Ray would not likely have said anything to him anyway, because he could not believe this was happening to him. He would get Pam back. People in the office saw very well what was happening to him, that he was losing weight and making mistakes at his work that no one would have believed Ray Matthews capable of. Most of all, they noted the haunting change in his face.

When things were at their worst, he heard Pam's voice in the kitchen one morning when he was shaving. It was months since he had seen or heard her and the sound of her voice made him shake so violently that he had to lay his razor down so as not to slash himself. Then it came to him what it was. Pam hadn't come home to him. She was being interviewed on the local CBC morning radio show.

Ray stood absolutely still, intent, and as he listened to the disembodied voice of his wife, something strange began to happen. He heard the electrical whir and chatter of wheels speeding over flimsy rails, the clink of ice rocking against the sides of a tumbler, his father shouting funny things to him in a raw voice, the laughter of a small boy who could not guess or imagine the harsh territory his father had crossed to find himself standing where he stood that night. Ray could guess now, having been on a similar journey, now completed.

Pam's voice returned from the other room, talking about some man called Ibsen. Over all the months of separation her voice had changed, or his way of hearing it had. Coming out of the void, how false, how insincere it sounded, how *actressy*. It struck Ray that the owner of such a voice might not know all there was to know. Something more *had* passed between him and his father, borne on his dead brother's train, than a mere exchange of drinks and loose change. What, was for him to decide.

With that thought, Ray picked up his razor and set about uncovering his face.

What Saffi Knows
CAROL WINDLEY

THAT SUMMER A BOY WENT missing from a field known as the old potato farm, although no one could remember anything growing there but wild meadow barley, thistles in their multitudes, black lilies with a stink of rotten meat if you brought your face too close or tried to pick them. There were white fawn lilies like stars fallen to earth and bog-orchids, also called candle-scent, and stinging nettles, blameless to look at, leaves limp as flannel, yet caustic and burning to the touch. Even so, nettle leaves could be brewed into a tea that acted on the system like a tonic, or so Saffi's aunt told her. She recited a little rhyme that went: *Nettle tea in March, mugwort leaves in May, and all the fine maidens will not go to clay.*

Imagine a field, untended, sequestered, grass undulating in a fitful wind. Then disruption, volunteer members of the search party arriving, milling around, uniformed police and tracking dogs, distraught relatives of the missing boy. No place for a child, Saffi's mother said, yet here Saffi was, holding tight to her aunt's hand, taking everything in.

All the people were cutout dolls. The sun hovered above the trees like a hot-air balloon cut free. Saffi's shoes were wet from walking in the grass; she was wearing a sundress that tied at the back of her neck and she kept scratching at mosquito bites on her arms and legs until they bled and her Aunt Loretta said she'd give herself blood poisoning, but Saffi didn't stop, she liked how it felt, it gave her something to do. She could see her daddy, standing a little apart from the others, drinking coffee from a paper cup. He was a young man then, tall, well-built, his hair a sprightly reddish-brown, his head thrown back, eyes narrowed in concentration, as if he hoped to be first to catch sight of any unusual movement in the woods, down near the river. Saffi looked where he was looking and saw a flitting movement in the trees like a turtledove, its silvery wings spread like a fan and its voice going coo-coo, the sound a turtledove would make when it was home and could rest at last. But there was no turtledove. Never would there be a turtledove. Saffi was the only one who knew. But who would listen to her?

July 1964, in a town on Vancouver Island, in the days before the tourists and land developers arrived and it was quiet, still, and everyone more or less knew everyone else. There was a pulp and paper mill, a harbour where the fishing fleet tied up, churches, good schools, neighbourhoods where children played unsupervised. Children were safe in this town. They did not go missing. But now, unbelievably, not one but two children were gone, one for nearly six weeks and then three days ago this other boy, his red three-speed bike found ditched at the edge of the old potato farm, where it seemed he liked to play, hunting snakes and butterflies, but never hurting anything, just catching things and letting them go.

His name was Eugene Dexter. His jacket had been found snagged in a hawthorn tree beside the Millstone River, at the far end of the old potato farm. Or else it was a baseball cap that was found. Or a catcher's mitt. You heard different stories. There was a ransom note. There was no such note. The police had a suspect, or, alternately, they had no suspects, although they'd questioned and released someone and were refusing to give out details. But, said Saffi's mother, wasn't that how they operated, secretly, out of the public eye, trying to conceal their own ineptness? She kicked at a pebble. A woman beside her spoke of premonition, showing the gooseflesh on her arms. Some men got into a scrum, like elderly, underfed rugby players, and began praying aloud.

One minute it was warm and then the wind made Saffi shiver. Behind the mountain dark clouds welled up, filled with a hidden, shoddy light. The boy's parents arrived in a police car, lights flashing. But maybe Saffi was remembering that wrong. Maybe they drove up in their own car, Mr. Dexter behind the wheel. In any case, there they were, Mr. and Mrs. Dexter, making their way over to tables borrowed from the high school cafeteria and set up in the field, with sandwiches and donuts and coffee and mimeographed instructions for the search party, so perhaps it wasn't surprising when Mr. Arthur Dawsley sidled up to Saffi's mother and said wasn't this turning into quite a three-ring circus? He was their neighbour. He lived on the other side of a tall hedge. Along the front of his yard was a picket fence painted green and on his front door was a sign that said: No Peddlers. When Saffi was small, less than two years old, she'd mispronounced his name, saying Arthur Daisy, and in her family it was the wrong name that had stuck. It didn't suit him; she wished she could take it back. Her parents teased her, calling Arthur Daisy her friend, but he wasn't. His hair the colour of a cooking pot sat in deep waves above his forehead. Under his windbreaker he was wearing a white shirt and a tie. He said he knew this gathering was no circus, that was merely a figure of speech, and not a good one, considering. He said he supposed he was too old to be of much help in the search, but surely he could lend a little moral support.

"Beautiful weather, all the same," he said, and then walked in his peculiar upright, stolid fashion over to Saffi's daddy, who averted his face slightly and emptied the dregs of his coffee onto the ground, as if the last thing he craved was a word with Arthur Daisy. At the same time the boy's father was handing an item of clothing over to the police, a green striped soccer shirt, it looked like, tenderly folded, and the police let their dogs sniff it and they strained at their leashes as if they'd been given a new idea and the sound of their baying came like a cheerless chorus off the mountain.

Later the wind died down and the clouds built up, dark clouds edged with a beautiful translucent white, dazzling to the eye, and just as Saffi and her mother and aunt got in the car to go home there came a violent drenching downpour, and everyone said it was almost a relief; it was turning out to be such a hot, dry summer.

THIS COULD BE SAID of her: as a child she noticed things, she took things in, and to this day she can't decide, is this a curse or a gift? A curse, she thinks, for the most part.

The child she was and the person she's become: in a way they're like two separate people trapped in the same head. Could that be? The child mystifies her. The child with her pallor, her baby-fine, dry hair; her solemn grey-blue eyes, her air of distraction and wariness. Her odd little name that her mother had got out of a book of names: Saffi, meaning "wisdom." *Who are you? I am Saffi, no one else.* She feels sympathy for that child, of course she does, and affection, impatience, anger, shame. And sorrow. Shouldn't someone have been looking out for her? Shouldn't someone have been watching over her? "Daddy's girl," her daddy called her, but daddy didn't have much time for her, not really.

WHEN SAFFI WAS IN her yard she made a game out of watching for Arthur Daisy to leave in his car, which he did sometimes, not every day, and as soon as he was gone she crawled through a gap in the hedge into his backyard. She knelt in the shade, looking out at the things he kept there: a wheelbarrow tipped up against a garden shed, a pile of buckets, a heap of steamy grass clippings buzzing with blue-bottles, a mound of composted dirt he made from dead leaves and egg shells and potato peelings, garbage from his kitchen.

At the foot of his porch steps there was a folding chair and an overturned washtub he used as a table, a coffee mug on it. Two of his shirts hung from the clothesline like guards he'd left on duty.

He had painted his cellar window black, but he'd missed a little place shaped like a star and she could get up close to it and see a shaded light hanging from the ceiling and beneath the light a table with a boy crouched on it. He was a real boy. She saw him and he saw her, his eyes alert and shining, and then he let his head droop on his chest. Don't be scared, she said; don't be. He was awake but sleeping, his arm twitching, his feet curled like a bird's claws on a perch. All she could see in the dim light was his hair, nearly white. He was wearing a pair of shorts.

She called him bird-boy. She whistled at him softly, as if he were a wild thing. She had to be careful. Since he'd got the bird-boy, Arthur Daisy never stayed away for long; he'd drive off and then almost at once he was back, slamming his car door and pounding up his front steps. Before he got that far, though, Saffi would have scrambled through the hedge, her hair catching in the branches so that she'd have to give it a cruel tug, but she never cried or uttered the least sound, and at last she was home free.

If Arthur Daisy didn't drive away in his car, if he happened instead to be working in his garden and saw her playing outside, he'd call to her. "Well, Saffi, what do you think I've got?" He kept calling to her. Your friend, Arthur Daisy, her daddy would tease her. She walked to his house on the side of the road, placing the heel of one foot in front of the toe of the other, her arms out for balance. "Hurry up, slowpoke," he would say, pushing his gate open to let her in.

He looked like the old troll that lived under the bridge in *Three Billy Goats Gruff*, one of Saffi's picture books. He wore an old brown cardigan, the pockets sagging with junk. "What do you think I've got?" he'd say, and he'd pull something out of a pocket and hold it in his clenched fist and if she stepped back he'd bend closer, closer, his colourless lips drawn back so that she could see his stained teeth, gums the bluish-pink of a dog's gums. She didn't want to guess, she was no good at it. She covered her eyes until he told her to look and it would turn out to be an old nail or a screw-driver or the sharp little scissors he used for cutting roses.

"Well?" he'd say. "What do you say? Has the cat got Saffi's tongue?" He slapped his hand on his trouser leg and laughed his old troll laugh and picked up his shovel and went back to work digging in his garden.

THAT SUMMER Saffi's mother got hired as an operator at the B.C. Telephone Co. on Fitzwilliam Street. Her first job, she said, since she got married. Her first real job, ever. If she had a choice, she wouldn't leave Saffi every day, but the truth was, she had no choice, she needed the extra income; she'd lost interest in being poor her entire life. She ran up some dresses for work on her old treadle sewing machine, dark blue dresses, in rayon or a serviceable poplin, something she said she could gussy up with a little white collar, or a strand of pearls.

Saffi remembered her mother wearing those dresses to work for years. When at last they'd gone completely out of style or had simply worn out, she'd cut them into squares and stitched them into a quilt for Saffi, and Saffi had it still, folded away in a cedar chest her husband's parents gave her for a wedding present. When she took it out and ran her fingers over the scraps of fabric, little cornfields, meadows of blue, she couldn't help returning in her mind to those long-ago summer mornings, bright and hot, dreamlike, almost, when she'd clung to her mother and begged her to stay home, and her mother had given her a weary, abstracted glance and pulled on the little chamois-soft gloves she wore for driving. She kissed Saffi on the top of her head and then she was gone, and Saffi heard her backing her car out onto the road and driving away. Aunt Loretta made Saffi sit at the table and eat her breakfast, but Saffi's throat ached from not crying and she couldn't swallow a spoonful. Aunt Loretta rinsed her uneaten porridge down the drain—what a terrible waste, she said—and then she wiped Saffi's face with a dishrag and sent her outside to play in the sun while she got on with tidying the house. Saffi sat on the front steps and looked at one of her books, with pictures of a frog prince, his blubbery mouth pursed for a kiss, a scraggly old witch with skinny fingers reaching out to grab anyone she could catch.

Even though she knew he couldn't see her, she imagined the bird-boy was watching, and so she turned the pages carefully. She was good at reading, but poor at arithmetic. It wasn't her fault. The numbers had their own separate lives, their own shapes, and refused to let her touch them. Nine in its soldier's uniform the colour of an olive with a double row of brass buttons. Three a Canterbury bell, a curled-up snail leaving a trail of slime, dragging its little clamshell house behind. Seven had a licking tongue of fire and smelled like a thunderstorm. Four was the sea coming in along the shore, it was a ship sailing, it was blue and white and stood on its one leg.

The numbers said: Leave us be! Be quiet! Don't touch! They kept themselves apart, like little wicked soldiers in a castle. The teacher held her worksheets up in class and said, Is this the work a grade one girl should be doing? Saffi had to cover her ears and sing to herself about the Pied Piper, how he made the rats skip after him out of town and then the children followed and the town got dark and the parents wrung their hands and lamented, Oh, what have we done?

When Aunt Loretta finished the housework she called Saffi inside and read her a story about a turtledove.

"I know what that is," Saffi said. "I seen a turtledove in the cellar at Arthur Daisy's house."

Aunt Loretta said she must have seen some other kind of bird. "All we have around here is pigeons," she said. "You know what a pigeon looks like, don't you? And it's *I saw*, not *I seen*."

"It looked like a boy," Saffi said. "It had white feathers on its head. It sang like this: *cheep, cheep, cheep*."

"Oh, Saffi," her aunt said. "You are a funny little thing."

OUTSIDE HER HOUSE the road was all churned up where her daddy parked his logging truck when he got home. Sometimes he'd swing her up into the cab and she'd sit behind the steering wheel and he'd get her to pretend she was the driver, telling her, "Start the engine, Saffi, or we'll still be sitting here when those logs sprout a whole new set of roots and branches." He made engine noises like a growling cat and she pretended to turn the wheel and he gave directions. "Turn left," he'd say. "Gear down for the hill, now shift into third, that's the way." It was hot in the truck and there was a sour smell of her daddy's sweaty work shirt, the smell of stale thermos coffee and engine oil, the beer her daddy drank. Her daddy always said he was a hard-working, hard-drinking man and people could take him or leave him. Leave him, was his preference. He liked a quiet life. He liked his home and when he got home he deserved a beer, didn't he? "Yes," said Saffi. "Yes, sir, you do."

"Who are you?" her daddy said. "Are you daddy's favourite girl?"

Her daddy. Danny Shaughnessy. He was away in the woods for days at a time, then he'd be home, he'd come into the kitchen, where Saffi was standing on a kitchen chair at the counter, helping Aunt Loretta coat chicken pieces with flour or peel potatoes, little tasks her aunt allotted her to fill in the last hour or so until her mother returned. Her daddy would go straight to the fridge for a beer and sometimes he gave Saffi a taste, the beer making her gag and trickling down her chin and her daddy laughed and kissed it away. Her aunt told him to leave her alone. He said Saffi was his kid, wasn't she? He didn't have to leave his own kid alone, did he? Aunt Loretta said he could at least take off his work boots and wash his hands.

"Don't you have a kitchen of your own to go to?" he'd say. "Isn't it time you got back to good old Vernon, Loretta?"

They fought like kids, the way kids at school went at each other, hands on their hips, faces thrust forward, then they agreed to an armistice and sat at the kitchen table and had a glass of beer together, Saffi with them, and her daddy praised her, saying what a doll she was, a real little lady. On the drive down from Campbell River, he said, he'd heard on the radio a boy was missing, ten years old, a slightly built boy, with white-blond hair, last seen wearing shorts, a blue jacket, running shoes. And then, just south of Royston, a boy who answered that description exactly was standing at the side of the highway. He'd blasted the horn at him, because kids never understood, they had no idea how much room a truck like that needed to stop, they'd run out without thinking. More than likely it was some other kid, but what if it was this Eugene Dexter and he'd just driven on by?

He had another beer. He talked about joining the search party, if they needed more volunteers. He had a sense for these things, he said, a kind of infallible sixth sense, which was why he never got lost in the woods or took a wrong turn driving the truck. He stood up and stretched his arms and said he was going to have a shower. What time was supper going to be, he wanted to know, and Aunt Loretta said it would be when it was ready and not a minute sooner.

"Daddy's girl!" her daddy said, sweeping Saffi off her feet, holding her high above his head, shaking her as if she were a cloth doll, her hair flopping in her eyes, and she laughed so hard she thought her sides would split open and the stuffing would fall out. I'll knock the stuffing out of you, her daddy said when he was angry. But he was teasing. He was never angry with her. She was his girl. He tossed her in the air and caught her safely, every time. His fingers dug hard into her ribs and she couldn't get a breath.

"Can't you see she's had enough?" her aunt said.

If she wasn't laughing so hard, if her daddy wasn't laughing and cursing Aunt Loretta, telling her she was a tight-assed old broad, she could tell him she had this bad secret in her head that hurt like blisters from a stinging nettle. In Arthur Daisy's cellar there was a bird-boy, a turtledove, its head tucked beneath its wing.

IT SEEMED TO HER a line divided her yard from Arthur Daisy's yard. Even after all these years she saw this line as a real thing, like a skipping rope or a length of clothesline or a whip, taut, then slack, then pulled tight again until it sang like a banjo string and nearly snapped in two. The line or the rope or whatever it was separated the dangerous elements, fire and air, from the more tolerable elements of earth and water. That was how she pictured it. She crept into Arthur Daisy's yard, holding her breath, mousey small, so small and quick no one could catch her. She pressed her hands to the window. She had to see if the bird-boy was still there, perched on his roost. He was. He scared her to death. His skull was luminous and frail as an egg, yet he seemed strong to her, his gaze cold, not beseeching but full of strength, as if nothing could hurt him. His eyes were dark, like a bird's eyes. What did he eat? Where did he sleep? She called to him, whistling a tune she'd made up. She told him not to be afraid. She cupped a black and yellow caterpillar in her hand. It was so small she felt her heart curl around it. She pictured the hawthorn tree near the river, light spilling in tatters through the leaves, the sun caught in its branches. She saw the boy's jacket hanging there still, as if no one cared enough to take it home.

She held the caterpillar up to the window, saying, look at this, look at this.

All around there was fire and air, scorching her hair and clothes, leaving her weak and sick and shaking with a chill, so that her mother would have to put her to bed and take her temperature and fuss over her and say, What have you done to yourself, Saffi? She put a cold cloth on Saffi's forehead and called her dumpling pie and gave her half a baby Aspirin and a little ginger ale to swallow it with.

WHAT DID SAFFI SEE? She saw Arthur Daisy in his garden, snipping at blood-red roses and sprays of spirea, telling Saffi he was on his way to visit the municipal cemetery to put flowers on his mother's grave. His dear old mother, who'd passed away twenty years ago this month, almost to the day, dead of a wasting disease, did Saffi know what that meant? It ate her body up, her skin, her flesh, and she never was a fleshy person. She shrivelled up to the size of an old lima bean, a dried pea. She'd scare the liver out of you, he said, and that's a fact. That was what happened when you got to be the age he was, he told Saffi. You ended up having to visit the dear departed on a regular basis. He placed his scissors and cut flowers on the ground.

"What's wrong with you?" he said. "Cat got your tongue, little girl?" He bent over his hands on his knees. He looked at her. He looked into her eyes and she knew he saw everything in her head; he knew how scared she was.

"Well, well," he said, straightening up and brushing a leaf off his sleeve. "Isn't Saffi a funny little monkey?" he said.

Before she could do a thing—run, or squirm away—he'd reached out and pinched her arm just above her elbow. It burned like a hornet's sting. "There, now," said Arthur Daisy, turning his face away. He picked up his flowers. He pocketed his scissors. Don't think anything, she told herself. Behind her in the house there was the bird-boy crouched in the cellar, eating crumbs from the palm of his hand. She saw him like that in her dreams. She couldn't get rid of him.

SLEEP: WHAT WAS *SLEEP?* Saffi's mother complained to Saffi that never before in her life had she suffered from insomnia, normally she didn't even dream, and now she was lucky if she got two or three hours of decent sleep a night. It could be the heat, she said. Or it could be that her head was crackling with the sound of voices, her own voice repeating endlessly, *Number, please,* and *One moment, please, while your call is completed,* and then the voices of strangers, people to whom she'd never in this life be able to attach a face or name. She was in her bedroom, the blind pulled down against the evening sun. Saffi stood beside her mother's dressing table, watching her take off her pearl earrings and put them away in a jeweller's box. Her mother pressed her hands to her head. She wasn't used to working, she said; her nerves were shot. She'd lie awake until dawn, her temples throbbing, and a feeling of unbearable sadness, of grief, would descend on her. It haunted her all day. She hated this summer, it was unlucky; it was a trial to her and everyone else.

The real reason she couldn't sleep, she said, was that she worried about life passing her by, about not getting the things she'd set her heart on, like a nicer house, with three bedrooms, in case she and Danny decided to have more kids, which they might, a little brother or sister for Saffi, or maybe one of each. Wouldn't that be fun? she said, picking up her comb and tugging it painfully through the snarls in Saffi's hair. In the mirror her eyes were resolute and bright, the skin around her mouth taut and pale.

Aunt Loretta always said that as far as babies went, it was her turn next. Who could doubt her? At her house she had a nursery prepared, the walls papered with kittens tangled up in balls of yarn. There were drawers full of handmade baby clothes and a bassinet with a silk coverlet and when Saffi visited she was allowed to lay her doll in it. Aunt Loretta patted the doll's tummy and said, What a fine baby you have there, and for a moment it truly did seem there was a real baby asleep in the bassinet, snoring and fat as a little cabbage.

On the drive home, Saffi's mother would say what a shame, what a shame, but not everyone could have what they wanted. She shifted gears with a brisk movement of her wrist. "You can have a perfectly fulfilled life without children, they say. Sometimes I almost wish …" She glanced at herself in the rear-view mirror, running a finger along the edge of her lip. "Well," she said. "I wish Loretta luck, that's all." Saffi understood that her mother didn't want Aunt Loretta to have a baby or anything else; she was afraid Aunt Loretta would use up all the available good luck, the small quantity of it there was in this world, thus stealing something irreplaceable from Saffi's mother. But knowing this didn't make Saffi love her mother less. If anything, it made her love her more, but from a little further off, like the time her daddy took her to watch Uncle Vernon's team playing baseball and they sat so high up in the bleachers her daddy said they needed high-powered binoculars to figure out who in the hell was on the pitcher's mound.

"You can make your life turn out any way you want," Saffi's mother said. "You can realize your dreams through persistence and hard work combined with just a smidgeon of good fortune. Just a smidgeon. That's all I ask."

She drove so fast, barely slowing at stop signs, that a police ghost car pulled her over and the officer gave her a ticket and Saffi's mother said, "Not again!" Then she told the police officer he had such a nice smile it was almost worth it. Son of a bitch, she muttered, letting the ticket fall to the floor of the car, where it got ripped in half when Saffi trod on it getting out. She knew she should have talked to the police officer. He was right there beside her mother's car. She could have said, Wait, I know where he is, I know where he's hiding, please listen, but she'd remained in her seat, glued to the upholstery, the heat making her sweaty and numb. She hated herself; stupid, stupid Saffi, what's the matter, *cat got your tongue?*

"We are all autonomous beings," her mother said, her hands on the steering wheel. "We all have free will. It's just a matter of getting a few lucky breaks, that's all."

Within a very few years, as it turned out, Aunt Loretta and Uncle Vernon were the parents of twin boys, and then less than two years later they had a baby girl, so Saffi had three cousins to love and help care for, but she never did get the brother or sister her mother had promised her. Life didn't work out as expected, not then, or, it seemed, at any other time. In 1968, when Saffi was eleven, her father was forced to quit work after developing chronic lower back pain, diagnosed variously as a herniated disc, sciatica, an acute inflammation at the juncture of the sacrum and the iliac, perhaps treatable with cortisone injections, perhaps not. Her father said it was all the same to him, he was fed up with the whole deal. He stayed at home, he watched TV and stared out the window at the rain, drumming his fingers on the glass, a prisoner, he said. Saffi's mother would come home from work and grab his prescription drugs up off the kitchen table and say in disgust, "Beer and painkillers? Not that I care. You're not a child, Danny Shaughnessy, are you? You can do what you damned well like."

Her father moved out of the house. He stayed at a dubious-looking motel on the island highway and collected sick pay until it ran out, and then he packed up and announced he was moving to Ontario. He said he was no good to anyone and Saffi's mother said she wasn't about to argue the point. His hair was prematurely grey; he walked with the slightest stoop, alarmingly noticeable to Saffi, if not to him. Take me with you, she had pleaded. Things went wrong all around her and she was helpless to prevent it. She wanted a normal, happy life, like other girls her age. Couldn't her daddy see that? She beat her fists against his chest and he caught her hands in his, still muscular, fit in spite of the injury to his back, and he said, "Hold on there, little girl, that's enough of that." Saffi swore she'd never speak to him again if he left and he said, "Well, Sugar, if that's how you feel." But she did speak to him. She kept in touch. Several years later, in Ontario, he got married for a second time, to someone called Liz, and then in the 1980s he went back to school and became a photocopier technician.

"What did you say your job was again?" Saffi would tease him on the phone. "Could you repeat that? Could you just run that by me again?" She made him laugh. He said she must have inherited his sick sense of humour.

"Daddy," she said. "I wish I could see you. I really miss you."

He mumbled something and then recovered and said, in his new brusque yet genial voice, the voice of a man in business, with business contacts and a little windowless office of his own, that she would always be his girl. Of course she would. "I know that," she said. "I know."

BUT THE SUMMER she was seven, a little girl in a sundress, her hair in pigtails, she didn't believe anything would change in her life. She wouldn't allow it. "I am not moving to any new house," she said, kicking at the table legs. She sat there crayoning the pictures in her colouring book black and purple. She gave the sun a mad face. Outside there was Arthur Daisy's house with its dark cellar and a bird-boy trapped in it. He had claws and a head full of feathers. If she stayed close nothing bad would happen to him, nothing bad; he would sleep and wake and sleep again and one day he'd fly up into the air, blinking at the light. Shoo, she'd say to him, and he'd fly off like a ladybug.

JULY 1964, there were dogs at the old potato farm, straining at their leashes, anxious to be let go, to pick up a scent and run with it along the banks of the Millstone River. Or who knows, maybe the dogs dreamed of steak dinners and only pretended to sniff the ground. In any event, they didn't seem to have much luck tracking anything down.

It was a day of brilliant sun eclipsed at intervals by dark clouds. And there was Arthur Dawsley, a man in his late sixties, a bachelor or perhaps a widower, a man seemingly without family of his own, a volunteer member of the search party, after all, in spite of his age. He was given a clipboard and a pencil and told to keep track of the other volunteers. At the end of the day his shoulders drooped a little with fatigue. He wasn't much help, really, more of a diversion, chatting to the police officers, reminiscing about a time when it was safe to leave your doors unlocked at night, you could forget your wallet in a public place and pick it up later, the bills still folded inside. People said that, they got nostalgic for a vanished code of ethics or morality; wishful thinking, in Arthur Dawsley's opinion. He was a likeable old guy, or maybe not so likeable, maybe more of a nuisance, full of questions and bright ideas, not that they were of any real value.

Not everyone appreciated him. A young cop by the name of Alex Walters gave him a hollow, exasperated stare and considered asking him why he was so darned curious and where he'd been, exactly, on the afternoon young Eugene Dexter was last seen, wearing a blue cotton jacket and carrying two Marvel comics, all of which had been recovered from the bottom of the field. Or were the comics found near the three-speed bicycle, red with gold and black decals, the kind of bicycle Alex Waters dreamed of buying for his own infant son some day? He'd have to check the report again to be sure. Questioning Arthur Dawsley was just a thought that came to him, a result of his increasing sense of fatigue and irritation, more than anything, although for a moment the thought felt right, felt germane, almost woke him up, then got pushed to the back of his mind.

WHAT KIND OF A BOY had he been? What kind of boy, before he was lost? It was said he was in the habit of wandering around on his own, that he had a passion for collecting butterflies and tadpoles, that he'd been a good student who had, at the assembly on the last day of school, received an award for academic achievement and a trophy for sportsmanship, his name inscribed for posterity on a little silver plaque. He was well-liked, mischievous, yet thoughtful, a little withdrawn at times, unexpectedly serious, old for his years, some said. For weeks, for months, there had been posters stapled to telephone poles, pictures of the missing boy, his fair hair sticking up a little in front, a wide smile, his teeth milk white and slightly protuberant, a small dimple at the corner of his mouth. An ordinary boy. His parents' only son. How was it possible he was there one day and gone the next? And how was it possible that not one but two boys had vanished within a few weeks of each other, as if they'd never existed, or as if they had existed merely to be each other's shadow image, a sad confirmation.

There were no answers, it seemed. It was a genuine and terrible mystery that infected the town like a virus and then suddenly cleared up, leaving as an after-effect an epidemic of amnesia. Not even the land appeared to remember: each spring the old potato farm erupted in a vigorous new crop of tufted grasses and coarse-leafed weeds drenched in dew, lopsided with spit-bug saliva. Tiny grey moths and butterflies patterned like curtains rose up in clouds. Birds nested in the trees. Children played there, running through the long grass, switching each other across the shins with willow branches. On the other side of the Millstone River the marsh got set aside as a park and bird sanctuary and Saffi walked there almost every day when her own children were young and even she didn't always remember. The field she glimpsed on the far side of the river did not seem like the same field. That was, it did and did not look the same. For one thing, the town had grown up around it, crowding at its outermost boundaries. Some of the alders and hawthorns near the river had been cut down. But it remained just a field, innocent, mild, apart.

For each separate person the Earth came into being. It began its existence anew and surprised everyone with its beauty. So Saffi believed. The loss of any individual, any single life, must, therefore, dull the perception of beauty. Wasn't that true? Loss was something you fought. But if it happened you got over it. What choice did you have? You recovered and went on. Wasn't that what the therapists meant, when they used the word "healing"? Wasn't that the promise implicit in therapy, and, for that matter, in religion? *And all the fine maidens will not go to clay!*

What did Saffi know? What had she seen and forgotten, or not forgotten, but remembered, shakily, in fragments that, once re-assembled, would make up a picture she could scarcely bear to contemplate? For a time she'd suffered with some kind of anxiety disorder, quite incapacitating and disagreeable. She no longer took medication; she had no need of it. But what a struggle! It was difficult to pinpoint a cause for the spells of depression and exhaustion and what she could only think of as an unnameable dread, a nearly living presence that did, at times, choose to haunt her. She'd gone through a hard time when she was first married, when the children were babies, but she'd recovered, hadn't she? She just didn't have the luxury of understanding every little thing that had happened in her life. How many people did? Memory was so imperfect. The habit of reticence, of keeping secrets, was, on the other hand, easily perfected; it was powerful and compelling, irresistible.

She was a vigilant parent. She couldn't help it. If she lost sight of her kids, even for the briefest time, she felt a bleak, enervating moment of inevitability and it was as if she herself had vanished, as if the world was simply gone, all its substance and splendour disintegrating into nothing. She wouldn't allow it. Just as her Aunt Loretta had taught her to love and respect nature, to study and give names to all things— trees, grasses, wildflowers, all growing things—Saffi passed on to her children what she laughingly called *my arcane secrets*. Because wasn't there something arcane and essentially troubling in wild plants—their brief tenure on Earth, their straggling, indiscriminate growth and contradictory natures, both healing and destructive, the small stink of decay at the heart of each flower like a reproach or accusation?

SHE TAUGHT HER CHILDREN to be observant, to see the wonderful, unexpected architecture of an ant's nest glistening like molten lava in the sun. Listen to the crickets, she said. Look at the mallard ducks, how they swim in pairs, peaceably. Look at the dragonflies, filled with light, primitive, unsteady, like ancient aircraft. Even: Look at this robin's egg, shattered, vacant, useless. Look at this dead raccoon, its paws stiff as hooks. Go ahead, look, she said. It won't hurt you to look.

SHE HAD A RECURRING DREAM, only it was more the memory of a dream that recurred, rather than the dream itself. In the dream she got up from her bed and went outside. She crawled through the hedge and crouched there in its shelter. She could see Arthur Daisy by his shed, the door swinging open, and inside the shed it seemed there was a greater darkness than the dark of night. There was Arthur Daisy, striking with his shovel at the ground, which had baked hard as clay after a long drought interrupted only by that one downpour the day the search party went out with the dogs and all the other useless things they took, sticks to beat down the grass and maps and walkie-talkie radios. All of them searching in the wrong place. Saffi was the only one who knew. But who would listen to her? *What was true and what was something else, a made-up story?*

It happened on the seventh day of the seventh month; Saffi was seven years old. She saw the sevens in a line, affronted, braced like sailors, their little tongues of flame licking at the air. They linked up and made a barbed-wire fence no one could get through. They made a prison house no one could enter.

A mist was rising over the yard. In the mist was a turtledove. The bird-boy wasn't lost anymore. He wasn't a boy waiting near a riverbank for a shape to appear comic and deceptive and dangerous as a troll. He was indeed a turtledove, soaring higher and higher, giving the night a sort of radiance that came from within, his soul or spirit shining out. In the dream Saffi spoke to herself kindly, saying, Hush, hush, it's all right. It will be all right. And the only sound that came to her from the soundless well of her dream was the ringing of a shovel against the unyielding earth.

Jhoomri's Window
ANITA RAU BADAMI

TODAY JHOOMRI IS WEARING her Meena Kumari tragedy-queen earrings. When she wears those earrings, even Amma cannot scold her for coming to work at ten o'clock instead of eight in the morning. If she does, Jhoomri will pounce fiercely on her words and spit them back like hard marbles, "Why am I late? Why am I late? My life is one big thorn that's why." On such days, Jhoomri can get away with flicking the broom across the floors without collecting any dirt. Sometimes Mother takes a chance and says, "Jhoomri there are tigers and bears growing behind the fridge, so long your broom hasn't touched that place."

Then Jhoomri throws down the broom, places her fists on her hips and says, "Look Bibi-ji, if you aren't happy with my work, tell me straight-straight. Going around the garden to pick one nimboo, I don't like that hanh!"

"Oh-ho," says my mother, "Now I am so afraid of a girl as high as my thumb that I can't even talk straight is it? Treat you like one of the family and see what happens?"

Jhoomri tosses her head, her long earrings flying gold and red.

MY MOTHER ALWAYS HAS SOMETHING to do in the house. Baba likes tea at six in the morning, as soon as he wakes up, so Amma has to be up early too. Once when Jhoomri was grumbling about having to be up every day of the year at six o'clock, Amma said, "And when have I slept later than that girl."

"True Bibi-ji, true, we are both servants are we not?"

Amma looked as if she was going to scold Jhoomri for calling her a servant, but instead she said, "Ah Jhoomri, at least you go out of your house every day and get paid to work."

And Jhoomri said, "Ah Bibi-ji, at least you have a posh-pash bungala with lots of windows."

JHOOMRI IS A STRANGE GIRL. Of the sixty rupees Amma pays her every month, she takes home only fifty.

"If I take it home, my brothers will snatch it all away to buy bidis and daaru," she says, stuffing the notes down the front of her blouse. She keeps her keys down her blouse too. When I try putting ten-paise coins from Amma's change bowl into my dress neck, they just slide down, tickling my tummy, and clatter to the floor. Sometimes a coin gets stuck in the elastic band of my bloomers and I let it stay there poky and hard against my stomach, my secret. I ask Jhoomri why her money doesn't slip down and she laughs, "Because, little kaboothar, I have pillows in my blouse and you don't."

Amma hears this and shouts at Jhoomri for teaching me bad things.

"Arrey Bibi-ji," says Jhoomri, scrubbing the big black pan with ash and mud, "She is also a girl na? Soon she will grow up and become like you and me. So why hide these things from her."

"No," says Amma, "She won't be like you and me. She will study hard and become a doctor."

"Okay Bibi-ji, your darling will become a doctor or an ingineer like babu-ji. But she will still be a woman one day."

I DON'T WANT to become anything when I grow up. I want to climb the jamoon tree like my friend Meenu, I want to stand and do soosoo like her big brother and I want to live in a house with twenty-hundred windows. I like windows and so does Jhoomri. That's why she leaves ten rupees of her money with Amma—to buy a window.

The first time she leaves money Amma says, "Why don't we go and open a bank account for you Jhoomri?"

"No, no, Bibi-ji, you keep it under your pillow or in your godrej. I don't want strange men to keep my money."

"What will you do with your savings? Buy silly earrings from Gadhbadh Jhaala?" asks Amma.

"Hah, I haven't gone to iskool, but I am not stupid Bibi-ji. I am going to buy a window with my money Bibi-ji."

I imagine Jhoomri taking money out of the pillows inside her blouse and bargaining for a window in the market. How will she carry the window home?

"Will you buy a square window or a round one, Jhoomri?" I ask, jumping up and down. No one I know has ever bought a window and I am excited.

Jhoomri taps her mouth with her fingers and nods her head so that her earrings dance in the long curls of hair she leaves loose only near her ears. "Maybe a round one with little flowers all around the edge hanh? Then every time I look out of my window, I will see a garden."

"Jhoomri, that's enough rubbish you are stuffing into the child's head. Window indeed, has anyone ever heard such foolish talk?"

"But it is true, it is true. My father is building a house Bibi-ji and I want a window of my own in it."

"Oh so now Jhoomri is going to have a palace," says Amma, looking up from the knitting she always has. We are in the verandah next to the dining room. It is cool here with its cage of morning-glory creepers. Our gardener Mungroo is clever with plants. He is the one who made our fern-house, as Amma calls it, because we keep all the potted plants in here. Only Chopra Aunty who never hears anything right tells everybody in the colony, with a sniff, that our "fun-house" is full of caterpillars and spiders. She is jealous, says Amma, because we are the only ones in the colony with a morning-glory cage. If you sit in there, nobody can see you, total privacy, says Amma. But you can't see anything either, except our own vegetable garden.

"No Bibi-ji, it is a small house," says Jhoomri. "Two rooms, a kitchen and a ghusal-khaana. One door and two windows—one will be mine."

"What colour will your window be?" I ask.

"What do you think?" says Jhoomri.

"Make it pink," I say, "Like your dupatta with the silver dots."

"Okay my kaboothar, for you I will have a pink window," says Jhoomri, "and then…."

"And then?" I ask giggling.

"And then a prince as handsome as an Ashoka tree will come and say, who lives behind this pretty pink window?" Jhoomri puffs out her chest and strokes an imaginary moustache with huge sweeping hands.

"And then?"

"And then I will look out with my Saira Bano earrings and pink dupatta with silver stars and the prince will say…."

"Hai, will you be my queen," I chorus along with Jhoomri.

All her stories end like this, even the scary one about the princess who stole fire from a bhooth and ran through a dark forest holding the fire in her sari pallu. When Jhoomri is angry with me she says softly so Amma cannot hear, "Now the fire-bhooth will come out of your toy cupboard and eat you up."

Then I can't sleep at night. I don't even like switching off the light, there might be a ghost under the bed waiting to catch me by the toes. I shout for Amma or Baba to turn off the lights, but Amma shouts back, "Such a big girl, seven years old. Do it yourself."

And Baba says, "Pray to God Hanuman, Sona, and you will be okay."

I've prayed and prayed but still there is a bhooth under my bed, I know it. So I build a bridge, first the little stool with a red cushion, then the black chair, then my small writing-table chair. There, now I can reach the light switch. But when it is dark, I can't see anything to find my way back to the bed. I open my eyes huge and my hands become cold. I feel like going to the bathroom, but Amma will slap me if I do it in my panties. I am a big girl now. I switch on the lights again and the ghost runs back to its hiding place under the bed. I go to sleep with the lights on. Baba always comes to check if my blanket is on. He will turn off the lights and Amma will tell me tomorrow that I am a naughty girl wasting electricity. But that is tomorrow.

I TELL JHOOMRI about the bhooth under my bed. She marches upstairs with a broom and says, "See now I will sweep it out."

She pushes the broom into the dark corners under my bed and thumps so hard that balls of cotton dust fly out. "There, now I've killed the bhooth," she says.

"What about the one in my toy cupboard? You said there was one there."

Jhoomri flings open the cupboard and swishes her broom inside. My toys clatter out and Jhoomri dusts them hard, saying, "Chhoo-manthar-anthar-banthar, bhooth-preth-chhoo-chhoo."

Her bangles go chhin-chhin and I laugh hard.

Amma comes running up the stairs, "What is all this noise?" she asks, two lines in the middle of her forehead.

"Nothing Bibi-ji, I just thought I would clean up the little one's cupboard," says Jhoomri winking at me. I cover my mouth with both hands so the giggles won't come running out.

"I see," says Amma, "And since you are in a cleaning mood, we can do the kitchen too. Dust that died ten years ago is sitting behind the shelves there."

Jhoomri makes a face as soon as Amma leaves.

"See," she says pulling my pony tail, "Your bhooth has given me extra work to do today."

I feel very bad. Poor Jhoomri, Amma always finds something for her to do. I go and tell Amma that we should give her a special present. Maybe one of our windows. We have a hundred million windows in our house.

"Amma, which window do you like best?" I ask.

"All of them," says Amma, running from here to there in the kitchen. Baba likes everything cooked a certain way. Amma has to make sure that bhindi is fried crisp, and that drumsticks are cut in one-inch pieces and tied together with a piece of string before being hung in the sambaar. I like them swimming like fish so I can grab them and suck out the crunchy seeds. Baba gets annoyed though, he thinks it is junglee to suck and chomp and make noises while eating. Amma is scared of Baba so she is always running around the house checking that everything is all right.

Now when I ask her which window she likes, she just says, "All of them."

"But which is your special, special favourite Amma?"

"I don't know you silly girl, out of the kitchen, go out," says Amma pushing me, "You'll touch something hot and then I will have that to worry about."

"But which is your favourite window," I ask from the doorway between the kitchen and the dining room. If I don't know how can I give Jhoomri the best one in the house?

"I don't like any of them," says Amma angrily, "I am the one who has to clean them every week, so much dust from so many windows."

"You don't clean them, Jhoomri does," I say.

Amma lifts her hand to slap me and I run out of the room quickly.

MY MOTHER IS SILLY, first she says she likes all the windows, then she says she doesn't like any. *My* favourite is the one in the dining room. From there I can look straight into Kalpu's window. Her mother puts her in a chair every morning and she sits there all day making faces. She is a big girl but her mother has to feed her still. Amma told me she is not all right in the head and I shouldn't stare. I know Kalpu doesn't mind, she likes it when I wave and make faces back at her.

The back bedroom window is nice too. Outside is the shady place under the neem tree where Mungroo gardener sleeps in the afternoon. If I climb on a chair and lean out of the window, I can watch the way he snores, khoon-phee, khoon-phee, phrr-

phrr-phrr. All the long hairs in his nose move in and out, in and out. In the afternoon Amma takes a nap, and when she is fast asleep, I pull a long piece of straw out of the broom and tickle Mungroo's nose. I have to lean far out to do this. With one hand I hold my frock down so that my panties don't show. If Amma comes in suddenly, she will get angry. One for being naughty and again for showing my panties.

"No shame," she will say, "No shame. Such a big girl, showing everything to the whole world. Rama-rama, why didn't I have a son instead of this wild monster."

Mungroo never wakes up though, only hits his nose and rubs it hard. I feel like laughing but he might get up and see me. Then he will go straight to Amma and complain, "Bibi-ji, the child doesn't even let me sleep. Whole day I am working in the sun."

That Mungroo is a chugal-kore, he tattles to Amma about everything. He told her that I was eating raw mangoes that's why my stomach was upset. Amma called me a shaitaan and told me to stay in my room all day. That is boring, I can't see anything nice from my window. Only a field. On Sundays boys play cricket there.

"Sixer!" they shout when someone hits a ball very hard. Then they run up and down in their fat pants swinging a bat and everyone else jumps and screams. Sometimes they have a match, St. Francis School against Vidhya School. The St. Francis boys wear shiny new clothes and caps and slap each other on the back when they are happy. The Vidhya School boys are more fun. They do funny dances and sing songs, "Yaaro, yaaro, ball ko maaro; sixer lagaao, team ko bachaao, yaaro, yaaro." Amma says they are goondas, the Vidhya School boys, they can't even speak English.

Lots of people in the colony come to watch these matches. Only my parents don't go because Baba thinks cricket is boring and Amma never goes anywhere without Baba. Everything in our house is decided by Baba. He decided that my name would be Sona and he never calls Amma by her name. For a long time I thought her name was Amma. But it is Malini. When I ask her why, she says I am a silly, nosy child. I ask Jhoomri and she says it is because Baba has six wives and can't remember all their names. I ask Jhoomri why my Baba has six wives, and she says it is because he is getting lots of white hair and needs six wives to pull them out. Then she quickly says, "Now don't you go and tell your mother this okay?"

ON CRICKET-MATCH DAYS, Jhoomri takes a different road to our house. She goes all the way around Type Six Quarters and right through the field. She dresses up like a princess in a shiny green skirt and blouse. With it she wears a red dupatta which Jhoomri says was made by a spider specially for her. She let me put it on my face so that I can see how soft it is. Jhoomri also wears ten green and ten red bangles on each hand and her special green and red earrings. She showed me a picture of film star Rekha wearing the exact same earrings.

"Why are you special-dressed today?" I ask.

And she laughs and says, "So that all the boys will look at me and say, 'Look there goes the red-dupatta waali.'" Then she shakes her bottom and walks up and down the room singing, "Lal dupatta waali, oh-ho-hoo," keeping a watch out for Amma at the same time.

On match days, Mungroo gardener behaves very funnily. He works only in the vegetable garden behind the kitchen where Jhoomri washes the vessels and hangs out the clothes to dry. And I have seen him, he only pretends to work like I do in Miss Massey's Moral Science class when she gives us god books to read. Mungroo sits at the cabbages, and says things to Jhoomri.

"Oh my heart is beating, beating, repeating," he sings. I know that song, it is from the new movie which my friend said is a bad one with lots of big people things in it. Sometimes Mungroo says, "Ohey Pyaari, come with me to the sanema today." That Mungroo can't even say cinema, I've told him and told him and he says I am a little English fly, go away.

Jhoomri never answers, she sits with her back to Mungroo and washes the vessels harder and harder.

"Jhoomri," I say, "Why don't you say anything to Mungroo. Don't you like him?"

"Hai shaitaan," yells Jhoomri, frightening me, "Have I bhoosa in my head that I should start liking a nalayak gardener?"

"Then why don't you tell him to keep quiet?"

"Because decent girls don't talk to villains like him."

"He has hair coming out of his nose Jhoomri, don't marry him."

Jhoomri giggles, "How do you know what he has in his nose?"

I tell her about my Mungroo window and she laughs till she is going to cry. "Oo ma, I think my blouse button has popped open," she says finally, wiping the laugh-water from her eyes.

"Are you going to tell Amma?" I ask, suddenly worried.

"Not if you don't tell her about your Baba's six wives," she says.

"I won't, cross my heart and hope to die," I say.

"What is all this Inglis-pinglis you are saying," says Jhoomri, "I won't tell your mother, but now I can have some fun with that Mungroo."

SO THE NEXT TIME Mungroo comes close to Jhoomri and says, "Oh my golden beauty, whose thummak-thummak walk makes my heart go dhummak-dhummak."

Jhoomri spits on the ground near his feet and says, "Oh one with the hairy nose, whose smell makes me vomit."

Mungroo catches Jhoomri's arm and says, "I know the way to your house, gori, and I know your father is looking for a man to tie you to."

Jhoomri spits again, this time on Mungroo's foot. He lifts his other hand and I scream for my mother, "Amma, Amma, Mungroo is bad, come quickly!"

Mungroo leaves Jhoomri's arm.

Amma comes running and picks me up. "What happened," she asks stroking my face, "What happened?"

"Mungroo was going to beat Jhoomri," I sob.

"She is a randi," says Mungroo making red eyes at Jhoomri.

Amma looks shocked. She drops me down hard on the ground and pushes me into the kitchen, "Run away child, go to your room and play."

She steps out into the backyard and I stay near the kitchen window. I want to see Amma scolding that bad hairy-nose.

"Okay now what is going on here?" asks Amma in a stern voice like when she sees me taking threads out of her stitching box.

"She is always teasing me, the randi," says Mungroo.

Amma holds up her hand, "Mungroo, I don't want to hear gutter language."

"Look at the way she dresses Bibi-ji," says Mungroo shaking a flat hand at Jhoomri, "Will any decent girl wear such things?"

"He thinks he is my father, telling me what to wear. Hah!" says Jhoomri throwing her head and making a face.

"If your father had any brains he wouldn't let you out of the house," says Mungroo.

"Hai-amma, now he is calling my father names, this Mungroo, half-wit son of a thieving she-ass."

"That's enough both of you," says Amma, her hands clenched together. "If I hear you Mungroo saying anything to this girl again, I'll tell Saab-ji and you won't have a job."

"It is a permanent job memsahib, saab-ji can't do anything," says Mungroo, "But you have been my mother and father, so I will listen to you."

He looks at Jhoomri, snaps his towel hard, throws it over his shoulder and walks off. He looks just like the rooster in Gopa Tailor's yard. I run out of the kitchen before Amma comes in.

ON DIWALI FESTIVAL DAY, Amma gives Jhoomri a new salwar-kameez. I chose it for her, I know the colours Jhoomri likes. The salwar is red and the kameez green with red and white flowers. Amma wanted to buy a black and white one, like all her own saris. I hate Amma's saris, but she wears them because Baba says she is a married lady and should wear only quiet colours. I think that is silly. Amma looks beautiful in her red and gold sari which she wears on special days. But she listens only to Baba, he doesn't even let her plait her hair. Amma always wears a bun and no flowers in her hair. One day when she was in a good mood, she told me that as a little girl she loved wearing long strings of jasmine. I love my Baba, but I am afraid that when I grow up he will make me wear ugly clothes and no flowers.

On Diwali day, Amma also gives Jhoomri twenty rupees. "Here, you can buy earrings and bangles to match your new clothes," she says.

But Jhoomri keeps only five and gives the rest back to Amma. "Bibi-ji, keep that in your godrej-cupboard with the rest of my window money," she says. "Next month we will be putting in doors and windows and I will have just enough for my window."

Amma smiles and says, "No this is for your earrings, I will put extra twenty from my side for your window."

Jhoomri is so happy she laughs and then cries and then bends down and touches Amma's feet. As if Amma is a god or something, she is only my mother.

I want to see Jhoomri laugh again so I ask her, "Will you buy Shabana Azmi earrings Jhoomri?"

"Chee-chee," says Jhoomri, "Her earrings have no shaan, can't even see them sometimes. I am going to buy anklets for my feet."

"Enough talk now, there's lots of work to do today," says Amma. She is in a good mood. Diwali is a special day and nobody can get angry.

AMMA WAKES ME UP at five o'clock, before the sun has risen, and gives me an oil bath. First I make a fuss about waking up but soon I can hear all our neighbours already letting off crackers. I jump out of bed and my skin pokes out in small bubbles in the cold. After my bath, Amma gives me my new panties and petticoat to wear. I begged her for panties with lace and flowers like my friends. I hate the long bloomers she always makes me wear. I have a new frock too, but that is for the evening when all the lamps will be lit.

Today Amma opens the windows in the house, every one of them, and the doors too. She isn't worried about dust on Diwali, though afterwards Jhoomri has to clean for ten days.

"Why?" I ask Amma. I know the answer, but I like asking anyway. It is my Diwali question. "Why do you have to leave all the doors and windows open?"

"Because, Sona," says Amma, "Today Goddess Lakshmi will be roaming around our colony going into homes to taste laddoo and burfi and jalebi. She will leave lots of happiness behind, so we can't close any doors. Who knows which one she will want to enter, no?"

"Will she go to everybody's house?"

"Yes, of course."

"Even Jhoomri's?"

"Yes, yes, so many questions from an inch-high girl."

"Even though her house has no doors or windows yet?"

"I don't know," says Amma. "Go now, go and clean out your toy cupboard. Goddess Lakshmi will run away if she sees the mess there."

"Will you wear your red sari today?"

"Yes child, yes!"

ON DIWALI DAY, the beggar man comes down the road earlier than usual.

"Hail, hail Goddess Durga, give, *give* to poor old Murga!" he shouts, and rattles his bowl after each word. He is a big man with long curly hair and a beard. Though he goes around the colony every Sunday, Murga stops at our house only on Diwali day. Amma gives him some money and sweets but on other days says that he is a healthy fellow and why can't he work for a living.

Murga bangs the latch on our gate and shouts again, "Jai Durga-maata, jai!"

I am playing in the front verandah and he calls to me, "O little one, go tell your mother that a hungry soul is at her gates."

I run inside quickly. He scares me. Murga looks just like the demon Raavan in my Ramayan story book. Amma tells me that story the night before Diwali. And when she comes to the part where Lakshman draws a line in front of Seetha's hut my heart starts beating fast.

"Sister Seetha," says Lakshman, "Don't step out of this line I have drawn or great evil will happen."

Then Amma turns the page and there is Raavan dressed like Murga the beggar.

"My daughter, alms for a hungry sage," he says and Seetha puts her foot out of Lakshman's line. Then Raavan turns into a demon with big teeth and drags Seetha away, laughing ha-ha-ha.

At the end of the story Amma snaps the book shut and says, "And if you don't listen to your mother, that's what will happen to you too."

"What happened to Seetha?"

"A bad person kidnapped her."

Kidnapped. Kidnapped. That is a scary word. It happens to little girls who do not listen to Amma. She told me not to eat the raisins, but I didn't listen.

"Amma, I ate all the raisins," I say. "I don't want to be kidnapped by Murga."

Amma looks at me puzzled, "What strange things you say child. Why should he kidnap you?"

"Because I didn't listen to you."

Amma just says tchuk-tchuk like a lizard and tells me not to let too much air fill my head or I will float away.

I like my mother on Diwali day, she laughs a lot and says nonsense things like Jhoomri. Maybe it is because she can wear her red sari and not worry about dust in the house. She isn't even angry with Mungroo when he asks for more baksheesh.

"Bibi-ji, what can a man do with ten rupees nowadays?" he asks when Amma hands him a new shirt and the money.

"What do you think I am? Wife of Birla millionaire?" says Amma, but she gives him another five rupees anyway.

"Do you like that shirt?" she asks.

"Yes Bibi-ji, I will keep it for my wedding day."

"What Mungroo, are you getting married?" asks Amma.

"Perhaps Bibi-ji, perhaps. I have seen the mare I want," says Mungroo laughing and I can see all his teeth orange with paan stains.

I wish Amma hadn't given him any presents for Diwali. He is a piggy man and he makes Jhoomri afraid. He wants to marry her, I know. He tells her that when Jhoomri is hanging out the clothes.

Mungroo is pulling out grass in the vegetable garden and singing a film song. I am colouring my picture-book in the morning-glory room and I can see Jhoomri shaking out the wet clothes with a snap.

"Ohey Jhoomri, do you like my song?" asks Mungroo.

"Howls like a donkey and calls it a song," says Jhoomri.

"Talk, talk all you want now," says Mungroo making small eyes in the sun, "When you are my wife all that will end."

Jhoomri drops the sheet she is about to hang out and it falls into the damp mud. Now she will have to wash it all over again.

"You dirty man," she says, "Who will marry a hairy nose like you?"

"I have a permanent job with the railways. Which father will say no to a proposal from me?" says Mungroo.

Jhoomri tosses her head, "If I tell my father what kind of a luchha you are, he won't even let your shadow cross our doorstep."

Mungroo just laughs and I can see that Jhoomri is scared.

I run to tell Amma. She will scold Mungroo and Jhoomri will smile again.

Amma is busy as usual. Baba phoned to say that he is bringing office people home for Diwali dinner. Amma does not like it when he brings people suddenly like that, but she never says anything. She only scolds me. Now when I tell her about Mungroo and Jhoomri, she catches my ear and twists it hard so water fills my eyes and nose.

"Stupid girl, poke your nose everywhere. One day it will get bitten off," she says, "I don't want to hear anymore about that gardener, and you stop listening to every-thing in the world, otherwise I'll tell Baba."

TWO WEEKS AFTER DIWALI, Jhoomri tells me, "Tomorrow I will take my money home, little one, tomorrow I will pay for my window."

Then she goes in and tells Amma that she will collect her money tomorrow and Amma smiles at her and says, "After you get your window, what are you going to collect money for, Jhoomri?"

And Jhoomri says, "I don't know Bibi-ji, I'll think of something nice."

The next day Jhoomri comes in late and is wearing her Meena Kumari tragedy-queen earrings. Before Amma can say anything, she starts crying.

Amma catches her by the shoulders and shakes her hard, "Arrey, Jhoomri what is the matter with you? Today you are going to buy your window and here you look like the sky has fallen on your head."

"What will I do with a window when I am going out of the house," says Jhoomri.

"What are you talking about?"

"Bibi-ji, my marriage has been fixed up," says Jhoomri wiping her face on her kameez sleeve like I do sometimes.

"Is that something to cry about, you silly girl?" asks Amma.

"Bibi-ji, I am to be tied to that Mungroo, my father didn't even ask me if I liked him."

"But he has a good job Jhoomri, what else do you want?"

"Amma, he has a hairy nose," I say eagerly, "How can Jhoomri marry him?"

Amma acts like she did not hear me and asks Jhoomri again, "Well Jhoomri, what is wrong with Mungroo?"

A great big smile spreads across Jhoomri's face, "Bibi-ji, he has a hairy nose," she says.

Amma frowns at her, "You still behave like a child, girl, and about to get married too."

"No Bibi-ji, I am no longer a child, am I?" says Jhoomri.

Amma pats her on the shoulder and says, "Don't worry, you'll be happy, you'll learn how to be happy with Mungroo."

"Yes," says Jhoomri.

"And your window?" I ask, totally confused now. How can Jhoomri be happy about marrying Mungroo? "Will you be getting your pink window today Jhoomri?"

"What will I do with a window now, child?" asks Jhoomri. And all of a sudden she sounds just like my mother.

Part 3

LUNCH
CONVERSATION

THE COMBINATION OF THE WORDS lunch *and* conversation *tends to bring to mind the words* casual *and* relaxed; *the lightly taken and the mildly observed. During Michael Ondaatje's family gathering in his memoir "Running in the Family," however, the opportunity to present various versions of events is seized upon in witty and ingenious ways. Exaggeration, embellishment, even lies are fair game: family histories can be changed, mysterious secrets revealed. It can also be a time (as it is in "Aunts") to table one's private observations of loved ones for future reference. In this world the small detail becomes large, revisioned, reimagined, and transformed into art.*

The stories in this section, then, are not set against the turbulence of great historic events; rather, they are a tale told in a canyon (Joseph Boyden), a memory of a first love (Sandra Birdsell) or a lost love (Wayne Johnston), or an account of a search for a gift (Carol Shields). And running throughout are the various patterns, the versions of how things might have been, should have been, or how things seemed to be in the minds of several characters, for everything that one recalls about life has been filtered through the twin lenses of one's own memory and imagination. After all, without such alteration, few narratives, whether told or written, could quicken. As Timothy Findley suggests, "real life writes real bad," and tragedy, when it is not shaped by art, can seem simply banal. When the shaping takes place, however, the smallest object can resonate with significance: the underside of a dining room table from a child's point of view, a cookbook, a scarf, the way a wrist disappears into the silk of a sari.

Lunch Conversation

MICHAEL ONDAATJE

WAIT A MINUTE, wait a minute! When did all this happen, I'm trying to get it straight ...

Your mother was nine, Hilden was there, and your grandmother Lalla and David Grenier and his wife Dickie.

How old was Hilden?

Oh, in his early twenties.

But Hilden was having dinner with my mother and you.

Yes, says Barbara. And Trevor de Saram. And Hilden and your mother and I were quite drunk. It was a wedding lunch, Babette's I think, I can't remember all those weddings. I know Hilden was moving with a rotten crowd of drinkers then so he was drunk quite early and we were all laughing about the drowning of David Grenier.

I didn't say a word.

Laughing at Lalla, because Lalla nearly drowned too. You see, she was caught in a current and instead of fighting it she just relaxed and went with it out to sea and eventually came back in a semi-circle. Claimed she passed ships.

And then Trevor got up in a temper and challenged Hilden to a duel. He couldn't *stand* everyone laughing, and Hilden and Doris (your mother) being drunk, two of them flirting away he thought.

But *why?*, your mother asked Trevor.

Because he is casting aspersions on you ...

Nonsense, I love aspersions. And everyone laughed and Trevor stood there in a rage.

And then, said Barbara, I realized that Trevor had been in love with your mother, your father always *said* there was a secret admirer. Trevor couldn't stand Hilden and her having a good time in front of him.

Nonsense, said your mother. It would have been incest. And besides (watching Hilden and Trevor and aware of the fascinated dinner table audience), both these men are after my old age pension.

What happened, said Hilden, was that I drew a line around Doris in the sand. A circle. And threatened her, "don't you dare step out of that circle or I'll thrash you."

Wait a minute, wait a minute, *when* is this happening?

Your mother is nine years old, Hilden says. And out in the sea near Negombo David Grenier is drowning. I didn't want her to go out.

You were in love with a nine year old?

Neither Hilden nor Trevor were *ever* in love with our mother, Gillian whispers to me. People always get that way at weddings, always remembering the past in a sentimental way, pretending great secret passions which went unsaid …

No No No. Trevor *was* in love with your mother.

Rot!

I was in my twenties, Hilden chimes in. Your mother was nine. I simply didn't want her going into the water while we tried to rescue David Grenier. Dickie, his wife, had fainted. Lalla—your mother's mother—was caught in the current and out at sea, I was on the shore with Trevor.

Trevor was there too you see.

Who is Hilden? asks Tory.

I am Hilden … your host!

Oh.

Anyway … there seems to be three different stories that you're telling.

No, *one,* everybody says laughing.

One when your mother was nine. Then when she was sixty-five and drinking at the wedding lunch, and obviously there is a period of unrequited love suffered by the silent Trevor who never stated his love but always fought with anyone he thought was insulting your mother, even if in truth she was simply having a good time with them the way she was with Hilden, when she was sixty-five.

Good God, I was there with them both, says Barbara, and *I'm* married to Hilden.

So where is my grandmother?

She is now out at sea while Hilden dramatically draws a circle round your mother and says "Don't you *dare* step out of that!" Your mother watches David Grenier drowning. Grenier's wife—who is going to marry three more times including one man who went crazy—is lying in the sand having fainted. And your mother can see the bob of her mother's head in the waves now and then. Hilden and Trevor are trying to retrieve David Grenier's body, carefully, so as not to get caught in the current themselves.

My mother is nine.

Your mother is nine. And this takes place in Negombo.

OK

So an hour later my grandmother, Lalla, comes back and entertains everyone with stories of how she passed ships out there and they tell her David Grenier is dead. And nobody wants to break the news to his wife Dickie. Nobody could. And Lalla says, alright, she will, for Dickie is her sister. And she went and sat with Dickie who was still in a faint in the sand, and Lalla, wearing her elaborate bathing suit, held her hand. Don't shock her, says Trevor, whatever you do break it to her gently. My grandmother waves him away and for fifteen minutes she sits alone with her sister, waiting for her to waken. She doesn't know what to say. She is also suddenly very tired. She hates hurting anybody.

The two men, Hilden and Trevor, will walk with her daughter, my mother, about a hundred yards away down the beach, keeping their distance, waiting until they see Dickie sitting up. And then they will walk slowly back towards Dickie and my grandmother and give their sympathies.

Dickie stirs. Lalla is holding her hand. She looks up and the first words are, "How is David? Is he alright?" "Quite well, darling," Lalla says. "He is in the next room having a cup of tea."

Aunts

MICHAEL ONDAATJE

HOW I HAVE used them…. They knit the story together, each memory a wild thread in the sarong. They lead me through their dark rooms crowded with various kinds of furniture—teak, rattan, calamander, bamboo—their voices whispering over tea, cigarettes, distracting me from the tale with their long bony arms, which move over the table like the stretched feet of storks. I would love to photograph this. The thin muscle on the upper arms, the bones and veins at the wrist that almost become part of the discreet bangle, all disappearing into the river of bright sari or faded cotton print.

My aunt Dolly stands five foot tall, weighing seventy pounds. She has not stopped smoking since the age of fifteen and her 80-year-old brain leaps like a spark plug bringing this year that year to life. Always repeating the last three words of your question and then turning a surprising corner on her own. In the large house whose wings are now disintegrating into garden and bush she moves frail as Miss Havisham. From outside the house seems incapable of use. I climb in through the window that frames her and she greets me with "I never thought I'd see you again," and suddenly all these journeys are worth it, just to be able to hug this thin woman who throws her cane onto the table in order to embrace me.

She and her brother Arthur were my father's close friends all his life. He knew that, whatever he had done, Arthur would be there to talk him out of madness, weakness, aloneness. They introduced most of the children of our generation to the theatre, dressing us up in costumes for *The Mikado, A Midsummer Night's Dream*—all of which Dolly made herself. Although her family was not excessive in their affairs, they shielded anyone who was in the midst of a passion. "Affairs were going on all around us, even when we were children … so we were well trained."

Today is one of Dolly's deaf days but the conversation rolls with the pure joy of the meeting. "Oh I looked after you several times when you were in Boralesgamuwa, do you remember?" "Yes, yes." "WHAT?" *"Yes."* The frailty does not stop her stories though she pauses now and then to say, "God if you quote me I'm dead. I'll be caught for libel and *killed*…. You see they liked their flirtations. All the wives met their beaux in the Cinnamon Gardens, that's where they went to flirt, then they'd come here and use us as an alibi. Your grandmother Lalla for instance had lots of relationships. We could never keep up with her. We almost had to write the names down to remember who she was seeing. My advice you see is to get on with everybody—no matter what they do."

The conversation is continually halted by a man lying just below the ceiling hammering nails into it—hoping to keep it propped up for a few more years.

Outside loud chickens fill in the spaces between Dolly's words. Eyes squint in the smoke. "I wish I could see you properly but my glasses are being fixed this week."

As I prepare to leave she walks with me, half deaf and blind, under several ladders in her living room that balance paint and workmen, into the garden where there is a wild horse, a 1930 car splayed flat on its axles and hundreds of flowering bushes so that her eyes swim out into the dark green and unfocussed purple. There is very little now that separates the house from the garden. Rain and vines and chickens move into the building. Before I leave, she points to a group photograph of a fancy dress party that shows herself and my grandmother Lalla among the crowd. She has looked at it for years and has in this way memorized everyone's place in the picture. She reels off names and laughs at the facial expressions she can no longer see. It has moved tangible, palpable, into her brain, the way memory invades the present in those who are old, the way gardens invade houses here, the way her tiny body steps into mine as intimate as anything I have witnessed and I have to force myself to be gentle with this frailty in the midst of my embrace.

Dinner at Noon

ETHEL WILSON

FAR AWAY AT THE END OF THE TABLE sat Father, the kind, handsome and provident man. At this end sat Mother, her crinoline spread abroad. On Mother's right was Mr. Matthew Arnold. On each side of the table the warned children ate their food gravely, all except Topaz on Mother's left. Topaz, who could not be squelched, was perched there on the top of two cushions, as innocent as a poached egg. Mother sat gracious, fatigued, heavy behind the majestic crinoline with the last and fatal child.

Said Mr. Matthew Arnold in large and musical tones, speaking across the children and three jellied fowls to Father who with divided attention carved, "It is now my hope to make a survey of the educational systems of France and Germany with a view to the establishment in this country of reasonable educational facilities for every child, rich or poor. You will agree with me, Mr. Edgeworth, that a modicum of education, given under healthy and happy conditions, is the right of every boy. This I would extend to girls also." Thus spoke Mr. Matthew Arnold.

Father, as he carved for ten people, made encouraging sounds, although he had not yet considered this novel idea. He was, however, prepared to do so. He looked forward to a pleasant afternoon with this agreeable and enlightened person who was a coming Inspector of Schools, a present poet, and a son of Arnold of Rugby.

Mother's quiet sombre gaze swept round the table, dwelt for a moment thoughtfully on the poet, rested on Father busy with the jellied fowls, rested on the two young grown-up daughters, on the four sons, on the little Topaz at her side, and on the ministering Cook and Emma.

Topaz was anxious to be noticed. But nobody was noticed today except Mr. Matthew Arnold. Not Annie, Mary, Blakey, George, John, nor Joe. She determined to be noticed immediately, so she spoke across the table to the guest.

As she was so unimportant no one paid her any attention at first until she was heard to say, "... and it's got a lovely yellow glass handle and you pull it and it goes woosh! Woosh, woosh!" she trumpeted, and smiled happily at Mr. Matthew Arnold.

"What goes woosh, my child?" he asked.

"Our new—"

"TOPAZ!" thundered Father, and Mother put out a grieved and loving hand. The outraged brothers and sisters looked across and downwards. Only Mr. Matthew Arnold regarded Topaz without horror.

"Topaz, eat your bread and butter," commanded Mother. But Topaz had succeeded. She had been noticed, although she had failed to tell Mr. Matthew Arnold about their new plumbing. All ordinary friends and relatives had witnessed the behaviour of the Edgeworths' revolutionary plumbing, which was the first of its kind to be installed in the town of Ware in North Staffordshire. Its fame had spread, and even strangers accosted Father in the street and asked him if it really worked. It was the joy of Topaz and the pride of the Edgeworths. It took the family a few moments to recover from the near-horror of the indelicate child.

The desire of Topaz to be noticed intoxicated her, and she went on. She looked only at the kind and unshocked face of Mr. Matthew Arnold, and she desired ardently to impress him now, at this very moment, while she still had the chance.

"Would you like me to say some poetry?" she asked.

"Topaz," said Mother half rising, "Emma shall take you upstairs to your room."

"Please, Mrs. Edgeworth," said Mr. Matthew Arnold, "let the child say her poetry, and I will then, if I may, expound a favourite theory of mine."

Topaz sparkled and began:

"Two are better far than one
For comfort or for fight.
How can one keep warm alone,

Or serve his God aright?"[1]

---

1. From an old Methodist hymnal.

"And I'll say you another," she said quickly, "'How doth the little busy—'"

"TOPAZ—THAT—WILL—DO," said Father in a terrible tone. Topaz looked at Father. His eyes and his whiskers looked larger and darker than usual. She hung her head. Dear Father was angry. She slithered down from her cushions, down from her chair, and vanished under the table. The outraged brothers and sisters waited.

Mr. Matthew Arnold took things in hand and addressed both Father and Mother. "This is an interesting little child of yours. Will you, as a favour to me, let her stay under the table? She has not really offended. She is young, and she wishes to entertain. Don't make her shy. Leave her to herself. She knows in her heart that she has been rather forward. Let her think about it. Now, on the subject of coercion, I feel strongly that ..."

Father listened. The children watched the good guest and the good food. Mother rested her graceful head on her hand. She gazed attentively and sweetly on the expounding Mr. Matthew Arnold, and did not hear a word that he was saying. Upstairs with the nurse was Hannah, the youngest, labouring with croup. Within Mother the last and fatal babe moved and moved. "It will be tonight," thought Mother, "I feel it will be tonight, and Joseph will be greatly disturbed. Dear Father. But I ..." She turned her troubled look on Father and on the food. Swish went the white cap-streamers as Emma set down the sweet. "Cream pudding," murmured Blakey, looking with greedy eyes across to George, unchecked. Mother looked upon George, upon all her brood. "Now, according to Rousseau ..." said Mr. Matthew Arnold.

UNDERNEATH THE HEAVY MAHOGANY TABLE sat Topaz in a world of shoes. She had recovered from fear and shame. Now she crawled from shoe to shoe. Each pair of shoes told Topaz a story. Mother had no shoes, no feet at all, just a beautiful rustling spread of purple silk, Topaz studied the silk without touching. Then she crawled to the large visiting boots of Mr. Matthew Arnold. Mr. Arnold wore elegant old-fashioned trousers which had straps under the feet. His feet were large, impeccable, neatly placed together. Topaz touched a leg with a friendly tickling finger. Above the table the great man checked his speech, smiled to himself, and continued. Topaz in the pleasing gloom of tablecloth, legs, and feet, crawled on.

Next to Mr. Arnold sat her nearest and favourite brother Joe. Joe's slippered feet curled round his chair legs. He listened, understanding a little, to the great man. Joe, gentle and frail, destined for early death, was never impatient with the chattering Topaz. Topaz dared to stroke Joe's ankle softly. Pussy pussy pussy. He gave no sign. She crawled on.

She put her head on one side and looked at Blakey's clodhoppers. What a smell! Blakey smelled of the stable and Father's horse. Topaz regarded Blakey and his boots coldly. He, the sharp-nosed boy, was already the farmer, the jockey. He was to sail cheerfully across an ocean and a half to Australia. Yes, Blakey said goodbye to the narrow streets of Ware and lived to be a happy horsey patriarch in a wide world of his own choosing. Happy Blakey. Topaz crawled on.

Here were the good shoes of Mary. Out she went to India, poor Mary, to marry a missionary. Glory surrounded the absent Mary who soon bore two little spinsters in the heat and died. Poor Mary, buried almost as her eyes closed, in that distant consuming heat. Topaz passed from Mary's shoes without interest and crawled on.

Here was Father. Two well-shod feet rested side by side on the thick carpet. Topaz looked at Father's boots with respect. Father never buttoned his own boots. Godlike he extended a foot, and his boot was put on and fastened by a reverent son, or daughter, or Emma, or Nurse, or Cook, or sometimes by Mother. Topaz dared not touch these hallowed and angry feet. She crawled on.

Oh, the beautiful slippers of Annie. Topaz made little passes with her hands over Annie's tiny feet. Annie was as pious as beautiful. She was eighteen and modestly in love. She was to marry James Hastings, Father's brilliant young man at the Works. She was to be the gentle and obeyed mother of nine. She was, in her charming matriarchal old age, to go far away across sea and land to join distant sons yet unborn. She was yet in mildness and in formidable and unquestioned piety to infuse the lives of her sons, of her daughters Laura and Rachel, of her orphaned granddaughter Rose, of a wicked Chinaman, of more, of more, unborn, unknown. She was to be the refuge and comfort of her bereft young sister Topaz. She was to die in Vancouver (yet undreamed of), tiny, ancient, beautiful, gently amused, pure in heart, greatly beloved. Here she sat, as yet the young and filial daughter, neat feet, tender eyes, unknown thoughts, and ringlets of brown. Topaz looked long at the slippers of Annie. She fingered Annie's grey silk dress with pleasure, and then she crawled on.

She did not stop at the plain and lumpish shoes of George. George was red of face, genial, soon to be ardent, to be much wived. George was kindly, lazy, earthy, petted, and at last to be tamed. Topaz was never to be tamed, never. She crawled on.

Here were the neat and respectable feet of John. John was pretty. When Topaz called John "pretty," Blakey and George were rude. But so he was. He grew more elegant and fastidious as years increased. It became inevitable that John should be called Giovanni, that he should marry an heiress, that he should mingle with lords, that he should move with conscious distinction through several decades of public service. These neat feet of John's globe-trotted. They carried him busily among the great and the near-great with correctness. These quiet feet will hasten to many a directors' meeting. ("Hear-hear. Hear-hear.") John, the correct one, who could make you feel sneaped.[2] John never felt sneaped. If you were a dog, being sneaped would be the same as going off with your tail between your legs. If you were Topaz, people tried to sneap you, but you were hard to sneap. Even the proud gentle Annie, the eldest, could be sneaped by a look, but never John. Those who cause others to feel sneaped are vulnerable. Brother John, your day will come. Topaz pondered the neatness of John's feet and then curled up and fell asleep.

Above the table the future hung implicit, almost palpable, around the family. Above the table Mother sighed, caught the adult eyes, smiled her sad smile, and arose.

It was the next night that Mother died.

The Buried Life
ETHEL WILSON

ROSE ENTERED AUNTY'S BEDROOM with a guilty feeling. Too long had passed since she had visited Aunt Topaz; but Aunty never showed resentment at this, however much she might, a few minutes later, provoke and enjoy a good tiff with you. She looked up from her book, and her face lighted with the particularly well-mannered winning look which always accompanied her greetings, which were never dull. Aunty was becoming rather attached to Rose, whom she had regarded until lately as still a person of fourteen who had accidentally been married and had no real status. She had suddenly begun to regard Rose as an adult and a genuine married person, indeed as a contemporary, but above all as a surviving symbol of Annie and Rachel. "What a many years of memory we share!" And it was true.

"So *there* you are!" she exclaimed joyously. "You're just in time to hear something. Listen to this! It's poetry. You like poetry, you know," as if this were Rose's odd peculiarity. And she read aloud from the book which she held in her left hand. She read in a very special voice:

"The unplumb'd, salt, estranging sea."

and again, more slowly;

"The unplumb'd, salt, estranging sea."

---

2. Sneaped—a good Staffordshire word. Used by William Shakespeare too.

"Mrs. Porter used to say," said Aunty, "that there was everything that anyone could think, know, or say about the sea in that line. And many's the time I've shaken the hand that wrote that line! He used to come to our house to dinner whenever he came to Ware, and very good he was to me once when he came to dinner. Matthew Arnold, you know. Nobody reads Matthew Arnold now, do they, but they should, they should. Listen to this," and she riffled the pages over until she came to her place. She raised her crooked little gemmed hand (something like a gemmed claw) and, the little crooked hand held up, said, "Listen! Mark this!" and Rose listened.

"How well Aunty reads poetry!" she thought. "With all her love of rattle and bang you'd think she would trumpet it, or read with windy eloquence. But her voice is slow and musical when she reads, and her tone is level and plain. She lets the words and phrases speak for themselves. This must be the training of the classical Mrs. Porter of whom I have heard; eighty years ago and more."

Aunty read, and her hand with its glittering rings remained upraised:

"Only—but this is rare—
When a beloved hand is laid in ours,
When, jaded with the rush and glare
Of the interminable hours,
Our eyes can in another's eyes read clear,
When our world-deafen'd ear
Is by the tones of a loved voice caress'd—
A bolt is shot back somewhere in our breast,
And a lost pulse of feeling stirs again …"

She raised her voice and dulcetly she read on:

"The eye sinks inward, and the heart lies plain,
And what we mean, we say, and what we would, we know.
A man becomes aware of his life's flow,
And hears its winding murmur; and he sees
The meadows where it glides, the sun, the breeze …
… And then he thinks he knows
The hills where his life rose,
And the sea where it goes."

There was quiet in the room, and then Aunty descended briskly from poetry. "That's from 'The Buried Life.' Read it. Read it. It's very good, a good man Matthew Arnold. My life rose in Staffordshire and I suppose it's going out into the Pacific Ocean. Well, well! But as for a Buried Life," said Aunty pertly, "I suppose some people have them. Couldn't say, I'm sure. I never did, myself, only for a time I suppose when I loved Unrequited for seven years. It isn't everyone who can love for seven years ... Unrequited," said Aunty complacently. "Could you do that?"

"No," said Rose honestly, "I don't believe I could."

"There, you see," said Aunty scornfully, "you and your happy marriages! Any simpleton can do *that*. But to love Unrequited," she continued with satisfaction, "your generation hasn't got the guts to do it. Not a one of you could do it! Have I told you about it before? ... Oh, I have." (Rose knew the story well.) "Well, here's tea! Good, good! You pour it out. And get down that picture of William Sandbach. That's him. Hasn't he got a handsome nose?"

"I'm always inclined to suspect a handsome nose," said her great-niece.

"What a ridiculous remark! Suspect a nose indeed! He was a widower, the hand-somest man in Parliament they used to say. They lost their only son and then she went a little queer before she died. I'm not surprised, I'm sure.

"He gave me that picture. In Court dress with a white ostrich feather along his hat. Oh, I *was* proud when he gave me that picture. No, another lump, I like it sweet. Why don't you take sugar in your tea? You'd be fatter. You'd be a deal better-looking if you were fatter. Well, whenever distinguished people came to the Potteries, Mr. Sandbach gave a dinner-party. And he always asked John and me until John married Annie-John. John and I used to drive there in the brougham and we always Dressed. No one Dressed in Ware except at Mr. Sandbach's dinner-parties. Oh, I met Gladstone there (I worshipped Gladstone) and the Prince and Princess Colonna and Burne-Jones and Sir Garnet Wolseley and Baroness Burdett-Coutts and all the Foreigners. I could always talk, you see, English and French, oh yes. I could always talk and so could John and so we were always asked. I never could bear to sit mum as a mouse. Very dull I call it. Just like Charles Lamb said, 'A party in a parlour, all silent and all damned!'"

"Wasn't it Wordsworth or wasn't it ..." interrupted Rose.

"Don't argue so much," said Aunty. "You argue. Very unattractive in a woman, arguing, anyone will tell you. But I'd as lief go to bed as sit mum as a mouse. That young woman here last week. Not a word did she say. I talked to her all afternoon and not a word did she utter."

"Well, Aunty ..." began Rose, defending.

"A bit more cake.... No, that one. And the result was that people said, 'You'll see, William Sandbach will marry Topaz Edgeworth!' Oh, it became very painful to me, very painful." Rose knew what was coming next. If she had not known, it would have shocked her, coming as a disclosure, a secret. But Aunty was enjoying herself. "Oh yes, I fell in love. How I suffered! Driving down with John to dinner and driving home again. My greatest joy and misery too. I loved him for seven years of my life, and it was wasted, wasted. I'm proud of it now, not everybody could do it!

But then I said to myself, 'No, it's over,' and it *was* over. And I well remember, in me bedroom I raised me fist to heaven and I CURSED HIM!"

If ever a face flashed, Aunty's face flashes now. If a crooked jewelled hand was raised and shaken to heaven, it is hers. She lives through the distant dreadful moment again. Her face is contorted in pleasurable rage. Rose, curled up in the armchair, watches. She has seen this before. She has heard it before. "Wherein is it," she wonders, "that our generation is different? I'd feel a fool, shaking my fist to heaven. Aunty doesn't feel a fool and, moreover, she doesn't look it. She's enjoying herself. Don't we feel as deeply? Yes, we do. But we're different."

"How strange!" thought Rose, looking at Topaz. She marvelled again at the unquenched vitality of the small ancient being who was her Great-Aunt. This vitality had been preserved and untroubled by Aunty's lack of awareness of the human relations which compose the complicated fabric of living. The limitless treasure and absorbing motions of a continuous hidden life had neither enriched nor depleted her. Rose began to admire the candour of Aunt Topaz, who now had passed the zenith of her wrath.

"But," said Aunty, "I'll never forget, when I came back to England in nineteen-twenty, I was driving up Port Hill in John's brougham and I saw William Sandbach walking up alone, and ill he looked, and very very old. And I bade the coachman stop the horse, and I leaned out of the brougham and said, 'Mr. Sandbach, may I offer you a lift home?' And he came up to the brougham and he took off his hat. We looked at each other. It was a strange moment," said Aunty gently, "very strange. And he got in. And as we talked I thought, 'How could I curse him? How could I be so wicked, and how could he make me suffer so?' It was all washed away except that I had cursed him. I regretted it bitterly, bitterly, when I saw him old and ill. We drove him home and I never saw him again, and I could not read his thoughts."

Aunty sat quiet for a moment, but not for long. "Well, and how's Charles? … Oh, here's someone. Who is it? Who? Visitors? Oh, good. I like visitors. Now … do I know …? Oh!" with delight. "Oh-h-h," in a downward ripple of pure joy. "It's Frank, I do declare! *And* Stephen! Well, I do declare!" And with her winning greeting face she offered a fresh welcome.

Jesus Christ, Murdeena
LYNN COADY

HER MOTHER WOULD TELL YOU it started with the walks. Just out of the blue, not too long after she got fired from the Busy Burger and had been kicking around the

house for a few days. Out comes Murdeena with, "I think I'll go out for a little walk."
Margaret-Ann was just finishing up the dishes and hurried to dry off her hands when
she heard it, thinking Murdeena was being sly about asking for a drive somewhere.

"Where do you want to go?" asks Margaret-Ann.

"I don't know, I'm just going to walk around."

"Where are you going to walk around?"

"I'll just go down by the water or somewhere."

"Here, I'll take you down," she says, reaching for the keys.

"Pick me up a Scratch and Win!" Mr. Morrisson calls from the couch, hearing
them jingle.

"No, no, no," goes Murdeena. "I'm just going for a walk, to look at the water."

"I'll drive you down, we can sit in the car and look at it," says Margaret-Ann. She
doesn't know what her daughter is on about.

"I want to go for a *walk*," says Murdeena.

"Who goes for *walks*?" points out Margaret-Ann. She's right, too. Nobody goes
for walks. The only people who go for walks are old women and men who have
been told by their doctors that they have to get more exercise. You can see them,
taking their turns around the block every night after supper, looking none too
pleased.

"What's the matter with you?" asks Margaret-Ann. She's thinking Murdeena is
feeling bad about getting fired and wants to go mope.

"Nothing, Mumma. It's a nice night."

"Go sit on the porch, you don't have to go traipsing about."

"I *want* to."

"Go on, I'll bring you a cup of tea."

"I don't want to drink any more tea. I want to walk."

Thinking of the seniors, it occurs to Margaret-Ann that walking is a healthy
pastime, and maybe she should encourage it.

"You're on some kind of new health kick, now, are you?"

"No."

"Well, if that's what you want to do," she says, doubtful. "Are you going to be all
right?"

"Yes." Meanwhile Murdeena's digging around in the porch, trying to find something to put on her feet.

"Do you need a jacket?"

"Yeah, I'll put on my windbreaker."

"Maybe you should wear mine," says Margaret-Ann, fidgety about the whole
performance.

"No, I'll be all right."

"What do you got on your feet?"

That's a bit of a problem. Nobody walks, so nobody has any walking shoes. Murdeena settles for a pair of cowboy boots she bought in Sydney back when they were in style.

"You can't walk in those."

"They're *made* for people to walk in. Cowboys. They walk all around the range."

"They ride around on their horses," protests Margaret-Ann.

"Well, they'll do for now." Murdeena puts on her windbreaker.

Then Ronald pipes up again. "She's not going out by herself, is she?" he calls from the couch.

"Yes. She wants to go for a *walk*."

"Where's she going to walk to?"

"Jesus Murphy, I'll bring you back a Lotto!" Murdeena hollers before the whole rigmarole can get under way again, and she clomps out the door in her boots. So there's Margaret-Ann left to do all the explaining.

Margaret-Ann will tell you that is where it all started, although it didn't seem like much of anything at first. Murdeena walking. By herself, in the evening. Perhaps it was getting fired, that's what Margaret-Ann thought. Murdeena had never been fired before, although the Busy Burger was only her second job—before that she was a cashier at Sobey's, for four years, right up until it closed down. She was great at it, and everybody liked her. She liked it too because she got to visit with everyone in town and catch up on their news. The Busy Burger wasn't so much her style because most of the people who came in were high school kids and Carl Ferguson who ran the place was a big fat shit. She used to get along so well with her manager at Sobey's, because they'd gone to school together, but Carl Ferguson was just this mean old bastard she couldn't relate to who didn't like girls and treated them all like idiots. He picked on Murdeena especially because she couldn't count. Even with the cash register there giving a read-out, she never gave anyone the right change. Murdeena could never do math, none of the teachers at school could figure her out because the math teacher assumed she was borderline retarded while the rest of them were giving her A's and B's. There must be some kind of condition where you can't do math, just like the one where you can't spell, and that's what Murdeena had. If you asked her anything having to do with numbers, she'd change the subject. If you asked her how many people lived in her town, she'd say, "Oh, quite a few," or else, "Oh, it's about the size of Amherst, I'd guess. Maybe more." If you'd try to pin her down on a figure, she might say something like, "Oh … maybe … a … couple of hundred." It was a good way to get her back in high school. We'd all laugh.

But her mind just didn't work that way, some people's minds don't. It didn't make her a moron, but Carl Ferguson treated her like one anyway. She was always careful to check the register and count out the change meticulously, but sometimes the bastard would stand there watching her making slow calculations as she moved the change from the register to her palm and he'd wear this disgusted smirk and make her all nervous. So one day, right in front of him, she handed Neil MacLean a twenty instead of a five. Neil said he could see her hand shaking as she did it, and he tried to nod to her or something, let her know in some way that the change was wrong. Before he could do a blessed thing, though, Carl Ferguson tears the twenty out of her hand. "For Christ's sake, woman," he goes. "You trying to make me go broke?" And Murdeena cried and Neil, probably trying to help out, told Carl he was an arsehole, but that's when Carl told her she was fired—probably just to shut Neil up and prove that he could do or say whatever he damn well pleased in his own establishment.

Everyone hated Carl after that because everyone liked Murdeena. Whenever she gave people back the wrong change at Sobey's, they'd just say, "Oops, dear, I need a bit more than that," or a bit less, or whatever, and then they'd help her to count out the right amount, and then everyone would have a big laugh together.

So then she was on UI again and there was talk in town about a big bulk-food store opening up, and Margaret-Ann kept telling her there was no need to worry.

"I'm not worried anyways," says Murdeena.

"Then why all the walks?" This was after the fourth walk of the week. Murdeena was going through all the shoes in the closet, trying to find the best pair for walking. Tonight she had auditioned a pair of her brother Martin's old basketball sneakers from eight years ago.

"I'm not walking because I'm worried about anything!" says Murdeena, surprised. And the way she says it is so clean and forthright that Margaret-Ann knows she's not lying. This makes Margaret-Ann more nervous than before.

"Well for the love of God, Murdeena, what are you doing stomping around out there all by yourself?"

"It's nice out there."

"It's nice, is it."

"Yes."

"Well, it seems like an awful waste of time, when I could be driving you anywhere you wanted to go."

Murdeena has never gotten her driver's licence. This is something else about her that's kind of peculiar. She says there isn't any point because she never goes anywhere. Margaret-Ann and Ronald like it because it means that she still needs them to do things for her from time to time.

"If I wanted to go for a drive," says Murdeena, "I'd go for a drive."

"It just seems so Jesus *pointless*!" bursts out Margaret-Ann, wishing Murdeena would quit fooling with her, pretending everything was normal. People around town were starting to make remarks. Cullen Petrie at the post office:

"Oh, I see your girl out going for the walks these days."

"Yes, it's her new thing, now."

"Well, good for her! I should be getting out more myself."

"Yes, shouldn't we all," says Margaret-Ann, officiously licking her stamps.

"Isn't she tough!"

"Yes, she is."

"Every night I see her out there," marvels Cullen Petrie. "Every night!"

"Yes." Margaret-Ann gathers up her mail in a pointed sort of fashion, so as to put Cullen in his place. "Yes, she's tough, all right."

Cullen calls after her to have Murdeena put in an application at the post office—he'd be happy to see what he could do for her. Margaret-Ann would like to kick him.

"You don't *need* a job right now, in any event," Margaret-Ann keeps telling her over and over again. "Your UI won't run out for a year, and you've got enough to keep you busy these days."

"That's right," agrees Murdeena, clomping around in an old pair of work boots to see how they fit, and not really paying much attention. "I've got lots to keep me busy."

Murdeena is always on the go, everyone says so. She plays piano for the seniors every weekend and always helps out at the church teas and bake sales. She'll do the readings in church sometimes, and plays on her softball team. It used to be the Sobey's softball team before it closed down, but they all enjoyed the games so much that the employees didn't want to disband. They ripped the cheap SOBEY'S logos off their uniforms and kept playing the other businesses in town anyway. Nobody minded. For a joke, they changed their name to the S.O.B.'s.

Some people are concerned that she doesn't have a boyfriend, but Margaret-Ann and Ronald are relieved, they like her where she is. She went out with a fellow in high school for three years, and it looked as if things were pretty much all sewn up for after graduation, but didn't he go off to university—promising they'd talk about the wedding when he came home for the summer. Well, you don't have to be a psychic, now, do you?

So Murdeena hasn't been seeing anyone since then—almost five years now. She has her own small group of friends, the same ones she had in school, and they all go out to the tavern together, or sometimes will take a trip over to the island or into Halifax. There are a couple of young fellows that she spends time with, but they're all part of the group, one with a girlfriend and one married.

So no one can think of anyone Murdeena might end up with. Murdeena knows everyone in town and everyone knows her. Everyone has their place and plays their part. So it's hard to think of changing things around in any sort of fundamental way. Like starting something up with someone you've known since you were two. It doesn't feel right, somehow.

"TO HELL WITH IT," she announces one evening after supper. She's got every pair of shoes in the house lined up across the kitchen floor.

"What is it now?" gripes Margaret-Ann, even though Murdeena hasn't said a word up until now. Margaret-Ann always feels a little edgy after suppertime, now, knowing Murdeena will be leaving the house to go God knows where. "What's the matter with you?"

"None of these are any good." She kicks at the shoes.

"What do you mean? Wear your nice deck shoes."

"No."

"Wear your desert boots."

"They're all worn out. I've worn them all. None of them feel right."

"Do they hurt your feet? Maybe you need to see a doctor."

"They don't hurt, Mumma, they just don't feel *right.*"

"Well, for Christ's sake, Murdeena, we'll go out and get you a pair of them hundred-dollar Nike bastards, if that'll keep you quiet."

"I'm going to try something else," says Murdeena, sitting down in one of the kitchen chairs. *Thank God!* thinks Margaret-Ann. *She's going to stay in and drink her tea like a normal person.*

But Murdeena doesn't reach for the teapot at all. What she does is take off her socks. Margaret-Ann just watches her, not really registering anything. Then Murdeena gets up and goes to the closet. She takes out her windbreaker. She puts it on. Margaret-Ann blinks her eyes rapidly, like a switch has been thrown.

"What in the name of God are you doing now?"

"I'm going for my walk."

Margaret-Ann collapses into the same chair Murdeena had been sitting in, one hand covering her mouth.

"You've got no *shoes!*" she whispers.

"I'm going to give it a try," says Murdeena, hesitating in the doorway. "I think it'll feel better."

"For the love of Jesus, Murdeena, you can't go walking around with no shoes!" her mother wails.

Murdeena makes her lips go thin and doesn't ask her mother why, because she knows why just as well as Margaret-Ann does. But she's stubborn.

"It'll be all right. It's not cold."

"There's broken glass all over the street!"

"Oh, Mother, there is not."

"At least put on a pair of sandals," Margaret-Ann calls, hoping for a compromise. She follows Murdeena to the door, because she's leaving, she's going out the door, she's doing it. And she's hurrying, too, because she knows if her mother gets hold of that windbreaker, she'll yank her back inside.

"I won't be long," Murdeena calls, rushing down the porch steps.

Margaret-Ann stands on the porch, blinking some more. She thinks of Cullen Petrie sitting on his own front porch across the street, taking in the evening breeze.

MURDEENA MORRISSON HAS BEEN PARADING all over town with no shoes on her feet, everyone says to everyone else. They marvel and chuckle together. They don't know what she's trying to prove, but it's kind of cute. People will honk their horns at her as they go by and she'll grin and wave, understanding. "You're going to catch cold!" most of them yell, even though it's the middle of summer. The only people who are kind of snotty about it are the teenagers, who are snotty to everyone anyway. They yell "hippie!" at her from their bikes, because they don't know what else to yell at a person without shoes. Sometimes they'll yell, "Didn't you forget something at home?"

Murdeena hollers back: "Nope! Thanks for your concern!" She's awfully good-natured, so nobody makes a fuss over it, to her face anyway. If that's what she wants to do, that's what she wants to do, they say, shaking their heads.

Margaret-Ann does her shopping with a scowl and nobody dares mention it to her. Murdeena won't wear shoes at all any more. She'll go flopping into the pharmacy or the seniors home or anywhere at all with her big, dirty feet. The Ladies Auxiliary held a lobster dinner the other night, and there Murdeena was as usual, bringing plates and cups of tea to the old ladies, and how anyone kept their appetites Margaret-Ann could not fathom. Murdeena stumbled with a teacup: "Don't burn your tootsies, now, dear!" Laughter like gulls.

"I DON'T WANT to hear another word about it!" Margaret-Ann announces one evening at the supper table. Murdeena looks up from her potatoes. She hasn't said a thing.

It is obviously a signal to Ronald. He puts down his fork and sighs and dabs his lips with a paper napkin. "Well," he says, searching for the right words. "What will you do in the winter? There'll be snow on the ground."

Margaret-Ann nods rapidly. Good sound logic.

Murdeena, still hunched over her plate—she's been eating like a football player these days, but not putting on weight, as she tends to—suddenly grins at the two of them with startling love.

"I'll put on *boots* when it's wintertime!" she exclaims. "I haven't gone crazy!" She goes to shovel in some potatoes but starts to laugh suddenly and they get sprayed across the table.

"Oh, for Christ's sake, Murdeena!" complains her mother, getting up. "You'd think you were raised by savages."

"That's politically incorrect," Ronald articulates carefully, having done nothing but watch television since his retirement.

"My arse," Margaret-Ann articulates even more carefully. Murdeena continues to titter over her plate. This quiet glee coming off her lately is starting to wear on Margaret-Ann. Like she's got some big secret tucked away that she's going to spring on them at any moment, giving them instant triple heart attacks. "And what's so Jesus funny inside that head of yours, anyway?" she stabs at Murdeena suddenly. "Walking around grinning like a monkey, like you're playing some big trick on everybody, showing off those big ugly feet of yours."

Offended, Murdeena peers beneath the table at them. "They're not ugly."

"They're ugly as sin!"

"Since when?"

"Since you decided you wanted to start showing them off to the world!"

"Why should anybody care about seeing my *feet*?" queries Murdeena, purely bewildered.

"Exactly!" shoots back her mother. "Why should anyone care about seeing your feet!"

It ends there for a while.

SHE HAD ALWAYS BEEN THE SWEETEST, most uncontentious little girl. Even as a baby, she never cried. As a child, never talked back. As a teenager, never sullen. She was their youngest and their best. Martin had driven drunk and had to go to AA or face jail, and Cora had gotten pregnant and then married and then divorced, and Alistair had failed grade nine. And all of them moved far away from home. But Murdeena never gave them any trouble at all. *Agreeable* was the word that best described Murdeena. She was always the most agreeable of children. Everybody thought so.

Gradually, however, she takes to speaking to Margaret-Ann like she believes her to be an idiot.

"Mother," she says, slow and patient, "there's things you don't understand right now."

"Mother," she murmurs, smiling indulgently, "all will be explained."

Margaret-Ann rams a taut, red fist into a swollen mound of bread dough. "Will you take your 'mothers' and stuff them up your hole, please, dear?"

"Ah, Mumma," Murdeena shakes her head and wanders away smiling, her bare feet sticking to the kitchen linoleum. Margaret-Ann fires an oven mitt at her daughter's backside, and feels around the counter for something more solid to follow it up with. She can't stand to be condescended to by Murdeena. The world seems on its head. She can hear her in the living room with Ronald, solemnly advising him to turn off the TV and listen to her tell him something, and Ronald is trying to joke with her, and play round-and-round-the-garden-like-a-teddy-bear on her hand to make her laugh. She won't give him her hand. Margaret-Ann can hear her daughter speaking quietly to her husband while he laughs and sings songs. Margaret-Ann feels dread. She goes to bed without asking Ronald what Murdeena had tried to say.

It is reported to Margaret-Ann later in the week. The folks at the seniors home were enjoying a slow and lovely traditional reel when the entertainer abruptly yanked her hands from the keys and slammed the piano shut. The loud wooden *thunk* echoed throughout the common room and the piano wires hummed suddenly in nervous unison. A couple of old folks yelped in surprise, and one who had been sleeping would have lurched forward out of his wheelchair if he hadn't been strapped in.

"Murdeena, dear, are you trying to scare the poor old souls out of their skins?" gasped Sister Tina, the events organizer, and Margaret-Ann's informant.

"There's just so much to tell you all," Murdeena reportedly answered, staring down at the shut piano, which looked like a mouth closed over its teeth. "And here I am playing reels!" She laughed to herself.

"Are you tired, dear?" Sister Tina asked in her little-girl's voice, always calculated to be soothing and inoffensive to those around her. She moved carefully forward, using the same non-threatening gestures she approached the seniors with.

With unnerving spontaneity, Murdeena suddenly cried, "There's so much news!"

"What's wrong with her?" barked Eleanor Sullivan, who loved a good piano tune. "Get her a drink of rum!"

"Give her some slippers, her feet are cold," slurred Angus Chisholm, groggy from being jolted out of his snooze.

"I have some good wool socks she can put on," Mrs. Sullivan, the most alert and officious of the bunch of them, offered. "Run and get them for her, Sister, dear." All of a sudden, all the seniors were offering to give Murdeena socks. A couple of them were beckoning for Sister Tina to come and help them off with their slippers— Murdeena obviously had more need of them than they did.

"I haven't been able to feel my *own* goddamned feet in years," Annie Chaisson was reasoning, struggling to kick off her pom-pommed knits.

"For the love of God, everyone keep your shoes on," commanded Sister Tina. "You'll all get the cold and there won't be enough people to look after you!"

"I don't need your footwear!" hollered Murdeena. "I need to be heard! I need to be believed and trusted and heard!"

It was an outlandishly earnest thing to say, and the old people looked everywhere but at the piano. Murdeena had swung around on the stool and was beaming at them. What came next was worse.

"I TAKE IT YOU'VE HEARD," says Murdeena to her mother. She'd gone for a walk after her time with the seniors and stayed out for two and a half hours. Margaret-Ann stands in the middle of the kitchen, practically tapping her foot like a caricature of an angry, waiting mother. You would think Murdeena was a teenager who had been out carousing all night. Ronald is sitting at the kitchen table looking apprehensive because Margaret-Ann told him to and because he is.

"I take it you have something you'd like to say," Margaret-Ann shoots back. "Your father tells me you've already said it to him. And now that you've said it to a bunch of senile incontinent old friggers, perhaps you can say it to your own mother."

"All right," says Murdeena, taking a breath. "Here she goes."

"Let's hear it, then," says Margaret-Ann.

"I am the Way and the Light," says Murdeena.

"What's that now?"

"I am the Way and the Light," says Murdeena.

"*You* are," says Margaret-Ann.

"I am."

"I see."

Ronald covers the lower part of his face with his hands and looks from one woman to the other.

"Now what way and what light is that?" asks Margaret-Ann with her hands on her hips.

"What—?"

"What way and what light is it we're talking about?"

Murdeena swallows and presses her lips together in that stubborn but uncertain way she has. "The way," she says, "to heaven."

Margaret-Ann looks to her husband, who shrugs.

"And the light," continues Murdeena, "of—well, you know all this, Mother. I shouldn't have to explain it."

"Of?"

"Of salvation."

Murdeena clears her throat to fill up the silence.

They are up all night arguing about it.

FIRST OF ALL, the arrogance. It is just plain arrogant to walk around thinking you are "the end-all and be-all," as Margaret-Ann insisted on putting it. She would acknowledge it in no other terms.

"What you're saying is you're better than the rest of us," was Margaret-Ann's argument.

"No, no!"

"You're walking around talking like you know everything. No one's going to stand for it."

"Not *everything*," said Murdeena. But she was smiling a little, you could tell she thought she was being modest.

"People aren't going to stand for it," Margaret-Ann repeated. "They're going to say: 'Murdeena Morrisson, who does she think she is?'"

"Oh, for Pete's sake, Mumma!" burst Murdeena with uncharacteristic impatience. "Don't you think back in Nazareth when Jes—I mean me, when I was telling everyone in Nazareth …"

Margaret-Ann covered her ears.

"… about how I was the Way and the Light back then, don't you think everyone was going around saying: 'Humph! Jesus Christ! He must think he's some good! Walking around, preaching at people.'"

"This is blasphemy," hollered Margaret-Ann over the sound of blood pumping through her head. She was pressing against her ears too tightly.

"That's what they said back then, too."

Margaret-Ann was right and Murdeena was wrong. Nobody wanted to hear it. Everyone liked Murdeena, but she was taking her dirty bare feet and tromping all over their sacred ground. Word spread fast.

POURING TEA FOR MRS. FOUGUERE in the church basement, she leans over to speak.

"Once upon a time, there was a little town on the water …" she begins.

"Oh, please, dear, not now," Mrs. Fouguere interrupts, knowing by now what's coming and everybody looking at her with pity.

"No, it's okay," says Murdeena, "I'm telling you a story."

"I just want to drink my tea, Murdeena, love."

"There was this whole town of people, you see … and they were all asleep! The whole town!"

"I don't believe I care for this story, dear," says Mrs. Fouguere.

"No, no, it's a parable! Just wait," Murdeena persists. "This whole town, they were all asleep, but the thing is … they were sleepwalking and going about their business just as if they were awake."

"I don't care to hear it, Murdeena."

"Yes, for God's sake, dear, go and have a little talk with the Father, if you want to talk," Mrs. MacLaughlin, seated at the next table and known for her straightforward manner, speaks up.

"But it's a parable!" explains Murdeena.

"It doesn't sound like much of a friggin' parable to me!" Mrs. MacLaughlin complains. The women nearby all grumble in agreement.

Murdeena straightens up and looks around at the room: "Well, I'm only starting to get the hang of it!"

The ladies look away from her. They take comfort, instead, in looking at each other—in their dresses and nylons and aggressive, desperate cosmetics. Someone snickers finally that it was certainly a long way from the Sermon on the Mount, and a demure wave of giggles ripples across the room. Murdeena puts her hands on her hips. Several of the ladies later remark on how like Margaret-Ann she appeared at that moment.

"To hell with you, then," she declares, and flops from the room, bare feet glaring.

Murdeena has never been known to say anything like this to anyone before, certainly no one on the Ladies Auxiliary.

SISTER TINA COMES to the house for a visit.

"Seeing as I'm the Way and the Light," Murdeena explains, "it would be wrong for me not to talk about it as often as possible."

"Yes, but, dear, it wasn't a very subtle story, was it? No one likes to hear that sort of thing about themselves."

"The point isn't for them to *like* it," spits Murdeena. "They should just be quiet and listen to me."

At this, Margaret-Ann leans back in her chair and caws. Sister Tina smiles a little, playing with the doily the teapot has been placed upon.

"They *should*," the girl insists.

"They don't agree with you, dear."

"Then they can go to hell, like I said."

"Wash your mouth out!" gasps her mother, furious but still half-laughing.

Sister Tina holds up her tiny hand with all the minute authority she possesses. "Now, that's not a very Christian sentiment, is it Murdeena?"

"It's as Christian as you can get," Murdeena counters. Scandalously sure of herself.

The next day, the Sister brings the Father.

"I hate the way she *talks* to everyone now," Margaret-Ann confides to him in the doorway. "She's such a big know-it-all." The Father nods knowingly and scratches his belly. The two of them, he and Murdeena, are left alone in the dining room so they can talk freely.

Crouched outside the door, Margaret-Ann hears Murdeena complain: "What are dining rooms for, anyway? We never even use this room. Everything's covered in dust."

"It's for *good*!" Margaret-Ann hollers in exasperation. Sister Tina gently guides her back into the kitchen.

The Father's visit is basically useless. Afterwards he keeps remarking on how argumentative little Murdeena has become. She would not be told. *She simply will not be told,* he keeps repeating. The Father has little idea how to deal with someone who will not be told. He makes it clear that his uselessness was therefore Murdeena's own fault, and goes off to give Communion to the next-door neighbour, Allan Beaton, a shut-in.

"Everyone's too old around here," Murdeena mutters once the priest is gone. She's watching him out the window as Allan Beaton's nurse holds the door open to let him in. The nurse is no spring chicken herself. The Father is mostly bald with sparse, cotton-ball hair and a face like a crushed paper bag.

"You're just full of complaints, these days," her mother fumes, hauling a dust rag into the dining room.

SO NOW MURDEENA is going around thinking she can heal the sick. She figures that will shut them up. In the parking lot at the mall, Leanne Cameron accidentally slams her seven-year-old boy's finger in the car door and Murdeena leaps from her mother's Chevette and comes running up, bare feet burning against the asphalt, a big expectant grin splitting her face. This scaring the piss out of the little boy, who starts to scream at the sight of her, twice as loud as before. Murdeena tries and tries to grab the hand, but Leanne won't let her anywhere near him. It is a scene that is witnessed and talked about. Margaret-Ann vows never to take Murdeena shopping with her again, or anywhere else, for that matter.

Margaret-Ann declares that she has officially "had it." She experiments with giving Murdeena the silent treatment, but Murdeena is too preoccupied to notice. This hurts Margaret-Ann's feelings, and so she stops experimenting and quits talking to her daughter altogether. Her days get angrier and quieter, as she waits for Murdeena to take notice of her mother and do the right thing. See to her.

"See to your mother," Ronald pleads with her at night, lowering his voice so that the television will keep it from carrying into the kitchen. "Please go in and see to her."

Murdeena's head snaps up as if she had been asleep and someone had clapped their hands by her ear. "Did she hurt herself? Is she bleeding?" She wiggles her fingers eagerly, limbering up.

She starts lurking around the children's softball games, hoping someone will get a ball in the face or sprain their wrist sliding into home. She hovers like a ghoul and the children play extra carefully all summer long as a result. Murdeena watches toddlers waddling away from their parents, toward broken bottles and the like, with her fingers crossed.

By now, though, people know to keep their kids away from Murdeena Morrisson. In the space of a couple of months it has become the community instinct. She stalks the adult softball games too, even though she has long since stopped playing for the S.O.B.'s.

NO ONE CAN very well tell Murdeena to stop coming to play piano, since she has been doing it since she was thirteen and on a volunteer basis—Margaret-Ann thought it would be a good way for her to get some practice and do something nice for the senile incontinent old friggers at the same time. So Murdeena headed over every Sunday after supper, and for the next ten years there never arose any reason for her to stop. It was a perfectly satisfactory relationship, if somewhat stagnant. The seniors asked for, and Murdeena played impeccably, the same songs, Sunday night after Sunday night. "Mairie's Wedding" and "Kelligrew's Soiree" and such. Some of the seniors who were there when she first started playing had died, but most of them were still around—living out the final years of their lives while Murdeena was experiencing practically the whole of her own, a bland and inoffensive local girl for them to tease about clothes and boyfriends, sucking up her youth.

But Murdeena will no longer be teased. Her friends have abandoned her in response to the "high and mighty" tone she's adopted with them, her mother is angry, and her father has never spoken to her much in the first place. The seniors are the only captive audience she has. For the first little while after the night she slammed the piano shut, she'd make a slight pretence of being there to play for them, but the tunes would usually trickle off after a few minutes. She'd stealthily start making inquiries about Angus Chisholm's knee, Annie Chaisson's hip, Eleanor Sullivan's arthritis.

"If you'd just let me hold your hands for a couple seconds, Mrs. Sullivan," she'd plead.

"My dear, I'd love for you to hold my hands, but not in the spirit of blasphemy."

They listened, though. The seniors are the most tolerant of the town, for some reason neither threatened nor scandalized by what Murdeena has to say. They don't tease her about the way she looks either—they don't mention her feet. Murdeena's lips are now always thin, and so is her body—she has finally lost all her baby fat from walking the streets for hours into the night and sometimes forgetting to eat supper. It's October, and there's no sign of shoes as yet. The seniors decide it's her own business and they don't say a word.

And so, stymied by the town, she gradually turns all her attention and efforts to the attentive oldies, stuck in their chairs every Sunday night until the nurses come along to help them to bed, waiting to hear Murdeena. Sister Tina—who writhes and jumps like she's being jabbed with hot pokers at every word out of Murdeena's mouth—soon realizes that she needn't be worried about the girl giving them offence. The seniors greet the blasphemy with more good humour than anyone else in town. Born in farmhouses, raised up on hills or in remote valleys, where to come across another human being, no matter who they were or what they had to say, was a deep and unexpected pleasure—therefore humble, charitable, and polite—the old folks listen, lined up side by side in front of the piano.

It's like Murdeena figures that the seniors represent the front lines—that if she can just plough her way through them, everything else might fall into place. The world will become reasonable again. So Sunday after Sunday she abandons the music in order to plead. Sunday after Sunday, now, she pleads with them until dark.

And they're good about it. They let her talk and hold out her hands to them. They don't complain or interrupt. They smile with their kind and patient old faces and refuse to let themselves be touched.

Abitibi Canyon

JOSEPH BOYDEN

WHEN RICHARD, my second cousin, told me he was here to arrest Remi for suspicion of involvement in the Abitibi dam getting blown up, I laughed at him till his red cheeks blushed purple. Richard's the tribal police sergeant, the big one sent when a drinking party turns violent or there's a standoff between an abusive husband and his wife's brothers. They send him when the situation calls for muscle. We call him the Equalizer. That he was here for Remi, his own blood, it didn't make sense. Remi's the first frog child. He can't comprehend what a dam is for, never mind how to blow it up.

Four of us on the reserve have frog children. You have to have one to be a member of our club. *Anigeeshe awasheeshuk.* The Cree word for them. My son Remi was the first. Born nineteen years ago. Big bulging eyes. Thick, muscled limbs. A long sloping back. His voice a croak. The old ones on the reserve, they named him first. *Aneegishush.* Little Frog. And when more came, over the years, to different women near the Abitibi Canyon, *anigeeshe awasheeshuk.* Frog children.

You see the Abitibi Canyon from the Little Bear Express, appearing like a *windigo*'s grave out of the trees, dipping slowly at first, then shooting straight down, the rock cliffs dropping for a lifetime until the brown water of the river licks them and swallows them up. Long fat pike there. Sturgeon big as my husband, Patrick. Old Isaac Tomatuk, who's dead now, lost part of his finger to a pike there, years back. The odd part is, Isaac swore till he was gone for good that the pike had a man's eyes. No one doubted him. If there's a sacred place still left for us, it's Abitibi Canyon.

Me, I didn't want another after Remi. Not because he looks like a frog. Children are too much work. My life is full enough. I sound selfish now, and I guess I am. I do love Remi. I've fought for Remi. Big fights. Hair pullers. Nose bleeders. Cheek bruisers. It got so that they called me the freight train. No man or woman was safe if they insulted Remi. It soon got, though, that he could defend himself. At least make others think twice when they saw the size of him.

ALL THE TROUBLE, Remi's trouble, began with work in the canyon. The tribal council had been battling over whether to let the hydro people build a dam for power. It was a big project being proposed. A year of construction. More money than I'd ever heard of was involved. How much the band would ever see was questionable. One side loved the idea—especially the chief, Jonah Koosees. Big money for all of us, he said. New schools. New houses. Prosperity. The down side is that thousands of hectares of traditional land will be swallowed up by water. No more hunting. No control in our own country. Negative environmental impact. My husband, Patrick, he's against. He's on council. *Hookimaw* of the ones who are against Jonah. Give the *wemestikushu* a little, he knows, and they find a way to take it all. Thing is, Patrick's got a lot of history, a lot of examples to back him up. We might lose hunting ground, Jonah said to Patrick at one meeting, but just think of all the new fishing area we'll gain. Jonah's humour isn't so funny.

This battle has been going on for two years. It's split the community. It's good for our side that more on the reserve are wary of giving so much land away in return for promises. We've seen it before. No one trusts handing over all we have in return for paperwork. That's what treaties are for. Jonah Koosees, he knows he's in a losing battle. Election for chief is in a few months and the majority here don't trust him. The way things are going, my man Patrick will be next chief.

Me, I'm against it for a more selfish reason. Me and Shirley and Mary and Suzanne, we get up there twice a year to camp with our *anigeeshe awasheeshuk,* where we keep the idea of the Abitibi Canyon Ladies Club alive. It's a simple club. We just leave the reserve behind for a little while and camp with our children up in the canyon. Where else could we meet that has the same meaning to all of us? Strong magic there.

It's pretty much an accepted fact around here. It's what the older ones refer to as a place of power, a place where the manitous live. Lots of boys been sent there by their fathers for a first fast and vision. Many girls for their first blood of womanhood, their strawberry ceremony. Strange lights have been seen there at night. Everybody here knows someone who's seen them. Government men in red parkas came to investigate that. Said it was the northern lights playing tricks. Wasn't no northern lights. It was manitous. Sky children. At least these manitous were. They come out and run around like that when they're unhappy. With what's been going on around the canyon lately, I expect people will see a lot more of them soon.

This one time when Remi was no bigger than a goose, I left him with my mother, his *kokum,* while I went to the bingo. I still remember winning a hundred dollars. Big money back then. Not any more. Pots in the thousands now. New cars, snowmobiles, trips to places where snow has never fallen. When I came back, Remi was sleeping on the couch, his sloped naked back shining in the lamplight like a wet piece of driftwood. My mother, she wasn't sleeping. She'd sat up watching Remi, waiting to tell me.

"He spoke," she said. Nothing new. He'd been putting his mouth around certain words in Cree and English for a whole year. "No," she said. "He spoke whole sentences. He spoke like that priest does, about water covering the land." At the time I didn't think much of it. I brought Remi to church since he was born. Had him pray right along with me to keep winning bingo. Maybe he had a gift for repeating. But mother—old school. From then on she had Remi to every medicine man, every circle, every feast, every sweat when his lungs got strong enough. It got so that I teased him, though he couldn't grasp that. Called him *aneegishush dekonun*. Little frog medicine man. He smiles and shows his crooked teeth when I call him this, even now. I like that he likes it.

He spoke strange words for a while, talking like a slow minister on a roll. I remember the first time I myself heard him speak like that. He was six. We'd just fitted him for glasses. Black, thick-rimmed things. He was angry and hated them. "The Lord says, Repent!" he shouted at Patrick and me when we got him home. "Heed my word and be saved!" Then he went back to talking like he always did. Slurred words and lots of smiling. I was never quite sure if he was acting or not, wasn't sure where it came from, but I got used to it. You get used to anything after a while. Right about the time he turned twelve, he quit talking like a minister. We don't know why. He just went back to being a handicapped kid, his tongue thick when he talked, his mind searching hard for the words.

Mary and Shirley and Suzanne are the three others with *anigeeshe awasheeshuk*. None of those kids ever talked like prophets, though. They are all younger than Remi. All born in the Abitibi Canyon. All of us lived in Abitibi Canyon when our husbands worked on the railroad crew. All of us who had frog children conceived them while we were living there. Doesn't take a genius. Again, government men came in to investigate. These ones had green parkas. Lots of needles. Lots of questions that made the other girls blush. Lots of prodding. Lots more blushing. Results are inconclusive, the government men finally said. Possible coincidence. Possibly eating the same fish poisoned by a sunken Soviet nuclear sub thirty-five hundred kilometres away. Lots of possibilities.

"What about the possibility that these children are gifts from manitous?" Mother says. "Lots of possibilities," I say like a government man. "Results are inconclusive."

When Remi started growing, he didn't stop. At eight, his frame curved like a bow, he was still a head taller than the others his age. At twelve he could carry twenty-five geese for kilometres, on a pole slung across his arched back. At fifteen he was as big as his father, one of the biggest men on the reserve. This in a band of big people. To top it off, Remi will always have to wear those thick black glasses that magnify his eyes. He breaks all the others. There's no getting past the fact he looks like a big, crazy Cree.

Remi's father is what they call an activist. He's always filled Remi's head with stories of how we're an Unceded First Nation, how our particular band never signed a treaty. I thought Remi didn't understand any of it till one night, just before all hell broke loose on the reserve, I told him to help me with dinner and he shot right back, "No. I'm not seeded." I sent him out hunting with his father. That trip changed things for good.

When they came back, my husband told the reserve of bulldozers being unloaded and work crews scurrying around like ants upriver of the canyon. Most were shocked that we hadn't been told of this latest venture on what everyone considers tribal land. But I wasn't. I've known Jonah Koosees for a long time. I knew as soon as my husband told me about new work crews up there that the OK had been given by Jonah, without council even knowing about it. Rumour is Jonah's got a bank account down south that would make the Pope jealous. It's obvious by his clothes mail-ordered from Toronto and his car that he lives by other means.

Jonah might as well have admitted his guilt when the next day he didn't show when half the band boated upriver to see for themselves and make a plan of action. My man was there, Remi beside him, grinning and drooling. Didn't fit the mood. I came too, sad to see my special place with so many people on it, white and Indian alike.

We set up camp and started cook-fires along the riverbank. Just like the old days. The workers watched nervously from their camp downriver, images of scalpings and savages dancing around campfires all night, I'm sure. Just like the old days. I make sure that Mary and Shirley and young Suzanne, the newest Abitibi club member, have their tents right by mine. Maybe if the four of us try hard enough, we can pretend there isn't anybody else around. Nobody's really got a plan at this point. The young warriors want to force a standoff and stop construction, with violence if necessary. Patrick heads back to the reserve, to a phone, so he can call lawyers and get an injunction until we can sort out exactly what's happening.

We sit and drink hot tea and cook bannock for our children over the cook-fires. The smell of the raisins and fresh dough makes me hungry. I watch Remi play with the other women's children, his big, awkward body hulking over the two little ones, his paw hands gently picking them up and dipping them, giggling, into the river like something I might have read in the Bible once. Remi does this over and over. Picks up Mary's little boy, Jacques, who's only six and round like a black-haired piglet, under the arms and raises him over his head until Jacques squeals. Then Remi, with a look of deep concentration and his tongue sticking a bit out of his mouth, dips Jacques into the cold stream of brown river up to his waist, Jacques' face contorting from a grin to the surprised O of shock, a whine like a fire truck coming from his mouth.

Remi then picks up Albert, who's thirteen and much bigger, and Remi must strain to do this. Albert is thick-limbed and stronger than he knows. Shirley is always complaining of bruised arms and strained muscles. Remi knits his brows, squats like a weightlifter, heaves Albert into the air, holding him there like a prize or an offering, then splashes him down into the cold water, where Albert moans with a child's happiness.

This is when Jacques runs up and Remi begins the whole process again. He would continue this cycle until he dropped from exhaustion if I didn't interrupt him. Remi needs these cycles, lives for the repetition of events and daily grind. Mother says he is the old Cree epitomized, his desire for cycles and seasons and the healing circle.

I see that there are a couple of white workers standing by a pickup truck on the new little gravel road that's been carved out of the bush in the last few weeks. They lean against the truck and watch what's becoming most of the reserve set up camp.

Suzanne's little boy, he's still just a tiny thing. Suzanne breastfeeds him discreetly and watches the boys play. She is scared of the intensity, the complete focus that Remi exhibits in his actions. He's like a machine. Or an alien, she thinks—I can see it in her eyes. Suzanne will get used to it. Maybe one day it will even become a calming thing for her.

I watch the two workers' eyes glide to Remi and the boys. First one man stares, then he nudges his friend in astonishment. Both talk and laugh, pointing like they are the only ones who exist here. I hope Mary doesn't notice this. She will stomp over, and then stomp over them. Mary's a hothead. Although one of the workers looks Swampy Cree, I don't think he is. He would never be so obvious in his rudeness. Suddenly I see that Mary does notice. My stomach tightens.

"What's this all about?" she growls, looking at the men. Mary stands up. The men see her. They stop laughing. She walks over to them and I can see her exchanging words. The two men look down at their workboots, hands in pockets. They nod and the Indian-looking one answers. He looks up into Mary's eyes briefly, then down again. She walks back, the two men following.

"Rather than them making fun, I told them to come meet the kids," she says, dropping her weight onto her haunches. The two are nervous. Scolded schoolboys. We women sit and look up, wait for them to introduce themselves.

"I'm Matthew," the skinny white one says.

"I'm Darren," the other says.

"You *Anishnabe*?" I ask Darren. He just looks at me. That answers it. "Are you Indian?" I ask.

"Oh," he answers. "No. My parents were born in Japan, but I'm Canadian."

"I'm not an Indian either," the skinny one says. No shit, *kemo sabe*.

"These are our children," Mary says. "Funny, eh?" The two men look down at their boots again.

"It's just that I've never seen retarded Indians before," Darren says. Mary stares at him.

"We don't call them retarded," I say. "We call their condition an environmentally induced mental handicap. The doctors came up with a name for this particular condition. Abitibi Canyon Syndrome."

"Yeah," Shirley says. "You work here long enough, your kids might turn out the same." Darren and Matthew stare at one another.

"Go play with them," Mary says, shooting her thumb towards our children. Suzanne looks up, panicked. Quiet girl isn't used to Mary's strong personality. Shirley laughs.

"Yeah, get yourselves acquainted," she says. The two really look nervous now, but they follow her command, not strong enough to resist her will.

For the first long while, the two men stand behind the children, not sure how to enter their circle of play. The children know they are there. I can see their sidelong glances. If you want in, they seem to say, we're not going to make it easy. Good boys. Eventually, Matthew sits and removes his boots and socks and rolls up his pants. He walks into the river carefully and says, "Hi," to the children. They ignore him. Matthew walks out a little deeper, then suddenly slips, disappearing into the water. Remi and Albert stare, concerned, but when Matthew's head pops up from the water, grinning, they begin to laugh, their laughing turning to howls, eyes squinting, mouths wide open. Makes the rest of us on the bank laugh too. Jacques looks at all of us, not sure what's so funny, but then joins in, not wanting to be left out. Matthew stands up and bows to us.

It isn't long before Darren is sitting with the boys, carefully explaining to them how the dam is going to be built. He uses the sand to construct a model, and the boys watch, transfixed. Remi looks from the sand model to Darren's face. He's completely mesmerized by the talk, by Darren. After a while, Remi grabs Darren's hand and holds it in his. Darren looks a little surprised, but continues talking. Remi's never taken so quick to a stranger before. Darren will say something, and Remi repeats the last word or two, squinting behind his glasses and smiling. "Dam," he repeats, and "construction," and "dynamite."

"Oh shit," Matthew says, tapping Darren's shoulder. "Here comes the asshole." They both turn their heads and watch a large man with blond hair stomp through the sand towards them. He carries a hard hat, wears a white T-shirt under a long-sleeved shirt. Looks important.

"What the hell are you two dipshits doing here playing with kids? You asking me to dock your pay?" Darren and Matthew turn their heads from him like it isn't important what he's saying. "Better yet," the hard hat says, "I'll stick you on that train and you can crawl back to wherever it is you crawled from." Matthew's eyes sparkle with hate. Darren continues to stare calmly out at the river. "Don't dare give me that look, son," the hard hat says.

"I ain't your son," Matthew spits back. Darren stands up and pats Matthew's shoulder to calm him before things go too far. They get up and follow the man back to work. Remi waves to Darren's back.

For the next days we all camp and burn great fires at night. We send sparks and smoke into the sky high as we can. My man remains away, working on an injunction. Small stones to stop a river. Rumours fly through the camp, worse when it turns dark. The government will flood our reserve and move us to a barren place down south. The army is being called in, fearful of another Oka. The dynamite will blast soon and the construction crews don't care whether we're in the way or not. The worst of it is that we all know these are real possibilities. The great fires at night, tree trunks stacked in teepees ten metres high, are our sign to the crews and the manitous watching that we are still out here in Abitibi Canyon, in the same bush by the same river we've lived by *mawache oshkach,* from the beginning.

Patrick visits on the third day to bring news and some supplies. He calls us all to a meeting on the riverside and tells us it's important to stay. "We have to slow down work in any way we can," he says. "In any lawful way we can." The warriors grumble. "It could be a week before we have an injunction," he shouts to our crowd. "Historically, the more work the crew does before an injunction, the smaller our chance of stopping the dam being built. If the court sees not much was built, they are much more likely to rule against more building."

"And what of Jonah Koosees?" one of the women calls out in Cree.

"He's still disappeared," my husband answers back in Cree. The crowd talk among themselves. "That is the best news we can have," Patrick shouts. "It will be a damning thing to see that the chief who secretly made this deal has run away. Just focus on ways to legally slow down their work. We can win this court battle."

So we devise ways to slow things down. One morning a barricade of trees appear on the work road leading to the river. Every evening we stay up late into the night, playing loud music and screaming and laughing like drunken Injuns until dawn to keep the workers awake and nervous in their beds. We are good actors, having outlawed liquor on our site. From what I can tell, everyone obeys. We invite workers who are brave enough to come for tea and bannock during their breaks, and keep them talking with us as long as we can. From what I can see, our plan is working. It is hard to tell of any progress, other than the work road that leads to the river and the litter lying around.

But on the sixth day all of us are shocked to see great mounds of dirt being bull-dozed into the river from either side. At first we think the fools are making a dam of mud, like children do in small streams, but we quickly find out that this is simply the first of many foundations to slow the river's course. One old fellow who's worked on dams before says that men would actually slow the great Abitibi to a trickle for a time by shutting dams farther up the river, and from these mounds of dirt that we now see built up and falling into the river they can build further foundations, and pour tons and tons of concrete. So this dirt is how it all starts. I can't picture my stretch of river here running dry. I push from my mind the image of a concrete monster lying in our river and controlling it like some greedy giant.

I sit with Mary and we debate how much slower the river runs now due to the mounds of dirt that stand like giant breasts on each side. "It isn't important that the river is slower right now," she says. "Just look at it." We both stare at the once pure water, running so muddy now that our children can no longer swim in it. "The silt by the reserve will continue to build up until all we are left with are shallows and sandbars," she says. "Not to mention no more place upriver for us girls to get away to."

Darren and Matthew continue visiting us when they can, playing with the children and talking with us. At first, we don't trust them—we never fully do in those days of camping—but they become a regular enough sight, and try to learn everything they can about how the dam is going to change things in big ways for us. We rely on the river for everything from transportation to food to drinking water. Now it is going to end up in someone else's control, its volume and even its course changed by the flick of some stranger's fingers on a couple of buttons. We've been cheated out of any say by one of our own and by strangers who don't care.

By the eighth day, I can see our camp is losing its focus. Some have packed up and left, and the ones who remain grumble more and more about what good we can possibly be doing. I admit that the shine of an unexpected camp-out is beginning to dull for me too. The ground is hard at night and there is little shade during the days. Unlike our autumn and spring outings, there is no anticipation of the arrival of geese and the happy work they bring, the gossip and laughter while plucking and cleaning and smoking. The one positive thing that remains is that Remi has made a new friend in Darren, and actually speaks to him. After Remi's brief stint as reserve prophet when he was young, it was like his tongue had thickened; he grunted more than he spoke as he grew older. But sitting near him and Darren as they lounge by the river, I hear him say words like "construction" and "Darren" and "Abitibi" as clearly as if he was never born a frog child. And I am happy for it. If only I knew what I am exposing my boy to.

We shout out on the tenth day when Patrick pulls up in his freighter canoe with the news that he's gotten an injunction. Work stops. Even the crew looks happy. But not the foreman. He walks down to where Matthew and Darren sit by us, and fires them on the spot.

"Don't come back when work starts up again," he spits at them. Remi looks as scared as I've ever seen him, staring up at that man.

"Fuck you," Matthew shouts at him, standing up and pushing him. The foreman snaps his arm out and drops Matthew with a solid punch in the mouth.

"You want some too, nip?" he says to Darren. Darren just looks away. "Hanging out with goddamn Indian retards," the foreman mutters, walking away. "We'll be back and working soon enough," he shouts at us. Mary stands to follow him, but I hold her back.

"We won," I told her. "All they got done in ten days are those stupid mounds." I point to them and all our eyes follow. Darren helps Matthew up and they walk away without a word to Remi. Within hours, we have broken camp and are on the river back to home.

That night word began trickling down to us that the foundations of the dam had been blown up. Some actually claimed they had heard the explosion, like distant thunder in the middle of the night. At first, talk was that the crew had done it on purpose, on orders of the government. They weren't going to bother fighting a long battle with us in court. But then word spread that the explosion had actually been a horrible accident and that was when we learned that the foreman had been killed in it. We felt bad for him, for his family if he had any. But that did seem to put an end to any talk of a dam. The way I figured it, the manitous were protecting special land. They were the ones responsible for the explosion.

THAT SUMMER'S EVENTS were quickly becoming local legend when a month later Richard, the Equalizer, came knocking for Remi.

"You're joking," I said to Richard.

He shook his head sadly. "RCMP's got two men in custody. They named Remi as an accomplice."

That's when I started laughing, when Richard blushed. I called for Remi and he came to the door, looking guilty. When he saw Richard he began to wail, and that's when I knew.

At first, Remi was held on reserve by the band's police force, in a little cell underneath the station. They let us see him only after Patrick threatened them with words I'd never heard come out of his mouth before. With Richard sitting nearby, we talked to our son, but he had gone somewhere deep into his mind—somewhere neither of us had seen him go before, and a place neither of us could get to.

"It's going to be OK, boy," his father told him.

"I'll have you home with me soon," I said. But Remi just stared down at his stocking feet, drooling. Richard had taken his shoes and belt for fear he'd hang himself. That was the strangest thing to me. Did my son have any idea about such things?

We stayed long as we could. Richard had to practically drag us out. Within a week, the OPP came and escorted Remi south by train to North Bay. Patrick and me, we followed, spent every penny we had on a hotel while we waited weeks for trial, and visited Remi every day.

I waited and worried, left with only little events and remembrances to try and piece it all together. There were dark places, shadows in all of this that I could only guess at. We got us a lawyer from Indian Services, a tiny little Crow woman from somewhere out west. Everyone who knew of her said there wasn't any better. Her name was Angela Blackbird. She finally began filling in some of the pieces for us.

"The accused are a Matthew Cross and a Darren Shin," she told us. We sat with Remi in a little meeting room in the institution he was being held at. Remi was still deep in his mind. "At first, these two tried to pin the whole thing on Remi here, but under questioning by police and the Crown attorney, one of them admitted that Remi only carried a box of explosives that was too heavy for them. This one, Darren

Shin, said on record that Remi didn't even know what he was carrying and that he's innocent of wrongdoing."

Patrick and me, we looked at each other and smiled for the first time in a long while.

"So what about Remi?" Patrick asked. "Why isn't he free to go?"

"That's the catch," Blackbird said. I watched Patrick's smile fade. "The OPP are still investigating and recommended that the Crown press charges of complicity so Remi doesn't disappear. He's going to have to go to trial. The good news is, I got him his own trial so he's not tied in with those other two. They're both being charged with first-degree murder, on top of explosives and theft charges. I wouldn't want to be those two."

Remi's trial came first. It made the papers. "Mentally Handicapped Cree Faces Charges for Abitibi Dam Explosion." Everyone showed up to support us—Mother, Mary, Shirley, Suzanne and their kids. Angela Blackbird fought like a warrior for us. Got Darren on the witness stand. Matthew refused, but Darren had already pleaded guilty to all of it, knew he was doomed. Angry as I was at him, I admired him for trying his best for Remi. The day Darren took the stand in court, handcuffed and with his feet chained, wearing an orange jumpsuit, was the first time since Remi's arrest that I saw Remi come out of himself a little. He stared at Darren, then waved to him.

"The accused had nothing to do with the planning, preparation or carrying out of the explosion on Abitibi River?" Angela asked Darren.

"Nothing," Darren answered.

"His only involvement was unwittingly carrying a box of explosives too heavy for the two of you, with no idea of the contents or of your purposes with those contents?"

"Correct," Darren answered.

Then it was the Crown's turn. "So why did your story change so much from statements at arrest as compared to a week later?"

"I couldn't live with myself for lying about Remi's involvement. I couldn't pin it on him when he was innocent," Darren answered. Every last person in the count knew he was damning himself by speaking those words.

"So what you're saying is that Remi had nothing to do with this, other than carrying a box, having no idea what it contained?"

"Correct," Darren answered. "We befriended him, and tricked him into helping. He's got an environmentally induced mental handicap, for chrissakes! How hard could it be to fool him?" As if on cue, Remi waved to Darren again, and the court broke out in quiet laughter.

In the end, it was the judge who was left with the decision. Angela was confident. So was Patrick. "It's clear to me that the accused was an unwitting accomplice in this act of terrorism and, may I add, murder," the judge said, his voice nasal. "But as small a role as he played, let us keep in mind the destruction to property and to human life. It leaves me to ask this question: where were the parents of this young, handicapped man that he could be befriended by admitted terrorists and, furthermore, made a pawn by them? I do not blame the child here. I place blame on the parents. With this in mind, I deem it necessary that Remi Chakasim be made a ward of the state until it can be proven beyond a reasonable doubt that his parents are fit for the duty of his complete welfare. The proper authorities will decide upon his new place of residence, as well as the terms for his release back to his parents' custody. Case closed." With that he dropped his hammer, and I watched Remi being escorted out of the court.

And that is what I'm left with. It has been two months now and Remi is in the North Bay Centre for the Mentally Challenged. I take the ten-hour train ride once a week and spend Saturdays with him. His father fights hard on the phone for his release.

Darren's and Matthew's trial was not much longer than Remi's. Darren pleaded guilty and got forty years, twenty-five for killing the foreman and fifteen for the explosives. Matthew pleaded not guilty even though the case was sealed shut against him, and got life with no chance of parole for his effort. There was no greater reason for what they did. No honourable plan to help us Cree fight the corporations and government. They simply hated the foreman so bad that they figured he'd lose his job if they blew up his work. Darren claimed in his trial that they didn't want to kill the foreman. It was just a severe case of wrong place at the wrong time. I believe him.

I received a letter from Darren the other day. He's in Kingston Pen and he's sorry for Remi. Darren wrote me that he hooked up with Indian inmates and is involved in their sweat lodges and ceremonies now. They took him as a brother, even though he told them he's Japanese. He's become a celebrity with some Indians for blowing up that dam.

All I can do is keep faith in Remi's release. No one's really talking to us. No one knows who's in charge, it seems, or what course to take in order to get him back to us. Remi just sank back into wherever that place is that he goes. Two weeks after he was sent away, I sat and talked to him. I held him in my arms and rocked him and hummed him some old songs I hummed for him as a baby. Suddenly he sat straight up and stared out the window and spoke. His voice sounded like someone else's I'd heard a long time ago.

"Our world will be covered with water," he said. "Repent now, sinners. Make plans and be saved."

I stared, frightened by my child. All I could do was hug him and cry.

Falling in Love

SANDRA BIRDSELL

I GET OFF THE BUS and I stand beside the highway at Jordon Siding, wondering what to do now. I've come to a dead end. Stopped by the reality of a churned-up landscape. For shitsake, as Larry, the past-love-of-my-life, would say. Today, in late June, while the fields around me are growing towards harvest, I am empty. I'm split in two. One part of me can think, what are you going to do? And the other is off somewhere, wandering through empty rooms, bumping into dusty furniture, hoping that this may be a dream. And that Larry is still here.

"I'm sorry you didn't know, ah," the bus driver searches for the correct word. Am I Miss or Ma'am? He pushes his cap back onto his chunky, sandy head and glances down and then away from my breasts which nudge out against Larry's denim shirt. No, I'm not wearing a bra. His glance is at once shifty and closed as though he, too, is guilty of betraying me. And immediately, I'm glad that at least I have not made the mistake of being pregnant. Grateful that I never gave in to those odd flashes of desire to make love without a contraceptive, to play a kind of roulette game with sex.

"Didn't they tell you when you bought the ticket that the road was under construction?" the bus driver asks. His eyes take in the shoebox I carry beneath my arm, tied closed with butcher string, air holes punched in it so Satan can breathe. A going-away present from Larry, a black rabbit. He has taken off, Larry has, has flown the coop and left me with the rabbit and one measly shirt to remind me of him. Larry, I'm remembering you in the briny smell of armpits.

I remember this morning, the acne-faced girl in the coffee shop at the bus depot in Manitou saying something about having to go to Winnipeg and then back south to get to Agassiz. But my mind wasn't paying attention. I was aware instead of her squinty mean eyes enjoying the lapsed state of my affair. Larry Cooper is wild, I'd been warned, and he's lazier than a pet coon. And I told myself that they were just jealous. There are no callipers wide enough to measure the scoured sides of my stupidity. This year, I have learned something about the eternal combustion engine, about love.

Before me, where I should be making my connection with another Grey Goose bus that will carry me thirty miles east across farming country to Agassiz and back into the bosom of my family, the road is a muddy upheaval of rocks, slippery clay and top-soil. Under destruction. The whole world is under destruction. Larry used the word "dead-end." And so he has turned the other way, headed down the highway to Montreal to work in his brother-in-law's car rental business.

If you love someone, let him go, Larry's mother said. And if he comes back, he's yours. Whatever you do, don't take this thing personal, okay? Larry's like that. Every spring, he takes off. Spring fever, it's in his blood, she said. And then she evicted me.

"You'd better get back on the bus and make your connection in Winnipeg," the driver says and it's clear from his tone that he's decided I'm a Miss which gives him certain authority. I'm aware of faces in the windows looking out at me, slight amusement at my predicament. I see in the window my greasy black hair tied up into a pony tail, Larry's shirt, my jeans held at the waist with safety pins because I have lost ten pounds. My luggage is an Eaton's shopping bag.

When I woke up and discovered Larry missing, I didn't worry at first because he often went out riding before dawn. He liked to be alone in the early morning. Larry liked to watch the sun rise. He's out ripping off truck parts, you mean, his mother said, raising an artfully plucked eyebrow and flicking cigarette ashes into her coffee cup. But she didn't know Larry the way I thought I did. He would come back to me, crawl beneath the sheets, hairy limbs still cool from the early morning air, breath minty and sweet, and he would wind himself around me and describe the colour of the sun on a barn roof, or the distinct clatter of a tractor starting up. On such a morning, he brought Satan to me because he said its shiny black coat, its constant nibbling reminded him of me. On such a morning, he came home and invented a gadget that cooked weiners electrically. He stuck wires into each end of the weiner, plugged it into the wall and instant, cooked weiner. Another morning, he was inspired to try to build a more effective water pump.

I lay in bed waiting for Larry, looking up at the new ceiling tiles overhead. His mother let us live rent-free in those three rooms above the butcher shop if we fixed the caved-in ceiling. I liked the suite the way it was when we first moved in, sawdust and shavings ankle-deep on the floor, ceiling slats dangling free, the lone lightbulb suspended by a single twined wire. It was early Canadian Catastrophe. It reminded me that when I met Larry, I was sitting in the hotel cafe in Agassiz, between jobs, waiting for the world to end. For a year, I'd had the feeling that a bomb was going to drop and that would be the end of us all. For this reason, I left school. I was filling in time, waiting, and then Larry walked in and I thought that if the bomb fell that day, I'd rather be dead with him than anyone else.

But Larry wouldn't live with a caved-in ceiling and when he'd fixed that, he enamelled the kitchen counters black. And the paint never quite dried and if we let a dish stand on it overnight, it became permanently stuck there. And then I went crazy and hand-stitched curtains for the windows in the front room. Larry nailed Christmas tree lights onto the wall above the couch and we made love in their multi-coloured glow. We made love every single day for six months.

I waited for Larry to return and listened at the same time to the rats thumping about in the butcher shop below, dragging bones from the bone box. (I never minded the rats, I figured they worked hard for what they got.) Above me, near the ceiling, a shaft of light came through the small window, spotlighting Larry's note taped to the closet door. I knew before reading it that Larry had left me. I have this built-in premonition for bad news. As I reached for the note, I could smell Larry, like alkali, dry, metallic, in the palms of my hands. And scattered in the sheets were his c-shaped blond pubic hairs. I read the note and it was as though a thick, black, woollen hood had fallen suddenly into place over my head.

Two days later, Larry's mother dropped by. She told me to get out of bed. She wanted her sheets back. She had me clean out the fridge. I have brought along the left-overs of our relationship in the shopping bag. Lettuce for Satan, a dimpled, wilted grapefruit and one beer. And resentment, which is a thick sludge clogging my chest. If Larry, by some miracle, showed up now, I would jump on his skinny back, grab hold of his blond hair and wrestle him to the ground. I would stomp on his adam's apple.

"Forget it," I say to the bus driver. "I'm not going all the way to Winnipeg. Just forget it."

He laughs. "I don't see what choice you have." He puts his sunglasses back on and I can see myself in them. And it seems to me that he, along with everyone else, conspires against me. That I have never had a choice.

"You looked at my ticket when I got on. Why didn't you say something?"

"I thought you knew."

I pick up the shopping bag and begin to walk away. "Well, I didn't. And I'm not spending three bloody hours on the bus. So, I guess I'll walk."

He blocks my way. "Whoa, Agassiz is thirty miles away. And it's going to be one hot day." He scans the cloudless sky.

Larry, you creep. This is all your fault. "What's it to you whether I walk or ride?"

The driver's thick neck flares red. He steps aside. "Right. It's no skin off my nose. If you want to walk thirty miles in the blazing sun, go ahead. It's a free country."

The bus roars down the highway, leaving me in a billow of hot sharp-smelling smoke. The sound of the engine grows fainter and then I'm alone, facing that churned-up muddy road where no vehicle could ever pass. Thirty bloody miles. God-damn you, Larry. I hear a meadowlark trilling and then a squealing rhythmic sound of metal on metal. It comes from a BA gas sign swinging back and forth above two rusting gas bowsers that stand in front of a dilapidated wood-frame building. Jordon Siding garage and store. Eureka. A telephone. I will call home and say, guess what? No, I'll say, it's your prodigal daughter, to get them thinking along charitable lines. I have seen the light. But all that is another issue, one I don't have the energy to think about. Plants fill the dusty store window and off to one side, a tiny yard, freshly laundered clothes flutter from a clothesline.

I enter the dim interior and feel surrounded. The atmosphere is dreary, relentlessly claustrophobic. It's a typical country store and yet it reminds me of old things, of fly-specked calendars, lambs and young girls in straw hats smiling with cherry-painted lips, innocent smiles. And me pulling a toboggan through the streets of Agassiz each New Year, collecting calendars, trekking through the fragile blue sphere of a winter night that seemed to embrace all ages so that as I bumped along ice and snow I thought, years ago, someone like me was doing this, may still be doing this. But at the same time, I felt the world dangling like a bauble about to shatter on the floor. I went to the garages, grocery stores, the bank. I needed many calendars because during the coming year each time a month ended, I wrote messages on the backs of the spent time and hid the messages in the garden, in flower pots, beneath stones, for people from another world to discover when I would be gone. A fly buzzes suddenly against the window, trapped between the foliage of the plants and the glass. Beyond, a counter, glass casing, but there's nothing inside it but shelf-lining, old newspapers.

"Hello, anyone here?" I call in the direction of the back rooms behind the varnished counter where I imagine potatoes boil in a pot, a child sleeps on a blanket on the floor while its mother ignores my voice, sits in an over-stuffed chair (the type Larry and I inherited with our suite, an olive green, scratchy velour couch and chair), reading a magazine. What is she reading? I wonder. I look about me. No telephone in sight.

Outside once again, I face that bleak landscape and begin walking in the direction of Agassiz. I face the sun and walk off to the side of the road, following the deep imprint left behind by one of the monstrous yellow machines that sits idle in the field beyond. Why aren't there any men on the machines? Why aren't they working today? I begin to feel uneasy. The sounds of the countryside rise up and Satan thumps violently against his box in answer. Around me stretch broad fields dotted with clumps of trees. In the distance a neat row of elms, planted as a windbreak, shade a small farmhouse and outbuildings. Overhead, the flat cloudless sky, no perspective, I cannot gauge distance. It's as though this is a calendar picture of a landscape and I have somehow entered it. Except for yellow grasshoppers sprinting up before my feet and the tireless hovering of flies above the ditches, there is no movement anywhere. I turn around. The garage is still the same distance. I can turn back and wait for a car and hitch a ride to Winnipeg. I could go back to Manitou. But it seems to me that I have been set in this direction, that it's inevitable. I walk for an hour. Satan continues to struggle. I stop to rest, lift the lid off the box a crack and push wilted lettuce through to him. I sit down, take Larry's note from my shirt pocket and unfold it on my knee.

Dear Lureen,
    I'm sorry if you got your hopes up. Like the song goes, you always hurt the one you love, the one you shouldn't hurt at all. That's life. But this town is a dead-end. You know what I mean. I think I'll take my sister up on her offer.

You are okay. Don't think I'm leaving because of you. I know you will get over me. Anyway, if it works out, I'll send you some money. I might send you enough to come to Montreal. I'll see. It just depends.

You can have Satan. I don't trust my mother to look after him anyway. Once, she forgot to feed my goldfish and they all turned belly-up. Notice, I am leaving you my denim shirt because you liked it so much.

Tell the old lady not to get in a sweat.

Luv U,
Larry.

Whatever you do, Larry's mother said when he introduced us, don't get married. A cigarette dangled from one corner of her mouth and she squinted at me hard through the blue smoke. She was blonde like Larry and I thought that at one time she must have been beautiful, you could see flashes of it sometimes when she wasn't being sarcastic. I'm only telling you for your own good, she said later when Larry was out of the room. He's like his father. Lazier than a pet coon.

Larry was not lazy. He could pull the head off a motor, ream out the cylinders, do a ring and valve job in two days flat. I'd tell him I wanted to go to the dance at Rock Lake and he'd rebuild the transmission that afternoon so we could go. He opened the housing, called me down the stairs to come and see the giant cogs, how the gears were supposed to mesh. And I couldn't help think that the combustion engine is a joke, or at least a hoax perpetrated on man to keep him busy tinkering so he can't think about what's really happening. Wheels moving wheels, moving pulleys, moving more metal and so much motion for so little effect, arms, lifters, valves, wheezing breathers, springs, filters, cylinders, shoes, things pressing against other things, grinding, particles of chewed-up metal sifting into other important parts. God, it was overwhelming. Faulty timing, a coughing, farting engine, a rotten swaying front-end, screeching wheel bearings, all these problems Larry and I faced and overcame in six months.

Okay Larry, I said, wanting to say, this is silly. There has got to be a much simpler way than the eternal combustion engine.

Internal, internal combustion engine, he said, and anyway, you are paid not to think, but to do. So, okay, I played the game. I soaked bolts and other metal shapes in my dishpan, brushed them down with Varsol, removed grease with a paring knife, had them looking like new. I learned how to install brushes in a generator. I took it apart in my lap. I thought the copper wires were beautiful. And then, that what I was doing was important. That maybe I'd like to have a part in the running of the internal combustion machine. And the next time Larry complained about having to wash his feet with his socks on, maybe I'd let him ride bareback for a while. Maybe the two of us could open a garage?

Larry flicked the end of my nose with a greasy finger and said no way would he put in four years getting his papers just to satisfy some government-hired jerk who had never taken apart anything more complicated than a Zippo lighter.

And always, we made it to the dance on time. That night, we'd be cruising down the highway, eating up the miles to Rock Lake, radio turned up full volume, Larry driving with two fingers and reaching with his other hand for me, naked beneath my sundress. And the gears would be meshing and the motor singing, the timing tuned just right and the radio playing all our favourite hits. And Larry would squeeze my breast and say, hey, honey bunch. Remind me to slow down long before we get to the corner, okay? I got no brakes.

Ancient history. Ancient bloody history. I rest my head against my knees and I don't want to cry, Larry's not worth it, but I do. And then I take the lid off the shoebox and I pet Satan for a few moments and then I carry him to the side of the road and drop him into the tall grass. He scurries away without a backward glance.

Do you think it's true, Larry said, turning away from me to examine his naked physique in the mirror, that a large ass means a short sex life? That's what my mother told me.

And I spent the next two hours convincing him that she was wrong and that he had the neatest, hardest, turned-in buttocks I had ever seen. Bullshit. I wish for Larry an extremely short sex life. May he never have sex again. I pick up the shopping bag, swing it back and forth a couple of times and let loose. It flies across the ditch and whacks against the telephone pole. Screw yourself Larry. Stick your scrawny dink in your ear.

Free now, I walk faster, arms swinging, following the fish-bone tire pattern pressed into the yellow clay. I will go to Winnipeg, look for work. Or I will go to bed and stay there. Or I could go back to school. And then I hear a sound, the sound of a motor geared down low—Larry? My heart leaps. I wouldn't put it past him. Larry can do anything. Even materialize out of thin air. I look up. There on the crest of the muddy graded mound is a pale blue car, the bullet-nosed shape of a '51 Studebaker. It slithers sideways first one way and then the other. It stops, starts, makes its way slowly towards me. I see a man behind the wheel, copper-red hair, a brushcut. Not Larry. The car comes to a stop and the man opens the door. I measure the distance to the farmhouse beyond. Could I outrun him? He unfolds from the seat. He's match-like, tall and thin. He stands up, shakes creases from his grey slacks, tiptoes across the ruts in shiny brown penny loafers and I begin to relax, he looks harmless. He stretches out a long pale hand to me, it looks fragile, like worn porcelain. I keep my hands behind my back. He doesn't seem to mind and folds his, one overtop the other across his stomach. He tilts back slightly on his heels and smiles down at me. "Well, well. Bless you. This is the day that the Lord hath made. Let's just take a moment to rejoice in it." He breathes deeply. "Thankyou Jesus."

God. A Pentecostal fanatic. One of the holy rollers.

"I saw you coming down from the corner and I said to myself, 'Now there's the reason God had for waking you up this morning.'" He lifts his hand suddenly, pokes a long finger into his red hair and scratches.

A grasshopper leaps up between us and lands on the roof of the car. I can see a resemblance between the insect and the man: long limbs, angles, ball-bearing shaped eyes.

"So, you're stranded then," he says.

"I didn't know about this." I indicate the upturned road.

"No matter," he says. He flutters his flimsy hand in my direction and catches himself on the chin in the process. I begin to like him. His smile is wide, lights up his steel grey eyes. "Everything works out for the good in the end. For those that trust in Him. Where are you hoping to get to?"

Life, I want to say. I am hoping to get through life, but I don't think I will. "Agassiz."

"Agassiz. Well, well. The heavenly Father has given me business just outside of Agassiz. I can get you close to it. Closer than this. Didn't I say everything would work out?"

He leads the way around to the passenger side, opens the door and suddenly I feel awkward. Larry would let me crawl through the window before he'd think to open a door for me. The car is like new inside. The seats are covered in clear plastic. A sheet of plastic lies on the floor. On the dash is what looks to be a deck of playing cards but the box says, "Thought for Today." Clipped to the sun visor is another card that reads, "I am a Flying Farmer."

He turns the car around in stages and soon we are bumping down the road, mud scraping against the bottom of the car. Despite the good condition of the car, there's a slight ticking and I want to tell him that he ought to watch the valves but I don't think it would be polite. I look over my shoulder and sure enough, tell-tale blue smoke billows from the exhaust. He's a clumsy driver, shifts gears too soon, strains the engine, rides the clutch. And then the tires grab hold of a groove of deep ruts and he speeds up, letting the car find its own path.

"So, what's your story?" he asks after a while.

"Story?"

"Sure. The Lord sends me lots of people. I know when someone has a story."

And so I begin the way I always do, with the question that makes people frown or shrug or walk away. "Have you ever thought that at this very moment, someone may be pressing a button and that the world may come to an end? And we'll all be instant cooked weiners?"

He laughs. "Now why would I want to waste my time thinking about that? I couldn't live with those negative thoughts hanging over my head all the time. I know that He is able to keep me against that day. Whatever a man thinks, that's what he is. And I think about all the good things we've got." He thumps the wheel for emphasis, sticks his head out the window. "Look around you, this country is *beaudyfull*. Good crops this year. The fields are white unto the harvest. Thankyou Jesus." He begins to hum to himself as we slither down the road. Then he sucks something loose from his teeth. "Cooked weiners, my, my. That just won't happen. Know how I know? Because I wouldn't be here right now if that was true. The Lord would have returned already if it was the end of the world and I wouldn't be here. I'd be with Him."

I know the story. I have been brought up on this. Graves opening, the rapture of the saints. People reaching towards a shining light. Whenever I heard the story, I would imagine grabbing hold of a tree on the way up so I could stay behind. "How do you know that's true?"

He laughs once again. "And how do you know that it isn't? It takes more faith to believe that it isn't true than to believe that it is. Know why? Because of hope. Man is born with hope right in him and you've got to go against the grain not to believe. Now tell me, what's the story behind the story? What brings you here today, to this place, this time?"

And suddenly, my tongue takes off and I tell him everything, about being young and hiding pieces of paper from the calendar that say, Whoever finds this, my name was Lureen Lafreniere, I lived in Agassiz, Manitoba. This month, when I was running, I slipped and fell and cut my hand on a sharp piece of ice. Five stitches.

"For a while, I stopped doing this, I thought it was a silly thing to do. But it came back to me, the feeling, so strong, that I couldn't sit still in school. I had to get up and move, just do something, because I felt that something terrible was going to happen that would prevent me from ... from...."

"From doing all the things you want to do even though you aren't even sure what it is you want to do."

"Yes."

"There's nothing new under the sun. I've heard that one before."

"Yes, but just when man says, nothing is new, everything is the same as yesterday, then comes the end. Therefore, watch and wait."

He smiles and his smile makes me smile. "You know your scripture. Bless you sister."

And then I tell him how I met Larry, about the past six months, about the feeling of impending doom leaving me. I talk to him as though I have known him for years and he doesn't ever interrupt, just says, "whoops" and "bless you" when we hit large clumps of mud. I talk non-stop, as though this man were sent for just this reason. And when I finish, he doesn't answer for a long time, just squints near-sightedly at the road and I think that I have made a mistake. I hold my breath and wait for his sermon. The Thou Shalt Nots.

"You love him," he says finally and puts a long, slender, cool hand overtop mine.

"Yeah." I realize this is true. That I am in love with Larry. While waiting for the world to end, I have fallen in love. I fell for Larry Cooper. I'm falling.

"Well, well. Love is great. Love is wonderful. The Lord knew what He was doing when He created Adam and Eve."

I wipe my eyes on Larry's denim shirt.

"That fella of yours will come back. You can be sure of that."

"He will?"

He squeezes my hand. "Believe it and it will happen. Tell yourself, Larry's coming back."

Shit. The power of positive thinking crap. "Larry's pretty stubborn, you don't know him like I do."

"Shh. I understand. You know Larry and you may be right. But that's only one side of it. Listen, this is my story. Long time ago, I was in a bad accident. A plane crash. I went down in the bush in northern Manitoba. I thought I was finished. I walked in circles for two days with a broken collarbone. When I came upon the plane the second time, I cried. Broke right down. And then a verse from the Bible came to me. It was, 'not by might, nor by power, but by my spirit.' It was the Lord telling me to trust Him. So I knelt in the bush and I prayed and I said, 'Okay God. I'm lost. I can't find the way myself. I've already tried. And I'm tired and I'm injured and so I have no choice. I'm going to trust you. Show me the way.' And I opened my eyes, got up, started walking and I hadn't walked more than five minutes and there in front of me was a road. A paved road. So you see, from my side of it, I was finished. There was nothing I could do. But from God's side, He had only just begun. And God knows Larry better than you do."

I want to say, I know how that happened. Often, when you try too hard, the answer escapes you. You have to give up and then the inner mind brings the answer to the surface. There wasn't anything supernatural about your experience. It happens all the time. I bite my tongue.

"That's very nice," I say.

He turns to me in astonishment. "Nice? I tell you about my wonderful experience, how the Lord delivered me and you say, 'that's nice'? It was more than nice, sister. It was a frigging miracle."

Would an angel swear? I ponder the question later that evening as I lie in bed in the front bedroom of my house in Agassiz. He dropped me off three miles from town, near the elevators, and when I turned to tell him, as a favour, that he'd better get the valves checked, the car had vanished. And I was shocked. I sat down beside the road to think about it. I rubbed my stiff calf muscles, my feet burned as though I had walked a great distance. And I came to the conclusion that I had imagined meeting that man. The mind can do that. It was a way of coping with the situation

I was in. But the question intrigues me. Would an angel swear? And was that swearing? I have always imagined swearing to mean to swear on something, to have to prove in some way the fact that you are telling the truth. The error of not being trustworthy.

The reception I received from my family was surprising. My mother was strangely tender, as though I had fallen ill with a fever. My younger brothers and sisters regarded me as someone who had come from a long way away, a distant relative, and they were guarded and shy. "Are you expecting?" my mother asked while the two of us changed the linen on the bed in the front bedroom. And I said no, but that I wished I was. She flicked the sheet and smoothed it straight. "No you don't," she said. "You just think you do, but you really don't."

As I lie in bed, the sounds around me are all familiar. The town siren blares out the ten o'clock curfew. The curtains on the window are the same ones I've had since I can remember. But I pull the sheet up around me and I feel like a guest, a visitor in the home I grew up in. How will I ever be able to sleep without Larry?

I remember our first date. Larry showing off, climbing up on a snowplow in the municipal yards, starting it and ripping through the chainlink fence before he could figure out how to stop it. And later, driving eighty miles to Manitou to crawl across the roof of the butcher shop, breaking a window to get into the suite. Still wearing our parkas, it was bitterly cold, I gave up my virginity while our breath hung in clouds of frost in the air above us and the beer we'd bought popped the caps and climbed up in frosty towers from the bottles. Afterward, teeth chattering, we chewed frozen malt and Larry warmed my hands in his armpits.

The memory climbs up the back of my throat, finds its way into my eyes, leaks down the sides of my face into the pillow. Okay God. I'll give you this one chance. This miracle involves another person, his own stubborn will. I clench my teeth. I feel as though I am levitating off the bed. This is it. Thanks for bringing Larry back to me.

I sigh. I'm calm. Tension seeps from me as I lie in the room where I have first thought of love and making it happen. And I hear the breeze in the trees outside the window. I have hidden many particles of time beneath their branches. I see the faint glow of the town. And if I got up, I would see the green watertower and the siren on it that orders the movement of my town. I would see the skating rink, my father coming down from the corner on his way home from the Hotel, to the news that Lureen's back home. And then I hear it, a jangle of keys that stiffens my spine, sends my heart jumping. Then a cough. I'm rigid, listening. A whistle. I leap down the bed, pull aside the curtains and below I see him, his narrow pale face turned up to the window. Larry in his white windbreaker, collar turned up, the glow of his cigarette.

"Larry?"

"For shitsake. What's keeping you?" he asks.

And I run barefoot down the stairs, through the rooms, out the front door and then Larry catches me by the wrist and pulls me to him, wraps me around his skinny shivering body.

"Blew a rod at Thunder Bay," he says. "I couldn't fix it."

Liar. "I'm sorry," I say. He kisses me. His mouth is chilly and warm at the same time. I wedge my tongue between his shivering lips.

He pulls away. "I caught a ride with a real weirdo. He offered me fifty bucks if I'd jerk him off. So I said to hell with it and I took the first bus going west."

"Hey honey bunch," I whisper into his neck, "let's go to the park. We can talk tomorrow."

"The park, what for?" But I can feel him growing hard against my stomach. "I haven't got anything on me. You know." His tongue answers mine and it's like the faint fluttering of a moth.

I link my arm through his and lead him in the direction I want to go. "Oh, by the way, I let the rabbit loose."

He stops walking, frowns. "What did you go and do that for?"

"Well, he was heavy, Larry. I suppose you never thought of that. And there I was, thirty miles from nowhere. I had to walk because the bloody road was under construction, so what was I supposed to do?"

"You've got all the brains," Larry says. "Why ask me?"

And we walk arm in arm down the road, Larry and me going to the park.

Catechism

WAYNE JOHNSTON

WHY DID HE COME to the city?

He was not yet ready to return to the one where his wife was waiting for him. He could never return to the one where he was born.

There was a snowstorm on Labour Day—the third of the 311 days that would comprise his stint as writer-in-residence at the Regina Public Library—which he hoped in vain the natives of Regina would assure him was anomalous or would seem even slightly disconcerted by.

Being a Newfoundlander, he thought of a familiar phrase that made him disinclined to even remark upon the occurrence of a snowstorm fifteen days before the end of summer: "People in glass houses should not throw stones."

His employers and the writers of the city were very helpful and welcoming when he arrived.

They found him an inexpensive basement apartment within walking distance of the library. They searched their attics and basements for pieces of furniture which they no longer used but which were still serviceable and saved him the bother and expense of buying his own.

One writer, whom he never saw again after their initial transaction, asked him, "Do you have your own brick or would you like me to get one for you?" To which he responded that he neither had a brick nor was able to think of why he might be thought to need one.

The writer came to his library office the next day bearing a red clay brick, assured him that, in ways that he did not have time to explain and which in any case a newcomer might not believe, it would prove useful, then left.

He took the brick home with him and put it in his closet.

Not until mid-winter did he discover its purpose. By then, the nights were so cold that not even by plugging one's car into a block heater could one ensure that it would start in the morning, a problem that was easily solved by keeping one's car running all night long by placing a brick on the gas pedal. On the coldest nights, the cars in the parking lot of his apartment building idled from eight at night to seven in the morning, row upon row of them with plumes of exhaust rising up like smoke from chimneys, engines running, windows opaque with frost.

But he decided that to keep his car running all night long, night after night, was, given the proximity of his workplace, more trouble than it was worth.

The sound of the idling cars just outside his basement apartment windows kept him awake at night, as did the exhaust fumes, which seeped into the building and made it, on the worst nights, all but impossible to breathe. By mid-winter, everything in the city, indoors and out, smelled of exhaust. A pall of blue-grey haze, such as he had once seen in Los Angeles, hung above the city.

Among the things with which the residents of the city diverted themselves throughout the long winters was a car called "Old Faithful," which was placed on the frozen lake near the university each January and left there until, with the melting of the ice in the spring or during an unexpected but not unheard-of winter thaw, it sank out of sight.

To raise money for some charity, people placed bets on when Old Faithful would sink through the ice.

For ten dollars he bought an entry form and guessed that Old Faithful would sink on March 17. On March 17 of that year, it was thirty-eight degrees below zero and the lake looked as if one could safely have driven across it a fleet of tractor-trailers.

Old Faithful sank not quite two months later, on May 11. It was not left at the bottom of the lake but was dragged from the lake by the chains, which, in January, had been fastened to its undercarriage. In this way, the number of cars in the lake did not increase by one each spring and it was possible to use Old Faithful over and over again.

WHAT WERE THE CITY'S most remarkable natural features?

An ash-coloured river, from which bubbles of sulphur erupted continuously, that wound its way through the neighbourhoods near the university and from which there came a stench that carried throughout the city—just such a stench as his high-school chemistry teacher had described as being like that of "last year's cabbage."

When hell freezes over it will look like that, he thought.

There was a kind of mud called "gumbo" that was so deep and volatile that it rendered pointless the laying of sidewalks in the outlying parts of the city, the parts where, not long after his arrival, he went for a walk and wound up with boots so encrusted that when he stood on the pavement to wipe them clean he found himself six inches taller than usual and his feet so gumbo-laden that he lurched along like Frankenstein's monster.

There was cold of a severity for which not even a childhood spent in Newfoundland was sufficient preparation. He was terrified by the early onset of this cold, by whose innocuousness the locals swore and attributed to its being "dry" and, which, by October, made it necessary for him to buy replacements for his winter clothes. He was terrified, too, by the wind chill, which was measured in "watts" and which, when it surpassed 2,000 watts, was, in spite of its "dryness," thought to be sufficient reason for warning people not to venture out of doors for more than thirty seconds at a time.

DID THE USERS of the library frequently consult with him in his capacity as writer-in-residence?

Throughout his ten-month tenure, he dealt with two people who wished him to help them with their writing.

There was a middle-aged woman who brought him what she described as "a children's novel, for preschoolers I think, whose main character is a little lamb named Flossie." It appeared to him, as he regarded the typescript, that it was about 150 pages long. He told her to leave it with him and to come back and see him in a week.

He began reading the book, which was called The Barnyard Adventures of Flossie McPhee. The first fifty pages were of the sort that the title led him to expect. Flossie began to grow up and made friends with other lambs. She drank milk from a bottle held by a succession of children who liked nothing better than to feed her and to pat her on the head. Flossie watched nervously while her mother was carefully shorn of wool by the kind farmer on whose land they grazed. Her mother smiled at her and told her that it didn't hurt a bit and that she needn't worry about what her first time would be like. At the bottom of page fifty appeared the following: "Flossie realized that her mother had been right. It hadn't hurt. Her wool was gone and if anything she felt better than before, not so warm but nice and cool even though it was nearly summer." He turned to page fifty-one, the first line of which read: "Flossie pecked at the ground with her beak."

At last, he thought, postmodernism has found the audience that it deserves.

He turned back to page fifty and then to page one to confirm that Flossie had begun the book as a lamb. He then returned to page fifty-one and continued reading. "She still hadn't learned the knack of picking up those little seeds. She tried to peck the way her mother did but every time the seed fell to the ground before she could get it in her mouth."

The woman came back to see him at his office and said, "Well, what do you think?"

He had always had great reserves of politeness, consideration, and forbearance, which were fatally combined with a desire to be liked, and so he had never been able to dismiss someone out of hand or offend them even when he knew that it would have served their interests even more than his if they were to never meet again.

He knew it would be with this woman as it had been with many other such people in his past. For fear of offending them, but especially for fear of incurring their dislike, he would for so long indulge their ambitions that when to do so was no longer possible they would be far more disappointed than was necessary and would never guess that he had not only foreseen their disappointment but, for his own sake, had done nothing to prevent it.

Solicitously, congenially, by prefacing his comments with the caveat that he had never evaluated a children's book before, that she was doubtless better versed in certain aspects of the genre than he would ever be, that he had heard that the audience for children's books was ten times that of the audience for adult books, and so on, he commended the woman on her writing.

She was pleased but eager to hear in more detail what he thought of Barnyard.

He complimented her on having "hit just the right tone" and for not condescending to an audience so young that Barnyard would have to be read to them out loud.

Unavoidably, he eventually got round to the narrative twist by which, in his reading of Barnyard, he was so nonplussed.

"What did you have in mind?" he said, "when, between the bottom of page fifty and the top of page fifty-one, you transformed Flossie from a lamb into a chicken?"

The woman looked mystified, embarrassed. She reached across the desk and took the book from him as if she believed he must have missed something. She looked at the bottom of page fifty and the top of fifty-one and put her hand over her mouth, from which he concluded that the transformation of Flossie from a lamb into a chicken had been unintentional.

His second client?

A voice on the telephone that saddened him the first time he heard it. The voice of a woman who told him she could not come to see him as she had not left her house in seven years. She told him she had "twentieth-century disease," or tcd, whose cause was unknown but which so completely compromised the immune system that the patient was allergic to "almost everything."

"My house is vacuumed five times a day, every inch of it. The windows of the house are always closed. The only foods I can eat are boiled white rice and bananas. I have two children and a husband but they keep to their own side of the house because of my allergies. I have a special machine for reading because I am very allergic to ink of any kind. My husband puts the books I want to read, as well as the short stories I work on, under a kind of bell jar and there is a lever that I use to turn the pages. I read everything through glass. I dictate what I write to my husband. I lived in Toronto for ten years, near a chemical plant. I think that's what made me sick, but no one believes me."

Her short stories were delivered to him by her husband, who was a Pentecostal minister and wordlessly handed him a manila envelope each week.

He had lotion-slick black hair brushed back from his forehead. Skin as pale as if it were he who had not been outside in seven years. Thin-framed silver glasses. A slight, ascetic build.

They never spoke. As if in solidarity with his wife who consisted of nothing but a voice, he consisted of everything except a voice. Each week, the minister's eyes seemed to say that he disapproved of the writing of short stories and of the man whose job it was to speak by phone to his wife about them but that she had so little in her life that he would not begrudge her this one bit of contact with the world.

He wished he could work up the nerve to tell her: you are ill because you do not love your husband and he does not love you; he does not consider love to be necessary to a marriage and he disapproves of happiness, his own, yours, his children's; you know this but will not end your marriage because you are afraid that he would get custody of the children and that you would be allowed only very limited access to them, if any; you are justifiably afraid that if you do not see your children you will die.

They spoke about her stories, the invariable subject of which was her disease, the setting of which was her "side" of the house, her bedroom, and her bathroom. The only characters were her, her husband, and her children, though she gave them other names, and, in her husband's case, other physical characteristics.

Unable to resist playing the role of therapist, he asked her why her characters, including the one that she denied was based on her, seemed to have no past and to be unable to conceive of any future. But all she wanted to talk about was the stories. "I'm looking for technical improvements, that's all," she said. "I don't expect anyone to enjoy these stories. I don't expect anyone to publish them. But I want to get them right technically. I know that I'm so withdrawn from the world that I have nothing to write about except myself."

He guessed that the stories, which were really just one story, were more difficult for him to read than they would have been for others, more difficult because his and hers were similar predicaments, though he could not bear to dwell for long on this observation.

He didn't know if it was the stories or the toneless sound of her voice or the fact that his own existence had, because of his unhappiness, become so limited, so cloistered, that made him feel as though they were both suffocating as they spoke.

He decided that, no matter what he said and despite the fact that it was she who had sought out this contact with him, there was no point in his trying to prod her toward some kind of self-knowledge, that it was presumptuous of him to think he could help someone so inscrutably ill, about whom he knew next to nothing and had never met, and that it would therefore be less taxing for both of them if all they spoke about was "technical improvements."

He wished he knew what she looked like. He could think of no way of asking her for a photograph that would not give her and her husband the wrong idea. She had no idea what he looked like, and for the same reason that he could not ask for her photograph he could not offer her one of himself.

WHAT, WHILE TURNING the Yellow Pages without purpose one winter night, did he conclude were more numerous in Regina than in any city he had ever lived in or visited?

On what he dearly hoped would prove to be the coldest night of the winter, while sitting at his kitchen table and leafing through the Yellow Pages because he could think of no more appealing way to pass the time, he noticed that two sorts of establishments were more numerous in Regina than any city of comparable size to which he had thus far travelled: adult-video stores and escort services.

Wearing so much clothing that perambulation of even so flat a city as Regina proved to be a challenge, his face covered with two scarves to protect him from frostbite and prevent him from being recognized, he concluded that the proliferation of adult-video stores in the city was at least equal to and perhaps greater than that of advertisements for same in the Yellow Pages.

He was unable to draw a similar conclusion regarding the proliferation in the city of escort services owing to the absence from the advertisements in the Yellow Pages of street addresses, the only means of contacting the escort services being the telephone numbers that accompanied the drawings of busty and curvaceous women.

Night after night he borrowed videos from the adult-video stores, always scarved but nevertheless feeling mortified and shameful, all the more so because of the unaffected nonchalance of the exclusively male clerks in the stores.

In his basement apartment, with all the lights turned off and the volume of his television set turned so low that he had to sit within inches of the screen to hear the sound, he watched the videos.

He had watched similar ones before but never ones so relentlessly explicit, so inclusive of all possible sexual positions and techniques, the effect of which on him was arousal that, after self-administration, always gave way to an oppressive guilt that dogged him night and day but in spite of which he was unable to resist further visits to adult-video stores, especially when he realized that because they were so numerous he would be able to frequent a different one each night for months and that therefore the clerks to whom the renting of adult videos seemed to be as reasonable and no more interesting an act than buying bread would never recognize him.

DID HE THINK often of the city in which he was born and in which he could no longer stand to live?

St. John's reminded him of things beyond recovery, beyond retrieval, of a promise and the breaking of that promise, and of a series of revelations that even now he thought could not be true yet knew they were, revelations that convinced him that not only was there such a thing as evil but that two people who were widely misperceived as being decent and respectable were living with untroubled consciences in spite of having freely chosen evil.

He thought about four daughters in St. John's who by those they trusted most had been destroyed. His wife, now waiting for him in Toronto, had been one of them.

As he sat alone in the library on that succession of afternoons, he thought of her, 1,500 miles away. And he thought of another woman twice that far away in St. John's.

He thought about the speculation of the woman from St. John's that, by her subtraction from it, his life would be improved, and about her further speculation that, by her subtraction from it, the world might be improved.

He remembered the faces of her two children. And he remembered her, a tall woman with shoulders slightly hunched, arms crossed as she looked out to sea on a sunny day from a hilltop where a hundred years before a church had stood.

On the nights he spent staring at his television set, he felt sorrow, lust, boredom, self-pity, guilt, nostalgia for a life unlived. Now and then a surge of what he thought might be despair. He pointlessly, over and over, reconsidered the choice that he had made, imagined how things would be, for him, for others, if he had chosen otherwise.

He drank and read and listened to music.

He did not even try to write.

Did there come a time when he availed himself of an escort service?

Yes, but only after having spent many consecutive nights dialing telephone number after telephone number and hanging up upon hearing, whispered in what he assumed were intended to be sultry, seductive, provocative tones, a non-committal, non-incriminating, informationless reply consisting of nothing but the word "hello."

One night he did not hang up when the voice said "hello."

He asked, "So how does this work?"

He was told that, assuming everything "to be in order," a "young lady" would be sent to his address, a masseuse whose hourly rate was fifty dollars, all charges for any "supplementary services" to be worked out between the "young lady and the customer."

He replied that he had only fifty-seven dollars.

The voice replied that she was certain he would find that fifty-seven dollars could still "buy a lot of things."

"OK," he said.

She asked him "what sort of young lady" he was interested in. He was unable to formulate even the semblance of an idea as to what she could possibly mean and therefore said nothing.

The voice informed him that he could normally have chosen from among "blonds, brunettes, redheads, and ravenheads," but that no blonds were currently available; that the "available" ranged in height from five feet two inches to five feet eleven inches.

Never having heard the noun "ravenhead" before, he chose a ravenhead and said that he would "like it if she was about five foot six."

After he furnished the voice with his address and phone number, he hung up and waited.

Standing at the window of his basement apartment, looking out at the frozen courtyard across which the ravenhead would have to make her way to reach the common hallway and the intercom, he waited ninety minutes until he saw her as she hurried down his walkway in a long fur or fur-like coat. She was, in spite of the voice that had indicated the unavailability of blonds, a blond, or at least appeared from that distance to be one, as she likewise appeared from that distance to be slightly over five feet tall despite the high heels on which she somehow managed to walk over months' worth of ice and snow.

When she rang the building's buzzer, he let her in and soon after heard her knock, twice, sternly, loudly, yet somehow discreetly.

He opened his apartment door. She stepped inside and told him to quickly close the door. She said: "Are you the sole tenant of this dwelling?" He replied that he was. "Is there anyone in this dwelling at the moment other than you?" He replied that there was not. "Are you expecting anyone?" When he shook his head, she told him to lock the door.

His first impression of her was that her first impression of him was unfavourable, that she knew that this was his first time, that she had hoped that he had lied about how much money he had, that she had seen many times before the sort of skewed and sheepish smile he imagined he was wearing.

"Fifty-seven dollars?"

He nodded.

"That's a hand job."

"For fifty-seven dollars?"

"You already owe me thirty, so it will only cost you twenty-seven."

He agreed. With hand out-held she demanded that he pay her first.

They lay side by side on his bed. She removed her coat and all but one of her upper garments, a kind of camisole, one of the straps of which was frayed. He removed his jeans and underwear but not his shirt or sweater. "Too cold," he said.

She reached beneath his shirt, took him in her hand, and began a jigging motion such as he had seen ice fishermen make.

"Your hand is cold," he said.

"Relax," she said, then made his doing so impossible by adding, "you haven't got much time left on your clock." She continued jigging, looking around the unlit room as she did, sighing loudly.

"Can you take off the rest of your clothes?" he said.

"Not for fifty-seven dollars."

"I think if I could see your breasts—"

"Jesus," she said, and with crossed arms removed the camisole.

"Can I touch them?" he said.

She sighed. "Only with your hands. Try anything else and there'll be someone at your door within five minutes."

He took one of her purple nipples between his thumb and forefinger.

"Ow," she said.

"Sorry, I barely—"

"I'm nursing," she said. At first he thought she meant she was in nursing or perhaps already a nurse who needed extra money. "Nursing a baby."

"Oh."

"We're not getting anywhere here. You got five more minutes."

"Perhaps if we stood up," he said, "and you stood behind me?"

She sighed and shrugged.

They stood. He took off his shirt and sweater, thinking they might somehow be impedimental.

She took him in her hand again, her hand that was no longer cold, and resumed the jigging motion as he closed his eyes and tried to concentrate.

A few minutes passed. He felt her breath, warm, on his bare back and heard her sigh, about once every ten seconds it seemed. He felt her lean her forehead against his back. He pictured her standing behind him, her forehead against his back, her eyes closed.

"You can stop," he said.

"I think you were getting hard there for a while."

"I didn't really care if anything happened," he said.

She shrugged.

"No, really," he said. "I'm a writer."

"So?" she said, looking at him as both of them put their clothes back on.

"No really, I'm a writer," he said. "I'll show you one of my books." He took a book from his top dresser drawer and handed it to her.

"You wrote this?" she said. "That's your name?"

He nodded. "And that's my picture, right there. See?"

"Yeah, that's you."

"All of this just now was—well, it wasn't really research, but I did want to find out what it was like. How it was all done, I mean, how it was all arranged. That kind of thing."

"You're not going to write about me?"

He shook his head.

"No. But you can have that book. I'll sign it for you." He took the book from her and found a pen atop his dresser. "What's your name?"

"Brandy," she said.

"Really?"

She smiled and shook her head.

For Brandy, he wrote. With best wishes. March 29, 1990, Regina.

She took the book from him.

As she was leaving, she paused in the open doorway and flipped slowly through the book.

She raised it, and, like a preacher exhorting a congregation with it, shook it several times.

"I'm going to read this," she said, as if she thought he doubted she could read.

She let the door close behind her. He thought of going to the window to watch her cross the courtyard in her spiked high heels but instead sat on the bed in the unlit room.

WHAT, YEARS LATER, reflecting on the months he spent in the city, would he remember fondly?

The clattering of leaves along the street outside his window on gusty autumn afternoons.

The zodiacal light that because of the flatness of the prairie he could see on the horizon for hours after sunset.

The street people, mostly men, who on winter mornings came into the library to escape the cold and slept undisturbed in the chairs outside his door like the congregants of some exclusive club who had nodded off while chatting over brandy and cigars.

He would remember remembering Newfoundland and how he had lied that it was because he could not write there that he had left the place for good.

He would remember remembering the day he wrote to the woman in St. John's that she would never hear from him again.

He would remember remembering the moment, months before he wrote the letter, when she told him it was time for him to leave; he would remember the tears that when she blinked spilled onto her cheeks while the wind roared against the walls of her house in which they lay supine, apart, silent and immobile and faithless on her bed; he would remember wondering how she remembered him and how she would remember him twenty years from now and thinking that such sentimental speculation would soon give way to sorrow; he would remember remembering her face, the way she looked away at first when he caught her looking at him and then looked back at him and how it seemed the colour of her eyes and the timbre of her voice changed when she smiled.

When did he leave the city?

In June, by car, faintly surprised to have survived what he hoped would prove to be the worst year of his life, he left for Toronto.

He thought about the two women.

The one whom out of vanity he would never leave.

The one he had been too cowardly to love.

A Scarf

CAROL SHIELDS

TWO YEARS AGO I wrote a novel, and my publisher sent me on a three-city book tour: New York, Washington and Baltimore. A very modest bit of promotion, you might say, but Scribano & Lawrence scarcely knew what to do with me. I had never written a novel before. I am a middle-aged woman, not at all remarkable-looking and certainly not media-smart. If I have any reputation at all it is for being an editor and scholar, and not for producing, to everyone's amazement, a "fresh, bright, springtime piece of fiction," or so it was described in *Publishers Weekly*.

My Thyme Is Up baffled everyone with its sparky sales. We had no idea who was buying it; I didn't know, and Mr. Scribano didn't know. "Probably young working girls," he ventured, "gnawed by loneliness and insecurity."

These words hurt my feelings slightly, but then the reviews, good as they were, had subtly injured me too. The reviewers seemed taken aback that my slim novel (two hundred pages exactly) possessed any weight at all. "Oddly appealing," the *New York Times Book Review* said. "Mrs. Winters' book is very much for the moment, though certainly not for the ages," the *New Yorker* said. My husband, Tom, advised me to take this as praise, his position being that all worthy novels pay close attention to the time in which they are suspended, and sometimes, years later, despite themselves, acquire a permanent luster. I wasn't so sure. As a long-time editor of Danielle Westerman's work, I had acquired a near-crippling degree of critical appreciation for the sincerity of her moral stance, and I understood perfectly well that there was something just a little bit *darling* about my own book.

My three daughters, Nancy, Chris and Norah, all teenagers, were happy about the book because they were mentioned by name in a *People* magazine interview. ("Mrs. Winters lives on a farm outside Lancaster, Pennsylvania, is married to a family physician, and is the mother of three handsome daughters, Nancy, Christine and Norah.") That was enough for them. Handsome. Norah, the most literary of the three—both Nancy and Chris are in the advanced science classes at General MacArthur High School—mumbled that it might have been a better book if I'd skipped the happy ending, if Alicia had decided on suicide after all, and if Roman had denied her his affection. There was, my daughters postulated, maybe too much over-the-top sweetness about the thyme seeds Alicia planted in her window box, with Alicia's mood listless but squeaking hope. And no one in her right mind would sing out (as Alicia had done) those words that reached Roman's ears—he was making filtered coffee in the kitchen—and bound him to her forever: "My thyme is up."

It won the Offenden Prize, which, though the money was nice, shackled the book to minor status. Clarence and Dorothy Offenden had established the prize back in the seventies out of a shared exasperation with the opaqueness of the contemporary novel. "The Offenden Prize recognizes literary quality and honors accessibility." These are their criteria. Dorothy and Clarence are a good-hearted couple, and rich, but a little jolly and simple in their judgments, and Dorothy in particular is fond of repeating her recipe for enduring fiction. "A beginning, a middle and an ending," she likes to say. "Is that too much to ask!"

At the award ceremony in New York she embraced Tom and the girls, and told them how I shone among my peers, those dabblers in convolution and pretension who wrote without holding the reader in the mind, who played games for their own selfish amusement, and who threw a mask of *noir* over every event, whether it was appropriate or not. "It's heaven," she sang into Tom's ear, "to find that sunniness still exists in the world." (Show me your fatwa, Mrs. Winters.)

I don't consider myself a sunny person. In fact, if I prayed, I would ask every day to be spared from the shame of dumb sunniness. Danielle Westerman has taught me that much, her life, her reflection on that life. Don't hide your dark side from yourself, she always said, it's what keeps us going forward, that pushing away from the unspeakable brilliance. She wrote, of course, amid the shadows of the Holocaust, and no one expected her to struggle free to merriment.

After the New York event, I said goodbye to the family and got on a train and travelled to Washington, staying in a Georgetown hotel that had on its top floor, reserved for me by my publisher, something called the Writer's Suite. A brass plaque on the door announced this astonishing fact. I, the writer in a beige raincoat, Mrs. Reta Winters from Lancaster, entered this doorway with small suitcase in tow and looked around, not daring to imagine what I might find. There was a salon as well as a bedroom, two full baths, a very wide bed, more sofas than I would have time to sit on in my short stay, and a coffee table consisting of a sheet of glass posed on three immense faux books lying on their sides, stacked one on the other. A large bookshelf held the tomes of the authors who had stayed in the suite. "We like to ask our guests to contribute a copy of their work," the desk clerk had told me, and I was obliged to explain that I had only a single reading copy with me, but that I would attempt to find a copy in a local store. "That would be most appreciated," she almost whistled into the sleeve of my raincoat.

The books left behind by previous authors were disappointing, inspiration manifestos or self-help manuals, with a few thrillers thrown in. I'm certainly not a snob—I read the Jackie Onassis biography, for example—but my close association with writers such as Danielle Westerman has conditioned me to hope for a degree of ambiguity or nuance, and there was none here.

In that great, wide bed I had a disturbing but not unfamiliar dream—it is the dream I always have when I am away from Lancaster, away from the family. I am standing in the kitchen at home, producing a complicated meal for guests, but there is not enough food to work with. In the fridge sits a single egg and maybe a tomato. How am I going to feed all these hungry mouths?

I'm quite aware of how this dream might be analyzed by a dream expert, that the scarcity of food stands for a scarcity of love, that no matter how I stretch that egg and tomato, there will never be enough of Reta Winters for everyone who needs her. This is how my friend Gwen, whom I am looking forward to seeing in Baltimore, would be sure to interpret the dream if I were so foolish as to tell her. Gwen is an obsessive keeper of a dream journal—as are quite a number of my friends—and she also records the dreams of others if they are offered and found worthy.

I resist the theory of insufficient love. My dream, I like to think, points only to the abrupt cessation, or interruption, of daily obligation. For twenty years I've been responsible for producing three meals a day for the several individuals I live with. I may not be conscious of this obligation, but surely I must always, at some level, be calculating the amount of food in the house and the number of bodies to be fed: Tom and the girls, the girls' friends, my mother-in-law next door, passing acquaintances. Away from home, liberated from my responsibility for meals, my unexecuted calculations steal into my dreams and leave me blithering with this diminished store of nourishment and the fact of my unpreparedness. Such a small dream crisis, but I always wake with a sense of terror.

SINCE MY THYME IS UP is a first novel, and since mine is an unknown name, there was very little for me to do in Washington. Mr. Scribano had been afraid this would happen. The television stations weren't interested, and the radio stations avoided novels unless they had a "topic" like cancer or child abuse.

I managed to fulfill all my obligations in a mere two hours the morning after my arrival, taking a cab to a bookstore called Politics & Prose, where I signed books for three rather baffled-looking customers and then a few more stock copies that the staff was kind enough to produce. I handled the whole thing badly, was overly ebullient with the book buyers, too chatty, wanting them to love me as much as they said they loved my book, wanting them for best friends, you would think. ("Please just call me Reta, everyone does.") My impulse was to apologize for not being younger and more fetching, like Alicia in my novel, and for not having her bright ingenue voice and manner. I was ashamed of my red pantsuit, catalogue-issue, and wondered if I'd remembered, waking up in the Writer's Suite, to apply deodorant.

From Politics & Prose I took a cab to a store called Pages, where there were no buying customers at all, but where the two young proprietors took me for a splendid lunch at an Italian bistro and also insisted on giving me a free copy of my book to leave in the Writer's Suite. Then it was afternoon, a whole afternoon, and I had nothing to do until the next morning, when I was to take my train to Baltimore. Mr. Scribano had warned me I might find touring lonely.

I returned to the hotel, freshened up and placed my book on the bookshelf. But why had I returned to the hotel? What homing instinct had brought me here when I might be out visiting museums or perhaps taking a tour through the Senate chambers? There was a wide springtime afternoon to fill, and an evening too, since no one had suggested taking me to dinner.

I decided to go shopping in the Georgetown area, having spotted from the taxi a number of tiny boutiques. My daughter Norah's birthday was coming up in a week's time, and she longed to have a beautiful and serious scarf. She had never had a scarf in all her seventeen years, not unless you count the woollen mufflers she wears on the school bus, but since her senior class trip to Paris, she had been talking about the scarves that every chic Frenchwoman wears as part of her wardrobe. These scarves, so artfully draped, were silk, nothing else would do, and their colours shocked and awakened the dreariest of clothes, the wilted navy blazers that Frenchwomen wear or those cheap black cardigans they try to get away with.

I never have time to shop in Lancaster, and, in fact, there would be little available there. But today I had time, plenty of time, and so I put on my low-heeled walking shoes and started out.

Georgetown's boutiques are set amid tiny fronted houses, impeccably gentrified with shuttered bay windows and framed by minuscule gardens, enchanting to the eye. My own sprawling, untidy house outside Lancaster, if dropped into this landscape, would destroy half a dozen or more of these meticulous brick facades. The placement of flowerpots was so ardently pursued here, so caring, so solemn, and the clay pots themselves had been rubbed, I could tell, with sandpaper, to give them a country look.

These boutiques held such a minimum of stock that I wondered how they were able to compete with one another. There might be six or seven blouses on a rod, a few cashmere pullovers, a table casually strewn with shells or stones or Art Nouveau picture frames or racks of antique postcards. A squadron of very slender saleswomen presided over this spare merchandise, which they fingered in such a loving way that I suddenly wanted to buy everything in sight. The scarves—every shop had a good half-dozen—were knotted on dowels, and there was not one that was not pure silk with hand-rolled edges.

I took my time. I realized I would be able, given enough shopping time, to buy Norah the perfect scarf, not the near-perfect and certainly not the impulse purchase we usually settled for at home. She had mentioned wanting something in a bright blue with perhaps some yellow dashes. I would find that very scarf in one of these many boutiques. The thought of myself as a careful and deliberate shopper brought me a bolt of happiness. I took a deep breath and smiled genuinely at the anorexic saleswomen, who seemed to sense and respond to my new consumer eagerness. "That's not quite her," I quickly learned to say, and they nodded with sympathy. Most of them wore scarves themselves around their angular necks, and I admired, to myself, the intricate knotting and colours of these scarves. I admired, too, the women's forthcoming involvement in my mission. "Oh, the scarf absolutely must be suited to the person," they said, or words to that effect—as though they knew Norah personally and understood that she was a young woman of highly defined tastes and requirements that they were anxious to satisfy.

She isn't really. She is, Tom and I always think, too easily satisfied and someone who too seldom considers herself deserving. When she was a very small child, two or three, eating lunch in her high chair, she heard an airplane go overhead and looked up at me and said, "The pilot doesn't know I'm eating an egg." She seemed shocked at this perception, but willing to register the shock calmly so as not to alarm me. She would be grateful for any scarf I brought her, pleased I had taken the time, but for once I wanted, and had an opportunity to procure, a scarf that would gladden her heart.

As I moved from one boutique to the next, I began to form a very definite idea of the scarf I wanted for Norah, and began, too, to see how impossible it might be to accomplish this task. The scarf became an idea; it must be brilliant and subdued at the same time, finely made, but with a secure sense of its own shape. A wisp was not what I wanted, not for Norah. Solidity, presence, was what I wanted, but in sinuous, ephemeral form. This was what Norah at seventeen, almost eighteen, was owed. She had always been a bravely undemanding child. Once, when she was four or five, she told me how she controlled her bad dreams at night. "I just turn my head around on the pillow," she said matter-of-factly, "and that changes the channel." She performed this act instead of calling out to us or crying; she solved her own nightmares and candidly exposed her original solution—which Tom and I took some comfort in but also, I confess, some amusement. I remember, with shame now, telling this story to friends, over coffee, over dinner, my brave little soldier daughter, shaping her soldierly life.

I seldom wear scarves myself; I can't be bothered, and besides, whatever I put around my neck takes on the configuration of a Girl Scout kerchief, the knot working its way straight to the throat, and the points sticking out rather than draping gracefully downward. I was not clever with accessories, I knew that about myself, and I was most definitely not a shopper. I had never understood, in fact, what it is that drives other women to feats of shopping perfection, but now I had a suspicion. It was the desire to please someone fully; even oneself. It seemed to me that my daughter Norah's future happiness now balanced not on acceptance at Smith or the acquisition of a handsome new boyfriend, but on the simple ownership of a particular article of apparel, which only I could supply. I had no power over Smith or the boyfriend or, in fact, any real part of her happiness, but I could provide something temporary and necessary: this dream of transformation, this scrap of silk.

And there it was, relaxed over a fat silver hook in what must have been the twentieth shop I entered. The little bell rang; the updraft of potpourri rose to my nostrils, and the sight of Norah's scarf flowed into view. It was patterned from end to end with rectangles, each subtly out of alignment: blue, yellow, green, a kind of pleasing violet. And each of these shapes was outlined by a band of black, coloured in roughly as though with an artist's brush. I found its shimmer dazzling and its touch icy and sensuous. Sixty dollars. Was that all? I whipped out my Visa card without a thought. My day had been well spent. I felt full of intoxicating power.

In the morning I took the train to Baltimore. I couldn't read on the train because of the jolting between one urban landscape and the next. Two men seated in front of me were talking loudly about Christianity, its sad decline, and they ran the words *Jesus Christ* together as though they were some person's first and second names—Mr. Christ, Jesus to the in-group.

In Baltimore, once again, there was little for me to do, but since I was going to see Gwen at lunch, I didn't mind. A young male radio host wearing a black T-shirt and gold chains around his neck asked me how I was going to spend the Offenden prize money. He also asked what my husband thought of the fact that I'd written a novel. (This is a question I've been asked before and for which I really must find an answer.) Then I visited the Book Plate (combination café and bookstore) and signed six books, and then, at not quite eleven in the morning, there was nothing more for me to do until it was time to meet Gwen.

Gwen and I had been in the same women's writing group back in Lancaster. In fact, she had been the informal but acknowledged leader for those of us who met weekly to share and "workshop" our writing. Poetry, memoirs, fiction: we brought photocopies of our work to these morning sessions, where over coffee and muffins—this was the age of muffins, the last days of the seventies—we kindly encouraged each other and offered tentative suggestions, such as "I think you're one draft from being finished" or "Doesn't character X enter the scene a little too late?" These critical crumbs were taken for what they were, the fumblings of amateurs. But when Gwen spoke, we listened. Once she thrilled me by saying of something I'd written, "That's a fantastic image, that thing about the whalebone. I wish I'd thought of it myself." Her short fiction had actually been published in a number of literary quarterlies, and there had even been one near mythical sale, years earlier, to *Harper's*. When she moved to Baltimore five years ago to become writer-in-residence for a small women's college, our writers' group first fell into irregularity, and then slowly died away.

We'd kept in touch, though, the two of us. I wrote ecstatically when I happened to come across a piece of hers in *Three Spoons* that was advertised as being part of a novel-in-progress. She'd used my whalebone metaphor; I couldn't help noticing and, in fact, felt flattered. I knew about that novel of Gwen's—she'd been working on it for years—trying to bring a feminist structure to what was really a straightforward account of an early failed marriage. Gwen had made sacrifices for her young student husband, and he had betrayed her with his infidelities. In the early seventies, in the throes of love and anxious to satisfy his every demand, she had had her navel closed by a plastic surgeon because her husband complained that it smelled "off." The complaint, apparently, had been made only once, a sour, momentary whim, but out of some need to please or punish she became a woman without a navel, left with a flattish indentation in the middle of her belly, and this navel-less state, more than anything, became her symbol of regret and anger. She spoke of erasure, how her relationship to her mother—with whom she was on bad terms anyway—had been erased along with the primal mark of connection. She was looking into a navel reconstruction, she'd said in her last letter, but the cost was criminal. In the meantime, she'd retaken her unmarried name, Reidman, and had gone back to her full name, Gwendolyn.

She'd changed her style of dress too. I noticed that right away when I saw her seated at the Café Pierre. Her jeans and sweater had been traded in for what looked like large folds of unstitched, unstructured cloth, skirts and overskirts and capes and shawls; it was hard to tell precisely what they were. This cloth wrapping, in a salmon colour, extended to her head, completely covering her hair, and I wondered for an awful moment if she'd been ill, undergoing chemotherapy and suffering hair loss. But no, there was a fresh, healthy, rich face. Instead of a purse she had only a lumpy plastic bag with a supermarket logo; that did worry me, especially because she put it on the table instead of setting it on the floor as I would have expected. It bounced slightly on the sticky wooden surface, and I remembered that she always carried an apple with her, a paperback or two and her small bottle of cold-sore medication.

OF COURSE I'd written to her when *My Thyme Is Up* was accepted for publication, and she'd sent back a postcard saying "Well done, it sounds like a hoot."

I was a little surprised that she hadn't brought a copy for me to sign, and wondered at some point, halfway through my oyster soup, if she'd even read it. The college pays her shamefully, of course, and I know she doesn't have money for new books. Why hadn't I had Mr. Scribano send her a complimentary copy?

It wasn't until we'd finished our salads and ordered our coffee that I noticed she hadn't mentioned the book at all, nor had she congratulated me on the Offenden Prize. But perhaps she didn't know. The notice in the *New York Times* had been tiny. Anyone could have missed it.

It became suddenly important that I let her know about the prize. It was as strong as the need to urinate or swallow. How could I work it into the conversation?— maybe say something about Tom and how he was thinking of putting a new roof on our barn, and that the Offenden money would come in handy. Drop it in casually. Easily done.

"Right!" she said heartily, letting me know she already knew. "Beginning, middle, end." She grinned then.

She talked about her "stuff," by which she meant her writing. She made it sound like a sack of kapok. A magazine editor had commented on how much he liked her "stuff," and how her kind of "stuff" contained the rub of authenticity. There were always little linguistic surprises in her work, but more interesting to me were the bits of the world she brought to what she wrote, observations or incongruities or some sideways conjecture. She understood their value. "He likes the fact that my stuff is off-centre and steers a random course," she said of a fellow writer.

"No beginnings, middles and ends," I supplied.

"Right," she said. "Right." She regarded me fondly, as though I were a prize pupil. Her eyes looked slightly pink at the corners, but it may have been a reflection from the cloth that cut a sharp line across her forehead.

I admire her writing. She claimed she had little imagination, that she wrote out of the material of her own life, but that she was forever on the lookout for what she called "putty." By this she meant the arbitrary, the odd, the ordinary, the mucilage of daily life that cements our genuine moments of being. I've seen her do wonderful riffs on buttonholes, for instance, the way they shred over time, especially on cheap clothes. And a brilliant piece on bevelled mirrors, and another on the smell of a certain set of wooden stairs from her childhood, wax and wood and reassuring cleanliness accumulating at the side of the story but not claiming any importance for itself.

She looked sad over her coffee, older than I'd remembered—but weren't we all?—and I could tell she was disappointed in me for some reason. It occurred to me I might offer her a piece of putty by telling her about the discovery I had made the day before, that shopping was not what I'd thought, that it could become a mission, even an art if one persevered. I had had a shopping item in mind; I had been presented with an unasked-for block of time; it might be possible not only to imagine this artifact, but to realize it.

"How many boutiques did you say you went into?" she asked, and I knew I had interested her at last.

"Twenty," I said. "Or thereabouts."

"Incredible."

"But it was worth it. It wasn't when I started out, but it became more and more worth it as the afternoon went on."

"Why?" she asked slowly. I could tell she was trying to twinkle a gram of gratitude at me, but she was closer to crying.

"To see if it existed, this thing I had in mind."

"And it did."

"Yes."

To prove my point I reached into my tote bag and pulled out the pale, puffy boutique bag. I unrolled the pink tissue paper on the table and showed her the scarf.

She lifted it against her face. Tears glinted in her eyes. "It's just that it's so beautiful," she said. And then she said, "Finding it, it's almost like you made it. You invented it, created it out of your imagination."

I almost cried myself. I hadn't expected anyone to understand how I felt.

I watched her roll the scarf back into the fragile paper. She took her time, tucking in the edges with her fingertips. Then she slipped the parcel into her plastic bag, tears spilling more freely now. "Thank you, darling Reta, thank you. You don't know what you've given me today."

But I did, I did.

But what does it amount to? A scarf, half an ounce of silk, maybe less, floating free in the world. I looked at Gwen/Gwendolyn, my old friend, and then down at my hands, my wedding band, my engagement ring, a little diamond thingamajig from the sixties. I thought of my three daughters and my mother-in-law and my own dead mother with her slack charms and the need she had to relax by painting china. Not one of us was going to get what we wanted. Imagine someone writing a play called

Death of a Saleswoman. What a joke. We're so transparently in need of shoring up our little preciosities and our lisping pronouns, her, she. We ask ourselves questions, endlessly, but not nearly sternly enough. The world isn't ready for us yet; it hurts me to say that. We're too soft in our tissues, even you, Danielle Westerman, Holocaust survivor, cynic and genius. Even you, Mrs. Winters, with your new, old useless knowledge. We are too kind, too willing, too unwilling too, reaching out blindly with a grasping hand, but not knowing how to ask for what we don't even know we want.

Smoke's Fortune

TIMOTHY TAYLOR

AFTER SOME TALKING, Fergie offered us forty dollars to shoot the dog. Smoke haggled with him, standing in that little screened porch tacked onto the front of Fergie's house, but he just said the dog was dying anyhow and swatted at a fly. Smoke said we wanted forty dollars each, and that we knew the dog had bitten a kid, and that the RCMP said kill it. But Fergie didn't budge even though we said we'd bury it and all. He said, "I know I can't kill the bastard anyway. Here's your forty dollars. You boys take it."

So we took it, Smoke and I. Then we got my Ruger 30-06 out of Smoke's truck and went to the shack by the yard where Fergie kept all his wrecks and parts of cars. He kept two dogs in there. They were fenced, but I guess there was one kid smarter than that fence. When Fergie found the kid, and then the dog with blood in her mouth even he knew what had to happen. And Fergie was a guy crazy for his dogs.

Frank Hall was in the shack propping up the desk with his feet, and he laughed when we came in.

"Here come the hunters," he said, and came over to the counter. "Don't get bit now, you hear?"

That was Frank, always winking and ribbing, but Smoke flipped a bit. He grabbed Frank's jacket and pulled him hard up into the counter so some coffee spilled. I was glad I was carrying the rifle so nothing went off or anything. Frank just laughed again like he couldn't care, and got a fresh toothpick out.

The yard was set out like a football field. Blocks on the fifteen-yard line, exhaust units on the forty, stacks of bodies on the forty-five. All with some roads for the trucks running out into the junk and then back into the corner by the Haffreys' land.

The dogs knew Smoke, but since I'd only started with Fergie in July, I carried a deer steak. This was Smoke's idea. I wasn't too sure really. If they didn't recognize me

I figured the steak might give them the wrong idea. So I hung back a bit while Smoke went ahead looking for the dog.

"This fucking heat," I heard him say.

"What," I said.

"I can't see through this heat," he said.

"It's hot, all right," I said swinging the steak.

We kept on walking through the blocks. There was about a half acre of them I guessed. Up ahead I could see the stacks of pipes, then the rads, bodies and smaller parts all grown up with weeds and grass. Fergie kept a yard for certain, everything neat and separated and lined with rosehips.

"Smoke," I said.

"What."

"Listen, I shouldn't be carrying the steak and the rifle. I mean, I can't shoot her one-handed. I figured maybe …"

But Smoke came back to where I stood and said to me slowly, like it didn't need saying, "We find her, you throw the steak, then you shoot her. It's easy."

I looked at him.

"I'm here to do the finding," he said. "They like me."

This was how Smoke got you to do things. He made it real obvious, and then kept on telling you anyway. So by the end of his telling, you were wishing he'd be quiet and let you do it.

We went on walking, through some trucks and into more blocks. I guess there might have been a thousand old engines there, all black and rust-coloured. Right where we were, the grass grew up through some of the cylinders. They looked pretty in all that junk, which was mostly just oily.

Smoke was poking on ahead, into the big stacks of bodies. It was well-known junkyard knowledge that you watched yourself in the stacks. Frank always told about Marcel, who came out from Quebec and was crushed under a stack. He was tugging at some piece of dirty junk and pulled about three trucks down on himself. Right out from Quebec, had a job for maybe three weeks, and pulling on something he was probably barely curious about and boom. So I was watching Smoke a bit because he would tug on stuff even though he'd probably been in a junkyard as long as Frank, or even Fergie. That was Smoke's way, tugging on things even when he was in the stacks.

"Here, here, here," I heard him say, like he was coaxing something, and then I saw him back out from under a big cab-over with his hand out. I stayed back near the blocks, holding the steak, ready to throw.

Smoke came back further and a dog came out of the grass. I could hear it panting and breathing all hanging with saliva the way they do when it's hot. This was all the sound, next to Smoke saying, "Here, here, here. Yes, yes. Easy boy."

When they were right in front of me Smoke just held his hand out, dangled it in the dog's face and waited. Then I'll be damned if the dog didn't start smiling, only all I saw was that whole face change, and the eyes squint back and tight, and the teeth drop out of the black lips, and the mouth crease back along the sides. I have to admit I dropped the steak and brought the Ruger right up fast thinking about squeezing not jerking the trigger, and letting the bastard move at you before you fire.

Smoke turned his hand over and cupped the dog under the muzzle and said, "Just show them slow, like that, see?"

Jesus, I was like a stone. I think I even turned grey-coloured.

"Hey, that's great Smoke," I said.

"What are you going to do? Shoot me or what?"

"No, hey," I said lowering the rifle and stooping to pick up the steak. "No."

"This here's the one that likes me," Smoke said, all grins.

"Yeah, well, I guess I can see you've met."

"Here, I'll go put this one in the pen so's we don't have to catch him another four times. Give me some steak."

I propped the rifle between my knees and managed to get my knife out. I hacked off a bit and tossed it.

"OK, I'll be back. Have a smoke or something. Don't wander around and get lost."

"Right," I said. And I sat down on the nearest block and smoked. It was too hot to smoke actually, but I was feeling like having one. Sometimes when I want a smoke the worst, I don't even like it when I light up. It'll even make me feel sick sometimes. I figure that's just like me to feel sick about something when you want it the most.

Smoke came back patting dust out of his pants, looking all keyed up again. He was glad to find the one dog. Now he was thinking about finding the bitch, and it wasn't getting any cooler.

"OK, OK, OK, huphuphup. Move it out!" he started shouting like a crazy person. "Here pup, here pup!"

"Jesus, Smoke, you'll get her all riled."

"Relax on the trigger, old son. I'm finding dogs. Come here, dog!"

So we went off further, looking. Right into the back parts of the yard where the real junk was. Some of Fergie's stuff back here didn't move too often, I figured. The back of some old Seville was rusting off to one side, fins slanting up through the weeds.

Smoke was poking, pulling on things like nothing could ever hurt him. Under a pile of fenders twenty, thirty feet high, he pulls up a piece of a radio or something and says, "Well, shit, look at this." I think a fender even fell off about a foot away and he just shuffled over and said, "Hey, easy now."

"Smoke."

"Yeah."

We had stopped again, I was getting dust down my shirt.

"Smoke, we're getting way the hell back here."

Smoke came over and took a drag off my cigarette and then took one out of the package in my shirt pocket, and lit it off an old Zippo he carried around. I've seen Smoke use about three of his own cigarettes over the years and that includes the one he keeps behind his ear. He's never without the Zippo though, he loves that old thing.

"Well, she's out there, son," he said.

Then, as he dragged on the cigarette, Smoke got to thinking and he sat down on the grass, quiet, and I slid down so my neck could crook between the manifold and the block on this old motor. There were clouds floating by really peacefully. Maybe forty clouds across the whole sky.

"Smoke, you figure that cloud's a hundred miles across?"

"Where?"

"There. That one that looks like a couch or something."

Smoke started craning his neck all around, trying to think of an answer.

"Well," he said finally, "you know, I think they're actually a whole lot smaller than people think. The sky's actually smaller than people think too. You take Fergie, say, thinks he's a smart guy. Now he'll tell you that this sky's so big you can't even start to understand it. But it isn't. It's really quite small to some scientists. And getting smaller every year."

Smoke kept on talking. I was remembering about last Saturday at the Tudor. There was a lady there I'd never seen before. Really pretty, in a skirt, looking around her like she was a little scared or something. Like maybe she got a flat going through town on her way to Red Deer and ended up here. Sitting at this bar, sipping a Coors, waiting for someone from the garage.

Well, Smoke caught one sight of her and went right up to her like she was waiting for him in particular. "Are you the lady with the flat?" he said, like Magnum P.I. or something. You know, here's a time when I'm thinking, Maybe this lady had a flat. Smoke, he's thinking, Maybe, maybe not, no difference. And I get to wondering sometimes why it is that Smoke thinks he can ask people right on if they have a flat just because they're pretty.

Then Smoke shifted over in the weeds and looked down at me. I noticed he had stopped talking.

"You entirely comfortable, son?" he said.

"Why yes, Smoke," I said. The exhaust manifold felt smooth and cool on my neck.

"Well, don't you wake up if you can kill that bitch sleeping."

"Oh, I'm not sleeping."

"Well, what do you think?"

I stalled a bit, wondering what I might have missed. I pulled myself up a bit, looking around for the steak. It was all ground with dirt and I wondered if a rabid dog would still like it.

"What about this steak?" I asked Smoke finally.

Smoke looked at it.

"Doesn't look too good, does it?"

"Not to me," I said.

Smoke shrugged and looked around.

"Say, I'm going to beat the brush around here a bit, maybe drive her back toward you so you can get a shot at her." He squinted a bit into the weeds.

"Uh, well, Smoke, I'm not too sure here ..."

He was on his feet, gliding into the grass.

"Smoke, Jesus!" I jumped up. Smoke stopped and turned slowly, following his nose around like he was finding me by smell.

"Listen, I mean, why don't we fan out together?" The idea of wandering around these stacks with both Smoke and a rabid dog cut loose seemed like craziness.

Smoke looked disgusted for a second, like I was about twelve years old for being spooked by a dog. "You got the fucking gun," he said. "You just use it when the time seems right."

I stood there for about a minute after he left. Not moving. Swearing quietly and keeping my breathing even and shallow. The grass stretched out around me, yellow and burnt, stained with oil so the heat made your head swim with fumes. The sun kept rising higher overhead like it wasn't planning to set that day.

I backed up, holding the Ruger against my thigh, feeling the rough patterned grip on the stock grab little tufts of my jeans. I was feeling backward with my left hand, until I felt the big stack of radiators behind me. I crouched down, watching the dry weeds and thinking.

The rads had a lot of sharp edges so I stopped and pulled on my hunting gloves, which let your trigger finger hang out. Then I slung the rifle flat across my shoulders and began looking for a place to start climbing. The rads were stacked in a huge pyramid, maybe forty feet high. I put my boot up on one and pushed, knocking one off higher up. It came sliding down the stack, and I rolled to one side. It hit my shoulder and then the ground.

I started again. Trying to stay on top of the metal pieces as I climbed. My boots gripped on the rough edges all right, but as I got higher I was knocking them off left and right, kicking twisted chunks of metal down into the lane. I kept thinking, Fergie will kill us if we don't clean this up.

When I got to the top, I was afraid to look down for a while. I pinched my eyes almost shut and wormed my way onto a flat area at the top of the stack. Here I shifted around and got myself cross-legged. Then I slung the Ruger off my back carefully, trying not to shake too much. I sat like that, with the rifle up, stock up against my cheek, elbows on my knees. Then I opened my eyes wider and started looking around the yard.

Smoke was pretty small from up there. He was moving up and down the lanes, cutting across the grassy bits between the bodies and the blocks, trying to sweep through the yard toward me, and flush her out. It was kind of hypnotic, like watching a spider wait out a fly. Only now I wondered whether Smoke was the spider or the fly or what.

He was right up to the exhaust pipes, all jumbled with the weeds. He was bobbing his head again like he was smelling something, taking a quiet step or two every so often. I nestled the rifle into my cheek. The wood was oily and hot from the sun. Through the scope I could see Smoke and about two feet all around him. With my other eye open, though, I could still see the rest of the yard. My dad taught me that. A lot of people think your scope eye stops working if you do that, but it doesn't. You start seeing better. As you stare and you don't blink, you suddenly start getting every little movement all over the yard. And in the middle, this circle of larger detail.

I could see Smoke breathing slowly, his cheek sucking in and out. I could see the brick-red sunburn across his neck and the line of dirt around his collar. Across the top of my sight, I could see a truck on the highway, maybe a mile away. You could barely hear it growling, but I could see it moving and see the black exhaust jump out the pipe every time he took another gear. I could see them both, Smoke and the truck.

Smoke kept on crawling through those pipes. Near the far side of the pile he slowed right down and froze. His one hand was up hanging over a tailpipe, the other behind his back, his nose pointing. I tracked the crosshairs of the scope over his shoulders into the grass, then back into his open hand. His hand went into a fist, my left eye was shaking, trying to see all over the yard and concentrate on Smoke at the same time.

Suddenly he jumped to the left, swinging his hand down and pulling the pipe with it. They crashed and rolled across the dirt and he leaped backwards and rolled on one shoulder, coming up in a squat with his hunting knife hovering in front of him, blade up. The crosshairs hung in open air for a moment, a foot in front of his face.

In that second when Smoke was still, I saw her. In my left eye, in the big picture. She was there, where we'd dropped the steak, maybe twenty yards from Smoke. She was muzzling the meat, pawing it. Trying to figure out why it smelled so good and looked so bad, I guess.

She wasn't looking too good herself. All matted and caked around the mouth, dripping drool on herself when she shook her black head. Her sharp snout had flecks of grey, her chest was muddy and her legs shook badly. Her hair was dull, and she panted as she pawed the meat, then jumped back and shook her head from side to side. Just a half-crazy old Doberman, mad at the world and hungry.

When she heard Smoke dump the exhaust pipes, she stopped and listened. She turned and thrashed on her back in the dust then stood up again. I didn't move the rifle too much, just let it coast over as Smoke started out down the lane again and cut into the weeds towards her. I was dead still except for that, that tiny movement of the barrel; Smoke walked along slowly, whistling softly, wondering where I was, maybe, crosshairs on his shoulder. When he crouched down, I'd freeze entirely. No breathing, both eyes locked open, I think my heart stopped even.

I guess I kept meaning to do something, but I didn't want to. I felt almost sleepy except for my face smeared into the Ruger. Pretty soon they were both moving again. Smoke in the scope. The bitch in the yard. I was seeing them both, eyes running with tears. When she saw Smoke through the weeds she went still and tight, low to the ground, like a piece of steel sitting with the others. I was thinking about shooting her then, but I was afraid the bullet would skip right off her, ricochet around, maybe hurt someone. Her lips went back into a grin; her teeth hung with dirt and saliva.

Smoke was batting at some weeds with an old antenna. I was looking at his scalp with my right eye, thinking I could feel the itch of the dirt and grass in it. I scratched it lightly with the crosshairs. From the back up across the top where it was tangled, down into the slick sideburns and the tuft in the ear.

And I was watching these two tangled bits of hair and dirt and saliva get closer together and thinking about how my finger, soft on the trigger, was going to do something soon, very small, and stop them from hurting each other, which seemed a shame, although also very natural.

And then she moved up fast, coming off the ground like a jet, real low at first and then wide and high. Her front legs in and close to her chest, her head forward, brows over and down to protect her eyes, her mouth lipless, showing every tooth and every rib on her black gums. Streaming saliva. And I just sat there until I saw her pass from my left eye into the light, and when she burst into my scope I shot her.

And then she seemed to vanish, and I lowered the Ruger, and Smoke had spun around like a drunken wrestler and was sitting in the grass, his knife still in his belt, his face blank, his mouth open a bit.

I climbed down and walked into the lane past the broken dog. Smoke was on his feet again, grinning. As we stood there he took a cigarette out of my pocket, lit it off the Zippo, and said, "Nice piece of shooting, son." And I guess I knew he'd say something like that.

The Madonna Feast

JOAN CLARK

MADGE AND NONIE check into the cabin late Saturday—they are getting an early start on Mother's Day. The cabin hugs a cliff overlooking a strip of sand the colour of wet cement. Giant logs washed ashore during winter storms lie on the rocks below like fallen monoliths.

Far out on the grey water, Nonie sees something dark rising out of the waves.

"A whale!" she says, squinting, she has forgotten to put on her glasses.

But Madge, who has become farsighted in middle age, tells her it's a fallen tree. "The root tip sticks up like a fin."

Rain drips off trees. Madge feels the moisture seeping into her pores. The dampness makes her joints ache, her bones feel brittle and stiff. She looks at Nonie. Drops of water cling to Nonie's cropped hair, yellow and coarse as wheat stubble from years of living on the prairie. Nonie tips her head back, parts her lips, welcoming the rain. She looks as if she could stand in the rain for days, a porous, bulky sponge.

Madge shivers. "Let's go inside and light a fire," she says.

They carry their suitcases and baskets into the cabin, return for firewood and kindling. A pink rhododendron blooms by the door. Nonie picks a blossom, carries it inside, and puts it in a bowl of water. Madge lights the fire. Nonie walks around the large room, the kitchen, the bathroom, returns to the window overlooking the sea.

"It's lovely," she says. "Better than I imagined."

"I wanted one of the cedar cabins," Madge says. "But they don't have phones. I need a phone in case she calls."

Nonie doesn't ask about Alison. Madge has already told her about Alison's anorexia, which surfaced two years ago when Alison moved east to look for work and became a teller for the Toronto Dominion Bank.

"I told Stuart we wouldn't be near a phone," Nonie says. "It's just as well. The boys wouldn't try to telephone, but Pauline might decide to call if she has a nightmare. She might get up and dial without Stuart knowing."

While the fire crackles, they unpack their bags and put away food. Nonie has brought a basket of food with her on the plane. In it are jars of marmalade and pear preserves, espresso, miniature bottles of liqueur, Camembert, cream cheese, caviar. Madge has brought applesauce, homemade bread, croissants, bagels, honey, candles. On their way from the airport they stopped at a fish market for smoked salmon and crabmeat, at the liquor store for wine, at a supermarket for fruit, vegetables, and cream.

"How about a celebratory drink?" Madge says.

They kick off their runners and sprawl on the floor, each holding a glass of wine.

Although they have lived apart since their girlhoods in Cape Breton during the fifties, Madge and Nonie have kept in touch through letters and visits. When Madge's marriage was breaking up, Nonie flew to Halifax for a week to help out. Madge and her children have camped in Nonie's backyard in Calgary. Last year, the two friends spent an afternoon in Stanley Park when Nonie accompanied Stuart to a geological conference. For two people who have been travelling different currents since leaving Cape Breton, they feel lucky to have once again drifted into the same cove.

Madge stares at the rhododendron. In the firelight the blossom is licked with gold. Her thoughts leave the West Coast. They wing over the prairies, travelling back to another coast, another island, to a rocky promontory jutting into the Atlantic, a scruffy hillside with barely enough soil on it to camouflage the coal mines tunnelled beneath.

"Do you remember the Mother's Day we went looking for mayflowers?" she says.

She and Nonie had begun in the graveyard on the edge of town. Leaning against two tombstones, they ate molasses sandwiches and swigged strawberry pop. Afterwards they walked around the graveyard, reading the inscriptions on the grave markers. This was when Madge and Nonie were fifteen, when their mothers were both alive.

"Susan Barton, aged 41 years / In Death's cold arms lies sleeping here, / A tender parent, Companion dear," Madge recites now.

"I remember thinking Susan was some sort of heroine," Madge says. "I had the idea Death was her abductor, that she half wanted to be carried off so the people left behind would pine for her."

"Beloved, lovely, she was but seven / A fair bird to earth, to blossom in heaven," Nonie says. Like Madge she can still remember poetry she memorized years ago. She takes a sip of wine. "It was the small white crosses that got to me. All those infant graves. Dozens and dozens."

Madge remembers the graveyard was where Otis Brogan did his drinking. Otis was a bald, shambling man, to whom nobody paid much attention. They could always tell when he'd been in the graveyard because, after he'd finished a bottle, he'd stick flowers from the grave into it and prop the bottle against a stone marker. Otis showed himself to young girls. Sometimes Madge and Nonie would taunt him into doing this, then run away. This made them feel daring, that they were flirting with the possibility of wrongdoing and chance.

"Babes in the woods, that's what we were," Madge says.

The afternoon of the mayflowers they didn't bother doing this. They saw Otis coming along the road with a brown paper bag and made for the woods.

Beyond the woods was a hill. On top of it was a disused powder magazine from the war. Inside it were dried weeds and empty liquor bottles. They sat on the grey cement walls and looked over the black coal heaps to the harbour ice. The afternoon sun poured gold onto the town, glazing the cinder streets, the rows of houses, in clear honeyed light. The cross on top of the Catholic church pierced the blue like an early star. Up there on the powder magazine, they felt a cool wind blowing off the ice. Nonie and Madge left the cement wall and started down the hillside, searching the tufted grass for rust-spotted leaves. Mayflowers grew under old grass, close to the ground. It was possible to walk right over them without knowing they were there, beneath the soles of your feet.

Madge can still recall how the possibility of not finding mayflowers and arriving home without them had filled her with panic. Mayflowers appeared in early spring, when there was leftover snow on the ground, when there was the likelihood of more snow to come. Sometimes the snow lasted until June and the time for mayflowers slipped past. You had to be lucky to find them. You had to move quickly. Together Madge and Nonie ripped apart the hillside, kicking at clumps of soil, tearing up fistfuls of grass, trying to uncover the tiny pink-white flowers whose fragrance was so exquisitely pungent that the presence of a small bouquet was everywhere inside the house.

"What I remember about that afternoon was how fierce you were," Nonie says. "You were in tears. You were frantic about the possibility of not finding mayflowers."

"Was I as serious as all that?" Madge says, though she knew she had been. She had been young enough then to feel desperate about pleasing her mother, something she grew out of later on.

"I remember we used to tiptoe around your mother," Nonie says. "We had to be careful not to close the fridge door because she was lying down." Nonie arranges herself cross-legged in front of Madge. "I never did understand that. I suppose because my mother never slowed down long enough to take a nap. She was always off playing the organ, doing church work or something. Was your mother sick or what?"

"She had high blood pressure," Madge says. "Before we moved to Cape Breton, she spent nearly a year in bed with TB. We treated her like a china doll locked inside a glass case."

"I can't remember my mother ever being sick," Nonie says.

"I used to think my mother was holding back something," Madge says. "I don't think she was. I just thought she was. Because of the glass case. We weren't allowed too close to her for fear of catching TB." Madge stares into the fire. "The fact is I was fascinated by her. I used to lie on her bed and watch her breathe. For some reason I found that interesting."

"Well, I certainly knew what made my mother tick," Nonie says. "She told me in spades. Many times. Maybe your mother left more to the imagination."

"Did I ever tell you I never wept when my mother died?" Madge says. "I always thought that was odd, considering how I felt about her."

"No, you never told me that," Nonie says. "You never said much about her death, beyond the fact that it was an accident. We never talked about it."

"She was hit by a truck when she was crossing the street. The young man who was driving the truck was back on the road the next day. He didn't even have his licence taken away. He nearly hit someone else two weeks later when he was driving the same truck. My mother's sister, Margaret, was there when the accident happened. She insisted that my mother had walked in front of the truck. She made it sound as if it was deliberate. I was so angry about all that going on that I couldn't cry."

"I don't think crying means much anyway," Nonie says. "Take me for instance. I'm so sentimental I cry over anything." Nonie tells Madge about the Saturday afternoon she dragged the ironing board in front of the TV so she could watch *Lassie Come Home* again, knowing full well she'd cry when the boy came out of the school and found the dog waiting for him. "I cried so much I didn't need to dampen the shirts." Nonie laughs. "Water, water, everywhere."

"Nor any drop to drink," Madge says, and pours more wine.

Nonie gets out lox, bagels, cream cheese, caviar. Rain drums on the roof. They hear the surf booming far below on the beach. Embers fall through the grate. There is a daybed on either side of the room and, eventually, after they've eaten the bagels and finished the wine, they tumble into bed. They close their eyes and, like fallen trees bobbing drunkenly on the waves, they drift toward the shore of sleep.

At three o'clock the phone shrills on the kitchen counter. Madge heaves herself out of sleep and stumbles over a chair on her way to answer.

"Christ," she mutters, "doesn't she know what time it is here?" *Of course she does.* Madge fumbles across the wall for the light switch, flicks it on and picks up the phone. *Steady now. You gave her the number, remember?*

"Hello."

"Mum, is that you?"

Who else would it be? "Yes, it's me."

"Mum?"

"Yes?"

"Mum. I've got to ask you something important."

Alison's voice is heavy and wet, dragged out of a swamp. Madge knows this means she's probably spent the night bingeing, that she's exhausted, her throat and stomach sore from throwing up. Madge's head throbs at one temple. She shifts the receiver to the left hand and presses her right hand against the pain.

"Fire away," she says.

"Mum." She hears Alison's intake of breath. "Mum, when Dad left, what was it that kept you alive? Was it us kids?"

There it is laid out on the ground like a dead animal, a doe. Her eldest daughter had been hunting in the woods, stalking this deer for months, maybe years, preparing to shoot it. And here it is. Thrown at Madge's feet.

Alison was the one who took over after Doug left and Madge went to bed for most of a year. The eldest of Madge's four children, Alison showed the forbearance of a saint. She was the one who was the most responsible, the most anxious and attentive, and she is now making up for it. Sometimes Madge thinks Alison is trying to find a way to sainthood, to punish and scourge herself into becoming selfless and pure-hearted. What saves Alison from going this far is righteous anger. At least this is what Madge tells herself when the anger is being directed toward her.

Madge pushes hard against her temple and concentrates on the doe. She wants to bury it but, if she does, Alison will only dig it up. Madge circles round and round, nudging the body with her foot, but it lies there lifeless on the ground.

She knows what Alison wants. She wants to be told that it was she, more than any of the others, who kept her mother alive, that when Madge's eyes finally focused on her children's faces, it was Alison's she saw most clearly. Madge has told Alison this many times. She's willing to repeat it if necessary. But if she does, Alison could say, once again, "What about me? I have no kids. Why should I stay alive?"

Madge slides to the floor and leans her head against the cold metal handle of the fridge.

"I guess," she says slowly, "I guess what kept me alive was not wanting to die."

In Death's cold arms.

"I was young. I had the rest of my life ahead of me." Madge stops. Then goes on, "Like you have."

Silence.

This is not enough.

"Since then, it's been easier," Madge corrects herself, "mostly easier, I'm fine now. Just fine." Madge feels the metal handle dig into her temple. "I have a satisfying life."

She stops, waits. Then she says, "And you can have a satisfying life too, Ally, once you get over this hump."

"Maybe I don't want a satisfying life," Alison says, and hangs up.

Pain shoots across Madge's forehead. She goes into the bathroom and rummages in her cosmetic kit for Aspirins. When she comes back, she sees Nonie lying awake watching her.

"What's her doctor say?"

"Ha! She refuses to talk to me. Weeks go by without me hearing a thing from her or from Alison. Then I'll get a call like tonight. I'm trying to stay out of it, but I feel at this stage I've got to hang in there, keep in close touch. Her doctor doesn't agree. Once I phoned and she said (Madge pitches her voice high), *'Mrs. Ogilvey, you must remember this is Alison's problem. You have to leave her alone to work it out.'"* Madge switches off the light. "I wonder if she's a mother," she says and gets into bed.

In the morning Madge wakens before Nonie. She dresses and goes outside. The storm has left behind a clear blue sky, an azure sea. She chooses a path through the woods, moist and green, lush with mossy trees and bracken. She passes one of the rustic cabins. Pink clematis climbs over the chimney, spills off the roof. Purple wisteria weeps onto the grass. A slug the colour of soapstone inches along the path. Madge rubs its back with a twig as she used to as a child and the slug stretches luxuriously. She begins picking the flowering shrubs: forsythia, copper broom, rhododendron. She takes her time, enjoying the cool drops of water spraying onto her bare, warm skin. She picks until her arms are overflowing. Then she carries the flowers back to the cabin, tiptoes inside, and fills two bottles and a jar with water. She arranges the flowers and places them around the room. She puts the jar on the floor beside Nonie.

Nonie wakens, sits up.

"Get back in bed." She speaks sternly. "I'll bring you coffee."

Years ago Madge used to crawl back to bed on Mother's Day to please her children. When they were school age, her children brought her clumsily wrapped mugs, soap, bath salts, notepaper, and handmade cards, settling themselves onto the bed covers to watch her open and exclaim.

Madge gets under the covers.

Nonie serves the espresso with glasses of Bailey's Irish Cream.

Madge props herself up with pillows, leans back against the wall.

"Oh my," she says. "This is something." There are dark circles beneath her eyes.

They drink their coffee and liqueur, staring at the sea.

Nonie lights a candle, carries it into the bathroom, and takes a bath, using the new bar of sandalwood soap she has brought along. Then, while Madge bathes, watching the candlelight flicker off the white-tiled walls, Nonie makes breakfast.

She serves warm pears with whipped cream. On top of the cream are two forsythia leaves dipped in crème de menthe. This is followed by eggs Benedict, croissants.

Nonie holds a croissant in front of Madge like a microphone.

"Ms. Ogilvey," Nonie says, dragging out the *Mizz,* "would you tell me what you think of Mother's Day after all these years? I'm sure our listeners would like to hear from one of our, ah, more *seasoned* mothers."

"Seasoned, my foot. *Broken in,* is more like it."

"But the day itself?"

Madge bites the end off a croissant.

"I like it," she grins, "especially the food."

"Seriously."

"Seriously, it's just another day, or almost, now that my kids are nearly grown. Naturally I'd like my kids to acknowledge the day with a card or a note, but no fuss.

A fuss embarrasses me. It reminds me of the mistakes I've made. What do *you* think of Mother's Day?"

"Well, the last few years, Mother's Day has been a charade. Except for Pauline. The boys usually forget about it. At least I think they do, especially now that they have girlfriends. I think Stuart buys the gifts and signs their names. Sometimes I think I should put a stop to such nonsense. Other times I think I'd miss it if I did. I have to admit I feel I deserve a bit of fuss." Madge dips the last of her croissant into honey and pops it into her mouth. She leans back in her chair, pats her belly, and says, "I'm absolutely stuffed."

They take their coffee outside to the deck chairs. They move the chairs into an enclosure of sunlight and sit listening to the waves far below the cliff. Madge closes her eyes.

"Pauline," she murmurs drowsily. "How's Pauline?"

After a while Nonie says, "Well she's given up thinking she's a daughter of a Czech princess, which is something."

Pauline's adopted. Nonie has already told Madge some of the difficulties she's had with Pauline. Not Stuart. Apparently Stuart and Pauline get along just fine.

"I think she was too young for the information I gave her," Nonie says. "She was only five years old when she asked me why her real mother didn't keep her."

Nonie and Pauline were lying together beside a lake in the mountains while Stuart was off fishing with the boys. Pauline had crawled into Nonie's sleeping bag. She began playing with Nonie's breasts, probing the soft flesh. She stuck a finger into Nonie's navel.

"Is that where I grew?"

"No. You grew inside someone else's belly."

"Oh. What was her name?"

"I don't know."

"If I came out of *her* belly, why didn't she keep me?"

Nonie told Pauline that her birth-mother had wanted to keep her but she couldn't. She was sixteen, still a girl herself. Nonie explained about the girl's parents, that the family managed to get out of Czechoslovakia before the Russians clamped down, that they had owned a house in Prague the size of a castle and a country place in the mountains, which they had to give up when they defected. (The social worker had told Nonie all this, it wasn't on the forms.) Nonie told Pauline the family had arrived in Canada penniless, with only the clothes on their backs. It was a large family, eight children. With all those mouths to feed the girl couldn't bring herself to tell her parents about her pregnancy. She ran away instead. Nonie told Pauline that the girl wanted to keep her but she couldn't. She didn't have a job. She was still in high school. There was no way she could support a tiny baby.

"I never should have used the word 'castle,'" Nonie says. "That's what got Pauline started on the princess business. I probably told her more than she wanted to know." Nonie sighs. "Just like my mother."

"Well, she might have imagined herself a princess without your help," Madge said. "When Theo was eight years old, he was convinced he was adopted because he didn't look like the others. He made up a story about his father being a hockey player."

"When the nightmares and the tantrums started, I went to a shrink," Nonie says. "He told me I should tell Pauline her birth-mother didn't want to keep her, that she would have to face the fact that not all mothers want their children. He told me there was nothing sacrosanct about giving birth. I told him I would never tell Pauline that her birth-mother didn't want her. She was simply trying to do what was best for her daughter."

Madge doesn't ask Nonie if she remembers the woman who threw her daughters into the Bow River because she failed to produce a son, then jumped in the water herself, holding her newborn daughter. Fortunately, Pauline's birth-mother wasn't that desperate.

Instead Madge says, "I once did a piece called the *Madonna Feast*. It was part of a series I did on eating, our food rituals: you know, the birthday party, the picnic, the tea party, the wedding banquet, the Last Supper. It was when I began to take sculpture seriously." It pleases Madge that she creates painted sculptures out of something as unassuming as papier mâché, that her apprenticeship evolved when she did art projects in the basement with her children. She feels proud and oddly defiant about this, that all the time she was mothering—and mismanaging her marriage— she was transforming a mess of wet, gluey paper into her own landscape, she was finding a way to rescue herself.

"You might say it was a round table of mothers," Madge says. "There was an artist, a nurse, a secretary, a quilt maker, a teacher, a cleaning lady, a cook." She laughs. "The Virgin Mary was pouring."

For a long time neither she nor Nonie speaks. They sit listening to the sea. The tide has gone out and the water laps soothingly against the sand. Eventually they get up and stroll down to the beach. Steps have been built down the cliffside. Salmonberry bushes arch overhead, making their descent one of alternating light and shade. They clamber across the rocks at the end of the beach, searching tidal pools for exotic underwater flowers.

When they tire of poking in rock pools, they sit on a giant log beneath a red alder. The tree leans over the sand, its long drooping branches protecting them from the sun. Behind them giant trees rock softly in the breeze.

"Let's play hopscotch," Nonie says. She picks up a sharp stick and draws two rows of squares at the tideline where the sand is firm. Madge collects two crab shells, hollow orange stones. She was never good at hopscotch. As a child she lacked fluidity, was all angles and bones. But she's willing to play hopscotch now, to humour Nonie. They play with cheerful determination, dragging their knees up for each jump, then thumping heavily onto the sand on thick, peasant ankles. As they play, the tide comes in, flattened waves looping across the sand.

Madge is surprised that she would like to win this game, that she cares. Why should either of them care, both of them cut loose, drifting ashore with the tide. This need to win is the quietest of impulses, an echo, yet it teases, pokes urgently in deepest corners. *You think you don't care if you win or lose, that you've moved beyond that, but you do care, you do.* Madge recognizes the point of origin, a harsher coast where there are icebergs and mayflowers, where she often felt she was coming from behind. She still feels this. Sometimes Madge is surprised she likes Nonie so much. Women who seem to have everything don't interest Madge. She thinks they are likely to be smug. She prefers a woman with a tougher edge, preferably a woman with plenty of mistakes in her past. A few setbacks. Disadvantages. Nonie hasn't made many mistakes. She hasn't had many setbacks. She has been lucky. Like Madge's sister, Ardith, Nonie has worked hard for advantages. They weren't handed to her, she went after them. Madge remembers Nonie used to be good at sports. She played volleyball and badminton, tennis. Even when she and Madge played cards Nonie usually won. Madge never tried to change this. If Nonie wanted to come out on top so badly (Nonie would often pull away, become aloof with concentration), then let her. If Madge had tried harder, if the odds had been on her side, she could have won oftener. Or so she thinks.

Madge watches as Nonie backs up for the final jump, crouches like a sprinter and makes a run for it. Nonie leaps over two squares, lands on one foot exactly in the middle square, bends down and picks up her shell before hopscotching lightly over the last three squares.

"I made it!"

Madge knows Nonie is so far ahead that beating her would require more energy than she is willing to give. Madge prefers to give in gracefully. That way she keeps her magnanimity intact. Madge is helped along by the rhythmic waves and moist scented air, which have entered her skin and made her lethargic and nirvanic. Lying there on the sand, she feels satiated, drugged, as if she's marooned on an enchanted isle.

"Do mermaids have children?" she asks.

"Probably," Nonie says. "After all, there are mermen."

"Then how come we don't see any merchildren?"

"They grow up fast and leave home early," Nonie says solemnly.

"Leaving their mothers free to swim the oceans," Madge says dreamily. She gets up, tosses her shell toward the middle square, and misses. When she leans over to pick up the shell, she loses her balance and flops down laughing. She rolls onto her back, leans on her elbows, and looks at her feet. There's a corn on the little toe of each foot.

"See what happens to a beached mermaid?" she says. "She grows feet with corns on them." She lies back and closes her eyes. "I think I might stay in lotus-land indefinitely."

"You do that," Nonie says briskly. "I'll bring us back some lunch."

Nonie goes back through the tunnel and up the cliff to the cabin. Madge feels no obligation to follow her up, to help in the kitchen. She feels like being indulged, fussed over, though not by her children. She will take whatever is being offered without apology or regret, to make up for possible inequities, disproportions. She languishes on the beach thinking *fresh crab on lettuce, Camembert, cold white wine.*

Real Life Writes Real Bad

TIMOTHY FINDLEY

I HAD AN ACCIDENT, once, and my dog was killed. This was a long time ago. I'd been riding my bike and the dog, whose name was Danny, had been running along beside me on the road. It was a country road and there was a lot of dust because it hadn't rained. A truck came by and it knocked me off my bike and Danny went under the wheels and he disappeared. The truck drove on and Danny's body went on with it.

Bud, my brother, came running—I don't remember where he'd been. I refused to leave the side of the road. My arm was fractured and my legs were pitted with gravel and they were bleeding—but this was nothing compared to my grief and the shock of Danny's disappearance. "I won't go home without him," I said. "I'd rather stay here and die."

Bud said: "Okay Neil. I'll go and get him." Just like that: an everyday occurrence.

One whole hour he was gone. I remember that afternoon precisely—every detail. I crouched beside the road and I brushed away the flies that were coming after my legs and I kept my eye on the long, hot road where Bud had gone out of sight beyond a railroad track. The heat—it was July 15th—made waves in the air and I think I was close to fainting when I finally saw him coming back.

I swear I saw him growing before my eyes, that day. He was like a man we had seen unfolding from a box at the circus, once. The box had been collapsed with the man inside and when the magician waved his wand, the box was whole again and the man came out. And that was Bud that afternoon. A miracle.

He was carrying Danny, dead, in his arms and he said: "We can go now. I found him." The dog had been lying in a ditch full of water, two miles down the road. I guess the driver had thrown him there.

We left my broken bike behind and we went back home to where our mother was waiting. It wasn't really home, but a farm where we'd been staying. This was the summer of 1941 when our dad was in the army and Bud was twelve and I was ten.

"Danny is dead," Bud told our mother. "But this dog's alive." He put his hand on my head and smiled.

Bud thought—even then—that each scene had to have its tag-line. *This dog is dead*, Errol Flynn had said in *Captain Farrago*. *But this dog is still alive....*

In spite of all that's happened since and all the hell he's put us through, I often recall the image of Bud unfolding along the road that afternoon, as if the magician had waved his wand and out had stepped my brother—whole—with Danny in his arms.

He might have thought he was Errol Flynn; who cares? To me, it's the only image I have of Bud the way he was before his dreams took over; the ones about the end of time and the ones about the box before it was collapsed.

I GUESS WE WERE ALL EXPECTING IT—all of us prepared for the worst—but everyone praying it wouldn't happen yet. This is what they call the Scarlett O'Hara syndrome. You know the one: *I'll think about that tomorrow.* The only trouble is, in real life, tomorrow has a funny way of turning up today.

Bud always had a love of books and a prodigious memory. The two, when combined, produced his unpleasant habit of dropping acid quotes into life's worst moments. Bud was the one who was always there to remind you how many times he'd told you not to play with matches, just when you'd burned the house down.

Sadly, he wasn't good at using this fund of plagiarized wisdom when it came to himself. For instance, the day we found him, a piece of paper was discovered—by the telephone—on which Bud had carefully written out for someone else's benefit a poem by Dorothy Parker. Here it is—but you have to imagine Bud's handwritten version of it, the way he made all the letters perfect because he was so afraid he'd lost his powers of concentration. In the margin he had written: *Hartley—484 9842—April 2.* And then:

Razors pain you;
Rivers are damp;
Acids stain you;

And drugs cause cramp.
Guns aren't lawful;
Nooses give;
Gas smells awful;
You might as well live.

Bud's oldest friend, Teddy Hartley, killed himself on April 9th.

IT MAY WELL BE that I'm maligning Bud by saying he never applied his found advice to himself. All I have to go on is my witness. And my witness was that Bud ignored all good advice—the way most desperadoes do—until it was too late. Maybe, on the other hand—just before his brain burned out—he did remember what he'd written down on that piece of paper for Teddy Hartley. And maybe it made him want to live. I'll never know, but my guess would be—it made him laugh.

WAS BUD, my brother, a true desperado?

Yes; I think he was. He lived his life strung out as far away from reality as he could get. Back when he was twenty-seven, Bud decided life had been best when he was twenty-six. Time must be made to stop if he was going to survive. And so he chose to live in a world rendered timeless by alcohol.

BUD WAS A DESTRUCTIVE MAN and people turned away from him in droves. He wasn't easy to take; he came, almost, to delight in driving you away. When I add up all there is to say, I'd have to say I didn't like my brother, Bud. I loved him, though.

If I had been a writer and if Bud had been a person in a story, this is where, in that story, there would be a description of Bud before the fall, in all his glory. That way, in stories, writers justify their failing heroes. The trouble is, Bud had no glory. What he had, instead, was anti-glory: fear and rage and disappointment.

All his life, Bud wanted out of being who he was. It wasn't so much that he hated being Thomas "Bud" Cable as the fact that Thomas "Bud" Cable hadn't been given "the breaks." Everyone else, according to Bud, had been given something at birth that made for an easy passage. Money, looks and talent were the main things he lacked. He also lacked what he called "a name to go by," meaning he might have managed getting by if his name, at birth, had been John Paul Getty.

Bud never knew this was funny, by the way. Once he retired from the world he never got the chance to see that everyone else might want a different birthright than the one they had. That even Errol Flynn might want to be Cary Grant.

Katie, Bud's wife, once asked him why he didn't go out and make his own fortune "instead of hanging around the house waiting for the money tree to bloom."

Bud said he couldn't do that.

"Why not?" said Katie. "Everybody else does."

"I know," said Bud. "But it takes them so *long....*"

When Katie told me this, I laughed out loud and said: "so much for money!"

"No," said Katie, "so much for work."

BUD NOT ONLY WANTED OUT of who he was, he wanted out of his body, too. He would stand in front of mirrors and curse the elongation of his bones.

"Look at my head," he would say, his voice always rising up the scale and getting louder. "Look at the shape of my fucking head! It's like a goddamned shoe box!" he'd yell. "A goddamned shoe box and the fucking shoes inside are goddamned size fourteen!"

Every time he looked, you might have thought he'd never seen himself in mirrors or photographs before. He was constantly appalled and panic-stricken by what he saw. He always cringed while peering at himself through narrowed eyes—a voyeur watching through a window. "Look at his hands!" he would say as if the person in the mirror wasn't him. "Look at the size of his bloody hands, Neil!"

This much was true: Bud stood so tall he had to crouch when passing through doorways, reaching up with his fingers to protect the top of his head. He stooped wherever he went and he even stooped when he was lying down—his middle caved, his legs drawn up, his back an arabesque. All his clothes were bought at what he called The Grotesquery on King Street East—a store for oversized men and women. Katie had to do the shopping. Bud had gone there once, but the size of the exaggerated mannikins had traumatized him. "I don't really look like that," he kept repeating. "Tell me I don't really look like that...." He didn't, of course, but nothing would persuade him of it.

He told me, once, he'd had a dream in which there was a spa for the oversized. "They can perform an operation there where they saw your bones in half," he said. "You go to sleep and wake up two feet shorter!" There were also magic baths in which you steamed your height away. *Contraction Waters,* they were called. *Shrinkage guaranteed!*

But the best thing of all, Bud said, was the fact they had "a magic shampoo for reducing the size of shoe-box heads...."

It was sad, I guess. Bud didn't like to walk in the streets. He became alarmed when the prospect opened up that he might be asked to meet a stranger. "What will they say," he would ask, "when they see me?"

Somehow, it never occurred to him they might just say *hello.*

DURING BUD'S EARLY REVELS, Katie would join him, lending her sense of fun to everything he did. She withdrew only when, at last, it came to be obvious that Bud had no intention of stopping. Ever. It took until they were in their early forties for this to happen—not until their money was running out and their friends had begun to turn down their invitations. The trouble was, Bud showed no inclination to believe that either dwindling funds or loss of friends had anything to do with how much he drank.

Neither was he inclined to support his drinking habit by getting a job. I'm talking about the early-to-mid-1970s here, and Bud had not set foot inside the workplace since 1962 when, for a month, he had answered a telephone somewhere downtown for one of those fly-by-night firms that used to sell household cleaning products after midnight on television. Bud, in fact, didn't answer anything. He listened to a recording device on which the potential customers were meant to leave their names and addresses. The reason he quit this job, so he told me at length in one of his endless monologues, was because so many of the recorded phone calls were obscene. *The world,* he informed me, *is a rotten apple and to hell with it!*

Bud was a man who could deliver a two-hour tirade on almost any given subject, drop of a hat. His diatribes were unencumbered by reason and as time went on they became his only mode of conversation. Increasingly the focus of these harangues was reality itself—though Bud, of course, would never have called it that. He would have called it *the great conspiracy* or *the universal menace* or *the sinister intruder.* Reality was anything—or anyone—that challenged the rightness of Bud's withdrawal from society. It was, of course, a psychotic withdrawal—but those who loved him, myself included, refused to see that. To us, Bud must not be thought of as insane—because he must always be seen as someone who, having gone astray, could return to the fold through an act of will. Our mother was always saying this in Bud's behalf. *His reason will bring him back to us,* she'd say. *He only needs to come to his senses and exercise his will.* But alcohol—if not the alcoholic—repudiates the will. It has no tolerance for anything connected with the self.

This way, as Bud went all the way downhill and finally took up residence at the bottom, I, too, became less tolerant of reality. I only mean where Bud was concerned. Reality was so predictable. It operated entirely without imagination. It might as well have been a textbook. Besides which, it had such bad taste. Imagine Thomas Cable, Jr.—Bud—ensconced in his suit and tie—his shoes highly polished—his hair and his fingernails impeccable—sitting in his darkened living-room at noon with his bottles of Beaujolais at hand—raising his glass to his lips and his gaze upon the flickering screen that has become his only companion.

"What are you watching?" I ask, when I telephone.

"Roger Ramjet," Bud informs me. "Don't interrupt me, now. I'll talk to you later on."

And he hangs up.

This was Bud, aged fifty-four.

WHEN KATIE DIED, I had to tell him over and over she was gone and in the grave. He simply did not believe me. Not because he was obtuse—(perhaps the alcohol was obtuse)—but because the image of Katie dead could not be made to fit into what he thought was reality. Death was not proper. It couldn't just walk in like that and take up residence. Bud had not accounted for it in his scheme of things.

He refused to come to the lying-in. He said it was a put-up job.

"You're lying, Neil," he said to me. "You're only trying to protect her because you've always taken her side in everything...."

"No, Bud," I'd say to him—(we had this conversation at least four times)—"Katie had cancer and died."

He would look at me then, as if I was a traitor. Katie wasn't dead. She wasn't even sick.

We had known she was dying for over eight months. The cancer was in her lung. Bud had not even gone to visit her in the hospital. He claimed she was "away somewhere."

"She's having an affair," he insisted.

The grave, I'm afraid, meant nothing to Bud. It was just another of Katie's wild excuses to ignore his needs.

HERE'S WHAT HAPPENED—and the only reason I'm telling you this is that I want to put it on record. I want someone to know. The way some lives work out, you'd think the King of Clichés came in to write them. Bud's life was like that: shabby; squalid, like Katie's death.

I am an actor—and because I am an actor, I have had—for almost forty years— contact with well-written lives. When an actor throws up his hands and cannot manage to play a role, his response is always going to be: *I can't do this because I don't believe it.*

Katie's death and the nominal "end" of my brother's life were like that. No one in their right mind could make them believable. The facts and the images are too banal for words. Embarrassing.

THE WORST OF KATIE'S CONDITION came when she needed oxygen and nursing care at home. All this was seen as an inconvenience of monumental proportions from Bud's point of view.

A nurse, whose name was Sandra Ossington, came to give Katie baths and to oversee the regimen of pills and the supply of oxygen. Sometimes, when very drunk, Bud wouldn't let Ms. Ossington come in. He'd lock the door and shout at her: *go away!* Katie then had to barricade herself in her room for fear that Bud would come in with a cigarette when she had the oxygen turned on.

The canisters of oxygen would be delivered by a man on schedule. He would always take away the expended tank and replace it with the new. He did this by rote according to a list that was given to him every day. He could hardly afford the time to say *hello,* let alone the time to argue about his right to enter the house. Once, when Katie was desperate to breathe and the oxygen man arrived, she had to phone the police in order to have Bud restrained. In the meantime, the oxygen man was forced to continue on his rounds because his other clients' needs were just the same as Katie's: a matter of life and death.

After that incident, Katie left Bud and their rented house in Scarborough and came down into Forest Hill, where she stayed with her cousin Jean. Jean gave me a call and said: "we're going to have to take Katie in. She can't go home again."

So a system was devised whereby—to all intents and purposes—Katie played the fugitive, "hiding out" first with Jean and then with me and then with a friend from work whose name was Gloria.

Gloria hated Bud with alarming vehemence. She once went up and threatened to burn the house down if Bud didn't let her in to collect Katie's things. This was about six weeks before Katie died and I guess we were all on Gloria's side and cheered her on. That's when Bud decided his wife was having an affair. He even went so far as to say she was having the affair with Gloria. Gloria had to be restrained.

The image of Bud and Gloria shouting on the lawn is funny, I suppose. Or it would be—perhaps—if Katie hadn't been so badly off. Shortly thereafter, she went into Sunnybrook Hospital—called every day for Bud—never heard from him and died.

THE LAST TIME I saw Katie myself before she went into Sunnybrook, she was standing off in the distance, unaware that I was there. This was at the White Rose Nursery out in Unionville, and I had gone to buy a fern or something. Katie always made a garden wherever she lived with Bud and she left behind about a dozen perfect flower beds filled with her need for sanity and peace. I guess that day in Unionville she was making up for the fact she would never walk in a garden again. I saw the look of loss on her face and turned around and walked away. It was unbearable: the loneliness.

I'VE ALREADY SAID Bud wouldn't come to the lying-in. A mass of others came instead—and that was the one good moment in all of this, the moment when all the twenty years of tension fell away and all the friends came through the door of the funeral home to say goodbye. I'm glad I was there; it gave me back—in that moment—something tangible of hope.

The burial itself was sad. Bud stood shaking when he saw the coffin. That was the moment when it dawned on him: *Katie is dead and gone forever.* He sat down hard on the ground beside the grave and his mouth fell open when he tried to speak. I had to go and lift him up and lead him away because, when he started to move, he seemed to want to follow her.

Later, though—and who am I to say it was not a blessing?—Bud denied being present at the funeral. How could he have been present when it hadn't even happened?

THE PHONE RANG twice every day all summer after that—(Katie died in May). By the fall, Bud was calling up at four o'clock in the morning, begging me to say he wasn't going to die. Somehow, if someone said it, he seemed to be genuinely reassured. Afterwards, he would natter on about what meals he'd eaten, where he'd been and who he'd seen.

The food was all-important. He could talk for hours about it.

I don't know why I believed him—but, like a fool, I did. He was so convincing, the way he told about the cuts of meat he would buy at Loblaws and the way he had cooked the potatoes—and all the herbs he used when making up the salad. His meals were almost poems to listen to. He loved the names of all the vegetables: *broccoli, spinach, zucchini* and he'd tell me which wines he'd drunk and he complained of all the prices.

He also had a lot to say about the friends who had begun to return his calls—the houses he had been in and the restaurants downtown. His social life was picking up. He was a normal human being again.

That was the trigger, of course: the word *again*. Bud had never been a normal human being in all his adult life.

Just about then it was getting on for a year since Katie's death and it was nearly May, Bud's birthday month. The phone calls—now that I wanted them—stopped. I had thought, since he was going about in the world, I would take him out for supper. Bud and I had not been out together for a century.

I waited for a week before I began the process in reverse. I called him three and four times a day. He didn't answer.

I telephoned our mother.

I didn't want to alarm her. I tried to say it diffidently, laughing because he was leaving me alone for a change. But I was interested … had she heard from Bud?

No.

Her story was more or less the same as mine. She had been receiving the same reports: the food—the outings—the friends. Now, for several days, there had been nothing.

"I'll go around and see what's happening," I told her. Finally, I was worried. Very.

LOOKING AT THE HOUSE, I knew there was something wrong. Some of the lights were on. The car was parked in the driveway. I turned around and went away. I couldn't bear the thought of finding him dead.

I got the police and they had to break down the door. I waited on the lawn while they called for an ambulance. Someone barely alive had been found inside the house: almost a skeleton.

THE CORRIDOR WAS DARK and filled with beds and between the beds a stream of people, most of them hospital staff, was flowing—it seemed—almost entirely in my direction. All of them were blank-eyed; busy. At the nursing station they had said that I would find my brother down this corridor somewhere near the end.

I was walking towards a patch of vivid sunlight streaming through a window—almost blinding because the corridor was like a cave. There were three or four wheelchairs parked with their backs to me—facing this window—draped with rugs and ostensibly containing passengers, although I could see no evidence of this. There weren't any legs or arms or the backs of any heads that I could see.

"I'm looking for my brother, Thomas Cable," I said to an orderly who had just been arranging the wheelchairs in the sunlight.

The orderly said, without inflection: "you're standing right beside him. That's his chair you have your hand on." I walked around and stood in front of Bud.

Before me sat a man of almost eighty—whose mouth was hanging open and whose hands lay helpless in his lap—whose legs were so weak and thin they lay against each other, caved in against the side of the chair. His neck would barely support his head and his chin was resting on his collar-bone. I knelt before this man and called him *Bud* and told him who I was.

He stirred—uneasy—and he tried to move his hands and lift his chin, but he couldn't. I did that for him.

Looking back at me, he struggled desperately to understand why I should know his name and why he should think I seemed to be someone he knew. But he could not manage this. I was a stranger to him.

"How old is he?" the orderly asked.

"He's fifty-six," I said.

The orderly grunted.

"He can't have eaten in almost a month," he said.

I smiled. I thought of all the meals that Bud had described—and all the restaurants and all the wine.

"He's been on a liquid diet," I said—as lightly as I could.

THE DOCTOR—a knowledgeable, pleasant little man whose sunny disposition somewhat threw me until I got to know him better—told me that Bud was suffering from something called Korsakov's syndrome. In short, this means that a part of Bud's brain has been destroyed and that, while he might live for many years, he will never recover the whole of his past and never quite understand who he is. He will know his name and he will recognize, from time to time, some specific incident from his life. Otherwise, Bud is locked—and will remain so—in a time zone from which he cannot escape.

He knows me, now, but every time I visit, he behaves as if we were at home and children and he wants to know where I have been.

You look so old, he will say to me. *Why have you grown so much older than me?*

I do not respond to this. I simply acknowledge that I am aberrant and Bud accepts this fact as being sufficient explanation. Sometimes, he smiles. I guess he knows what aberrant means.

He wants to see our parents and I have to tell him—every visit—that our mother has been ill and cannot come, just now, to see him. And then I have to tell him— every visit—that our father is dead and Bud is not surprised, but merely curious that his father could die and Bud not know it. *He must have died while I was away,* he will say. And I say nothing.

Every visit, too, he asks me where he is and who *these people* are. I do not tell him he is in a clinic for the aged because this would distress him. He does not know that he will not be leaving. He recognizes it must be some kind of rest home because the nurses and the doctors come and go and, time to time, somebody dies and is taken away.

On one occasion he asks me; "am I mad?"

I tell him: "no. You have been ill and we don't know why."

"Will you come and see me?"

"Yes."

"I get very lonely here," he says. "But the food is good."

I smile.

He looks at me, crooked—Bud grown old, a very old man—and he says: "I'm missing someone, Neil. And I don't know who it is."

I hold his hand. He is greatly distressed and he rides along the edge of what remains of memory—peering out into the dark and trying desperately to see who might be there and to remember.

"Never mind," I tell him. "Honestly; no one is missing. Everything's fine."

"Where has our father gone?" he says.

I tell him. And I leave.

EVERY SO OFTEN—maybe fifteen times a year—we will hold this meeting until he dies.

THE DAY THE POLICE broke down the door and found him, I went with him to the hospital and gave him up in all his blankets and sheets to the doctors and the nurses in the Emergency Ward. Being told there was nothing to be done but wait and see if he would survive, I decided to return and await the news in Bud and Katie's rented house.

When I got there, it was nearing four o'clock in the afternoon and Katie's black cat was sitting on the porch. His name was Bubastis and we had met before.

Bubastis, however, would not come into the house. He seemed confused and wary and he kept his distance. I supposed he must be after food—he looked so thin—and I guessed that Bud had given up feeding him. Perhaps he had been coming for days to sit on the porch in the hopes that Bud would open the door and put down his meal.

I wished then, fervently, that we could talk to animals. How else could I explain to this beast that Katie was dead and Bud was probably going to die—as I thought that afternoon—and I would be more than happy to take Bubastis back with me to my house….

But no. He would have to wonder, perhaps forever, where all his people had gone and why they had deserted him. He went away and sat in the yard and I went into the house.

I opened a can of cat food and put the whole thing, dumped on a plate, onto the porch and called him.

"Bubastis!"

He did not come while I was standing there, but he must have come in the next half-hour because when I returned to the porch both the cat and all the food had disappeared.

Inside the house I found a wilderness of bottles and glasses and a maze of unmade beds, undusted furniture and piled-up cardboard boxes.

I looked and saw where Bud had been found. He had been lying—dressed in slacks and shirt, bare-footed, facing Katie's bed—in the hallway between their rooms. His own dark bedroom was behind him and the sheets on his bed were grey with age. On Katie's pillow, a note was pinned with a safety-pin and the note was in Katie's hand and it said: *Bud—Honey—I am going now and I won't be back. I've left a hundred dollars hidden in the hall closet. Look in the usual place and it will be there. I'm scared, right now, and I guess the thing is, soon I'm going to die. I wish you would come and see me. I will always love you, honey. Thank you for everything. Katie.*

She could only have written this before she made her escape to her cousin Jean, and that had been over a year ago. In all that time, the note had remained on Katie's pillow—and her bed exactly as she left it: the coverlet thrown back—the nightdress abandoned—her glass of water spilled and fallen to the floor.

In the kitchen, the smell was that of an abattoir; all the raw meat was so far gone it was alive with maggots. Bags of potatoes were sprouting in the corner. The sink was filled with dishes and the only evidence of food Bud might have truly eaten was a brace of opened and empty cans of Habitant pea soup. Four or five wide, flat boxes indicated that pizza had been delivered—but none of it had been removed and all of it was now a rotted sequence of red-and-yellow wheels.

Bud must have had some temper tantrums. Several dishes were broken—cigarettes and ash had been scattered over the floor and a case of beer appeared to have been struck a dozen blows by a hammer.

The living-room, which had once been charming under Katie's hand, was the wilderness already described of opened and unopened liquor bottles and glasses. Ashtrays were sprouting mould. A mouse had drowned in a vase of flowers. The telephone sat beside Bud's chair—unanswered all those days—and the television set was playing one of the soaps. I turned it off.

There by the telephone, neatly printed in Bud's distinctive hand, were Teddy Hartley's telephone number, the date—April 2—and Dorothy Parker's poem.

I hoped, in that moment, for everyone's sake—especially his own—that Bud would die. That was the option he had chosen. And I had screwed it up by sending in the police.

I GOT DOWN off the porch where the cat had finished the food and I went along the driveway past the garbage cans and into the large backyard.

Here, I was confronted by what I can only call the last bloody straw.

Katie's beloved flower beds had all spilled out across the uncut lawn—and the only thing in bloom was a mile-and-a-half wide carpet of forget-me-nots.

Forget-me-nots.

I ask you!

And sitting right in the middle, black as the ace of spades, was the cat, Bubastis—staring at me—asking me: *why?*

ON EITHER SIDE OF THE FIREPLACE, back in the living-room, all of Bud's books had been lined up in rows on shelves. When I thought of them, I thought how Bud had loved them and been nourished by them all those years and years ago when he was young and had wanted to be a writer. That was when he'd progressed from Erle Stanley Gardner to Joseph Conrad, Evelyn Waugh and F. Scott Fitzgerald. And I thought how unjust it was that all the mad and alcoholic heroes of whom these men had written should pass along through time forever, with their tragedies perfectly formed around their names and their lives set out in lucid prose with all the points well made and all the meanings clear. And I thought if only some great, compassionate novelist had been assigned to flesh out Bud and Katie's tragedy, they might have had a better ending to their lives than this.

Really, I thought, as I stood that afternoon and stared at Bubastis down among the forget-me-nots—*real life writes real bad. It should take lessons from the masters.*

An Easy Life

BRONWEN WALLACE

RIGHT NOW, Marion is giving her kitchen its once-a-year major cleaning, right down to that little crack where the gunk builds up between the counter and the metal edge of the sink. She's going at it with Comet and an old toothbrush, singing along to the Talking Heads on her Walkman, having a great time. She smoked a joint with her coffee before she started this morning. It helps. She's already done the fridge, the stove *and* the oven, wiped down the walls. Just the counters and drawers to go, really. Then the floor. Marion does a little dance over to the cupboard for the Lysol.

It's a beautiful day. The patio door is half open and the air that blows in is real spring air without that underscent of snow. Crocuses glow in creamy pools of purple and gold, all along the stone path to the garden. Soon, there'll be daffodils, tulips. And hyacinths, Marion's favourite, their sweet, heavy scent filling the kitchen, outrageous, it always seems to Marion, like the smell of sex.

Marion has thick auburn hair and the fine, almost translucent complexion that often goes with it. These days, she's got it cut short with longer wisps over her forehead and at the back of her neck. She has always been beautiful, not in any regular, classic way, certainly, but because she has the kind of bone structure that can give a face movement. At forty-two, her beauty seems deeper, more complex than it ever was, as if it's just beginning to discover all its possibilities. Everyone who knows Marion acknowledges how beautiful she is. The other thing they say is that she seems to have a very easy life.

She was born Marion Patterson, the youngest of three, the only daughter of a Home Economics teacher and a high school principal. Her health was always excellent, her teeth straight. She watched "Howdy Doody" and "Father Knows Best" and saw the first-time appearances on "The Ed Sullivan Show" of both Elvis Presley and The Beatles. In school she was one of those people who manage to get high marks without being a browner and at the same time is pretty, popular and good at sports.

All of this had its predictable effect when she entered university. After her first class, English 101, Marion walked directly to the centre of the campus where a long-haired boy with deep-set, deep-brown eyes was handing out leaflets. END CANADIAN COMPLICITY IN VIETNAM, they said. Below that was the time and place of a meeting. Marion took a leaflet. She also went to the meeting.

By Christmas she was spending most of her time in the coffee shop reading *Ramparts* and *I.F. Stone's Biweekly,* and talking to anyone who would listen about what she read. She wore short skirts, fishnet stockings and turtleneck sweaters in dark colours. Her hair was long then, straight down her back, almost to her waist, and her face was sharper than it is now, vibrant in an almost aggressive way that some men found intimidating.

One man who was not intimidated was Carl Walker, a second-year art student who spent his afternoons in the coffee shop smoking and sketching. Marion had one of the strongest profiles he'd ever seen. In April, Carl and Marion were arrested at a demonstration outside the U.S. Embassy in Toronto.

That summer they were married. Marion wore a long, red Indian cotton skirt, a tie-dyed T-shirt and a crown of daisies and black-eyed Susans. Carl wore blue jeans, a loose white shirt and a button that said, L.B.J. L.B.J. HOW MANY KIDS DID YOU KILL TODAY? Back at school, their tiny apartment was the favourite hangout of campus politicos. Carl made huge pots of chili, Marion rolled the joints and everyone argued with their mouths full. Over the stereo was a poster showing the profiles of Karl Marx, Mao Tse Tung and Ho Chi Minh. SOME PEOPLE TALK ABOUT THE WEATHER, it said above the profiles. And below, in larger letters, WE DON'T.

When Marion got pregnant, she and Carl decided to quit university and find a place in the country. They could grow their own food, Carl would continue paint-ing, Marion would read.

"Who needs a degree?" Marion said.

"Just you wait," replied Marion's women friends, among whom feminism (or Women's Lib as it was then called) was making rapid advances. "Wait'll you have a colicky baby and it's thirty below outside. Carl'll go on painting the great male masterpiece and you'll be up to your elbows in shit."

Not so, however. Jason Dylan Walker was rapidly followed by Benjamin Joplin and Joshua Guthrie. All of Marion's labours were short, the boys were born undrugged, screaming red and perfectly formed. Carl was always there. He was— and still is—an enthusiastic parent, willing to do his share. He also kept on painting and managed to mount two highly acclaimed shows in six years. His paintings began to sell for very respectable prices.

Both Marion and Carl took pride in their organic vegetable garden and were keenly involved in a protest that stopped Ontario Hydro from building transmit-ter towers through a strip of choice farmland in their community. Marion raised chickens, Carl baked bread and they both spent hours taking the boys for walks in the woods around their farm. When Josh was five, Marion decided to go back to school. Carl's growing reputation got him an excellent faculty position in the art department of a small community college, they moved into the city and Marion got her Masters in Psychology and Education. For the last five years, she has been a guidance counsellor at Centennial Secondary School. She is good at what she does. Not only do most of the kids like her, they sometimes listen to some of what she has to say. What's more, some of what she has to say is actually relevant to their lives as they see them.

Of course, Marion and Carl argue, who doesn't. And sometimes they both wonder what it would have been like if they'd waited awhile, met other people, maybe travelled a little, if they hadn't been, well, so *young*. On the other hand, they also believe you have to go with what's happening at the time. Surprising as it may seem, this attitude still works for them.

Or so Marion says.

"Oh, Marion," her friends reply, only half laughing. "Wake up. Look around. The sixties are over."

Marion knows what they're getting at, of course. For every Marion Walker, married at eighteen and having three kids bang, bang, bang, who ends up cleaning her spacious kitchen in her tasteful house on her tasteful street, a little stoned and more beautiful than she was twenty years ago, there are thousands of others with their teeth rotted and their bodies gone to flab on Kraft Dinner and Wonder Bread, up to their eyeballs in shit. Women whose husbands left them (as, in fact, Marion's own brother, Jeff, left his first wife, Sandra, with a three year old and a set of twins, with no degree because she'd worked to put him through med school and with support payments based on his last year as a resident rather than his present salary as a pediatrician), or, worse yet, women whose husbands are still around, taking it out on them, women who are beaten, whose kids end up in jail or ruined by drugs or …

OR TAKE TRACEY HARPER, for example. She's just come home from her Saturday afternoon shift at Harvey's. The kitchen is scrupulously clean, as it always is, and on the table, in exactly the same spot as last Saturday and the Saturday before and every day after school for as long as she can remember, is a note in her mother's thick, wavery writing: *"Your supper's in the fridge. Just heat and eat. Love, Leslie."*

In the living room, the television is on full-blast, as always, "Wheel of Fortune" is half over and Leslie is sprawled on the couch, sound asleep, mouth open, snoring. On the table beside her, in a row, is a bottle of Maalox, a bottle of Coke, a bottle of rum, an empty glass and an empty package of Export "A"s. If Leslie were still awake, which would be unusual, she would light a cigarette, take two drags, put it in the ashtray, take two sips of rum and Coke, a sip of Maalox, two more drags of her cigarette and so on, never breaking her pattern until she ran out or passed out, whichever came first. It's by the same rigorous adherence to a system that she manages to keep her kitchen clean and food on the table for her daughter.

In so doing, she has done one helluva lot better—and she would be the first to tell you this—than her own mother. Like Tracey, Leslie came home to her mother passed out on the couch and the television blaring. Where Tracey stands in the doorway and watches men and women win glamorous merchandise and large sums of money on "Wheel of Fortune," Leslie would stand and watch women's wildest dreams come true, right there, on "Queen For a Day." What's changed (besides the television shows, of course) is that Tracey comes home to a clean kitchen and a meal, whereas Leslie came home to a shithole and nothing to eat. The other thing that's changed is that she, Leslie, has managed to keep her boyfriends out of Tracey's bed, which is more than her mother ever did for her.

What hasn't changed (besides the idea that winning something will improve your life): Tracey's eyes and her way of standing in the doorway, both of which are exactly like her mother's. Already she has the look and posture of someone whose parents abandoned her early. It doesn't matter to what—drugs, alcohol, violence, madness or death—she has that look. That particular sadness which starts in the eyes and goes bone-deep, displacing all traces of the child she was, leaving the shoulders stiff and thin, all their suppleness and softness gone for good. The softness that some of us are allowed to carry (that Marion Walker carries, for example) a good distance into our lives.

So Tracey is standing in the doorway of the living room, waiting for her supper to heat up, watching her mother sleep. Her mother is only seventeen years older than she is, which makes her thirty-four, but she looks about sixty. Her belly bloats out over the waistband of her jeans and the skin that shows, in the space between her jeans and her T-shirt, is grey and puckered. If statistics are anything to live by (and surely they're as reliable as game shows), Leslie will be dead in five to ten years. *How* is still being decided by her cells. Will it be her stomach, where the ulcer has already made its presence known? Her heart or her lungs, whose complaints she hears but manages to ignore? Right now, her cells are deciding her future.

As indeed Tracey's cells are deciding hers. If she goes back to her boyfriend Kevin's tonight after the movies, as she usually does, she will get pregnant. Everything in her body (the delicate balance of hormones controlled by her pituitary gland, the ripened ovum swimming in her right fallopian tube) is ready. In one sense, her pregnancy has already been decided. Statistically, it's almost inevitable. If it actually occurs, then, given that course of events which are so usual as to seem almost natural, Tracey may replace Leslie in a few years, exactly as she is—passed out, bloated on the couch.

Lately, though, Tracey is beginning to think that maybe it isn't such a great idea after all, dropping out of school and living together, which is what she and Kevin are planning to do as soon as he gets on at Petro-Can.

What she is hearing, under the chatter of the TV and her mother's snoring and the sausages hissing in the pan behind her and her own confused thoughts, is the voice of her guidance counsellor at school, Mrs. Walker, who is one of the weirdest people Tracey has ever met. Sometimes they don't even *talk*, for fuck sake, they go to the mall and try on clothes. Seriously.

But what Mrs. Walker is saying now inside Tracey's head is: *Well, really, Tracey, your marks aren't that bad, you know. And you've got more experience of life than most kids your age. What you've gotta decide is how you're going to use that to your advantage. Any ideas?*

And then Tracey is amazed to hear her own voice, there, inside her head. As amazed as she was last Wednesday, when she heard herself say: *Well, I always thought I might like to be a physiotherapist.*

Physiotherapist. Yeah, right. She'd just read it on one of those stupid pamphlets they have outside the guidance office.

That's not a bad idea, Tracey, Mrs. Walker is saying now, *I think you'd be really good at that. In some ways working with people who've been injured might be a little like helping your mom. Now you'd have to go to university, so we're going to have to figure out some money schemes but I …*

And then she goes on, laying it all out like it's possible, and now Tracey sometimes thinks that maybe it just is. She walks over to the TV, turns it off, goes to the couch and picks up the empty glass and the cigarette pack, butts the last cigarette, which is stinking up the ashtray. She takes the glass, the full ashtray and the empty pack to the kitchen counter, comes back and eases her mother's body gently along the couch a little ways so that her neck isn't cramped over the arm like that. Then she gets her sausages and macaroni from the stove and heads for her room.

Already, she's thinking she might tell Kevin she doesn't want to go out tonight, though it's hard to imagine having the nerve to actually say that to him. Right now, it's just sort of there, like a buzzy place, inside her head. Right now, she's just going to eat her supper and study for her math exam. Then she'll see.

MARION FILLS THE SINK with hot water, adds detergent and a few drops of Javex and dumps in the contents of the left-hand middle drawer, the one where she keeps all the stuff she hardly ever uses. Tea strainers, pie servers, cookie cutters, two ice picks and a couple of those things you use to make little scoops of melon for fruit salads.

"Melon ballers," the boys call them.

Outside, she can see Ben and Josh sorting stuff for a garage sale tomorrow, hauling everything into the driveway and organizing it into piles. Hockey sticks and skates, a huge box of Lego, Jason's old ten-speed, a bunch of flippers and some diving masks, tennis racquets, a badminton set, ski poles. They lift and carry the awkward bundles with ease, competent and serious. Even Josh is almost passed the gangly stage, almost completely at home in the body he'll live in for the rest of his life.

A body that seems so much like a stranger's to Marion these days, even as she watches him, his every movement familiar. It's hard to believe she used to take it so for granted. All of it. The rooting motions their mouths made when she picked them up to nurse. The ease with which she oiled and powdered their bums, handling their penises as casually as she'd handle her own breasts, pushing back their foreskins to check for redness, helping them aim over the potty when she was training them. It doesn't seem possible.

Marion wipes out the drawer with a damp cloth, empties the sink, starts drying the stuff and putting it back, automatically, still watching the boys. Sometimes she doesn't know and it scares her. She can feel it, inside, what she doesn't know. It's like when she miscarried between Jason and Ben and how, even before the blood came, from the very beginning, she knew something was wrong, terribly wrong and there was nothing she could do about it even though it was there, right there, inside her own body. She can feel the cold sweat of it, the way she felt it then, all over her.

And no one else seems to notice, that's what really gets to her, they seem to see her as, well, *finished,* somehow. Carl and the boys. Or the kids she sees at work, other people's kids, as precious and impossible as her own. That she should be expected, should get *paid,* to sit in an office and tell other people's kids what to do with their lives seems crazy to her sometimes. Crazier that they listen.

Ben and Josh turn suddenly and see her in the window. They wave vigorously and Ben gets onto his old skateboard, mouthing something Marion can't hear with the Walkman on and the window between them. She shakes her head, but he keeps on, tilting the skateboard wildly, his arms waving a crazy semaphore, insisting on her attention. It reminds her of when they were little, all crowded around her, and she'd send them outside, just long enough for a coffee or to talk to Carl for a few minutes. How every two seconds they'd be at the door, wanting her to watch something or do something.

It used to drive her crazy sometimes. Still does. Even now as she waves, shaking her head again, vigorously this time, she can feel that familiar pulse of irritation at her temples, quick and absolute as the swell of love that comes with it.

Anger and tenderness. That she can feel so many conflicting things, that she can know so little about anything she feels and still manage to appear a competent adult. Sometimes it scares her. Knowing there's no end to feeling like this, ever.

THE BEST TRACEY HARPER CAN DO right now is to crouch behind the chest of drawers in her bedroom and listen as Kevin bangs and bangs and bangs on the door to the apartment. Before, it was the phone ringing and ringing and ringing. Her mother has slept through it all, which, even for her, is amazing.

"All right, bitch. I know you're in there." Kevin gives the door a kick.

Silence.

Then Tracey hears him stomp down the stairs, she hears the outer door bang shut. In a few minutes his car squeals off down the street. Tracey can see it perfectly, the dark blue, rusted-out '78 Firebird and Kevin inside, his knuckles white around the steering wheel, really fuckin' pissed off.

For a minute she thinks of getting up, going out, trying to find him. It would be a lot easier than this is. She wishes she'd never met that fucking bitch Walker. Now she's going to have to spend her time avoiding Kevin, who will be on her ass every goddamn minute. Phoning her at all hours, following her to and from school. All she'll be able to do is ignore him and keep on walking.

Even when he grabs her arm, hard, next Friday afternoon and pulls her towards him. Even when she has to kick him, she won't speak, she'll just get the fuck out of there and keep on going. It's all she can do.

And it isn't Kevin's fault, either. Though he's acting like a jerk right now, he's an okay guy. Next week he'll get on at Petro-Can, and had he and Tracey gone through with their plan, everything might have worked out fine for them, statistics be damned.

As it is, Tracey will spend the next three weeks sitting silent in Marion Walker's office, not even looking at her, arms clamped around her chest as if it takes her whole strength to hold its contents in.

She will look a lot the way she looks now, crouching against the wall of her bedroom, hugging her knees to her chest as if the effort of keeping them from jumping up, running into the hallway and never stopping till she finds Kevin, wherever he is, takes everything she's got.

Which it does.

DRAWERS AND COUNTERS DONE, Marion goes to the cupboard for the pail and sponge mop, but before she starts the floor, she fills the coffeemaker and turns it on so that it will be ready when she is. She puts a new tape—*Patsy Cline's Greatest Hits*—into the Walkman and gets down on her knees to do the tough spots near the sink and under the edge of the stove. A whiff of Lysol stings her nose. Once the hard stuff's loosened, she does the rest with the mop, singing again, having a great time.

Sometimes what Marion thinks is simply that she's lucky to have such an easy life. "Karma" some of their friends used to call it, hanging out at the farm, smoking black hash, letting the boys run naked through the fields.

Other times she knows damn well it's because of Carl and their double income, her education, her parents' double income even, everything that's made her luck possible. Political, not spiritual, and she should damn well face up to what that means. Whatever that means.

Sometimes she just doesn't know, and it scares her.

Besides, who knows what will happen next, even in an easy life. In five minutes, for example, Jason will be driving in from the mall where he works part-time as a clerk at Music World, speeding, already late to pick up his girlfriend, Karen. While in an apartment nearby, someone else knocks back his last beer and climbs into his car to go get more before his friends show up. Two cars, both driven by teenage boys, hurtle towards each other, like sonar blips on a great map of possibilities, like cells gone haywire. Marion's own death ticks in her cells as it does in anybody's. Anything can happen, any time.

STILL CROUCHING behind her dresser, Tracey Harper has fallen asleep. She is dreaming. In the dream she is in a red Corvette convertible, moving very fast along a highway which is like a highway in a cartoon show, with flowers springing up on all sides, and birds and rainbows filling the sky. Mrs. Walker is driving and the two of them are laughing and eating triple-scoop French chocolate ice-cream cones from Baskin-Robbins. The dream is so vivid that Tracey can taste the cold chocolate on her tongue and feel the wind in her hair. She can hear herself laughing and laughing, and in the dream she reaches over and puts her hand, just there, for a moment, on Mrs. Walker's arm. In the dream, she has no idea where they are going.

MEANWHILE, a few blocks away, Jason pulls up in front of Karen's place, gets out of the car and goes around to the back porch where she is waiting for him in brand-new, acid-washed jeans and a yellow sweatshirt, one of her mother's daffodils stuck behind her ear.

Meanwhile, Marion's kitchen gleams, the sun shines through the window, the crocuses pulse and shimmer as the afternoon wanes. Marion pushes the mop and pail into the corner and tiptoes around the edge of the floor to the coffeemaker, pours herself a cup and tiptoes back towards the patio door.

The breeze feels wonderful on her hot face. She wipes the sweat off her forehead with the back of her hand as she steps out, and that for some reason makes her think of the day she took Tracey Harper to the mall because she couldn't think of anything else to do and how they'd tried on clothes and makeup in The Bay. Tracey wanted to do Marion's face and she let her though she never wears makeup. Now, she can feel Tracey's fingertips again on her eyelids and her cheeks. They stick slightly, pulling at her skin, as if Tracey is pressing too hard, exasperated with something she sees there, something she can't erase or alter. And at the same time, they flutter and soothe, almost as a lover's would.

Anger and tenderness. From nowhere, Marion feels the tears start. On the Walkman Patsy Cline is singing one of those songs that someone sings when they've been ditched, trying to cram a lifetime of pain into every note.

And so Marion just stands there, on her patio, with a cup of coffee in her hand, crying like an idiot. Partly because of the song. Partly because it's finally spring and she's a little stoned. Because of her kids and her job. Because she's like that, Marion, soft and open, in her easy life.

But not only because.

The Art of Cooking and Serving

MARGARET ATWOOD

THE SUMMER I WAS ELEVEN I spent a lot of time knitting. I knitted doggedly, silently, crouched over the balls of wool and the steel needles and the lengthening swath of knitwear in a posture that was far from easy. I'd learned to knit too early in life to have mastered the trick of twisting the strand around my index finger—the finger had been too short—so I had to jab the right-hand needle in, hold it there with two left-hand fingers, then lift the entire right hand to loop the wool around the tip of the needle. I'd seen women who were able to knit and talk at the same time, barely glancing down, but I couldn't do it that way. My style of knitting required total concentration and caused my arms to ache, and irritated me a lot.

What I was knitting was a layette. A layette was a set of baby garments you were supposed to dress the newborn baby in so it would be warm when it was brought home from the hospital. At the very least you needed to have two thumbless mittens, two stubby booties, a pair of leggings, a jacket, and a bonnet, to which you could add a knitted blanket if you had the patience, as well as a thing called a soaker. The soaker looked like a pair of shorts with pumpkin-shaped legs, like the ones in pictures of Sir Francis Drake. Cloth diapers and rubber baby pants were prone to leaks: that's what the soaker was for. But I was not going to knit the soaker. I hadn't yet got around to visualizing the fountains, the streams, the rivers of pee a baby was likely to produce.

The blanket was tempting—there was one with rabbits on it that I longed to create—but I knew I had to draw the line somewhere because I didn't have all the time in the world. If I dawdled, the baby might arrive before I was ready for it and be forced to wear some sort of mismatched outfit put together out of hand-me-downs. I'd started on the leggings and the mittens, as being fairly simple—mostly alternate rows of knit and purl, with some ribbing thrown in. That way I could work up to the jacket, which was more complicated. I was saving the bonnet to the last: it was going to be my *chef d'oeuvre*. It was to be ornamented with satin ribbons to tie under the baby's chin—the possibilities of strangulation through ties like this had not yet been considered—and with huge ribbon rosettes that would stick out on either side of the baby's face like small cabbages. Babies dressed in layettes, I knew from the pictures in the Beehive pattern book, were supposed to resemble confectionery—clean and sweet, delicious little cakelike bundles decorated with pastel icing.

The colour I'd chosen was white. It was the orthodox colour, though a few of the Beehive patterns were shown in an elfin pale green or a practical yellow. But white was best: after it was known whether the baby was a boy or a girl I could add the ribbons, blue or pink. I had a vision of how the entire set would look when finished—pristine, gleaming, admirable, a tribute to my own goodwill and kindness. I hadn't yet realized it might also be a substitute for them.

I was knitting this layette because my mother was expecting. I avoided the word *pregnant*, as did others: *pregnant* was a blunt, bulgy, pendulous word, it weighed you down to think about it, whereas *expecting* suggested a dog with its ears pricked, listening briskly and with happy anticipation to an approaching footstep. My mother was old for such a thing: I'd gathered this by eavesdropping while she talked with her friends in the city, and from the worried wrinkles on the foreheads of the friends, and from their compressed lips and tiny shakes of the head, and from their *Oh dear* tone, and from my mother saying she would just have to make the best of it. I gathered that something might be wrong with the baby because of my mother's age; but wrong how, exactly? I listened as much as I could, but I couldn't make it out, and there was no one I could ask. Would it have no hands, would it have a little pinhead, would it be a moron? *Moron* was a term of abuse, at school. I wasn't sure what it meant, but there were children you weren't supposed to stare at on the street, because it wasn't their fault, they had just been born that way.

I'D BEEN TOLD about the expectant state of my mother in May, by my father. It had made me very anxious, partly because I'd also been told that until my new baby brother or sister had arrived safely my mother would be in a dangerous condition. Something terrible might happen to her—something that might make her very ill—and it was all the more likely to happen if I myself did not pay proper attention. My father did not say what this thing was, but his gravity and terseness meant that it was a serious business.

My mother—said my father—was not supposed to sweep the floor, or carry anything heavy such as pails of water, or bend down much, or lift bulky objects. We would all have to pitch in, said my father, and do extra tasks. It would be my brother's job to mow the lawn, from now until June, when we would go up north. (Up north there was no lawn. In any case my brother wouldn't be there: he was heading off to a camp for boys, to do things with axes in the woods.) As for me, I would just have to be generally helpful. More helpful than usual, my father added in a manner that was meant to be encouraging. He himself would be helpful too, of course. But he couldn't be there all the time. He had some work to do, when we would be at what other people called *the cottage* but we called *the island*. (Cottages had iceboxes and gas generators and water-skiing, all of which we lacked.) It was necessary for him to be away, which was unfortunate, he continued. But he would not be gone for very long, and he was sure I would be up to it.

I myself was not so sure. He always thought I knew more than I knew, and that I was bigger than I was, and older, and hardier. What he mistook for calmness and competence was actually fright: that was why I stared at him in silence, nodding my head. The danger that loomed was so vague, and therefore so large—how could I even prepare for it? At the back of my mind, my feat of knitting was a sort of charm, like the fairy-tale suits of nettles mute princesses were supposed to make for their swan-shaped brothers, to turn them back into human beings. If I could only complete the full set of baby garments, the baby that was supposed to fit inside them would be conjured into the world, and thus out of my mother. Once outside, where I could see it—once it had a face—it could be dealt with. As it was, the thing was a menace.

Thus I knitted on, with single-minded concentration. I finished the mittens before we went up north; they were more or less flawless, except for the odd botched stitch. After I got to the island, I polished off the leggings—the leg that was shorter could be stretched, I felt. Without pause I started on the jacket, which was to have several bands of seed stitch on it—a challenge, but one I was determined to overcome.

Meanwhile my mother was being no use at all. At the beginning of my knitting marathon she'd undertaken to do the booties. She did know how to knit, she'd knitted in the past: the pattern book I was using had once been hers. She could turn heels, a skill I hadn't quite mastered. But despite her superior ability, she was slacking off: all she'd done so far was half a bootie. Her knitting lay neglected while she rested in a deck chair, her feet up on a log, reading historical romances with horseback riding and poisoning and swordplay in them—I knew, I'd read them myself—or else just dozing, her head lying slackly on a pillow, her face pale and moist, her hair damp and lank, her stomach sticking out in a way that made me feel dizzy, as I did when someone else had cut their finger. She'd taken to wearing an old smock she'd put away in a trunk, long ago; I remembered using it for dressing up at Halloween once, when I was being a fat lady with a purse. It made her look poor.

It was scary to watch her sleeping in the middle of the day. It was unlike her. Normally she was a person who went for swift, purposeful walks, or skated around rinks in winter at an impressive speed, or swam with a lot of kicking, or rattled up the dishes—she called it rattling them up. She always knew what to do in an emergency, she was methodical and cheerful, she took command. Now it was as if she had abdicated.

When I wasn't knitting, I swept the floor diligently. I pumped out pails and pails of water with the hand pump and lugged them up the hill one at a time, spilling water down my bare legs; I did the washing in the zinc washtub, scrubbing the clothes with Sunlight soap on the washboard, carting them down to the lake to rinse them out, hauling them up the hill again to hang them on the line. I weeded the garden, I carried in the wood, all against the background of my mother's alarming passivity.

Once a day she went for a swim, although she didn't swim energetically, not the way she used to, she just floated around; and I would go in too, whether I wanted to or not: I had to prevent her from drowning. I had a fear of her sinking down suddenly, down through the cold brownish water, with her hair fanning out like seaweed and her eyes gazing solemnly up at me. In that case I would have to dive down and get my arm around her neck and tow her to shore, but how could I do that? She was so big. But nothing like that had happened yet, and she liked going into the water; it seemed to wake her up. With only her head sticking out, she looked more like herself. At such times she would even smile, and I would have the illusion that everything was once again the way it was supposed to be.

But then she would emerge, dripping—there were varicose veins on the backs of her legs, I couldn't avoid seeing them, although they embarrassed me—and make her way with painful slowness up to our cabin, and put together our lunch. The lunch would be sardines, or peanut butter on crackers, or cheese if we had any, and tomatoes from the garden, and carrots I'd dug out and washed. She didn't appear much interested in eating this lunch, but she chewed away at it anyway. She would make an effort at conversation—how was my knitting coming along?—but I didn't know what to say to her. I couldn't understand why she'd chosen to do what she'd done— why she'd turned herself into this listless, bloated version of herself, thus changing the future—my future—into something shadow-filled and uncertain. I thought she'd done it on purpose. It didn't occur to me that she might have been ambushed.

IT WAS MID-AUGUST: hot and oppressive. The cicadas sang in the trees, the dry pine needles crackled underfoot. The lake was ominously still, the way it was when thunder was gathering. My mother was dozing. I sat on the dock, slapping at the stable flies and worrying. I felt like crying, but I could not allow myself to do that. I was completely alone. What would I do if the dangerous thing—whatever it was— began to happen? I thought I knew what it might be: the baby would start to come out, too soon. And then what? I couldn't exactly stuff it back in.

We were on an island, there were no other people in sight, there was no telephone, it was seven miles by boat to the nearest village. I would have to start the outboard motor on our clunky old boat—I knew how to do this, though pulling the cord hard enough was almost beyond my strength—and go all the way to the village, which could take an hour. From there I could telephone for help. But what if the motor wouldn't start? That had been known to happen. Or what if it broke down on the way? There was a tool kit, but I'd learned only the most elementary operations. I could fix a shear pin, I could check a gas line; if those things didn't work I would have to row, or wave and yell at passing fishermen, if any.

Or I could use the canoe—put a stone in the stern to weight it down, paddle from the bow end, as I'd been taught. But that method would be useless in a wind, even a light wind: I wasn't strong enough to hold a course, I would be blown sideways.

I thought of a plan of last resort. I would take the canoe over to one of the small offshore islands—I could get that far, no matter what. Then I would set fire to the island. The smoke would be seen by a fire ranger, who would send a float plane, and I would stand on the dock in full view and jump up and down and wave a white pillowcase. This could not fail. The risk was that I would set the mainland on fire as well, by accident. Then I would end up in jail as an arsonist. But I would just have to do it anyway. It was either that, or my mother would … Would what?

Here my mind cut out, and I ran up the hill and walked softly past my sleeping mother and into the cabin, and got out the jar full of raisins, and made my way to the large poplar tree where I always went when I'd come to the edge of an unthinkable thought. I propped myself against the tree, crammed a handful of raisins into my mouth, and plunged into my favourite book.

This book was a cookbook. It was called *The Art of Cooking and Serving*, and I'd recently thrown over all novels and even *The Guide to Woodland Mushrooms* and devoted myself to it entirely. It was by a woman called Sarah Field Splint, a name I trusted. *Sarah* was old-fashioned and dependable, *Field* was pastoral and flowery, and *Splint*—well, there could be no nonsense and weeping and hysteria and doubts about the right course of action with a woman called Splint by your side. This book dated from the olden days, ten years before I was born; it had been put out by the Crisco company, a manufacturer of vegetable shortening, at the beginning of the Depression, when butter had become expensive—said my mother—so all the recipes in it had Crisco in them. We always had lots of Crisco on the island, because butter went bad in the heat, Crisco on the other hand was virtually indestructible. In the long ago, before she'd started expecting, my mother had used it to make pies, and her writing could be found here and there among the recipes: *Good!!* she'd written. Or, *Use half white, half brown.*

It wasn't the recipes that held me in thrall, however. It was the two chapters at the front of the book. The first was called "The Servantless House," the second "The House with a Servant." Both of them were windows into another world, and I peered through them eagerly. I knew they were windows, not doors: I couldn't get in. But what entrancing lives were being lived in there!

Sarah Field Splint had strict ideas on the proper conduct of life. She had rules, she imposed order. Hot foods must be served *hot*, cold foods *cold*. "It just *has* to be done, however it is accomplished," she said. That was the kind of advice I needed to hear. She was firm on the subject of clean linen and shining silver. "Better never to use anything but doilies, and keep them immaculately fresh, than to cover the table for even one meal with a cloth having a single spot on it," she ordered. We had oilcloth on our table, and stainless steel. As for doilies, they were something beyond my experience, but I thought it would be elegant to have some.

Despite her insistence on the basics, Sarah Field Splint had other, more flexible values. Mealtimes must be enjoyed; they must have charm. Every table must have a centrepiece: a few flowers, an arrangement of fruits. Failing that, "some tiny ferns combined with a bit of partridge vine or other coloured woodsy thing in a low bowl or delicate wicker basket" would do the trick.

How I longed for a breakfast tray with a couple of daffodils in a bud vase, as pictured, or a tea table at which to entertain "a few choice friends"—who would these friends be?—or, best of all, breakfast served on a side porch, with a lovely view of "the winding river and the white church spire sailing out of the trees on the opposite bank." *Sailing*—I liked that. It sounded so peaceful.

All of these things were available to the house with no servant. Then came the servant chapter. Here too Mrs. Splint was fastidious, and solidly informative. (You could tell she was *Mrs.* Splint; she was married, though without sloppy consequences, unlike my mother.) "One can transform an untidy, inexperienced girl into a well-groomed, professional servant if one is patient and kind and fair," she told me. *Transform* was the word I seized on. Did I want to transform, or to be transformed? Was I to be the kind homemaker, or the formerly untidy maid? I hardly knew.

There were two photographs of the maid, one in daytime dress, with white shoes and stockings and a white muslin apron—what was muslin?—and the other in an afternoon tea and dinner outfit, with black stockings and organdy collar and cuffs. Her expression in both pictures was the same: a gentle little half-smile, a straight-ahead, frank, but reserved gaze, as if she was waiting for instructions. There were faint dark circles under her eyes. I couldn't tell whether she looked amiable, or put-upon, or merely stupefied. She'd be the one to get blamed if there was a spot on the tablecloth or a piece of silver less than gleaming. All the same, I envied her. She was already transformed, and had no more decisions to make.

I finished the raisins, closed the book, wiped my sticky hands on my shorts. Now it was time for more knitting. Sometimes I forgot to wash my hands and got brown raisin stains on the white wool, but that could be corrected later. Ivory Soap was what Mrs. Splint always used; it was good to know such a thing. First I went down to the garden and broke off some pea vine and a handful of red flowers from the scarlet runner beans, for the centrepiece it was now my duty to arrange. The charm of my centrepiece would not however cancel out the shabbiness of our paper napkins: my mother insisted they be used at least twice, to avoid waste, and she wrote our initials on them in pencil. I could imagine what Mrs. Splint would think of this grubby practice.

HOW LONG did all of this go on? It seemed forever, but perhaps it was only a week or two. In due course my father returned; a few maple leaves turned orange, and then a few more; the loons gathered together, calling at night before their fall migration. Soon enough we went back to the city, and I could go to school again in the normal way.

I'd finished the layette, all except the one bootie that was the responsibility of my mother—would the baby have the foot of a swan?—and I wrapped it in white tissue paper and put it in a drawer. It was a bit lopsided and not entirely clean—the raisin smears lingered—but you couldn't tell that when it was folded.

MY BABY SISTER was born in October, a couple of weeks before I turned twelve. She had all the right fingers and toes. I threaded the pink ribbon into the eyelets in the layette and sewed together the rosettes for the bonnet, and the baby came home from the hospital in the proper manner and style. My mother's friends came over to visit, and admired my handiwork, or so it appeared. "You did all this?" they said. "Almost all," I said modestly. I didn't mention my mother's failure to complete her own minor task.

My mother said she'd hardly had to lift a finger. I'd gone at the knitting just like a beaver. "What a good little worker," said the friends; but I got the impression they thought it was funny.

The baby was cute, though in no time flat she outgrew my layette. But she didn't sleep. As soon as you put her down she'd be wide awake and wailing: the clouds of anxiety that had surrounded her before she was born seemed to have entered into her, and she would wake up six or seven or eight or nine times a night, crying plaintively. This didn't go away in a few months, as Dr. Spock's *Baby and Child Care* said it would. If anything, it got worse.

From having been too fat, my mother now became too thin. She was gaunt from lack of sleep, her hair dull, her eyes bruised-looking, her shoulders hunched over. I did my homework lying on my back with my feet up on the baby's crib, jiggling it and jiggling it so my mother could get some rest. Or I would come home from school and change the baby and bundle her up and take her out in her pram, or I would pace back and forth, pressing her warm, fragrant, wriggling flannelette body against my shoulder with one hand while holding a book up with the other, or I would take her into my room and rock her in my arms and sing to her. Singing was particularly effective. *Oh my darling Nellie Gray, they have taken you away, and I'll never see my darling any more*, I would sing. Or else the "Coventry Carol" from junior choir:

Herod the King, in his raging,
Charged he hath this day,
His men of might, in his own sight,
All children young, to slay.

The tune was mournful, but it put her right to sleep.

When I wasn't doing those things, I had to clean the bathroom or do the dishes.

My sister turned one, I became thirteen; now I was in high school. She turned two, I became fourteen. My girlfriends at school—some of them were fifteen already—were loitering on the way home, talking to boys. Some of them went to the movies, where they picked up boys from other schools; others did the same at skating rinks. They exchanged views on which boys were real dolls and which were pills, they went to drive-ins on double dates with their new steadies and ate popcorn and rolled around in the back seats of cars, they tried on strapless dresses, they attended dances where, drowning in swoony music and the blue light of darkened gymnasiums, they shuffled around mashed up against their partners, they necked on the couch in their rec rooms with the TV on.

I listened to the descriptions of all this at lunch hour, but I couldn't join in. I avoided the boys who approached me: somehow I had to turn away, I had to go home and look after the baby, who was still not sleeping. My mother dragged around the house as if she was ill, or starving. She'd been to the doctor about the baby's sleeplessness, but he'd been no help. All he said was, "You've got one of *those*."

From being worried, I now became surly. I escaped from the dinner table every night as soon as I could, I shut myself in my room and answered questions from my parents with grudging monosyllables. When I wasn't doing homework or chores or baby-tending I would lie on my bed with my head hanging over the edge, holding up a mirror to see what I looked like upside down.

One evening I was standing behind my mother. I must have been waiting for her to get out of the bathroom so I could try out something or other on myself, a different shampoo most likely. She was bending over the laundry hamper, hauling out the dirty clothes. The baby started to cry. "Could you go and put her to sleep?" she said, as she had done so often. Ordinarily, I would trudge off, soothe, sing, rock.

"Why should I?" I said. "She's not *my* baby. I didn't have her. You did." I'd never said anything this rude to her. Even as the words were coming out of my mouth I knew I'd gone too far, though all I'd done was spoken the truth, or part of it.

My mother stood up and whirled around, all in one movement, and slapped me hard across the face. She'd never done that before, or anything remotely like it. I didn't say anything. She didn't say anything. We were both shocked by ourselves, and also by each other.

I ought to have felt hurt, and I did. But I also felt set free, as if released from an enchantment. I was no longer compelled to do service. On the outside, I would still be helpful—I wouldn't be able to change that about myself. But another, more secret life spread out before me, unrolling like dark fabric. I too would soon go to the drive-in theatres, I too would eat popcorn. Already in spirit I was off and running—to the movies, to the skating rinks, to the swooning blue-lit dances, and to all sorts of other seductive and tawdry and frightening pleasures I could not yet begin to imagine.

Part 4

PAPER
SHADOWS

AS A CHILD *Wayson Choy was often taken by his mother into the magical world of Vancouver's Chinese theatre, with its tapestry of exotic sounds, vivid colour, and heart-breaking drama. It was an art whose radical removal from the quotidian could inspire joy; an art that was spellbinding in the true sense of the term: one was deliciously bound by the sights and sounds until the end of the drama set one free.*

The stories in this section break the bonds imposed by what we believe to be "reality." Whether a fable inspired by a fairy tale (Sheila Heti) or the imagined voyage of a glass sphere through the globe's waterways (Sean Virgo), these stories take us out of ourselves and our known domain. This kind of writing has a long history in Canada, as evidenced by Stephen Leacock's time-travelling train, and often involves journeys into Canada's or another country's past, or into nations not of this world. Imagination is the key word here: children float, lovers meet in dark and unusual places, time collapses, historical figures are reimagined. And almost everyone, one way or another, runs away with the gypsies.

Paper Shadows

WAYSON CHOY

THE YELLOW BACKDROP CURTAIN of the Sing Kew Theatre shimmered in a sudden blaze of light. Speaking formal Cantonese, a plump man in a drab suit stood erect on stage and pleaded with the packed house to buy the new 1942 issues of the Republic of Free China and Dominion of Canada war bonds. I licked my fish-shaped caramel all-day sucker to the rhythm of his talking.

"Ally victory over our common enemies!" he said suddenly in English for the benefit of some white officials in the audience, then translated the statement into Chinese, raising his fingers in a Churchillian V. Fifth Aunty told me there was always someone who was appeasing these visiting officials during the opening ceremonies. They were often invited by Chinatown's politicians to stay a few minutes to witness the community's loyalty to the Crown.

Vancouver's Chinatown crowd politely applauded. Pinkish Chinese gold and mutton-coloured jade bracelets jangled on the slender wrists of Mother's companions. I grew restless at the speech-making and climbed onto Mother's lap.

My four-year-old mind wanted cartoons, like the Bugs Bunny ones I saw with *Dai Gung, Great Uncle,* who for the first time, last week, had taken me to the Lux movie house on Hastings Street. (Bugs Bunny was all I got to see; Mother told me I was too excitable and had to be taken out of the theatre, pants wet.) Finally, the man read aloud the names of all the performers, stiffly bowed and left the stage.

"Eeeih-yah! Gum daw yan!," Mother said, in her Sze Yup dialect. *"So many people!"* Her lady friends on either side clucked their tongues in agreement. Mother reached over my shoulder and wiped my mouth of candy residue. One of the ladies ambushed my sticky fingers with her handkerchief.

As the front-of-house double doors opened to accommodate a last rush of ticket-holders, a draught of night air swept through the auditorium, bringing noxious chemical smells from the False Creek refineries a block away. Some Great Northern Railway trains coupled with an abrupt *BANG,* causing the three-storey Shanghai Alley building to vibrate. Most of the audience continued to chat, unconcerned; the only people disturbed by the noises and smells of *Tohng Yahn Gaai, China-People Street,* were tourists.

Mother held me tightly on her lap and leaned back against a stiff wooden seat to let a young couple bump by us. The chattering audience began pointing to the rectangle of light and the billowing back curtain; people sighed with expectation, shook off their drenched raincoats, and sat down.

A foghorn bellowed once, twice, and the doors of the Sing Kew slammed shut. Stubborn latecomers were now directed through the side entry. The opera was to begin. The houselights dimmed. I wiggled forward onto Mother's boney knees. The brightly lit yellow curtains made me suddenly squint-eyed.

To the right of the stage—a stage bare except for a plain brown carpet; a small, rectangular table covered with a red cloth; and two plain wooden chairs—an eight-man orchestra began to play. The crowd applauded.

The rising notes of a dulcimer stilled the audience; the pliant notes of the two-stringed *hu chin* and the violin dispensed quivering half melodies. Cymbals shivered; gongs and drumbeats throbbed; a pair of woodblocks clacked.

My all-day sucker slipped out of my hand. All at once, I felt my heart pounding to a rhythm outside of myself. I was thunderstruck. I clenched my four-year-old legs, tightened my candy-stained fists: I wanted to pee.

"Hi-lah!" Mother said to me in Toisanese. *"Hi-lah, look!"*

Balanced on the edge of her knees, feverishly swallowing the pungent air, I pushed forward, stretched my neck and *hi-lah*ed between the big heads and shoulders in front of us.

The door-sized side curtain parted. A burst of colour struck my eyes. In sequinned costumes of forest green and gold, jolting cobalt blue and fiery red, living myths swayed onto the stage, their swords slashing the air, their open ornate fans snapping.

Mother whispered into my ear who each was as, one by one, the performers made a few stylized movements to introduce their character, briefly sang their histories, and danced away before my amazed eyes: that's the *Hsiao-sheng*, the *Scholar-Prince;* there, the Princess with pretty eyes; now the grand King with his servants; last, with orchestral roars, the fierce South Wind General, his soldiers swirling behind him, tumbling like madmen. I could tumble, too. I could even stand at attention, like a soldier, arms stiffly by my side. Some of the older boys had taught me that. But these soldiers were different from the ones I saw walking on the streets of Vancouver.

Mesmerized by the tumbling warriors, I didn't care about the growing dampness on my pant leg, but Mother made a clucking noise to signal her disgust and lifted me off her knees. I stood beside her on the box provided for children, my knees bending and straightening as if I myself were majestically stomping about the stage.

A maternal hand pressed against the buttoned-up fly of my woollen pants.

"You just went ten minutes ago!"

Mother's Chinese words were pitched high above the clamorous music.

"I should chop you to death!"

"Ngoh m'pee-pee!" I said, afraid she would snatch me up and take me away from the magic. *"I not pee-pee!"*

"Stand still!" Mother's lipstick-sweet breath tickled my ear, her dialect as lush as the whining strings of the orchestra. "Look. Look at the warriors."

I stood on my tiptoes and lifted my head to peer between the adults in front of me. The strangers felt my fingers urgently pushing against them and, used to children in the theatre, shifted their shoulders to let me see better.

In my excitement, I took big breaths and caught in my nose the exhaled puffs of the men's Export or Bull Durham, the women's Black Cat or Sweet Caporal. The tobacco smell was seasoned by the aromas of salt-sweet savoury dumplings and roasted red or black melon seeds. Whenever hunger pangs hit me, I nudged Mother, or her lady friends on either side of us, and the smoky air was made sweeter by yellow-eyed egg tarts lifted up from B.C. Royal Café pastry boxes.

On the stage, poised at opposite ends, painted faces fierce in blood red and cobalt blue, the King and General made threatening gestures towards each other's kingdoms: fists shook; swords waved menacingly. The King uttered stylized shrieks that melded with the majestic singing of the bold young Prince. With hypnotic force, the General sang counterpoint. When the Prince left the stage, the King and the General broke into soliloquies of talk-patter, then dipped and darted at each other. With a clash of cymbals and drums, they both stormed away.

The audience roared their approval.

A Princess dashed onto the stage, waving her long white sleeves. Her eyebrows made an exaggerated arch above her crimson cheeks, and, I thought, she looked like Mother. She began to sing in shrill veering rhythm. I impatiently sucked my thumb and held my breath, my fish-shaped sucker now forgotten in the darkness at my feet.

"She's in love," Mother said.

The Princess sang on and on. For ever.

"Doesn't she stop?" I asked.

"Stand still," Mother said.

"She just keeps singing."

"Hmmo cho! Be quiet!" Mother gently tapped my head to get my attention. "She's supposed to sing. She's happy. Sit here."

I climbed back on to Mother's lap. I might have closed my eyes then; I might even have napped. Eventually her aria concluded and I sat up, sleepily rubbing my eyes. The prolonged applause was comforting: everyone else was just as relieved as I was that the lady had stopped singing. The man in front of us was even shouting *"Hou yeh, hou yeh! Excellent, excellent!"* Others cried out *"Ho-ho, ho-ho! Bravo, bravo!"*

The lovesick Princess bowed twice. I thought she was looking very sorry that she had wailed so long. One more bow and she scurried off stage with her maidservant. Everyone clapped to see them leave.

Next, the sound of drums stirred my interest. The King was returning from hunting, Mother explained. His elaborate headdress, made of long, exotic feathers, fluttered elegantly in the air, like antennae. His servants carried carcasses of deer and fowl across the stage. The royal court followed, their sequinned gowns and mirrored robes throwing coins of light into the audience.

IT WAS LATE SPRING, 1942, and the Sing Kew Theatre, a warehouse at 544 Shanghai Alley, played host nightly to a clamorous Chinatown crowd. For years, Mother went regularly with her friends to the Sing Kew, the Royal on Hastings, or the Yun Dong (Oriental) Theatre on Columbia Street; she thought nothing of taking me, even when I was only a few months old. Other mothers had their children with them, too, and newborns nursed indifferently at breasts wet with milk.

Tonight's fundraiser had been advertised for weeks, and featured all the Canton and Hong Kong professional touring actors stranded in North America by the war in China. Vancouver devotees also performed in these operas, talented men and women recruited from three clubs: the Sing Kew Dramatic Society, the Ching Won Society and the Jin Wah Sing Troupe.

Agile young men would volunteer to be soldiers, and lithe Lim Mark Yee, one of the stars, would coach them in the acrobatic art of sword- and spear-dancing. Even some of Mother's friends played bit parts, though she herself was too shy to volunteer. The theatre men were handsome, the women beautiful; aside from being shy, Mother never felt she was suitable.

Usually, the Sing Kew admitted toddlers and children free; adults paid from twenty-five cents to a dollar-fifty, depending on what time they entered the smoky theatre and which stars were singing that evening (one female star was said to earn as much as three hundred dollars a week, a small fortune). Every adult knew the opera stories by heart, so between shifts at work—or rounds of mah-jong or fan-tan—opera devotees could stop by for their favourite arias. Those who walked in after nine o'clock paid much less—an appealing option, given that a typical performance began at seven and often lasted until midnight, long enough to test the endurance of the most dedicated fan.

Before the Chinatown crowds, Tam Bing Yeun played the clown; Kwei Ming Yeong and Sui Kwung Lung performed as warriors, lovers or kings; Gee Ding Heung and the lovely Mah Dang Soh ... they all sang to ovations. (At eighty-two, Mother's younger friend, Betty Lee, could still recall for me the performances of the most famous stars, the handsome heroics of Kwei Ming Yeong and Gee Ding Heung, the exquisite singing of tiny Mah Dang Soh.)

Some nights, white people, such as city inspectors or Chinatown-friendly politicians, would be given free seating. They never stayed beyond an hour. With her lady friends, Mother always stayed until midnight.

From the beginning, I was enchanted. I fell in love with the dramatic colours, and the clowning, for I believed the whole opera was a clown show: didn't clowns paint their faces and jump about?

"Look, look," Mother said, pointing at the stage. "Buddha is laughing at Monkey."

I looked, only dimly aware that other eyes followed my every move. On either side of us, well-to-do lady friends rattled their new gold-coin bracelets from Birks, turned their amused heads to see how my eyes widened, how I kicked into the air—the same kick Buddha gave to naughty Monkey. When Buddha laughed, I laughed. When Monkey rubbed his bum in regret, I rubbed my bum in sympathy. The comic hijinks bewitched me.

At first, when the actors vaulted violently about the stage, and the orchestra produced an explosion of drumming and ringing gongs, I clung to Mother and peeked at the menacing antics through her enfolding arms, and used my fingers to plug my ears against the actors' yowling.

"First time at Sing Kew," Fifth Aunty told me years later, "you bunched up like a jack-in-the-box. But you keep looking."

As the evening performances and matinées paraded by me, these same ferocious faces quickly grew into familiar kings and warriors, into matchmaking clowns and an aberrant Monkey-King; I began to see—aided by Mother's simple narrations—that actual *continuing* stories were being played out.

One of the operas told the story of the Monkey-King who defied Buddha's warning not to eat the Peaches of Long Life. His adventures were often told to me by my Chinatown aunties and uncles.

"See the Monkey-King grab the Peaches of Long Life," Mother said, and I saw all of it, as if the stage were a living book.

As the orchestra at one side of the stage raised a clamour, my body rocked with a sensual pleasure, my fear for Monkey's safety flaming my cheeks. Monkey pushed against his long staff and pole-vaulted over Buddha's humble, rag-dressed buffoon. Clown was sent by Buddha to test the Monkey-King, to see if he would keep his promise to be a good monkey and not steal the forbidden peaches, I sat up. Monkey and Clown began to stalk each other, just like cousin Donald and I did when we played Catch You! on my birthday, in front of Aunty Freda's house.

Clown dove at Monkey and snatched away Monkey's long pole. With it, the round-faced fool poked and pointed at the ripe sacred fruit that hung from a branch way above their heads. The orchestra was silent, except for the woodblocks—and my heart—*knock-knocking* in unison. Would the Monkey-King be tempted?

Monkey shook his head, thinking hard. He stopped, looked out at the audience, skipped—winked at *me*—then suddenly hopped up like a spring onto the startled clown's shoulders.

Perched there like a tipsy bird, Monkey reached up, as if to spread his wings and fly. Instead, he came crashing down, a juicy peach clutched in each paw. Buddha's clown went tumbling backwards, raising puffs of dust from the stage carpet. Monkey, chortling and triumphant, ran off.

"Naughty Monkey!" Mother said. *"Hai m'hai ah!"*

"Silly Monkey!" I said. *"Hai! Yes!"* And Mother laughed. I laughed, too. Buddha's faithful servant could never have fooled me!

I very quickly caught on to the many characters' ritual gestures. Whenever a great king stroked his long black beard and pounded his chest, I knew there was trouble. Mother curled her fingers to my ear and whispered the story to me.

"That's the bad King," she said, pitting her Toisanese against the thundering drums and the squeal of strings. "He's jealous of the young scholar who loves the princess."

The Student-Prince ambled onto the stage, unaware that the jealous King was hiding behind trees. The handsome Prince, looking like my father, touched his forehead, then patted his heart, a heart clearly struck by love. Then he sang.

"The Prince sings too much," I complained. But Mother just held me tightly, rocking. By this point I had acquired a furious dislike of arias.

Still, I was left with some defences against the tedium. If tortured with an overlong aria, I could shut my ears with my palms, fight sleepiness and fervently hum, or even sing, my own songs. (Mother said I could do that, "if not too loud.")

I whisper-sang songs Aunty Freda played for me on her phonograph, songs like "Old MacDonald Had a Farm, EEE EYE, EEE-EYE, OHHH!" Sometimes I heard Mother sing, *oohh-ahhh, oohh-ahh-laah,* and I vowed to teach her the real words.

When the drums began, and the cymbals and gongs—*chang, chang, chang*—I stopped singing, and lifted my head and opened my eyes, my senses on alert.

If I turned my head in any direction, I could observe men, women and children eating and drinking. Whenever there was a lull at the Sing Kew—that is, when a third-level star was attempting to sing, or a local talent was apprenticing on stage—out came thermos cups of steaming tea. I loved the life that blossomed all over the auditorium, as if it were a busy village square. Those who were skilful enough used their front teeth to crack open tiny melon seeds, scattering the *quai gee* shells at their feet. Vendors offered small bags of dried apricots, dumplings and salted plums, and children ran up and down the aisles. Old men sometimes bowed their heads and spat neatly into round brass spittoons placed along the aisles.

A chattering kind of freedom filled the space, which Chinatown citizens treated more like an open-air teahouse than a formal theatre. In the traditional Canton and old village way, the Sing Kew was a place to "be home," as in back home in Old China—a place to pass the time, to meet friends, to gossip, and now and again to focus on the stage.

GUARDED BY TWO LOYAL SERVANTS, the Gentlewoman, played by Mah Dang Soh, stood ready to sing a challenging aria.

"Oh, those opera love stories just like *Wuthering Heights,*" one of Mother's oldest friends, Betty Lee, recently told me. The opera may have been *The Beauty on the Lake,* or the popular *Lay Toy Woo, The Romance at the Bridge.*

The star tilted her proud, confident head to one side. The audience stirred. I was mesmerized by the lengths of pure white silk cascading from the embroidered sleeves of her emerald-green dress. Her elegant hands rose like the wings of a swan, and the silk "water sleeves" swept backwards. She seemed to be brushing tears from her eyes. Mother told me the lady lived in exile, and was aching to see again her long-lost family, just like all of Chinatown was longing for their own families in faraway China.

"She's going to sing of her village," Chulip Sim told me in a more formal Chinese dialect. *"Hm'mo cho-lah. You be quiet now."*

"Kay-dee. Stand up," Mother said. "You be her guard."

I stood up, ramrod-stiff like a soldier, at attention.

With long fingers now resting against her cheek, the actress began to pierce the air with her falsetto voice, and the audience—suddenly—responded with silence. We children knew we were not to run about, but to tiptoe, and not to utter even a whisper.

Listening to the sing-song evocation of Old China, the lyrics conjuring up images of a genteel country life and lost family, of the Gentlewoman's dream to be in her village home again, our elders and our parents sat transfixed; then, after a defiant vibrating note, which escaped wildly from her throat, and after a final sweep of her water sleeves, the words she sang turned into a call to arms—*Oh, no, never give up hope!*—and the actress stood frozen in a heroic pose. Brushing aside their own tears, the audience gave her a thunderous ovation.

"It's so Chinese to long for home," the elders said to each other. Others said, "Oh, for the children to be still Chinese and go back to China!"

Her headdress shimmering with gemstones and pearls, the star bowed to the shouting audience. I bowed back.

IT WAS MANY YEARS before I understood that, although Mother always wore her bracelet of gold and her jade pendant, my parents were not as well off as many of their friends. I never thought of my parents as a working-class, no-citizenship family, despite the fact that they were each working long hours and earning only minimum wage. Whatever daily struggles my parents faced, the Cantonese opera at night bestowed upon me such a wealth of high drama, of myth, that I lacked for nothing in the ordinary world. The booming drums thrilled me. Mother half-shouted in my ear, *"Huang-Dai loy-lah! The great King comes!"* and gods and royalty sang before me.

Sometimes the thundering sounds and the imagined action were so beautiful that I nearly stopped breathing. I wanted to become what I saw before me: the General, the warriors, and the frightened guard who led the way to the prison.

"Here come South-Wind General's one hundred warriors and horses!" Mother's talk-story words blew into my ear, her Toisanese breathless. The plot was like *King Lear*. A good princess, not unlike the faithful Cordelia, was to be rescued.

"Hi-lah! The Princess can see their dust rising from the valley!" Mother held my hand and pointed to the action. *"Hi-lah! Hi-lah! See! See!* The General and his soldiers will rescue her!"

Two tasselled riding crops wielded by an emerald-costumed warrior guided invisible horses across the stage. In my mind's eye, I could see the steeds—their tall, sloped-back bodies, their crested manes and proud tails shaking in the valley wind, more splendid than any horses I saw in cowboy movies. The General came behind, shook his head at the herd and galloped forward on his splendid charger. He dismounted, raising one leg, then the other. Behind his jewelled headdress, two outstretched peacock plumes quivered in the air: the horses, the General knew, could climb no further. With an angry tilt of his head, South Wind General dismissed the horsemen: he and his footsoldiers would climb the steep slopes of the mountain—a chair and a table—left unguarded by the false King. Sound and fury thundered from the stage orchestra as they climbed, and the ordinary world vanished.

"See, see!"—I grabbed Mother's wrist—*"All the soldiers are climbing up!"*

I saw them, in their hundreds, just as Mother told me, though only six men in gold-braided maroon costumes stormed onto the stage. The front soldier scooted forward and swung a pole topped with long, scarlet pennants. The Sing Kew audience saw a whole regiment before them, every man climbing upwards. In minutes, two actors, arms linked, stood precariously atop a single chair, itself balanced on a pyramid of two wooden benches, the longer bottom bench sitting on two chairs. The two actors mimed reaching down to haul the South Wind General skyward. The four footsoldiers, each representing a garrison at least, moved their arms in unison as they scaled higher and higher into the glittering light of the mountain sun.

At last, they reached the summit. The two warriors somersaulted into the air and the chairs and two benches were quickly removed. The General, stroking his long beard, now stood on the table draped with a slate-grey cloth embroidered to look like clouds and rocks—the mountain's pinnacle. Teetering dangerously, he looked far below him, surveying the treacherous slopes he had conquered. He stepped back, and his feathered headdress shivered in the mountain winds.

I lifted my head higher to see more, to hear more. If I had first supposed the theatre was a strange dream, thought the tales unfamiliar, there came a moment when I no longer felt separated from the stage. Suddenly, nothing about the opera was foreign to me: I belonged. I could not make out the words spoken or sung on stage, but my mind could trace the stories like a magician tracing fire in the air.

The beautiful Princess was saved from the wicked King. The audience shouted their approval. But Mother told me she now had to pass a test to prove she was the real princess.

"She's going to perform a trick," Mother said.

The beautiful lady was offered a gold cup from an ebony tray held by a soldier. The soldier trembled with expectation; a stream of wine was poured until the cup was full. He carefully lowered the tray to the level of the royal lady's knees. Would the Princess know what to do? The only sound was the steady tap of a woodblock.

The beautiful lady turned away from the tray and slowly bent over backwards. Her spine arched, and her head dipped lower and lower, until, using only her teeth, she lifted the gold vessel off the tray. Still backward bent, she slowly tilted her head and tipped the wine down her throat. If she was the true princess, not a drop would be spilled. The audience held its breath; the woodblock beat a rhythm that matched her careful swallowing. Mother stopped me from talking.

The actress bent her head lower and lower, until she was almost doubled-over backwards. She unclenched her teeth, and the cup clicked back onto the tray, almost tipping over. The audience gasped. The servant lifted the tray. The General looked into the gold goblet. After a beat, he triumphantly turned the cup upside down to show the audience that every drop had vanished. The General now knew that she was the long-lost Princess he had loved when he was a young scholar. At last, they were reunited.

Mother and her lady friends wept and broke into applause. Now the General took the Princess by the hand and sang, his voice rousing and deep. Then he let her go, then grabbed his gilded belt, as if in anguish, and wept.

"Why is he crying?" I asked Mother. "Has he a tummy ache?"

"He's very happy," she said. "After all their struggles, the South Wind General is singing that they will now be blessed with good fortune. His tummy doesn't hurt. He cries for happy."

Unfortunately, he also sang for happy—sang and sang; then the Princess cried, tearing at her long hair and spinning about.

"She's happy, too," Mother told me. "She cry for happy."

Mother cried, too. Everyone was crying for happy.

It would be many years before I finally understood why every one of those melo-dramatic operas ended in happiness.

"They cry for happy," Mother had told me. But Mother lied. It was easier for her to deceive me, easier to weep in peace than to explain to a small child the dire outcome of the romantic tragedy on stage.

In fact, the beautiful Princess had just been told her poor father, the real King, believing her dead, had gone mad; and her lover, in despair, had committed suicide.

"They cry," Mother said, "they happy."

I remember sensing *something* was amiss; not knowing any better, I grew to dread happy endings. To this very day, if ever I wish for anything, I never wish for happiness.

"No, no, no, *no*," Fifth Aunty protested when I told her my memory is saturated with weeping. "You got it all wrong, Sonny. In those days, Chinatown so damp. So many hankies because everyone has so many colds. Eyes watery. Bad flu! Always sniffing. Polite to use hankies, not sleeves!"

What I did not know for sure until I was almost seven was that Mother had over-simplified and recast all those opera stories; that many of these epic dramas ended tragically. Twists of fate, not luck, condemned heroines to suicide; drunken heroes were murdered by watchful villains.

I knew only Mother's versions of these stories, and so came to believe that the mythic forces of good eventually won out over evil; Luck always conquered Bad Fortune. Crossing my fingers, I told myself in a dozen different ways, "Good luck will be my life."

Whenever I worry about whether my good fortune will last, I think of those drowsy nights at the warehouse theatre on old Shanghai Alley. I hear again the encircling tales of my mother, her Toisanese rising above a cloud of sleep, each narrated episode a happy one. I never saw the same opera everyone else did.

I now understand that my perceptions in life grew out of the fables told to me by my mother. Her whispered narratives constructed within me a permanent barrier against pessimism, perhaps even against adversity.

If I turn my head at a certain angle, I can still see Mother crying, her perfumed hankie above me, her face streaked with tears. And, in some other sphere, I see Mother laughing like the Buddha, her spirit unyielding, her mythic lies flying between us like bright pennants.

The Glass Sphere

SEAN VIRGO

THE GLASS SPHERE had drifted on the Pacific for almost two hundred years. It had gone so far south that the ground swell of the Hawaiis had drawn it in, but then a southwester drove it back to the open sea and it went with the currents, northwest, riding high on the surface, entering wave troughs and skimming the swells and rollers, light as a seabird.

The birds had ridden it, too. Gulls, terns, and once—a thousand miles from land—an exhausted storm petrel, one of those brown life-sparks which American whalers called Mother Carey's chickens and believed were the souls of drowned seamen.

For years at a time it had been host to barnacles; their miniature atolls of lime had altered its balance, so that the boss of its closure had lifted clear of the water and it had spun anti-clockwise. The barnacle colonies came and went; they left crusts on the glass like faint, cryptic lettering U's, C's, and O's.

It had ridden the verge of a warm current, a wide ocean road for migrating fish and aimless flotsam like itself. It had bobbed past a bleached wooden boat where a stiff hand dangled and brushed against it, and dead eyes stared from the gunwales into its mirroring skin.

The light of the sun, moon and stars shone milky-green through it. In a kelp-raft below Alaska it had been for a season the plaything of sea otters, lounging in seaweed hammocks as they preened and suckled.

And for nearly two years it was beached up in the Aleutians, nudged further by every tide up a thin shell beach to a cleft in the basalt cliffs. The sun and salt had lustred its flanks with iridescent streaks. One dawn the sea crept in utter silence to the top of the island, carrying the glass sphere up through the trees, and then it withdrew in a fury, tearing the forest down with it, and for half the day a nest of young eagles had floated behind the sphere, till the nest disintegrated.

The sphere had frozen, and baked. The air inside it, which was the breath of a man, had made frost-flowers upon its walls, and had filled it with mist.

At the start it had been one in a chain, buoying a net between rudderless fishing junks, caught in a squall with a full catch. One boat had had time to cut itself loose, and had watched its partner dragged by the weight of the net into the wind's face and under the waves.

The boat fell slowly, the net pluming up behind it, into the stillness a furlong below the storm, leaving the colours of red, orange, yellow, suspended in that blue silence by the mass of dead fish and the glass spheres, and by the body of one of the sailors which had floated up into the net.

They hung there, lifting and sinking for almost a month, till the great grey fishes came, tearing into the swollen net. One of them got itself trapped and its death struggles ripped a whole skein of the net free. The catch floated back to the surface, the weight of the dead shark joined that of the boat and they slipped together, with the ruin of the seine, faster away from the light. A last strand of the net broke free, and the sphere that was bound to it flew to the surface, the pressure slackening inside it like the lungs of a desperate swimmer. It floated again, under a cloudless sky, trailing a rag of meshes.

The shawl of netting became a world, sustained by the glass sphere. Algae, then weeds, then molluscs and fingerling fishes lived wholly within its shadow, feeding each other and multiplying, suspending their eggs and shells from the weakening fibres. Beside and below moved the golden-eyed, watchful predators. The sphere lay heavier in the water, dragged at by colder currents, immune now to the shifts of the wind, till the netting rotted and that world fell away to extinction. The sphere rode high again, skating before the winds.

An infinitesimal orb on the ocean's face, it was almost inviolate. Minute abrasions, small shifts in refraction and texture, a milkier light. In the law book of western physics the sphere is as much a liquid as the sea that it drifts upon. In that book the windows of Chartres and York are in flux, they pour like still waterfalls between their frames, through the centuries, achieving such magical shades and harmonies as their makers could not have imagined.

But whether the sphere's creator would have accepted, or understood, the rules of our science is unknown. His touchstone was an obsidian blade, washed out from the bank of the Yalu; its formal design and refractive perfection were a message and consolation to him from the first glass-breeders. He was master of his craft but to him glass was nature transformed and restated, and the art was in permanence, not change. His physics, and chemistry, were the suspension of Time, and to harness that science and matter to a thing like a fishing-float was for him, degradation.

He lived in the prison of exile. The barbarians had come, as they'd come in each generation since his great grandfather's father, the atelier's founder, had watched Hideyoshi's armada in rout off Pusan. In the third year of his own mastery, he saw the atelier burned and the village with it. Saw the nose and ears of his Lord paraded down to the shore on a leather cushion, and was chained himself, with the porcelain makers, the ivory-carvers and jewellers, in the hold of a ship and brought to the land of borrowed manners and clothes, a bastard language, unspeakable food. Here where they worshipped power and ghosts, he was put to work.

The noble Satsuma who owned him was in debt to a merchant. The glassmaster went with a daughter, as part of her dowry, to discharge the debt.

His dreams were a vacuum; his grandfather's hands appeared to him no more. From dawn till the last watch he walked among labourers, debt-slaves with minimum talent, overseeing the vats of cheap, molten glass, trying to teach consistency in a place where the glass was blown into moulds. His life was an insult, but unlike the barbarians he feared his own death.

He dreamed, but they were empty daydreams. His son might be living yet, his owner might be persuaded in time to open a fine-glass workshop. He was aging and broken in spirit. He wondered sometimes if he had forgotten—if six generations of craft and judgement had died in him while he still lived.

The merchant cared only for property, and the growth of his fishing fleet, but he had no pretensions and he honoured success. He was shrewd, too, and guessed at the glass-master's anguish. Trade for the moment had overridden hostilities with Korea; he made enquiries.

One evening in March, when the larch buds were scarlet and the wolfbane had turned the headlands yellow, the merchant's son called the old foreman to his office. He held out a letter. It came from the master's wife, in the hand of a scribe for the women of his class pretended illiteracy. The young man watched as he read, and saw nothing. The glass-master bowed slightly, thanked him, and returned to the foundry.

His son and grandson were dead. He breathed in the stench of the place, the coals and the schist-tainted glass, the sweat and the rice wine; for a moment, by the young merchant's window, he had smelled the Spring.

He snatched the blowpipe from the hands of the labourer nearest him and twirled its end through the surface of the vat. He took a great breath; all that was in his heart at that moment was grief and rage; he blew through the iron pipe.

Some of the labourers there would deny what they'd seen; others, in time, embroidered the truth. The man who had yielded the blowpipe would never forget, though. The old Korean had blown out a perfect float, without need of a mould, had walked down the gangway and plunged the sphere into the whale-oil vat, had fished it out with his hand and, after holding it up to his face, had thrown it down. It had not broken. He had come back and returned the pipe, without taking his eyes off the door at the end of the warehouse, and had gone out into the street. He was not seen again.

He did not die, though his mind might be said to have died. He disappeared into the floating world of Kagoshima.

His breath went out and survived him, drifting through space he could not have imagined, in its prison of glass. Five generations after his abdication it lay in a cul-de-sac of the ocean, passed back and forth by the currents from Japan and California, skirting the islands of Canada, outlasting the changing jetsam of the times.

In the month of July, a mile out of Naden Harbour, a girl's hands reached down from the stem of a fish boat and lifted the glass sphere from the water. The sea dripped back from it over her wrists, her face was curved and distorted in it, it was flushed through by the red sky in the west.

The boat moved on round the headland and drifted into the bay with its engines cut. "You should see this place," the fisherman said. "I like to stop in on my way home. My grandad was born here." He was an old man himself, though wonderfully active. He might have grown heavy in his middle years, but now he'd shrunk back to something like the muscularity of his youth. The boat ran gently onto the low-tide sand. He threw out a mud-anchor and they climbed into knee-deep water. He drew breath, his elbow on the gunwale. "It's called *K'ung*," he said. "*K'ung* means Moon in our language." He chuckled, and hauled a sack over the side: "It means knife, too. Who knows?" The girl reached for the blankets and clutched them to her chest. They waded ashore.

All she could see were the tumbles of moss-cloaked logs among the spruce trees, and two bleached houseposts, with animal-human faces, sagging above the sand.

There was a fire-blackened ring of stones below a projecting branch, and a stack of wood at the tree's base. She threw down the blankets and stretched. "It's so good to be back on land," she cried, "out in the open." She jogged on the spot for a moment, shaking her wrists out loosely "And *this*," she said, twirling around, "god, this must be the most peaceful spot on earth!"

The fisherman squatted by the stone ring, building a tent of kindling from his sack. "A lot of people died here," he said. He was matter-of-fact; there was no reproof. She came and stood over him: "After we came, the whites, you mean?" He put a match to an old cigarette pack under the sticks. "Uh-huh," he said, squinting against the smoke, "Disease and all that, you know. It was Scarlet Fever mostly." As the fire licked upwards the light seemed to die from the sky, and the trees closed in.

"Are they all buried here?" The sticks crackled, her voice seemed hushed. Their shadows were flat against the trees and the housepost faces, dancing up with the flames.

The man poured some water into his billy can. "Surely," he said, and grinned up at her: "There's skulls and bones all over, best watch where you walk!" He gestured for her to pass him some logs from the pile. "There's a gravestone or two, as well, but they're Swedes."

"Swedes?"

"Hmm. There was a whaling station here, for thirty years. After the people gave up on the village. We called them Swedes but they come from Norway I believe. They went home for the winter, I guess. Just made a little world of their own here, never got around." He brushed his hands on his thighs. "And so some of them died here."

It was not cold but she squatted and held out her hands to the flames. "Don't matter to us," he said, with one of his droll, teasing faces: "Us Haidas come back again a few times, I told you that. Everyone got his *hoonts*."

"*His* hoonts? Only the men?"

He laughed to himself, a sort of benign, soft cackle. "Ohh, ladies too. We are a very advanced people!"

"But look," she said, "there's a light on the boat."

He turned and squinted down the beach: "Now what could that be?" he said. "Ohh, I reckon it's that fishing float of yours, catching our firelight."

She stirred up the fire, and watched the answering flare above the water. "It looks like an eye," she said. "Do you find a lot of them?" He nodded: "Used to be; not so much anymore. I guess those Japanese using plastic now. Those bleach jugs do the job just as good."

"I think I'll go for a swim," she said, and stood up. "Okay?"

"It's safe," he said. "I'll heat up some grog while you're out."

Out of sight down the shore she took off her clothes and waded in. The tide had come in a little; the boat was shifting on its chain. The glass ball at the stem winked up and down. The water felt silken and safe; she was aware of the sweat and fish-grease, the fumes of the cabin from two months at sea drifting away from her on the surface. She swam round behind the boat and clambered over the side, got a towel and a clean sweater from the cabin, and came back to shore on her back, kicking lazily through the shallows, keeping the cloth dry.

The smoke was blowing towards her as she came to the fire. He looked up at her, took in the long sweater, almost to her knees, and held out a cup. "Sit next to me, girlie," he said. She hesitated—in the nine weeks she'd crewed for him, for all the jokes she'd put up with from the guys on the packer's barge, he had never made a pass, or a suggestion, or even looked at her that way.

She sat beside him, towelling her legs, huddled in front of the fire like a child. The mug of hot rye and sugar was innocent as cocoa. "There were ten big houses," he said. "Dancing, feasts. And all of the food that we needed right here." The sweep of his hand embraced the whole bay behind her.

"It must have been paradise," she said.

"It was good, yes. But people died then, too; people was hurt. People is people," he said. His hand touched her knee and began to caress it in little strokes, just the fingertips. They moved down, lifting her calf muscle, came back over her knee. She looked down at the hand, dark upon her thigh. "Were you ever with a white woman?" she said.

"Ohh," he laughed quietly, and took back his hand. "I'll not talk such foolishness with a lady like you." Back on shore, and on the ice-barge, he spoke pretty much like the other fishermen, but here he'd slipped into the near monotone of the older natives, hypnotic and lisping between the tide-lap and the settling coals.

"A lady!" she laughed, awkward now.

"Sure," he said. "You are getting an education."

"Oh come on!" she said. He held up his hand: "Now don't act ashamed of that," he said. "That *would* be foolishness." The hand fell back upon her thigh.

He was very gentle. She leaned back on her elbows; her eyes were closed. His voice was as soft as his touches: "We didn't lose near as much as it looks. We keep going," he said. "The changes are part of us too."

And then, "You are a smart girl, a pretty girl," he said, and turned over and lay on his side. Out at sea he had lain, stretched out in his bunk, on his back, lightly snoring; now he curled in like a child, hands thrust between his knees, his breathing inaudible. Yet she realized, almost at once, that he was asleep. He could have had her, and he left her. She would remember all of her life what did not happen.

She finished her drink and reached for one of the blankets. She lay on her back for a while, while branches shifted and fell in the forest, the sea hushed towards them, the anchor chain rasped. There was a mockery somewhere, hidden from her, like the faces up on the houseposts she could no longer see.

He gave her a small slate carving he'd done on the boat. A bear with her two, human cubs. It sat on the shelf above her bed in the residence, with her other summer trophies. A vase full of eagle feathers, an orange and yellow agate, the green fishing float with its barnacle runes.

The day after registration her boyfriend got back from hockey camp. They could scarcely wait for each other. Down the hall co-eds were shrieking and a dozen competing musics boomed out at the afternoon. They tugged off their clothes, laughing, rolling upon the bed. They could scarcely wait.

She thought, in the moment before he entered her, that she'd keep the old fisherman to herself. She was starved of this; it was strangely flagrant, and private too, making love while people ran shouting past her door and danced on the grass outside.

Here it came at last. She was both in control and beyond it. She was running, backwards, up the mountain, the valley beside it rolled over upon her. "Oh jesus," she cried, and her left hand flew from her lover's shoulder. It struck the shelf over their heads, the vase teetered and fell. Eagle feathers came down in a sheaf on their faces.

The glass sphere rolled from the shelf and dropped, from the pillow to the floor. A quick, high note rang back from the walls. The glass sphere shattered. The girl gasped for breath.

Napoleon in Moscow

MATT COHEN

I

Napoleon is dead and everyone wants to know: How did it happen? Was it death by poison, from the boredom of exile, the heartbreak of a last absurd campaign to build a last futile empire? Napoleon is dead, but I prefer to remember Napoleon in his days of glory, Napoleon at his most mysterious. Napoleon in Moscow.

We are in the square outside his winter palace. Stella's excited breath tickling my ear as she clutches my arm and we kick our booted feet in the thick snow. Above us, Napoleon's window, heavy with golden candlelight, glows into the dark night.

WHILE THE MOON RECOVERS from last night's eclipse, snow falls hard from the sullen sky, and otters lie dreaming in their riverbank homes. On the lonely road that passes by my cabin, a snowplough moans; its blue revolving light flashes through my window and across the room.

Snow swirls and beats against the window. I am Napoleon in Moscow. My soldiers occupy the squares and swarm through the twisted streets in search of food. Nothing will be safe from me.

I AM LISTENING to Japanese music. I am trying to make sense of my life. My plan is to get the life problem structured, then carry on the way I used to, your normal greedy, selfish, manic-depressive person.

What I'm looking for now is a new master plan. I always used to have goals. For example, when I was a real estate salesman, which in a half-hearted way I still am, my goal first expressed itself in the number of houses I sold. After a while I dropped the pretence and it was just a matter of making a certain amount of money. Excuses: wife, children, mortgage, etc. I'm not talking anything fancy.

The old life was Stella. The children. The nights we spent trying to make the numbers balance. Afterwards, but not always, we would go upstairs and balance on each other. Even on nights like this, with the snow falling heavy and the revolving blue light of the snowplough like a searchlight sweeping our white bellies.

I AM NAPOLEON IN MOSCOW. "Napoleon in Moscow!" Stella laughed. This was after she had left, not necessarily forever, just a "trial separation" as she said, a holiday during which she would take the children and stay in town with her sister whose house was too big anyway—guess who sold it to her!—and since then, to tell the truth, the trial has been dragging on.

"That's me," I said, "Napoleon in Moscow."

"How do you know?"

"Demons called me on the telephone. I thought it was some kind of police association lottery. But they insisted. The next morning I found the word 'Napoleon' tattooed on my left palm."

"I think you're letting yourself go," Stella said.

As Napoleon I faced a different configuration. I could lie on Stella and use her body to trace out my campaigns. But the truth is that despite his reputation, Napoleon was more interested in snow. That is why he had his men die there, rather than while making love with their loved ones.

2

My deeds will be recorded. Museums will rise in my name. The earth will be torn apart, shovels and pickaxes wielded in a chorus louder than any marching band to extract the lead from which millions of toy soldiers will be made in my image. Small boys the world over will turn me in their fingers. They will marvel at the splendour of my uniform, the bizarre cannonball shape of my head, the way I keep one hand warm by holding it inside my jacket. "Napoleon," those young voices will whisper in the night. The way my soldiers have always whispered my name. In the night. Full of admiration, dread and wonder. Why does he do it? they ask themselves. Who is it winds up this tiny conquest machine? With what light burns that brain which keeps inventing ways to raise and then exhaust armies on the world's battlefields? Etc.

The truth is, I have no answers. First I created the Empire, then the Empire created me. World history is a ping-pong match between my inscrutable unstoppable self and the marvels that self has created. And I? The *moi* behind the mask? Just another orphan soul tossing on the seas of destiny, even though those seas move to the tides I myself have caused.

The truth is that like all great French generals and statesmen, I am a man of action by default. My real vocation was to be a writer but my early stories were rejected by corrupt monarchist editors who wished to suppress the truth about Corsica. Before they went to the blade, my poems were taped to their mouths. Now I feel most myself in the night silence of my tent, the candles sputtering, the white paper stretching out in creamy reams softer than the eyeball of an empress. My letters to Josephine, my diaries of war, but most of all the words unwritten, the vast armies of prose I would send marching across untold pages—those unwritten armies that have sunk into the whiteness of paper like my troops into the snow of the endless Russian plains.

Lost, yes, because words cannot equal the splendour of these pre-dawn hours, the wonder of being alone in a tent near tomorrow's battlefield. Outside my canvas the starry sky sparkles over the heads of my sleeping troops, four hundred thousand men lurching towards the dawn, towards the first light that will jerk them awake, full of fear and hunger and that wild chaos only I can harness, only I can turn into an orderly hurricane of violence that will send them flying into the enemy, hacking and being hacked until their skins split, their bones shatter, their blood masses in stinking pools slowly draining to dark patches on the earth so at the end of the day, as the sun sets on the dead and the dying, as the cries of the wounded rise above the surgeons' saws and the hasty whispered prayers of my priests, I, Napoleon, repulsed, sated, sick at heart, fulfilled, I will mourn that great unconscious mass of men who sleep around me now; I will mourn their dead and crippled horses, their orphans, the rivers of wine they will never drink, the aging flesh their hands will never know. Monster, yes, that is the title with which history will reward me, but I am most at home in my lonely simple tent, doing the job that has been left to me, the manufacture of dreams and nightmares, sending my word-rich armies onto their pages of snow, letting them cancel and slaughter each other until all that remains is a brief and elegant poem, a few nostalgic blood-tinted lines limping towards eternity, yes, that's how I want to be remembered, bleeding and limping in rags across the snow, or even forget the blood, the rags, the snow, the limp. Just me.

3

When the blackness of night expands blue and yellow, I step outside and strap on my skis. At this hour snow creaks. Branches snap. My troops stir amongst the leafless ghostly poplars that rise with the sun from the snow, arch their frozen branches into the cold liquid light pouring up from the eastern horizon. A few strides and the cabin is behind me, the pale hint of a lantern, a whiff of woodsmoke, then nothing at all as I glide into the soft belly of my marsh, coast down into the dark piny bush that waits to embrace me.

4

My bucking bronco bucks and bronks. My two-hundred-and-eighty-six-horse cavalry moans, then roars and whinnies beneath the snow-covered hood, white stuff flies in all directions as we power our way towards the road, leaving behind us the great rutted tracks of our charge.

The empire of the sun is back. Its weak light shines through veils of swirling snow, low half-convinced clouds that lie crouched along the horizon. The black asphalt of the highway has been scraped clean. The school buses have already passed to pick up their roadside cargoes of ski-jacketed children. Now all that remains in front of each house is its pile of lopsided green garbage bags and blue recycling boxes, waiting for the yellow township trucks.

On the way to my office I pass the dump. Despite last night's snow, the air is still and clearing. They're having a little burn off; smoke rises straight and orderly towards the washed-out dome of the sky. The dump is where I open my thermos. I love the way the steam rises into my face, the bittersweet coffee scalds my waiting tongue.

Twenty minutes later and I'm at my office, a cube in a plaza off the main highway. Frank has been and gone. The office smells of baseboard heaters, wet wool, prehistoric pizza crusts. When the red light starts blinking I pick up the phone. It's Stella, unusually.

"You all right?"

"Of course."

"Frank said …"

"Frank called you?"

"Last night, of course, after …"

Last night after work Frank and I went to Aunt Lucy's, grabbed something to eat in the sports bar. Frank is always going for the nachos, pure grease, but even if it is crazy to worry about vegetables I like a plate of crunchies with the cheese dip. Then a hamburger. Not exactly a health spa special but at least the kind of meal you could admit to your doctor. A few beers and maybe this is crazy but after a certain number it's not that good for you so I switch to Scotch and water. At least you know what you're getting and where you are.

Last night after the switch I told Frank, nothing intended, that his face was starting to look like the nachos he was eating, tomato red with yellow stuff bubbling around the edges. "Look at your nose," I now remembered saying, Stella's silence bringing it all back, "one big glob of pepperoni."

"I didn't mean to hurt his feelings," I told Stella.

"He fired you," Stella said.

We'd been yelling in the parking lot and then Frank had screamed something about my not coming back. I'd picked him up by the coat, not really meaning to hurt him. That was when he'd let me have it in the face. Wouldn't have thought he could. Left me there with my nose spouting like a hydrant.

"Wanted me to call and apologize for him. Ask you to come back."

"Here I am."

"Well, I'm here," Stella said.

"The kids at school?"

"That's right."

A questioning silence settled in. Stella's sister was in Florida. The kids were gone for hours. My nose was fine and I had my job back. "You hoping for a visit?"

"*Hoping?*" Stella repeated, giving the word a half twist and just enough vinegar to let me know she could have drowned it if she wanted to.

I put my hand in my jacket. I'd lost the opening skirmish, but as every general knows, you can't win a battle unless you manage to engage the enemy.

"Well," I said, sounding a note of defeat and withdrawal.

"I'm out of coffee," Stella said. "You could pick some up on the way."

It is easier to conquer a country than a heart. Napoleon said that. Or perhaps it was me. It's amazing what I can come out with, mostly by accident, when I've had an extra cup of coffee or a few glasses of Scotch and a few thousand brain cells are tipped into mass suicide. Stella of course, Stella doesn't appreciate these little dictums. She doesn't want to play Josephine to my Napoleon. "Well, then, you can be my Stella," I once offered her, but she didn't realize what I meant, she never takes the long view, Stella, the backward glance from the future that allows us to know that what we're going through is just so much history waiting to be corrected by a little make-up, ~us lies and omissions, various inventions pointless to try to guess in advance.
~+ bluntly, that what's happening right now is some kind of
~d sometimes even try to convince myself, but

in the end I'm back to the long view, the realization Stella is but one of a number of campaigns, a point, perhaps even the high point, of my life-to-be with her as-yet-unencountered successors. "Stella," I'll one day sigh, possibly with the same bitter regret and loss I often feel for her even now. She'll have forgotten me. She'll be in some new present, some new "reality." Her life with me will be summed up by a few pictures in an album and the odd memory that catches her unexpectedly in the ribs.

We start off in the kitchen. To show goodwill I myself put the water in the kettle, though my hands begin to tremble and it spills before I can even get it to the stove. "You might as well come upstairs," Stella then says, not unkindly.

I follow her up. She's wearing a soft white sweater of wool so fine I can't imagine it between my fingers, dark pants stretched tight over the bum I also want to touch. While I sit on the edge of her sister's bed Stella goes into the bathroom to undress, then comes back in her white terry-cloth robe, the one I bought her last Christmas.

We climb in. In the morning winter light our skin is grainy, helpless. Soon we're under the sheets, humping and groaning. Do we love each other or are we just condemned to this weird sweet need? Afterwards we're lying side by side, and I'm looking up at my sister-in-law's pink stuccoed ceiling wondering if she too has inspected this dubious touch in the afterglow of sex, and then the whole need comes on us again. This time, hovering above Stella, I open my eyes and look down on her. Her white legs are spread in a perfect V, and I suddenly remember when Crystal was born: just before the final contractions Stella was lying this way, her legs splayed, exhausted, then suddenly her knees jerked up, her face and throat turned scarlet, her huge belly banded with muscle and effort—

In the shower my nose starts to bleed again, though not as badly as when Frank hit me. To save the towels I stand above the sink, holding toilet paper to my face. When I come back into the bedroom Stella is lying where I left her, hands clasped behind her head, making her own study of the pink stucco.

"You could stay for supper," Stella says.

I want to see the children. I want Stella. I want to slip into this pink stucco cocoon and sleep away my life until I come out dead on the other side.

But there's something in this I can't do. I can't burden the brightness of their living with the awkward shadow of my death, of my long view in which after all the dazzling campaigns, the retreats, the exiles, the empires constructed out of countries not yet named, the years spent in dungeons not yet built, I'll be lying in the ground somewhere and they'll be standing over me, not sure whether to weep or just be relieved.

"Don't make it into a big thing," Stella says.

I sit down on the edge of the bed. Outside the snow is sheeting against the windows. "Look at it," I say.

Stella pulls the sheets and covers up to her neck. "At least you could bring me some of the coffee you promised."

"I also got some wine."

"The corkscrew's in the drawer beside the fridge."

Soon all the windows are plastered with snow. We're plastered too, not really, just dizzy with all the times we keep going back to Stella's sister's bed. By the time we make it down to the kitchen, more or less dressed, to find something to eat, it's mid-afternoon and according to the radio, the highways and the schools are closing.

When school lets out we're both there. Crystal and Robbie have their scarves wrapped round their faces, the snow is blowing into everyone's eyes, we stagger into my bucking Bronco and drive the few blocks home without anyone doing anything but clapping their hands and panting.

I help Crystal, who is seven, out of her snowpants. She looks at me curiously at first, it's been weeks, then just goes along as though everything is normal, as though I've been here every night for the past several months kissing her beet-red cheeks, helping her in and out of clothes, reading her stories while she waits for her bath. Robbie, five, stays in the circle of his mother's arms, watching suspiciously. But when I pick him up he throws his arms around my neck and presses his face into my chest so hard that it hurts.

When all the coats and boots are piled up they run off to the family room I was so careful to point out to Carrie when she bought the house. Sprawled out on the apricot shag wall-to-wall that was featured in the ad, they watch the big colour television Carrie's husband Cal bought for the Stanley Cup a few years ago. Stella and I can see them from the kitchen. While she makes hot chocolate I look in the freezer and cupboards. "I'll do spaghetti," I announce, as though about to distribute a cordon bleu meal to my troops stranded knee-deep on the Russian steppes.

"Great," Stella says. "A night off cooking. That calls for another bottle of wine."

The house I sold Carrie is warm. There's real central heating, a gas furnace that blasts hot air through the house with Desert Storm efficiency, along with a living-room gas fireplace the designer built in as part of the guaranteed romance such a palace inspires. While I hack away at the onions, Stella opens a new bottle, turns on the fireplace so the flames start making their gassy blue dance. The living-room carpet isn't shag, just a dark broadloom meant to hide the dirt. The ceiling is stucco, like the ones in the bedrooms upstairs and the family room, but since we're down-stairs it's not pink but white. I wonder what it would be like to lie here, naked, in front of the romantic fireplace, looking up at the white stucco. Stella has already poured the wine. If the kids weren't here, I think to myself, we could try it right now. But of course the kids are here, because we tried it right now before, and so—etc., etc. Anyway, what kind of father am I, wanting my own children whom I don't really take care of to disappear so I can make more neglected children?

Stella now has on the kind of slacks women wear these days, wide hips, narrow little cuffs that hug their tiny ankles. One of those tiny ankles is crossed over her knee. She's sitting on one of the two matching white corduroy couches, reading a psychology textbook. That book, the master's degree program it's part of, was one of the reasons Stella gave for moving to town. It's basic to her plan, her master master's plan, at the end of which she'll have her own cube, not in a doughnut plaza off the highway but in a tastefully renovated downtown house, in which she'll "help women help themselves." She won't bother helping men help themselves, it goes without saying, because they already have, pigs at the trough, and if now they're sad and confused, well, it's just like a kid who steals too many candies and then gets sick from eating too much. Or is disappointed because they stop tasting sweet. Or angry that the people he robbed no longer like him.

While Stella reads her psychology text I dive into one of Carrie's magazines. It falls open to an article on composting vegetables. Almost every line is highlighted. I wish I could ask her how a person who lives in a house with stucco ceilings could spend her life composting vegetables but first of all she only lives in this house because she bought it to please Stella and second I've already asked her this kind of question and she doesn't even try to answer.

I switch to coffee and by the time I'm laying the steaming plates of spaghetti out on the table, I'm stone sober. Stella, meanwhile, has flaked out on one of the white corduroy sofas. I find her lying on her back, one leg hooked over the back of the sofa, one hand flung out to the coffee table, still wrapped around her wine glass. Her cheeks are flushed, her face in unusual and angelic repose. Feeling like Santa Claus I rearrange her a bit and cover her with one of Carrie's fuzzy angora blankets.

During dinner I quiz the children about life in their new school. As though I am some interested relative who just dropped in from Mars, not the unstable father because of whom their mother had to move the children out of their natural home and into this new school where they had to make all new friends and get used to different teachers.

Afterwards they show me their new room. Their pink stucco. They sleep in twin wood-framed beds that can be stacked to make bunks. On their beds are their favourite quilts, their stuffed toys, a few picture books I recognize. When I sit down on Crystal's bed she immediately snuggles up to me, demands that I read her a story about a brave worm, one I've read to her a thousand times before. Robbie pretends to be above all this. But he stretches out on his own bed and listens as I read.

One at a time I get them into their pyjamas, teeth and hair brushed, faces washed, the whole routine. Wind and snow are still rattling the windows. It is so warm here, so whole. I imagine the cabin, half-frozen and dark. As always, when I'm not there for the night, I feel uncomfortably disloyal, as though I've deserted my post.

When the children are ready I take them downstairs to kiss their mother good night. Stella is awake again, sipping a cup of coffee and reading in front of the fire. The children crowd around her. She draws them under the blanket. Soon they're chattering away, animated and oblivious.

That night we go to bed together as though I'd never left. So strange-familiar, Stella's body next to mine. This time when we make love it's like animals opening to each other in their cave. Stella falls asleep, holding me. When I wake up, she's still wrapped around my back. I listen to the snow and wind. There are night lights in the hall and bathroom for the children, and when I close my eyes I can imagine those lights glowing outside, in the storm. My future self—or one of Stella's lovers—could be standing on the street, seeing the glow of these lights, speculating on the mystery behind the windows.

For hours I lie there, imagining myself being imagined. I am trying to believe I am really real, really here, really asleep in Stella's arms. But every time I close my eyes I float up above the house. First I see us, yes, the happy family happily ensconced in our gas-powered central-heated warmth. But then I go higher; the whole town is just a red-yellow smear of lights, and I am floating north, up the frozen ribbons of highway and then into the back country thick with scrub and beaver ponds. Until I come to the cabin, stranded and battered by snow, deserted by the only one who can love and watch over it.

5

In the morning I leave early, as the children are preparing for school. The snow-ploughs have passed in the night, my bucking Bronco has no problem blasting its way out of the driveway and into the street. I go to a restaurant for bacon and eggs, double brown toast no butter, a newspaper and endless coffee until my nerves set up a high whining chatter.

When I arrive at the office Frank immediately starts talking about the Redway deal we've been working on for months—a strip plaza location for which we levered the land, fought for all the clearances and permits, and are now trying to unload in order to fill our bank accounts. Or at least pay our rent. Or something. It's so long since we've made a deal I can hardly remember the name of our lawyer.

This morning Frank is full of optimism. He's got on his lucky blue selling jacket, his face is shaved so close he looks like he's had his skin peeled. The blueprints are spread out on his desk and, this is how good Frank is, once he gets talking even I believe I can smell the fresh doughnuts and coffee from the little shop he's got marked out on the corner.

We're meeting the potential buyers in a downtown restaurant at noon, and just as we're getting ready to leave, Stella calls. Frank, giving me a big wink as though I'm about to pop the question, passes me the phone. I've just come out from our little washroom, my own face scraped raw by one of those disposable razors that you keep using for one more shave.

"How are you?" she asks.

"Nervous," I say. "We're trying to unload the plaza this morning."

Frank frowns. He doesn't like negative remarks except when he's into the nachos and beer.

"Good luck," Stella says, her voice empty. Of course she wasn't calling to ask about what I was or wasn't selling.

"I'll let you know how it goes later," I say, evading everything, leaving everything open. This is, as I often lecture my troops, known as taking possession of the high ground.

Stella responds with a direct and immediate attack. "Later?"

This is what it is to be Napoleon. This is what it is.

"I'll call you from the cabin," I concede, digging my own grave.

6

When I get home the snow is red with the setting sun. I go straight to the woodpile and let my splitting axe say it all, its huge iron head rearing back in the darkness, then descending into the frozen wood with a loud mourning shriek.

Later that night I am out in the snow. The bucking Bronco is a dark outline in the moonlight, my own windows cast their golden glow like abandoned tears. As my skis scream softly on the frozen snow I am free to imagine that behind those gold-lit windows Napoleon is gathering his forces, charting out his marches, planning the conquests of new far-flung empires, vast frozen hearts.

I move towards the pine woods. Thorns tear at my legs and face. Until finally I am safe in the darkness, dying to the shrill cries of winter owls, slivers of moonlight feasting on my blood.

The Woman Who Lived in a Shoe
SHEILA HETI

SHE WAS ONLY A WOMAN living in a shoe, and she didn't understand the ways of the world. Didn't know how to act at every specific social gathering. Wasn't invited to many anymore, not even museum openings.

One day a man came to her shoe and knocked on the front door. She went to open it and saw an older fellow who was quite charming-looking. He was holding a huge burst of roses and smiling at her, and she smiled back from inside.

"Why …" she said.

"I love you Dora," said the man, and he held out the flowers, and they were so grand and vast that they blocked her face entirely.

She was a modest woman and did not know what to say.

"Say you'll marry me."

"I can't," said the woman. She had said this before. "There's only room for me in the shoe, and if I leave, it will disappear and fall to the ground out of sorrow and uselessness."

The man turned and went away.

"Wait!" she called after him, waving her hand, but he kept walking in such a sorrow because he really did love Dora, and it was not good enough if she just kind of liked him back. He was the one she had to worry about falling to the ground out of sorrow and uselessness, not the shoe.

Well, there were a number of opportunities for the woman to have fun, and go to public events and make herself known to the world as the woman she was. But whenever she was invited she would just look at the card and shake her head. "I'd have nothing to wear," she'd say to herself, placing her hand against the leather walls. "And who would I meet there? And if I did, then what?"

Then the woman who lived in a shoe would go outside and sit on the toe and watch as the world went by in all its busy activity: the cities making money and the sun as it so very quickly went up in the sky and down in the sky and up and down and up and down like a yo-yo.

"My," she would say to herself. "I don't know how anybody finds any time to do anything in a day." And she'd go back inside her shoe where it was one colour of light and smelled of leather, and she'd knit or stitch or wring her hands, or not, or play cards with herself, or not.

One day the woman put up a notice on the door of the shoe. When the mailman came by he shook his head and walked away, saying to himself, "It's a changing world. Without the shoe it'll be any normal street, any normal city, any normal day. There will be a great tall tower put up there, and it will be the burial ground of the shoe. And I'll never see another woman who lives in a shoe ever again, and every shoe I see forever more will be just a shoe, just a shoe."

Then the baker came by with a loaf of bread that he had been making every week for twenty years, perfectly sized for the woman who lived in a shoe. "No shoe!" he exclaimed, and hugged the bread in close to his chest. As the tears welled up in his eyes he started to pull off nibbles. And when the milkman came by to drop off a milk bottle, something he did only for the woman who lived in a shoe, he took several stunned steps back, shaking his head like all the rest. His heart was filled with an inexpressible sorrow, and he looked at the shoe, and at the horizon, and back at the shoe, and back at the horizon.

That was all very well. When the woman came out she found no bread, she found no mail, she found no milk, and she found no men. So she took down the sign, picked up her suitcase, and looked into the distance at the city with the watch setting over the hill. She left the door open as she walked from the shoe, and walked and walked and walked and walked and walked and walked and walked and walked. There was little one could do in a day, in the outside world, outside the shoe.

Constance

VIRGIL BURNETT

More than one knight from Montarnis succumbed to the temptation of pilgrimage, or to its more bellicose sibling, crusade. Many commoners too followed the Cross in one way or another eastward. The experience of these peregrinations altered the men who indulged in them. Many were so changed that they were never again seen in the place of their origin. Those who did go back bore with them the burden of their new attitudes, their new tastes and vices. These foreign influences infiltrated the community that Montarnis had been, eroded it, transformed it. The population of the town increased and became more heterogeneous. The society became more complex. New wealth caused allegiances to shift and ostentation to flourish. Fine houses proliferated, whether aristocratic or bourgeois, episcopal or abbatial, with each of them designed to outshine the others in elaboration and elegance. It was much the same with manners. An alien courtliness insinuated itself into all intercourse. Native candour was swept aside by a tide of more devious ways, and intrigue, both political and amorous, was so generally practised as to become almost routine.

NO ONE HAD EVER PRETENDED that Constance shared her husband's bed. Thibault of Montarnis was a good, gentle man but a very ancient one, and long before their marriage the mutilations of age had unsuited him for a lover's role. Time had drained and reduced him until he was like a matted cobweb on a dry twig. His sharp bones poked through his black serge gown at oddly inhuman angles, and his head, when he thrust it from his cowl, was so overlaid with wrinkles, knotted veins, and broken blood vessels that his features were completely obscured by a dark veil of decrepitude.

The old lord had always been more monk than master. He had married late in life to appease Constance's ambitious father, a close and threatening neighbour, by embellishing that nobleman's family tree with his own illustrious name. Since the wedding Thibault had scarcely been seen outside his library, where he was engaged in a study of certain documents concerning his ancestors and his fief, documents of no interest to the rest of the world. His devotion to this study was incomprehensible to the members of his little court and to his wife as well. No one questioned his behaviour, however. Thibault was the head of the most important family in Montarnis and the direct descendant of Hugues the Pious. Thibault was expected to do as he pleased. Besides, no one really missed him. In her father's house Constance had lived a restricted and solitary life; her existence was altered very little by moving to Thibault's palace.

Whole months would go by without a meeting of the couple. Sometimes they would encounter one another in a corridor as the old man shuffled from his bedroom to his books, but his absorbing conversations with himself, as well as the extremity of his stoop, made it difficult for him not to overlook other presences. If he did happen to notice the tall form of his wife drifting quietly past him in the hall, he remembered to greet her, dimly but affectionately. As often as not on these rare occasions, he called her Berthe, his dead cousin's name.

This unnatural situation inspired a keen, almost competitive, curiosity among the courtiers. If Constance had been plain or herself advanced in years, they might have accepted the incongruity of their patrons' *ménage,* but Constance was not yet thirty and was admitted to be a beauty by even the least charitable of her ladies-in-waiting. She was a fair woman, very pale, since she never left the palace, never exposed herself to the sun or open air. She had a strong waist, stately hips that sloped to full flanks, and neat breasts that rose from her fine torso like twin domes of blue-veined marble. Her head might have been a model for a cathedral sculptor, and her hair was as remarkable for its mass as for its colour, a blend of amber and topaz. It hung down her back to her thighs, like a voluptuous, silky garden of Babylon. She was intelligent and polite, if rather remote. Except for the fact of her marriage to an octogenarian, nothing about Constance suggested that she was fashioned for a passionless life.

Although the courtiers pried industriously into Thibault's wife's affairs, they were never able to attribute to her even the slightest evidence of misbehaviour. The part of each morning that she spent in their society was an inquisition; the courtiers studied her as avidly as Thibault studied his crumbling codices. Daily they scanned her person for some telltale keepsake or talisman, but she dressed soberly and wore as decoration only the family heirlooms of her station. Daily they brought forth insinuating queries about her private hours and pastimes, but she parried their questions with answers as decorous as her costume. That Constance was neither a promiscuous nor even a flirtatious woman, the courtiers were forced to concede. Her apparent virtue, however, was intolerable to them, and rather than accept what seemed to be, they took what mean pleasure they could in speculating on the lascivious escapades she must enjoy in secret.

The identity of the partner in the sins of which Constance was suspected by the court gossips was a subject of endless discussion. A multitude of theories was advanced, factions developed, and the probability of each candidate for her affections was debated hotly and with utter frankness. One group insisted that the culprit must be a palace lackey, or a squad of them. Another imagined, more chivalrously, that some daring outsider nightly penetrated the palace defences and scaled the wall to Constance's apartment. Guardsmen and grooms were accused. Even her confessor and the old scholar who gave her lessons in Latin came in for their share of suspicion, though they were as old and ugly as the count. In reference to this possibility, an especially sharp-tongued lady suggested, much to the courtiers' amusement, that perhaps Constance enjoyed her husband after all, and other old men as well. An eleven-year-old page and a pretty hairdresser were denounced, but the ladies who pointed them out were obviously guilty of confusing their own desires with those of their lady, and no one took them seriously. Of all the theories put forward, the most persistent one held that some member of the court, one of their own number, was Constance's paramour. The least lovely of the courtiers found this possibility especially annoying, as painfully nagging as a splinter beneath a fingernail, and it was they who were most tireless in the search.

Evidence was collected by every imaginable means. Servants were threatened, bribed, beaten. Patrols were organized along the ramparts so that Constance's windows could be constantly observed. Informing, eavesdropping, and spying became as prevalent in the palace as gossip had always been. This diligence was rewarded by the exposure of a score of entertaining scandals, but none of them involved Thibault's wife.

The courtiers were completely justified in their suspicions. Constance *did* have a lover, a young and handsome and very wealthy knight named Roscelin de Saint-Phal. This Roscelin had until recently been very little known at Thibault's court. He had spent his childhood in the country and had been educated abroad. Since the death of his father and his assumption of the older man's responsibilities, he had visited the palace only on those occasions when his presence was demanded by politesse. His behaviour there was correct but scarcely enthusiastic. He was habitually tardy and was as quick to depart as slow to arrive. During the ceremonies and festivals that he felt obliged to attend, he stood apart from the assembly, yawning and gazing vaguely at the ceiling. His peers, without exception, despised him.

Roscelin's jousting feats made him particularly hated among the more pugnacious gentlemen of Montarnis. In the arena, as in the great hall, he was often late. He thought nothing of keeping his opponents waiting fully armed and mounted in the hot sun while he dawdled over his weapons or adjusted his elaborate plumage. Even more infuriating than his tardiness was his invincibility. He was a limp and casual horseman, but he had a way of urging his charger suddenly forward at the moment of the impact of the lances, so that his adversary's thrust struck air and his own had added force. On foot, fighting with long sword, short sword, axe, or mace, his unorthodox style and exasperating changes of pace won him victory after victory. At the end of each encounter, he left his challenger lying dazed, dented, and dusty on the turf. He took no interest in competitions between other knights and, between his own fights, passed the time alone in his cloth-of-gold pavilion, sipping wine and reading foreign verse.

The nicer gentlemen of the town hated him almost as ardently as the athletic ones because of the splendour of his dress. His appearances at the palace were rare but impressive. Whenever it was known that he was to be present, a burst of activity quickened the court fops. All their efforts with ribbons, sashes, feathers, furs, and chains were wasted, however, for Roscelin's costumes were inevitably more gorgeous and distinguished than theirs, and at the end of every audience they were left gnawing their lips with envy.

Among the ladies of Montarnis, Roscelin was even less popular than he was with the men. He methodically avoided their society, and if he happened by chance to meet one of them, he limited their discourse to a few formal words and a brief departing bow. He had never been known to indulge in gallantries or flattery. He made it perfectly apparent to everyone that these women did not in the least attract or interest him. His haughtiness naturally infuriated them, and they avenged themselves with calumnies against him. They never tired of pointing out to whoever would listen that a man so insensitive to their charms must be either impotent or perverse. If they had been less provincial, they would have heard stories to quiet their rumour-mongering, for Roscelin's amorous exploits had made him notorious in courts from Burgos to Czerwinck. He was neither cold to women nor incapable of serving them; he was merely fastidious.

This very air of superiority placed Roscelin above, or perhaps beneath, suspicion of adultery with Constance. The courtiers were unanimously of the opinion that he was far too self-obsessed to devote his time and energy to a love affair, particularly one so demanding as this one must necessarily be. They were mistaken, misled by the exaggeration of Roscelin's manner and the poverty of their own imaginations. What they interpreted as ridiculous vanity was in fact an artful pose. Behind the masque of egotism Roscelin concealed the depth of his feelings and the complete seriousness of his intentions.

Shortly after returning home from his years of wandering, Roscelin had been invited to Thibault's wedding. His first sight of Constance was in church, as she knelt in her bridal robes, patiently reciting to the aged lord the words that were to make a prison of her life. Throughout the tedious ceremony, Roscelin watched her blond head softly reflecting the light of the altar candles. When finally the new wife and the old husband rose and passed in stately procession out of the church, Roscelin remained behind. For hours he paced the dim ambulatory, studying, it seemed, the infinite complexities of its cosmatesque pavement. Behind his regular footfall, his cloak, a vast sail of gold brocade and wolf pelts, hissed intermittently across the tesserae. He stood still at last on the grave slab of a knight from some immemorial epoch. Still visible in the worn stone was an effigy, a faint engraving polished in places to perfect blankness. Roscelin, motionless for the first time since the church had emptied, pondered the wan image in the floor and seemed to recognize in it a colleague. Before he left he spoke to it, confided in it, explained to it his impossible but irrevocable passion for the Lady Constance.

For more than a year Roscelin did not approach her. He occupied himself with riding and exercising with his weapons or, more dangerously, with sour brooding in his house. During these painful months he saw her only five times—in the great hall on feast days. The spectacle of the countess's natural beauty splendidly embellished with the richest of her finery filled Roscelin with alternating sensations of longing and self-reproach. On the fifth day she appeared at the long banquet table in regalia more various and magnificent than any she had worn before. Her bright hair was braided and bound with gold. Precious pendants of silver filigree and intagliated gems dangled in radiant profusion about her throat and breast. Her robe was a bazaar of oriental fabrics. Above her heart a fibula decorated with a battling pair of ruby-eyed enamel monsters fixed a mantle so heavy with baroque pearls, carved ivory, and brilliants that she could scarcely hold herself erect beneath it. Like a sublime work of art, more chryselephantine goddess than woman, she posed beside her husband. Her face was as pure and expressionless as the great diamond that hung between her brows.

As he studied her from his place at the far end of the table, Roscelin felt his resist-ance to her beauty weaken and crumble, as if some temple in his brain had been exploded to dust by the advent of a new and superior religion. He would not, indeed he could not, restrain himself any longer. To do so, he admitted at last, would be to attempt to deny all the precepts of destiny.

The following morning Constance found a strange book beside her bed. It was a small volume of Latin verse bound between covers of gold granulation and cloisonné. Puzzled and vaguely disturbed, she turned its parchment pages and deplored for a moment her ignorance of classical tongues. She was certain that her table had been bare except for a candle when she had retired the night before. How had the book come, and from where? No one else slept in her apartment; no one was allowed to enter without her permission. Her eyes turned uneasily toward the open window that pierced the palace wall a hundred feet above the moat.

She thought of questioning her maids and the guards in the corridor, but in the end she was silent, without knowing why. She returned the book to her table. During the day she wondered often at this odd epiphany and that night she fell asleep contemplating its jewelled beauty in the moonlight.

The days passed and Constance's curiosity about the book increased. The mysteries of its text both annoyed her and excited her imagination. She memorized the illuminations and the historiated capitals. She scanned again and again the lines of calligraphy, as if to compensate for her lack of learning with visual familiarity. When, at the end of a week, a petition arrived from a Latinist in the town who offered instruction in return for a small pension, she sent for him directly.

The scholar, of course, was Roscelin in fancy dress, a preposterous parody of the bookish count. His body appeared bent and palsied inside a musty gown, his face shrivelled and pouched around a purple beak. His hair, dusted with cornstarch and disarrayed, escaped from beneath a decayed fur hat that clung to his head like a mangy cat. Along the corridor that led to Constance's apartment, he shed a trail of leaves from a ruptured folio dictionary, and when he crossed her threshold, he was already in full discourse.

Roscelin's long-planned strategy abandoned him when he was at last alone with Constance. He had intended to proceed diplomatically from the classics to his suit, but in the middle of his opening disquisition on a favourite fragment of Ovid, he let his eyes stray from the page and looked too long at his lovely student's lips. Before he quite knew it, he had plucked off his putty nose and kissed her lavishly on the mouth. A short time later his outrageous eyebrows, his gown, and ultimately his entire scholarly costume joined the false nose on the floor. On the floor, too, eventually lay the lady's elegant dress, and beside the heap their mingled garments made, lay Constance herself, holding hard to her naked lover. She clung to him until the day was spent, her breast heaving, her loins streaming, her soul reeling before the force of her rioting passion.

At last, however, the sun set, and she rose and disappeared into the more private rooms of her apartment. When she returned to her place beside Roscelin, a single candle burned on the back of a black iron goat near their heads.

"It was your book, then?" she said.

He stirred, shaking off heavy layers of sweet sleepiness and satisfaction. "My lady, it was."

"But how? …"

He laughed softly. "By the roof, of course, with a length of cord."

"You were in my bedroom and watched me sleep?"

"I was and did."

"And did you think of waking me?"

"To climb down the wall to your window was a game for a boy. To leave after I had seen you was the most difficult thing I have ever done."

She shook her head. "You might have stayed. I have been waiting for you since my wedding."

"You saw me there?"

"I saw no one else," she answered as she laid her forefinger on his thigh.

Roscelin kissed her arm where it lay against her breast. His mouth spanned the boundary between the two warm volumes of flesh. As the slight affectionate gesture of his lips joined the cylinder and the sphere, he saw, in an instant of metaphysical illumination, their united flesh stretching out before him to infinity.

The white moment passed; his daily mind returned. He lay back, sighing, and began to tell her stories of his travels and to build for her the cities she had never seen. Through the agency of his memory, she saw Caen, with its two abbeys like a wedding couple, tall and white above the meadows of the Orne. She saw Fougères and grim Josselin and beyond them Merlin's forest watered by a multitude of dark, linked lakes. She saw spotted trout under Colmar's bridges and dove-coloured, dove-tempered cows in Autun's pagan circus. Fulda's church, Sion's fort, Krakow's market, and Bari's sparkling marble port flickered through her imagination and left their residue of fantasy.

And then their time was up. They restored Roscelin's costume and in a tender, melancholic mood resumed the masquerade. They went to the door together and stood for a while, discussing grammar for the benefit of the servant in the corridor.

"Your ladyship's grasp of the subjunctive is, if I may speak frankly, deplorable," wheezed the old pedant in an absurd voice.

"Professor," Constance replied, "you may be certain that I shall try to strengthen it."

"Allow me also to remark, my lady, that your declensions are imprecise. I shall go so far as to say that they are untidy."

Constance lowered her eyes. "Orderliness, I am afraid, has never been one of my virtues."

"Nevertheless," the scholar continued, remembering to temper the scolding with praise, "your conjugation shows promise."

"For that my teacher must take credit."

"Not at all, madame. You are distinctly gifted in this area of your study. Review today's lesson seriously, and we shall both profit from it next week."

"Fortunately, my dear professor, I did not neglect to take some mental notes."

As Constance withdrew, the old scholar made a deeper bow than was usual for one of his age and remained gallantly bent before the closing door until its latch snapped home. The guards joked about him as he passed through the palace gate. The Lady Constance, they agreed, had engaged an odd tutor, a ridiculous old bird who hummed, tottered, doddered, quoted aloud, and occasionally skipped like a schoolboy as he went away in the dusk.

That night Constance tried to read, but her crowded mind rejected the quiet challenge of the page; her book fell forgotten to her lap as she contemplated the logs blazing on the hearth. In a pleasantly reflective state she sat for some time, seeing Roscelin's cities in the flames. Suddenly, as in an optical illusion, her vision shifted; instead of looking into the fire she was looking through it—through it at a small iron door. At first she doubted her eyes, but as the fire died she could make out more clearly, in spite of the camouflage of years of soot, the door's smooth texture and its thin rectangular outline. Fascinated, she watched it until the embers cooled; then she stepped over the ashes and pushed with her silver-slippered toe against the panel of iron. It grated briefly back across a stone sill. A second, stouter kick forced it open.

Constance had that courage which solitude inspires. Without hesitating to wonder what lay beyond, she fetched a candelabrum and slipped into the darkness beyond the hearth. She found herself in a small stone chamber at the bottom of a stairway. Fearlessly she mounted the narrow, cobweb-choked passage. Whole cities of gossamer, weighted with the corpses of roasted spiders, flared away in the heat of her tapers as she climbed.

At the top of the stair, she stepped through a second door and stood inside a more modest replica of the fireplace in her own apartment. A long, empty hall flanked by shuttered lancets opened before her. Moonlight filtered through the roof slates that clung like fish scales to the grandiose carpentry overhead. The room's population of rats chirped an unwholesome protest as her light advanced through their dim and fetid domain.

Constance reached the end of the hall and passed through yet another door into an abandoned wing of the castle, a section of the rude original structure that had been made obsolete by the architectural endeavours of Thibault's grandfather. The attic room in which she stood had been an arsenal, and the storeys below it a barracks for the palace guard. The walls around her were tapestried with blades of Bordeaux steel: swords of every description, daggers, axes, and perversely curving falchions. Shields and studded bucklers hung in ranks from the rafters. Sallets and hawk-beaked bascinets, breastplates, greaves, and liquid chain mail were spread at random across the floor. At the centre of the room, like an iron baldachin, rose a great inverted cone of pikes. Over all these tools of war, steel's nemesis, rust, had crept and with it rust's grey comrade, dust.

It was in this abandoned hall that Constance spent her free hours between the first and second of her lessons in Latin. Each day she climbed the chimney stair and worked in the arsenal like an ordinary housewife. For the first time in generations the room was swept clean and put in order. The scattered weapons were collected into tall pyramidal trophies in each of the room's four corners. Helmets were fitted with candles and converted into phantasmagoric lanterns around the steel-lined walls. Mirrors were polished until they gleamed brighter than the blades they mirrored. The pikes were draped with banderoles, and the circular area inside them was heaped with furs and stuffs. Against the door that led into the barracks below, an unsteady mound of axes was built, so that anyone who slipped its bolt would be instantly carried away in an avalanche of honed blades.

When Roscelin returned, Constance took him by the hand and led him up the spider-infested flue to the chamber she had prepared for their studies. The knight made a delighted circuit of the place, pausing here and there to admire an antique weapon or to inspect an armorial device. His interest was held for several moments by the simple ingenuity of the deadfall against the bolted door. He turned back to Constance full of a new kind of admiration. She curtsied in response to his congratulations, took his hand again, and pulled him down beside her under the steel canopy.

They repeated their earlier lesson with excurses and elaborations. Constance was untutored but eager to learn; she went to her lover as avidly as a backcountry scholar to his first great library and advanced rapidly in the academy of lust. Roscelin took his pleasure gently and applauded the least of his mistress's lascivious experiments. In time her initial courage blossomed into a proud sensual virtuosity that provided them both with pleasures more ample and intense than had been held out to them in even their most complicated fantasies.

It was inevitable that their lovemaking, if it were to last at all, would be exceptional. At the outset the omnipresent dangers of the liaison established around them an atmosphere of a strange melodrama. If they had heeded the myriad threats confronting them, the affair would have quickly expired in a net of suspicion and fear. The danger was irrefutable, but after their first embrace they elected to ignore it. Outside Constance's door, extreme caution was necessary, but, when they were together in their secret bedchamber, they let the tone of the room permeate their sensibilities, and every moment they shared seemed as unreal and grotesque as the abandoned armoury itself.

Thus their afternoons became a bizarre succession of charades. Partly in an attempt to obscure all that was ominous in their situation, and partly in recognition of its extravagance, they competed in displays of libertine caprice and vanity. They mimed and danced among the trophies. They devised sinister games of hide and seek. They dressed in nightmarish costumes culled from Thibault's wardrobes and the lockers of dead guardsmen. On one brilliant occasion, Roscelin delighted his lady by stepping from behind an arras wearing the skin of a bear; on another even more memorable day, Constance greeted her lover clad magnificently in nothing but her jewels.

When their theatrical invention flagged, they armed themselves with clubs and hunted rats in the empty hall outside. They beat through the archaic trash that littered the floor until their rooting weapons found a heap of huddled bodies. The rats were wary but when one was goaded it would come out and rush, bare-fanged and squealing, into the hunters' range. Sometimes a whole assembly of the creatures would be aroused. In the stampede that followed, the clubs were inefficient and the hunters would leap among the tumbling grey bodies and stamp on as many spines as possible before the frantic pack scattered to new cover. At first the small bodies jerking beneath her feet disgusted Constance, but after several sorties her squeamishness passed, and she became far more proficient in the sport than Roscelin. She began to take pride in her hits and developed a peculiar balletic finesse in what they called her rat-dancing. In the end she scorned any weapon but her toes and killed only by stepping on the tiny heads. On her best days Roscelin stood aside in wonder, as she skipped across the scampering hordes to the accompaniment of minute skulls popping like holiday squibs.

When they tired of games, they feasted on the supply of dainties Constance had filched from her table during the week. She spread a picnic on a drum, and they sat like barbarians cross-legged on the floor, gorging without the convenience of cutlery or plate and swilling Thibault's *vin de Beaune* from a long-dead trumpeter's horn. After the feast they made love—sometimes brusquely beside the picked bones and twisted parings of their meal, sometimes lingeringly on the couch under the steel canopy, and sometimes, almost ceremonially, standing upright at the centre of the baldachin.

The affair between Lady Constance and the knight Roscelin continued through three precarious years. It was unknowingly brought to an end by the combined efforts of the envious courtiers and the agents of the Inquisition. Since Roscelin's return to Montarnis, his enemies had been circulating rumours about him. Many of these stories hinted at the obscene and heretical nature of the books in his library. One evening as he returned to his house from a day's riding, he found a detachment of heavily armed men waiting for him in his study. Their chief, a fat man with a deformed ear like a baby's fist and a nose that tilted up repulsively to expose his nostrils, sat behind his lectern. As the knight entered, a book was held out to him.

"Does this belong to you?" demanded the fat man without any introduction or explanation of his presence.

Roscelin took the volume, studied its ornate binding, and turned through several of its pages. Then he walked to a shelf and slipped it into the dark slot that was its usual place.

"You know it is my book, since you took it from one of my shelves," he replied.

Another volume was thrust toward him; it was an exquisite herbal illustrated with portraits of poisonous plants. "And this?"

Roscelin acknowledged it fondly. It was one of his proudest acquisitions. He rubbed its cover with his sleeve and laid it carefully on the table.

"Do you know who I am?" asked the fat man.

Roscelin surveyed him with exaggerated interest.

"In spite of your curiosity about books," he said, deliberately, "I do not think you are a connoisseur."

The man squinted and leaned a little forward in his seat. He was not used to irony.

"Nor do I think," Roscelin went on, "that you are an illuminator or any other sort of craftsman. Your fingers are short and fat, wholly unsuited to fine work. Neither do you have the look of a scholar."

The inquisitor flushed. The pale, crumpled scar tissue of his bad ear stood out like a lump of tallow against the alizarin of his face. He got ponderously to his feet.

"I think I know you now," Roscelin said as the fat man was about to speak. "You are a parchment pedlar, a sheep butcher. But you are mistaken in coming to me. I buy books, not skin."

Later that night Roscelin and his library were taken to a low building behind the bishop's palace. Both the knight and the books arrived in somewhat damaged condition, as if they had been tossed together in the same sack and dragged along the paving stones to prison.

News of Roscelin's arrest spread rapidly through the court. It reached Constance at her morning meeting with her ladies-in-waiting. No gesture or exclamation betrayed her emotion at what she heard. She went on quietly with her needlework, her hands obediently adding bright threads to a pattern that her brain denied with a chorus of voiceless screams.

Several weeks later the prison was emptied. In the square in front of the church of Saint Arnoul, a scaffold was erected and buttressed with firewood. A great crowd gathered, as if the day were a high festival. Shops were closed, fields were abandoned, and spectators arrived from all parts of the country. Farmers rode aimlessly about on oxen. Merchants paraded their large families and bargained casually with their competitors. Contingents from monasteries stood here and there, in neat black and brown squads. In honour of the nobleman who was to be executed that day most of the courtiers were present. They rented upper rooms in houses on the square and had light, winy luncheons spread on trestle tables near the window. The more daring of them masked themselves and descended into the mob to get a closer view of the proceedings at the scaffold. A temper of bright wantonness enlivened the whole congregation. No one except the city's thieves thought of work. Burglars in the deserted streets called greetings to one another as they stripped the unattended houses, while eager pickpockets toiled among the multitude before the church.

When the prisoners were led into the square, a chorus of jeers and obscenities met them. They, for the most part, were old women and idiots—mad, miserable creatures who had been proven by the Inquisition to be traffickers with incubi or succubi, familiars of dark beasts, dealers with the devil himself. Roscelin was among them. He was emaciated and filthy, but his manner was as indifferent, as lazily defiant, and as infuriating as ever. He had carefully combed his hair and beard with his split fingernails and he had tied the tatters that hung about him into ingenious and elaborate bows.

Like greedy carp worrying bread crusts in a pond, the mob closed around the prisoners, shoving them, cursing them, showering them with filth and blows. The leader in this assault was one of the courtiers, a tall figure whose identity was obscured by a full cloak and a rusty helmet of antiquated design. He carried a long wand bound with silver ribbons and tipped with a bear's claw. With grim, methodical cruelty he slashed his way through the crowd, inflicting as many welts and gashes on his comrades, the tormentors, as on the tormented. A space cleared around him, and he advanced alone on the segment of the column in which Roscelin marched. The helmeted figure paused, poised, before the knight. Some words, low, intense, and unintelligible to the mob, passed between them. Then the courtier's fury, which seemed for a moment to have abated, returned, and the decorated quirt darted forward. Roscelin, struck in the face, flinched and raised his manacled hands, as if to protect himself from a second blow. The mob cheered to see him shaken at last from his indifference, and then went suddenly silent as he fell to the pavement. From the brief hush rose a howl of disappointment. The tormenter's hand had been too heavy; the thrust that should have bloodied Roscelin's cheek had driven through his eye socket to the brain.

The masked courtier was quickly lost in the confusion surrounding the fallen prisoner. So great was the noise of the moment that no one in the crowd heard the sobs that were echoing inside the steel helmet.

Thus the heretic knight was cheated of his chance at repentance and ultimate absolution; thus, too, the crowd was cheated of the contest between living flesh and living flame that made such a popular spectacle of the auto-da-fé.

Roscelin was carried by a pair of grumbling sergeants to the scaffold and tossed like another piece of firewood on the mound of timbers beneath it. He sprawled on his back among the logs as he might have done on one of the couches in his library. As the execution proceeded, he was forgotten in the hysteria generated by the prayers and screams that constitute the rhetoric of capital punishment. One man, a young artisan who discovered to his embarrassment that the drama on the scaffold made him queasy, looked down and noticed Roscelin's corpse among the flames. Later, in a reassuring tavern with his friends, he said that it had seemed as if the knight were watching him, as ironically as he might have in life, through an eye fitted with a crimson monocle.

The days following the public execution were odd ones at the palace. For the first time since her wedding, Constance failed to appear among her ladies. Her absence was first attributed to some slight illness, but after a week of waiting for her the courtiers decided to investigate. Her servants were questioned, but none of them had seen her, none of them had been inside her apartment all week. Curiosity grew into alarm and a delegation was sent to her door. No amount of knocking or shouting brought a response. At last the door was forced; the apartment was empty.

The courtiers went off in a band to tell the count. They found him in his library. He was reading and seemed to be in a more than usually abstracted state of mind. When he was finally made to understand that the countess had disappeared, he groaned and shook his old head. "Gentlemen, gentlemen," he said through the rain of tears that splashed down his ruined cheeks, "it is unkind of you to tease an old man. Which of us will not disappear in time? Poor Berthe—thirty years in her grave."

They gave him up and returned to Constance's rooms. The apartment was carefully searched. Nothing was missing except the lady herself and the jewels she was privileged to wear. Constance, the outraged courtiers concluded, had bolted with her mysterious lover.

She never returned. Although spies were sent by the courtiers throughout the country, and to many foreign cities as well, no report of her was heard, and no trace was found. Her disappearance was never acknowledged outside the palace, in part because of the feelings of the old, and ultimately raving, Thibault and in part because of the scandal that the theft of his family's jewels would have caused. Nothing was said, and nothing was ever learned. Except for sporadic rumours, the whole affair slowly died, along with the childless noble's dynasty and the generation of courtiers that had served and tormented that dynasty's last and loveliest lady.

ON THE TWELFTH DAY of the siege a wall was breached. An assault followed immediately, a rush of well-armed men who managed to enter the town almost before the smoke cleared from the cannonade. The subsequent carnage was appalling. Most of the fighting was done at close quarters where pistols and muskets and grenades had devastating effect. The grim advance of the invaders drove the defending garrison slowly back through the narrow streets toward the church of Saint Arnoul. Its porch was the scene of a valiant stand. Liberated by the collapse of the defence from the main chores of the day, the victorious attackers stormed through the town, slaughtering citizens or raping them, torching barns, looting shops and houses. Minor pockets of resistance, wherever they were encountered, were systematically and ruthlessly reduced. Mercy was called for many times, but very little was granted.

Late in the afternoon the marauders arrived at the palace that once had belonged to a scholarly old baron called Thibault. His famous library had survived intact, but on this day it was burned. The whole house was ransacked, and whatever did not suit the looters was destroyed. They were very thorough. They burst open every door, rummaged through every closet and cupboard. They even entered the wing of the building, shut up for more than a century, where Thibault's lady, Constance, had once sported with her lover, Roscelin. There was little of worth in those dust-muffled barracks rooms. Feeling cheated by the paucity of what they found, the angry soldiers stamped about, coughing and swearing, smashing more than they tried to carry, until one of them discovered a stair leading to an upper floor. Several of the grenadiers sprang instantly up the steps and wrenched open the door at the top. Their reward for their greedy enthusiasm was a cascade of axes, for they had sprung the trap that Constance had set for them so many years before.

When the other soldiers recovered from the shock of seeing their comrades hacked to bits by an invisible enemy, they too advanced up the steps, but more warily, with their long rapiers held out before them. Inside the shadowy armoury they found the lady Constance, hanging by the neck at the end of a long silver chain, beneath the baldachin of pikes. Her long skeleton, immaculate after the attention given it by her old enemies the rats and radiant beneath a treasury of antique jewels, shivered in the sudden draft from the open door, and swung slowly in the unfamiliar light to face the intruders.

Sad Stories in Patagonia

ERIC MCCORMACK

The stony Patagonia wilderness south of the Rio Negro has always been renowned as a dinosaur graveyard. But nowadays several reported sightings of a live Mylodon (ancestor of the South American sloth) have led to a number of expeditions from various countries bent upon capturing this last survivor of the Age of Dinosaurs.

P. Hudwin, *Monsters of Patagonia*, Edinburgh, 1903

WHEN THE MEMBERS OF THE EXPEDITION squatted round the campfire on that first summer night ashore in Patagonia, the hiss of the fine drizzle on the logs reminded us, sitting on the wet grass, of damp summer nights in our own country, and the telling of sad stories began. The leader of the expedition, the distant gloom of the Andes behind him, spoke first. He was commander of our great endeavour to find the last mylodon alive, this cautious man, his balding skull pimpled with rain, this admirer of whisky, a man who wept, if anything, too easily.

"I am no authority myself on sadness" (we did not disagree, though his misfortunes were legendary—the aristocratic wife whose affairs scandalized society; the pistol-cleaning "accident" which perforated his left ear; the addiction to cards that led to the dissipation of an inheritance one warm night in Monte Carlo), "but I do remember seeing something pitiful when I was heading an expedition to the Mparna range in Lower Borneo.

"While we were provisioning to ascend the Central Massif, we were living in a village in the foothills. In the centre of the village a large bamboo cage stood, curtained with coconut matting. The villagers told us that a young boy, or what was *once* a young boy, was in that cage. We could all hear frightening snorts and hisses coming from it all day and all night.

"The boy was being trained as Guardian of the shrine of Rimso, the spider-god of the region. They always keep a few apprentices in training in case the official Guardian should die suddenly.

"The witch-doctors acquire these apprentices by raiding villages out in the bush where male infants have been newly born. The witch-doctors in their devil-masks descend on a village in the dawn mists. It must be an eerie sight. The wailing of the mothers is a waste of time. No one dares to defy the witch-doctors. If a baby looks strong, fit to withstand the training, they tear him away from his mother and bring him to a cage like the one we saw in that village.

"All of his bodily training takes place here for seven years. The training is aimed at completely reversing many of the child's natural physical instincts.

"They know a way of restructuring the body. It is the same method they use to train the branches of the banyan tree. In the first months of the child's captivity, they twist his upper body a little at the waist, so that the shoulders are turned slightly out of alignment with the hips and feet. Then they clamp it in position with vines and an ironwood frame, until, after a few months, the child becomes used to that posture. Then they twist him a little further, using the same clamping method for another few months, and then a little further, and so on. They do this again and again until the torso is turned one-hundred and eighty degrees around, and the boy's face is directly over his buttocks. So, when he bows his head, he is looking directly down at his own heels, his right arm dangles beside his left hip, and his left arm by his right hip. His spinal column is permanently coiled, like a spring, or like a plastic doll twisted out of shape by an angry child. The process takes about five years in a normal boy.

"The villagers often hear howls of anguish from the apprentice Guardian in the middle of the night. This is caused by the operations the witch-doctors perform upon him at each full moon to give him the walk of a spider, in the image of the god. They have a method of grafting four thick membranes of human flesh (no one dares ask where they find the material) onto his arms and legs. The membranes form a webbing at the angles of his knees and armpits, so that he cannot ever straighten out his limbs. He is forced to crouch, on all fours, like a monstrous spider, with his genitalia exposed to the skies, his chest and haunted face to the ground.

"I saw this apprentice only once, on the morning he left the cage. It was, as usual, misty in the jungle dawn. All of the villagers and the expedition-members were watching from the safety of the compounds, for we knew that by now the apprentice's teeth had been replaced with bamboo fangs full of spider venom.

"Through my binoculars, I saw four witch-doctors in spider-masks come up to the cage armed with long goads. They unfastened the gate and poked through the bars at whatever was in there, driving it towards the opening. Something tumbled out. A huge form, entirely covered in matted hair, lay there quivering for a moment, then shook itself and scuttled quickly into the fringes of the bush, grunting inhumanly, the four witch-doctors jogging behind it, jabbing it with their goads. I never wanted to see such a creature again, and I was glad that our expedition would soon be setting out into the mountains.

"In this way the witch-doctors train the body of an apprentice Guardian in public, to frighten the people. How they train the boy's mind I do not know. That part of the training takes another three years: no outsider may witness it and live.

"But these apprentices do not disappear from public view completely. After the final three years of training, they are often seen again. Some of the men on the Mparna expedition swear that while we were setting up camp one night in the rain forest under the mountain, a monster unlike anything they had ever come across shuffled out of the undergrowth towards them, grunting brutally, cowing the hunting dogs, silencing all the jungle creatures. They could see insane red eyes under a wilderness of hair. For some reason, it suddenly stopped and slithered back into the bush. If what they saw really was an apprentice, they were lucky, for, according to the villagers, its appetite for inflicting pain, either on itself or on others who stumble onto it in jungle paths, is insatiable. Its only food is living flesh."

That was the end of the leader's story. Darkness was eliminating the world around us, the Andes had vanished, even the nearby bushes were barely clutching shreds of their reality. We could see quite large bats wheeling on the edges of extinction. The leader squinted rapidly at us, tears flooding the outer deltas of his eyes. He slid a Mickey of whisky from the pea-jacket under his sou'wester, unscrewing the cap with unerring left hand whilst lifting the bottle to his open mouth with his right.

In spite of his own popularity, the leader's narrative did not please all of those assembled in their dripping oilskins around that roaring Patagonian fire. Some of these men who would rise next morning to pursue the last living mylodon criticized the story for its lack of relevance to their situation in Patagonia. They demanded realism, not the kind of primitivist fantasy they detected all too often for their tastes, they said, in the leader's stories. Not the cook, however, with his scraggy red beard and flaking skin. He praised the story's "organic structure, its thematic integrity, and its attention to the unities of time and place." No one else was willing to go that far, but there was general acknowledgement of the requisite element of sadness in the story. The discussion was all very revealing, all very useful.

JOHNNY CHIPS, ship's carpenter and expedition handyman, had a sad story to tell. He rocked back and forth on a small barrel, which, because of his weight (he was a heavy man) had already hollowed a smooth indentation in the wet, reddish earth beneath him. For all his drooping moustache and long face, Chips had seen us through hard times—many a lifelike female miniature he had carved for the comfort of the lonely men before the mast on a long voyage.

He himself, however, was above everything a scholar, his cabin stowed to the gunwales with books that took precedence over his carpenter's tools. He always kept his nose covered with a little black leather cone tied behind his head with black shoelaces. When he was telling a story, his eyes would become unstable, strobing wildly in time with his words. The rasp of the wood file was in his voice:

"Thomas à Kempis was a medieval Dutchman who never went to sea, who never knew of Patagonia's existence. He was the man who wrote *Imitatio Christi*, known to us as *The Imitation of Christ*.

"He lived out his long life and died in due course, everyone agreeing that he was the holiest man of the age. Soon, miracles began happening around his grave: missing legs and arms sprouted back, eyesight and hearing were restored. He was especially good with piles and syphilis—decayed noses would grow on again."

The men around the fire did not doubt that the plight of Chips's own nose was the result of a carpentry accident long ago, as he had often assured them.

"Because of the miracles, the Church set out to make Thomas à Kempis a saint, they didn't begrudge him that. They delegated a team of specialists led by a cardinal to see to the exhumation of his body six months after his death as part of the canonizing procedure. The body would have to be completely uncorrupted to satisfy them. Even better if it had a very nice smell coming from it, a sure sign that the man buried there was a saint.

"On the day of the exhumation, a wet wintry day, a big crowd gathered, it being a Saturday afternoon, and not much else going on. Some of the people who claimed Thomas à Kempis had cured them (along with the usual quota of phonies) took the occasion to show off their shiny new eyes, or lily-white legs (no one seems to have received teeth, the most frequently requested and most rarely granted miracle in those days and since, according to researchers). The grave-diggers started shovelling the heavy earth, and after they had penetrated the topsoil, the most aromatic of smells filled all the air of that graveyard, sweeter than any rose, or even any tulip they had ever smelt.

"Then, bump! The long-handled shovels clanged against the coffin! The diggers looped ropes around it and a gang of workmen jerked it up to the surface, all sheathed in lead, the damp clay sticking to it. It had been in that hole, by then, almost seven months.

"The cardinal ordered the soldiers to keep the crowd back. The coffin was laid out on trestles, and one of the team began to jimmy off the lid. The people were hushed now, though some of them were already praying quietly to Thomas à Kempis, hoping to impress the saint-to-be with their confidence.

"The lid squealed ajar. The cardinal and his team moved closer to have a good look at the disinterred saint. 'Oh Christ!' shouted the cardinal, cowering back at what he saw inside that half-open coffin.

"He saw that the interior of the lid of the coffin was grooved with deep scratches. That Thomas à Kempis's dead face was indeed perfectly preserved, but his eyes were bulged open. That his fingers were curled like the claws of a vulture and his finger-nails were all broken with wooden splinters to the quick. That his winding sheet was stained around his middle with urine and excrement.

"Poor Thomas à Kempis. The cardinal who had witnessed the opening of the coffins of hundreds of candidates for sainthood understood. The body had not been fully dead when they buried him, but had been in a deep coma. Who could know when he woke up out of it and into his nightmare? One of the men who had been at the funeral half a year before said he was sure he had heard noises from the coffin on that day, but was afraid it was the devil's work.

"Well. That was it for Thomas à Kempis. The cardinal ordered the coffin closed and put back in the earth. No one needed to be told that Thomas couldn't be made a saint, for what curses might he not have howled in that narrow coffin? The scratches told everything. Wouldn't a real saint have been content with his fate, even if he had been buried a little too early?

"No. That was it for Thomas à Kempis. His book was marvellous, the whole world agreed. But the author was only human after all."

Chips rocked gently on his barrel, his eyes resuming their usual orbits. His story was over.

The rain fell a little more heavily now in Patagonia, and even the bushes near the fire had lost their battle with the night.

Debate immediately began over Chips's story. Some of the men were indignant over the way Thomas à Kempis had been treated, and insisted that anyone in their right minds would try to get out of a coffin if they'd been buried alive. The case only reconfirmed their worst suspicions about institutions and regulations generally. Chips rocked gently on his barrel.

One of the men objected to the *way* in which Chips told the story. He charged that, in deliberately delaying the final revelation for so long, Chips had indulged in the most hackneyed of attention-holding devices. The leader himself came to life at this point. He disengaged himself a moment from his bottle to argue that Chips ought to have begun with the ending, rather than toying with their feelings in what the leader, now weeping helplessly, considered to be a heartless fashion, and one that he himself would never have used. Chips refused to be baited.

Some men quibbled over the historical factuality of the story: in their minds, Chips ought to have made it clear right from the start that he was dealing in speculation, at best, and certainly not in history. This criticism startled one of the little cabin-boys, a great favourite of Chips, who had been allowed to stay up late. He said that Chips was always telling him such stories about historical figures, and that he'd never doubted their truth. On hearing this, a few of the men reckoned Chips ought to be ashamed of himself.

The cook, however, had been biding his time. His red beard challenged all opposition. He congratulated Chips on "his refusal to be intimidated by history," and praised him for "the intransigent penetration of his metaphor."

This comment effectively ended the discussion.

Chips rocked backwards and forwards on his barrel, backwards into the flickering darkness, forwards into the light of the blazing fire, and said nothing, nothing at all. Just smiling, in that damp Patagonian night, the tense smile of a man not given to smiling.

Hundreds of bats, it seemed, were now swooping in and out of the firelight above us. The leader pulled out his pocket-watch and dangled it in the light. He yawned.

"Time for one more," he said.

We all turned towards the chief engineer. He was a man from the islands, who would occasionally take over medical duties when the ship's doctor was ill (an illness brought on by whisky). The chief's hands were familiar with bunker oil and heavy steel piping, yet he had the elegant fingers of a pianist or a surgeon, the milky blue eyes of a dreamer. He spoke into the silence:

"A thing happened in my home town when I was a young boy. A new doctor with a strong foreign accent came up to practise at our end of the island, bringing his wife and four children, two boys and two girls all under ten years of age. The man was thin with a head like a snake. The wife was beautiful.

"After only a month, the thing happened. On a sunny September morning, this new doctor stumbled through the door of the police station looking very upset, and said that his wife was missing, having gone for her daily walk the day before and not come back. He had looked everywhere.

"The police made sure she had not boarded the ferry for the mainland, then organized a search for her. They searched day and night for two days, but there was no sign of her.

"The children showed up at school as usual. They did not look well, they were all pale and washed out as though they had been crying. What was most noticeable was the way they walked. All of them walked the stiff walk of an old man.

"The island children did not know them well, and were shy about asking what was the matter, thinking it must have something to do with their mother's disappearance.

"But on their second day back at school, one of the little girls, who was six years old, turned very sick and fell over from her desk onto the floor in convulsions, holding her stomach.

"The old schoolmistress made her comfortable in the staff room with blankets and a pillow and phoned her father, the doctor, to come right away.

"The little girl kept on groaning in agony, and the schoolmistress tried to coax her to show where the pain was. The little girl was not willing at first, but she was in pain and saw the schoolmistress wanted to help. So she began to unbutton her dress. But her father, the doctor, came rushing into the staff room shouting, 'No! No!' and lifted her away in his arms out into his car. He then came back for the other three children, and took them all away with him.

"But the old schoolmistress had seen enough, and phoned the police station.

"Without any delay, the sergeant and his constable drove to the doctor's house on the cliffs overlooking the ocean. They knocked, and had to wait a few minutes before the doctor, looking nervous, came to the door. The sergeant said he'd like to look at the children. The doctor at first said they were too sick to be disturbed, but had to let them in.

"All the children were lying in their beds in one large room on the ocean side of the house and anyone could see how sick they were. The sergeant knew what he had to do. He asked them to open up their clothing for him. They all did so, with groans and gasps of pain.

"He understood the reason for their suffering.

"The sergeant saw that each of those four children had a large incision along the centre of their abdomens, the sutures fresh, the wounds inflamed.

"Their father, the doctor, stood watching all of this, sobbing loudly. When the sergeant asked him why the children had been operated upon, he would say nothing.

"The sergeant took all four children to the hospital at the other end of the island.

"The resident surgeon there, a kind man, saw the sergeant's concern, and ordered the little girl who had been in the greatest pain to be taken into the operating theatre where he was about to conduct a class in pathology for some nurses. The little girl was anaesthetized, and the resident showed the nurses how pus mixed with the blood was oozing from the wound. No wonder she had been in agony.

"The resident then cut the sutures and lifted them away. He slid his fingers into the wound and groped around. He said he could feel a lump of some sort. He managed to grip part of it with his calipers, and carefully fished it out, holding it up in the air.

"All of those assembled round that table saw something they would never forget. The resident had snared in the calipers a severed human hand, dripping blood and pus. He was holding it by its thumb, and they could all see, quite clearly, the gold wedding ring on its middle finger, and the scarlet polish on the long fingernails."

No one stirred around that camp-fire in Patagonia. The night had turned chilly, the members of the expedition crouched nearer to the fire's heat. The chief engineer continued:

"That was how they found out that the new doctor had killed his wife. He had cut off parts of her and buried them inside the children. Each of the four children contained a foot or a hand. Later, the family pets, a Highland collie and a big ginger cat, were found lying in the house cellar, half alive. They too had abdominal incisions. The local veterinarian discovered the woman's eyes in the dog and her ears in the cat.

"The resident testified later that he hoped never to perform such a salvage operation again. He was sure that if the man had had enough children and pets, he'd have managed to conceal every part of her. As it was they found the rest of her body under some rocks by the shore.

"The resident said the father's workmanship was a marvel, he had never seen such skill. The murderer himself was silent. He was later sentenced to death, though his children pleaded for his life. The islanders would never allow hangings on the island for fear of bad luck. They did not object, however, to his being hanged on the mainland."

The chief engineer's story was ended. The Patagonian darkness silenced the men for a while. Then Chips, rocking smoothly on his barrel, said in his grating voice that he thought the story was well enough done, but that it was disgusting rather than sad, and therefore not really suitable to the occasion.

The cook rarely liked the chief's stories. He could hardly wait, his scraggy beard bristling, to denounce this one as "another rather boring instance of the metaphysical/erotic struggle for authenticity and freedom in daily life, and of the problems of coping with the dichotomy of the Word/word, its abstract and concrete dimensions in experience and language."

No one seemed enthusiastic about pursuing this particular line of analysis.

One of the men, a friend of the chief, tried to be diplomatic, suggesting that perhaps the story should be understood symbolically rather than literally. He doubted, anyway, that the human body could be used as a repository of dead limbs.

The chief engineer answered this last objection, and all objections in a very simple manner. He rose to his feet in the Patagonian night before the smouldering fire, and pulled the front of his shirt up from his waist. There, just above the waistline, we could all see a long horizontal scar, a white corrugation about nine inches long dissecting his pale, northern skin.

That seemed to settle everything. The leader, a man of habit, never commented on the final story of an evening. Yet his tearful eyes told all. A man of habit, he yawned, nevertheless, his ritual last yawn, his mouth bracketed by flowing tears, and he stood up.

"Time to turn in," he said. "Tomorrow morning bright and early it will be our task to ensnare the last mylodon on this earth."

Without reluctance, we all arose now, drowsy with pleasure at the sadness of the world, anticipating the warmth of sleeping bags, the shelter of canvas against the rain which whispered noisily to the failing logs. Soon the fire would be dead, and the darkness would extinguish us all, here in Patagonia.

Presbyterian Crosswalk

BARBARA GOWDY

SOMETIMES BETH FLOATED. Two or three feet off the ground, and not for very long, ten seconds or so. She wasn't aware of floating when she was actually doing it, however. She had to land and feel a glowing sensation before she realized that she had just been up in the air.

The first time it happened she was on the church steps. She looked back down the walk and knew that she had floated up it. A couple of days later she floated down the outside cellar stairs of her house. She ran inside and told her grandmother, who whipped out the pen and the little pad she carried in her skirt pocket and drew a circle with a hooked nose.

Beth looked at it. "Has Aunt Cora floated, too?" she asked. Her grandmother nodded.

"When?"

Her grandmother held up six fingers.

"Six years ago?"

Shaking her head, her grandmother held her hand at thigh level.

"Oh," Beth said, "when she was six."

When Beth was six, five years ago, her mother ran off with a man down the street who wore a toupee that curled up in humid weather. Beth's grandmother, her father's mother, came to live with her and her father. Thirty years before that, Beth's grandmother had had her tonsils taken out by a quack who ripped out her vocal cords and the underside of her tongue.

It was a tragedy, because she and her twin sister, Cora, had been on the verge of stardom (or so Cora said) as a professional singing team. They had made two long-play records: "The Carlisle Sisters, Sea to Sea" and "Christmas with the Carlisle

Sisters." Beth's grandmother liked to play the records at high volume and to mouth the words. "My prairie home is beautiful, but oh …" If Beth sang along, her grandmother might stand next to her and sway and swish her skirt as though Beth were Cora and the two of them were back on stage.

The cover of the "Sea to Sea" album had a photograph of Beth's grandmother and Aunt Cora wearing middies and sailor hats and shielding their eyes with one hand as they peered off in different directions. Their hair, blond and billowing out from under their hats, was glamorous, but Beth secretly felt that even if her grandmother hadn't lost her voice she and Cora would never have been big stars because they had hooked noses, what Cora called Roman noses. Beth was relieved that she hadn't inherited their noses, although she regretted not having got their soft, wavy hair, which they both still wore long, in a braid or falling in silvery drifts down their backs. Beth's grandmother still put on blue eye shadow and red lipstick, too, every morning. And around the house she wore her old, flashy, full-length stage skirts, faded now— red, orange or yellow, or flowered, or with swirls of broken-off sequins. Beth's grandmother didn't care about sloppiness or dirt. With the important exception of Beth's father's den, the house was a mess—Beth was just beginning to realize and be faintly ashamed of this.

On each of Beth's grandmother's skirts was a sewed-on pocket for her pencil and pad. Due to arthritis in her thumb she held the pencil between her middle finger and forefinger, but she still drew faster than anyone Beth had ever seen. She always drew people instead of writing out their name or their initials. Beth, for instance, was a circle with tight, curly hair. Beth's friend Amy was an exclamation mark. If the phone rang and nobody was home, her grandmother answered it and tapped her pencil three times on the receiver to let whoever was on the other end know that it was her and that they should leave a message. "Call," she would write, and then do a drawing.

A drawing of a man's hat was Beth's father. He was a hard-working lawyer who stayed late at the office. Beth had a hazy memory of him giving her a bath once, it must have been before her mother ran off. The memory embarrassed her. She wondered if he wished that she had gone with her mother, if, in fact, she was supposed to have gone, because when he came home from work and she was still there, he seemed surprised. "Who do we have here?" he might say. He wanted peace and quiet. When Beth got rambunctious, he narrowed his eyes as though she gave off a bright, painful light.

Beth knew that he still loved her mother. In the top drawer of his dresser, in an old wallet he never used, he had a snapshot of her mother wearing only a black slip. Beth remembered that slip, and her mother's tight black dress with the zipper down the back. And her long red fingernails that she clicked on tables. "Your mother was too young to marry," was her father's sole disclosure. Her grandmother disclosed nothing, pretending to be deaf if Beth asked about her mother. Beth remembered how her mother used to phone her father for money and how, if her grandmother answered and took the message, she would draw a big dollar sign and then an upside-down v sitting in the middle of a line—a witch's hat.

A drawing of an upside-down v without a line was church. When a Presbyterian church was built within walking distance, Beth and her grandmother started going to it, and her grandmother began reading the Bible and counselling Beth by way of biblical quotations. A few months later a crosswalk appeared at the end of the street, and for several years Beth thought that it was a "Presbyterian" instead of a "Pedestrian" crosswalk and that the sign above it said Watch for Presbyterians.

Her Sunday school teacher was an old, teary-eyed woman who started every class by singing "When Mothers of Salem," while the children hung up their coats and sat down cross-legged on the floor in front of her. That hymn, specifically the part about Jesus wanting to hold children to His "bosom," made Beth feel that there was something not right about Jesus, and consequently it was responsible for her six months of anxiety that she would end up in hell. Every night, after saying her prayers, she would spend a few minutes chanting, "I love Jesus, I love Jesus, I love Jesus," the idea being that she could talk herself into it. She didn't expect to feel earthly love; she awaited the unknown feeling called glory.

When she began to float, she said to herself, "This is glory."

SHE FLOATED ONCE, sometimes twice a week. Around Christmas it began to happen less often—every ten days to two weeks. Then it dwindled down to only about once a month. She started to chant "I love Jesus" again, not because she was worried any more about going to hell, she just wanted to float.

By the beginning of the summer holidays she hadn't floated in almost seven weeks. She phoned her Aunt Cora who said that, yes, floating was glory all right, but that Beth should consider herself lucky it had happened even once. "Nothing that good lasts long," she sighed. Beth couldn't stop hoping, though. She went to the park and climbed a tree. Her plan was to jump and have Jesus float her to the ground. But as she stood on a limb, working up her courage, she remembered God seeing the little sparrow fall and letting it fall anyway, and she climbed down.

She felt that she had just had a close call. She lay on her back on the picnic table, gazing up in wonder at how high up she had been. It was a hot, still day. She heard heat bugs and an ambulance. Presently she went over to the swings and took a turn on each one, since there was nobody else in the park.

She was on the last swing when Helen McCormack came waddling across the lawn, calling that a boy had just been run over by a car. Beth slid off the swing. "He's almost dead!" Helen called.

"Who?" Beth asked.

"I don't know his name. Nobody did. He's about eight. He's got red hair. The car ran over his leg *and* his back."

"Where?"

Helen was panting. "I shouldn't have walked so fast," she said, holding her hands on either side of her enormous head. "My cranium veins are throbbing." Little spikes of her wispy blond hair stood out between her fingers.

"Where did it happen?" Beth said.

"On Glenmore. In front of the post office."

Beth started running toward Glenmore, but Helen called, "There's nothing there now, everything's gone!" so Beth stopped and turned, and for a moment Helen and the swings seemed to continue turning, coming round and round like Helen's voice saying, "You missed the whole thing. You missed it. You missed the whole thing."

"He was on his bike," Helen said, dropping onto a swing, "and an eyewitness said that the car skidded on water and knocked him down, then ran over him twice, once with a front tire and once with a back one. I got there before the ambulance. He probably won't live. You could tell by his eyes. His eyes were glazed." Helen's eyes, blue, huge because of her glasses, didn't blink.

"That's awful," Beth said.

"Yes, it really was," Helen said, matter-of-factly. "He's not the first person I've seen who nearly died, though. My aunt nearly drowned in the bathtub when we were staying at her house. She became a human vegetable."

"Was the boy bleeding?" Beth asked.

"Yes, there was blood everywhere."

Beth covered her mouth with both hands.

Helen looked thoughtful. "I think he'll probably die," she said. She pumped her fat legs but without enough energy to get the swing going. "I'm going to die soon," she said.

"You are?"

"You probably know that I have water on the brain," Helen said.

"Yes, I know that," Beth said. Everyone knew. It was why Helen wasn't supposed to run. It was why her head was so big.

"Well, more and more water keeps dripping in all the time, and one day there will be so much that my brain will literally drown in it."

"Who said?"

"The doctors, who else?"

"They said, 'You're going to die'?"

Helen threw her an ironic look. "Not exactly. What they tell you is, you're not going to live." She squinted up at a plane going by. "The boy, he had ... I think it was a rib, sticking out of his back."

"Really?"

"I *think* it was a rib. It was hard to tell because of all the blood." With the toe of her shoe, Helen began to jab a hole in the sand under her swing. "A man from the post office hosed the blood down the sewer, but some of it was already caked from the sun."

Beth walked toward the shade of the picnic table. The air was so thick and still. Her arms and legs, cutting through it, seemed to produce a thousand soft clashes.

"The driver was an old man," Helen said, "and he was crying uncontrollably."

"Anybody *would* cry," Beth said hotly. Her eyes filled with tears.

Helen squirmed off her swing and came over to the table. Grunting with effort, she climbed onto the seat across from Beth and began to roll her head. "At least *I'll* die in one piece," she said.

"Are you really going to?" Beth asked.

"Yep." Helen rotated her head three times one way, then three times the other. Then she propped it up with her hands cupped under her chin.

"But can't they do anything to stop the water dripping in?" Beth asked.

"Nope," Helen said distantly, as if she were thinking about something more interesting.

"You know what?" Beth said, swiping at her tears. "If every night, you closed your eyes and chanted over and over, 'Water go away, water go away, water go away,' maybe it would start to, and then your head would shrink down."

Helen smirked. "Somehow," she said, "I doubt it."

From the edge of the picnic table Beth tore a long sliver of wood like the boy's rib. She pictured the boy riding his bike no-hands, zigzagging down the street the way boys did. She imagined bursting Helen's head with the splinter to let the water gush out.

"I'm thirsty," Helen sighed. "I've had a big shock today. I'm going home for some lemonade."

Beth went with her. It was like walking with her grandmother, who, because of arthritis in her hips, also rocked from side to side and took up the whole sidewalk. Beth asked Helen where she lived.

"I can't talk," Helen panted. "I'm trying to breathe."

Beth thought that Helen lived in the apartments where the immigrants, crazy people and bums were, but Helen went past those apartments and up the hill to the new Regal Heights subdivision, which had once been a landfill site. Her house was a split-level with a little turret above the garage. On the door was an engraved wooden sign, the kind that Beth had seen nailed to posts in front of cottages. No Solicitors, it said.

"My father is a solicitor," Beth said.

Helen was concentrating on opening the door. "Darn thing's always stuck," she muttered as she shoved it open with her shoulder. "I'm home!" she hollered, then sat heavily on a small mauve suitcase next to the door.

Across the hallway a beautiful woman was dusting the ceiling with a mop. She had dark, curly hair tied up in a red ribbon, and long, slim legs in white short shorts.

To Beth's amazement she was Helen's mother. "You can call me Joyce," she said, smiling at Beth as though she loved her. "Who's this lump of potatoes," she laughed, pointing the mop at Helen.

Helen stood up. "A boy got run over on Glenmore," she said.

Joyce's eyes widened, and she looked at Beth.

"I didn't see it," Beth told her.

"We're dying of thirst," Helen said. "We want lemonade in my room."

While Joyce made lemonade from a can, Helen sat at the kitchen table, resting her head on her folded arms. Joyce's questions about the accident seemed to bore her. "We don't need ice," she said impatiently when Joyce went to open the freezer. She demanded cookies, and Joyce poured some Oreos onto the tray with their coffee mugs of lemonade, then handed the tray to Beth, saying with a little laugh that, sure as shooting, Helen would tip it over.

"I'm always spilling things," Helen agreed.

Beth carried the tray through the kitchen to the hallway. "Why is that there?" she asked, nodding at the suitcase beside the front door.

"That's my hospital suitcase," Helen said. "It's all packed for an emergency." She pushed open her bedroom door so that it banged against the wall. The walls were the same mauve as the suitcase, and there was a smell of paint. Everything was put away—no clothes lying around, no games or toys on the floor. The dolls and books, lined up on white bookshelves, looked as if they were for sale. Beth thought contritely of her own dolls, their tangled hair and dirty dresses, half of them naked, some of them missing legs and hands, she could never remember why, she could never figure out how a hand got in with her Scrabble letters.

She set the tray down on Beth's desk. Above the desk was a chart that said "Heart Rate," "Blood Pressure" and "Bowel Movements" down the side. "What's that?" she asked.

"My bodily functions chart." Helen grabbed a handful of cookies. "We're keeping track every week to see how much things change before they completely stop. We're conducting an experiment."

Beth stared at the neatly stencilled numbers and the gently waving red lines. She had the feeling that she was missing something as stunning and obvious as the fact that her mother was gone for good. For years after her mother left she asked her father, "When is she coming back?" Her father, looking confused, always answered, "Never," but Beth just couldn't understand what he meant by that, not until she finally thought to ask, "When is she coming back for the rest of her life?"

She turned to Helen. "When are you going to die?"

Helen shrugged. "There's no exact date," she said with her mouth full.

"Aren't you afraid?"

"Why should I be? Dying the way I'm going to doesn't hurt, you know."

Beth sat on the bed. There was the hard feel of plastic under the spread and blankets. She recognized it from when she'd had her tonsils out and they'd put plastic under her sheets then. "I hope that boy hasn't died," she said, suddenly thinking of him again.

"He probably has," Helen said, running a finger along the lowest line in the chart.

The lines were one above the other, not intersecting. When Beth's grandmother drew one wavy line, that was water. Beth closed her eyes. Water go away, she said to herself. Water go away, water go away …

"What are you doing?" The bed bounced, splashing lemonade out of Beth's mug as Helen sat down.

"I was conducting an experiment," Beth said.

"What experiment?"

More lemonade, this time from Helen's mug, poured onto Beth's leg and her shorts. "Look what you're doing!" Beth cried. She used the corner of the bedspread to dry herself. "You're so stupid sometimes," she muttered.

Helen drank down what was left in her mug. "For your information," she said, wiping her mouth on her arm, "it's not stupidity. It's deterioration of the part of my brain lobe that tells my muscles what to do."

Beth looked up at her. "Oh, from the water," she said softly.

"Water is one of the most destructive forces known to mankind," Helen said.

"I'm sorry," Beth murmured. "I didn't mean it."

"So what did you mean you were conducting an experiment?" Helen asked, pushing her glasses up on her nose.

"You know what?" Beth said. "We could both do it." She felt a thrill of virtuous resolve. "Remember what I said about chanting 'water go away, water go away'? We could both chant it and see what happens."

"Brother," Helen sighed.

Beth put her lemonade on the table and jumped off the bed. "We'll make a chart," she said, fishing around in the drawer of Helen's desk for a pen and some paper. She found a red pencil. "Do you have any paper?" she asked. "We need paper and a measuring tape."

"Brother," Helen said again, but she left the room and came back a few minutes later with a pad of foolscap and her mother's sewing basket.

Beth wrote "Date" and "Size" at the top of the page and underlined it twice. Under "Date" she wrote "June 30," then she unwound the measuring tape and measured Helen's head—the circumference above her eyebrows—and wrote "27 1/2." Then she and Helen sat cross-legged on the floor, closed their eyes, held each other's hands and said, "Water go away," starting out in almost a whisper, but Helen kept speeding up, and Beth had to raise her voice to slow her down. After a few moments both of them were shouting, and Helen was digging her nails into Beth's fingers.

"Stop!" Beth cried. She yanked her hands free. "It's supposed to be slow and quiet!" she cried. "Like praying!"

"We don't go to church," Helen said, pressing her hands on either side of her head. "Whew," she breathed. "For a minute there I thought that my cranium veins were throbbing again."

"We did it wrong," Beth said crossly. Helen leaned over to get the measuring tape. "You should chant tonight before you go to bed," Beth said, watching as Helen pulled on the bedpost to hoist herself to her feet. "Chant slowly and softly. I'll come back tomorrow after lunch and we'll do it together again. We'll just keep doing it every afternoon for the whole summer, if that's what it takes. Okay?"

Helen was measuring her hips, her wide, womanly hips in their dark green Bermuda shorts.

"Okay?" Beth repeated.

Helen bent over to read the tape. "Sure," she said indifferently.

WHEN BETH GOT BACK to her own place, her grandmother was playing her "Sea to Sea" record and making black bean soup and dinner rolls. Talking loudly to be heard over the music, Beth told her about the car accident and Helen. Her grandmother knew about Helen's condition but thought that she was retarded—in the flour sprinkled on the table she traced a circle with a triangle sitting on it, which was "dunce," and a question mark.

"No," Beth said, surprised. "She gets all A's."

Her grandmother pulled out her pad and pencil and wrote, "Don't get her hopes up."

"But when you *pray*, that's getting your hopes up," Beth argued.

Her grandmother looked impressed. "We walk by faith," she wrote.

There was a sudden silence. "Do you want to hear side two?" Beth asked. Her grandmother made a cross with her fingers. "Oh, okay," Beth said and went into the living room and put on her grandmother's other record, the Christmas one. The first song was "Hark! the Herald Angels Sing." Beth's father's name was Harold. The black bean soup, his favourite, meant he'd be home for supper. Beth wandered down the hall to his den and sat in his green leather chair and swivelled for a moment to the music. "Offspring of a Virgin's womb ..."

After a few minutes she got off the chair and began searching through his wastepaper basket. Whenever she was in here and noticed that the basket hadn't been emptied, she looked at what was in it. Usually just pencil shavings and long hand-written business letters with lots of crossed-out sentences and notes in the margins. Sometimes there were phone messages from his office, where he was called Hal, by

Sue, the woman who wrote the messages out.

"PDQ!" Sue wrote. "ASAP!"

Today there were several envelopes addressed to her father, a couple of flyers, an empty cigarette package, and a crumpled pink note from her grandmother's pad. Beth opened the note up.

"Call," it said, and then there was an upside-down v. Underneath that was a telephone number.

Beth thought it was a message for her father to call the church. Her mother hadn't called in over four years, so it took a moment of wondering why the phone number didn't start with two fives like every other phone number in the neighbourhood did, and why her father, who didn't go to church, should get a message from the church, before Beth remembered that an upside-down v meant not "church" but "witch's hat."

In the kitchen Beth's grandmother was shaking the bean jars to "Here We Come a-Wassailing." Beth felt the rhythm as a pounding between her ears. "My cranium veins are throbbing," she thought in revelation, and putting down the message she pressed her palms to her temples and remembered when her mother used to phone for money. Because of those phone calls Beth had always pictured her mother and the man with the toupee living in some poor place, a rundown apartment, or one of the insulbrick bungalows north of the city. "I'll bet they're broke again," Beth told herself, working up scorn. "I'll bet they're down to their last penny." She picked up the message and crumpled it back into a ball, then opened it up again, folded it in half and slipped it into the pocket of her shorts.

Sticking to her promise, she went over to Helen's every afternoon. It took her twenty minutes, a little longer than that if she left the road to go through the park, which she often did out of a superstitious feeling that the next time she floated, it would be there. The park made her think of the boy who was run over. On the radio it said that his foot had been amputated and that he was in desperate need of a liver transplant. "Remember him in your prayers," the announcer said, and Beth and her grandmother did. The boy's name was Kevin Legg.

"Kevin *Legg* and he lost his *foot*!" Beth pointed out to Joyce.

Joyce laughed, although Beth hadn't meant it as a joke. A few minutes later, in the bedroom, Beth asked Helen, "Why isn't your mother worried about us getting your hopes up?"

"She's just glad that I finally have a friend," Helen answered. "When I'm by myself, I get in the way of her cleaning."

Beth looked out the window. It hadn't occurred to her that she and Helen were friends.

Beth's best friend, Christine, was at a cottage for the summer. Amy, her other friend, she played with in the mornings and when she returned from Helen's. Amy was half Chinese, small and thin. She was on pills for hyperactivity. "Just think what

I'd be like if I *wasn't* on them!" she cried, spinning around and slamming into the wall. Amy was the friend that Beth's grandmother represented with an exclamation mark. Whatever they were playing, Amy got tired of after five minutes, but she usually had another idea. She was fun, although not very nice. When Beth told her about Helen dying, she cried, "That's a lie!"

"Ask her mother," Beth said.

"No way I'm going to that fat-head's place!" Amy cried.

Amy didn't believe the story about the doctor ripping out Beth's grandmother's tonsils, either, not even after Beth's grandmother opened her mouth and showed her her mutilated tongue.

So Beth knew better than to confide in Amy about floating. She knew better than to confide in anybody, aside from her grandmother and her Aunt Cora, since it wasn't something she could prove and since she found it hard to believe herself. At the same time she was passionately certain that she *had* floated, and might again if she kept up her nightly "I love Jesus" chants.

She confided in Helen about floating, though, on the fifteenth day of *their* chanting, because that day, instead of sitting on the floor and holding Beth's hands, Helen curled up on her side facing the wall and said, "I wish we were playing checkers," and Beth thought how trusting Helen had been so far, chanting twice a day without any reason to believe that it worked.

The next day, the sixteenth day, Helen's head measured twenty-seven inches.

"Are you sure you aren't pulling the tape tighter?" Helen asked.

"No," Beth said. "I always pull it this tight."

Helen pushed the tape off her head and waddled to the bedroom door. "Twenty-seven inches!" she called.

"Let's go show her," Beth said, and they hurried to the living room, where Joyce was using a nail to clean between the floorboards

"Aren't you guys smart!" Joyce said, sitting back on her heels and wiping specks of dirt from her slim legs and little pink shorts.

"Come on," Helen said, tugging Beth back to the bedroom.

Breathlessly she went to the desk and wrote the measurement on the chart.

Beth sat on the bed. "I can't believe it," she said, falling onto her back. "It's working. I mean I *thought* it would, I *hoped* it would, but I wasn't absolutely, positively, one hundred per cent sure."

Helen sat beside her and began to roll her head. Beth pictured the water sloshing from side to side. "Why do you do that?" she asked.

"I get neck cramps," Helen said. "One thing I won't miss are these darn neck cramps."

The next day her head lost another half inch. The day after that it lost an entire inch, so that it was now down to twenty-five and a half inches. Beth and Helen demonstrated the measurements to Joyce, who acted amazed, but Beth could tell that for some reason she really wasn't.

"We're not making it up," Beth told her.

"Well, who said you were?" Joyce asked, pretending to be insulted.

"Don't you think her head *looks* smaller?" Beth said, and both she and Joyce considered Helen's head, which *had* looked smaller in the bedroom, but now Beth wasn't so sure. In fact, she was impressed, the way she used to be when she saw Helen only once in a while, by just how big Helen's head was. And by her lumpy, grown-up woman's body, which at this moment was collapsing onto a kitchen chair.

"You know, I think maybe it *does* look smaller," Joyce said brightly.

"Wait'll Dr. Dobbs sees me," Helen said in a tired voice, folding her arms on the table and laying her head down.

Joyce gave Helen's shoulder a little punch. "You all right, kiddo?"

Helen ignored her. "I'll show him our chart," she said to Beth.

"Hey," Joyce said. "You all right?"

Helen closed her eyes. "I need a nap," she murmured.

WHEN BETH RETURNED HOME there was another message from her mother in her father's wastepaper basket.

This time, before she could help herself, she thought, "She wants to come back, she's left that man," and she instantly believed it with righteous certainty. "I *told* you," she said out loud, addressing her father. Her eyes burned with righteousness. She threw the message back in the wastepaper basket and went out to the back yard, where her grandmother was tying up the tomato plants. Her grandmother had on her red blouse with the short, puffy sleeves and her blue skirt that was splattered with what had once been red music notes but which were now faded and broken pink sticks. Her braid was wrapped around her head. "She looks like an immigrant," Beth thought coldly, comparing her to Joyce. For several moments Beth stood there looking at her grandmother and feeling entitled to a few answers.

The instant her grandmother glanced up, however, she didn't want to know. If, right at that moment, her grandmother had decided to tell her what the messages were about, Beth would have run away. As it was, she ran around to the front of the house and down the street. "I love Jesus, I love Jesus," she said, holding her arms out. She was so light on her feet! Any day now she was going to float, she could feel it.

Her father came home early that evening. It seemed significant to Beth that he did not change into casual pants and a sports shirt *before* supper, as he normally did. Other than that, however, nothing out of the ordinary happened. Her father talked about work, her grandmother nodded and signalled and wrote out a few conversational notes, which Beth leaned over to read.

After supper her father got around to changing his clothes, then went outside to cut the grass while Beth and her grandmother did the dishes. Beth, carrying too many dishes to the sink, dropped and smashed a saucer and a dinner plate. Her grandmother waved her hands—"Don't worry, it doesn't matter!"—and to prove it she got the Sears catalogue out of the cupboard and showed Beth the new set of dinnerware she intended to buy anyway.

It wasn't until Beth was eating breakfast the next morning that it dawned on her that if her mother was coming back, her grandmother would be leaving, and if her grandmother was leaving, she wouldn't be buying new dinnerware. This thought left Beth feeling as if she had just woken up with no idea yet what day it was or what she'd just been dreaming. Then the radio blared "… Liver …" and she jumped and turned to see her grandmother with one hand on the volume knob, and the other hand held up for silence. "Doctors report that the transplant was a success," the announcer said, "and that Kevin is in serious but stable condition."

"Did they find a donor?" Beth cried as the announcer said, "The donor, an eleven-year-old girl, died in St. Andrew's hospital late last night. Her name is being withheld at her family's request."

Her grandmother turned the volume back down.

"Gee, that's great," Beth said. "Everybody was praying for him."

Her grandmother tore a note off her pad. "Ask and it shall be given you," she wrote.

"I know!" Beth said exultantly. "I know!"

Nobody was home at Helen's that afternoon. Peering in the window beside the door, Beth saw that the mauve suitcase was gone, and the next thing she knew, she floated from Helen's door to the end of her driveway. Or at least she thought she floated, because she couldn't remember how she got from the house to the road, but the strange thing was, she didn't have the glowing sensation, the feeling of glory. She drifted home, holding herself as if she were a soap bubble.

At her house there was a note on the kitchen counter; a drawing of an apple, which meant that her grandmother was out grocery shopping. The phone rang, but when Beth said hello, the person hung up. She went into her bedroom, opened the drawer of her bedside table and took out the message with her mother's phone number on it. She returned to the kitchen and dialled. After four rings, an impatient-sounding woman said, "Hello?" Beth said nothing. "Yes, hello?" the woman said. "Who's calling?"

Beth hung up. She dialled Helen's number and immediately hung up.

She stood there for a few minutes, biting her knuckles.

She wandered down to her bedroom and looked out the window. Two back yards away, Amy was jumping off her porch. She was climbing onto the porch railing, leaping like a broad jumper, tumbling on the grass, springing to her feet, running up the stairs and doing it again. It made Beth's head spin.

About a quarter of an hour later her grandmother returned. She dropped the groceries against a cupboard door that slammed shut. She opened and shut the fridge. Turned on the tap. Beth, now lying on the bed, didn't move. She sat bolt upright when the phone rang, though. Five rings before her grandmother answered it.

Beth got up and went over to the window again. Amy was throwing a ball up into the air. Through the closed window Beth couldn't hear a thing, but she knew from the way Amy clapped and twirled her hands between catches that she was singing, "Ordinary moving, laughing, talking ..."

She knew from hearing the chair scrape that her grandmother was pulling it back to sit down. She knew from hearing the faucet still run that her grandmother was caught up in what the caller was saying. Several times her grandmother tapped her pencil on the mouthpiece to say to the caller, "I'm still listening. I'm taking it all down."

Where Is the Voice Coming From?

RUDY WIEBE

THE PROBLEM is to make the story.

One difficulty of this making may have been excellently stated by Teilhard de Chardin: "We are continually inclined to isolate ourselves from the things and events which surround us ... as though we were spectators, not elements, in what goes on." Arnold Toynbee does venture, "For all that we know, Reality is the undifferentiated unity of the mystical experience," but that need not here be considered. This story ended long ago; it is one of finite acts, of orders, of elemental feelings and reactions, of obvious legal restrictions and requirements.

Presumably all the parts of the story are themselves available. A difficulty is that they are, as always, available only in bits and pieces. Though the acts themselves seem quite clear, some written reports of the acts contradict each other. As if these acts were, at one time, too well known; as if the original nodule of each particular fact had from somewhere received non-factual accretions; or even more, as if, since the basic facts were so clear perhaps there were a larger number of facts than any one reporter, or several, or even any reporter had ever attempted to record. About facts that are still simply told by this mouth to that ear, of course, even less can be expected.

An affair seventy-five years old should acquire some of the shiny transparency of an old man's skin. It should.

Sometimes it would seem that it would be enough—perhaps more than enough—to hear the names only. The grandfather One Arrow; the mother Spotted Calf; the father Sounding Sky; the wife (wives rather, but only one of them seems to have a name, though their fathers are Napaise, Kapahoo, Old Dust, The Rump)—the one wife named, of all things, Pale Face; the cousin Going-Up-To-Sky; the brother-in-law (again, of all things) Dublin. The names of the police sound very much alike; they all begin with Constable or Corporal or Sergeant, but here and there an Inspector, then a Superintendent and eventually all the resonance of an Assistant Commissioner echoes down. More. Herself: Victoria, by the Grace of God etc., etc., QUEEN, defender of the Faith, etc., etc.; and witness "Our Right Trusty and Right Well-beloved Cousin and Councillor the Right Honorable Sir John Campbell Hamilton-Gordon, Earl of Aberdeen; Viscount Formartine, Baron Haddo, Methlic, Tarves and Kellie, in the Peerage of Scotland; Viscount Gordon of Aberdeen, County of Aberdeen, in the Peerage of the United Kingdom; Baronet of Nova Scotia, Knight Grand Cross of Our Most Distinguished Order of Saint Michael and Saint George, etc., Governor General of Canada." And of course himself: in the award proclamation named "Jean-Baptiste" but otherwise known only as Almighty Voice.

But hearing cannot be enough; not even hearing all the thunder of A Proclamation: "Now Hear Ye that a reward of FIVE HUNDRED DOLLARS will be paid to any person or persons who will give such information as will lead ... (etc., etc.) this Twentieth day of April, in the year of Our Lord one thousand eight hundred and ninety-six, and the Fifty-nineth year of Our Reign ... etc. and etc.

Such hearing cannot be enough. The first item to be seen is the piece of white bone. It is almost triangular, slightly convex—concave actually as it is positioned at this moment with its corners slightly raised—graduating from perhaps a strong eighth to a weak quarter of an inch in thickness, its scattered pore structure varying between larger and smaller on its perhaps polished, certainly shiny surface. Precision is difficult since the glass showcase is at least thirteen inches deep and therefore an eye cannot be brought as close as the minute inspection of such a small though certainly quite adequate, sample of skull would normally require. Also, because of the position it cannot be determined whether the several hairs, well over a foot long, are still in some manner attached or not.

The seven-pounder cannon can be seen standing almost shyly between the show-case and the interior wall. Officially it is known as a gun, not a cannon, and clearly its bore is not large enough to admit a large man's fist. Even if it can be believed that this gun was used in the 1885 Rebellion and that on the evening of Saturday, May 29, 1897 (while the nine-pounder, now unidentified, was in the process of arriving with the police on the special train from Regina), seven shells (all that were available in Prince Albert at that time) from it were sent shrieking into the poplar bluffs as night fell, clearly such shelling could not and would not disembowel the whole earth.

Its carriage is now nicely lacquered, the perhaps oak spokes of its petite wheels (little higher than a knee) have been recently scraped, puttied and varnished; the brilliant burnish of its brass breeching testifies with what meticulous care charmen and women have used nationally advertised cleaners and restorers.

Though it can also be seen, even a careless glance reveals that the same concern has not been expended on the one (of two) .44 calibre 1866 model Winchesters apparently found at the last in the pit with Almighty Voice. It also is preserved in a glass case; the number 1536735 is still, though barely, distinguishable on the brass cartridge section just below the brass saddle ring. However, perhaps because the case was imperfectly sealed at one time (though sealed enough not to warrant disturbance now), or because of simple neglect, the rifle is obviously spotted here and there with blotches of rust and the brass itself reveals discolorations almost like mildew. The rifle bore, the three long strands of hair themselves, actually bristle with clots of dust. It may be that this museum cannot afford to be as concerned as the other; conversely, the disfiguration may be something inherent in the items themselves.

The small building which was the police guardroom at Duck Lake, Saskatchewan Territory, in 1895 may also be seen. It had subsequently been moved from its original place and used to house small animals, chickens perhaps, or pigs—such as a woman might be expected to have under her responsibility. It is, of course, now perfectly empty, and clean so that the public may enter with no more discomfort than a bend under the doorway and a heavy encounter with disinfectant. The door-jamb has obviously been replaced; the bar network at one window is, however, said to be original; smooth still, very smooth. The logs inside have been smeared again and again with whitewash, perhaps paint, to an insistent point of identity-defying characterlessness. Within the small rectangular box of these logs not a sound can be heard from the streets of the, probably dead, town.

Hey Injun you'll get hung for stealing that steer
Hey Injun for killing that government cow you'll get three weeks on the woodpile
Hey Injun

The place named Kinistino seems to have disappeared from the map but the Minnechinass Hills have not. Whether they have ever been on a map is doubtful but they will, of course, not disappear from the landscape as long as the grass grows and the rivers run. Contrary to general report and belief, the Canadian prairies are rarely, if ever, flat and the Minnechinass (spelled five different ways and translated sometimes as "The Outside Hill," sometimes as "Beautiful Bare Hills") are dissimilar from any other of the numberless hills that everywhere block out the prairie horizon. They are bare; poplars lie tattered along their tops, almost black against the straw-pale grass and sharp green against the grey soil of the plowing laid in half-mile rectangular blocks upon their western slopes. Poles holding various wires stick out of the fields, back down the bend of the valley; what was once a farmhouse is weathering into the cultivated earth. The poplar bluff where Almighty Voice made his stand has, of course, disappeared.

The policemen he shot and killed (not the ones he wounded, of course) are easily located. Six miles east, thirty-nine miles north in Prince Albert, the English Cemetery. Sergeant Colin Campbell Colebrook, North West Mounted Police Registration Number 605, lies presumably under a gravestone there. His name is seventeenth in a very long "list of non-commissioned officers and men who have died in the service since the inception of the force." The date is October 29, 1895, and the cause of death is anonymous: "Shot by escaping Indian prisoner near Prince Albert." At the foot of this grave are two others: Constable John R. Kerr, No. 3040, and Corporal C.H.S. Hockin, No. 3106. Their cause of death on May 28, 1897 is even more anonymous, but the place is relatively precise: "Shot by Indians at Min-etch-inass Hills, Prince Albert District."

The gravestone, if he has one, of the fourth man Almighty Voice killed is more difficult to locate. Mr. Ernest Grundy, postmaster at Duck Lake in 1897, apparently shut his window the afternoon of Friday, May 28, armed himself, rode east twenty miles, participated in the second charge into the bluff at about 6:30 p.m., and on the third sweep of that charge was shot dead at the edge of the pit. It would seem that he thereby contributed substantially not only to the Indians' bullet supply, but his clothing warmed them as well.

The burial place of Dublin and Going-Up-To-Sky is unknown, as is the grave of Almighty Voice. It is said that a Métis named Henry Smith lifted the latter's body from the pit in the bluff and gave it to Spotted Calf. The place of burial is not, of course, of ultimate significance. A gravestone is always less evidence than a triangular piece of skull, provided it is large enough.

Whatever further evidence there is to be gathered may rest on pictures. There are, presumably, almost numberless pictures of the policemen in the case, but the only one with direct bearing is one of Sergeant Colebrook who apparently insisted on advancing to complete an arrest after being warned three times that if he took another step he would be shot. The picture must have been taken before he joined the force; it reveals him a large-eared young man, hair brush-cut and ascot tie, his eyelids slightly drooping, almost hooded under thick brows. Unfortunately a picture of Constable R. C. Dickson, into whose charge Almighty Voice was apparently committed in that guardroom and who after Colebrook's death was convicted of negligence, sentenced to two months hard labour and discharged does not seem to be available.

There are no pictures to be found of either Dublin (killed early by rifle fire) or Going-Up-To-Sky (killed in the pit), the two teenage boys who gave their ultimate fealty to Almighty Voice. There is, however, one said to be of Almighty Voice, Junior.

He may have been born to Pale Face during the year, two hundred and twenty-one days that his father was a fugitive. In the picture he is kneeling before what could be a tent, he wears striped denim overalls and displays twin babies whose sex cannot be determined from the double-laced dark bonnets they wear. In the supposed picture of Spotted Calf and Sounding Sky, Sounding Sky stands slightly before his wife; he wears a white shirt and a striped blanket folded over his left shoulder in such a manner that the arm in which he cradles a long rifle cannot be seen. His head is thrown back; the rim of his hat appears as a black half-moon above eyes that are pressed shut in, as it were, profound concentration; above a mouth clenched thin in a downward curve. Spotted Calf wears a long dress, a sweater which could also be a man's dress coat, and a large fringed and embroidered shawl which would appear distinctly Dukhobour in origin if the scroll patterns on it were more irregular. Her head is small and turned slightly towards her husband so as to reveal her right ear. There is what can only be called a quizzical expression on her crumpled face; it may be she does not understand what is happening and that she would have asked a question, perhaps of her husband, perhaps of the photographers, perhaps even of anyone, anywhere in the world if such questioning were possible for an Indian lady.

There is one final picture. That is one of Almighty Voice himself. At least it is purported to be of Almighty Voice himself. In the Royal Canadian Mounted Police Museum on the Barracks Grounds just off Dewdney Avenue in Regina, Saskatchewan, it lies in the same showcase, as a matter of fact immediately beside, that triangular piece of skull. Both are unequivocally labelled, and it must be assumed that a police force with a world-wide reputation would not label *such* evidence incorrectly. But here emerges an ultimate problem in making the story.

There are two official descriptions of Almighty Voice. The first reads: "Height about five feet, ten inches, slight build, rather good looking, a sharp hooked nose with a remarkably flat point. Has a bullet scar on the left side of his face about 1? inches long running from near corner of mouth towards ear. The scar cannot be noticed when his face is painted but otherwise is plain. Skin fair for an Indian." The second description is on the Award Proclamation: "About twenty-two years old, five feet ten inches in height, weight about eleven stone, slightly erect, neat small feet and hands; complexion inclined to be fair, wavey dark hair to shoulders, large dark eyes, broad forehead, sharp features and parrot nose with flat tip, scar on left cheek running from mouth towards ear, feminine appearance."

So run the descriptions that were, presumably, to identify a well-known fugitive in so precise a manner that an informant could collect five hundred dollars—a considerable sum when a police constable earned between one and two dollars a day. The nexus of the problems appears when these supposed official descriptions are compared to the supposed official picture. The man in the picture is standing on a small rug. The fingers of his left hand touch a curved Victorian settee, behind him a photographer's backdrop of scrolled patterns merges to vaguely paradisiacal trees and perhaps a sky. The moccasins he wears make it impossible to deduce whether his feet are "neat small." He may be five feet, ten inches tall, may weigh eleven stone, he certainty is "rather good looking" and, though it is a frontal view, it may be that the point of his long and flaring nose could be "remarkably flat." The photograph is slightly over-illuminated and so the unpainted complexion could be "inclined to be fair"; however, nothing can be seen of a scar, the hair is not wavy and shoulder-length but hangs almost to the waist in two thick straight braids worked through with beads, fur, ribbons and cords. The right hand that holds the corner of the blanket-like coat in position is large and, even in the high illumination, heavily veined. The neck is concealed under coiled beads and the forehead seems more low than "broad."

Perhaps, somehow, these picture details could be reconciled with the official description if the face as a whole were not so devastating.

On a cloth-backed sheet two feet by two and one-half feet in size, under the Great Seal of the Lion and the Unicorn, dignified by the names of the Deputy of the Minister of Justice, the Secretary of State, the Queen herself and all the heaped detail of her "Right Trusty and Right Well Beloved Cousin," this description concludes: "feminine appearance." But the pictures: any face of history, any believed face that the world acknowledges as *man*—Socrates, Jesus, Attila, Genghis Khan, Mahatma Gandhi, Joseph Stalin—no believed face is more *man* than this face. The mouth, the nose, the clenched brows, the eyes—the eyes are large, yes, and dark, but even in this watered-down reproduction of unending reproductions of that original, a steady look into those eyes cannot be endured. It is a face like an axe.

IT IS NOW EVIDENT that the de Chardin statement quoted at the beginning has relevance only as it proves itself inadequate to explain what has happened. At the same time, the inadequacy of Aristotle's much more famous statement becomes evident: "The true difference [between the historian and the poet] is that one relates what *has* happened, the other what *may* happen." These statements cannot explain the storyteller's activity since, despite the most rigid application of impersonal investigation, the elements of the story have now run me aground. If ever I could, I can no longer pretend to objective, omnipotent disinterestedness. I am no longer *spectator* of what *has* happened or what *may* happen: I am become *element* in what is happening at this very moment.

For it is, of course, I myself who cannot endure the shadows on that paper which are those eyes. It is I who stand beside this broken veranda post where two corner shingles have been torn away, where barbed wire tangles the dead weeds on the edge of this field. The bluff that sheltered Almighty Voice and his two friends has not disappeared from the slope of the Minnechinass, no more than the sound of

Constable Dickson's voice in that guardhouse is silent. The sound of his speaking is there even if it has never been recorded in an official report:

hey injun you'll get
hung
for stealing that steer
hey injun for killing that government
cow you'll get three
weeks on the woodpile hey injun

The unknown contradictory words about an unprovable act that move a boy to defiance, an implacable Cree warrior long after the three-hundred-and-fifty-year war is ended, a war already lost the day the Cree watch Cartier hoist his gun ashore at Hochelaga and they begin the long retreat west; these words of incomprehension, of threatened incomprehensible law are there to be heard just as the unmoving tableau of the three-day siege is there to be seen on the slopes of the Minnechinass. Sounding Sky is somewhere not there, under arrest, but Spotted Calf stands on a shoulder of the Hills a little to the left, her arms upraised to the setting sun. Her mouth is open. A horse rears, riderless, above the scrub willow at the edge of the bluff, smoke puffs, screams tangle in rifle barrage, there are wounds, somewhere. The bluff is so green this spring, it will not burn and the ragged line of seven police and two civilians is staggering through, faces twisted in rage, terror, and rifles sputter. Nothing moves. There is no sound of frogs in the night; twenty-seven policeman and five civilians stand in cordon at thirty-yard intervals and a body also lies in the shelter of a gully. Only a voice rises from the bluff:

We have fought well
You have died like braves
I have worked hard and am hungry
Give me food

but nothing moves. The bluff lies, a bright green island on the grassy slope surrounded by men hunched forward rigid over their long rifles, men clumped out of rifle-range, thirty-five men dressed as for fall hunting on a sharp spring day, a small gun positioned on a ridge above. A crow is falling out of the sky into the bluff, its feathers sprayed as by an explosion. The first gun and the second are in position, the beginning and end of the bristling surround of thirty-five Prince Albert Volunteers, thirteen civilians and fifty-six policemen in position relative to the bluff and relative to the unnumbered whites astride their horses, standing up in their carts, staring and pointing across the valley, in position relative to the bluff and the unnumbered Indians squatting silent along the higher ridges of the Hills, motionless mounds, faceless against the Sunday morning sunlight edging between and over them down along the tree tips, down into the shadows of the bluff. Nothing moves. Beside the second gun the red-coated officer has flung a handful of grass into the motionless air, almost to the rim of the red sun.

And there is a voice. It is an incredible voice that rises from among the young poplars ripped of their spring bark, from among the dead somewhere lying there, out of the arm-deep pit shorter than a man; a voice rises over the exploding smoke and thunder of guns that reel back in their positions, worked over, serviced by the grimed motionless men in bright coats and glinting buttons, a voice so high and clear, so unbelievably high and strong in its unending wordless cry.

THE VOICE OF "GITCHIE-MANITOU WAYO"—interpreted as "voice of the Great Spirit"—that is, The Almighty Voice. His death chant no less incredible in its beauty than in its incomprehensible happiness.

I say "wordless cry" because that is the way it sounds to me. I could be more accurate if I had a reliable interpreter who would make a reliable interpretation. For I do not, of course, understand the Cree myself.

The Man with Clam Eyes
AUDREY THOMAS

I CAME TO THE SEA because my heart was broken. I rented a cabin from an old professor who stammered when he talked. He wanted to go far away and look at something. In the cabin there is a table, a chair, a bed, a woodstove, an aladdin lamp. Outside there is a well, a privy, rocks, trees and the sea.

(The lapping of waves, the scream of gulls.)

I came to this house because my heart was broken. I brought wine in green bottles and meaty soup bones. I set an iron pot on the back of the stove to simmer. I lit the lamp. It was no longer summer and the wind grieved around the door. Spiders and mice disapproved of my arrival. I could hear them clucking their tongues in corners.

(The sound of the waves and the wind.)

This house is spotless, shipshape. Except for the spiders. Except for the mice in corners, behind the walls. There are no clues. I have brought with me wine in green bottles, an eiderdown quilt, my brand-new *Bartlett's Familiar Quotations.* On the inside of the front jacket it says, "Who said: 1. In wildness is the preservation of the world. 2. All hell broke loose. 3. You are the sunshine of my life."

I want to add another. I want to add two more. Who said, "There is no nice way of saying this"? Who said, "Let's not go over it again"? The wind grieves around the door. I stuff the cracks with rags torn from the bottom of my skirt. I am sad. Shall I leave here then? Shall I go and lie outside his door calling whoo—whoo— whoo like the wind?

(The sound of the waves and the wind.)

I drink all of the wine in one green bottle. I am like a glove. Not so much shapeless as empty, waiting to be filled up. I set my lamp in the window, I sleep to the sound of the wind's grieving.

(Quiet breathing, the wind still there, but
soft, then gradually fading out. The passage
of time, then seagulls, and then waves.)

How can I have slept when my heart is broken? I dreamt of a banquet table under green trees. I was a child and ate ripe figs with my fingers. Now I open the door—

(West-coast birds, the towhee with
its strange cry, and the waves.)

The sea below is rumpled and wrinkled and the sun is shining. I can see islands and then more islands, as though my island had spawned islands in the night. The sun is shining. I have never felt so lonely in my life. I go back in. I want to write a message and throw it out to sea. I rinse my wine bottle from last night and set it above the stove to dry. I sit at the small table thinking. My message must be clear and yet compelling, like a lamp lit in a window on a dark night. There is a blue bowl on the table and a rough spoon carved from some sweet-smelling wood. I eat porridge with raisins while I think. The soup simmers on the back of the stove. The seagulls outside are riding the wind and crying ME ME ME. If this were a fairy tale, there would be someone here to help me, give me a ring, a cloak, a magic word. I bang on the table in my frustration. A small drawer pops open.

(Sound of the wind the waves lapping.)

Portents and signs mean something, point to something, otherwise—too cruel. The only thing in the drawer is part of a manuscript, perhaps some secret hobby of the far-off professor. It is a story about a man on a train from Genoa to Rome. He has a gun in his pocket and is going to Rome to kill his wife. After the conductor comes through, he goes along to the lavatory, locks the door, takes out the gun, then stares at himself in the mirror. He is pleased to note that his eyes are clear and clam.   *Clam?* Pleased to note that his eyes are clear and clam?   I am not quick this morning. It takes me a while before I see what has happened. And then I laugh. How can I laugh when my heart is cracked like a dropped plate? But I laugh at the man on the train to Rome, staring at himself in the mirror—the man with clam eyes. I push aside the porridge and open my *Bartlett's Familiar Quotations*. I imagine Matthew Arnold—"The sea is clam tonight ..." or Wordsworth—"It is a beauteous evening, clam and free ..."

I know what to say in my message.   The bottle is dry. I take the piece of paper and push it in. Then the cork, which I seal with wax from a yellow candle. I will wait until just before dark.

(The waves, the lapping sea. The gulls, loud
and then gradually fading out. Time passes.)

Men came by in a boat with a pirate flag. They were diving for sea urchins and when they saw me sitting on the rocks they gave me one. They tell me to crack it open and eat the inside, here, they will show me how. I cry No and No, I want to watch it for a while. They shrug and swim away.   All afternoon I watched it in pleasant idleness. I had corrected the typo of course—I am that sort of person—but the image of the man with clam eyes wouldn't leave me and I went down on the rocks to think. That's when I saw the divers with their pirate flag; that's when I was given the gift of the beautiful maroon sea urchin. The rocks were as grey and wrinkled as elephants, but warm, with enormous pores and pools licked out by the wind and the sea. The sea urchin is a dark maroon, like the lips of certain black men I have known. It moves constantly back/forth, back/forth with all its spines turning. I take it up to the cabin. I let it skate slowly back and forth across the table. I keep it wet with water from my bucket. The soup smells good. This morning I add carrots, onions, potatoes, bay leaves and thyme. How can I be hungry when my heart is broken? I cut bread with a long, sharp knife, holding the loaf against my breast. Before supper I put the sea urchin back into the sea.

(Sound of the wind and the waves.)

My bottle is ready and there is a moon. I have eaten soup and drunk wine and nibbled at my bread. I have read a lot of unfamiliar quotations. I have trimmed the wick and lit the lamp and set it in the window. The sea is still tonight and the moon has left a long trail of silver stretching almost to the rocks.

(Night sounds. A screech owl.
No wind, but the waves lapping.)

I go down to the sea as far as I can go. I hold the corked bottle in my right hand and fling it towards the stars. For a moment I think that a hand has reached up and caught it as it fell back towards the sea. I stand there. The moon and the stars light up my loneliness. How will I fall asleep when my heart is broken?

(Waves, then fading out. The sound
of the wild birds calling.)

I awoke with the first bird. I lay under my eiderdown and watched my breath in the cold room. I wondered if the birds could understand one another, if a chickadee could talk with a junco, for example. I wondered whether, given the change in seasons and birds, there was always the same first bird. I got up and lit the fire and put a kettle on for washing.

(The iron stove is opened and the wood lit.
It catches, snaps and crackles.
Water is poured into a large kettle.)

When I went outside to fling away the water, he was there, down on the rocks below me, half-man, half-fish. His green scales glittered like sequins in the winter sunlight. He raised his arm and beckoned to me.

(Sound of the distant gulls.)

We have been swimming. The water is cold, cold, cold. Now I sit on the rocks, combing out my hair. He tells me stories. My heart darts here and there like a frightened fish. The tracks of his fingers run silver along my leg. He told me that he is a drowned sailor, that he went overboard in a storm at sea. He speaks with a strong Spanish accent.

He has been with the traders who bought for a pittance the sea-otters' pelts which trimmed the robes of Chinese mandarins. A dozen glass beads would be bartered with the Indians for six of the finest skins.

With Cook he observed the transit of Venus in the cloudless skies of Tahiti.

With Drake he had sailed on "The Golden Hind" for the Pacific Coast. They landed in a bay off California. His fingers leave silver tracks on my bare legs. I like to hear him say it—Cal-ee fórn-ya. The Indians there were friendly. The men were naked but the women wore petticoats of bulrushes.

Oh how I like it when he does that.

He was blown around the Cape of Good Hope with Diaz. Only they called it the Cape of Storms. The King did not like the name and altered it.   Oh.   His cool tongue laps me. My breasts bloom in the moonlight. We dive—and rise out of the sea, gleaming. He decorates my hair with clamshells and stars, my body with sea-lettuce. I do not feel the cold. I laugh. He gives me a rope of giant kelp and I skip for him in the moonlight. He breaks open the shells of mussels and pulls out their sweet flesh with his long fingers. We tip the liquid into our throats; it tastes like tears.   He touches me with his explorer's hands.

(Waves, the sea—loud—louder. Fading out.)

I ask him to come with me, up to the professor's cabin. "It is impóss-ee-ble," he says. He asks me to go with him. "It is impóss-ee-ble," I say. "Not at all."

I cannot breathe in the water. I will drown. I have no helpful sisters. I do not know a witch.

(Sea, waves, grow louder, fade,
fading but not gone.)

He lifts me like a wave and carries me towards the water. I can feel the roll of the world. My legs dissolve at his touch and flow together. He shines like a green fish in the moonlight. "Is easy," he says, as my mouth fills up with tears. "Is nothing." The last portions of myself begin to sift and change.

I dive beneath the waves! He clasps me to him. We are going to swim to the edges of the world, he says, and I believe him.

I take one glance backwards and wave to the woman in the window. She has lit the lamp. She is eating soup and drinking wine. Her heart is broken. She is thinking about a man on a train who is going to kill his wife. The lamp lights up her loneliness. I wish her well.

Gypsy Art

LEON ROOKE

YOUNG FAZZINI WAS APPRENTICED to an artist who made incredible boxes that were like airy castles, each with a thousand rooms and baffling appendages. One day the master said to Fazzini, "You don't understand art, or boxes, or castles. You need to run with gypsies and lose yourself in amazing adventures." At home Fazzini's parents were ever bickering at him. "Grow up," they said. "Avail yourself of every opportunity. Let not the smallest blade of grass go unnoticed." In other words, hit the road. So Fazzini struck off on the road, eager for any adventure. On the road Fazzini met a gypsy woman, big-boned and unruly. The woman took Fazzini to her encampment. He was the love of her life, she said, and requested the other gypsies refrain from spitting at him. Within the hour they were married. Fazzini could not believe his luck. He had been in love before, though never so deliriously. His wife tired herself out, proclaiming her love. They fell asleep entwined. All the gypsies were entwined one with another, Fazzini and his own gypsy somewhere in the middle. Then the gypsies hit the road. Fazzini had a headache. He wondered why it was he had awakened under the sour apple trees and where the gypsies had gone. Later on he realized his toe must be broken, since walking was such a difficulty. The sun was unbearable and the only shade in the vicinity was taken up with wild animals which hissed at him when he neared. Fazzini fashioned crude crutches from the branches of the apple tree. The crutches hurt, his underarms were raw, but at least he could walk. Fazzini had been warned as a youth to avoid gypsies, but hadn't paid attention. He had felt contempt in those days for anyone so arrogant as to believe their calling in life was to issue advice. How many the times his mother had slapped his face? He did not want to go home again, but now he was going home because this adventure on the road had not worked out as planned. He had taken the wrong road. Next time he met a gypsy woman on the road he would know better. He wouldn't be so easy to fool. From time to time he rested by the road under the shade of more sour apple trees. Life would be all right, God, he thought, if you will deliver me a little food. A nice prosciutto would be divine. A bottle of vino, dear God, as well. Lately Fazzini had been talking to God as though God was a sweet woman. It paid to compliment Her, although in his personal opinion a good cattolico should not advertise the fact. Deeply religious people should keep their feelings to themselves. The crutches felt fine now; such an ungrateful fellow he had been, complaining endlessly of every triviality. His toe had miraculously healed. It was a magic toe. People he passed on the road were of two sorts, civil or uncivil. They spat at him, or sought to set him off in opposing directions. More than one person offered the opinion that he appeared able-bodied. Why did he not secure meaningful employment? Fazzini trudged on; he had many a mile to traverse, and ambition was his guide. He was a mature fellow now—no longer the crass fool. If his family saw him they would be amazed. On a high meadow Fazzini discerned an encampment of gypsies. He hid behind bushes, throwing rocks into their camp. When they ran at him he also ran. Fazzini and gypsies just did not get along. "You gypsies," he said to them, "are the dregs of the earth." The maddened gypsies threw Fazzini in the river. This was round about the Spesso Fumo lowlands where the Spesso Fumo River finally allows itself to be seen. The gypsies jumped into the river themselves. They washed themselves, they sang. A gypsy with an ugly bruise on his forehead embraced Fazzini constantly. "Your stones have knocked sense into my head," this man said. "You shall henceforth be known as the King of the Gypsies." But once Fazzini was in their camp the gypsy women swore at him. They spat. They made him cook their gypsy food and wash their gypsy clothes. Even their gypsy feet. They made him tend the horses and dogs. They were at him every minute. The gypsies not badgering him were singing gypsy songs. Fazzini, in all his life, had never heard such ugly, uninspiring songs. One night when all the gypsies were asleep Fazzini crawled away from the gypsy camp on his hands and knees. He crawled until his knees bled. All along the escape route he was pursued by an insane crew of black flies. After a time he no longer bothered with the ticks pricking at his scalp. He was hungry and cold. He talked sweetly to his sweetheart God, complimenting Her at length on Her fine dress, but God wasn't fooled. She knew he was speaking only to hear his own voice. He changed his voice, which did not fool Her either. She wore fine jewels, though, and was quite radiant. She looked to him like She was on Her way to a party. His hands burned. All that lye soap that the gypsies had made him boil. So many boiling pots, so many pots that Fazzini was made to stir. Gooey stuff, hard on the limbs. His very elbows ached. The gypsies simply did not know how to live. They knew no other life. The refineries of life were unknown to them. Plus, babies everywhere, always crying, and only Fazzini to care for them. Crawling babies that went about on all fours until on their own accord they uprighted themselves and pranced about as mature gypsies yodelling senseless gypsy songs. It was sickening, if you wanted to know the truth. But what did Fazzini care? He was free of their lot now. He'd learned a thing or two. He had experience under his belt which he meant to put to good use. He wished his family could see him now. They would be amazed. Finally Fazzini decided he would stand up. Why all that crawling anyway? He guessed he'd crawled a million miles. Now it was raining; the heavens pouring down. What's that? Oh my God, yes, there's a road! Now, Fazzini thought, I know where I am. No more of this bush life for me. Immediately upon taking to the road, Fazzini found himself intercepted by an unruly gang of men who appeared out of nowhere. They wore slickers, carried umbrellas, did not heed the ferocious heavens, the pelting rain. This gang wanted right out to know whether Fazzini had seen anywhere in the vicinity a dirty band of roving gypsies. "Speak up," they said, "and we'll go easy on you." They slapped Fazzini around. They punched him one way and another. This gang, truly they were enraged. You trust a gypsy at your peril, they told him. They were on foot, they said, because the gypsies had stolen their wagons. Oh, and their horses too. And the womenfolk. The gypsies had set fire to their haystacks. They'd raided every hen coop and carried away good God-fearing children, to raise these children as mangy gypsies. The gang had been on the gypsies' trail for weeks. Now they were close. They could smell gypsies nearby. Come to that, Fazzini smelt like a gypsy himself. "If you want to know why we are swatting you, that is why." Fazzini objected. "I hate gypsies more than you," he said. "Those gypsies just have no respect for the common decencies. They are godless creatures. You would not believe the bizarre acts they had me perform. Chickens? Who was made to pluck those chickens? Your womenfolk? Forget your womenfolk. Already they are more the gypsy than the gypsies are themselves." Fazzini felt proud of himself. His tale of woe worked this gang of roughcuts into a frenzied state. They proclaimed their own virtues endlessly, firing off muskets right and left. Fazzini raised one finger in the air, and pointed the way the wind was blowing. Go that way, he said. You'll find those scurvy gypsies before the sun goes down. The gang was so enlivened by this news they decided then and there to have a party. To celebrate this turn in their fate, why not? Unloosen the jugs. Everybody have a good drink to make us mean, then it's onward to sweet revenge. One jug led to another and soon all were so wildly drunk not one of them, including Fazzini, could stand up. Fazzini did not know how it happened: one second he was by the river, his pee grandly arching, and the next second he was in the drink. He was in the Spesso Fumo River, which had finally showed itself. Fazzini had to swim like a rat. Agony, you want to know the truth. So many times he nearly perished. Glubglub, Fazzini the drowned rodent. The river at flood stage, current sweeping him along. Debris flowing by him: rooftops, pigs, cows, fowl. The whole of the once dry earth flowing with him. He clutched at mud and wet grass, ferns, katydids, sprig of daffodil; not so easy was it getting ashore. He drifted miles and miles and no longer knew where he was. Finally the heavens relented, the rain softened, he was at eddy in a swirling pool. Fazzini cried out; the object he had been clinging to over the past hours, clinging to for dear life, was a swollen dead man. Oh, dear God, Fazzini said. Oh, my Lord, I love Your shoes. What pretty feet! Bella! Bella! He tried pushing the dead man away—*go! go!*—but the eddy repeatedly floated the dead body back at him. The arms of the dead man flung themselves over his shoulders, the face time and time again tried kissing him. It tried crawling itself up over him. Rape! Fazzini thought. That dead man means raping me. What a come-down. May I never know tranquillity? All I wanted from this world was a dignified life. A little something to eat now and then. A warm bed. Flotsam, foam, and the dead man encircled him. Fazzini's legs dangled uselessly in the river's depths. "What's that?" Fazzini asked. "There, swimming by?" A giant turtle. Well, dear God. Fazzini threw himself at the turtle, catching its shell on either side. Astonished, the turtle whipped back its head. Its jaws clamped entirely through one of Fazzini's hands. The turtle dived and twisted in a frenzy of disbelief. Its feet clawed; it dived, it surfaced, it flipped over and over and over. It was a turtle thoroughly deranged. Fazzini's head reposed on the shell's muck. The turtle was now away from the eddy. Fazzini had courage; he was fighting for his life; he held on. He must have slept. When he opened his eyes the sun was bright, he felt warmth. He was akimbo upon the silent earth. Don't just lie there. Show your mettle, Fazzini told himself. You've endured the worst patch. Trudge, Trudge. A thicket? A thicket, yes, so many vines and trees. So many squirrels jumping tree to tree. So many snakes. "And who," Fazzini asked of the black flies, "invited you?" Eventually Fazzini, trudging, saw a campfire at blaze within a clearing; he trudged towards it. He looked first for wagons but saw no wagons. The campers were not gypsies, then; his luck was looking up. In fact, the campfire was deserted, despite the flaring fire, cinders volleying to the heavens. I'll just warm myself, Fazzini thought. Yoo-hoo! I wonder if they have any grub. Fazzini warmed himself. He felt so much better now. Someone had been even nice enough to leave a nice green tent, neatly propped. My lucky day, Fazzini thought. He lifted the tent flap, and immediately felt faint. In a swoon, hot all over. Oh, God, he said, I love Your ears, Your nose, Your beautiful lips. Have I spoken of Your most incredible knees, Your ankles, Your fine, firm buttocks? "Grr and crunch," the beast in front of him said. Yikes! A giant black, grunting, creature stared back at him. Fazzini smelt it. It had a terrible smell reminiscent of smelly feet. The creature was busy eating something. It looked him over closely, but went on eating. A small fold-up desk had been set up inside the tent. On the desk was spread a large map. An explorer's jacket hung from a nail on the centre pole. Fazzini took the jacket; he took the map, which felt oily. Oh, my God, English biscuits! He quickly took these; he filled his mouth with biscuits. "Just go on," he told the beast, "with what you are doing." The creature nodded sagely. He and the beast were pals. The beast seemed not to mind what Fazzini took. It went on eating. It slurped and chomped, blood and gore dribbling from its chin and paws; the beast flung out one arm, offering Fazzini a long, dripping bone. Want some? Fazzini wasn't tempted. The biscuits had filled him. The beast watched him steadily, ever with a benign air. Afterwards, when the beast endeavored to embrace him, Fazzini ran. That beast is worse than the gypsies, Fazzini thought. I'm not coupling with bears. Oh, Mother in heaven, how many pedestals must I set You upon? Never mind, my Darling. I will scour the land, mend each broken toe, or nose, or thumb. Each eyelid. He blundered through the thicket. He felt brave. Renewed. He wished his family could see him now; they'd take back more than one of their previous harsh words. Soon Fazzini realized he was hearing music. He turned one direction and another. He whipped his head about. He dropped down and laid first one ear and then another against the cold earth. Music wafted his way from every direction. It was all the same music, gypsy music. By my life, Fazzini thought, those gypsies are everywhere! Well, he'd avoid them. A person could only accept gypsy company for so long. Gypsies are entirely too demanding. One desires one's own kind, Fazzini thought. That is how God has made the earth. Let the gypsies stay to their domain and I will cling to mine. Fazzini went on talking to himself like that. After his ordeals, why not? Plus, black flies were after him again. Ticks burrowing. Big fat pussy ticks in his scalp, mean black flat buggers everywhere else. His hand numb from the turtle's snapping jaws. His hand ugly, throbbing, heated up big as a drum. I'll get that tended to, Fazzini thought. You need not worry on my account. "I like Your hat, God," Fazzini said. "That's a splendid hat. Let no one tell You different. Create Your own fashion, I say. Pay no attention to what the rabble say. Your hair looks wonderful too. And such lovely skin. I'll grant You the rouge is heavy, someone would say overdone, but I like it. Please Yourself, that's what Fazzini says." He fell silent. No need to get carried away; no need to layer on the compliments with a spoon. There was something to be said for straight talk. But why run the risk? When had straight-talking got him anywhere? It had landed him with gypsies, that's what straight talk had done. Onwards now. Trudge, trudge. In his new jacket. You'd think just once God would compliment him. *Say, now, Fazzini, lad! That's a spiffy jacket! Aren't you the cheeky one! Brava, brava!* Indeed, Fazzini's view was that he cut a fine figure. Who wouldn't think so? Anyone with a fair gaze would be bound to be impressed. When he reached society, the quality people would see at a glance the kind of man he was. Style would carry the day. A soldier of fortune, yes! Tides betide. Before the moon set, without a doubt he would meet and marry a beautiful woman, marry and settle down. High time too, Fazzini thought. Time to shy away from this rover life, this existence without meat or merit. Yes, high time. It had taken him a long time to recognize the flaws in his character; now he was determined to set himself to mending these flaws. Youth, what did youth know? Sooner or later a person had to grow up. You had to work your way through it, didn't you? "Well, mother dear," Fazzini said, "that's my advice." Black flies coated his face; why flit here and there when already they'd found hospitable lodging for the night? First order of business, when he reached the city, was to do something about those flies. Then to the vineyard to slacken his thirst. To the Music Hall. All those high kicks, those heaving bosoms, all those naked legs! Yes, yes, if you would be so kind! *Cacciucco alla livornese,* why not? He'd want a good song to cheer him up. Not this crude gypsy zing-a-ling. Then to the studio of his artist friend, to re-apprentice himself. He too could build incredible boxes now, boxes each with a thousand rooms and anterooms, catacombs and towers, cat walks connecting one tower to another, and a thousand secret chambers holding incredible adventure behind every door. But, wait, here he was limping again. Those old war wounds, his broken toe, the bloated arm, each aching like the very devil. And beasts of the wild over there under sour apple trees consuming every inch of shade. Plus here came a caravan of unruly gypsies gypsies astride mules, riding creaking wagons, herding along an endless sweep of ponies, lambs, swine, acrobatic goats, caged monkeys, plumed birds that hopped on one leg. Up there, putting bite to the lead reins, a fine, slinky-eyed woman, bare-breasted, under a wilderness of hair, one and then another luscious eye winking wickedly at him.

"Tell your fortune, good-looking. Read your future? Today only, special price!"

"Why, hello there," Fazzini said. "Gypsies, are you? Oh, I've known a gypsy or two in my life. Salt of the earth. My heavens, I even married one. Big-boned and unruly, brimming over with love. Are you by chance going my way?"

"Sure, sure," the gypsies said. "Going here, going there! Today only, we are on our way to our airy castle in the sky. Much gold there, pig roasts, love eternal, wine that flows as from a waterfall."

The gypsies saw he was a nervy deluded fellow, the innocent romantic. His face encrusted, possibly suffering a fracture of the larynx; just a plain pasty-faced boy too long adrift from home.

They placed him inside a cage filled with chickens, outfitting him with a long blade, a sack to catch the feathers.

Art, Fazzini thought. Art is my life.

I love Your smile, he said to God. I love the rustle of Your skirts, the sun in Your hair, Your gay laughter, the fragrance of Your lilac-scented skin.

He would pluck feathers from the confused hysterical birds; he would go at this task feather by feather. The simple life is not to be disavowed.

Save me, my Darling. I lick the very sweat of Thy hand.

The Baby in the Airmail Box
THOMAS KING

Okay, so on Monday

THE BABY ARRIVES in a cardboard box with a handful of airmail stamps stuck on top and a label that says, "Rocky Creek First Nations."

Orena Charging Woman brings the box to the council meeting and sets it in the middle of the table. "All right," she says, after all of the band councillors have settled in their chairs, "who ordered the baby?"

"Baby?" says Louis Standing, who is currently the chief and gets to sit in the big chair by the window. "What baby?"

Orena opens the airmail box and bends the flaps back so everyone can get a good look.

"It's a baby, all right," says Jimmy Tucker. "But it looks sick."

"It's not sick," says Orena, who knows something about babies. "It's White."

"White?" says Louis. "Who in hell would order a White baby?"

And just then

Linda Blackenship walks into Bob Wakutz's office at the Alberta Child Placement Agency with a large folder and an annoyed expression on her face that reminds Bob of the various promises he has made Linda about leaving his wife.

"We have a problem," says Linda, who says this a lot, and she holds the folder out at shoulder level and drops it on Bob's desk. Right on top of the colour brochure for the new Ford trucks.

"A problem?" says Bob, which is what he says every day when Linda comes into his office and drops folders on his desk.

"Mr. and Mrs. Cardinal," says Linda.

When they were in bed together, Bob could always tell when Linda was joking, but now that they've stopped seeing each other (which is the phrase Bob prefers) or since they stopped screwing (which Linda says is more honest) he can't.

"Have they been approved?"

"Yes," says Linda.

"Okay," says Bob, in a jocular sort of way, in case Linda is joking. "What's the problem?"

"They're Indian," says Linda.

Bob pushed the truck brochure to one side and opens the file. "East?"

"West."

"Caribbean?"

"Cree."

"That's the problem?" says Bob, who can't remember if giving babies to Indians is part of the mandate of the Alberta Child Placement Agency, though he is reasonably sure, without actually looking at the regulations, that there is no explicit prohibition against it.

Linda stands in front of Bob's desk and puts her hands on her hips. "They would like a baby," she says, without even a hint of a smile. "Mr. and Mrs. Cardinal would like a White baby."

Meanwhile

Orena takes the baby out of the airmail box and passes it around so all the councillors can get a good look at it.

"It's White, all right," says Clarence Scout. "Jesus, but they can be ugly."

"They never have any hair," says Elaine Sweetwater. "Got to be a mother to love a bald baby."

Now, the baby in the airmail box isn't on the agenda, and Louis can see that if he doesn't get the meeting moving, he is going to miss his tee time at Wolf Creek, so when the baby is passed to him, he passes it directly to Orena and makes an executive decision.

"Send it back," he says.

"Not the way it works," says Emmett Black Rabbit. "First you got to make a motion. Then someone has to second it."

"Who's going to bingo tonight?" says Ross Heavy Runner. "I could use a ride."

"Maybe it's one of those free samples," says Narcisse Good. "My wife gets them all the time."

"Any chance of getting a doughnut and a cup of coffee?" says Thelma Gladstone. "I didn't get breakfast."

"We can't send it back," says Orena, "There's no return address."

"Invoice?" asks Louis.

"Nope," says Orena.

"All right," says Louis, who is not happy with the start of his day, "who wants a baby?"

"Got four of my own," says Bruce Carving.

"Three here," says Harmon Setauket.

"Eight," says Ross Heavy Runner, and he holds up nine fingers by mistake.

"You caught up on those child support payments yet?" Edna Hunt asks him.

"Coffee and doughnuts?" says Thelma, "Could we have some coffee and doughnuts?"

"Could someone come up with an idea?" Louis checks his watch.

"What about bingo?" says Ross.

"Perfect," says Louis. "Meeting adjourned."

At the same time

Bob Wakutz is shaking hands with Mr. and Mrs. Cardinal. "Would you like some coffee?" he says. "Maybe a doughnut?"

"Sure," says Mr. Cardinal. "Black, no sugar."

"Thank you," says Mrs. Cardinal. "One cream, no sugar."

Bob smiles at Linda.

Linda smiles back.

"Maybe we should get down to business first," says Bob, and he opens the file. "I see you've been approved for adoption."

"That's right," says Mrs. Cardinal.

"So, when can we expect to get a baby?" says Mr. Cardinal.

Bob looks at Linda. He still finds her attractive, and, if he's being honest with himself, he has to admit that he misses their get-togethers. "Don't we have several Red babies ready for immediate placement?"

"Yes, we do," says Linda, who has no idea what she saw in Bob.

"Perfect," says Bob.

"That's nice," says Mr. Cardinal, "but we don't want a Red baby."

"No," says Mrs. Cardinal, "what we want is a White baby."

"That's understandable," says Bob. "White babies are very popular."

Indeed

"White babies are very popular," says Louis.

"That's a dumb idea," says Orena, who has heard plenty of dumb ideas in her life, mostly from men.

"Everybody comes to bingo, don't they," says Louis, who has heard plenty of dumb ideas in his life, too, mostly from politicians.

"You can't give the baby away as a bingo prize."

"Why not?"

"Nobody wants to win a baby," says Orena. "Babies are a dime a dozen."

"This isn't just any baby," says Louis, who knows this is the best idea he is going to come up with. "This is a White baby. You make up the posters. I'll call the newspapers."

While

Bob has to get the coffee and the doughnuts himself. Black with no sugar and one cream with no sugar.

"We try to match our babies with our families," says Bob. He folds his hands in front of his face so he can smell his fingertips. "I think you can see why."

"Sure," says Mrs. Cardinal. "But lots of White people have been adopting Red babies."

"Yes," says Mr. Cardinal. "You see Black babies with White parents, too."

"And Yellow babies with White parents," says Mrs. Cardinal.

"Don't forget Brown babies with White parents," says Mr. Cardinal.

"That's true," says Bob, who is trying to remember why his left index finger smells the way it does. "And my administrative assistant Ms. Blackenship can tell you why."

"Sure," says Linda, who is particularly grumpy today and who has never liked the thing that Bob does with his fingers. "It's because we're racist."

Which explains why

Louis is late for his golf game and has to drive the golf cart to the third hole at speeds well above the posted limit. He arrives just as Del Weasel Fat hooks his drive into the trees.

"Where the hell you been?" says Vernon Miller, who tells people his handicap is eighteen when it's really ten.

"Council meeting," says Louis. "Usual game?"

"Dollar a hole," says Moses Thorpe. "Greenies, sandies, and snakes. What's in the box?"

"Baby," says Louis, and he grabs his driver.

"Baby what?" says Del, who is thinking about using one of his three mulligans on this hole.

"Baby baby," says Louis. "Everybody hit?"

Moses looks in the box. "Jesus, it is a baby. But it's White."

So everyone has to have a look, and Louis can't hit until everyone is finished looking.

"This one of yours?" asks Vernon.

"Of course not," says Louis. "It came in the mail."

"Are we going to play golf, or what?" says Del, who has decided against taking a mulligan so early in the round.

Louis hits his drive straight down the fairway. He hits the green with his second shot. And then, with everyone looking, he sinks a thirty-five-foot putt for a birdie. By the time they finish the front nine, Louis is up seven dollars.

"Jesus," says Vernon, "damn thing must be a rabbit's foot."

"Hope you plan to feed it," says Del. "Cause I don't want it crying on the back nine."

"You know what White babies eat?" says Moses, trying to remember a really good joke he heard last week.

"Put on a few more pounds," Vernon tells Louis, "and you'll be able to nurse it yourself."

Everybody has a good laugh, even Moses who can't remember the rest of the joke.

"Come out to bingo tonight," says Louis, holding up seven fingers just to remind everyone how well he's playing. "Maybe you'll get lucky."

"We're not racist," says Bob. "It's simply a matter of policy."

"So, race isn't a consideration?" asks Mr. Cardinal.

"Absolutely not," says Bob. "We're not allowed to discriminate on the basis of race, religion, or sexual orientation."

"So," says Mrs. Cardinal, "how do you discriminate?"

"Economics and education," says Bob.

"Well," says Mr. Cardinal, "we're rich."

"Great," says Bob. "We're always looking for rich parents."

"And we're well educated," says Mrs. Cardinal. "Mr. Cardinal has a master's in business administration and I have a doctorate in psychology."

"Terrific," says Bob. "I'm a college graduate, too."

"We love children," says Mrs. Cardinal. "But we also want to make a contribution."

"To society," says Mr. Cardinal. "White people have been raising our babies for years. We figure it's about time we got in there and helped them with theirs."

"Admirable," says Bob.

"Both of us speak Cree," says Mrs. Cardinal. "Mr. Cardinal sings on a drum, and I belong to the women's society on the reserve, and we know many of the old stories about living in harmony with nature, so we have a great deal we can give a White baby."

Bob chats with the Cardinals, who reassure him that they would make sure that a White baby would also have ample opportunities to participate in White culture.

"We'd sign up for cable," Mr. Cardinal tells Bob.

"Spectacular," says Bob, and he assures the Cardinals that their case is his number-one priority. "Call me in a week."

After the Cardinals have gone, Linda comes into the office with a fax and drops it on Bob's desk from shoulder level. "There's a big bingo game on the reserve this weekend."

"Fabulous," says Bob, who is running out of adjectives and who is sorry that Linda has started dropping things from shoulder level instead of bending over the way she used to when she wanted him to look at her breasts.

"One of the prizes," says Linda, "is a White baby."

So

When Louis gets to the bingo hall that night with the baby in the airmail box, there's not a single seat left. "I told you this was a good idea," he tells Orena.

"They came for the truck."

"Isn't the truck next week?"

"No," say Orena, "the truck is this week."

"So we have a truck and a White baby tonight."

"Technically," say Orena, "that's correct."

"Okay, so we double up and put the baby with the truck," says Louis, who is pleased to have come up with this without even thinking.

Orena is about to tell Louis that this is another one of his bad ideas, when she sees Bob Wakutz and his administrative assistant, Linda Blackenship, come into the bingo hall.

"Did I tell you I shot an eighty-one today," says Louis. "Maybe you should give *The Herald* a call."

"Forget golf," says Orena. "We've got a problem."

Yes

"We've got a problem," Linda tells Bob. "If you move this way a little and look to the right of the stage, you'll see a heavy-set Indian guy in a gold golf shirt standing next to an Indian woman in jeans and a white top, who is, if I'm not mistaken, related to that Indian woman from Red Deer whose baby we apprehended last month and are in the process of putting up for adoption."

Bob has never been fond of long, compound/complex sentences, but he does support the use of neutral terms such as "apprehended" and non-emotional phrases such as "in the process of putting up for adoption." However, he does not like problems.

"Claimed we had the wrong family," says Linda. "How many times have we heard that one?"

"Hey, look," says Bob. "The grand prize is a new Ford truck."

"What about the baby?" says Linda.

"We'll apprehend it right after the game for the truck," says Bob, and he puts the warrant back in his pocket, stops one of the bingo girls, and buys four cards.

While

Orena and Louis stand by the truck with the baby in the airmail box.

"Those are the two assholes from the Alberta Child Placement Agency who took my cousin's little boy," says Orena. "They must be here for the White baby."

"Problem solved," says Louis.

"You can't give them the baby," says Orena.

"Why not?" says Louis.

"Precedence," says Orena. "We can't let government agencies kidnap a member of the tribe."

"The baby's a member of our tribe?"

"That's probably why it was sent to us," says Orena.

"It doesn't look Indian," says Louis, even though he knows that not all Indian babies look Indian.

"Maybe it's part Indian," says Orena.

"Just great," says Louis. "Things were certainly easier when we were in harmony with nature."

And then

Linda turns to Bob and says, "What if I were to tell you that that baby was ours."

Bob knows that there is a right answer to this question, but he can't remember what it is.

"The White baby?"

"Yes."

"You're kidding," he says, and he's pretty sure that this is not the right answer.

"What if I were to tell you that you got me pregnant," says Linda, "and that, after I gave birth, I mailed it to the reserve in order to punish you?"

Bob puts his fingers in his nose and takes a deep breath.

"Our child?"

"What would you say?"

"Wonderful," says Bob, who hasn't run out of adjectives after all. "Look, there's the truck you can win. God, is it gorgeous!"

"Yes," said Linda. "That's exactly what I thought you would say."

And just then

The game begins. Louis hands the baby in the airmail box to Orena and goes to the microphone to drum up business.

"All right," he says. "Here's the game you've been waiting for. Blackout bingo. First prize is … a brand new Ford pickup and a White baby. Any questions?"

Martha Red Horse holds up her hand. "Is there a cash equivalent for the baby?"

"Good luck," says Louis, and he signals Bernie Strauss to start the game before someone else can ask a question.

Linda nudges Bob. "We better do something."

"Linda," says Bob, and he says this in a fatherly way without the hint of reprimand, "look around."

"What's that supposed to mean?" says Linda.

"We're surrounded by Indians."

And with that

Bob sits down next to Mr. and Mrs. Cardinal, who have twenty bingo cards spread out between them.

"Hello," says Mr. Cardinal. "I'll bet you came for that new Ford pickup."

"Hi," says Bob, trying to sound nonchalant. "You here for the truck, too?"

"No," says Mrs. Cardinal.

Bob taps Linda on the hip, though it's more of a pat than a tap. "Look who's here."

"Wish us luck," says Mrs. Cardinal.

And quick as you please

Bernie Strauss begins calling numbers. At first Bob doesn't get any, but then he hits a run of numbers, and before he knows it, he has only two left. Three of Mr. and Mrs. Cardinal's cards also have two numbers left and one of their cards has only one number left. And then one of Bob's numbers is called and he has only one to go.

Even Linda is getting excited.

Okay

"Okay," Louis says to Orena, as he watches the number come up on the big board, "what's the worst that can happen?"

This is a question that Louis asks all the time. This is the question that Louis asks when he hasn't a clue how bad things can get. And this time, he asks it just as a squad of RCMP comes storming into the hall.

"Oh, great," says Orena. "Now you've done it."

"B-8," Bernie shouts.

"Bingo!" shouts Bob, and he leaps out of his chair. "Bingo, bingo, bingo!"

And then

The RCMP confiscate the new Ford pickup.

"You don't have a permit," the RCMP tells Louis. "If you don't have a permit, this is an illegal gambling activity."

"It's my truck," says Bob, holding up his card. "See, I have a bingo."

"We have a permit," Louis tells the RCMP, but when he turns to find Orena to ask her to show the RCMP the permit, he finds that she is gone.

"We also heard that you were giving away a White baby," says the RCMP.

"I suppose we need a permit for that, too," says Louis.

"What about my truck?" says Bob. "What about my truck?"

Well, then

Two weeks after the raid on the bingo game, Orena's cousin calls to thank her for the White baby. "Where in the world did you get it?"

"In the mail."

"And they say *we* don't know how to look after our kids."

"You can keep it if you want," Orena tells her cousin.

"We've filed a suit against the Alberta Child Placement Agency," says Orena's cousin. "The idiots had me mixed up with a woman in Medicine Hat. Should have my son back by the weekend."

"So, you don't want the White baby?" says Orena.

"Come on, cuz," says Orena's cousin. "You know any skins who want a White baby?"

"It's tough," says Orena. "They just aren't that appealing."

"I suppose you can get used to them," says Orena's cousin. "What do you want me to do with it?"

"Drop it in the mail," says Orena. "I'll figure out something."

In the meantime

Bob gets out of jail, while the Crown reviews the case.

"Can you believe it," he tells Linda. "They take my truck, and they arrest me."

"You hit an RCMP officer."

"I didn't hit him," says Bob. "I stumbled into him by mistake."

"Is that what you tell your wife?" says Linda, who is not ready to let bygones be bygones.

"I'm going to leave her," says Bob, who finds that he is sexually aroused by Linda's reluctance and condemnation. "You just have to be patient."

"And what about that White baby?"

"What about my truck?" says Bob. "The White baby thing was probably just a gimmick to get people to come to bingo."

Okay, so on Monday

Joe in the Afterlife

ANNABEL LYON

JOE HAS BEEN KICKING his daughter out of the house since she was three. He can't help it, she's annoying. He shouts, but she whips books and cups at his head. Now, twenty years on, she's retreated to the bathroom as usual—violent, shaking, trying to get back inside herself. He likes it when Gaby loses control of her body like this, when she's angry.

Ellie, Joe's wife, has asked him to stop evicting the child. "I'm leaving anyway!" shouts the brat in the bathroom. This is not news. Gaby lives half packed, waiting for the planets to align and the bluebirds to sweep her to a bachelor with hardwood and cable for four-fifty a month, in a gingerbread house with a chocolate landlord, on a major bus route through the enchanted wood. "I'm serious," Joe tells Ellie.

Still, they have this fiction, or he does, that she is leaving tomorrow or the next day.

The days have been coming up hot. Six a.m. generally finds Joe in the back garden with tea and *New Yorkers*, in the tiny cooling slivered between night and day. He sleeps poorly, melancholic that he is, but enjoys the weightlessness of dawn. He floats up on it, and spends the rest of the day falling.

This morning Gaby appeared, eyes poached from sleep, airy-fairy in her little-girl nightie, with its ribbons and stitching. Had he woken her, nabbed her magazine, scored her mug?

"I dreamt a man was having his arms chainsawed off," she said.

"Oh, please," Joe said.

He knows what she needs. Her progress was arrested, he reckons, back in the creature stage, when she was supposed to learn to socialize with the other little crawlers at play school. But she got to books early and became a person while other people's offspring were still engaging little geckos. Now she won't leave the house. The stuff she collects for her apartment might as well furnish a tomb for the afterlife. Nothing gets used.

"You don't like anyone," he said once.

"I like Sam Cooke and the Hollies," she said. "I like Gandhi."

It's 1999. She needs a little push.

LATER THAT MORNING, Joe steps out to taste the air. Gaby has her futon frame on chairs in the garage. She's stirring a pot of urethane with a foam brush. The milky liquid looks too thin to have a purpose. "Don't come stand over me, Daddy," she says.

"Mum thinks you might like our bread knife for the new place. Is this true?"

Gaby wants to start painting, doesn't want to be looked at. Joe knows. "Oh, it's no secret I covet that knife," she says.

"What is that stuff, milk?" Joe asks, turning back to the house.

"That's right," she says.

Reaching for the doorknob, a pain in his arm stops him like a question. Are you sure? it asks. He's on his knees before he knows it, on his face. He or Gaby is laughing. Both, he thinks afterwards. Both, please?

LIVE ON TELEVISION, tethered astronauts are aloft, soundlessly patching their craft. The film lurches—intimate, faintly obscene—like film of insects.

Gaby sits beside him, absorbing images from the set. He's in her room, in her bed. He never allowed her to move her bed from her ground floor room to the attic loft and now he's in it, so.

An English nurse, bright and worthy as a new penny, comes and goes like a toy. She reminds him of the ambulance. That was a sunny day. A black flower had bloomed in his brain.

But will you look at this, Joe thinks, picking at an old, ongoing argument in his head. His daughter is an ascetic and a cold, cool woman. The walls and curtains are blue, the bookshelves are another blue. The girl herself slumps in a wicker armchair, puffed with cushions styled from a blue silk sari—*Ellie's* craft and thrift. Blue shadows puddle the corners. Otherwise the room is picked clean of personality, like a hotel room between guests.

And here sits Gaby, in her sandals and army surplus pants and the inevitable white T-shirt, no makeup, no jewellery, no graces at all, hugging her legs to her, mouth mashed to a knee, eyes on the set. He finds her easier to love in the summertime—small, impatient, muscled like a boy, strung up and down with blue veins. But she has an r.r.s.p., which he finds ghoulish in a young girl with good skin.

He's so sick, he realizes.

The pennyworth nurse wears a cardigan, pink or green. After she leaves Gaby makes fun of her. She takes Joe's pulse. "Bloody marvellous!" she says. "Now touch your pain." He can't much move, can't smile, although she's doing it for him. "Brilliant!" she says.

Ellie brings food for each of them on a tray. She and Gaby eat spaghetti with chicken and olives. Joe sips the spoonfuls of gelatine she slips between his teeth. There is a machine in the corner between the bed and the wall, heavy and square, set down like a piece of luggage. No one pays it heed except Joe, who would like to know if he is attached to it.

Days have been flipping past, like cards; and their black backs.

The sickroom curtains are drawn; the TV is alive. His wife and daughter wear lovely flickering masks. He wonders where the astronauts are going. When he makes a sound to ask they slowly turn, they look at him in wonder.

THE SPEECH THERAPIST wears a smart, creamy little summer suit with a daft sleeveless polka-dot blouse. When she removes her jacket he sees her arms are richly tanned, all the way up to the shoulders. He approves. She is after his heart with her careless skin—not like his own pair, with their fears of sun and estrogen and God knows. Although, to be fair, both he and his wife come from cancerous families. Barring the unforeseen, Gaby can expect to go that way, as Joe himself had expected, until now.

The speech therapist sits beside him on the bed and makes a business with flash cards and tape recorder, propping items on his leg. He feels placid and coddled, unfocused by her lovely skin. He senses her growing urgency—his hand squeezed, names repeated. His eyes swim in the dots on her blouse. Her throat too is nutty, her jaw, ears. Silver knots peg the lobes. What a lovely, babbling brook of a stupid woman. All right, he thinks. Just a minute.

He watches her mouth form shapes and his tongue butts tooth, trying to wet his dry lips. She disappears behind his head. *It's too soon,* or *It's no use.* The astronauts, stiff as big gingerbread men, don't speak clearly either. Their efforts emerge as radio cracklings in Houston. "Roger that," says Houston.

Gaby never turns the set off. She seems to need CNN like morphine. Is this what she does, long hours alone of a Saturday night?

I don't care, I think she's a lesbian, Joe told Ellie last month. It's fine with me. Safer in every direction when you think about it. All I'm saying is, at her age, she should be getting *out.* The astronauts give way to the death of a rock star, shot once accurately by the husband of a deranged fan. The fan had abandoned her family to stalk the singer, although at one time the whole family had been fans.

His daughter seems to hunger for this stuff. It lights her up, makes her laugh. When they play the rock star's famous song she hums along, snapping her fingers to the beat. "This is for my dad," she says, and sings the chorus into the microphone of her thumb. When the shot cuts back to the astronauts, she pounces towards the set, pointing. "The empyrean!" she cries.

Ellie looks in. "Gaby," she says.

At first, Ellie is there at night, eating raisins and reading *Anna Karenina* and books about paint. The phone rings, giving her a start. "Curses," she says, picking raisins off the carpet. The phone rings too many times—won't she answer? The TV stays off at night and he misses it—imagines the pulse behind its bland black eye. *Stay,* he thinks often, of no one particular. Shapes in his mouth, sweet and pepper—*stay.* Nights are as usual the worst, a despair of small sounds. It's summertime, again or still, the progress of summertime, and the insects—their fine Swiss mechanisms—

bother his reason. Gaby emblazons them to the walls with a slipper, not often enough. Saltwater sleep—he tries to get back under. But a mosquito has found his name and is repeating it, in its tiny tight language, over and over.

GABY HAS STARTED A DIET, a thing he has never permitted. His mind's eye follows her to the kitchen—ripping up lettuces, drinking water as an appetite suppressant. Thinner than *what?*, he thinks, fretting.

The astronauts are down. There have been brochures, lately. Lately she has been showing him pictures, too close to his nose. "It's a dorm, Dad," she says, shaking her head. "There's gonna be ivy."

Now she upends a sack from the drugstore onto his knees. Small, shaped items click against each other, coloured sticks and circles. She opens a compact and shows him a neat flat square of, apparently, hot chocolate mix. "Eleven ninety-five for dust," she says. She powders her nose, then his. She pops a lid and squirrels up a tube of lipstick. In a minute she looks like a small child who's been eating fruit. "All right?" she says. She wipes it off and tries again.

And then it's liquor store boxes, boxes, boxes. She and Ellie have spent the day on the floor taking kettles in and out of paper, it seems like, telling each other to put the books in small boxes and where is the list and thank you, thank you, you're sure I can take it?

"No one drinks coffee here any more anyway," Ellie says.

I can buy a better one, Joe tells himself. I'm sick and I'm rich. I can have anything I want.

TIME FLOWS AND OVERFLOWS. "Goofs wear makeup," says the brat at the mirror, expertly now at the mirror, pinking in her lips. He looks at the loot from her jeans pockets, the precious piles—pennies, nickels, starfish of keys. She puts it all on and takes it all off, with tissues and puffs and costly waters, until her face is pure again. She sorts her boxes. The TV is alive.

"WHAT DID THE DOCTOR SAY?"

He hates his own voice, such as it is now—the animal speaking-sound he makes, all sonorous wadded tongue.

"I'm anaemic, for one thing," she says. "He says it's like I gave blood, but every day. He says I have to take supplements and eat, basically, more."

"*Uh,*" says Joe.

"There's nothing like a soiled urinal to get you thinking about the future," Gaby says. "Personal hygiene is a long and winding road."

Ads. She rises to a protest of bones, body static, and lopes, stretching, to the bathroom.

On the television, beautiful women are selling creams with their beauty and naughtiness. They wink and lightly finger their faces. Their decadence is ancient and irresistible. Even Gaby is a sucker for their balms. He once hated her—*hated* her— for buying a little cake of complexion soap for thirty dollars when she was fifteen and her skin was poor. Imagining *what*? But he thinks now of the old woman's body she carries about within her gradually revealing itself. Take care of her! She's here now! Eyes, voice, baby pudge, eaten by aliens! Skin tortured, voice transposed down, hands buckled and sheathed with arthritis, sure as Christmas. He wants her to get out there, get married, now, soon. What's your problem? he thinks to his child. Marry a man, marry a woman, what are you waiting for?

He seems to recall his own wedding, but with a deluxe, five-star wealth of detail that falsifies the memory. Ellie in her wedding dress, spitting in the garden. Guests flinging palmfuls of pins. Ellie in her wedding dress, in the hotel room, talking on the phone, nibbling her bouquet. Gaby already known, there in her little spaceship, inside Ellie. A single black seed, like a kiwi seed, lodged in his brain, behind his left ear.

Either he's getting better or he's getting worse. That, he realizes, is the answer.

KISS. Doors slam. Gaby leaves.

After she's gone, Ellie decides to stencil the walls around him, to keep him company. She has low-odour paint. On the second day she abandons the template and goes freehand. *She's drawing on the walls,* flowers and such, twining lines up near the ceiling. She stands on his bed to reach her pencil into the corner, tracking and trailing graphite down the blue walls, her foot nudging his hip. On day five, frowning like an artist, she abandons her paints for a single colour, gold.

A SPEECH THERAPIST comes to the house, a West Indian woman in a white suit with a giddy tropical blouse. They make sounds at each other, smiling, and she leaves him with exercises. She will come each week until he is better.

Ellie no longer sits with him at night. It's cool and dark and dry in this painted room, with the whirr of jewelled insects exploring his daughter's woks and socks. Tonight they watched a program about space exploration. The narrator was lucid and seemed to peel back the mysteries of distance and light; Joe hoped children everywhere were watching. When it was over he felt like a steady ship. But then he asked, "How long have I been down?"

Ellie looked at him. "Three weeks," she said. "Including today." What was she waiting for?

A door opened in his mind. "Where does Gaby sleep?"

"At the dorm."

Now, alone in the dark, this answer he finds familiar, although he knows it to be false. She is in the next room, of course, or the next; he can hear her fidgeting at night, like the princess bedded down with her golden pea. Her tiny sounds, tiny rages and incoherencies. Presently she will come and watch TV with him, as she has always done, cool in her skin, his little alien. He has her now.

Comforted, he floats on down summer's river, royalty inspecting the desert.

The Man Doll

SUSAN SWAN

I MADE THE DOLL for Elizabeth. I wanted to build a surrogate toy that would satisfy my friend so completely I would never have to listen to her litany of grievances against the male sex again.

I constructed the doll by hand. I am a bio-medical engineer, but at that time I was still an intern. I couldn't afford to buy Elizabeth one of the million-dollar symbiotes called Pleasure Boys which the wealthy women and gay men purchase in our exclusive department stores.

I didn't like these display models anyhow. Their platinum hair and powder-blue eyes (identical to the colouring of Pleasure Girls) looked artificial and their electronic brains had overdeveloped intellects. I wanted something different from the run-of-the-mill life form for Elizabeth. I wanted a deluxe model that would combine the virility component of a human male with the intuitive powers of the female. In short, I wanted a Pleasure Boy whose programming emphasized the ability to give emotional support.

I made my doll in secret, requisitioning extra parts whenever some limbs or organs were needed at the Cosmetic Clinic in human repairs where I worked. So it was easy for me to get the pick of anatomical bargains. I particularly liked the selection of machine extensions offered by the Space Force Bank. After careful consideration, I chose long, sinewy hands, arms and legs, and made sure they were the type that could be willed into action in a twinkling. The Space Force Bank agreed to simulate the doll's computer brain from mine for $1,500. The exterior of the doll was made out of plastic and silicone that was lifelike to the touch. I placed a nuclear reactor the size of a baseball in the chest cavity, just where the heart is in the human body. The reactor warmed the doll by transmitting heat to a labyrinth of coils. The reactor uses a caesium source that yields an 80 per cent efficiency rate with a life expectancy of just over thirty years. The doll was activated by a handheld switch.

I smuggled the materials home from the Clinic and each night in my flat I worked on the doll. I wanted it to be a perfect human likeness, so exact in detail that

Elizabeth wouldn't guess it was a symbiote. I applied synthetic hair in transplants (matched with my own hair colour) and shaped its face with the help of liquid silicone. My money had almost run out by the time I got to the sex organs, but luckily I was able to find a cheap set from a secondhand supplier. For $250 I bought an antique organ that belonged to a 180-year-old Pleasure Boy. I hoped it would work under pressure.

Our laws forbid symbiotes to waste human food. But I gave the doll a silicone esophagus and a crude bladder because I wanted it to have something to do on social occasions. Its body was able to ingest and pass out a water and sugar solution. Of course, the doll didn't defecate. Its nuclear waste products were internally controlled and required changing once every ten years.

At the last moment I realized I had forgotten to add dye to the pupils, so its eyes were almost colourless. But in all other aspects, my doll looked normal.

When I installed its reactor, the doll came to life, lolling contentedly in my apartment, ignoring the discomfort of its mummy case and its helmet of elastic bandages and gauze. The doll called me "Maker" and, despite its post-operative daze, began to display a talent for understanding and devotion.

It could sense when I was in a blue mood and sighed sympathetically behind its bandages. When I came home, exhausted from catering to the scientists at the Clinic, the doll would be waiting for me at the door of my apartment, ready to serve me dinner. Soon, I was unable to keep my hands off it. I decided it wouldn't spoil my present to Elizabeth if I tried it out ahead of time. Playfully I stroked and kissed the symbiote, and showed it how to peel back its groin bandage so we could have sex. To my delight, the doll operated above normal capacity, thanks to its desire to give pleasure.

Like any commercial symbiote, my doll was capable of orgasm but not ejaculation. It is illegal for a doll to create life. The sole function of a symbiote must be recreational.

At the end of five months I removed its protective case and found myself staring at a symbiote who gazed back with a remarkable calm, loving air. It had red hair and freckles, just like me, and a pair of cute pear-shaped ears.

My desire to give the doll to Elizabeth vanished.

I fell in love with my creation.

I called the doll Manny.

The next year with Manny was happy. I felt confident; I worked at the Clinic with zeal and diligence, knowing that at the end of the day I would be going home to Manny; his cooking and his kisses! (Something about the way I had juxtaposed his two oricularis oris muscles made the touch of his lips sensational.)

Secretly, I worried Manny might harbour resentment about a life built around ministering to my needs. Pleasure Boys have no rights, but Manny was still an organism with a degree of self-interest. If I neglected his programmed needs, he might deteriorate. When I confessed my fear, the doll laughed and hugged me.

"I want to be the slave," he said. "I need to be in service."

Over the next six months I began to see less of my doll. I had graduated to the rank of engineer in facial repairs and was neglecting our home life.

I decided it was time to give Manny some social experiences, so I asked Elizabeth to the flat for a meal.

I felt a thrill of pride when Elizabeth walked in and didn't give Manny a suspicious look. Manny wore an ascot and a tweed sports suit. He beamed at the two of us as he placed a spinach quiche on the table.

"You look familiar," Elizabeth mused.

"Everybody says I look like Tina," the doll said breezily.

"You do," Elizabeth said. "Where did you meet Tina anyhow?"

"I'd rather hear about you," the doll replied. "Are you happy?"

Elizabeth started and looked at me for an explanation. I grinned.

"Go on. Tell him about your troubles with men."

"Tina, my problems would bore Manny," Elizabeth said nervously.

"No they wouldn't," Manny said. "I like to help people with their troubles."

Elizabeth laughed and threw up her hands.

"I can't find a man who is decent, Manny. Every affair starts off well and then I find the guy has feet of clay."

I saw Manny glance down at his plastic feet. He was smiling happily.

"I must be too much of a perfectionist," Elizabeth sighed, "but there are days when I'd settle for a good machine."

I nodded and noticed Manny's colourless eyes watching Elizabeth as if he were profoundly moved. I thought he could be a little less sympathetic. If he knew Elizabeth like I did, Manny would realize Elizabeth enjoyed feeling dissatisfied.

Suddenly, Manny reached over and patted Elizabeth's hand. Elizabeth burst into tears and Manny continued to hold her hand, interlocking his fingers with hers in a deeply understanding way. In profile, the doll looked serene. Elizabeth was staring at him through her tears with an expression of disbelief. I knew Elizabeth was waiting for the doll to frown and suggest that she pull herself together.

Of course, the doll's programming prohibited uncaring reactions. Manny was unique, not only among male symbiotes, but among men. What man loved as unselfishly as my doll?

During dinner, Elizabeth quizzed Manny about his background and the doll gracefully handled her questions.

"I'm Tina's invention," he quipped. "I call her 'Maker.' It's our private joke."

Elizabeth giggled and so did Manny. I winced. Why did my doll sound so happy? The understanding look on Manny's face, as Elizabeth whined about her love life, was a bit sickening! I noticed the doll lightly brush against Elizabeth's shoulder when he replenished the wine, and in disgust, I stood up and cleared away the dishes. When I came out of the kitchen, Manny was standing by the door holding hands with Elizabeth.

"Elizabeth needs me now, Tina," the doll said. He paused to help my friend on with her coat. Then he gave her shoulder a loving squeeze. "Elizabeth, I feel as if I were made just for you."

My doll leaned over and offered her his sensational oricularis oris muscles, and suddenly I felt angry.

"You can't leave me, Manny," I said. "I own you."

"Tina. You don't mean what you say," Manny replied sweetly. "You know dolls have rights too."

"Who says?" I cried. "You can't procreate. You can't eat. And your retinas are colourless."

"Manny eats," Elizabeth said. "I saw him."

"He just drinks," I said, starting to shout. "Elizabeth, Manny is my doll. Don't you dare walk out of my apartment with my possession."

"Manny is not a doll," Elizabeth said. "You're making it up because you're jealous."

"Manny, I'm warning you. If you leave me, I'll deactivate your program."

"My Maker is not the sort of human to be petty," Manny replied. Hand-in-hand, my doll and Elizabeth walked out of the apartment. "Goodbye, Tina dear," Manny called in an extremely sincere tone. I threw myself at the closed door, beating my fists against it, screaming my doll's name. Then I sank to my knees. I had made the doll for Elizabeth, but decided to keep him for myself. For the first time, I realized it didn't matter. My programming ensured that Manny would be drawn to whoever had most need of him.

For the next month, I was too depressed to see Elizabeth and Manny. I felt angry with my friend for taking my doll, although I scolded myself for being irrational. Now that Manny was gone, I regretted the way I had neglected him. I daydreamed nostalgically about the activities we might have done together. Why hadn't we gone shopping, or out to the movies? It made me sad to think we had never strolled arm-in-arm in the park like a normal couple.

True to his programming, Manny called me every day to see how I was doing. My pride stopped me from listening to his concerned inquiries and I slammed the phone down. Then one evening my symbiote phoned late and caught me offguard. I'd had an argument with my Clinic supervisor. This time, I was glad to hear my doll's friendly baritone.

"Tina, I'm worried about you," Manny chided. "The grapevine says you're working too hard."

"Hard enough," I agreed, relieved that someone cared.

"Dinner here this Tuesday. I won't take no for an answer."

That Tuesday, I changed out of my lab coat and headed for Elizabeth's apartment. At the entrance to the building, three dolls were talking to the doorman. One of the dolls, a Pleasure Girl with shoulder-length platinum hair, asked the doorman to let them in so they could see a friend. The doorman shook his head.

"No dolls allowed in before six," the doorman said. "ASTARTE TOWERS is a respectable space block." He made a slashing motion in the air with his gloved hand. Then he pushed the female doll on its chest. The doll groaned as if it were hurt and tottered backwards. For a second, it looked like it was going to fall. Then it slumped onto the curb and began to weep pitifully. The two male dolls rushed over to comfort it. Except for the unactivated models in store windows, I had never observed dolls in a group before. The sight of the symbiotes acting like humans made me uneasy. I hurried past the sobbing doll and her companions, and ran into the lobby.

In the apartment, I found Elizabeth reading a newspaper. Manny was setting the table. Elizabeth looked relaxed. But Manny! Why, the doll looked beatific! His synthetic curls shone with a copper glow and a suntan had brought out more large brown freckles. Then I remembered hearing that Elizabeth had gone on a Caribbean cruise.

"How wonderful to see you, Tina," Manny said. "Are you still mad at your old symbiote?"

I shook my head.

Joyfully, he embraced me. He told me about his holiday and asked about my new job. I immediately began to describe the way I had engineered a dish-face deformity. When I finished, I realized that Elizabeth had been listening intently too; apparently, she had no interest in going into her usual litany of grievances against the male sex.

Suddenly, Elizabeth said, "Did you see any dolls at the door?"

"One or two," I admitted. "What are they doing here?"

"A few come, every day. They sometimes bring a human. If they can get by the doorman, Manny lets them come in and talks to them." Elizabeth sighed and shrugged. "I suppose there's nothing wrong with it. Except I worry that they tire Manny."

"Elizabeth, I am tireless," Manny laughed, bending over and kissing my friend on the nape of her neck. I remembered just how tireless Manny could be.

Elizabeth grabbed his silicone hand and kissed it hungrily. "Selfless, you mean." She looked dreamy. "Tina, where did you find this paragon?"

"I already told you. I made him for you." I smiled.

"Do you think I'm going to believe that line of yours?" Elizabeth laughed. "It's time you forgave me for being with Manny."

"What are you talking about?" I asked.

"Elizabeth thinks I'm human," Manny smiled. "I've tried to show her I'm a doll, but she goes out of the room and refuses to listen." He paused, bewildered. "The dolls think I'm human, too."

"No doll could make *me* happy," Elizabeth giggled.

"Serving your needs fulfils my function," Manny replied.

"Isn't Manny funny?" Elizabeth said. "He says the cutest things!"

Before I could answer, the door opened and the symbiotes who had been arguing with the doorman rushed in uttering cries of glee.

"Pleasure Girl #024 found a way in through the back entrance," one of the male dolls said triumphantly.

The female doll kissed Manny fiercely on both his cheeks.

"Pleasure Boy #025 is the one who suggested we try another door," she said. "Aren't we clever for sex toys?" Then she noticed Elizabeth and me, and she blushed guiltily. "Excuse me. I forgot humans were listening."

"Don't apologize," said the other male doll. "We have the right to breathe like anybody else."

The dolls murmured agreement and then turned back to Manny, who was holding up a jug of liquid. I guessed it contained a sugar and water solution. Manny poured the liquid into glasses. The dolls lifted the glasses in a toast and pretended to drink Manny's solution.

I stared at the dolls without speaking to them. Once again, I felt uneasy. The symbiotes were claiming human privileges. Not only were they acting as if they had the right to consume precious food resources, but the dolls were also appropriating human metaphors. I wasn't certain about the design type of the other symbiotes, but no air passed through Manny's system. His lungs were a tiny non-functional sac next to the caesium reactor. I had stuck in the sac to designate lung space in case I decided later to give Manny a requirement for oxygen.

Now the dolls began to complain loudly about their lot as pleasure toys. My doll listened solemnly, stroking each of their hands in turn while Elizabeth and I looked on blankly. Then one of the male dolls threw himself at Manny's feet.

"Why are we discriminated against, Manny?" the doll wailed. "Why can't we procreate like humans do?"

Tears slowly dripped from Manny's clear eyes. He held out his arms and embraced the dolls, who in turn cried and embraced each other. In the midst of the hubbub I slipped out and left Elizabeth with the emotional dolls. Then I hurried back to the Clinic and calmed myself by working until dawn repairing a pair of cauliflower ears.

Three months went by. This time Elizabeth rang up and asked me to meet her at the Earth Minister's television studio. Elizabeth said that Manny had left her to become a spokesman for a political lobby of humans and symbiotes.

Manny's group could be heard in the background of the Earth Minister's daily broadcasts shouting their demands. Elizabeth wanted me to persuade Manny to give up politics. She wanted Manny back so they could start a family. She said that she would do "something unthinkable" that evening unless she could convince Manny to return.

Gently, I tried to point out that Manny was only a doll, but the more I pleaded with her to forget about my symbiote, the more desperate she sounded. I agreed to meet her at the studio. Just before I left my apartment, I stuck my handheld switch into my pocket. I decided the time had come to deactivate Manny. It was illogical for the symbiotes to think dolls had rights. I felt sympathy for them as organisms, but their aspirations were making pests out of what were once perfectly good recreational objects.

The studio was ten minutes by air, but it took me over half an hour to force my way through the crowd at the studio door. I noticed with a start that there were hundreds of human heads among the masses of synthetic ones.

Finally, I found a seat at the back of the auditorium. At that moment the lights dimmed and then flared brightly as the Earth Minister walked out onto a dais at the front of the room, followed by a television crew pushing cameras. The crowd immediately began to chant, "Manny for Earth Minister" and "Symbiotes are humans too."

I heard a noise at the front of the room and Manny was lifted onto the platform. Then Manny shook hands with the Earth Minister, a stocky human with an anxious smile. Now the crowd cheered more wildly than before, and Manny turned and lifted up his arms as if he wanted to embrace them all. He looked striking in his deep-magenta safari suit.

Just then, Elizabeth appeared by my side, weeping.

"Isn't it awful?" she whispered. "This swarm of dolls? Oh, Tina, I was just too busy with other things, so Manny went into politics. But I can't live without him."

"Sure you can," I sighed and looked over the crowd at Manny's synthetic head. "You already are."

Manny spotted me and waved. I hesitated, then smiled and waved back.

"Tina, you're not paying attention," Elizabeth sniffed. "I want Manny back. I want to have children with him."

"Look, Elizabeth," I said. I felt in my pocket for the switch. "Manny is a doll—a do-it-yourself model. His brains cost over a thousand dollars and his sex organs were two-fifty."

Elizabeth blushed. "Manny has talked about the help you gave him, but no symbiote could do what he does."

"He's a Pleasure Boy," I argued. "I should know. I made him. Haven't you noticed he doesn't eat or defecate? And that's not all. He can't procreate either."

"Nothing you say will make me believe Manny is a doll," Elizabeth shouted, and then she slapped my face!

Angrily, I grabbed her and dragged her towards the dais. "I'll show you his extensions, his hair strips, his silicone mouth …!"

"Tina! Please! Don't hurt Manny!" Elizabeth cried, ducking her head as if she expected me to hit her. Even though I am bigger than Elizabeth, I was surprised at how easily cowed she was.

I tightened my grip on my friend's arm. "I'm going to take you up there," I yelled, "and deactivate him in front of everyone. Manny the doll has come to an end."

"No, Tina! I'll do what you want! I'll forget him!" Elizabeth said and plucked at my arm. "I know Manny's a doll, but I love him. I've never loved anybody before."

She bowed her head, and for a second I relaxed my grip. At that moment, a great gust of sighs filled the studio and the oscillating physical mass knocked us apart as it pushed towards the dais where Manny sat. The Earth Minister toppled from his seat and the crowd hoisted Manny into the air.

Suddenly, the doll looked my way. His placid, colourless eyes met mine. I pulled the switch out of my pocket and threw it away. In the next moment, the mass of dolls and humans carried Manny off on a sea of hands. I wasn't surprised—as I strained for a last glimpse—to see a blissful look on my doll's face.

L'Envoi. The Train to Mariposa
STEPHEN LEACOCK

IT LEAVES THE CITY every day about five o'clock in the evening, the train for Mariposa. Strange that you did not know of it, though you come from the little town—or did, long years ago.

Odd that you never knew, in all these years, that the train was there every afternoon, puffing up steam in the city station, and that you might have boarded it any day and gone home. No, not "home,"—of course you couldn't call it "home" now; "home" means that big red sandstone house of yours in the costlier part of the city. "Home" means, in a way, this Mausoleum Club where you sometimes talk with me of the times that you had as a boy in Mariposa.

But of course "home" would hardly be the word you would apply to the little town, unless perhaps, late at night, when you'd been sitting reading in a quiet corner somewhere such a book as the present one.

Naturally you don't know of the Mariposa train now. Years ago, when you first came to the city as a boy with your way to make, you knew of it well enough, only too well. The price of a ticket counted in those days, and though you knew of the train you couldn't take it, but sometimes from sheer homesickness you used to wander down to the station on a Friday afternoon after your work, and watch the Mariposa people getting on the train and wish that you could go.

Why, you knew that little train at one time better, I suppose, than any other single thing in the city, and loved it too for the little town in the sunshine that it ran to.

Do you remember how when you first began to make money you used to plan that just as soon as you were rich, really rich, you'd go back home again to the little town and build a great big house with a fine verandah,—no stint about it, the best that money could buy, planed lumber, every square foot of it, and a fine picket fence in front of it.

It was to be one of the grandest and finest houses that thought could conceive; much finer, in true reality, than that vast palace of sandstone with the porte cochère and the sweeping conservatories that you afterwards built in the costlier part of the city.

But if you have half forgotten Mariposa, and long since lost the way to it, you are only like the greater part of the men here in this Mausoleum Club in the city. Would you believe it that practically every one of them came from Mariposa once upon a time, and that there isn't one of them that doesn't sometimes dream in the dull quiet of the long evening here in the club, that some day he will go back and see the place.

They all do. Only they're half ashamed to own it.

Ask your neighbour there at the next table whether the partridge that they sometimes serve to you here can be compared for a moment to the birds that he and you, or he and some one else, used to shoot as boys in the spruce thickets along the lake. Ask him if he ever tasted duck that could for a moment be compared to the black ducks in the rice marsh along the Ossawippi. And as for fish, and fishing,—no, don't ask him about that, for if he ever starts telling you of the chub they used to catch below the mill dam and the green bass that used to lie in the water-shadow of the rocks beside the Indian's Island, not even the long dull evening in this club would be long enough for the telling of it.

But no wonder they don't know about the five o'clock train for Mariposa. Very few people know about it. Hundreds of them know that there is a train that goes out at five o'clock, but they mistake it. Ever so many of them think it's just a suburban train. Lots of people that take it every day think it's only the train to the golf grounds, but the joke is that after it passes out of the city and the suburbs and the golf grounds, it turns itself little by little into the Mariposa train, thundering and pounding towards the north with hemlock sparks pouring out into the darkness from the funnel of it.

Of course you can't tell it just at first. All those people that are crowding into it with golf clubs, and wearing knickerbockers and flat caps, would deceive anybody. That crowd of suburban people going home on commutation tickets and sometimes standing thick in the aisles, those are, of course, not Mariposa people. But look round a little bit and you'll find them easily enough. Here and there in the crowd those people with the clothes that are perfectly all right and yet look odd in some way, the women with the peculiar hats and the—what do you say?—last year's fashions? Ah yes, of course, that must be it.

Anyway, those are the Mariposa people all right enough. That man with the two-dollar panama and the glaring spectacles is one of the greatest judges that ever adorned the bench of Missinaba County. That clerical gentleman with the wide black hat, who is explaining to the man with him the marvellous mechanism of the new air brake (one of the most conspicuous illustrations of the divine structure of the physical universe), surely you have seen him before. Mariposa people! Oh yes, there are any number of them on the train every day.

But of course you hardly recognize them while the train is still passing through the suburbs and the golf district and the outlying parts of the city area. But wait a little, and you will see that when the city is well behind you, bit by bit the train changes its character. The electric locomotive that took you through the city tunnels is off now and the old wood engine is hitched on in its place. I suppose, very probably, you haven't seen one of these wood engines since you were a boy forty years ago—the old engine with a wide top like a hat on its funnel, and with sparks enough to light up a suit for damages once in every mile.

Do you see, too, that the trim little cars that came out of the city on the electric suburban express are being discarded now at the way stations, one by one, and in their place is the old familiar car with the stuff cushions in red plush (how gorgeous it once seemed!) and with a box stove set up in one end of it? The stove is burning furiously at its sticks this autumn evening, for the air sets in chill as you get clear away from the city and are rising up to the higher ground of the country of the pines and the lakes.

Look from the window as you go. The city is far behind now and right and left of you there are trim farms with elms and maples near them and with tall windmills beside the barns that you can still see in the gathering dusk. There is a dull red light from the windows of the farmstead. It must be comfortable there after the roar and clatter of the city, and only think of the still quiet of it.

As you sit back half dreaming in the car, you keep wondering why it is that you never came up before in all these years. Ever so many times you planned that just as soon as the rush and strain of business eased up a little, you would take the train and go back to the little town to see what it was like now, and if things had changed much since your day. But each time when your holidays came, somehow you changed your mind and went down to Naragansett or Nagahuckett or Nagasomething, and left over the visit to Mariposa for another time.

It is almost night now. You can still see the trees and the fences and the farmsteads, but they are fading fast in the twilight. They have lengthened out the train by this time with a string of flat cars and freight cars between where we are sitting and the engine. But at every crossway we can hear the long muffled roar of the whistle, dying to a melancholy wail that echoes into the woods; the woods, I say, for the farms are thinning out and the track plunges here and there into great stretches of bush,— tall tamarack and red scrub willow and with a tangled undergrowth of brush that has defied for two generations all attempts to clear it into the form of fields.

Why, look, that great space that seems to open out in the half-dark of the falling evening,—why, surely yes,—Lake Ossawippi, the big lake, as they used to call it, from which the river runs down to the smaller lake—Lake Wissanotti,—where the town of Mariposa has lain waiting for you there for thirty years.

This is Lake Ossawippi surely enough. You would know it anywhere by the broad, still, black water with hardly a ripple, and with the grip of the coming frost already on it. Such a great sheet of blackness it looks as the train thunders along the side, swinging the curve of the embankment at a breakneck speed as it rounds the corner of the lake.

How fast the train goes this autumn night! You have travelled, I know you have, in the Empire State Express, and the New Limited and the Maritime Express that holds the record of six hundred whirling miles from Paris to Marseilles. But what are they to this, this mad career, this breakneck speed, this thundering roar of the Mariposa local driving hard to its home! Don't tell me that the speed is only twenty-five miles an hour. I don't care what it is. I tell you, and you can prove it for yourself if you will, that that train of mingled flat cars and coaches that goes tearing into the night, its engine whistle shrieking out its warning into the silent woods and echoing over the dull still lake, is the fastest train in the whole world.

Yes, and the best too,—the most comfortable, the most reliable, the most luxurious and the speediest train that ever turned a wheel.

And the most genial, the most sociable too. See how the passengers all turn and talk to one another now, as they get nearer and nearer to the little town. That dull reserve that seemed to hold the passengers in the electric suburban has clean vanished and gone. They are talking,—listen,—of the harvest, and the late election, and of how the local member is mentioned for the cabinet and all the old familiar topics of the sort. Already the conductor has changed his glazed hat for an ordinary round Christie and you can hear the passengers calling him and the brakesman "Bill" and "Sam" as if they were all one family.

What is it now—nine thirty? Ah, then we must be nearing the town,—this big bush that we are passing through, you remember it surely as the great swamp just this side of the bridge over the Ossawippi? There is the bridge itself, and the long roar of the train as it rushes sounding over the trestle work that rises above the marsh. Hear the clatter as we pass the semaphores and the switch lights! We must be close in now!

What? it feels nervous and strange to be coming here again after all these years? It must indeed. No, don't bother to look at the reflection of your face in the window-pane shadowed by the night outside. Nobody could tell you now after all these years. Your face has changed in these long years of money-getting in the city. Perhaps if you had come back now and again, just at odd times, it wouldn't have been so.

There,—you hear it?—the long whistle of the locomotive, one, two, three! You feel the sharp slackening of the train as it swings round the curve of the last embankment that brings it to the Mariposa station. See, too, as we round the curve, the row of the flashing lights, the bright windows of the depôt.

How vivid and plain it all is. Just as it used to be thirty years ago. There is the string of the hotel 'buses, drawn up all ready for the train, and as the train rounds in and stops hissing and panting at the platform, you can hear above all other sounds the cry of the brakesmen and the porters:

"MARIPOSA! MARIPOSA!"

And as we listen, the cry grows fainter and fainter in our ears and we are sitting here again in the leather chairs of the Mausoleum Club, talking of the little Town in the Sunshine that once we knew.

Part 5

MY GRANDFATHER'S HOUSE

THE PAST IS ALWAYS *developing around us. And when it comes to narrative, it is almost impossible to exist in the present with any kind of real authority since, arguably, once the tale begins to be told, the event it describes has come to completion.*

The less recent past, however, and that which we sometimes call the distant past, is something else altogether. Seemingly more solid as it becomes established by collective memory, it is also ironically more illusory simply because fewer and sometimes no witnesses remain to verify the facts. And then there is the literary memoir: personal, coloured by sentiment, and shaded by loss, it is the past described in a eulogistic manner. Old roads and vanished houses are recalled, close friends and beloved relatives are remembered, previous selves are revisited, mutability is acknowledged.

The stories in this section all deal in one way or another with this country's past. Either the action takes place long ago or the story itself was written in a previous time. Created by our literary mothers and fathers (some of whom, happily, continue to delight us with their work), these stories, it could be said, have helped shape us. And there is something else. These are the stories that gave us permission to be writers, for the path to publication for Canadian authors, though not entirely obstacle-free today, was at one time much more hazardous.

Charles Ritchie's evocative memoir of his grandfather's colonial house in Halifax, its dark, empty rooms, old daguerreotypes, drawers filled with yellowing letters, and splendid, plunging staircases—a house in the past that was itself concerned with the past—seems to me to be the most fitting introduction to this section. Ritchie, remembering the night when his grandfather—just short of a hundred years old—died, writes the following:

> *The dense night silence reverberated around me; then there swept over me the tide of the past rising from the sleeping house below me.... When I went back to my bed it was to fall into a sleep as deep as the stairwell where the dead children had played.*

Vanished houses and dead children, weather that has come and gone—these stories move us because they bring to mind the transience so beautifully articulated by Mavis Gallant's title "Voices Lost in Snow."

My Grandfather's House

CHARLES RITCHIE

THE STREETS OF THE TOWN were steep as toboggan slides up to the granite Citadel and down to the harbour wharves. People were accustomed to walking on the perpendicular. The houses clung at odd angles to the spine of the hill, so that a roof or a protruding upper window showed out of alignment, as in a crooked drawing. The effect was disturbing to the sense of balance. The houses were of indeterminate age—some eighteenth-century, others Victorian, built of wood or stone beneath their coating of dun-coloured shingle. They were narrow houses, bigger than they looked from the front, with an air of reticence, almost of concealment. Nothing was for show. One sees such houses in Scottish towns. The poor lived in squat, bug-ridden wooden boxes, the windows sealed tight, winter and summer. A charnel whiff of ancient dirt issued from the doorways where the children thronged.

The Citadel crowned Halifax. It was flanked by army barracks built from London War Office blueprints, oblivious of climate or situation. Toy-sized cannon made a pretence of protection. Neat paths of painted white stones spaced with military precision and planted with a straggle of nasturtiums led to the officers' quarters. Barracks and brothels, the one could not live without the other. The brothels were at the foot of the hill near the waterfront and the naval dockyard. One could fancy that these rickety old structures would one day collapse from the vibration of the rutting that went on within their walls. From the wharves the stink of fish was wafted up the streets and the fog rolled in from the harbour, bringing with it a salty taste to the lips. The sound of the fog-horn was the warning melancholy music of the place.

Past my grandfather's house the trams rumbled, in front of it were three elm trees, behind it was a garden ending in abandoned stables. It was a tall, dark house. Inside, steep stairs went up and up; it made one gasp to look down from the top-floor landing into the hall-well far below. The stair banisters were narrow and dangerous to slide on. The house was lit by gas; pop! went the jets when lighted, and they gave off a pungent smell.

Each year my mother came to spend a winter month with her father in Halifax, and she brought me with her, first when I was six, then seven, then eight. My grandfather was a few years short of a hundred. When my mother was out shopping or visiting friends, I would be left playing with toys or reading in my grandfather's sitting-room while he fussed and fumbled about his desk. He was a small, cheerful, impatient man, with the white mutton-chop whiskers of another era, his hands mottled with brownish spots.

The sitting-room was hot and airless. Affixed to the panels of the door were strips of canvas on which bloomed sunflowers and lilies painted by my aunt Geraldine in an outburst of aestheticism in the 1890s. Over the mantelpiece were arranged photographs sepia with age. Some were groups of officers in which my uncle Harry figured boldly in his Highland uniform.

At times my grandfather seemed to have forgotten that I was in the room. The hours slid by unnoticed. Then, as though by a common impulse, we would both pause in what we were doing, he would subside with a sigh into his leather armchair before the fire, and I would break off my game or book. It was as though we were listening for something scarcely audible in the distance, but the only sounds were the shifting coals in the grate and the intermittent plashing of the snow as it slid from the window-panes to the ledge outside. Abruptly he would explode into talk: "When the Fenian raids threatened this country I led my boys into action. I charged up the hill waving my sword" (here, seizing the poker, he made to charge at me across the hearthrug) "and the Irish ruffians fled before us." My mother said that there was no charge and no hill, that my grandfather had raised a company to fight the Fenians but the raids were over before he could take to the field. I preferred my grandfather's version; his stories were like the stories I told myself or the games I invented. They were rambling and repetitious, and depended on the imagination.

When my mother came into the sitting-room, her cheeks flushed from the cold, she would fling off her sealskin coat and say, "Oh, how stuffy it is in here, what have you two been doing? Charlie, you ought to be out playing in the snow, it is a lovely sunny day. Father, you just have time for half an hour's rest before lunch."

There were many empty rooms in my grandfather's house, empty but furnished. The emptiest of all was my grandmother's bedroom, which had been left as it was when she was alive. The bed was made up; her hand-mirror, her hairbrush, and her Bible with a marker in it were on the table beside her bed. No one but my grandfather was allowed to enter the room. Once I looked in and felt a breath of cold enclosed air on my face.

My grandfather's bedroom I visited every morning while he was still in bed in a flannel nightshirt, and he would give me a dusty lemon-drop out of a circular wooden box. The room smelled of old age—and of other things. He kept a ham and a bottle of stout under the bed, to conceal them from the doctor who had put him on a diet.

My grandfather had had twelve children. But he had outlived all of them but my mother and her brother Charlie. What had become of all those children? Most of them had died young, some in infancy, as so many used to in those days. Except for my mother, those who did grow up were not long-lived.

Of all the children who had played and called to each other in those rooms, two were to be met with at every turn. As soldiers they marched and countermarched along the garden paths, as Red Indians they put each other to the torture, as horses they galloped or trotted up and down to the stables. All their games and exploits were more real to me than my own. They were my mother and my uncle Charlie. These were the tales my mother told me, "Charlie and I, Charlie and I." He had been bold and adventurous; feats of nerve and truant defiance were his, and my mother had been his accomplice and his imitator.

What was he really like, Uncle Charlie? I still tease myself with the question. But he is nearly seventy years dead, killed leading his regiment at Bourlon Wood in 1918, against real enemies, not like my grandfather's phantom Fenians. The letters from the regiment after his death read, "The men would follow him anywhere; he seemed to bear a charmed life." Yet what was his life until the War gave him his chance? A life of adventure wearing down into plain middle-aged failure. Expelled from the Royal Military College for gambling, dismissed from the Mounted Police for striking a bullying corporal, disappearing for months into the Yukon, drifting into jobs and bars in Calgary or Edmonton, eking out his earnings by his gains at poker, he left a trail of legends and stories. A few old men still recount them, but his magnetism has evaporated and the point is gone.

His women were come-by-chance encounters doubled with romantic entanglements, for he had the attraction of the undomesticated man, restless and susceptible. He made husbands and other aspirants seem tame. The women who knew him felt they had a card up their sleeves. He never married. In a letter to my mother on the day before the battle in which he was killed, he wrote, "You are the only one I have ever loved." On the night that she was handed the telegram telling her of his death she saw, or thought she saw, him at her bedside. He wore a torn scarf knotted around his neck and there was a button missing on the left pocket of his tunic. Afterwards my mother wrote to the sergeant who had been with him when he was killed and he confirmed these details.

To my grandparents my uncle Charlie had always been a worry and a disappointment, sharpened by contrast with his elder brother Harry. Harry was their idol, a dashing soldier, startlingly handsome, cutting a figure in fashionable London, married to an Earl's daughter. But the idol was expensive to maintain. They paid his debts and waited for his letters, which came rarely—except when he needed money.

My grandparents were old-fashioned, innocent snobs. Innocent, in the sense that they never thought of themselves in this way. They believed that they had a Position to keep up (though what that Position was it would be hard to say). What made it more difficult to keep up was that my grandfather all his life drank in bursts of drunkenness, when he vanished from his wife and home for days at a time. My grandmother covered and concealed the outrage in the Victorian manner. Sometimes it was not easy. Once when she was presiding over a dinner party for some local dignitary, her husband, "unfortunately ill" upstairs, appeared at the dining-room door in his nightshirt, pleading for whisky. She rose from the table and majestically swept him away. He was smaller than she, and she so enveloped him in her amplitude that the guests could hardly believe, when she resumed her place, that he had ever been there.

Never in the course of nearly a century had my grandfather done a day's work. This, and his heavy drinking, may have accounted for his healthy old age. Although he was always prone to fits of gloom, his spirits revived quickly. The gloom was usually associated with money. He had inherited what used to be called "private means" from his father. Being generous and hospitable, he overspent his income. He and my grandmother found it difficult to retrench. My mother as a girl had no patience with their financial forebodings. "Why give dinner parties when we are in debt? Why import a spotty English boy and call him a footman?" My grandparents did not take these probings in good part. "Your father and I," my grandmother announced, "are pained, grieved, and disappointed in you, Lilian."

When I came to my grandfather's house as a child all this was long in the past. My grandmother's drawing-room was shuttered, its armchairs and sofas under dust-covers. The little papier-mâché chairs, almost too fragile to sit on, were pushed to the wall. The room was crowded with objects which seemed to me of inestimable rarity and strangeness. There was a picture of a boy in peasant costume holding an alpenstock; a souvenir from Switzerland, it was painted on cobweb. I held my breath when looking at it, believing that the picture would dissolve if I breathed on it. There was a silver horse trotting over a field of silver grass and flowers. In one corner of the room, enclosed in a large box, was a pile of old daguerreotypes. I would cautiously unfasten the rusty clasps of their black cases and bring to light a whole shadowy population. Men with fan-shaped whiskers and top hats, leaning gloomily against cardboard balustrades, behind which hung a drop-curtain of majestic parks and castle towers out of proportion with watch-fob and frock-coat; women voluminously robed, bent pensively over a family album, one arm gracefully arched to support a languid head. All the denizens of this ghostly world wore the same expression of grave impassivity; even the children looked unnaturally solemn in their strange garb. They might have been the priests and priestesses of some fantastic and forgotten cult, the secret of which had perished with them. When I snapped the clasps of their cases to once again, it was as if I enclosed these dim beings in their tombs.

A marble group of the Three Graces stood on a red velvet pedestal under a glass case. Once when alone in the drawing-room I lifted the glass case with guiltily trembling hands and ran my fingers over the cold breasts of the Graces. I knew that I was committing sacrilege, but the desire for the unattainable was too strong for me to resist.

Over the drawing-room fireplace hung the portrait of a lady, her hair parted in the style of the Empress Eugénie, her dark eyes smiling, her pink scarf floating away from her shoulders into an azure sky. It was my grandmother. But not the stout old woman in a black silk dress whom I could just remember. This was she as a young bride, painted in Paris on her honeymoon in the 1850s.

Beyond the drawing-room was a small, damp library, also now disused. Here stood a desk, its drawers brimming with packets of letters yellowed by age, tied with faded ribbons. They were the letters of my great-grandfather to the girl he was to marry, written during their courtship. They folded inward on their broken seals of red wax. I unfolded them one after another. In one was a pressed mayflower that they had picked together in a wood. It was odourless and almost colourless. In another was a twist of hair, a living chestnut colour, leaving an oily stain upon the paper. The writing scrawled and hurried in haste or excitement, as though the nerves in the writer's hand were still alive. Bursts of feeling, scoldings, secret endearments, zigzagged across the pages. These letters were not meant for me. I was spying out of childish eyes.

Under the hall stairs swung a green baize door leading to the kitchen. Roxie was the cook. She had been with my grandparents all her grown-up life. She saw through them and she served them with cross-grained fidelity. She was red-haired and rough-tongued. When she finally retired to her family farm in Stewiacke, Nova Scotia, my brother and I used to spend a week with her there each year. She had no high opinion of me. "That there Charlie, when he is with you you would think butter would melt in his mouth, but just wait till your back is turned." They did not mince their words on the farm—"pee or get off the pot" was a favourite expression (and one which in later life I found to apply to many situations—social, political, and even amorous). Once when I returned from our annual visit my language surprised my mother. She was walking restlessly up and down in her bedroom smoking a cigarette when I suddenly said, "Why don't you sit down on your arse?" She came to a standstill, staring at me in disbelief. "What did you say?" "Well, that's what they say in Stewiacke." My mother was not genuinely shocked; she had little use for the genteel, and what she despised most, apart from cowardice, was what she called "affectation."

How far can one reach back into the past? Farther than the sound of a voice? My mother was a natural mimic. Her ear was a tuning-fork for voices and accents; the least actressy of women, she had a face as mobile as that of an actress. She could bring before you not only the absent, but also the dead—those whom she had known in her childhood. They might just have left the room, and one could catch the inflections of their voices, hear their laughter just before the door closed on them. So, I saw and heard those people of the past not as they might have been described in books, but in the flashes of her mimicry.

There was still a handful of survivors of my grandfather's generation living, among them Mr. and Mrs. Lorrimer. They were no favourites of my grandfather, particularly Mrs. Lorrimer, who had been a leading light in teetotal circles. She was one of the innumerable Queen Victorias who once peopled the Empire, modelling themselves on the Great Original. She had the lost Victorian art of putting one not at one's ease, but at one's unease. She dressed her part: a white cap perched on her severely parted white hair, and she was encased in an armature of whalebone. When she approached, there was a rustle of skirts, and the tap of her ivory-handled stick on the floor. She trundled rather than walked across a room; there appeared to be no leg action involved. She had a chilly little laugh, miles away from mirth.

The Lorrimers lived in the country not far out of town. I remember as a child going there once with my mother to lunch with them. We arrived somewhat late. "Dear Lilian," Mrs. Lorrimer greeted us with the little laugh. "I hear you were delayed by rain. How *very* extraordinary that we have had no rain here only a mile away, but it is no matter. Here you are at last." We went in to lunch preceded by a very old and smelly Newfoundland dog. Mrs. Lorrimer turned to my mother: "How is your father? Always so cheery. I am sorry your brother Charlie should be causing him so much concern. Your dear mother was always so indulgent to him, too much so, I fear." At that moment the dog growled and stirred under the table where he had crouched, and on a sharp note of rage my mother cried out "Damn!" There was a pause as if the clock had stopped. "He nipped my ankle," my mother explained. "Ha ha," guffawed Mr. Lorrimer, "she said a big D, she said a big D." Our hostess's laugh was like the rustling of dry leaves. "I am sure she said nothing of the kind, but if," turning to my mother, "you had said 'poor doggie' instead of the expression which you did employ, it would have been preferable." In front of my place at the table was a glass of milk. "We had it brought straight from the barn for you as a treat. It is warm from the cow." With revulsion I downed a swallow of the milk. It had a distastefully intimate taste.

The luncheon-table conversation continued. "So dreadfully sad," observed Mrs. Lorrimer, "for the poor Brumleys that their only son should have become a pervert" (the reference was not to his sex preferences but to his conversion to the Roman Catholic Church), "but our own High Church so often leads the way to error." We rose to depart. "Dear Lilian," she said, "I remember you so well as a child and what a naughty little thing you were!" and, bending down to me, "Bonnie Prince Charlie, you didn't drink up your milk." A boy of six cannot suffer from the menopause, but my symptoms were those since described to me; a surge of heat flushed through my veins, and embarrassment dripped from me like sweat. Even today the words "Bonnie Prince Charlie" set up a queasy sensation in me as of the taste of warm milk.

My grandfather and his remaining contemporaries belonged to a breed now long extinct. They were Colonials. The word carries a whiff of inferiority, but they were not to know this. They thought of themselves as belonging to the British Empire, than which they could imagine nothing more glorious. They did not think of themselves as English. Certainly everything British was Best, but they viewed the individual Englishman with a critical eye. If the English patronized the Colonials, the Colonials sat in judgment on the English. The Colonial was an ambivalent creature, half in one element, half in another; British, but not English, cantankerously loyal. These were Nova Scotian Colonials. The earthy subsoil of Nova Scotia gave a tang to their personalities and an edge to their tongues. For many years they and those like them had managed the colony under the rule of British governors whom, in turn, they managed. It was a comfortable arrangement as long as it lasted, and not unprofitable. It enjoyed the blessings of the Church— the Church of England, of course. They were men of standing and standards, honourable men within the bounds of their monopoly. They were kind to their poor relations and moderately charitable to the poor who were not their relations and who lived in the slums. They began to think of themselves as an aristocracy, since there was no aristocracy on the spot to tell them differently. But they were small-town people, and they never escaped from the miasma of the small town. They woke to the apprehension of what the neighbours would say; they knew that, as always in Nova Scotia, ostentation was made to be undermined. There would be a dozen who would doubt the crests on their silver or the sources of their fortunes. So that they never achieved perfect complacency, a commodity hard to come by in that rocky land where misfortune revives friendship and where the worst word is "in trouble he let me down."

Halifax had been a garrison and a naval base for 150 years. Had not Kipling cele-brated it as the "Warden of the honour of the North"? British regiments and sailors of the Royal Navy had come and gone in all those years and had set their stamp upon the town. No ball, picnic, or sleighing party was complete without them. They carried off the prettiest girls, and many a local man resented and hated them. They brought with them rumours of wars in the days when wars seemed an adventure, an honourable escape for the spirited and restless from home-grown tedium. Some found forgotten glory in those wars of Empire. Theirs were the tunes that went whistling up and down the steep hills of the town, "We're the soldiers of the Queen, my boys, the Queen, my boys, the Queen, my boys," and there were boys, like my uncles Harry and Charlie, to listen and serve.

When I came to my grandfather's house the British soldiers had marched down the streets for the last time and the little world in which my grandfather had grown up had long ago vanished. "I have lived too long, I have lived too long," he used to declaim in melodramatic tones. Yet all the sorrows and losses, the drinking, the fathering, the loving, and the talking (and he was a great talker) had not worn him out. He had been born in 1817 and was already a middle-aged man when Nova Scotia ceased to be a colony and became a province of Canada, an event that did not seem to have penetrated very far into his consciousness. He had never set foot in "Upper Canada," as he called it. His journeys had been those taken from Halifax to

England, weeks spent in rolling, pitching, smelly little steamers, with shipwreck off the Grand Banks or Sable Island an accepted risk.

My grandfather never reached his hundredth year; he died ten days short of it. It was his impatience that killed him. Rather than waiting for help, he seized the heavy copper coal scuttle in his sitting-room and, in trying to pour the coal into the grate, he staggered, hit his head against the marble mantelpiece, and never recovered consciousness. My mother, my brother, and I were staying in the house at the time. By then it was 1917, and I was eleven years old. To me it was not the same house as it had been on my visits as a small child. I saw it with different and disparaging eyes.

On the day of my grandfather's death I was sent to the local cinema, I suppose to get me out of the way. When I went to bed that night in my bedroom at the top of the house I was not thinking of my grandfather. His death had not much moved me. He had come to seem no longer quite real to me, but like an old man on the stage who dies when the curtain falls.

At some moment in the night I woke to an intensity of listening. I got out of bed and stood at the top of the stairs, looking down to the gully where the banisters curved. The dense night silence reverberated around me; then there swept over me the tide of the past rising from the sleeping house below me. A constriction choked my throat. Had I heard a muffled sigh like a warning? What was it? Some signal from the frontier between childhood and old age where my grandfather and I had shared those timeless hours? When I went back to my bed it was to fall into a sleep as deep as the stairwell where the dead children had played.

Strayed

CHARLES G.D. ROBERTS

IN THE CABINEAU CAMP, of unlucky reputation, there was a young ox of splendid build, but of a wild and restless nature.

He was one of a yoke, of part Devon blood, large, dark red, all muscle and nerve, and with wide magnificent horns. His yoke-fellow was a docile steady worker, the pride of his owner's heart; but he himself seemed never to have been more than half broken in. The woods appeared to draw him by some spell. He wanted to get back to the pastures where he had roamed untrammelled of old with his fellow-steers. The remembrance was in his heart of the dewy mornings when the herd used to feed together on the sweet grassy hillocks, and of the clover-smelling heats of June when they would gather hock-deep in the pools under the green willow-shadows. He hated the yoke, he hated the winter; and he imagined that in the wild pastures he remembered it would be forever summer. If only he could get back to those pastures!

One day there came the longed-for opportunity; and he seized it. He was standing unyoked beside his mate, and none of the teamsters were near. His head went up in the air, and with a snort of triumph he dashed away through the forest.

For a little while there was a vain pursuit. At last the lumbermen gave it up. "Let him be!" said his owner, "an' I rayther guess he'll turn up agin when he gits peckish. He kaint browse on spruce buds an' lung-wort."

Plunging on with long gallop through the snow he was soon miles from camp. Growing weary he slackened his pace. He came down to a walk. As the lonely red of the winter sunset began to stream through the openings of the forest, flushing the snows of the tiny glades and swales, he grew hungry, and began to swallow unsatisfying mouthfuls of the long moss which roughened the tree-trunks. Ere the moon got up he had filled himself with this fodder, and then he lay down in a little thicket for the night.

But some miles back from his retreat a bear had chanced upon his footprints. A strayed steer! That would be an easy prey. The bear started straightway in pursuit. The moon was high in heaven when the crouched ox heard his pursuer's approach. He had no idea what was coming, but he rose to his feet and waited.

The bear plunged boldly into the thicket, never dreaming of resistance. With a muffled roar the ox charged upon him and bore him to the ground. Then he wheeled, and charged again, and the astonished bear was beaten at once. Gored by those keen horns he had no stomach for further encounter, and would fain have made his escape; but as he retreated the ox charged him again, dashing him against a huge trunk. The bear dragged himself up with difficulty, beyond his opponent's reach; and the ox turned scornfully back to his lair.

At the first yellow of dawn the restless creature was again upon the march. He pulled more mosses by the way, but he disliked them the more intensely now because he thought he must be nearing his ancient pastures with their tender grass and their streams. The snow was deeper about him, and his hatred of the winter grew apace. He came out upon a hill-side, partly open, whence the pine had years before been stripped, and where now grew young birches thick together. Here he browsed on the aromatic twigs, but for him it was harsh fare.

As his hunger increased he thought a little longingly of the camp he had deserted, but he dreamed not of turning back. He would keep on till he reached his pastures, and the glad herd of his comrades licking salt out of the trough beside the accustomed pool. He had some blind instinct as to his direction, and kept his course to the south very strictly, the desire in his heart continually leading him aright.

That afternoon he was attacked by a panther, which dropped out of a tree and tore his throat. He dashed under a low branch and scraped his assailant off, then, wheeling about savagely, put the brute to flight with his first mad charge. The panther sprang back into his tree, and the ox continued his quest.

Soon his steps grew weaker, for the panther's cruel claws had gone deep into his neck, and his path was marked with blood. Yet the dream in his great wild eyes was not dimmed as his strength ebbed away. His weakness he never noticed or heeded. The desire that was urging him absorbed all other thoughts—even, almost, his sense of hunger. This, however, it was easy for him to assuage, after a fashion, for the long, grey, unnourishing mosses were abundant.

By and by his path led him into the bed of a stream, whose waters could be heard faintly tinkling on thin pebbles beneath their coverlet of ice and snow. His slow steps conducted him far along this open course. Soon after he had disappeared, around a curve in the distance there came the panther, following stealthily upon his crimsoned trail. The crafty beast was waiting until the bleeding and the hunger should do its work, and the object of its inexorable pursuit should have no more heart left for resistance.

This was late in the afternoon. The ox was now possessed with his desire, and would not lie down for any rest. All night long, through the gleaming silver of the open spaces, through the weird and checkered gloom of the deep forest, heedless even of his hunger, or perhaps driven the more by it as he thought of the wild clover bunches and tender timothy awaiting him, the solitary ox strove on. And all night, lagging far behind in his unabating caution, the panther followed him.

At sunrise the worn and stumbling animal came out upon the borders of the great lake, stretching its leagues of unshadowed snow away to the south before him. There was his path, and without hesitation he followed it. The wide and frost-bound water here and there had been swept clear of its snows by the wind, but for the most part its covering lay unruffled; and the pale dove-colours, and saffrons, and rose-lilacs of the dawn were sweetly reflected on its surface.

The doomed ox was now journeying very slowly, and with the greatest labour. He staggered at every step, and his beautiful head drooped almost to the snow. When he had got a great way out upon the lake, at the forest's edge appeared the pursuing panther, emerging cautiously from the coverts. The round tawny face and malignant green eyes were raised to peer out across the expanse. The labouring progress of the ox was promptly marked. Dropping its nose again to the ensanguined snow, the beast resumed his pursuit, first at a slow trot, and then at a long, elastic gallop. By this time the ox's quest was nearly done. He plunged forward upon his knees, rose again with difficulty, stood still, and looked around him. His eyes were clouding over, but he saw, dimly, the tawny brute that was now hard upon his steps. Back came a flash of the old courage, and he turned, horns lowered, to face the attack. With the last of his strength he charged, and the panther paused irresolutely; but the wanderer's knees gave way beneath his own impetus, and his horns ploughed the snow. With a deep bellowing groan he rolled over on his side, and the longing, and the dream of the pleasant pastures, faded from his eyes. With a great spring the panther was upon him, and the eager teeth were at his throat—but he knew nought of it. No wild beast, but his own desire, had conquered him.

When the panther had slaked his thirst for blood, he raised his head, and stood with his fore-paws resting on the dead ox's side, and gazed all about him.

To one watching from the lake shore, had there been anyone to watch in that solitude, the wild beast and his prey would have seemed but a speck of black on the gleaming waste. At the same hour, league upon league back in the depth of the ancient forest, a lonely ox was lowing in his stanchions, restless, refusing to eat, grieving for the absence of his yoke-fellow.

The Painted Door

SINCLAIR ROSS

STRAIGHT ACROSS THE HILLS it was five miles from John's farm to his father's. But in winter, with the roads impassable, a team had to make a wide detour and skirt the hills, so that from five the distance was more than trebled to seventeen.

"I think I'll walk," John said at breakfast to his wife. "The drifts in the hills wouldn't hold a horse, but they'll carry me all right. If I leave early I can spend a few hours helping him with his chores, and still be back by suppertime."

She went to the window, and thawing a clear place in the frost with her breath, stood looking across the snowswept farmyard to the huddle of stables and sheds. "There was a double wheel around the moon last night," she countered presently. "You said yourself we could expect a storm. It isn't right to leave me here alone. Surely I'm as important as your father."

He glanced up uneasily, then drinking off his coffee tried to reassure her. "But there's nothing to be afraid of—even supposing it does start to storm. You won't need to go near the stable. Everything's fed and watered now to last till night. I'll be back at the latest by seven or eight."

She went on blowing against the frosted pane, carefully elongating the clear place until it was oval-shaped and symmetrical. He watched her a moment or two longer, then more insistently repeated, "I say you won't need to go near the stable. Everything's fed and watered, and I'll see that there's plenty of wood in. That will be all right, won't it?"

"Yes—of course—I heard you—" It was a curiously cold voice now, as if the words were chilled by their contact with the frosted pane. "Plenty to eat—plenty of wood to keep me warm—what more could a woman ask for?"

"But he's an old man—living there all alone. What is it, Ann? You're not like yourself this morning."

She shook her head without turning. "Pay no attention to me. Seven years a farmer's wife—it's time I was used to staying alone."

Slowly the clear place on the glass enlarged: oval, then round, then oval again. The sun was risen above the frost mists now, so keen and hard a glitter on the snow that instead of warmth its rays seemed shedding cold. One of the two-year-old colts that had cantered away when John turned the horses out for water stood covered with rime at the stable door again, head down and body hunched, each breath a little plume of steam against the frosty air. She shivered, but did not turn. In the clear, bitter light the long white miles of prairie landscape seemed a region alien to life. Even the distant farmsteads she could see served only to intensify a sense of isolation. Scattered across the face of so vast and bleak a wilderness it was difficult to conceive them as a testimony of human hardihood and endurance. Rather they seemed futile, lost, to cower before the implacability of snow-swept earth and clear pale sun-chilled sky.

And when at last she turned from the window there was a brooding stillness in her face as if she had recognized this mastery of snow and cold. It troubled John. "If you're really afraid," he yielded, "I won't go today. Lately it's been so cold, that's all. I just wanted to make sure he's all right in case we do have a storm."

"I know—I'm not really afraid." She was putting in a fire now, and he could no longer see her face. "Pay no attention. It's ten miles there and back, so you'd better get started."

"You ought to know by now I wouldn't stay away," he tried to brighten her. "No matter how it stormed. Before we were married—remember? Twice a week I never missed and we had some bad blizzards that winter too."

He was a slow, unambitious man, content with his farm and cattle, naively proud of Ann. He had been bewildered by it once, her caring for a dull-witted fellow like him; then assured at last of her affection he had relaxed against it gratefully, unsuspecting it might ever be less constant than his own. Even now, listening to the restless brooding in her voice, he felt only a quick, unformulated kind of pride that after seven years his absence for a day should still concern her. While she, his trust and earnestness controlling her again:

"I know. It's just that sometimes when you're away I get lonely.... There's a long cold tramp in front of you. You'll let me fix a scarf around your face."

He nodded. "And on my way I'll drop in at Steven's place. Maybe he'll come over tonight for a game of cards. You haven't seen anybody but me for the last two weeks."

She glanced up sharply, then busied herself clearing the table. "It will mean another two miles if you do. You're going to be cold and tired enough as it is. When you're gone I think I'll paint the kitchen woodwork. White this time—you remember we got the paint last fall. It's going to make the room a lot lighter. I'll be too busy to find the day long."

"I will though," he insisted, "and if a storm gets up you'll feel safer, knowing that he's coming. That's what you need, maybe—someone to talk to besides me."

She stood at the stove motionless a moment, then turned to him uneasily. "Will you shave then, John—now—before you go?"

He glanced at her questioningly, and avoiding his eyes she tried to explain, "I mean—he may be here before you're back—and you won't have a chance then."

"But it's only Steven—we're not going anywhere."

"He'll be shaved, though—that's what I mean—and I'd like you too to spend a little time on yourself."

He stood up, stroking the heavy stubble on his chin. "Maybe I should—only it softens up the skin too much. Especially when I've got to face the wind."

She nodded and began to help him dress, bringing heavy socks and a big woollen sweater from the bedroom, wrapping a scarf around his face and forehead. "I'll tell Steven to come early," he said, as he went out. "In time for supper. Likely there'll be chores for me to do, so if I'm not back by six don't wait."

From the bedroom window she watched him nearly a mile along the road. The fire had gone down when at last she turned away, and already through the house there was an encroaching chill. A blaze sprang up again when the draughts were opened, but as she went on clearing the table her movements were furtive and constrained. It was the silence weighing upon her—the frozen silence of the bitter fields and sun-chilled sky—lurking outside as if alive, relentlessly in wait, mile-deep between her now and John. She listened to it, suddenly tense, motionless. The fire crackled and the clock ticked. Always it was there. "I'm a fool," she whispered, rattling the dishes in defiance, going back to the stove to put in another fire. "Warm and safe—I'm a fool. It's a good chance when he's away to paint. The day will go quickly. I won't have time to brood."

Since November now the paint had been waiting warmer weather. The frost in the walls on a day like this would crack and peel it as it dried, but she needed something to keep her hands occupied, something to stave off the gathering cold and loneliness. "First of all," she said aloud, opening the paint and mixing it with a little turpentine, "I must get the house warmer. Fill up the stove and open the oven door so that all the heat comes out. Wad something along the window sills to keep out the draughts. Then I'll feel brighter. It's the cold that depresses."

She moved briskly, performing each little task with careful and exaggerated absorption, binding her thoughts to it, making it a screen between herself and the surrounding snow and silence. But when the stove was filled and the windows sealed it was more difficult again. Above the quiet, steady swishing of her brush against the bedroom door the clock began to tick. Suddenly her movements became precise, deliberate, her posture self-conscious, as if someone had entered the room and were watching her. It was the silence again, aggressive, hovering. The fire spit and crackled at it. Still it was there. "I'm a fool," she repeated. "All farmers' wives have to stay alone. I mustn't give in this way. I mustn't brood. A few hours now and they'll be here."

The sound of her voice reassured her. She went on: "I'll get them a good supper—and for coffee after cards bake some of the little cakes with raisins that he likes.... Just three of us, so I'll watch, and let John play. It's better with four, but at least we can talk. That's all I need—someone to talk to. John never talks. He's stronger—doesn't need to. But he likes Steven—no matter what the neighbours say. Maybe he'll have him come again, and some other young people too. It's what we need, both of us, to help keep young ourselves.... And then before we know it we'll be into March. It's cold still in March sometimes, but you never mind the same. At least you're beginning to think about spring."

She began to think about it now. Thoughts that outstripped her words, that left her alone again with herself and the ever-lurking silence. Eager and hopeful first, then clenched, rebellious, lonely. Windows open, sun and thawing earth again, the urge of growing, living things. Then the days that began in the morning at half-past four and lasted till ten at night; the meals at which John gulped his food and scarcely spoke a word; the brute-tired stupid eyes he turned on her if ever she mentioned town or visiting.

For spring was drudgery again. John never hired a man to help him. He wanted a mortgage-free farm; then a new house and pretty clothes for her. Sometimes, because with the best of crops it was going to take so long to pay off anyway, she wondered whether they mightn't better let the mortgage wait a little. Before they were worn out, before their best years were gone. It was something of life she wanted, not just a house and furniture; something of John, not pretty clothes when she would be too old to wear them. But John of course couldn't understand. To him it seemed only right that she should have the clothes—only right that he, fit for nothing else, should slave away fifteen hours a day to give them to her. There was in his devotion a baffling, insurmountable humility that made him feel the need of sacrifice. And when his muscles ached, when his feet dragged stolidly with weariness, then it seemed that in some measure at least he was making amends for his big hulking body and simple mind. Year after year their lives went on in the same little groove. He drove his horses in the field; she milked the cows and hoed potatoes. By dint of his drudgery he saved a few months' wages, added a few dollars more each fall to his payments on the mortgage; but the only real difference that it all made was to deprive her of his companionship, to make him a little duller, older, uglier than he might otherwise have been. He never saw their lives objectively. To him it was not what he actually accomplished by means of the sacrifice that mattered, but the sacrifice itself, the gesture—something done for her sake.

And she, understanding, kept her silence. In such a gesture, however futile, there was a graciousness not to be shattered lightly. "John," she would begin sometimes, "you're doing too much. Get a man to help you—just for a month—" but smiling down at her he would answer simply, "I don't mind. Look at the hands on me. They're made for work." While in his voice there would be a stalwart ring to tell her that by her thoughtfulness she had made him only the more resolved to serve her, to prove his devotion and fidelity.

They were useless, such thoughts. She knew. It was his very devotion that made them useless, that forbade her to rebel. Yet over and over, sometimes hunched still before their bleakness, sometimes her brush making swift sharp strokes to pace the chafe and rancour that they brought, she persisted in them.

This now, the winter, was their slack season. She could sleep sometimes till eight, and John till seven. They could linger over their meals a little, read, play cards, go visiting the neighbours. It was the time to relax, to indulge and enjoy themselves; but instead, fretful and impatient, they kept on waiting for the spring. They were compelled now, not by labour, but by the spirit of labour. A spirit that pervaded their lives and brought with idleness a sense of guilt. Sometimes they did sleep late, sometimes they did play cards, but always uneasily, always reproached by the thought of more important things that might be done. When John got up at five to attend to the fire he wanted to stay up and go out to the stable. When he sat down to a meal he hurried his food and pushed his chair away again, from habit, from sheer work-instinct, even though it was only to put more wood in the stove, or go down cellar to cut up beets and turnips for the cows.

And anyway, sometimes she asked herself, why sit trying to talk with a man who never talked? Why talk when there was nothing to talk about but crops and cattle, the weather and the neighbours? The neighbours, too—why go visiting them when still it was the same—crops and cattle, the weather and the other neighbours? Why go to the dances in the schoolhouse to sit among the older women, one of them now, married seven years, or to waltz with the work-bent, tired old farmers to a squeaky fiddle tune? Once she had danced with Steven six or seven times in the evening, and they had talked about it for as many months. It was easier to stay at home. John never danced or enjoyed himself. He was always uncomfortable in his good suit and shoes. He didn't like shaving in the cold weather oftener than once or twice a week. It was easier to stay at home, to stand at the window staring out across the bitter fields, to count the days and look forward to another spring.

But now, alone with herself in the winter silence, she saw the spring for what it really was. This spring—next spring—all the springs and summers still to come. While they grew old, while their bodies warped, while their minds kept shrivelling dry and empty like their lives. "I mustn't," she said aloud again. "I married him— and he's a good man. I mustn't keep on this way. It will be noon before long, and then time to think about supper.... Maybe he'll come early—and as soon as John is finished at the stable we can all play cards."

It was getting cold again, and she left her painting to put in more wood. But this time the warmth spread slowly. She pushed a mat up to the outside door, and went back to the window to pat down the woollen shirt that was wadded along the sill. Then she paced a few times round the room, then poked the fire and rattled the stove lids, then paced again. The fire crackled, the clock ticked. The silence now seemed more intense than ever, seemed to have reached a pitch where it faintly moaned. She began to pace on tiptoe, listening, her shoulders drawn together, not realizing for a while that it was the wind she heard, thin-strained and whimpering through the eaves.

Then she wheeled to the window, and with quick short breaths thawed the frost to see again. The glitter was gone. Across the drifts sped swift and snakelike little tongues of snow. She could not follow them, where they sprang from, or where they disappeared. It was as if all across the yard the snow were shivering awake—roused by the warnings of the wind to hold itself in readiness for the impending storm. The sky had become a sombre, whitish grey. It, too, as if in readiness, had shifted and lay close to earth. Before her as she watched a mane of powdery snow reared up breast-high against the darker background of the stable, tossed for a moment angrily, and then subsided again as if whipped down to obedience and restraint. But another followed, more reckless and impatient than the first. Another reeled and dashed itself against the window where she watched. Then ominously for a while there were only the angry little snakes of snow. The wind rose, creaking the troughs that were wired beneath the eaves. In the distance, sky and prairie now were merged into one another linelessly. All round her it was gathering; already in its press and whimpering there strummed a boding of eventual fury. Again she saw a mane of snow spring up, so dense and high this time that all the sheds and stables were obscured. Then others followed, whirling fiercely out of hand; and, when at last they cleared, the stables seemed in dimmer outline than before. It was the snow beginning, long lancet shafts of it, straight from the north, borne almost level by the straining wind. "He'll be there soon," she whispered, "and coming home it will be in his back. He'll leave again right away. He saw the double wheel—he knows the kind of storm there'll be."

She went back to her painting. For a while it was easier, all her thoughts half-anxious ones of John in the blizzard, struggling his way across the hills; but petu-lantly again she soon began, "I knew we were going to have a storm—I told him so—but it doesn't matter what I say. Big stubborn fool—he goes his own way anyway. It doesn't matter what becomes of me. In a storm like this he'll never get home. He won't even try. And while he sits keeping his father company I can look after his stable for him, go ploughing through snowdrifts up to my knees—nearly frozen—"

Not that she meant or believed her words. It was just an effort to convince herself that she did have a grievance, to justify her rebellious thoughts, to prove John responsible for her unhappiness. She was young still, eager for excitement and distractions; and John's steadfastness rebuked her vanity, made her complaints seem weak and trivial. She went on, fretfully, "If he'd listen to me sometimes and not be so stubborn we wouldn't still be living in a house like this. Seven years in two rooms—seven years and never a new stick of furniture.... There—as if another coat of paint could make it different anyway."

She cleaned her brush, filled up the stove again, and went back to the window. There was a void white moment that she thought must be frost formed on the window pane; then, like a fitful shadow through the whirling snow, she recognized the stable roof. It was incredible. The sudden, maniac raging of the storm struck from her face all its pettishness. Her eyes glazed with fear a little; her lips blanched. "If he starts for home now," she whispered silently—"But he won't—he knows I'm safe—he knows Steven's coming. Across the hills he would never dare."

She turned to the stove, holding out her hands to the warmth. Around her now there seemed a constant sway and tremor, as if the air were vibrating with the shudderings of the walls. She stood quite still, listening. Sometimes the wind struck with sharp, savage blows. Sometimes it bore down in a sustained, minute-long blast, silent with effort and intensity; then with a foiled shriek of threat wheeled away to gather and assault again. Always the eave-troughs creaked and sawed. She stared towards the window again, then detecting the morbid trend of her thoughts, prepared fresh coffee and forced herself to drink a few mouthfuls. "He would never dare," she whispered again. "He wouldn't leave the old man anyway in such a storm. Safe in here— there's nothing for me to keep worrying about. It's after one already. I'll do my baking now, and then it will be time to get supper ready for Steven."

Soon, however, she began to doubt whether Steven would come. In such a storm even a mile was enough to make a man hesitate. Especially Steven, who was hardly the one to face a blizzard, for the sake of someone else's chores. He had a stable of his own to look after anyway. It would be only natural for him to think that when the storm blew up John had turned again for home. Another man would have— would have put his wife first.

But she felt little dread or uneasiness at the prospect of spending the night alone. It was the first time she had been left like this on her own resources, and her reaction, now that she could face and appraise her situation calmly, was gradually to feel it a kind of adventure and responsibility. It stimulated her. Before nightfall she must go to the stable and feed everything. Wrap up in some of John's clothes—take a ball of string in her hand, one end tied to the door, so that no matter how blinding the storm she could at least find her way back to the house. She had heard of people having to do that. It appealed to her now because suddenly it made life dramatic. She had not felt the storm yet, only watched it for a minute through the window.

It took nearly an hour to find enough string, to choose the right socks and sweaters. Long before it was time to start out she tried on John's clothes, changing and rechanging, striding around the room to make sure there would be play enough for pitching hay and struggling over snowdrifts; then she took them off again, and for a while busied herself baking the little cakes with raisins that he liked.

Night came early. Just for a moment on the doorstep she shrank back, uncertain. The slow dimming of the light clutched her with an illogical sense of abandonment. It was like the covert withdrawal of an ally, leaving the alien miles unleashed and unrestrained. Watching the hurricane of writhing snow rage past the little house she forced herself, "They'll never stand the night unless I get them fed. It's nearly dark already, and I've work to last an hour."

Timidly, unwinding a little of the string, she crept out from the shelter of the doorway. A gust of wind spun her forward a few yards, then plunged her headlong against a drift that in the dense white whirl lay invisible across her path. For nearly a minute she huddled still, breathless and dazed. The snow was in her mouth and nostrils, inside her scarf and up her sleeves. As she tried to straighten a smothering scud flung itself against her face, cutting off her breath a second time. The wind struck from all sides, blustering and furious. It was as if the storm had discovered her, as if all its forces were concentrated upon her extinction. Seized with panic suddenly she threshed out a moment with her arms, then stumbled back and sprawled her length across the drift.

But this time she regained her feet quickly, roused by the whip and batter of the storm to retaliative anger. For a moment her impulse was to face the wind and strike back blow for blow; then, as suddenly as it had come, her frantic strength gave way to limpness and exhaustion. Suddenly, a comprehension so clear and terrifying that it struck all thoughts of the stable from her mind, she realized in such a storm her puniness. And the realization gave her new strength, stilled this time to a desperate persistence. Just for a moment the wind held her, numb and swaying in its vise; then slowly, buckled far forward, she groped her way again towards the house.

Inside, leaning against the door, she stood tense and still a while. It was almost dark now. The top of the stove glowed a deep, dull red. Heedless of the storm, self-absorbed and self-satisfied, the clock ticked on like a glib little idiot. "He shouldn't have gone," she whispered silently. "He saw the double wheel—he knew. He shouldn't have left me here alone."

For so fierce now, so insane and dominant did the blizzard seem, that she could not credit the safety of the house. The warmth and lull around her was not real yet, not to be relied upon. She was still at the mercy of the storm. Only her body pressing hard like this against the door was staving it off. She didn't dare move. She didn't dare ease the ache and strain. "He shouldn't have gone," she repeated, thinking of the stable again, reproached by her helplessness. "They'll freeze in their stalls—and I can't reach them. He'll say it's all my fault. He won't believe I tried."

Then Steven came. Quickly, startled to quietness and control, she let him in and lit the lamp. He stared at her a moment, then flinging off his cap crossed to where she stood by the table and seized her arms. "You're so white—what's wrong? Look at me—" It was like him in such little situations to be masterful. "You should have known better—for a while I thought I wasn't going to make it here myself—"

"I was afraid you wouldn't come—John left early, and there was the stable—"

But the storm had unnerved her, and suddenly at the assurance of his touch and voice the fear that had been gripping her gave way to an hysteria of relief. Scarcely aware of herself she seized his arm and sobbed against it. He remained still a moment unyielding, then slipped his other arm around her shoulder. It was comforting and she relaxed against it, hushed by a sudden sense of lull and safety. Her shoulders trembled with the easing of the strain, then fell limp and still. "You're shivering,"— he drew her gently towards the stove. "It's all right—nothing to be afraid of. I'm going to see to the stable."

It was a quiet, sympathetic voice, yet with an undertone of insolence, a kind of mockery even, that made her draw away quickly and busy herself putting in a fire. With his lips drawn in a little smile he watched her till she looked at him again. The smile too was insolent, but at the same time companionable; Steven's smile, and therefore difficult to reprove. It lit up his lean, still-boyish face with a peculiar kind of arrogance: features and smile that were different from John's, from other men's— wilful and derisive, yet naively so—as if it were less the difference itself he was conscious of, than the long-accustomed privilege that thereby fell his due. He was erect, tall, square-shouldered. His hair was dark and trim, his lips curved soft and full. While John, she made the comparison swiftly, was thickset, heavy-jowled, and stooped. He always stood before her helpless, a kind of humility and wonderment in his attitude. And Steven now smiled on her appraisingly with the worldly-wise assurance of one for whom a woman holds neither mystery nor illusion.

"It was good of you to come, Steven," she responded, the words running into a sudden, empty laugh. "Such a storm to face—I suppose I should feel flattered."

For his presumption, his misunderstanding of what had been only a momentary weakness, instead of angering quickened her, roused from latency and long disuse all the instincts and resources of her femininity. She felt eager, challenged. Something was at hand that hitherto had always eluded her, even in the early days with John, something vital, beckoning, meaningful. She didn't understand, but she knew. The texture of the moment was satisfyingly dreamlike: an incredibility perceived as such, yet acquiesced in. She was John's wife—she knew—but also she knew that Steven standing here was different from John. There was no thought or motive, no under-standing of herself as the knowledge persisted. Wary and poised round a sudden little core of blind excitement she evaded him, "But it's nearly dark—hadn't you better hurry if you're going to do the chores? Don't trouble—I can get them off myself—"

An hour later when he returned from the stable she was in another dress, hair rearranged, a little flush of colour in her face. Pouring warm water for him from the kettle into the basin she said evenly, "By the time you're washed supper will be ready. John said we weren't to wait for him."

He looked at her a moment, "You don't mean you're expecting John tonight? The way it's blowing—"

"Of course." As she spoke she could feel the colour deepening in her face. "We're going to play cards. He was the one that suggested it."

He went on washing, and then as they took their places at the table, resumed, "So John's coming. When are you expecting him?"

"He said it might be seven o'clock—or a little later." Conversation with Steven at other times had always been brisk and natural, but now all at once she found it strained. "He may have work to do for his father. That's what he said when he left. Why do you ask, Steven?"

"I was just wondering—it's a rough night."

"You don't know John. It would take more than a storm to stop him."

She glanced up again and he was smiling at her. The same insolence, the same little twist of mockery and appraisal. It made her flinch, and ask herself why she was pretending to expect John—why there should be this instinct of defence to force her. This time, instead of poise and excitement, it brought a reminder that she had changed her dress and rearranged her hair. It crushed in a sudden silence, through which she heard the whistling wind again, and the creaking saw of the eaves. Neither spoke now. There was something strange, almost frightening, about this Steven and his quiet, unrelenting smile; but strangest of all was the familiarity: the Steven she had never seen or encountered, and yet had always known, always expected, always waited for. It was less Steven himself that she felt than his inevitability. Just as she had felt the snow, the silence and the storm. She kept her eyes lowered, on the window past his shoulder, on the stove, but his smile now seemed to exist apart from him, to merge and hover with the silence. She clinked a cup—listened to the whistle of the storm—always it was there. He began to speak, but her mind missed the meaning of his words. Swiftly she was making comparisons again; his face so different to John's, so handsome and young and clean-shaven. Swiftly, helplessly, feeling the imperceptible and relentless ascendancy that thereby he was gaining over her, sensing sudden menace in this new, more vital life, even as she felt drawn towards it.

The lamp between them flickered as an onslaught of the storm sent shudderings through the room. She rose to build up the fire again and he followed her. For a long time they stood close to the stove, their arms almost touching. Once as the blizzard creaked the house she spun around sharply, fancying it was John at the door; but quietly he intercepted her. "Not tonight—you might as well make up your mind to it. Across the hills in a storm like this—it would be suicide to try."

Her lips trembled suddenly in an effort to answer, to parry the certainty in his voice, then set thin and bloodless. She was afraid now. Afraid of his face so different from John's—of his smile, of her own helplessness to rebuke it. Afraid of the storm, isolating her here alone with him. They tried to play cards, but she kept starting up at every creak and shiver of the walls. "It's too rough a night," he repeated. "Even for John. Just relax a few minutes—stop worrying and pay a little attention to me."

But in his tone there was a contradiction to his words. For it implied that she was not worrying—that her only concern was lest it really might be John at the door.

And the implication persisted. He filled up the stove for her, shuffled the cards— won—shuffled—still it was there. She tried to respond to his conversation, to think of the game, but helplessly into her cards instead she began to ask, Was he right? Was that why he smiled? Why he seemed to wait, expectant and assured?

The clock ticked, the fire crackled. Always it was there. Furtively for a moment she watched him as he deliberated over his hand. John, even in the days before they were married, had never looked like that. Only this morning she had asked him to shave. Because Steven was coming—because she had been afraid to see them side by side—because deep within herself she had known even then. The same knowledge, furtive and forbidden, that was flaunted now in Steven's smile. "You look cold," he said at last, dropping his cards and rising from the table. "We're not playing, anyway. Come over to the stove for a few minutes and get warm."

"But first I think we'll hang blankets over the door. When there's a blizzard like this we always do." It seemed that in sane, commonplace activity there might be release, a moment or two in which to recover herself. "John has nails to put them on. They keep out a little of the draught."

He stood on a chair for her, and hung the blankets that she carried from the bedroom. Then for a moment they stood silent, watching the blankets sway and tremble before the blade of wind that spurted around the jamb. "I forgot," she said at last, "that I painted the bedroom door. At the top there, see—I've smeared the blankets."

He glanced at her curiously, and went back to the stove. She followed him, trying to imagine the hills in such a storm, wondering whether John would come. "A man couldn't live in it," suddenly he answered her thoughts, lowering the oven door and drawing up their chairs one on each side of it. "He knows you're safe. It isn't likely that he'd leave his father, anyway."

"The wind will be in his back," she persisted. "The winter before we were married—all the blizzards that we had that year—and he never missed—"

"Blizzards like this one? Up in the hills he wouldn't be able to keep his direction for a hundred yards. Listen to it a minute and ask yourself."

His voice seemed softer, kindlier now. She met his smile a moment, its assured little twist of appraisal, then for a long time sat silent, tense, careful again to avoid his eyes.

Everything now seemed to depend on this. It was the same as a few hours ago when she braced the door against the storm. He was watching her, smiling. She dared not move, unclench her hands, or raise her eyes. The flames crackled, the clock ticked. The storm wrenched the walls as if to make them buckle in. So rigid and desperate were all her muscles set, withstanding, that the room around her seemed to swim and reel. So rigid and strained that for relief at last, despite herself, she raised her head and met his eyes again.

Intending that it should be for only an instant, just to breathe again, to ease the tension that had grown unbearable—but in his smile now, instead of the insolent appraisal that she feared, there seemed a kind of warmth and sympathy. An understanding that quickened and encouraged her—that made her wonder why but a moment ago she had been afraid. It was as if the storm had lulled, as if she had suddenly found calm and shelter.

Or perhaps, the thought seized her, perhaps instead of his smile it was she who had changed. She who, in the long, wind-creaked silence, had emerged from the increment of codes and loyalties to her real, unfettered self. She who now felt his air of appraisal as nothing more than an understanding of the unfulfilled woman that until this moment had lain within her brooding and unadmitted, reproved out of consciousness by the insistence of an outgrown, routine fidelity.

For there had always been Steven. She understood now. Seven years—almost as long as John—ever since the night they first danced together.

The lamp was burning dry, and through the dimming light, isolated in the fastness of silence and storm, they watched each other. Her face was white and struggling still. His was handsome, clean-shaven, young. Her eyes were fanatic, believing desperately, fixed upon him as if to exclude all else, as if to find justification. His were cool, bland, drooped a little with expectancy. The light kept dimming, gathering the shadows round them, hushed, conspiratorial. He was smiling still. Her hands again were clenched up white and hard.

"But he always came," she persisted. "The wildest, coldest nights—even such a night as this. There was never a storm—"

"Never a storm like this one." There was a quietness in his smile now, a kind of simplicity almost, as if to reassure her. "You were out in it yourself for a few minutes.

He'd have it for five miles, across the hills.... I'd think twice myself, on such a night before risking even one."

LONG AFTER HE WAS ASLEEP she lay listening to the storm. As a check on the draught up the chimney they had left one of the stovelids partly off, and through the open bedroom door she could see the flickerings of flame and shadow on the kitchen wall. They leaped and sank fantastically. The longer she watched the more alive they seemed to be. There was one great shadow that struggled towards her threateningly, massive and black and engulfing all the room. Again and again it advanced, about to spring, but each time a little whip of light subdued it to its place among the others on the wall. Yet though it never reached her still she cowered, feeling that gathered there was all the frozen wilderness, its heart of terror and invincibility.

Then she dozed a while, and the shadow was John. Interminably he advanced. The whips of light still flickered and coiled, but now suddenly they were the swift little snakes that this afternoon she had watched twist and shiver across the snow. And they too were advancing. They writhed and vanished and came again. She lay still, paralysed. He was over her now, so close that she could have touched him. Already it seemed that a deadly tightening hand was on her throat. She tried to scream but her lips were locked. Steven beside her slept on heedlessly.

Until suddenly as she lay staring up at him a gleam of light revealed his face. And in it was not a trace of threat or anger—only calm, and stonelike hopelessness.

That was like John. He began to withdraw, and frantically she tried to call him back. "It isn't true—not really true—listen, John—" but the words clung frozen to her lips. Already there was only the shriek of wind again, the sawing eaves, the leap and twist of shadow on the wall.

She sat up, startled now and awake. And so real had he seemed there, standing close to her, so vivid the sudden age and sorrow in his face, that at first she could not make herself understand she had been only dreaming. Against the conviction of his presence in the room it was necessary to insist over and over that he must still be with his father on the other side of the hills. Watching the shadows she had fallen asleep. It was only her mind, her imagination, distorted to a nightmare by the illogical and unadmitted dread of his return. But he wouldn't come. Steven was right. In such a storm he would never try. They were safe, alone. No one would ever know. It was only fear, morbid and irrational; only the sense of guilt that even her new-found and challenged womanhood could not entirely quell.

She knew now. She had not let herself understand or acknowledge it as guilt before, but gradually through the wind-torn silence of the night his face compelled her. The face that had watched her from the darkness with its stonelike sorrow—the face that was really John—John more than his features of mere flesh and bone could ever be.

She wept silently. The fitful gleam of light began to sink. On the ceiling and wall at last there was only a faint dull flickering glow. The little house shuddered and quailed, and a chill crept in again. Without wakening Steven she slipped out to build up the fire. It was burned to a few spent embers now, and the wood she put on seemed a long time catching light. The wind swirled through the blankets they had hung around the door, and then, hollow and moaning, roared up the chimney again, as if against its will drawn back to serve still longer with the onrush of the storm.

For a long time she crouched over the stove, listening. Earlier in the evening, with the lamp lit and the fire crackling, the house had seemed a stand against the wilderness, a refuge of feeble walls wherein persisted the elements of human meaning and survival. Now, in the cold, creaking darkness, it was strangely extinct, looted by the storm and abandoned again. She lifted the stove lid and fanned the embers till at last a swift little tongue of flame began to lick around the wood. Then she replaced the lid, extended her hands, and as if frozen in that attitude stood waiting.

It was not long now. After a few minutes she closed the draughts, and as the flames whirled back upon each other, beating against the top of the stove and sending out flickers of light again, a warmth surged up to relax her stiffened limbs. But shivering and numb it had been easier. The bodily well-being that the warmth induced gave play again to an ever more insistent mental suffering. She remembered the shadow that was John. She saw him bent towards her, then retreating, his features pale and overcast with unaccusing grief. She re-lived their seven years together and, in retrospect, found them to be years of worth and dignity. Until crushed by it all at last, seized by a sudden need to suffer and atone, she crossed to where the draught was bitter, and for a long time stood unflinching on the icy floor.

The storm was close here. Even through the blankets she could feel a sift of snow against her face. The eaves sawed, the walls creaked, and the wind was like a wolf in howling flight.

And yet, suddenly she asked herself, hadn't there been other storms, other blizzards? And through the worst of them hadn't he always reached her?

Clutched by the thought she stood rooted a minute. It was hard now to understand how she could have so deceived herself—how a moment of passion could have quieted within her not only conscience, but reason and discretion too. John always came. There could never be a storm to stop him. He was strong, inured to the cold. He had crossed the hills since his boyhood, knew every creek-bed and gully. It was madness to go on like this—to wait. While there was still time she must waken Steven, and hurry him away.

But in the bedroom again, standing at Steven's side, she hesitated. In his detachment from it all, in his quiet, even breathing, there was such sanity, such realism. For him nothing had happened; nothing would. If she wakened him he would only laugh and tell her to listen to the storm. Already it was long past midnight; either

John had lost his way or not set out at all. And she knew that in his devotion there was nothing foolhardy. He would never risk a storm beyond his endurance, never permit himself a sacrifice likely to endanger her lot or future. They were both safe. No one would ever know. She must control herself—be sane like Steven.

For comfort she let her hand rest a while on Steven's shoulder. It would be easier were he awake now, with her, sharing her guilt; but gradually as she watched his handsome face in the glimmering light she came to understand that for him no guilt existed. Just as there had been no passion, no conflict. Nothing but the sane appraisal of their situation, nothing but the expectant little smile, and the arrogance of features that were different from John's. She winced deeply, remembering how she had fixed her eyes on those features, how she had tried to believe that so handsome and young, so different from John's, they must in themselves be her justification.

In the flickering light they were still young, still handsome. No longer her justification—she knew now—John was the man—but wistfully still, wondering sharply at their power and tyranny, she touched them a moment with her fingertips again.

She could not blame him. There had been no passion, no guilt; therefore there could be no responsibility. Looking down at him as he slept, half-smiling still, his lips relaxed in the conscienceless complacency of his achievement, she understood that thus he was revealed in his entirety—all there ever was or ever could be. John was the man. With him lay all the future. For tonight, slowly and contritely through the day and years to come, she would try to make amends.

Then she stole back to the kitchen, and without thought, impelled by overwhelming need again, returned to the door where the draught was bitter still. Gradually towards morning the storm began to spend itself. Its terror blast became a feeble, worn-out moan. The leap of light and shadow sank, and a chill crept in again. Always the eaves creaked, tortured with wordless prophecy. Heedless of it all the clock ticked on in idiot content.

THEY FOUND HIM the next day, less than a mile from home. Drifting with the storm he had run against his own pasture fence and overcome had frozen there, erect still, both hands clasping fast the wire.

"He was south of here," they said wonderingly when she told them how he had come across the hills. "Straight south—you'd wonder how he could have missed the buildings. It was the wind last night, coming every way at once. He shouldn't have tried. There was a double wheel around the moon."

She looked past them a moment, then as if to herself said simply, "If you knew him, though—John would try."

It was later, when they had left her a while to be alone with him, that she knelt and touched his hand. Her eyes dimmed, it was still such a strong and patient hand;

then, transfixed, they suddenly grew wide and clear. On the palm, white even against its frozen whiteness, was a little smear of paint.

Horses of the Night

MARGARET LAURENCE

I NEVER KNEW I had distant cousins who lived up north, until Chris came down to Manawaka to go to high school. My mother said he belonged to a large family, relatives of ours, who lived at Shallow Creek, up north. I was six, and Shallow Creek seemed immeasurably far, part of a legendary winter country where no leaves grow and where the breath of seals and polar bears snuffled out steamily and turned to ice.

"Could plain people live there?" I asked my mother, meaning people who were not Eskimos. "Could there be a farm?"

"How do you mean?" she said, puzzled. "I told you. That's where they live. On the farm. Uncle Wilf—that was Chris's father, who died a few years back—he got the place as a homestead, donkey's years ago."

"But how could they grow anything? I thought you said it was up north."

"Mercy," my mother said, laughing, "it's not *that* far north, Vanessa. It's about a hundred miles beyond Galloping Mountain. You be nice to Chris, now, won't you? And don't go asking him a whole lot of questions the minute he steps inside the door."

How little my mother knew of me, I thought. Chris had been fifteen. He could be expected to feel only scorn towards me. I detested the fact that I was so young. I did not think I would be able to say anything at all to him.

"What if I don't like him?"

"What if you don't?" my mother responded sharply. "You're to watch your manners, and no acting up, understand? It's going to be quite difficult enough without that."

"Why does he have to come here, anyway?" I demanded crossly. "Why can't he go to school where he lives?"

"Because there isn't any high school up there," my mother said. "I hope he gets on well here, and isn't too homesick. Three years is a long time. It's very good of your grandfather to let him stay at the Brick House."

She said this last accusingly, as though she suspected I might be thinking differently. But I had not thought of it one way or another. We were all having dinner at the Brick House because of Chris's arrival. It was the end of August, and sweltering. My grandfather's house looked huge and cool from the outside, the high low-sweeping spruce trees shutting out the sun with their dusky out-fanned branches. But inside it wasn't cool at all. The woodstove in the kitchen was going full blast, and the whole place smelled of roasting meat.

Grandmother Connor was wearing a large mauve apron. I thought it was a nicer colour than the dark bottle-green of her dress, but she believed in wearing sombre shades lest the spirit give way to vanity, which in her case was certainly not much of a risk. The apron came up over her shapeless bosom and obscured part of her cameo brooch, the only jewellery she ever wore, with its portrait of a fiercely bearded man whom I imagined to be either Moses or God.

"Isn't it nearly time for them to be getting here, Beth?" Grandmother Connor asked.

"Train's not due until six," my mother said. "It's barely five-thirty, now. Has Father gone to the station already?"

"He went an hour ago," my grandmother said.

"He would," my mother commented.

"Now, now, Beth," my grandmother cautioned and soothed.

At last the front screen door was hurled open and Grandfather Connor strode into the house, followed by a tall lanky boy. Chris was wearing a white shirt, a tie, grey trousers. I thought, unwillingly, that he looked handsome. His face was angular, the bones showing through the brown skin. His grey eyes were slightly slanted, and his hair was the colour of couchgrass at the end of summer when it has been bleached to a light yellow by the sun. I had not planned to like him, not even a little, but somehow I wanted to defend him when I heard what my mother whispered to my grandmother before they went into the front hall.

"Heavens, look at the shirt and trousers—must've been his father's, the poor kid."

I shot out into the hall ahead of my mother, and then stopped and stood there.

"Hi, Vanessa," Chris said.

"How come you knew who I was?" I asked.

"Well, I knew your mother and dad only had one of a family, so I figured you must be her," he replied, grinning.

The way he spoke did not make me feel I had blundered. My mother greeted him warmly but shyly. Not knowing if she were expected to kiss him or to shake hands, she finally did neither. Grandmother Connor, however, had no doubts. She kissed him on both cheeks and then held him at arm's length to have a proper look at him.

"Bless the child," she said.

Coming from anyone else, this remark would have sounded ridiculous, especially as Chris was at least a head taller. My grandmother was the only person I have ever known who could say such things without appearing false.

"I'll show you your room, Chris," my mother offered.

Grandfather Connor, who had been standing in the living room doorway in absolute silence, looking as granite as a statue in the cemetery, now followed Grandmother out to the kitchen.

"Train was forty minutes late," he said weightily.

"What a shame," my grandmother said. "But I thought it wasn't due until six, Timothy."

"Six!" my grandfather cried. "That's the mainline train. The local's due at five-twenty."

This was not correct, as both my grandmother and I knew. But neither of us contradicted him.

"What on earth are you cooking a roast for, on a night like this?" my grandfather went on. "A person could fry an egg on the sidewalk, it's that hot. Potato salad would've gone down well."

Privately I agreed with this opinion, but I could never permit myself to acknowledge agreement with him on anything. I automatically and emotionally sided with Grandmother in all issues, not because she was inevitably right but because I loved her.

"It's not a roast," my grandmother said mildly. "It's mock-duck. The stove's only been going for an hour. I thought the boy would be hungry after the trip."

My mother and Chris had come downstairs and were now in the living room. I could hear them there, talking awkwardly, with pauses.

"Potato salad," my grandfather declaimed, "would've been plenty good enough. He'd have been lucky to get it, if you ask me anything. Wilf's family hasn't got two cents to rub together. It's me that's paying for the boy's keep."

The thought of Chris in the living room, and my mother unable to explain, was too much for me. I sidled over to the kitchen door, intending to close it. But my grandmother stopped me.

"No," she said, with unexpected firmness. "Leave it open, Vanessa."

I could hardly believe it. Surely she couldn't want Chris to hear? She herself was always able to move with equanimity through a hurricane because she believed that a mighty fortress was her God. But the rest of us were not like that, and usually she did her best to protect us. At the time I felt only bewilderment. I think now that she must have realized Chris would have to learn the Brick House sooner or later, and he might as well start right away.

I had to go into the living room. I had to know how Chris would take my grandfather. Would he, as I hoped, be angry and perhaps even speak out? Or would he, meekly, only be embarrassed?

"Wilf wasn't much good, even as a young man," Grandfather Connor was trumpeting. "Nobody but a simpleton would've taken up a homestead in a place like that. Anybody could've told him that land's no use for a thing except hay."

Was he going to remind us again how well he had done in the hardware business? Nobody had ever given him a hand, he used to tell me. I am sure he believed that this was true. Perhaps it even was true.

"If the boy takes after his father, it's a poor lookout for him," my grandfather continued.

I felt the old rage of helplessness. But as for Chris—he gave no sign of feeling anything. He was sitting on the big wing-backed sofa that curled into the bay window like a black and giant seashell. He began to talk to me, quite easily, just as though he had not heard a word my grandfather was saying.

This method proved to be the one Chris always used in any dealings with my grandfather. When the bludgeoning words came, which was often, Chris never seemed, like myself, to be holding back with a terrible strained force for fear of letting go and speaking out and having the known world unimaginably fall to pieces. He would not argue or defend himself, but he did not apologize, either. He simply appeared to be absent, elsewhere. Fortunately there was very little need for response, for when Grandfather Connor pointed out your shortcomings, you were not expected to reply.

But this aspect of Chris was one which I noticed only vaguely at the time. What won me was that he would talk to me and wisecrack as though I were his same age. He was—although I didn't know the phrase then—a respecter of persons.

On the rare evenings when my parents went out, Chris would come over to mind me. These were the best times, for often when he was supposed to be doing his homework, he would make fantastic objects for my amusement, or his own— pipecleaners twisted into the shape of wildly prancing midget men, or an old set of Christmas-tree lights fixed onto a puppet theatre with a red velvet curtain that really pulled. He had skill in making miniature things of all kinds. Once for my birthday he gave me a leather saddle no bigger than a matchbox, which he had sewn himself, complete in every detail, stirrups and horn, with the criss-cross lines that were the brand name of his ranch, he said, explaining it was a reference to his own name.

"Can I go to Shallow Creek sometime?" I asked one evening.

"Sure. Some summer holidays, maybe. I've got a sister about your age. The others are all grown up."

I did not want to hear. His sisters—for Chris was the only boy—did not exist for me, not even as photographs, because I did not want them to exist. I wanted him to belong only here. Shallow Creek existed, though, no longer filled with ice mountains in my mind but as some beckoning country beyond all ordinary considerations.

"Tell me what it's like there, Chris."

"My gosh, Vanessa, I've told you before, about a thousand times."

"You never told me what your house is like."

"Didn't I? Oh well—it's made out of trees grown right there beside the lake."

"Made out of trees? Gee. Really?"

I could see it. The trees were still growing, and the leaves were firmly and greenly on them. The branches had been coaxed into formations of towers and high-up nests where you could look out and see for a hundred miles or more.

"That lake, you know," Chris said. "It's more like an inland sea. It goes on for ever and ever amen, that's how it looks. And you know what? Millions of years ago, before there were any human beings at all, that lake was full of water monsters. All different kinds of dinosaurs. Then they all died off. Nobody knows for sure why. Imagine them—all those huge creatures, with necks like snakes, and some of them had hackles on their heads, like a rooster's comb only very tough, like hard leather. Some guys from Winnipeg came up a few years back, there, and dug up dinosaur bones, and found footprints in the rocks."

"Footprints in the *rocks*?"

"The rocks were mud, see, when the dinosaurs went trampling through, but after trillions of years the mud turned into stone and there were these mighty footprints with the claws still showing. Amazing, eh?"

I could only nod, fascinated and horrified. Imagine going swimming in those waters. What if one of the creatures had lived on?

"Tell me about the horses," I said.

"Oh, them. Well, we've got these two riding horses. Duchess and Firefly. I raised them, and you should see them. Really sleek, know what I mean? I bet I could make racers out of them."

He missed the horses, I thought with selfish satisfaction, more than he missed his family. I could visualize the pair, one sorrel and one black, swifting through all the meadows of summer.

"When can I go, Chris?"

"Well, we'll have to see. After I get through high school, I won't be at Shallow Creek much."

"Why not?"

"Because," Chris said, "what I am going to be is an engineer, civil engineer. You ever seen a really big bridge, Vanessa? Well, I haven't either, but I've seen pictures. You take the Golden Gate Bridge in San Francisco, now. Terrifically high—all those thin ribs of steel, joined together to go across this very wide stretch of water. It doesn't seem possible, but it's there. That's what engineers do. Imagine doing something like that, eh?"

I could not imagine it. It was beyond me.

"Where will you go?" I asked. I did not want to think of his going anywhere.

"Winnipeg, to college," he said with assurance.

The Depression did not get better, as everyone had been saying it would. It got worse, and so did the drought. That part of the prairies where we lived was never dustbowl country. The farms around Manawaka never had a total crop failure, and afterwards, when the drought was over, people used to remark on this fact proudly, as though it had been due to some virtue or special status, like the Children of Israel being afflicted by Jehovah but never in real danger of annihilation. But although Manawaka never knew the worst, what it knew was bad enough. Or so I learned later. At the time I saw none of it. For me, the Depression and drought were external and abstract, malevolent gods whose names I secretly learned although they were concealed from me, and whose evil I sensed only superstitiously, knowing they threatened us but not how or why. What I really saw was only what went on in our family.

"He's done quite well all through, despite everything," my mother said. She sighed, and I knew she was talking about Chris.

"I know," my father said. "We've been over all this before, Beth. But quite good just isn't good enough. Even supposing he managed to get a scholarship, which isn't likely, it's only tuition and books. What about room and board? Who's going to pay for that? Your father?"

"I see I shouldn't have brought up the subject at all," my mother said in an aloof voice.

"I'm sorry," my father said impatiently. "But you know, yourself, he's the only one who might possibly—"

"I can't bring myself to ask Father about it, Ewen, I simply cannot do it."

"There wouldn't be much point in asking," my father said, "when the answer is a foregone conclusion. He feels he's done his share, and actually, you know, Beth, he has, too. Three years, after all. He may not have done it gracefully, but he's done it."

We were sitting in the living room, and it was evening. My father was slouched in the grey armchair that was always his. My mother was slenderly straight-backed in the blue chair in which nobody else ever sat. I was sitting on the footstool, beige needlepoint with mathematical roses, to which I had staked my own claim. This seating arrangement was obscurely satisfactory to me, perhaps because predictable, like the three bears. I was pretending to be colouring into a scribbler on my knee, and from time to time my lethargic purple crayon added a feather to an outlandish swan. To speak would be to invite dismissal. But their words forced questions in my head.

"Chris isn't going away, is he?"

My mother swooped, shocked at her own neglect.

"My heavens—are you still up, Vanessa? What am I thinking of?"

"Where is Chris going?"

"We're not sure yet," my mother evaded, chivvying me up the stairs. "We'll see."

He would not go, I thought. Something would happen, miraculously, to prevent him. He would remain, with his long loping walk and his half-slanted grey eyes and his talk that never excluded me. He would stay right here. And soon, because I desperately wanted to, and because every day mercifully made me older, quite soon I would be able to reply with such a lightning burst of knowingness that it would astound him, when he spoke of the space or was it some black sky that never ended anywhere beyond this earth. Then I would not be innerly belittled for being unable to figure out what he would best like to hear. At that good and imagined time, I would not any longer be limited. I would not any longer be young.

I WAS NINE when Chris left Manawaka. The day before he was due to go, I knocked on the door of his room in the Brick House.

"Come in," Chris said. "I'm packing. Do you know how to fold socks, Vanessa?"

"Sure. Of course."

"Well, get folding on that bunch there, then."

I had come to say goodbye, but I did not want to say it yet. I got to work on the socks. I did not intend to speak about the matter of college, but the knowledge that I must not speak about it made me uneasy. I was afraid I would blurt out a reference to it in my anxiety not to. My mother had said, "He's taken it amazingly well—he doesn't even mention it, so we mustn't either."

"Tomorrow night you'll be in Shallow Creek," I ventured.

"Yeh." He did not look up. He went on stuffing clothes and books into his suitcase.

"I bet you'll be glad to see the horses, eh?" I wanted him to say he didn't care about the horses any more and that he would rather stay here.

"It'll be good to see them again," Chris said. "Mind handing over those socks now, Vanessa? I think I can just squash them in at the side here. Thanks. Hey, look at that, will you? Everything's in. Am I an expert packer or am I an expert packer?"

I sat on his suitcase for him so it would close, and then he tied a piece of rope around it because the lock wouldn't lock.

"Ever thought what it would be like to be a traveller, Vanessa?" he asked.

I thought of Richard Halliburton, taking an elephant over the Alps and swimming illicitly in the Taj Mahal lily pool by moonlight.

"It would be keen," I said, because this was the word Chris used to describe the best possible. "That's what I'm going to do someday."

He did not say, as for a moment I feared he might, that girls could not be travellers.

"Why not?" he said. "Sure you will, if you really want to. I got this theory, see, that anybody can do anything at all, anything, if they really set their minds to it. But you have to have this total concentration. You have to focus on it with your whole mental powers, and not let it slip away by forgetting to hold it in your mind. If you hold it in your mind, like, then it's real, see? You take most people, now. They can't concentrate worth a darn."

"Do you think I can?" I enquired eagerly, believing that this was what he was talking about.

"What?" he said. "Oh—sure. Sure I think you can. Naturally."

Chris did not write after he left Manawaka. About a month later we had a letter from his mother. He was not at Shallow Creek. He had not gone back. He had got off the northbound train at the first stop after Manawaka, cashed in his ticket, and thumbed a lift with a truck to Winnipeg. He had written to his mother from there, but had given no address. She had not heard from him since. My mother read Aunt Tess's letter aloud to my father. She was too upset to care whether I was listening or not.

"I can't think what possessed him, Ewen. He never seemed irresponsible. What if something should happen to him? What if he's broke? What do you think we should do?"

"What can we do? He's nearly eighteen. What he does is his business. Simmer down, Beth, and let's decide what we're going to tell your father."

"Oh Lord," my mother said. "There's that to consider, of course."

I went out without either of them noticing. I walked to the hill at the edge of the town, and down into the valley where the scrub oak and poplar grew almost to the banks of the Wachakwa River. I found the oak where we had gone last autumn, in a gang, to smoke cigarettes made of dried leaves and pieces of newspaper. I climbed to the lowest branch and stayed there for a while.

I was not consciously thinking about Chris. I was not thinking of anything. But when at last I cried, I felt relieved afterwards and could go home again.

Chris departed from my mind, after that, with a quickness that was due to the other things that happened. My Aunt Edna, who was a secretary in Winnipeg, returned to Manawaka to live because the insurance company cut down on staff and she could not find another job. I was intensely excited and jubilant about her return, and could not see why my mother seemed the opposite, even though she was as fond of Aunt Edna as I was. Then my brother Roderick was born, and that same year Grandmother Connor died. The strangeness, the unbelievability, of both these events took up all of me.

When I was eleven, almost two years after Chris had left, he came back without warning. I came home from school and found him sitting in our living room. I could not accept that I had nearly forgotten him until this instant. Now that he was present, and real again, I felt I had betrayed him by not thinking of him more.

He was wearing a navy-blue serge suit. I was old enough now to notice that it was a cheap one and had been worn a considerable time. Otherwise, he looked the same, the same smile, the same knife-boned face with no flesh to speak of, the same unresting eyes.

"How come you're here?" I cried. "Where have you been, Chris?"

"I'm a traveller," he said. "Remember?"

He was a traveller all right. One meaning of the word *traveller* in our part of the world, was a travelling salesman. Chris was selling vacuum cleaners. That evening he brought out his line and showed us. He went through his spiel for our benefit, so we could hear how it sounded.

"Now look, Beth," he said, turning the appliance on and speaking loudly above its moaning roar, "see how it brightens up this old rug of yours? Keen, eh?"

"Wonderful," my mother laughed. "Only we can't afford one."

"Oh well—" Chris said quickly, "I'm not trying to sell one to you. I'm only showing you. Listen, I've only been in this job a month, but I figure this is really a going thing. I mean, it's obvious, isn't it? You take all those old wire carpet-beaters of yours, Beth. You could kill yourself over them and your carpet isn't going to look one-tenth as good as it does with this."

"Look, I don't want to seem—" my father put in, "but, hell, they're not exactly a new invention, and we're not the only ones who can't afford—"

"This is a pretty big outfit, you know?" Chris insisted. "Listen, I don't plan to stay, Ewen. But a guy could work at it for a year or so, and save—right? Lots of guys work their way through university like that."

I needed to say something really penetrating, something that would show him I knew the passionate truth of his conviction.

"I bet—" I said, "I bet you'll sell a thousand, Chris."

Two years ago, this statement would have seemed self-evident, unquestionable. Yet now, when I had spoken, I knew that I did not believe it.

The next time Chris visited Manawaka, he was selling magazines. He had the statistics worked out. If every sixth person in town would get a subscription to *Country Guide,* he could make a hundred dollars in a month. We didn't learn how he got on. He didn't stay in Manawaka a full month. When he turned up again, it was winter. Aunt Edna phoned.

"Nessa? Listen, kiddo, tell your mother she's to come down if it's humanly possible. Chris is here, and Father's having fits."

So in five minutes we were scurrying through the snow, my mother and I, with our overshoes not even properly done up and our feet getting wet. We need not have worried. By the time we reached the Brick House, Grandfather Connor had retired to the basement, where he sat in the rocking chair beside the furnace, making occasional black pronouncements like a subterranean oracle. These loud utterances made my mother and aunt wince, but Chris didn't seem to notice any more than he ever had. He was engrossed in telling us about the mechanism he was holding. It had a cranker handle like an old-fashioned sewing machine.

"You attach the ball of wool here, see? Then you set this little switch here, and adjust this lever, and you're away to the races. Neat, eh?"

It was a knitting machine. Chris showed us the finished products. The men's socks he had made were coarse wool, one pair in grey heather and another in maroon. I was impressed.

"Gee—can I do it, Chris?"

"Sure. Look, you just grab hold of the handle right here."

"Where did you get it?" my mother asked.

"I've rented it. The way I figure it, Beth, I can sell these things at about half the price you'd pay in a store, and they're better quality."

"Who are you going to sell them to?" Aunt Edna enquired.

"You take all these guys who do outside work—they need heavy socks all year round, not just in winter. I think this thing could be quite a gold mine."

"Before I forget," my mother said, "how's your mother and the family keeping?"

"They're okay," Chris said in a restrained voice. "They're not short of hands, if that's what you mean, Beth. My sisters have their husbands there."

Then he grinned, casting away the previous moment, and dug into his suitcase.

"Hey, I haven't shown you—these are for you, Vanessa, and this pair is for Roddie."

My socks were cherry-coloured. The very small ones for my brother were turquoise.

Chris only stayed until after dinner, and then he went away again.

AFTER MY FATHER DIED, the whole order of life was torn. Nothing was known or predictable any longer. For months I lived almost entirely within myself, so when my mother told me one day that Chris couldn't find any work at all because there were no jobs and so he had gone back to Shallow Creek to stay, it made scarcely any impression on me. But that summer, my mother decided I ought to go away for a holiday. She hoped it might take my mind off my father's death. What, if anything, was going to take her mind off his death, she did not say.

"Would you like to go to Shallow Creek for a week or so?" she asked me. "I could write to Chris's mother."

Then I remembered, all in a torrent, the way I had imagined it once, when he used to tell me about it—the house fashioned of living trees, the lake like a sea where monsters had dwelt, the grass that shone like green wavering light while the horses flew in the splendour of their pride.

"Yes," I said. "Write to her."

The railway did not go through Shallow Creek, but Chris met me at Challoner's Crossing. He looked different, not only thinner, but—what was it? Then I saw that it was the fact that his face and neck were tanned red-brown, and he was wearing denims, farm pants, and a blue plaid shirt open at the neck. I liked him like this. Perhaps the change was not so much in him as in myself, now that I was thirteen. He looked masculine in a way I had not been aware of, before.

"C'mon, kid," he said. "The limousine's over here."

It was a wagon and two horses, which was what I had expected, but the nature of each was not what I had expected. The wagon was a long and clumsy one, made of heavy planking, and the horses were both plough horses, thick in the legs, and badly matched as a team. The mare was short and stout, matronly. The gelding was very tall and gaunt, and he limped.

"Allow me to introduce you," Chris said. "Floss—Trooper—this is Vanessa."

He did not mention the other horses, Duchess and Firefly, and neither did I, not all the fortnight I was there. I guess I had known for some years now, without realizing it, that the pair had only ever existed in some other dimension.

Shallow Creek wasn't a town. It was merely a name on a map. There was a grade school a few miles away, but that was all. They had to go to Challoner's Crossing for their groceries. We reached the farm, and Chris steered me through the crowd of aimless cows and wolfish dogs in the yard, while I flinched with panic.

It was perfectly true that the house was made out of trees. It was a fair-sized but elderly shack, made out of poplar poles and chinked with mud. There was an upstairs, which was not so usual around here, with three bedrooms, one of which I was to share with Chris's sister, Jeannie, who was slightly younger than I, a pallid-eyed girl who was either too shy to talk or who had nothing to say. I never discovered which, because I was so reticent with her myself, wanting to push her away, not to recognize her, and at the same time experiencing a shocked remorse at my own unacceptable feelings.

Aunt Tess, Chris's mother, was severe in manner and yet wanting to be kind, worrying over it, making tentative overtures which were either ignored or repelled by her older daughters and their monosyllabic husbands. Youngsters swam in and out of the house like shoals of nameless fishes. I could not see how so many people could live here, under the one roof, but then I learned they didn't. The married daughters had their own dwelling places, nearby, but some kind of communal life was maintained. They wrangled endlessly but they never left one another alone, not even for a day.

Chris took no part at all, none. When he spoke, it was usually to the children, and they would often follow him around the yard or to the barn, not pestering but just trailing along in clusters of three or four. He never told them to go away. I liked him for this, but it bothered me, too. I wished he would return his sisters' bickering for once, or tell them to clear out, or even yell at one of the kids. But he never did. He closed himself off from squabbling voices just as he used to do with Grandfather Connor's spearing words.

The house had no screens on the doors or windows, and at meal times the flies were so numerous you could hardly see the food for the iridescent-winged blue-black bodies squirming all over it. Nobody noticed my squeamishness except Chris, and he was the only one from whom I really wanted to conceal it.

"Fan with your hand," he murmured.

"It's okay," I said quickly.

For the first time in all the years we had known each other, we could not look the other in the eye. Around the table, the children stabbed and snivelled, until Chris's older sister, driven frantic, shrieked, *Shut up shut up shut up*. Chris began asking me about Manawaka then, as though nothing were going on around him.

They were due to begin haying, and Chris announced that he was going to camp out in the bluff near the hayfields. To save himself the long drive in the wagon each morning, he explained, but I felt this wasn't the real reason.

"Can I go, too?" I begged. I could not bear the thought of living in the house with all the others who were not known to me, and Chris not here.

"Well, I don't know—"

"Please. Please, Chris. I won't be any trouble. I promise."

Finally he agreed. We drove out in the big hayrack, its slatted sides rattling, its old wheels jolting metallically. The road was narrow and dirt, and around it the low bushes grew, wild rose and blueberry and wolf willow with silver leaves. Sometimes we would come to a bluff of pale-leaved poplar trees, and once a red-winged blackbird flew up out of the branches and into the hot dusty blue of the sky.

Then we were there. The hayfields lay beside the lake. It was my first view of the water which had spawned saurian giants so long ago. Chris drove the hayrack through the fields of high coarse grass and on down almost to the lake's edge, where there was no shore but only the green rushes like floating meadows in which the open lake stretched, deep, green-grey, out and out, beyond sight.

No human word could be applied. The lake was not lonely or untamed. These words relate to people, and there was nothing of people here. There was no feeling about the place. It existed in some world in which man was not yet born. I looked at the grey reaches of it and felt threatened. It was like the view of God which I had held since my father's death. Distant, indestructible, totally indifferent.

Chris had jumped down off the hayrack.

"We're not going to camp *here*, are we?" I asked and pleaded.

"No. I just want to let the horses drink. We'll camp up there in the bluff."

I looked. "It's still pretty close to the lake, isn't it?"

"Don't worry," Chris said, laughing. "You won't get your feet wet."

"I didn't mean that."

Chris looked at me.

"I know you didn't," he said. "But let's learn to be a little tougher, and not let on, eh? It's necessary."

Chris worked through the hours of sun, while I lay on the half-formed stack of hay and looked up at the sky. The blue air trembled and spun with the heat haze, and the hay on which I was lying held the scents of grass and dust and wild mint.

In the evening, Chris took the horses to the lake again, and then he drove the hayrack to the edge of the bluff and we spread out our blankets underneath it. He made a fire and we had coffee and a tin of stew, and then we went to bed. We did not wash, and we slept in our clothes. It was only when I was curled up uncomfortably with the itching blanket around me that I felt a sense of unfamiliarity at being here, with Chris only three feet away, a self-consciousness I would not have felt even the year before. I do not think he felt this sexual strangeness. If he wanted me not to be a child—and he did—it was not with the wish that I would be a woman. It was something else.

"Are you asleep, Vanessa?" he asked.

"No. I think I'm lying on a tree root."

"Well, shift yourself, then," he said. "Listen, kid, I never said anything before, because I didn't really know what to say, but—you know how I felt about your dad dying, and that, don't you?"

"Yes," I said chokingly. "It's okay. I know."

"I used to talk with Ewen sometimes. He didn't see what I was driving at, mostly, but he'd always listen, you know? You don't find many guys like that."

We were both silent for a while.

"Look," Chris said finally. "Ever noticed how much brighter the stars are when you're completely away from any houses? Even the lamps up at the farm, there, make enough of a glow to keep you from seeing properly like you can out here. What do they make you think about, Vanessa?"

"Well—"

"I guess most people don't give them much thought at all, except maybe to say—*very pretty*—or like that. But the point is, they aren't like that. The stars and planets, in themselves, are just not like that, not *pretty*, for heaven's sake. They're gigantic—some of them burning—imagine those worlds tearing through space and made of pure fire. Or the ones that are absolutely dead—just rock or ice and no warmth in them. There must be some, though, that have living creatures. You wonder what *they* could look like, and what they feel. We won't ever get to know. But somebody will know, someday. I really believe that. Do you ever think about this kind of thing at all?"

He was twenty-one. The distance between us was still too great. For years I had wanted to be older so I might talk with him, but now I felt unready.

"Sometimes," I said, hesitantly, making it sound like *Never*.

"People usually say there must be a God," Chris went on, "because otherwise how did the universe get here? But that's ridiculous. If the stars and planet go on to infinity, they could have existed forever, for no reason at all. Maybe they weren't ever created. Look—what's the alternative? To believe in a God who is brutal. What else could He be? You've only got to look anywhere around you. It would be an insult to

Him to believe in a God like that. Most people don't like talking about this kind of thing—it embarrasses them, you know? Or else they're not interested. I don't mind. I can always think about things myself. You don't actually need anyone to talk to. But about God, though—if there's a war, like it looks there will be, would people claim that was planned? What kind of a God would pull a trick like that? And yet, you know, plenty of guys would think it was a godsend, and who's to say they're wrong? It would be a job, and you'd get around and see places."

He paused, as though waiting for me to say something. When I did not, he resumed.

"Ewen told me about the last war, once. He hardly ever talked about it, but this once he told me about seeing the horses in the mud, actually going under, you know? And the way their eyes looked when they realised they weren't going to get out. Ever seen horses' eyes when they're afraid, I mean really berserk with fear, like in a bush-fire? Ewen said a guy tended to concentrate on the horses because he didn't dare think what was happening to the men. Including himself. Do you ever listen to the news at all, Vanessa?"

"I—"

I could only feel how foolish I must sound, still unable to reply as I would have wanted, comprehendingly. I felt I had failed myself utterly. I could not speak even the things I knew. As for the other things, the things I did not know, I resented Chris's facing me with them. I took refuge in pretending to be asleep, and after a while Chris stopped talking.

CHRIS LEFT SHALLOW CREEK some months after the war began, and joined the Army. After his basic training he was sent to England. We did not hear from him until about a year later, when a letter arrived for me.

"Vanessa—what's wrong?" my mother asked.

"Nothing."

"Don't fib," she said firmly. "What did Chris say in his letter, honey?"

"Oh—not much."

She gave me a curious look and then she went away. She would never have demanded to see the letter. I did not show it to her and she did not ask about it again.

Six months later my mother heard from Aunt Tess. Chris had been sent home from England and discharged from the Army because of a mental breakdown. He was now in the provincial mental hospital and they did not know how long he would have to remain there. He had been violent, before, but now he was not violent. He was, the doctors had told his mother, passive.

Violent. I could not associate the word with Chris, who had been so much the reverse. I could not bear to consider what anguish must have catapulted him into that even greater anguish. But the way he was now seemed almost worse. How might he be? Sitting quite still, wearing the hospital's grey dressing-gown, the animation gone from his face?

My mother cared about him a great deal, but her immediate thought was not for him.

"When I think of you, going up to Shallow Creek that time," she said, "and going out camping with him, and what might have happened—"

I, also, was thinking of what might have happened. But we were not thinking of the same thing. For the first time I recognized, at least a little, the dimensions of his need to talk that night. He must have understood perfectly well how impossible it would be, with a thirteen-year-old. But there was no one else. All his life's choices had grown narrower and narrower. He had been forced to return to the alien lake of home, and when finally he saw a means of getting away, it could only be into a turmoil which appalled him and which he dreaded even more than he knew. I had listened to his words, but I had not really heard them, not until now. It would not have made much difference to what happened, but I wished it were not too late to let him know.

Once when I was on holiday from college, my mother got me to help her clean out the attic. We sifted through boxes full of junk, old clothes, school-books, bric-a-brac that once had been treasures. In one of the boxes I found the miniature saddle that Chris had made for me a long time ago.

"Have you heard anything recently?" I asked, ashamed that I had not asked sooner.

She glanced up at me. "Just the same. It's always the same. They don't think there will be much improvement."

Then she turned away.

"He always used to seem so—hopeful. Even when there was really nothing to be hopeful about. That's what I find so strange. He *seemed* hopeful, didn't you think?"

"Maybe it wasn't hope," I said.

"How do you mean?"

I wasn't certain myself. I was thinking of all the schemes he'd had, the ones that couldn't possibly have worked, the unreal solutions to which he'd clung because there were no others, the brave and useless strokes of fantasy against a depression that was both the world's and his own.

"I don't know," I said. "I just think things were always more difficult for him than he let on, that's all. Remember the letter?"

"Yes."

"Well—what it said was that they could force his body to march and even to kill, but what they didn't know was that he'd fooled them. He didn't live inside it any more."

"Oh Vanessa—" my mother said. "You must have suspected right then."

"Yes, but—"

I could not go on, could not say that the letter seemed only the final heartbreaking extension of that way he'd always had of distancing himself from the absolute unbearability of battle.

I picked up the tiny saddle and turned it over in my hand. "Look. His brand, the name of his ranch. The Criss-Cross."

"What ranch?" my mother said, bewildered.

"The one where he kept his racing horses. Duchess and Firefly."

Some words came into my head, a single line from a poem I had once heard. I knew it referred to a lover who did not want the morning to come, but to me it had another meaning, a different relevance.

Slowly, slowly, horses of the night—

The night must move like this for him, slowly, all through the days and nights. I could not know whether the land he journeyed through was inhabited by terrors, the old monster-kings of the lake, or whether he had discovered at last a way for himself to make the necessary dream perpetual.

I put the saddle away once more, gently and ruthlessly, back into the cardboard box.

Meneseteung

ALICE MUNRO

I

Columbine, bloodroot,
And wild bergamot,
Gathering armfuls,
Giddily we go.

Offerings the book is called. Gold lettering on a dull-blue cover. The author's full name underneath: Almeda Joynt Roth. The local paper, the *Vidette*, referred to her as "our poetess." There seems to be a mixture of respect and contempt, both for her calling and for her sex—or for their predictable conjuncture. In the front of the book is a photograph, with the photographer's name in one corner, and the date: 1865. The book was published later, in 1873.

The poetess has a long face; a rather long nose; full, sombre dark eyes, which seem ready to roll down her cheeks like giant tears; a lot of dark hair gathered around her face in droopy rolls and curtains. A streak of grey hair plain to see, although she is, in this picture, only twenty-five. Not a pretty girl but the sort of woman who may age well, who probably won't get fat. She wears a tucked and braid-trimmed dark dress or jacket, with a lacy, floppy arrangement of white material—frills or a bow— filling the deep V at the neck. She also wears a hat, which might be made of velvet, in a dark colour to match the dress. It's the untrimmed, shapeless hat, something like a soft beret, that makes me see artistic intentions, or at least a shy and stubborn eccentricity, in this young woman, whose long neck and forward-inclining head indicate as well that she is tall and slender and somewhat awkward. From the waist up, she looks like a young nobleman of another century. But perhaps it was the fashion.

"In 1854," she writes in the preface to her book, "my father brought us—my mother, my sister Catherine, my brother William, and me—to the wilds of Canada West (as it then was). My father was a harness-maker by trade, but a cultivated man who could quote by heart from the Bible, Shakespeare, and the writings of Edmund Burke. He prospered in this newly opened land and was able to set up a harness and leather-goods store, and after a year to build the comfortable house in which I live (alone) today. I was fourteen years old, the eldest of the children, when we came into this country from Kingston, a town whose handsome streets I have not seen again but often remember. My sister was eleven and my brother nine. The third summer that we lived here, my brother and sister were taken ill of a prevalent fever and died within a few days of each other. My dear mother did not regain her spirits after this blow to our family. Her health declined, and after another three years she died. I then became housekeeper to my father and was happy to make his home for twelve years, until he died suddenly one morning at his shop.

"From my earliest years I have delighted in verse and I have occupied myself— and sometimes allayed my griefs, which have been no more, I know, than any sojourner on earth must encounter—with many floundering efforts at its composition. My fingers, indeed, were always too clumsy for crochetwork, and those dazzling productions of embroidery which one sees often today—the overflowing fruit and flower baskets, the little Dutch boys, the bonneted maidens with their watering cans—have likewise proved to be beyond my skill. So I offer instead, as the product of my leisure hours, these rude posies, these ballads, couplets, reflections."

Titles of some of the poems: "Children at Their Games," "The Gypsy Fair," "A Visit to My Family," "Angels in the Snow," "Champlain at the Mouth of the Meneseteung," "The Passing of the Old Forest," and "A Garden Medley." There are other, shorter poems, about birds and wildflowers and snowstorms. There is some comically intentioned doggerel about what people are thinking about as they listen to the sermon in church.

"Children at Their Games": The writer, a child, is playing with her brother and sister—one of those games in which children on different sides try to entice and catch each other. She plays on in the deepening twilight, until she realizes that she is alone, and much older. Still she hears the (ghostly) voices of her brother and sister calling. *Come over, come over, let Meda come over.* (Perhaps Almeda was called Meda in the family, or perhaps she shortened her name to fit the poem.)

"The Gypsy Fair": The Gypsies have an encampment near the town, a "fair," where they sell cloth and trinkets, and the writer as a child is afraid that she may be stolen by them, taken away from her family. Instead, her family has been taken away from her, stolen by Gypsies she can't locate or bargain with.

"A Visit to My Family": A visit to the cemetery, a one-sided conversation.

"Angels in the Snow": The writer once taught her brother and sister to make "angels" by lying down in the snow and moving their arms to create wing shapes. Her brother always jumped up carelessly, leaving an angel with a crippled wing. Will this be made perfect in Heaven, or will he be flying with his own makeshift, in circles?

"Champlain at the Mouth of the Meneseteung": This poem celebrates the popular, untrue belief that the explorer sailed down the eastern shore of Lake Huron and landed at the mouth of the major river.

"The Passing of the Old Forest": A list of all the trees—their names, appearance, and uses—that were cut down in the original forest, with a general description of the bears, wolves, eagles, deer, waterfowl.

"A Garden Medley": Perhaps planned as a companion to the forest poem. Catalogue of plants brought from European countries, with bits of history and legend attached, and final Canadianness resulting from this mixture.

The poems are written in quatrains or couplets. There are a couple of attempts at sonnets, but mostly the rhyme scheme is simple—*a b a b* or *a b c b*. The rhyme used is what was once called "masculine" ("shore"/"before"), though once in a while it is "feminine" ("quiver"/"river"). Are those terms familiar anymore? No poem is unrhymed.

II

White roses cold as snow
Bloom where those "angels" lie.
Do they but rest below
Or, in God's wonder, fly?

In 1879, Almeda Roth was still living in the house at the corner of Pearl and Dufferin streets, the house her father had built for his family. The house is there today; the manager of the liquor store lives in it. It's covered with aluminum siding; a closed-in porch has replaced the veranda. The woodshed, the fence, the gates, the privy, the barn—all these are gone. A photograph taken in the eighteen-eighties shows them all in place. The house and fence look a little shabby, in need of paint, but perhaps that is just because of the bleached-out look of the brownish photograph. The lace-curtained windows look like white eyes. No big shade tree is in sight, and, in fact, the tall elms that overshadowed the town until the nineteen-fifties, as well as the maples that shade it now, are skinny young trees with rough fences around them to protect them from the cows. Without the shelter of those trees, there is a great exposure—back yards, clotheslines, woodpiles, patchy sheds and barns and privies—all bare, exposed, provisional-looking. Few houses would have anything like a lawn, just a patch of plantains and anthills and raked dirt. Perhaps petunias growing on top of a stump, in a round box. Only the main street is gravelled; the other streets are dirt roads, muddy or dusty according to season. Yards must be fenced to keep animals out. Cows are tethered in vacant lots or pastured in back yards, but sometimes they get loose. Pigs get loose, too, and dogs roam free or nap in a lordly way on the boardwalks. The town has taken root, it's not going to vanish, yet it still has some of the look of an encampment. And, like an encampment, it's busy all the time—full of people, who, within the town, usually walk wherever they're going; full of animals, which leave horse buns, cow pats, dog turds that ladies have to hitch up their skirts for; full of the noise of building and of drivers shouting at their horses and of the trains that come in several times a day.

I read about that life in the *Vidette*.

The population is younger than it is now, than it will ever be again. People past fifty usually don't come to a raw, new place. There are quite a few people in the cemetery already, but most of them died young, in accidents or childbirth or epidemics. It's youth that's in evidence in town. Children—boys—rove through the streets in gangs. School is compulsory for only four months a year, and there are lots of occasional jobs that even a child of eight or nine can do—pulling flax, holding horses, delivering groceries, sweeping the boardwalk in front of stores. A good deal of time they spend looking for adventures. One day they follow an old woman, a drunk nicknamed Queen Aggie. They get her into a wheelbarrow and trundle her all over town, then dump her into a ditch to sober her up. They also spend a lot of time around the railway station. They jump on shunting cars and dart between them and dare each other to take chances, which once in a while result in their getting maimed or killed. And they keep an eye out for any strangers coming into town. They follow them, offer to carry their bags, and direct them (for a five-cent piece) to a hotel. Strangers who don't look so prosperous are taunted and tormented. Speculation surrounds all of them—it's like a cloud of flies. Are they coming to town to start up a new business, to persuade people to invest in some scheme, to sell cures or gimmicks, to preach on the street corners? All these things are possible any day of the week. Be on your guard, the *Vidette* tells people. These are times of opportunity and danger. Tramps, confidence men, hucksters, shysters, plain thieves are travelling the roads, and particularly the railroads. Thefts are announced: money invested and never seen again, a pair of trousers taken from the clothesline, wood from the wood-pile, eggs from the henhouse. Such incidents increase in the hot weather.

Hot weather brings accidents, too. More horses run wild then, upsetting buggies. Hands caught in the wringer while doing the washing, a man lopped in two at the sawmill, a leaping boy killed in a fall of lumber at the lumberyard. Nobody sleeps well. Babies wither with summer complaint, and fat people can't catch their breath. Bodies must be buried in a hurry. One day a man goes through the streets ringing a cowbell and calling, "Repent! Repent!" It's not a stranger this time, it's a young man who works at the butcher shop. Take him home, wrap him in cold wet cloths, give him some nerve medicine, keep him in bed, pray for his wits. If he doesn't recover, he must go to the asylum.

Almeda Roth's house faces on Dufferin Street, which is a street of considerable respectability. On this street, merchants, a mill owner, an operator of salt wells have their houses. But Pearl Street, which her back windows overlook and her back gate opens onto, is another story. Workmen's houses are adjacent to hers. Small but decent row houses—that is all right. Things deteriorate toward the end of the block, and the next, last one becomes dismal. Nobody but the poorest people, the unre-spectable and undeserving poor, would live there at the edge of a boghole (drained since then), called the Pearl Street Swamp. Bushy and luxuriant weeds grow there, makeshift shacks have been put up, there are piles of refuse and debris and crowds of runty children, slops are flung from doorways. The town tries to compel these people to build privies, but they would just as soon go in the bushes. If a gang of boys goes down there in search of adventure, it's likely they'll get more than they bargained for. It is said that even the town constable won't go down Pearl Street on a Saturday night. Almeda Roth has never walked past the row housing. In one of those houses lives the young girl Annie, who helps her with her housecleaning. That young girl herself, being a decent girl, has never walked down to the last block or the swamp. No decent woman ever would.

But that same swamp, lying to the east of Almeda Roth's house, presents a fine sight at dawn. Almeda sleeps at the back of the house. She keeps to the same bedroom she once shared with her sister Catherine—she would not think of moving to the large front bedroom, where her mother used to lie in bed all day, and which was later the solitary domain of her father. From her window she can see the sun rising, the swamp mist filling with light, the bulky, nearest trees floating against that mist and the trees behind turning transparent. Swamp oaks, soft maples, tamarack, bitternut.

III

Here where the river meets the inland sea,
Spreading her blue skirts from the solemn wood,
I think of birds and beasts and vanished men,
Whose pointed dwellings on these pale sands stood.

One of the strangers who arrived at the railway station a few years ago was Jarvis
Poulter, who now occupies the next house to Almeda Roth's—separated from hers
by a vacant lot, which he has bought, on Dufferin Street. The house is plainer than
the Roth house and has no fruit trees or flowers planted around it. It is understood
that this is a natural result of Jarvis Poulter's being a widower and living alone. A man
may keep his house decent, but he will never—if he is a proper man—do much to
decorate it. Marriage forces him to live with more ornament as well as sentiment, and
it protects him, also, from the extremities of his own nature—from a frigid parsi-
mony or a luxuriant sloth, from squalor, and from excessive sleeping or reading,
drinking, smoking, or freethinking.

In the interests of economy, it is believed, a certain estimable gentleman of our town
persists in fetching water from the public tap and supplementing his fuel supply by picking
up the loose coal along the railway track. Does he think to repay the town or the railway
company with a supply of free salt?

This is the *Vidette,* full of shy jokes, innuendo, plain accusation that no newspaper would get away with today. It's Jarvis Poulter they're talking about—though in
other passages he is spoken of with great respect, as a civil magistrate, an employer,
a churchman. He is close, that's all. An eccentric, to a degree. All of which may be a
result of his single condition, his widower's life. Even carrying his water from the
town tap and filling his coal pail along the railway track. This is a decent citizen,
prosperous: a tall—slightly paunchy?—man in a dark suit with polished boots. A
beard? Black hair streaked with grey. A severe and self-possessed air, and a large pale
wart among the bushy hairs of one eyebrow? People talk about a young, pretty,
beloved wife, dead in childbirth or some horrible accident, like a house fire or a
railway disaster. There is no ground for this, but it adds interest. All he has told them
is that his wife is dead.

He came to this part of the country looking for oil. The first oil well in the world
was sunk in Lambton County, south of here, in the eighteen-fifties. Drilling for oil,
Jarvis Poulter discovered salt. He set to work to make the most of that. When he
walks home from church with Almeda Roth, he tells her about his salt wells. They
are twelve hundred feet deep. Heated water is pumped down into them, and that

dissolves the salt. Then the brine is pumped to the surface. It is poured into great evaporator pans over slow, steady fires, so that the water is steamed off and the pure, excellent salt remains. A commodity for which the demand will never fail.

"The salt of the earth," Almeda says.

"Yes," he says, frowning. He may think this disrespectful. She did not intend it so. He speaks of competitors in other towns who are following his lead and trying to hog the market. Fortunately, their wells are not drilled so deep, or their evaporating is not done so efficiently. There is salt everywhere under this land, but it is not so easy to come by as some people think.

Does this not mean, Almeda says, that there was once a great sea?

Very likely, Jarvis Poulter says. Very likely. He goes on to tell her about other enterprises of his—a brickyard, a limekiln. And he explains to her how this operates, and where the good clay is found. He also owns two farms, whose woodlots supply the fuel for his operations.

Among the couples strolling home from church on a recent, sunny Sabbath morning we noted a certain salty gentleman and literary lady, not perhaps in their first youth but by no means blighted by the frosts of age. May we surmise?

This kind of thing pops up in the *Vidette* all the time.

May they surmise, and is this courting? Almeda Roth has a bit of money, which her father left her, and she has her house. She is not too old to have a couple of children. She is a good enough housekeeper, with the tendency toward fancy iced cakes and decorated tarts that is seen fairly often in old maids. (Honourable mention at the Fall Fair.) There is nothing wrong with her looks, and naturally she is in better shape than most married women of her age, not having been loaded down with work and children. But why was she passed over in her earlier, more marriageable years, in a place that needs women to be partnered and fruitful? She was a rather gloomy girl—that may have been the trouble. The deaths of her brother and sister, and then of her mother, who lost her reason, in fact, a year before she died, and lay in her bed talking nonsense—those weighed on her, so she was not lively company. And all that reading and poetry—it seemed more of a drawback, a barrier, an obsession, in the young girl than in the middle-aged woman, who needed something, after all, to fill her time. Anyway, it's five years since her book was published, so perhaps she has got over that. Perhaps it was the proud, bookish father encouraging her?

Everyone takes it for granted that Almeda Roth is thinking of Jarvis Poulter as a husband and would say yes if he asked her. And she is thinking of him. She doesn't want to get her hopes up too much, she doesn't want to make a fool of herself. She would like a signal. If he attended church on Sunday evenings, there would be a chance, during some months of the year, to walk home after dark. He would carry a lantern. (There is as yet no street lighting in town.) He would swing the lantern to light the way in front of the lady's feet and observe their narrow and delicate shape. He might catch her arm as they step off the boardwalk. But he does not go to church at night.

Nor does he call for her, and walk with her *to* church on Sunday mornings. That would be a declaration. He walks her home, past his gate as far as hers; he lifts his hat then and leaves her. She does not invite him to come in—a woman living alone could never do such a thing. As soon as a man and woman of almost any age are alone together within four walls, it is assumed that anything may happen. Spontaneous combustion, instant fornication, an attack of passion. Brute instinct, triumph of the senses. What possibilities men and women must see in each other to infer such dangers. Or, believing in the dangers, how often they must think about the possibilities.

When they walk side by side, she can smell his shaving soap, the barber's oil, his pipe tobacco, the wool and linen and leather smell of his manly clothes. The correct, orderly, heavy clothes are like those she used to brush and starch and iron for her father. She misses that job—her father's appreciation, his dark, kind authority. Jarvis Poulter's garments, his smell, his movements all cause the skin on the side of her body next to him to tingle hopefully, and a meek shiver raises the hairs on her arms. Is this to be taken as a sign of love? She thinks of him coming into her—*their*— bedroom in his long underwear and his hat. She knows this outfit is ridiculous, but in her mind he does not look so; he has the solemn effrontery of a figure in a dream. He comes into the room and lies down on the bed beside her, preparing to take her in his arms. Surely he removes his hat? She doesn't know, for at this point a fit of welcome and submission overtakes her, a buried gasp. He would be her husband.

One thing she has noticed about married women, and that is how many of them have to go about creating their husbands. They have to start ascribing preferences, opinions, dictatorial ways. Oh, yes, they say, my husband is very particular. He won't touch turnips. He won't eat fried meat. (Or he will only eat fried meat.) He likes me to wear blue (brown) all the time. He can't stand organ music. He hates to see a woman go out bareheaded. He would kill me if I took one puff of tobacco. This way, bewildered, sidelong-looking men are made over, made into husbands, heads of households. Almeda Roth cannot imagine herself doing that. She wants a man who doesn't have to be made, who is firm already and determined and mysterious to her. She does not look for companionship. Men—except for her father—seem to her deprived in some way, incurious. No doubt that is necessary so that they will do what they have to do. Would she herself, knowing that there was salt in the earth, discover how to get it out and sell it? Not likely. She would be thinking about the ancient sea. That kind of speculation is what Jarvis Poulter has, quite properly, no time for.

Instead of calling for her and walking her to church, Jarvis Poulter might make another, more venturesome declaration. He could hire a horse and take her for a drive out to the country. If he did this, she would be both glad and sorry. Glad to be beside him, driven by him, receiving this attention from him in front of the world. And sorry to have the countryside removed for her—filmed over, in a way, by his talk and preoccupations. The countryside that she has written about in her poems actually takes diligence and determination to see. Some things must be disregarded. Manure piles, of course, and boggy fields full of high, charred stumps, and great heaps of brush waiting for a good day for burning. The meandering creeks have been straightened, turned into ditches with high, muddy banks. Some of the crop fields and pasture fields are fenced with big, clumsy uprooted stumps; others are held in a crude stitchery of rail fences. The trees have all been cleared back to the woodlots. And the woodlots are all second growth. No trees along the roads or lanes or around the farmhouses, except a few that are newly planted, young and weedy-looking. Clusters of log barns—the grand barns that are to dominate the countryside for the next hundred years are just beginning to be built—and mean-looking log houses, and every four or five miles a ragged little settlement with a church and school and store and a blacksmith shop. A raw countryside just wrenched from the forest, but swarming with people. Every hundred acres is a farm, every farm has a family, most families have ten or twelve children. (This is the country that will send out wave after wave of settlers—it's already starting to send them—to northern Ontario and the West.) It's true that you can gather wildflowers in spring in the wood-lots, but you'd have to walk through herds of horned cows to get to them.

IV

The Gypsies have departed.
Their camping-ground is bare.
Oh, boldly would I bargain now
At the Gypsy Fair.

Almeda suffers a good deal from sleeplessness, and the doctor has given her bromides and nerve medicine. She takes the bromides, but the drops gave her dreams that were too vivid and disturbing, so she has put the bottle by for an emergency. She told the doctor her eyeballs felt dry, like hot glass, and her joints ached. Don't read so much, he said, don't study; get yourself good and tired out with housework, take exercise. He believes that her troubles would clear up if she got married. He believes this in spite of the fact that most of his nerve medicine is prescribed for married women.

So Almeda cleans house and helps clean the church, she lends a hand to friends who are wallpapering or getting ready for a wedding, she bakes one of her famous cakes for the Sunday-school picnic. On a hot Saturday in August, she decides to make some grape jelly. Little jars of grape jelly will make fine Christmas presents, or offerings to the sick. But she started late in the day and the jelly is not made by nightfall. In fact, the hot pulp has just been dumped into the cheesecloth bag to strain out the juice. Almeda drinks some tea and eats a slice of cake with butter (a childish indulgence of hers), and that's all she wants for supper. She washes her hair at the sink and sponges off her body to be clean for Sunday. She doesn't light a lamp. She lies down on the bed with the window wide open and a sheet just up to her waist, and she does feel wonderfully tired. She can even feel a little breeze.

When she wakes up, the night seems fiery hot and full of threats. She lies sweating on her bed, and she has the impression that the noises she hears are knives and saws and axes—all angry implements chopping and jabbing and boring within her head. But it isn't true. As she comes further awake, she recognizes the sounds that she has heard sometimes before—the fracas of a summer Saturday night on Pearl Street. Usually the noise centres on a fight. People are drunk, there is a lot of protest and encouragement concerning the fight, somebody will scream, "Murder!" Once, there was a murder. But it didn't happen in a fight. An old man was stabbed to death in his shack, perhaps for a few dollars he kept in the mattress.

She gets out of bed and goes to the window. The night sky is clear, with no moon and with bright stars. Pegasus hangs straight ahead, over the swamp. Her father taught her that constellation—automatically, she counts its stars. Now she can make out distinct voices, individual contributions to the row. Some people, like herself, have evidently been wakened from sleep. "Shut up!" they are yelling. "Shut up that caterwauling or I'm going to come down and tan the arse off yez!"

But nobody shuts up. It's as if there were a ball of fire rolling up Pearl Street, shooting off sparks—only the fire is noise; it's yells and laughter and shrieks and curses, and the sparks are voices that shoot off alone. Two voices gradually distinguish themselves—a rising and falling howling cry and a steady throbbing, low-pitched stream of abuse that contains all those words which Almeda associates with danger and depravity and foul smells and disgusting sights. Someone—the person crying out, "Kill me! Kill me now!"—is being beaten. A woman is being beaten. She keeps crying, "Kill me! Kill me!" and sometimes her mouth seems choked with blood. Yet there is something taunting and triumphant about her cry. There is something theatrical about it. And the people around are calling out, "Stop it! Stop that!" or "Kill her! Kill her!" in a frenzy, as if at the theatre or a sporting match or a prizefight. Yes, thinks Almeda, she has noticed that before—it is always partly a charade with these people; there is a clumsy sort of parody, an exaggeration, a missed connection. As if anything they did—even a murder—might be something they didn't quite believe but were powerless to stop.

Now there is the sound of something thrown—a chair, a plank?—and of a woodpile or part of a fence giving way. A lot of newly surprised cries, the sound of running, people getting out of the way, and the commotion has come much closer. Almeda can see a figure in a light dress, bent over and running. That will be the woman. She has got hold of something like a stick of wood or a shingle, and she turns and flings it at the darker figure running after her.

"Ah, go get her!" the voices cry. "Go baste her one!"

Many fall back now; just the two figures come on and grapple, and break loose again, and finally fall down against Almeda's fence. The sound they make becomes very confused—gagging, vomiting, grunting, pounding. Then a long, vibrating, choking sound of pain and self-abasement, self-abandonment, which could come from either or both of them.

Almeda has backed away from the window and sat down on the bed. Is that the sound of murder she has heard? What is to be done, what is she to do? She must light a lantern, she must go downstairs and light a lantern—she must go out into the yard, she must go downstairs. Into the yard. The lantern. She falls over on her bed and pulls the pillow to her face. In a minute. The stairs, the lantern. She sees herself already down there, in the back hall, drawing the bolt of the back door. She falls asleep.

She wakes, startled, in the early light. She thinks there is a big crow sitting on her windowsill, talking in a disapproving but unsurprised way about the events of the night before. "Wake up and move the wheelbarrow!" it says to her, scolding, and she understands that it means something else by "wheelbarrow"—something foul and sorrowful. Then she is awake and sees that there is no such bird. She gets up at once and looks out the window.

Down against her fence there is a pale lump pressed—a body.

She puts a wrapper over her nightdress and goes downstairs. The front rooms are still shadowy, the blinds down in the kitchen. Something goes *plop, plup,* in a leisurely, censorious way, reminding her of the conversation of the crow. It's just the grape juice, straining overnight. She pulls the bolt and goes out the back door. Spiders have draped their webs over the doorway in the night, and the hollyhocks are drooping, heavy with dew. By the fence, she parts the sticky hollyhocks and looks down and she can see.

A woman's body heaped up there, turned on her side with her face squashed down into the earth. Almeda can't see her face. But there is a bare breast let loose, brown nipple pulled long like a cow's teat, and a bare haunch and leg, the haunch showing a bruise as big as a sunflower. The unbruised skin is greyish, like a plucked, raw drumstick. Some kind of nightgown or all-purpose dress she has on. Smelling of vomit. Urine, drink, vomit.

Barefoot, in her nightgown and flimsy wrapper, Almeda runs away. She runs around the side of her house between the apple trees and the veranda; she opens the front gate and flees down Dufferin Street to Jarvis Poulter's house, which is the nearest to hers. She slaps the flat of her hand many times against the door.

"There is the body of a woman," she says when Jarvis Poulter appears at last. He is in his dark trousers, held up with braces, and his shirt is half unbuttoned, his face unshaven, his hair standing up on his head. "Mr. Poulter, excuse me. A body of a woman. At my back gate."

He looks at her fiercely. "Is she dead?"

His breath is dank, his face creased, his eyes bloodshot.

"Yes. I think murdered," says Almeda. She can see a little of his cheerless front hall. His hat on a chair. "In the night I woke up. I heard a racket down on Pearl Street," she says, struggling to keep her voice low and sensible. "I could hear this— pair. I could hear a man and a woman fighting."

He picks up his hat and puts it on his head. He closes and locks the front door, and puts the key in his pocket. They walk along the boardwalk and she sees that she is in her bare feet. She holds back what she feels a need to say next—that she is responsible, she could have run out with a lantern, she could have screamed (but who needed more screams?), she could have beat the man off. She could have run for help then, not now.

They turn down Pearl Street, instead of entering the Roth yard. Of course the body is still there. Hunched up, half bare, the same as before.

Jarvis Poulter doesn't hurry or halt. He walks straight over to the body and looks down at it, nudges the leg with the toe of his boot, just as you'd nudge a dog or a sow.

"You," he says, not too loudly but firmly, and nudges again.

Almeda tastes bile at the back of her throat.

"Alive," says Jarvis Poulter, and the woman confirms this. She stirs, she grunts weakly.

Almeda says, "I will get the doctor." If she had touched the woman, if she had forced herself to touch her, she would not have made such a mistake.

"Wait," says Jarvis Poulter. "Wait. Let's see if she can get up."

"Get up, now," he says to the woman. "Come on. Up, now. Up."

Now a startling thing happens. The body heaves itself onto all fours, the head is lifted—the hair all matted with blood and vomit—and the woman begins to bang this head, hard and rhythmically, against Almeda Roth's picket fence. As she bangs her head, she finds her voice and lets out an openmouthed yowl, full of strength and what sounds like an anguished pleasure.

"Far from dead," says Jarvis Poulter. "And I wouldn't bother the doctor."

"There's blood," says Almeda as the woman turns her smeared face.

"From her nose," he says. "Not fresh." He bends down and catches the horrid hair close to the scalp to stop the head-banging.

"You stop that, now," he says. "Stop it. Gwan home, now. Gwan home, where you belong." The sound coming out of the woman's mouth has stopped. He shakes her head slightly, warning her, before he lets go of her hair. "Gwan home!"

Released, the woman lunges forward, pulls herself to her feet. She can walk. She weaves and stumbles down the street, making intermittent, cautious noises of protest. Jarvis Poulter watches her for a moment to make sure that she's on her way. Then he finds a large burdock leaf, on which he wipes his hand. He says, "There goes your dead body!"

The back gate being locked, they walk around to the front. The front gate stands open. Almeda still feels sick. Her abdomen is bloated; she is hot and dizzy.

"The front door is locked," she says faintly. "I came out by the kitchen." If only he would leave her, she could go straight to the privy. But he follows. He follows her as far as the back door and into the back hall. He speaks to her in a tone of harsh joviality that she has never before heard from him. "No need for alarm," he says. "It's only the consequences of drink. A lady oughtn't to be living alone so close to a bad neighbourhood." He takes hold of her arm just above the elbow. She can't open her mouth to speak to him, to say thank you. If she opened her mouth, she would retch.

What Jarvis Poulter feels for Almeda Roth at this moment is just what he has not felt during all those circumspect walks and all his own solitary calculations of her probable worth, undoubted respectability, adequate comeliness. He has not been able to imagine her as a wife. Now that is possible. He is sufficiently stirred by her loosened hair—prematurely grey but thick and soft—her flushed face, her light clothing, which nobody but a husband should see. And by her indiscretion, her agitation, her foolishness, her need?

"I will call on you later," he says to her. "I will walk with you to church."

At the corner of Pearl and Dufferin streets last Sunday morning there was discovered, by a lady resident there, the body of a certain woman of Pearl Street, thought to be dead but only, as it turned out, dead drunk. She was roused from her heavenly—or otherwise—stupor by the firm persuasion of Mr. Poulter, a neighbour and a Civil Magistrate, who had been summoned by the lady resident. Incidents of this sort, unseemly, troublesome, and disgraceful to our town, have of late become all too common.

V

I sit at the bottom of sleep,
As on the floor of the sea.
And fanciful Citizens of the Deep
Are graciously greeting me.

As soon as Jarvis Poulter has gone and she has heard her front gate close, Almeda rushes to the privy. Her relief is not complete, however, and she realizes that the pain and fullness in her lower body come from an accumulation of menstrual blood that has not yet started to flow. She closes and locks the back door. Then, remembering Jarvis Poulter's words about church, she writes on a piece of paper, "I am not well, and wish to rest today." She sticks this firmly into the outside frame of the little window in the front door. She locks that door, too. She is trembling, as if from a great shock or danger. But she builds a fire, so that she can make tea. She boils water, measures the tea leaves, makes a large pot of tea, whose steam and smell sicken her further. She pours out a cup while the tea is still quite weak and adds to it several dark drops of nerve medicine. She sits to drink it without raising the kitchen blind. There, in the middle of the floor, is the cheesecloth bag hanging on its broom handle between the two chairbacks. The grape pulp and juice has stained the swollen cloth a dark purple. *Plop, plup,* into the basin beneath. She can't sit and look at such a thing. She takes her cup, the teapot, and the bottle of medicine into the dining room.

She is still sitting there when the horses start to go by on the way to church, stirring up clouds of dust. The roads will be getting hot as ashes. She is there when the gate is opened and a man's confident steps sound on her veranda. Her hearing is so sharp she seems to hear the paper taken out of the frame and unfolded—she can almost hear him reading it, hear the words in his mind. Then the footsteps go the other way, down the steps. The gate closes. An image comes to her of tombstones— it makes her laugh. Tombstones are marching down the street on their little booted feet, their long bodies inclined forward, their expressions preoccupied and severe. The church bells are ringing.

Then the clock in the hall strikes twelve and an hour has passed.

The house is getting hot. She drinks more tea and adds more medicine. She knows that the medicine is affecting her. It is responsible for her extraordinary languor, her perfect immobility, her unresisting surrender to her surroundings. That is all right. It seems necessary.

Her surroundings—some of her surroundings—in the dining room are these: walls covered with dark-green garlanded wallpaper, lace curtains and mulberry velvet curtains on the windows, a table with a crocheted cloth and a bowl of wax fruit, a pinkish-grey carpet with nosegays of blue and pink roses, a sideboard spread with embroidered runners and holding various patterned plates and jugs and the silver tea things. A lot of things to watch. For every one of these patterns, decorations seems charged with life, ready to move and flow and alter. Or possibly to explode. Almeda Roth's occupation throughout the day is to keep an eye on them. Not to prevent their alteration so much as to catch them at it—to understand it, to be a part of it. So much is going on in this room that there is no need to leave it. There is not even the thought of leaving it.

Of course, Almeda in her observations cannot escape words. She may think she can, but she can't. Soon this glowing and swelling begins to suggest words—not specific words but a flow of words somewhere, just about ready to make themselves known to her. Poems, even. Yes, again, poems. Or one poem. Isn't that the idea— one very great poem that will contain everything and, oh, that will make all the other poems, the poems she has written, inconsequential, mere trial and error, mere rags? Stars and flowers and birds and trees and angels in the snow and dead children at twilight—that is not the half of it. You have to get in the obscene racket on Pearl Street and the polished toe of Jarvis Poulter's boot and the plucked-chicken haunch with its blue-black flower. Almeda is a long way now from human sympathies or fears or cozy household considerations. She doesn't think about what could be done for that woman or about keeping Jarvis Poulter's dinner warm and hanging his long underwear on the line. The basin of grape juice has overflowed and is running over her kitchen floor, staining the boards of the floor, and the stain will never come out.

She has to think of so many things at once—Champlain and the naked Indians and the salt deep in the earth, but as well as the salt the money, the money-making intent brewing forever in heads like Jarvis Poulter's. Also the brutal storms of winter and the clumsy and benighted deeds on Pearl Street. The changes of climate are often violent, and if you think about it there is no peace even in the stars. All this can be borne only if it is channelled into a poem, and the word "channelled" is appropriate, because the name of the poem will be—it *is*—"The Meneseteung." The name of the poem is the name of the river. No, in fact it is the river, the Meneseteung, that is the poem—with its deep holes and rapids and blissful pools under the summer trees and its grinding blocks of ice thrown up at the end of winter and its desolating spring floods. Almeda looks deep, deep into the river of her mind and into the tablecloth, and she sees the crocheted roses floating. They look bunchy and foolish, her mother's crocheted roses—they don't look much like real flowers. But their effort, their float-ing independence, their pleasure in their silly selves do seem to her so admirable. A hopeful sign. *Meneseteung.*

She doesn't leave the room until dusk, when she goes out to the privy again and discovers that she is bleeding, her flow has started. She will have to get a towel, strap it on, bandage herself up. Never before, in health, has she passed a whole day in her nightdress. She doesn't feel any particular anxiety about this. On her way through the kitchen, she walks through the pool of grape juice. She knows that she will have to mop it up, but not yet, and she walks upstairs leaving purple footprints and smelling her escaping blood and the sweat of her body that has sat all day in the closed hot room.

No need for alarm.

For she hasn't thought that crocheted roses could float away or that tombstones could hurry down the street. She doesn't mistake that for reality, and neither does she mistake anything else for reality, and that is how she knows that she is sane.

VI

I dream of you by night,
I visit you by day.
Father, Mother,
Sister, Brother,
Have you no word to say?

April 22, 1903. At her residence, on Tuesday last, between three and four o'clock in the afternoon, there passed away a lady of talent and refinement whose pen, in days gone by, enriched our local literature with a volume of sensitive, eloquent verse. It is a sad misfortune that in later years the mind of this fine person had become somewhat clouded and her behaviour, in consequence, somewhat rash and unusual. Her attention to decorum and to the care and adornment of her person had suffered, to the degree that she had become, in the eyes of those unmindful of her former pride and daintiness, a familiar eccentric, or even, sadly, a figure of fun. But now all such lapses pass from memory and what is recalled is her excellent published verse, her labours in former days in the Sunday school, her dutiful care of her parents, her noble womanly nature, charitable concerns, and unfailing religious faith. Her last illness was of mercifully short duration. She caught cold, after having become thoroughly wet from a ramble in the Pearl Street bog. (It has been said that some urchins chased her into the water, and such is the boldness and cruelty of some of our youth, and their observed persecution of this lady, that the tale cannot be entirely discounted.) The cold developed into pneumonia, and she died, attended at the last by a former neighbour, Mrs. Bert (Annie) Friels, who witnessed her calm and faithful end.

January, 1904. One of the founders of our community, an early maker and shaker of this town, was abruptly removed from our midst on Monday morning last, whilst attending to his correspondence in the office of his company. Mr. Jarvis Poulter possessed a keen and lively commercial spirit, which was instrumental in the creation of not one but several local enterprises, bringing the benefits of industry, productivity, and employment to our town.

So the *Vidette* runs on, copious and assured. Hardly a death goes undescribed, or a life unevaluated.

I LOOKED FOR Almeda Roth in the graveyard. I found the family stone. There was just one name on it—Roth. Then I noticed two flat stones in the ground, a distance of a few feet—six feet?—from the upright stone. One of these said "Papa," the other "Mama." Farther out from these I found two other flat stones, with the names

William and Catherine on them. I had to clear away some overgrowing grass and dirt to see the full name of Catherine. No birth or death dates for anybody, nothing about being dearly beloved. It was a private sort of memorializing, not for the world. There were no roses, either—no sign of a rosebush. But perhaps it was taken out. The grounds keeper doesn't like such things; they are a nuisance to the lawnmower, and if there is nobody left to object he will pull them out.

I thought that Almeda must have been buried somewhere else. When this plot was bought—at the time of the two children's deaths—she would still have been expected to marry, and to lie finally beside her husband. They might not have left room for her here. Then I saw that the stones in the ground fanned out from the upright stone. First the two for the parents, then the two for the children, but these were placed in such a way that there was room for a third, to complete the fan. I paced out from "Catherine" the same number of steps that it took to get from "Catherine" to "William," and at this spot I began pulling grass and scrabbling in the dirt with my bare hands. Soon I felt the stone and knew that I was right. I worked away and got the whole stone clear and I read the name "Meda." There it was with the others, staring at the sky.

I made sure I had got to the edge of the stone. That was all the name there was—Meda. So it was true that she was called by that name in the family. Not just in the poem. Or perhaps she chose her name from the poem, to be written on her stone.

I thought that there wasn't anybody alive in the world but me who would know this, who would make the connection. And I would be the last person to do so. But perhaps this isn't so. People are curious. A few people are. They will be driven to find things out, even trivial things. They will put things together. You see them going around with notebooks, scraping the dirt off gravestones, reading microfilm, just in the hope of seeing this trickle in time, making a connection, rescuing one thing from the rubbish.

And they may get it wrong, after all. I may have got it wrong. I don't know if she ever took laudanum. Many ladies did. I don't know if she ever made grape jelly.

Let Me Promise You

MORLEY CALLAGHAN

ALICE KEPT ON RETURNING to the window. Standing with her short straight nose pressed against the window pane, she watched the rain falling and the sidewalk shining under the streetlight. In her black crêpe dress with the big white nun-like collar and with her black hair drawn back tight from her narrow nervous face she looked almost boldly handsome.

Earlier in the evening it had started to snow, then it had begun to drizzle and now the rain was like a sharp sleet. As Alice stood at the window, she began to wish that the ground had been covered with an unbroken layer of fine thin snow, a white sheet that would remain undisturbed till Georgie came, his single line of footprints marking a path up to her door. Though her eyes remained open, she began to dream of a bitterly cold dry evening, of Georgie with a red scarf and a tingling face bursting in on her, his arms wide open. But the wind drove the sleet steadily against the pane. Sighing, she thought, "He won't come in such weather. But he would if it weren't for the weather. I can't really expect him tonight." She walked away from the window and sat down.

Then her heart began to thump so slowly and heavily she could hardly move, for someone was knocking. Opening the door in a rush, she cried, "Georgie, I'm so glad you came," and she put out her hands to help him off with his dripping coat. In the light belted coat he looked very tall and he had a smooth round face that would never look old. The wind and the rain had left his face wet and glowing, but he was pouting because he was uncomfortable in his damp clothes. As he pushed his fair wavy hair back from his eyes, he said, "This isn't exactly a night for visiting." He sat down, still a bit embarrassed by her enthusiasm, and he looked around the room as if he thought that he had made a mistake in coming and didn't expect to be very comfortable. "It's rotten out on a night like this when it can't make up its mind to snow or rain. Maybe you didn't think I'd come."

"I wanted you to come, and because I wanted it, I thought you would, I guess," she said candidly. So many days seemed to have passed since she had been alone with Georgie that now she wanted to take his head in her hands and kiss him. But she felt too shy. A year ago, she knew, he would have been waiting anxiously for her to kiss him.

"Alice," he said suddenly.

"What's bothering you, Georgie, frowning like that?"

"What did you want me for? You said you wanted to speak about something in particular."

"Such curiosity. You'll just sit there unable to rest till you find out, I suppose," she said. She knew he was ill at ease, but she wanted to pretend to herself that he was just impatient and curious. So her pale handsome face was animated by a warm secret delight as she went across the room to a chest of drawers and took out a long cardboard box which she handed to him after making a low girlish curtsey. "I hope you like it … darling," she said shyly.

"What's this? What's the idea?" Georgie said, as he undid the box and pulled out the tissue paper. When he saw that she was giving something to him, he became embarrassed and almost too upset to speak, and then, because he did not want to hurt her, he tried to be full of enthusiasm, "Lord, look at it," he said. "A white, turtle-neck sweater. If I wore that I'd look like a movie actor in his spare time." Grinning at her, he took off his coat and pulled the white sweater over his shirt. "Do I look good? How about a mirror, Al?"

Alice held the mirror in front of him, watching him with a gentle expression of devotion and feeling contentment she had hardly dared to hope for. The high-necked sweater made his fair head look like a faun's head.

"It's pretty swell, Al," he said, but now that he couldn't go on pleasing her with enthusiasm, his embarrassment increased. "You shouldn't be giving me this, Al," he said. "I didn't figure on anything like this when you phoned and said you wanted to see me."

"Today is your birthday, Georgie."

"Imagine you remembering that. You shouldn't be bothering with birthday presents for me now."

"I thought you'd like the sweater," she said. "I saw it this afternoon. I knew it would look good on you."

"But why give me anything, Al?" he said.

"Supposing I want to?"

"You shouldn't waste your money on me."

"Supposing I have something else, too," she said teasing him.

"What's the idea, Al?"

"I saw something else, something you used to want an awful lot. Do you remember? Try and guess."

"I can't imagine," he said, but his face got red and he smiled awkwardly at being forced in this way to remember a time which only made him feel uncomfortable when he recalled it.

Laughing huskily because she was able to tease him as she used to do, she moved lazily over to the chest of drawers, and this time took out a small leather watchcase. "Here you are," she said.

"What is it, let me see," he said, for he couldn't help being curious. He got up. But when he held the watch in his hand, he had to shake his head to conceal his satis-faction. "It's funny the way you knew I always wanted something like that, Al," he said. All his life he had wanted an expensive wristwatch and he was so pleased now that he smiled serenely.

But after a moment he put the watch irresolutely on the table. "You're a great girl, Al," he was saying, "I don't know anybody like you." He added, "Is it never going to stop raining? I've got to be on my way."

"You're not going now, George, are you?"

"I promised to see a fellow. He'll be waiting."

"George, don't go. Please don't," she said. He was ashamed to be going, especially if he picked up the watch from the table, but he felt if he stayed it would be like beginning everything all over again. He didn't know what to do about the watch. He put out his hand, knowing she was watching him, and picked it up.

"So you're just coming here like this and then going?" she said.

"I've got to."

"Have you got another girl?"

"I don't want another girl."

"Yet you won't stay a little while with me?"

"That's over, Al. I don't know what's the matter with you. You phoned and wanted me to drop in for a moment."

"It wasn't hard to see that you liked looking at the watch more than at me," she said moodily.

"Here, if you don't want me to take the watch, all right," he said, and with relief he put it back on the table, and smiled.

For a moment she stared at the case, almost blinded by her disappointment, and hating his smile of relief, and then she cried out, "You're just trying to humiliate me. Take it out of my sight." She swung the back of her hand across the table, knocked the case to the floor and the watch against the wall where the glass broke, and trying not to cry, she clenched her fists and glared at him.

He didn't look at her. With his mouth open, he looked longingly at the watch, for he realized how much he wanted it now that he saw it smashed on the floor. He had always wanted such a watch. His blue eyes were innocent with the sincerity of his full disappointment. "Al," was all he said.

The anger began to go out of her, and she felt how great was his disappointment. She felt helpless. "I shouldn't have done that, Georgie," she said.

"It was a crazy thing to do. It was such a beauty," he said. "Why did you do it?"

"I don't know," she said. She knelt down and started to cry. "Maybe it's not broken much," she faltered, on her knees and picking up the pieces of glass carefully. In her hand she held the pieces but her eyes were blinking so that she could not see them. "It was a crazy thing to do," she was thinking. "It helps nothing. Why does he stand there like that? Why doesn't he move?" She looked up at him and saw his round smooth chin above the white neck of the sweater, and her dark eyes were shining with tears, for it seemed, as he watched her without speaking or moving, that everything ought to have turned out differently. They both looked at the broken pieces of glass she held in her hand in such abject despair, and for that moment while they looked, they began to share a common, bitter disappointment which made Georgie gravely silent and drew him close to her. "Never mind, Al," he said with tenderness. "Please get up."

"Go away. Leave me alone."

"You've got to get up from there. I can't stand here like this with you there."

"I know I'm mean and jealous. I wish someone would shake me and hurt me. I'm a little cat."

"No, you're not, Al. Who'd want to shake you? Please get up," he said, putting his hand on her shoulder.

"Say you'll stay, Georgie," she said, holding on to his hand. "It's so warm here. It's miserable outside. Just listen to the wind. I'll get you something to eat."

"It's no worse than when I came," he said, but his sudden tenderness for her was making him uneasy. He had known Al so well for a long time, she had been one of his girls, one he could feel sure of and leave at any time, but now he felt that he had never looked right at her and seen her before. He did not know her. The warmth of her love began to awe him. Her dark head, her pale oval face seemed so close to him that he might have put out his hand and touched her and felt her whole ardent being under the cloth of her dress. Faltering, he said, "Al, I never got you right. Not in this way. I don't want to go. Look how I want to stay."

"Georgie, listen to me," she said eagerly. "I'll get that watch fixed for you. Or I'll get a new one. I'll save up for it. Or I'll get you anything else you say."

"Don't think about it," he said shamefaced.

"But I want so much to do it, and you can look forward to it. We both can look forward. Please let me promise it to you."

She was still crouched on the carpet. He glanced at her handsome dark face above the white nun-like collar and at her soft pleading eyes. "You look lovely right now, Al," he said. "You look like a wild thing. Honest to God you do."

Touched by happiness, she smiled. Then with all her heart she began to yearn for something more to give him. If there were only more things she had and could give, she thought; if she could only give everything in the world and leave herself nothing.

The Road Past Altamont
GABRIELLE ROY

I

One fine sunny day when we were driving, my mother and I, across the prairie in my little car and for hours had seen the vast, always flat horizons unwind before our slightly weary eyes, I heard Maman complain gently beside me, "Why is it, Christine, that in all this immense plain God never thought of putting at least a few hills?"

She had talked to us a great deal in the last years of the hills in the old province of Quebec where she was born: a severe little range with peaks and notches prolonged by spruce trees, an almost hostile troupe guarding the impoverished backwoods region. There was nothing in this, I felt, to be so much missed. Yet we were still deeply involved with this countryside that had been left behind at the beginning of our family, as if a mysterious and troubled relationship persisted between us and the abandoned hills that had never been quite settled. My own knowledge of it was slight: one day Grandfather saw in his imagination—because of the closed-in hills perhaps?—an immense open plain. At once he was ready to set out, for such was his nature. Grandmother, herself as stable as her hills, resisted for a long time. At last she was overcome. It is almost always, in a family, the dreamer that prevails. This then was what I understood about this matter of the lost hills.

And on this particular day again, not knowing that I was hurting Maman, I said, "Now come, Mother old dear. Your hills were just like all the other hills. It's only because your imagination has embroidered your childhood memories that they seem so attractive to you today. If you were to see them again, you'd be disappointed."

"Ah no," said Maman, who was always irritated when anyone tried to disparage the hills that had been lost to her sight for almost sixty years. And she firmly denied that her splendid imagination could have touched up the faded contours of such a faraway landscape.

And she began to tell me about it again as we crossed the flattest country in the world, the vast plain of southern Manitoba, which is so bare that a single lonely tree can be seen from a great distance and the least things appearing far away upon its surface take upon themselves a unique and pathetic value. Even the flight of a bird, suspended in so much space, twists the heart.

"Imagine," said Maman, "that everything was suddenly turned upside down. We'd see debris, a great mass of bare rocks, others thinly covered with moss. Next would come some low wooded hills, and the folds between them are the most curious thing in the world. One keeps going on, Christine, to discover what can be between them. But once again the escarpment opens out. One is compelled to explore another fold. One is always in suspense."

"Yes, perhaps," I said.

I myself passionately loved our open plains. I didn't think I would have the patience for those closed-in regions that keep drawing us forward by one trick after another. It was undoubtedly the prairie's lack of secretiveness that delighted me most, its lofty and open countenance—although, all of infinity reflected in its boundless extent, is it not itself the most secret country? I could not conceive of there being any hills between me and this reminder of the total enigma, nor any other fleeting accident against which my eye might strike. It seemed to me that this would have thwarted and diminished the vague but powerful summons toward a thousand possibilities that my being received from it.

"Ah, you don't understand," said Maman. "It's the unexpected height, when you attain it, that gives meaning to all the rest."

But she seemed to have forgotten her old longing, which had returned to her for an instant, so fresh and so piercing. It was September, one of those beautiful days that are still warm but to which the resigned, slightly greyish sky and the stripped earth give an indefinable and touching air of gentle sadness. These are the abandoned days, which belong neither to summer nor yet to winter, and my mother began to look eagerly about her. At heart she was still too much alive, too much in love with life, to prefer a time already fixed in her memory to one that was still on its way to lose itself there, like a tributary to the ocean. She agreed with me that the uniformly golden color of the cropped straw and the uniform blue-grey of the sky formed a grave and profound beauty, although too unvarying perhaps for the needs of the heart. But what fine weather for travelling, she said. Yes, autumn was admirably suited to journeys, to all journeys....

Then, just when I thought she was over her regret, I heard her sigh, "But this lack of trees everywhere—trees and water. In my little hills, Christine, the elements are mixed, the aspens, the birches, the maples.... Oh our sugar maples that turned so red in the autumn ... the beeches also flamed with colour. And below, flowing from cove to cove, capturing all the colours, was our little Assomption River."

I was astonished to see Maman pass over her adult existence in Manitoba to go to the most remote part of her life in search of those images, unknown to me yesterday and now seemingly more pleasing to her than any others. I was perhaps even somewhat vexed.

We arrived then at a crossroads, and I thought of something else; I reflected for a moment, or perhaps, on the contrary, did not reflect at all. Today again a sort of light mist seems to lie across that day and I am still unable to be quite clear about what happened to us when I reached that lonely branching of the roads.

2

Do you know the rectilinear and inflexible narrow roads that crisscross the Canadian prairie, making of it a huge chessboard, above which the pensive sky seems to have been deliberating for a long time over which piece it will move, if indeed it will move any. One can get lost there; one often does get lost. Before me, meeting and parting in the same instant, stretched flat upon the grass like the arms of a huge cross, were two little dirt roads, absolutely identical and without signposts, as taciturn as the sky and the silent prairie all around, which absorbed only the rustle of the grasses and, from time to time, the far-off trilling of an unseen bird.

I had completely forgotten the directions my uncle had given me when we set out: turn to the left, then to the right, then to the left. These roads, I assure you, form a sort of vast confusing game and, if one goes wrong a single time, the error will multiply itself to infinity. But perhaps this was precisely what I wanted. At this lonely crossroads I may have been bewitched to the point of not wishing to decide anything for myself, unknown roads having always drawn me as do certain anonymous faces glimpsed in the middle of a crowd. I committed myself, I think, to chance—and yet was it chance that brought such prodigious things to pass that day? I committed myself then to the one of the two roads that seemed to me the most completely strange. Yet actually both were equally strange. Can it be that one, similar as it was to the other, gave me a sort of intelligible signal?

We had not been driving for more than a quarter of an hour along this out-of-the-way road, always flat upon the fields, when it crossed another of its fellows, leading into the distance. Once again, it seemed to me, I refused to choose and let myself be guided by caprice or intuition, by whatever it is we prefer to rely upon at times rather than our own judgment alone.

Now we were lost, of that there could be no doubt. If I had decided to retrace my steps at that point, it is doubtful if I could have repeated a journey that had been guided so entirely by caprice. So I might as well continue to go on. This I did, quickened, I think, by a secret delight at finding ourselves lost on this immense prairie that had no hiding place at all.

These roads in the depths of rural Manitoba, which I had taken to save time, as a short cut to the highway, we call section roads, and there are no others like them for going farther and nowhere. Tedious roads that cut the back country into a thousand squares, in those faraway, unimaginably lonely places—I miss them still today. I see once more their silent meeting under that enigmatic sky; the wind, lightly playing with them, raises dust from their surfaces and makes it turn in a lasso. I recall their soundless greeting, their astonishment at coming together and parting again so soon—and for what destination? For of whence they have come and where they are going they never say a word. When I was young, it seemed to me that they existed for no practical purpose, but only for the strange excitement the wind obtains from playing with them in childish and fascinating games.

So I drove on at random. It was quite necessary, anyway, for who was there in this dead region from whom I could ask the way? For more than an hour we had not seen even as much as the roof of a barn lost in the distance. There were not even any power lines across this wild country. I was happy for the instant as I have rarely been in my life.

I have never been sure what the source of this happiness was. No doubt it was a matter of confidence, unlimited confidence in a future that seemed itself to be unlimited. Whereas my mother had to return to the past for her joys, mine were all ahead, almost all of them intact—and is it not a marvellous moment when everything life has to give can be seen intact upon the horizon, through the charm and magic of the unknown?

MAMAN WAS HALF ASLEEP. Her head nodded slightly. From time to time she partly opened her eyes, undoubtedly struggling against her tiredness with that fear I had known in her all her life, the fear that if she rested for a minute or even dozed off, in that precise instant she would miss the best and most interesting thing that could happen. The heat and the monotony overcame her curiosity in spite of her. Her head fell forward again, her eyelids beat heavily, and, as they slipped over her eyes, I noticed in their expression a physical weariness so great that soon perhaps all Maman's eagerness and love of life would no longer be able to prevail against it. And I remember I said to myself something like: I mustn't wait too long to give Maman happiness. She may not be able to wait for it much longer. At that time I imagined that it was on the whole rather easy to make someone happy, that a tender word, a caress, or a smile could be enough. I imagined that it was in our power to fulfill the deepest needs of the heart, not yet knowing that tragic desires for perfection haunt some people till the end or, on the other hand, desires of such purity and simplicity that even the best will in the world would not know how to satisfy them.

I was perhaps slightly annoyed with my mother for wishing something other than what I considered it right to wish for her. If the truth be told, I was astonished that, old and sometimes weary as she was, Maman still entertained desires that seemed to me to be those of youth. I said to myself: Either one is young and it is time to strike out to know the world or one is old and it is time to rest and give up.

So a hundred times a day I said to Maman, "Rest. Haven't you done enough? It's time for you to rest."

And, as if I had insulted her, she would reply, "Rest! Believe me, it will soon enough be time for that."

Then, becoming thoughtful, she would say, "You know, I spoke that way to my own mother when she seemed to me to be growing old. 'When are you ever going to give up and rest?' I used to say to her, and only now can I see how provoking it must have been."

OUR QUIET, HAPHAZARDLY CHOSEN ROAD had seemed for some time to be climbing, without perceptible strain, by slight and very gentle slopes, no doubt. However, the motor was puffing a little, and, if this hadn't been enough to tell me, I would have realized from the drier, more invigorating air that we were gaining altitude, sensitive as I have always been to the slightest atmospheric variation. With closed eyes, I think, I would recognize from the first breath the air of the ocean, the air of the plain, and certainly that of the high plateaus, because of the delightful feeling of lightness it communicates to me, as if I shed weight as I climbed—or mistakes.

Then, as we continued to rise, I seemed to see, spread against the sky, a distant, half-transparent range of small blue hills.

I was accustomed to the mirages of the prairies and this was the time of day when they arose, extraordinary or completely reasonable—sometimes great stretches of shimmering water, heavy, lifeless lakes. Often the Dead Sea itself appeared among us, level with the horizon; at other times phantom villages around their grain elevators. And once in my childhood an entire city rose from the ground at the end of the prairie especially for me, a strange city with cupolas.

Those are only clouds, I told myself, nothing more—and yet I pressed on as if to reach those gentle little hills before they were effaced.

But they did not melt away, like an illusion, sooner or later. Time and again, when I had rested my glance elsewhere, I found them still there when I looked back. They seemed to sharpen, to increase in size, and even perhaps become more beautiful. Then—did I dream all this? In so many things in our life an element of the imprecise and inexplicable persists, which makes us doubt their reality—the prairie, which since the beginning of the ages had been level and submissive, appeared to revolt. First it exploded in swellings, in crevices, in eroded cracks; boulders broke the surface. Then it split more deeply; ridges sprang up, took on height and came rushing from every side as if, delivered from its heavy immobility, the land was beginning to move and was coming toward me in waves quite as much as I was going toward it. Finally, there was no more doubt possible. Little hills formed on either side of us; they accompanied us at a fixed distance, then suddenly drew near and now we were completely enclosed.

Now, moreover, the dirt road was perceptibly climbing, without pretense, with a sort of elation, in joyous little bounds, in leaps like a young dog straining at the leash, and I had to change gears in mid-hill. From time to time as we passed, a liquid voice, some flow of water over the rocks, struck my ear.

Ah, Maman is right, I thought. Hills are exciting, playing a game of waiting and withholding with us, keeping us always in suspense.

And soon, just as my mother had wished, they showed themselves to be covered with dry bushes, with small trees insecurely rooted on inclining slopes but warmed by the sun, shot with ardent light, the luminous tones of their foliage trembling in the sunlit air. All this—the patches of scorched rock, the red berries on their slender branches, the scarlet leaves of the underbrush—was delightfully tangled together, almost dead, and yet meanwhile what a shout of life it gave!

Then, abruptly, my mother woke up.

HAD SHE BEEN INFORMED during her sleep that the hills had been found again? At any rate, when the landscape was at its most beautiful, she opened her eyes, just as I was about to pull her by the sleeve and say, "Look, just look what's happened to you, Mamatchka!"

At first she appeared to be sunk in a profound bewilderment. Did she believe she had been carried back to the land of her childhood, returned to her starting point with her whole long life to be lived over again? Or did it seem to her that the landscape was mocking at her desires, offering her only an illusion?

But I still didn't know her. Always prompter to faith and to reality than I was, Maman soon realized the simple, delightful truth.

"Can you believe it, Christine!" she cried. "We're in the Pembina Mountains. You know—the only range of mountains in southern Manitoba. I've always wanted to see them. Your uncle assured me there was no way in. But there is, there is, and you, dear child, have discovered it!"

HOW WOULD I DARE to touch her joy that day, much less try to take it apart to grasp its inmost spring? All joy is so mysterious that I am always most conscious in its presence of the clumsiness of words and of the impiety of wishing to be always analyzing, trying to take the human heart by surprise.

And then everything that took place between Maman and the little hills was so silent. I went slowly to let her look at them at her ease, watching the way her eyes flew from one side of the road to the other. We were still climbing, and the hills continued to hurry to the right, then to the left, as if to see us pass, since they in their isolation could not have seen human beings any oftener than we saw hills. Then I stopped; I turned off the engine. In her anxiety to get out, Maman no longer knew which handle to turn to open the door. I helped her. Then, without a word, she set out alone into the hills.

She began to climb, between the dry bushes that caught for an instant at her skirt, surprisingly agile, with the movements of a young goat, raising her head from time to time toward the height ... then I lost sight of her. When she reappeared a short time later, she was right on top of one of the steepest hills, a silhouette diminished by the distance, completely alone on the farthermost point of the rock. Beside her leaned a small twisted fir tree, which had found its niche up there among the winds. And the curious thought came to me as I saw them there side by side, Maman and the tree, that it is perhaps necessary to be quite alone at times in order to find oneself.

What did they say to each other that day, Maman and the little hills? Did the hills really give Maman back her joyous childhood heart? And why is it that a human being knows no greater happiness in old age than to find in himself once more the face he wore as a child? Wouldn't this be rather an infinitely cruel thing? Whence comes the happiness of such an encounter? Perhaps, full of pity for the vanished youthful soul, the aged soul calls to it tenderly across the years, like an echo. "See," it says, "I can still feel what you felt ... love what you loved...." And the echo undoubtedly answers something … but what? I knew nothing of this dialogue at that time. I merely wondered what could hold my mother for so long, in the open wind, on the rock. And if it was her past life she was finding there, how could there be happiness in this? How could it be good at seventy to give one's hand to one's childhood on a little hill? And if this is what life is, to find one's childhood again, at that moment then, when in their own good time childhood and old age come together again, the round must be almost finished, the festival over. I was suddenly terribly eager to see Maman back with me once more.

At last she came down from the hill. To conceal her emotion, she plucked a branch of red glowing leaves from a half-dead bush and, as she came toward me, caressed her bowed cheek with this. For she kept her eyes hidden from me as she approached and did not reveal them to me till quite a long time later, when there was no longer anything but ordinary things between us.

She sat down beside me without saying a word. We drove on in silence. From time to time I looked at her stealthily; I saw joy sparkling in her eyes like far-off water and even, for an instant, break to the surface in real moisture. So what she had seen was so disturbing? I was anxious all at once. The hills seemed different now, humped and rather cheerless; I longed to find the frank clear plain again.

Then Maman seized my arm in agitation.

"Christine," she asked, "did you just find this marvellous road by mistake?"

"So the thoughtlessness of youth is good for something!" I said jokingly.

But I saw that she was really troubled.

"In fact," she said, "you may not be able to find it again when we're coming back from your uncle's next year. You may never be able to find it again. There are roads, Christine, that one loses forever."

"What would you have me do?" I teased her gently. "Scatter bread crumbs like Tom Thumb?"

At that moment the hills opened out a little and, lodged completely in a crevice between fir trees, a tiny settlement appeared, rather like a mountain village with its four or five houses clinging at different levels to the uneven ground. On one of them shone a red Post Office sign. We had scarcely glimpsed the poor hamlet before it was hidden from our sight, though the singing of a stream, somewhere on the rocks, followed us for a moment longer. Maman had had time to catch the name of the place from the Post Office sign, a name that had, I think, fixed itself like an arrow in her spirit.

"It's Altamont," she said, glowing.

"Well, there's your landmark," I said, "since you're determined to have something definite about the journey."

"Yes," she said, "and let's never forget it, Christine. Let's engrave it in our memories. It's our only key to these hills, all we know for certain, the Altamont road."

And as she was speaking, our hills abruptly subsided, dwindled into scarcely raised mounds of earth, and almost at once the prairie received us, stretching away on every side in its obliterating changelessness, denying everything that was not itself. With one accord Maman and I turned to look behind us. Of the hills that were already beginning to withdraw into the night almost nothing remained, only a faint contour against the sky, a barely perceptible line such as children make when they amuse themselves drawing the earth and the sky.

3

Once again, next year in the autumn, the season of harvesting that she loved so well, I set out with my mother for our annual visit to her brothers. There were always two periods in the year when my mother was absolutely unable to be still, when her spirit, which was always close to the seasons, received from them the most irresistible summons—when it was time to sow and when it was time to reap. She would be informed, it seems to me, in a mysterious way. In the middle of the city, walking along the sidewalk or perhaps in a store, Maman would sniff the air, raise her head, and announce, "Cléophas will have begun to plant his wheat today...." She would endure two or three days of agitation and restlessness, undertaking at one and the same time her spring house cleaning, some dressmaking, trips into town, and countless other things, to trick her migratory instinct, no doubt—for if ever one of us was possessed by it, it was certainly she, before she realized that it would attack us all in turn, her children, and snatch us from her.

We arrived at Uncle Cléophas's house in the midst of the threshing.

What activity used to prevail at that season on our Manitoba farms! Twelve to fifteen men lodged at the farm, some of them in the big house, others sleeping in small sheds fitted out as dormitories, furnished with camp beds, and with sometimes, it seems to me, a window pierced in their sides, unless there was only a door left constantly open to admit air.

These people, at once hired men, guests, and friends—but how to define the excellent relations we had with each other?—came from every corner of Canada, I should perhaps say of the world, for that was the most astonishing thing of all, that men of such diverse nationalities and characters were gathered together in our remote farms to harvest the wheat. There were young students fresh from the university, whom we heard talking all day long about reforms and changes; old fellows without an illusion about anything; rovers and born storytellers who seemed to live only for the evenings, when they held the floor; immigrants of all sorts, of course; in short, sad people and roisterers, and all of them, no matter what they told us, told us a little of their lives.

As I think now of those evenings long ago at my uncle's, in his house in the middle of the night on the prairie, it seems to me that I have my ear pressed against one of those conch shells from which a tireless murmur is to be heard. In that out-of-the-way farmhouse something of the universe vibrated. For these men were never so tired that they did not attempt, when night came and the whining of the machines was silenced for a few hours, to share something unique to each of them that might draw them for a moment closer to each other.

It is from those evenings, unfolding like competitions of songs and stories, that my desire, which has never since left me, to learn to tell a story well undoubtedly dates, so much was I impressed at that time by the poignant and miraculous power of this gift.

Maman, it is true, had always given me an example of it, but never so much so as at these times of powerful stimulation when the past lived again in her with particular force, for this farm of my uncle's, which was actually modern for the period, had come to him from Grandfather, who broke the virgin soil himself.

The old theme of my grandparents' arrival in the west had been to my mother a sort of canvas on which she had worked all her life as one works at a tapestry, tying threads and commenting upon events like fate, so that the story varied, enlarged, and became more complex as the narrator gained age and perspective. Now when my mother related it again, I could scarcely recognize the lovely story of times past that had so enchanted my childhood; the characters were the same, the route was the same, and yet nothing else was as it used to be.

Sometimes we interrupted her.

"But that detail didn't appear in your first versions. That detail is new," we said with a hint of resentment perhaps, so anxious were we, I imagine, that the past at least should remain immutable. For if it too began to change ...

"But it changes precisely as we ourselves change," said Maman.

I had gone out that evening, I remember, to breathe the scented air for a few minutes. Two paces from the house, a sort of impenetrable night began, just as in the times so often described to us by Maman. I went down to the end of the farm road, to the edge of the immense plateau, so sombre at that hour and rustling like a great cloak spread out in the wind. How easy it was, with the darkness blotting out all traces of habitation, to imagine these places in the primitive reverie that had so excited my grandfather but always rebuffed my grandmother. On those nights of mild and vaguely plaintive wind, I was always aware of those two profoundly divided spirits. And my own adventurous heart perhaps divided them even further by inclining me so strongly toward the one who had so loved adventure.

I retraced my steps and, before I could see the lights of the house at the end of the wood, I heard, from another direction, an indistinct, muffled, vaguely happy sound. It was the rumination of the big farm horses in the stable full of animals exhausted by the labours of the day—a slow weary rhythm that had in it also, I thought, something of the contentment of repose.

In the big living room, where a few of our people were lingering, I found my mother and Uncle Cléophas, sitting a little to one side and engaged at this very moment in calling to mind the character of my grandmother.

"Do you remember the sudden anger she turned on us, Eveline," said my uncle, "that first night on the wagon trail when we couldn't find a house to stop in and had to camp out under the stars? Was it because the fire wouldn't catch? Or in fear of the naked prairie all around? She stood up, calling us gypsies, and said threateningly, 'All right. I've had enough of following you, you band of strangers. You go your way then. I'll go mine.'"

Maman smiled rather sadly.

"Those are the sorts of threats one makes when one is at the end of one's tether. Before she left her village, she probably didn't realize how different everything would be. The night you speak of must have been when she finally saw all the implications."

"But to call us strangers!"

"Weren't we, in a sense," said Maman, "when we all turned against her to extract her consent by force?"

"We had to," my uncle insisted. "We had to leave. Back in the hills, you remember, Eveline, it was nothing but rocks, thin soil...."

"No doubt," said Maman. "But she was attached to it, and you must know now yourself that one doesn't only become attached to what is soft and easy."

Hidden in a corner of the room, a very young man was softly playing a harmonica. The slightly languid air formed a discreet accompaniment to their speech and perhaps urged them a little toward nostalgia.

"What could we have done but what we did?" my uncle continued. "The west was calling us. It was the future then. Besides, it proved to be right."

"It was the future," said Maman. "Now it's our past. At least let's try, in the light of what we've learned by living, to understand what it was like for her to have to leave her past when she was no longer young. Would you, Cléophas, willingly leave this farm you've inherited?"

"That's not the same thing," said my uncle defensively. "I've worked so hard here."

Maman appeared to be listening to someone invisible, a soul that had vanished perhaps but had not yet stopped trying to make itself heard. She raised her eyes to her brother and gave him a smile of indulgent rebuke.

"Cléophas, haven't you ever understood how hard she had to work on that wretched farm in order to make a life for us that was pleasant on the whole?"

"That's true," said my uncle, somewhat ashamed. "But I was so young when we left the hills. I scarcely remember them. What about you? Do you remember?"

Maman stared dreamily at her clasped hands.

"I remember them, yes, quite well."

But what was she recalling exactly? The bygone hills she had not seen since child-hood? Or the quite unexpected ones in Manitoba, which we had one day discovered, which had restored so much else to her memory and which must have been the source of the change I had observed in her, for, come to think of it, it was only since the reappearance of hills in our life that I had noticed that attention to voices from the past that I found so bewildering and that took her to some extent away from me.

Suddenly I had had enough of all this chiaroscuro. After all, since hills were in some way involved in all this, we might as well speak of them openly, settle the matter once for all. It occurred to me that she had not spoken of them to me even once in this whole year, although she thought of them incessantly, I was convinced.

I broached the subject.

"Uncle Cléophas," I said, "do you know the village of Altamont? Less than a village, actually—just a few houses …"

"Altamont!" my uncle repeated, tranquilly smoking his pipe. "Queer little spot, isn't it? It's been half dead for a long time. I've never liked that region. It's too cramped and narrow. I've never been able to understand why, with the choice of homesteads on the level easy prairie, anyone would look at that clump of hills. Yet it happened some fifty years ago. At least the region attracted some Scottish immi-grants who, I imagine, found there a smaller edition of the country they had left. But what folly! The Highlanders didn't make a go of it and scattered after a short while, some returning home, others going to the towns. An experiment that turned into a disaster, that's Altamont."

"Nevertheless," I said, hearing myself speak on Maman's behalf, "there are some extraordinary views to be seen when you cross the entire little range."

"Do you say there's a road right across the range? If so, it must be in a bad state of repair, for almost no one, to my knowledge, ever goes there now."

I noticed then that Maman was watching me nervously, as if she feared I might let my uncle too far into our secrets, and with her eyes she cautioned me against it. Good and affable as he was, my uncle was not much given to flights of the imagina-tion and knew how to squelch them sometimes with a single, too concrete word. It was curious: the true son, at heart, of my grandmother, the one most exactly like her, with his realistic spirit and his attachment to what he possessed, he was because of his lack of imagination the one least capable of understanding her. The conversation took another turn. A little old Norwegian, hired by my uncle, often close-mouthed and yet loquacious in his own good time, suddenly began in his strong rough accent to describe the mountains of his native land and the great fjords profoundly open to the sea.

On these evenings of memories and melancholy, many times we found thus, at dreamy distances, lost horizons.

The time came for us to be on our way. I sensed, without her saying a word, that Maman was preoccupied again by the thought of the hills, perhaps by the tender look on her face, that absently tender look a face wears when it is withdrawn from the present.

We set out in silence. After passing through a few villages, along still slightly travelled roads, we reached an almost uninhabited prairie at the end of which a slight rise of land was outlined in faint relief.

And once again, by narrow taciturn roads, from crossing to silent crossing, without considering, without hesitation, as if the place to which I was going was not on the map but only somewhere at the limit of faith, between the sighing grasses and the dust rising in melancholy spirals on either side, proceeding as if in a dream from intersection to intersection, I drove my mother directly into the hills. But she did not waken to find them there complete, because she had been watching for them for some time, sitting on the edge of the seat, and saw them approach with a sort of peaceful joy that contrasted strongly with her agitation of the previous trip. But this happy reassurance, which came undoubtedly from the awareness that the hills were indeed real, was tinged with a tender melancholy, perhaps because, finding them so real, she would have to say to them as well a sort of good-by.

I don't know why I began to question her about Grandmother.

"Was she quarrelsome all her life?" I asked. "Or did that just come upon her later on?"

Maman seemed to rouse herself from a dream.

"It's curious that you should speak of her at the exact moment I was thinking how lonely she must have been among us, her husband and her children, who were all, you might say, of a different breed. I would have liked to call her back to earth, for a moment at least, and try to set things right with her."

"But Grandfather, with his dreams she didn't wish to share, must also have been lonely...."

"Yes, undoubtedly ... It's strange," she went on, "what takes place in us as we live, the way the beings who gave us life continue, in us and through us, to struggle against each other, each wishing to have us completely on his side."

"That's a rather frightening thing you're saying."

"Frightening? Why no, quite fair from their point of view, though for the one who has to suffer this division it isn't always easy."

Her eyes lit up slightly as she admitted, "When I was very young I recognized myself perfectly in my father. We were allies, he and I. Maman used to say of us, with some rancour perhaps, 'As thick as thieves.' I believed I took entirely after him and I think I was glad of it.... I loved him almost to the exclusion of everyone else."

"And then?"

"Later," said Maman, "with the first disillusionments of life, I began to detect in myself a few small signs of the personality of my mother. But I didn't want to resemble her, admirable as she was, poor old thing, and I fought against it. Only with middle age did I catch up with her, or she caught up with me—how can you explain this strange encounter outside time? One day, imagine my stupefaction, I caught myself making one of her gestures, which from the first time I made it came to me as naturally as breathing. Even my face began to change. When I was young, I was said to be the living image of your grandfather. Then little by little, from day to day, I saw my face alter as if as the result of an invisible, determined, and boundless will. And now can you honestly say that I don't bear an astonishing resemblance to that picture we have of Grandmother when she was just my present age?"

I gave her a troubled look and could not help admitting that there was something in what she said.

"In your face perhaps, but not in your character."

"In my character too, believe me. Besides, I'm no longer angry about it, since, having become her, I understand her. Ah, that is certainly one of life's most surprising experiences. We give birth in turn to the one who gave us birth when finally, sooner or later, we draw her into our self. From then on she lives in us just as truly as we lived in her before we came into the world. It's extremely singular. Every day now as I live my own life it's as if I were giving her a voice with which to speak. So, instead of saying to myself, 'This is what I feel, this is what is happening to me ...' I think instead, with a sort of sad astonishment, but with joy too in the discovery, 'So this is what she experienced, poor soul, this is what she suffered.' We come together," she said. "We always do finally come together, but so late!"

Slightly crushed by this confidence, in which I saw, rather than a miraculous coming together, some sort of irksome interference with the personality and individual freedom, I began to speak against Grandmother in my turn.

"You scarcely resemble her at all, thank God. In the first place, you're a trotting horse like Grandfather. You're not in the least a stay-at-home.... And in the second place, you're not yet too quarrelsome...."

She received my gentle teasing with a sidelong smile.

"That may come," she said, and began to defend Grandmother bitterly. "And anyway, she wasn't as quarrelsome as it is said. She became so when we all pushed her to the limit."

"How was that?"

"By resisting her love. There are two sorts of love. One closes the eyes and is easygoing. The other keeps the eyes open. That was her way, and it was exacting and difficult."

"But if it's true, as you say, that she loved Grandfather so much, how is it that in the long run she never completely forgave him for dragging her into the western adventure?"

"Simply because love finds it hard to forgive the slightest lack of love."

"And it was a lack of love on Grandfather's part to be determined to transfer his family at all costs?"

"Ah, I no longer know," Maman admitted. "Fundamentally they were both right. No doubt it's this that keeps us so far from each other in this life. There's always something to say on both sides."

"Really," I said, "if love and marriage are as you say, they seem to tend rather to diminish the human being...."

"Diminish!" Maman exclaimed. "Then you can't have understood a word of what I've been trying to explain to you—that it's the only way, on the contrary, to get a little outside one's self.... But you're young," she said, with a sudden tender indulgence. "Stay young," she begged me, as if this were in my power. "Stay young and always with me, little Christine, so I won't become too old and quarrelsome too soon."

With one accord we burst out laughing. Then Maman turned her eyes back to the hills and I saw them fill with that joyous freedom the soul knows before it feels any need to possess, when the world and things offer themselves as if for the first time and to it alone. I understood somewhat better the attraction this road held for my aged mother. This freedom to receive everything, since no important choice has yet broached the possibilities, this infinite and yet at times troubling freedom must itself be youth. And no doubt it was upon this source of ephemeral freedom that Maman was still able to draw. Ah, no matter what she might say about human love and how much we learn from its restraints, I felt clearly as I watched her that it is only in solitude that the soul tastes release.

Then I heard her exclaim beside me, "How charming these hills are ... and young, don't you think?"

"Young? I don't know. It is claimed, on the contrary, that they are extremely old formations...."

"Oh you don't say!" she said, a trifle vexed, and went on chidingly, "You know, Christine, you ought to draw a map of these tangled roads, since you refuse to ask directions when you set out or on the way, saying that it's contrary to the spirit of the journey, that we must trust entirely to the road. That's all very well, but why couldn't you make a map of our little country? Otherwise, one of these days," she concluded on a note of rather tart reproach, "you'll end up by losing my Altamont road."

I burst into laughter. What melancholy and mistaken idea could I have got into my head! Maman was neither threatened, nor aged, nor diminished. At heart she was scarcely fifteen.

5

I had already heard at times the summons, insistent and alien—coming from no one but myself, however—that, in the midst of my games and my friendships, commanded me to set out to measure myself against some challenge, vague as yet, that the world flung to me or I flung to myself.

I had succeeded until then in freeing myself from this stranger. Then, without his speaking much more clearly, I began to hear him hounding me at every turn. (I say *he,* for how else can I name the one who became little by little my tyrannical possessor?) Were I for a moment happy in my heedlessness, my small reasonable plans for the future, I would hear his remonstrances again: Why do you put off going? Sooner or later you'll have to do it.... I was tempted to ask, "Who are you who pursues me so?" but I did not dare, for I knew that this foreign being within me, who was quite insensitive, if need be, to the sorrow he would cause to me and to others, was also myself.

Yet my life pleased me and my work as a teacher was high enough surely to fill it. Besides, I had my mother and she had no one but me.

And then this life I was living, as if it felt itself threatened, began to cover me with caresses and seemed more tender and precious to me than ever before. It is always when we love life that it loves us best in return, as if in a marvellous accord.

How well I remember that year of my life, the last perhaps when I lived quite close to people and things, not yet somewhat withdrawn, as happens inevitably when one yields to the intention to set things down in words. Everything still existed simply for me that year, because of the precise and reasonable duties that stitched me to life. It snowed, and quite artlessly I received the sensation of moist cold upon my cheek. The wind blew, and I ran to see from which direction it came. Our town was not an enigma to me, an invitation to lift up the roofs and see what was hidden within. It was a small town of friendly houses, whose people I knew, as well as all their habits, the hour at which they went out, where they went. I remained for some time at ease in life ... not slightly to one side. Seldom since then have I been able to return completely to this or to see things and human beings otherwise than through words, once I had learned to use them as fragile bridges for exploration ... and, it is true, sometimes for communication also. I became by degrees a sort of watcher over thoughts and human beings, and this passion, however sincere, uses up the insouciance that is needed for life.

For a short time longer, then, I knew the free play of my own thoughts—and do those who still possess it sufficiently realize their good fortune? They did not seem important enough for me to stop them in their tracks, impose a halt upon them, retain them, make use of them. Free still, they went their modest joyous way.

Now, as soon as they come to me, I fancy that they are for others, too, to some extent. I search them, work over them. In this way they have become a weariness to me.

NOT MUCH LATER, the sense and warmth of reality, to which I was attached as to my dearest possession, were taken from me and I have never dreaded anything as much since then as to see this deprivation recur.

I walked in our town and it had become as insubstantial and pale to my eyes as a cinema town. The houses on either side of the street were of papier-mâché, the streets themselves empty, for when passers-by brushed against me, I seemed scarcely to hear them come or realize that they had fates. When it snowed, I seemed scarcely to be aware that snow fell on me. I myself, moreover, was filled with a sort of emptiness, if it may be so expressed.

Sometimes a strange question rose from within me, as if from the bottom of a well: What are you doing here? Then I would cast my eyes around me. I would try to attach myself to something, familiar to me yesterday, in this world that was fleeing from me. But the troubling sense persisted that I was here only by chance and that I had to discover the place in the world, as yet unknown to me, where I might feel rather more at home. The thought, seemingly so trivial and yet disturbing, accompanied me everywhere: This is over. This is no longer your place. Now you are a stranger here.

One day, exhausted by all this, I tried to speak to my mother about what I was feeling.

"Maman, in your own life, have you sometimes had the impression that you are here by mistake, that you're a stranger?"

"Often," she said, as if projected by this simple question into that vast and terrible reverie where we are so alone with our own knowledge of ourselves. "Do you believe there are many people who are so satisfied with their lives that they never feel confined—or strangers, if you prefer?"

"You never let us know that you …"

"What would have been the good? You know that in my youth I was eager to learn and travel and raise myself as much as I could…. But I was married at eighteen. My children came quickly. I haven't had very much time for myself. Sometimes even now I dream of an infinitely better person I might have been able to be … a musician, for instance—isn't that foolish?" Then she added quickly, as if to put me off the track, prevent herself from being revealed to me, "Everyone has such dreams—everyone, I tell you."

"If you had it to do over again, would you get married just the same?"

"Certainly. For I look at you and tell myself that nothing is lost, that you will do everything I wished to do in my place and better than I could."

"Then that compensates?"

"It does more than compensate. Haven't you understood yet that parents truly live over again in their children?"

"I thought you chiefly relived the lives of your own parents."

"I relive their lives and I also live over again with you."

"That must be exhausting! You can't have much time to be yourself."

"At any rate, it's perhaps the most illuminated part of one's life, situated between those who came before us and those who follow after us, right in the middle...."

But all this, I thought, did not bring us to the subject I wished to broach.

"Listen, Maman," I said, "would you approve if I told you that very soon perhaps ...?"

"What do you mean? You're not also thinking of going away?"

"Yes, Maman, for a year or two."

She considered me for a long time, as if withdrawing all the while, withdrawing terribly from me. It was unbearable to me that, simply because I had told her I wished to go away, I should see her go on ahead, retire first. Then she burst into vehement reproaches.

"So you're going away too. That's what you're plotting. I should have suspected it."

Even more disturbing to me than this sudden violence was the effort I could see her making to calm and control herself.

In a toneless voice she asked, "Going away? But where?"

"To Europe, Maman."

"Europe!" she repeated, the remoteness of this word renewing her indignation. "But why? Why? What will you do over there? In those old tormented countries, so different from ours."

"But that very difference, Maman, should be enlightening. Anyway, it's chiefly to France that I want to go."

"To France!" she cried, as if in scorn, she who had always spoken of it to us in a tone of the highest respect.

"Where else?" I said. "After all, I was brought up to believe that France was our ancestral country and that I'd feel perfectly at home there."

"Well, it's not true. That's the greatest of all the chimeras we've ever fostered."

"Perhaps so, but wouldn't it be better to go and see, before one says it's a chimera?"

"Oh you don't say!" she said derisively, then tried to compose herself, like one who perceives that there is a hard battle to be fought. "In the first place, if you want to write, you don't need to rush to the ends of the earth to do it. Our town is made up of human beings. Here as elsewhere there is joy to be described, sorrows, atonements...."

"But to see it, shouldn't I first go away from it?"

"Go away! All my life I've heard those words! From the mouths of all my children! Where did you all get that passion for going away?"

"From you, perhaps."

"Perhaps—but I didn't go."

"Try to be reasonable."

"Reasonable!"

And she continued stubbornly, "A writer really needs nothing but a quiet room, some paper, and himself...."

"Himself, that's just it."

"So to be yourself, you propose to break everything?"

Before the intemperance of our speech, our defences fell for an instant and we looked at one another in grief.

"To think that only yesterday I believed you were happy," she lamented.

"Remember, Maman," I said, "if you and Grandfather discovered the prairie on your way west, it was because you'd first abandoned something."

"Would you dare to tell me that in order to discover you must abandon everything?"

"Some things, anyway. When you were younger you understood."

"Understood!" she cried. "Do you think one understands when one is young? Understanding is a matter of experience, of a lifetime...."

"Well, since you understand everything better than I do ..."

"That's right, turn my own weapons against me. Do you mean to wear me down as we all combined in the old days to wear down my poor mother?"

"You're beginning to be like her, as a matter of fact," I said unkindly, to which her only reply was a wounded look.

It was useless. She could not or would not yield to my arguments. And yet, pathetically, I continued to believe that arguments could be effective against a tortured spirit. We became to some extent enemies, my mother and I. She had the sorrow in her old age of holding hostile feelings against me. How could it be otherwise? When parents oppose their children, are they not often struggling against the audacity of their own youth, come back to harass them when they are tired out and through with adventure?

For almost a whole year Maman, incessantly vanquished, incessantly beginning again, faced the part of me that was most similar to herself as she had been, discouraging it with a bitter thrust, mocking at it, and sometimes, quite unexpectedly, pitying it.

Neither she nor I, during those cruel months, was attentive to the world and the seasons.

Sometimes, if I went for a few weeks without speaking of my plan or if I merely seemed to be interested in something else, she would draw some sort of timid hope from this. I would see her eyes watching mine, as if spying out the lie of the land, ready to flee at a moment's notice or become reconciled.

Spring came this time without her noticing it. She observed the renewal of life belatedly when it was already far advanced, almost complete. On an already warm day she raised her eyes in astonishment toward the sky and sighed, "Cléophas must have sowed his fields a long time ago. His fields ..." she repeated, as if lost in a dream.

Then the summer was behind us. I was to leave at the beginning of October. I had booked third-class passage to Paris. From the depths of Manitoba to the City of Light, as I naïvely expressed it, is a great step. I trembled at the thought of embarking upon it now that the journey before me was taking on the appearance of certainty. I was beginning to dread that exhilarating moment of departure that is also the moment when we take our exact measurement in the world and find it so small that our hearts almost fail us. Yet this extreme vulnerability seemed to me then, and seems to me now, one of the most necessary stages to self-knowledge.

Grandfather must have experienced it when he plunged into the still savage territories of the west. Perhaps we were not, after all, so far from each other—the pioneer heedful of the call of a land still to be created and I, who heard, from a young and half-formed country, the summons of the exacting ancient cities.

Besides, it has always been like this in our family. One generation goes to the west; the next makes the journey in reverse. We are always in migration.

MAMAN WAS PERHAPS close to admitting that she felt herself to be too old to lose me, that there is a time when one can bear to see one's children go away but after that it is truly as if the last rag of youth were being taken from us and all the lamps put out. She was too proud to hold me at this price. But how insensitive my lack of assurance made me. I wanted my mother to let me go with a light heart and predict nothing but happy things for me.

Sometimes she dared to offer me a word of warning, at which I bristled.

"Perhaps you'll have a hard time there. What will you live on?"

"My savings will be enough for a year ... perhaps two. After that, I'll manage."

"I'll be anxious," she said.

To which I replied, slightly provoked, "But why? There's no need for you to be anxious."

Then a day came when I suggested, "Before I sell my car, would you like us to make our trip to see Uncle Cléophas? On our way back, we'll go by your Altamont road."

6

Just what was it that happened that day? The hills seemed to me less high, less shapely, almost insignificant. Was I so far ahead with my departure that I was comparing them already with the mountains I was to see, those mountains whose names I had been saying to myself since childhood—the Alps, the Pyrenees?

It's true that it wasn't really sunny that day and the autumn didn't glow as it usually did. The familiar colours were there, if you will, but subdued. At any other time Maman would have told me that this was through lack of frost, for at least one night of it was needed to put nature on the alert and make it assume its burning shades. But she said nothing. This was the most painful part of it, that we had to avoid almost all the subjects that had pleased us in the old days and keep to banalities. After a moment I turned toward her and saw that her face was creased with disappointment.

"These aren't our hills, Christine. You must have taken the wrong road."

"Still ..."

"Our hills were closer together, more attractively grouped, higher too."

"We must have become accustomed to them."

"But the second time we passed through them, they still seemed charming, you remember."

"Well, perhaps we're only seeing them today as they've always been."

"Ah, do you think so?"

I had succeeded in shaking her, and she began to scrutinize the landscape with a doubtful expression that was pathetic to see. Just what was missing from our trip today? Something in the hills themselves? Or in the way we looked at them? In Maman's eyes, at any rate, I saw no return of that young and released expression I had observed on our previous trips. I already knew, of course, that remembered happiness does not come at our bidding, that it belongs to a different world from that of the will; but I was stubborn, I was determined that Maman should grow young before me once again.

"Still, these knolls are beautiful," I said.

"Perhaps, but they're not ours."

In a sense it was the same landscape we had travelled through and loved, but as if blurred. It gave us the same painful impression as does an imperfect photograph of a beloved face.

The mounds continued to slip past, without much spirit. A great shut-in heat prevailed between them. Maman finally granted them only a vague and slightly indifferent glance, as if she were quite prepared to lose everything now and indeed didn't much care. Now indifference is the one thing that all my life I have found it least possible to bear. I did not know that old people must have at least a trace of it, however, if they are to withstand the blow of seeing something taken from them each day.

"Maman," I said, "are you going to fall asleep right in the middle of the hills?"

She started, looked quickly around her and then, noticing a hillock that was a little higher and more shapely than the others, began to smile, not at this knoll perhaps but at something it suggested to her, something enchanting and young that came to her from far away but intact. Then her hope fell; her eyes grew dull.

She reproached me a little fretfully, "I told you you'd end up by losing my Altamont road."

Had I lost it?

In my mind I set about retracing my usual itinerary as well as I could. I passed again by the silent crossroads. Had I not hesitated at the first of them and taken a different direction from that of our previous journeys? How could I be sure? This Altamont road was like a dream—did I really know it? I had found it twice, chanced upon it, without searching. Was it not one of those roads one never finds again when one wills it too strongly? I had never, in any case, detected the least trace of it on the maps, though it is true that most of these maps do not take account of hamlets of less than ten houses or of the roads that lead to them. And meanwhile I was asking myself: Hasn't Maman aged enormously all at once? Will she even be able to wait till I am ready to show her what I can do? And if she is not, will what I am so anxious to accomplish have any value in my eyes?

Then I heard myself say in somewhat impatient tones, "What road do you think it is then, if it isn't the Altamont road?"

But was it another road?

Could there, in fact, be two roads into these hills where almost no one went any more—one lighthearted and happy, crossing the peaks, and another, lower down, which would skirt, but never enter, the little secret country?

Once again Maman began to scrutinize the sides of the road. She did it with a sharp but unhappy vigilance in which I believed I could distinguish a fear that she might no longer be able to recognize what landscapes had once had to offer her. Because she was too old now? Too weary? Because her memory was failing? Or her sensitivity? Because it was lost to her forever perhaps?

As on the previous occasions, we looked behind us for a moment as we emerged once more upon the plain. Against the already dark horizon no slightest undulating line of hills stood out, not even one of those clouds that imitate them so often in our Manitoba sky. But it was late, it is true; almost no light remained.

WE REACHED THOSE TALL, bright yellow signposts on which the likeness of a buffalo appears. Once Lord of the Prairies, roving at will across these open spaces, now, on these metal plaques, he points out the main roads of Manitoba, which he maintains in the most direct line possible from town to town.

We had been rolling bumper to bumper along the monotonous highway for some time when Maman lifted her head and said defiantly, "No, Christine, that wasn't the Altamont road."

"How do you know?"

"Because we didn't see the village of Altamont."

"Such a tiny village," I said. "If we'd just chanced to look on the wrong side of the road while we passed it, we'd have missed it. You remember it's all on the same side of the road."

She seemed for a moment disconcerted and confused but almost at once began to search for arguments against me.

"I certainly looked at both sides of the road at once," she said.

Ahead of us, planted squarely on the prairie grass, loomed the cement factory, blanching and stifling everything with its chalky breath. Then came the new developments, identical cottages ranged sadly in long similar avenues on the edge of the ancient meditative plain. The young cities of my country have not had time yet to make themselves personalities to match the grandeur of the landscape that encompasses them. But it occasionally seems that the prairie is offering to our imagination these cities of tomorrow perhaps, ideal and in its own image, when it raises them on the rim of the horizon in mirages of marvellous completeness, perfectly in place.

"It's not your fault," Maman resumed, "but how sad it is that today of all days we should miss the Altamont road."

What did she mean by "today of all days"? Wishing to be kind and to atone perhaps for some momentary flash of joy, I said, calling her by her first name, as I did sometimes when I wished, I suppose, to bind her to me more closely and at the same time defend my young and unsure independence, "Next time, Eveline, I'll find your Altamont road. I'll come back from Paris. You'll always be an ardent traveller. We'll set out for Altamont together. When I have money, we'll take lots of other trips besides. Why shouldn't we go some day, for instance, and see the real family hills, in Grandmother's village in Quebec?"

She gave me then such a bitter, forlorn, and desolate look that I didn't dare go on. And perhaps it was not after all so important that she didn't see the Altamont road that day.

IMMOBILIZED BY AGE and circumstances, she did not travel much more. When she did so occasionally, it was only to go to help one or another of her children scattered over this vast country. But was this really travelling? Was it even living, to wait and wait, alone in the depth of Manitoba, while I went in search of myself along the great roads of the world: to Paris, London, Bruges, and Provence; and also along the little roads, known to those who are unable to do without solitude, across another range of hills, for instance, to Ramatuelle in the Maures, and along the coast of Cornwall to Saint Ives and Tintagel?

I sent her postcards, with a few words scrawled on their backs: "Mother, if only you could see Notre-Dame of Paris …" "Kew Gardens on a day in spring …" "Mother, you can't imagine anything more perfect than Chartres Cathedral glimpsed from a distance across the plain of Beauce…."

The waiting emptiness, the lonely, slightly poignant expanses of my own country had not returned to me yet to pluck at my heart. Nor did modest existences in small provincial cities greatly disturb as yet the intoxication of my youth. Moreover, to learn to know myself and to write was a far longer task than I had thought at first.

My mother replied with long patient letters, tender, meticulous, and deceitful, so deceitful. She assured me that she had plenty to live on, no longer having many needs or even, really, the desire to travel. Once only did she write to me about hills, and then about the earliest ones of her life, those that attached us to the memory of my grandmother. "When you return to this country," she entreated, "if you're not too far away, go and see them. They're not so far really from Montreal. You go to Joliette. Then you take a road that goes up …"

What a strange dialogue we exchanged across the ocean, I speaking of not much else besides my discoveries, my mother of such modest landmarks that they could not have moved me much at that time.

She approved of me now: "You were right to go. The winter has been hard. I see that you are discovering, discovering! It must be exhilarating! See all you can while you are in France and take as much time as you need…. Why yes, my health is good…. That cold I had is almost better. I found the story you wrote extremely interesting…."

It was nothing compared to what I would do for her if only she would give me time. But I was always and forever only at the beginning. As yet unaware that it could never be otherwise on this way I had taken, I hurried, I pushed myself; years passed; I hurried, I continued to think of myself as being on the edge of what I wished to become in her eyes before I returned to her. And I am sure that my eagerness for what I would become hid all the rest from me.

My mother failed very quickly. No doubt she died of illness, but, as so many people do fundamentally, of grief too, a little.

Her capricious and youthful spirit went to a region where there are undoubtedly no more difficult crossroads and no more starting points. Or perhaps there are still roads there but they all go past Altamont.

Dog Monday's Vigil

LUCY MAUD MONTGOMERY

DOG MONDAY was the Ingleside dog. He really belonged to Jem, but he was very fond of Walter also. Monday was not a collie or a setter or a hound or a Newfoundland. He was just, as Jem said, "plain dog"—"*very* plain dog," uncharitable people added. Certainly Monday's looks were not his long suit. Black spots were scattered at random over his yellow carcass, one of them apparently blotting out an eye. His ears were in tatters, for Monday was never successful in affairs of honour. But he possessed one talisman. He knew that not all dogs could be handsome or eloquent or victorious, but that every dog could love. Inside his homely hide beat the most affectionate, loyal, faithful heart of any dog since dogs were, and something looked out of his brown eyes that was nearer akin to a soul than any theologian would allow. Everybody at Ingleside was fond of him, even Susan, although his one unlucky propensity of sneaking into the spare room and going to sleep on the bed tried her affection sorely.

On the morning when Jem Blythe left Glen St. Mary for Valcartier, Dog Monday went to the station with him. He kept close to Jem's legs and watched every movement of his beloved master.

"I can't bear that dog's eyes," said Mrs. Meredith.

"The beast has more sense than most humans," said Mary Vance.

Then the train was coming—mother was holding Jem's hand—Dog Monday was licking it—everybody was saying good-bye—the train was in—the train was pulling out—everybody was waving—Dog Monday was howling dismally and being forcibly restrained by the Methodist minister from tearing after the train—they were gone!

The Ingleside folks were half way home when they missed Dog Monday. Shirley went back for him. He found Dog Monday curled up in the shipping shed near the station and tried to coax him home. Dog Monday would not move. He wagged his tail to show he held no hard feelings, but no blandishments availed to move him. "Guess Monday had made up his mind to wait there until Jem comes back," said Shirley, trying to laugh as he rejoined the others.

Which was exactly what Dog Monday had done. His dear master had gone; he, Monday, had been deliberately and of malice aforethought prevented from going with him by a demon disguised in the garb of a Methodist minister; wherefore he, Dog Monday, would wait there until the smoking, snorting monster which had carried his hero off, carried him back.

For weeks the Ingleside family tried to coax Dog Monday home—and failed. Once Walter went down and brought him home by main force in the buggy, and shut him up for three days. Monday went on a hunger strike and howled like a banshee night and day. They had to let him out or he would have starved to death. So they decided to let him alone, and Dr. Blythe arranged with the butcher near the station to feed him with bones and scraps. Dog Monday lay curled up in the shipping shed, and every time a train came in he rushed over to the platform, wagging an expectant tail, and tore around to everybody who came off the train. Then, when the train was gone, and he realized that Jem had not come, he trotted dejectedly back to his shed, with the funny little sidelong waggle that always made his hind legs appear to be travelling in a totally different direction from his front legs, and lay patiently down to wait for the next train. When cold weather came, Walter built a little kennel in the corner of the shed for him. Monday became quite famous. A Charlottetown reporter came out and photographed him and wrote up the story of Monday's vigil for his paper. It was copied all over Canada. But earthly fame mattered not to Monday. Jem had gone away—Monday didn't know where or why—but he would wait until he came back. Somehow, this comforted the Ingleside folks; it gave them an irrational feeling that Jem would come back, or Monday wouldn't keep on waiting for him.

"Fancy the faithful little beggar watching for me like that," Jem wrote home. "Honestly, dad, on some of these cold, dark nights in the trenches it heartens and braces me up to no end to think that thousands of miles away, at the old Glen station, there is a small spotted dog sharing my vigil."

Walter went away the next year and Dog Monday sent messages by him to Jem. Still another long year went by and still Dog Monday waited. On the September morning after Courcellette Rilla Blythe wakened at dawn and heard distinctly a dog howling in a melancholy way down in the direction of the station. Was it Dog Monday? Rilla shivered—the sound had in it something ominous and boding. She remembered hearing some one say once, "When a dog howls like that the Angel of Death is passing." Rilla listened with a curdling fear at her heart. It *was* Dog Monday—she felt sure of it. Whose dirge was he howling? To whose hovering spirit was he sending that anguished greeting and farewell? Rilla went down to the station after breakfast, and the station master said: "That dog of yours howled from midnight to sunrise something weird. I dunno what got into him. He kept the wife awake, and I got up once and went out and hollered at him; but he paid no 'tention to me. He was sitting all alone in the moonlight out there at the end of the platform, and every few minutes the poor little beggar'd lift his nose and howl as if his heart was breaking. He never did it afore—always slept in his kennel quiet and canny from train to train. But he sure had something on his mind last night."

Rilla went home anxiously. For four long days she waited. And when the word came that Walter had been killed in action at Courcellette she knew why Dog Monday had cried.

Three years went by—three years that seemed as long as an ordinary life time. Dog Monday, grown old and rheumatic, still kept faithful vigil. And one spring day, when wind and sunshine frolicked in Rainbow Valley, and the maple grove was golden-green, and the harbour all blue and dimpled and white-capped, the news came about Jem. There had been an insignificant little trench raid on the Canadian front, and Lieut. James Blythe was reported "wounded and missing."

That night, when Rilla was lying on her bed in the moonlight praying desperately for a little strength, Susan stepped in like a gaunt shadow and sat down beside her.

"Rilla, dear, do not worry. Little Jem is not dead."

"Oh, how can you believe that, Susan?"

"Because I *know*. Listen to me. When that word came this morning the first thing I thought of was Dog Monday. And to-night, I went down to the station. There was Dog Monday waiting for the night train, just as patient as usual. Now, Rilla dear, that trench raid was last Monday, and I said to the station agent, 'Can you tell me if that dog howled or made any kind of a fuss last Monday night?' He thought it over a bit and then he said, 'No, he did not.' 'Are you sure?' I said. 'There's more depends on it than you think.' 'Dead sure,' he said. 'I was up all night last Monday night because my mare was sick, and there never was a sound out of him.' Now, Rilla, dear, those were the man's very words. And you know how that poor little dog howled all night after the battle of Courcellette. Yet he did not love Walter as much as he loved Jem. If he mourned for Walter like that, do you suppose he would sleep sound in his kennel the night after Jem had been killed? No, Rilla, dear, little Jem is not dead, and that you may tie to. If he were, Dog Monday would have known, just as he knew before, and he would not still be waiting for the trains."

It was absurd and irrational and impossible. But Rilla believed it for all that; and Mrs. Blythe believed it; and the doctor, though he smiled faintly in pretended derision, felt an odd confidence replace his first despair; and foolish and absurd or not, they all plucked up heart and courage to carry on just because a faithful little dog at the Glen station was still watching for his master to come home. Common sense might scorn; incredulity might mutter "mere superstition"; but in their hearts the folks of Ingleside stood by their belief that Dog Monday knew—a belief that was justified six months later when word came that Jem Blythe had escaped from his German prison.

One spring day, when Rainbow Valley was sweet with white and purple violets, the little lazy afternoon accommodation train pulled into the Glen station. It was very seldom that passengers came by that train; so nobody was there to meet it except the new station agent and a small black and yellow dog, who for four and a half long years had met every train that had steamed into Glen St. Mary. Thousands of trains had Dog Monday met, and never had the boy he waited and watched for returned. Yet still Dog Monday watched on with eyes that never quite lost hope. Perhaps his dog heart failed him at times; he was growing old and rheumatic; when he walked back to his kennel after each train he never trotted, but went slowly, with a drooping head, and a depressed tail that had quite lost its old saucy uplift.

One passenger stepped off the train—a tall fellow in a faded lieutenant's uniform, who walked with a barely perceptible limp. He had a bronzed face and there were some grey hairs in the ruddy curls that clustered round his forehead. The new station agent looked at him curiously. He was used to seeing the khaki-clad figures come off the train, some met by a tumultuous crowd; others, who had sent no word of their coming, stepping off quietly like this one. But there was a certain distinction of bearing and feature in this soldier that caught his attention and made him wonder a little more interestedly who he was.

A black and yellow streak shot past the station agent. Dog Monday stiff? Dog Monday rheumatic? Dog Monday old? Never believe it! Dog Monday was a young pup gone clean mad with rejuvenating joy.

He flung himself against the tall soldier, with a bark that choked in his throat from sheer rapture. He flung himself on the ground and writhed in a frenzy of welcome. He tried to climb the soldier's khaki legs and slipped down and grovelled in an ecstasy that seemed as if it must tear his little body to pieces. He licked his boots, and when the Lieutenant had, with laughter on his lips and tears in his eyes, succeeded in gathering the little creature up in his arms, Dog Monday laid his head on the khaki shoulder and licked the sunburned neck, making queer sounds between barks and sobs.

The station agent had heard the story of Dog Monday. He knew now who the returned soldier was. Jem Blythe had come home.

One Mile of Ice
HUGH GARNER

DOWN HERE IN OUR PART of New Brunswick we have a great respect for winter, but not much liking for it. Snow has its uses: it makes easily traversed winter roads through the woods and covers the earth to keep the frost from penetrating too deep, but, to us, it is not formed of the gossamer flakes that fall upon a poet's window. Sometimes it is blinding and cruel and impenetrable, and its dainty little patterns when multiplied a billion times can kill a man, and often do. And there are those of us who are afraid of the winter as some people are of lightning or fire or high places.

It was about a week before Christmas when, with his brother-in-law Pete, Ralph

Marsden set out for town with the mare and sleigh to buy a few things for the children. Gilbert Moncet, who lives back at the settlement, had dropped into his place to thaw out on his way home the evening before and had mentioned that LeFevre, the taxi driver, had crossed the new ice of the river on foot that afternoon.

Ralph was born and raised on the little clearing in the woods seven miles back from the river, and had married an Acadian girl, a Doucette from somewhere down the North Shore. He worked on the drive in the spring and cut pulp on contract most of the winter like everybody else in this part of the world. With the help of his wife Cecille he was already the father of eight young Marsdens, although only thirty-one. His brother-in-law, Pete, who had been married to Ralph's sister Anna before she died, had come down from Montreal to stay with him for the holidays. He was twenty-five, taller than Ralph, but not as lean and hard. When they stood side by side, Pete wearing Ralph's best mackinaw, they could have been brothers except for the difference in their ways. For our ways aren't the ways of those from the city.

They started out about ten o'clock in the morning. The air was crisp and clear, and before long they buttoned up their collars and pulled the ear flaps down on their caps. The mare needed little urging and she trotted through the soft new snow, the steam rising from her flanks.

Going along the narrow road through the trees they were out of the wind, and they took turns trotting behind the sleigh. The rabbit tracks were everywhere, through the woods, marking their winter runs, sometimes following the road for several yards before swinging off into the young fir and spruce.

"It's getting colder," Ralph said once. "It must be forty below."

"The wind has gone down anyway," Pete replied.

"I don't like it," Ralph said, and turned to look up at the narrow ribbon of northwest sky visible through the trees. "The wind dropped too suddenly. I wouldn't be surprised if we had a big blow later in the day."

They made good time through the woods, and a half hour later came out on the edge of the flats near the sawmill. Madame Cousineau came to the window of her shack and waved at them to stop. Pete drew rein on the mare and waited. Her husband came out and handed them a letter to post in town.

"How's the crossing?" asked Pete.

"I don't know. LeFevre crossed yesterday afternoon, they say. Lots of open water yet. Ice formed too quick this year. Too much air underneath. You figurin' on takin' the sleigh acrost?"

"We will if it looks good enough."

"Risky so early in the year. Frosty today, eh?"

"It's cold," Pete answered.

"I better go in before I freeze," Cousineau said. *"Bonne Chance!"*

Through the open flatlands the snow had drifted across the road, and driving over the soft white hummocks was like riding on a shallow roller-coaster. In the fields the white mantle of snow had been etched into fantastic shapes by the action of the wind, and it was powdered fine in the eddies behind the fence posts and trees.

The cold had rarefied the bitter air so that they gasped sometimes as each in turn ran behind in the runner tracks, holding on to the tailboard of the long *portage* sleigh.

When they reached the small cluster of houses at the summer ferryboat landing the wind had risen again, and the fine powdered snow stung their faces like a sandblast. The ice near the shore was covered with two or three inches of water pushed up by the action of the tide. Beyond it the ice looked firm enough, although several hundred yards out from the land there were two or three wide pools of clear water, each one topped by a rising film of steam.

"Well, what do you say? Are you game to try it?" Ralph asked.

Pete stared at the wide expanse of white ice, partly obscured now by the driving snow. Across the river the smoke rose from the railroad yards at the edge of town. He thought, I'm not going to be turned back now after driving this far and with the goal in sight. In another five minutes they would be across, and he would be able to buy the Christmas presents for the kids and have a nice hot dinner at the Chinaman's. "Might as well," he answered. "We'll be the first to cross by sleigh this year."

"I've always wanted to be first!" Ralph said, his wide brown face splitting with a grin at the thought.

They drove along the shoreline until they found an easy slope to the surface of the ice. The mare was nervous, tossing her head and balking as her feet came in contact with the tidal slush. Ralph slapped her on the rump with the reins and they slid down the bank and through the shallow water. The mare stretched her neck and set out for the opposite shore.

Except for a few ominous cracks at first the ice seemed solid enough, and they set a diagonal course from the end of the ferry wharf towards the town, one mile away across the frozen river. The mare was only lightly shod so Ralph drove her over the snow patches as much as possible.

With the wind at their back they made good time on the ice. Giving the largest of the water holes a fifty-yard berth they turned downriver again in the direction of the town's landing ramp. They crossed a low ice ridge and eased the mare to walk through the snow of the shoreline, then headed up a lane to the street.

Ralph was smiling. "How did you like it?"

"I'm glad it's over," Pete answered, glowing now that they were sheltered from the wind by the waterside buildings.

"There's nothing to be afraid of. If she'd have broken through I'd have made sure you got out while I tried to help the mare."

"That's nice to know," Pete said, "but we might both have gone down."

"Not with a long sleigh like this. So long as there are two of you, and you keep your heads, nobody needs to get drowned in an ice-hole."

"My cheeks sting a bit," said Pete. "I don't know whether this is my own nose or not. How does it look?"

"It's not frozen. How's your feet?"

"They're all right as long as I keep them under the buffalo robe."

"Those low shoes and galoshes may be all right for town, but you should have worn my gum-rubbers or mukluks."

They drove into the livery stable yard and unhitched the mare. Pete led her to a stall and removed her bridle. The manager came out of his office. "Good morning," he said. "You fellows come around by Shannonville?"

Ralph said, "No, we crossed the river."

"Eh!" the man exclaimed.

"We came across on the ice," Ralph reiterated. "I guess we're the first by sleigh, eh?"

"You're the first any way at all."

"I thought LeFevre the taxi driver from the Point crossed it yesterday on foot?" asked Ralph.

The man shook his head. "He didn't get within five hundred yards of this side. You're not going back that way today, are you?"

"I guess not," answered Ralph, laughing with relief and excitement. "We're the first and I'm satisfied with that."

THEY HAD THEIR LUNCH and posted Madame Cousineau's letter at the station. Pete bought some magazines for himself, and some toys and Christmas tree decorations for the kids. Ralph suddenly remembered that he wanted to place an order with the mail-order office for some wallboard to finish his kitchen, so he moved on up the street while Pete went back to the combination hotel and livery stable to wait for him.

When Ralph returned they had supper at the Chinaman's. Ralph had been drinking; he was bragging that he and some friends he met had drunk one bottle of brandy, and he had returned to the store and bought another one.

"I don't want to stay here tonight," he said. "What do you say we go home?"

Pete stared at his brother-in-law. When Ralph had a drink, which was seldom, all the loneliness and frustrations of being a pulp-cutter were brushed aside, and for the length of time the liquor lasted he became a new Ralph Marsden, cocky, argumentative, and ready to take a chance on anything.

"Don't be a fool, Ralph," Pete said. "Let's go back tomorrow morning in the daylight. Maybe the blizzard will have died down by then."

"I'm going anyway; I don't like leaving Cecille and the kids alone at night this time of year. If you're scared, you can stay here."

Despite all his arguments Pete could not change the other's mind.

The livery stable manager said, "It's none of my business, but I wouldn't take a chance if I were you. Those water holes shift with the tide. She ought to be good crossing by morning, and you'll be able to see your way then. You'll be bucking head-winds too, and don't forget it's over forty below."

As he was harnessing the mare to the sleigh Ralph turned once more to Pete. "Are you coming or not?"

Pete remembered what Ralph had said earlier in the day about two men being able to help one another out if the sleigh went into a hole. "I'll come, I guess, but I don't like it."

"It'll be a cinch," Ralph said.

Before they reached the edge of the river the darkness was closing in like a heavy blanket blown across the ice by the moaning wind. After the warmth of the livery stable the cold snow-laden blasts edged through their clothing and scratched at their skin like small sharp spears.

Ralph halted the sleigh at the shoreline and walked around the mare, checking the harness and reassuring her with his hands along her withers. When he returned to the seat they tucked the robe around their legs and fastened their collars high over their chins. "Feel like changing your mind?" asked Ralph, turning his face out of the wind to speak.

Pete stared ahead without answering. There was nothing in front but a black void crossed by vapourlike wisps of erratically driven snow. It was awesome and lonely-looking, and he felt a fear creep up his back. It was the fear of darkness, and the going forward into the unknown.

"Well, what do you say?" Ralph asked again, as if he too felt the nameless dread of the ice-covered river.

"Sure, let's get going," Pete answered, afraid that in another minute he would change his mind and run back to the lights and warmth.

Ralph clucked to the mare, and she stretched her head towards home, stepping out gingerly on the soft shore slush. When she felt the sleigh settle down on her heels she tucked her head into her chest and loped into the wind.

The ice was soft and mushy for fifty yards out from shore where the incoming tide of the afternoon had seeped through. The river crossing was only ten miles in from the open sea.

As they gained the hard surface farther out, Pete felt the uncertainty pressing in on him, and the town was suddenly fifty miles away instead of fifty yards. He felt the sleigh lift over the ice ridge and settle down for the long pull to the opposite side. When the mare faltered in her stride his fingers gripped the seat through his heavy mitts, and he shoved his body forward as though to help her. The darkness was frightening, and he fought an urge to hide his head under the robe as a child will do. Once or twice he glanced ahead and felt his heart stand still as he saw what at first he took to be open water, but it was only the sheen of wind-scarred patches of clear ice.

Ralph gave him the lines after a few minutes ⌐   ⌐ turned his head away from the wind, rubbing his face briskly witʰ ⌐

"How much farther is it?" Pete shoⁱ

"Three-quarters."

It was impossible to telⁱ   ⌐ers of the way to go, or that they hⁿ ⌐   ⌐ getting too cold to worry ⌐ⁱ   ⌐zen tears from the cⁱ   ⌐m fran- tically againsⱼ   ⌐, and they let the maⱼ

Looking behiⱼ.   ⌐ʸ the driving snow. ⌐ managed to see two ⌐ pitch darkness framed iⱼ   ⌐ve, and when his brother-in-ⱼⱼ   ⌐gripping his tongue like a vise, "Theⱼ   ⌐n the river!"

Ralph straightened up as iⱼ   ⌐ of cold water. Pete dragged at the lines and the maⱼ

Now that the sound of hooveⱼ   ⌐rs had ceased they were in the centre of a world turned into a frigiⁿ   ⌐acophony by the elements. The wind screamed in a falsetto from the north ⌐ore breaking into small gusts, each with a wail of its own, as it plucked at their clothes and shattered itself against the horse and sleigh.

Before they had been motionless a minute the fine snow began to drift against them, filling the creases of their clothing and cutting across their bare faces like a million tiny whiplashes.

"The mare is lost!" Pete shouted again. "We should have been across long ago!" He suddenly realized that his shout was a cry.

Ralph struggled to his feet, trying to shake the liquor from his head, and stepped from the box of the sleigh. He turned his back to the wind and asked, "Do you know where we are?"

Pete remembered the lights he had seen. With an effort he shouted back, "We're heading down the river. The town is on our right and the Point is over to our left!"

"How far?"

"I saw some lights a few minutes ago … a half mile!"

"Can't be," Ralp[h]

He pushed again[st] [c]ould see
his arms scraping at [he said,]
"Got to keep movin[g]

Pete nodded his [here they]
were no more than [who were]
eating supper, goin[g] [he Legion]
Hall, and yet they [ ] [dst of the]
frozen tundra.

They swung h[e] [her head]
almost touching [ ] [ut instead]
strained his eyes t[ ] [me before.]
Heedless of the bl[ ] [Where the]
lights should have been was now nothing [ ].

"No lights!" he screamed at Ralph. "No lights!" He beat at the other's arm with
his fist.

Ralph turned his head towards him, and in the slight phosphorescence that
surrounded them he noticed that his brother-in-law's face had stiffened into an ugly
grimace. "Your face is frozen!" he cried.

Ralph did not understand at first.

"Your face!"

Ralph pulled his hand from his mitt and rubbed it over his cheeks. Then he began
punching desperately at his nose and mouth. Pete took the lines once more and
tugged at them until the mare stopped. Then he reached over the side of the sleigh,
scooped up some snow, and began to rub it over his brother-in-law's cheeks. Ralph
sputtered and shook him off. "The brandy!" he shouted.

Pete reached beneath the seat and groped around in the hay until he found the
bottle. Keeping it under the robe he unscrewed the top and poured some through
the other's stiffened lips. Ralph choked and fought against him. Taking off one of his
mitts he rubbed his hand against Ralph's cheeks. Ralph slapped his hand away. "Got
to get warm," he whispered through chattering lips.

Pete pulled him into the bottom of the sleigh and placed his head between his own
knees, covering him completely with the robe. When he tried to re-cap the brandy
bottle he found that his hands had become too stiff from their slight exposure to the
air. The cap rolled away, and he let it go, no longer caring whether the bottle was
covered or not. He took a long gulp of the liquor before standing the uncapped bottle
in a corner and bracing it with some of the parcels which were lying at his feet.

When he gave his attention to the mare he saw that she was crouched almost to
her knees, and he whipped at her frenziedly with the lines. She shivered but refused
to budge. Crying and cursing with desperation he climbed out of the sleigh and felt

his way along her flank, grabbing the bridle. By dint of much tugging he got her into motion again, and they headed into the wind.

His exertions and the brandy began to warm him and he shouted encouragement to the mare while trying to get his bearings. Glancing back over the sleigh he picked out a pinpoint of light that flashed momentarily through the darkness.

He knew that if the light was one of those he had glimpsed earlier, they must have swung to the right from their original course, and must now be facing in the opposite direction. Wherever they were (unless they had travelled three or four miles down the river, which was unthinkable) they could not be more than a half mile away in one of two directions. He tried to reduce everything to its logical perspective. Somewhere in the darkness lay the town they had left—how long before? It was obvious that the flickering light he could see was not from the town because it would have been accompanied by many more. Therefore it could only mean they had almost traversed the river in the direction of the north shore before getting turned around and heading out again.

He grasped the mare by the bridle and swung her around. She struggled weakly, but plodded along at his side as they again pressed into the blizzard toward the flickering pinpoint of brightness.

They crept on for what he judged to be thirty or forty yards before he became conscious of a loss of feeling in his feet. He fought against the mounting panic that greeted this realization. Everything now depended on his not losing his head.

His mind worked with the strange clarity that accompanies danger and hardship, and he stamped upon the ice, jumping up and down in a vain attempt to cause a reassuring stab of feeling. Despite all his efforts his feet were like two blocks of wood. He knew then with the certainty of despair, that his only hope was to reach some haven of warmth.

He was not only cold in a sensory way, his face, legs and hands, but deep inside him the freezing wind seemed to have penetrated and reduced the temperature of his whole body. He began to fear for his life, no longer philosophical or logical, but aching with an urge to live. His breath came in great searing gasps which chilled and burned his throat and teeth....

The mare was enmeshed in a dull lethargy that all his blows and curses could not overcome. No matter how hard he tried he could not keep the light dead ahead, and sometimes it appeared to be swinging steadily to the left.

He was afraid his face was freezing, and he dragged the horse to a stop and buried his head in the shelter of her neck and rubbed his cheeks against the cold roughness of her hide. When he looked again for his landmark it had moved several degrees to the left of where it had been a moment before. With a sudden shock he realized that the light was not the fixed one of a window on the north side of the river, but the reflection of the headlight of a train.

It was too much. He turned back to the sleigh sobbing with fear and frustration. He gave up hope there and then of ever making a landfall alive. When he reached for the brandy bottle he found that it had tipped over and was now rattling emptily along the floorboards at his feet.

There was nothing else to do but climb under the buffalo robe alongside the comatose form of his brother-in-law and let the mare follow her head. He groped around until he found the lines, and slapped them across her haunches. She began moving slowly against the storm.

Later—he did not know how much later it was—he experienced one of those climatic happenings visited on man once in a lifetime by the devil himself. A gust of wind, stronger than the rest, plucked his cap from his head and flung it over the side of the sleigh. In a temperature of forty degrees below zero, and exposed as he was to the wind, the loss of a head covering meant certain death within minutes. He stood up to try to retrieve it, but stopped as he realized that it was yards away by then.

Before he could settle down again into the seat there was a high-pitched, almost human scream from the mare. As he stood rooted to the floor in terror she reared back in the shafts and slipped sideways into a water hole. He grabbed at Ralph's head, shouting something in a crazed scream, and then threw himself over the sideboard, landing on his back upon the ice. As soon as he fell he sprang to his feet, using the last reserves of energy that even an exhausted man can muster against death, and stood there clutching Ralph's cap in his hand.

With a dull splash the heavy sleigh followed the horse into the water. It floated for a long minute on the surface, and as Pete watched it, horror-stricken, he saw his brother-in-law raise himself on his hands and knees, his bare head shoved out from beneath the robe, his eyes staring at him from his frozen features.

It was impossible to tell whether his expression was one of remorse, hate or resignation. Pete wanted to blot out the stare of those eyes, and he hoped—yes, and prayed—that the sleigh would quickly sink.

Slowly—Oh God, how slowly!—it dipped and twisted before it filled with water and tilted into the cold black depths, bearing away that frozen grinning face.

The water churned and bubbled in the narrow hole, and several objects appeared for a minute on the surface: the buffalo robe, a parcel or two, and the empty brandy bottle. They swirled in the vortex and were lost again beneath the ice.

He backed away from the hole and ran before the wind in the direction from which they had come. He was no longer aware of distance or purpose in his flight, and his head was light with the fever of approaching death. When he could no longer run, he walked, after pulling Ralph's cap around his ears, looking like a ghostly scarecrow wandering around on the ice. After his legs gave out he crawled on frozen hands and knees through the drifting snow, falling on his face every few yards, going God knows where....

The search party didn't find him until he and Ralph had been gone over three hours, and a phone call to the opposite shore brought back the information that they had not arrived over there. He was lying at the edge of the water hole which had swallowed his brother-in-law and the sleigh, and he was screaming in delirium about a stolen cap.

Ralph's body was found the following spring almost twenty miles down the shore. Pete is still alive, but he lost both his legs at the knees.

He wanted to stay around the district after he came out of the hospital, and do what he could for Cecille and the children, but with the first fall of snow he went away. He wrote to Gilbert Moncet and told him that on cold winter nights he sometimes saw a vision of a frozen grimacing face, and he wanted to tear away its impenetrable mask…. He still wonders if Ralph went to his death bearing a hatred for him because he had thought only of himself. It frightens him, so that he is afraid of the winter as some people are of lightning or fire or high places.

Rough Answer
SHEILA WATSON

MARGARET STOOD at the door of the cabin. She watched the thin blue light of evening merge into the dark blue green of coming night. She heard the plaintive honking of some geese as they passed overhead, an arrow of blackness in the translucent sky. Somewhere in the black hills a coyote barked. "Joe will be coming soon," she thought. "The school lady will be tired."

She strained forward into the darkening evening, listening. The silence surged around her, cut off all contact with reality. The long drawn wail of the coyote wrenched her back to life. She went into the house and stirred up the fire. She lit the lamp. She looked once more into the little room which Joe had built by putting up a thin partition down the length of their one room. As she turned back to the fire she heard the rattle of wagon wheels coming over the culvert.

"Ho Major! Ho Colonel!" Joe's voice rang clear with laughter. "They couldn't hurt you nowise. We're here all right and Margaret'll make you comfortable."

Margaret went to the door with the lamp.

"Come in," she said. "Joe'll put the horses in and bring your things."

She watched Joe help the girl down from the high wagon. "She's pretty," she thought, "pretty like you don't see around here."

The girl pulled her fur jacket close about her and let Joe help her to the door.

"You must be cold," said Margaret, letting her eyes travel down the slim length of silk-clad leg, letting them rest for a moment on the queer strapped slippers. Her voice rang with a half suppressed note of disapproval.

"It's cold," the girl said with a slight shudder as she went into the house.

"Pretty," the girl thought to herself. "Pretty enough but old looking. I suppose they grow old living here—like this."

She felt a little frightened. She wouldn't let her thoughts rest on those months of boredom.

"God knows what I'll find to do," she thought.

Margaret took her into her bedroom. She lit a candle. The light flickered on the white spread, the work table and the frilled dresser.

"It looks like a hermit's cell," thought the girl.

"I hope you'll be comfortable," said Margaret. "Ask for anything you want. I'll give you warm water and Joe he'll fetch you a tubful Friday nights."

Good heavens! the girl hadn't thought of that. "In these places they didn't bathe, did they?" She had known that before. She was just beginning to realize, though, what she'd done. She could stick it anyway if things didn't pall too much. Joe—that was the man's name, wasn't it?—had asked her if she could ride. She had lied about it. Said she loved it. Perhaps he'd take her out sometime. He wasn't bad looking in his own way. A little rough—but then—he'd be much more amusing than Margaret. "She looks," the girl's thoughts hesitated—"she looks good."

At supper Joe seemed to be in a very good humour. He told several stories. Joe didn't talk much as a rule. When he spoke it was of the price of beef or irrigating or fencing or of the new corral he was going to build.

"Trying to cheer the girl up," thought Margaret. She, too, spoke more than was her wont. She and Joe didn't need to speak much. They knew. A third person changed things somehow. Broke the contact. Silence seemed a little shameless, a little naked.

"They're right glad to have a lady teacher," she said. "We've had men so long. It'll be nice to have a woman about."

"I'll let you have the bay mare to ride," said Joe. "Then you can come and go as you like. Margaret'll show you round."

The girl's eyelids fluttered slightly. She hadn't thought of that. Margaret would ride. Ride with Margaret—she might have saved herself the trouble of a lie.

"You must be tired," said Margaret. "Joe'll take you to school in the morning to get you acquainted with the way."

The girl went into her room. She felt a little depressed, a long way from nowhere. She shut the flimsy door and opening the window, lit a cigarette.

"The man's rather nice looking," she thought. She yawned and stared out into the darkness.

Margaret and Joe looked at each other.

"She's pretty," said Margaret, "but I think she'll find it quiet here."

"Don't know," said Joe. He felt a little disturbed. He'd never felt that way before, not that he could remember. He couldn't just say. He felt he should say something. He didn't know what. A third person always made a difference he guessed. He began to whistle under his breath.

The week hadn't been so bad, thought the girl on Friday night as she sat curled round in the corrugated tub of warm water which Joe had fetched for her. She was getting used to things. She dried herself and slipped into a thin white dress which showed the curves of her slim body. She sat down on the bed and polished her nails.

"Margaret's a funny woman," she thought. "Cuts her nails straight across as if she didn't care." Joe noticed those things, too. She was conscious of his eyes following her sometimes. Her thoughts hurried on, slipping over things she wouldn't really think about. "He's really nice," she thought, "not the kind of man ..." She rose abruptly and, putting on a sweater, went out.

Margaret was peeling the vegetables for supper.

"Going to watch Joe feed?" she asked. "He's going to take you up to see the critters tomorrow. Thought you'd like to tell them at home about it, he did. We don't want you to be lonely like."

"That will be nice. I can write them a long letter." The girl went out and down towards the yard.

Margaret went into her room and opened the window. She didn't like the smell of smoke. She went back and began to cut the turnips into squares. She set the table, putting a side plate and napkin for the girl.

"I suppose she's different to me, that's all," she thought. "Her way's not my ways."

She felt resentment rising in her throat. Her silence had been shattered. The presence of the girl in the house rang through the silence, the vibrant reality which was her only refuge, the tacit understanding she had with life. She couldn't have explained it, but she knew.

Joe was different too. He sang sometimes and talked, as if to clothe the silence which had been theirs, the understanding which they had arrived at without words the first night she had come home with him.

Joe looked up. He saw the girl coming. "Slim and white like them lilies on the mountain," he thought. Then he checked himself. He was thinking too much about that girl, he was, the way she moved, the helpless look in her eyes when she asked him to do anything, the soft white skin disappearing down her dress at the back of her neck. He didn't think of Margaret like that. She was a fact, was Margaret, a mighty pleasant fact, too, with her long, unbroken silence and her quiet ways; but still, a man—he liked the flowers, didn't he?—sort of made your throat ache to see them standing straight, their cups filled with sunlight.

The girl came up to him as he tossed down the hay. "You seem busy," she said.

"It's nice out here." She leant against the bars of the fence. Joe tossed down more hay. He began to whistle. She leant there, looking up the hill lonesome like. He saw the sunlight glint on her pale hair. His hand ached to touch the soft skin at her throat. "Wonder what it would feel like," he thought, "soft and warm like a horse's nostrils." But he shouldn't think that way. He knew that.

"He seems queer," thought the girl. "Don't think he'll ever be the real thing." She thought of the stories she had read—silent men, strong and passionate. Her own experience had not led her beyond the college boy type. She felt lonesome again. She was definitely bored but slightly expectant.

The next day Joe saddled the mare and his own fancy-looking stud. He felt himself possessed by a new sort of vanity, a desire to look smart. He had shaved and put on a clean shirt. Margaret had lent the girl a pair of overalls and Joe buckled her into his chaps.

"It'll be windy there," he said, bending closer as he tugged at the buckle, close enough to catch her fragrant warmth.

The mare was gentle but he went slowly. Anyone with half an eye in his head could see that the girl couldn't ride. Margaret sat a horse well. Rode like a man.

It gave Joe a protective feeling, a feeling twin brother to his new vanity to see her sitting slim and helpless on the mare. She bumped up and down in the saddle.

"Press yourself against the cantle," he suggested. "You'll ride easier."

When they reached the top of the hill the girl looked uncomfortably tired.

"Let's rest for a bit," he suggested. He knew he shouldn't suggest it. He felt that his feet were on marshy ground. His feeling of vanity was oozing away, but the protective feeling became stronger.

"It's a long way, isn't it," she said. He helped her down from the mare. Her hair brushed across his mouth. He let his hand rest on her shoulder for a moment. He wouldn't—not he, but the next moment she had let her head slip forward on his shoulder.

"I'm so tired." Her voice had a plaintive ring.

"We could go back," he said, knowing that he should go back at once. Margaret was his woman. The girl moved a little closer.

"I'm so lonely," she said, and began to whimper a little.

Joe knew what he should do—what you did to mares when they get a little skittish. He knew, but he stood gazing over the level stretch of the range. He thought of Margaret.

"You do tempt a man to pity," he said, "like young mares in the spring or yearling heifers."

She sprang back as if struck, her face crimson.

"How could you say that," she cried out. She felt perhaps it was true, but she wouldn't think, not for anything. He was crude, crude beyond belief.

"Let's go—back," she said.

He helped her to mount. He felt indifferent now. He looked out to where the blue sky and the yellow hills met. He felt the power of their silence.

That night the girl spoke to Margaret.

"I'm going," she said. "It's lonesome here. I shouldn't have come. I'm not made your way."

She wanted desperately to think. Joe had wakened in her a feeling, a stirring of realization which she could not comprehend. She felt different towards Margaret somehow. Yet she wanted to go. She wasn't ready to meet herself yet.

The next morning Joe drove her to the station.

"They'll have to get another girl for the school," Margaret said.

"I think they'll get a man again," said Joe.

They sat down to supper. Margaret's thoughts moved slowly. Joe's my man, she thought. He's life. Like rain for plants or hay for critters. The girl's gone. She thought of the slim length of the girl's supple legs.

"Beef's gone up," said Joe. "They told me at the station."

The light flickered on the plates. Margaret rose and stirred the fire. She felt at peace once more.

"We won't board no more school-teachers," said Joe.

"No," said Margaret.

A coyote howled in the hills. The dog barked. They did not notice it. They sat each wrapped in his own thoughts, their silence unbroken.

The Locket

ERNEST BUCKLER

I WAS RUNNING AWAY from home that night. I waited until the house was still.

The still moonlight was outside. The heavy June moonlight that lay like a waiting over the growth-full fields. The leaves of all the growing moved a little all the time, but there was no breeze you could feel, and they moved as if they were drowsy and burdened, not shivering bright the way the sun had made shot silk of the swimming grass in the still-hot afternoon. The only sound outside was the patient sound of the cowbells, muffled because the clapper barely touched the sides of the bell, but it carried close and near into the room.

I lay there, loving all that now that I must leave it and a little frightened now that the time had come to go, but having to go just the same.

My father and my brother Michael were sound asleep. They didn't lie awake and remember the way the sun had moved over the grass, because they belonged here. I noticed those things because I was a stranger.

I lay with my clothes on, and waited, and now, I thought, it is safe. My heart was beating fast when I tiptoed by the door of the room where my father and mother slept. And suddenly I thought, I can't do it after all. It was like stealing, somehow, because they were asleep. They are sleeping because they are tired, I thought, and I can't go away without a word, when they are tired. I thought, I'll wait till morning and tell them then and maybe they will see.

But how could I do that? In the morning the sun would be bright again and everything solid and real, and how could you speak suddenly to your father and Michael, standing to listen with the milk pails in their hands, or to your mother, stopping her work at the stove to listen, and tell them you did not belong in this place, when for them the thought of any other place in the world as home would be almost as strange and shameful as a lie? How could you look at their faces then? You couldn't. You would put it off till noon, but at the dinner table your breath would come too fast with just the thought of beginning to speak and you would put it off till evening, but then when evening was come, the thing would be dulled with the silting of the day's work through your mind and your muscles so you could find no tongue for it at all.

Not until you lay down on the bed at night would the shimmer of the sea and the places beyond it stir in you again like a madness.

I could never explain a thing like that to my father, I thought. It was not that there was no love between us, but when we were silent our minds were not moving alongside each other; and if I spoke this secret thing of mine to him in words, so it would always be there then, spoken, between us, every time we were angry or alone together it would come back.

I whispered softly, "Goodbye, mother and dad," and passed by their door to Michael's. I whispered to myself, "Goodbye, Michael, we had good times."

I could have told Michael and it would not be like trying to tell my father. Michael and I had felt that first strange lightness inside us to see a girl's dress cling to her in the wind, the same first secret summer, and talked about it together, and after that we could talk about anything at all. But he wouldn't understand this. He wouldn't understand a thing that was stronger even than girls. He wouldn't understand that your home was not where you were born, that it was some place you had to find.

I couldn't bear to think of telling my mother at all, the way her face would be.

I tiptoed downstairs and the guilt went away a little, until I came to my grandmother's door. I thought, the others ... but I will never see her again. And she is old and blind. She has never seen me.

And suddenly I thought, if she were young I could tell her. I know she of them all would understand. I thought, when she was young I know she was restless too sometimes, and sometimes she must have been struck still in the midst of her work and scared, for a minute, because the circle of trees everywhere she looked seemed small and closing about her and she was young and there were so many things her eyes would never see and her heart would never find out.

And now she was old and blind, and she had never been on a train. A thing like that could happen. The thought frightened me, so I wanted to hurry.

But she stirred. "David," she said softly, "what is it?"

I stepped into the room quickly and stood by her bed. "Nothing," I whispered. And then I couldn't lie. I said, "I'm going away."

"Away?" she said. "Where?"

She spoke softly too, as if it were already a secret thing between us.

"I don't know," I said.

I didn't. I didn't know which place would be home. I had money for the train. And then there would be ships. A ship was like a dream, then. The land was still and rooted like the noon of the day, but the sea was running and free like wide thoughts that came in the night.

"Why?" she said.

"I don't know," I said.

I didn't. I didn't know what it was I was looking for. If it weren't in one place it would be in another. There were all kinds of places and it must be in one of them.

"Will you tell them," I said, "the others …?"

I knew she could tell them all right. Far better than I. There are some people who can tell things, and some who can't. She could tell things and you couldn't see where her words were much different from the words another would use, but you would forget you were listening to a story, you were there.

I think that's why she had never seemed old to me. She had told me stories since I was a child. I think it was the way she told the stories that made me believe when she was young she had felt as I felt. Because sometimes she seemed to forget I was listening, it was as if she were telling these things to herself. A story of hers had started my thoughts of leaving, although I did not think of that now. It was a secret story between us, a story she had told to no one else. I can only give the facts. I cannot tell it the way she told it.

One day she'd been helping my grandfather in the fields and when she came in to kindle the fire for supper, before she reached the house she had a funny feeling that someone was inside. There was. A man was standing in the kitchen, by the wall near the window, where he could watch to know that she came alone. He was very young, no older than she, but the sailor's middy he wore was clothing so strange that he was like someone from another world.

She didn't scream. She said she stepped back to the bake oven where the great poker for turning the firewood lay, but although the house was alone by itself and the woods ran up behind it, somehow she was not afraid.

He spoke to her and told her she must hide him. Until his ship sailed. The port where his ship lay was only fifty miles from home, but that was as five hundred then, and he told her they would not come searching for him there.

He told her why he must hide. It was a strange reason, but she said she knew it was true. And she listened, because she was so startled she couldn't find her voice to deny him yet.

He had gone with his captain on some errand to a great house in the city. It was funny how she could make you see what a great house in the city was like as plainly as if she'd lived in one all her life. In the garden there had been a peacock. And she could make you see what a strange and wonderful thing a peacock was in the cool garden of a house in the city. The peacock had fascinated him. He had thought, if I could just have one feather from its tail. To carry to Bermuda in my blouse, to show them there.

He had managed to sneak into the garden while the captain was inside the house, and stealing close to the great bird he'd given its tail a sharp wrench. The bird screamed. He had never heard a peacock scream. He had no idea a bird could scream so loudly. The captain had rushed out and there he stood, with the feathers in his hand.

He knew as soon as they were back on ship he would be whipped. She told me what it was like to be whipped on a ship and my own body could almost feel it. Her eyes were angry and hurt. "The heavy thongs would have split his soft flesh like the blow of an axe lays open a maple's flesh when the sap is running ..."

He had run away while the captain was in a shop, on the way back to ship, and travelled through the woods by night and now he was here and he said she must hide him.

When she found her voice she said no, go away at once, she couldn't do it. I know she was thinking of my grandfather. He was a good man, and in his heart a kind one, he was like my father; but he would never be party to hiding a man, although giving him up might be a harder thing to do than to feel the lashes on his own flesh. If you were guilty you must be punished according to the rules that stood, and there could be no tampering with justice as it was written, even if you might not understand it.

She was thinking that there was no way of making my grandfather see about a thing like that. It would have been like trying to make my father see why I must go away. He would listen patiently, but words that went against the things that were strict and plain would mean nothing to him at all.

She told the young sailor no, but he kept saying yes, you must, you will, and at last she said, for one night.

I have looked at the picture of my grandfather that hung over the organ in the parlour and I know what that decision must have been like for her, who had never kept anything from him before in her life.

I think she must have said yes because the sailor was so young. My grandfather's age was almost twice hers then. I know she never loved anyone else and had been happy. But I think that afternoon, after all the years when there'd been so little youth about her that she'd ceased almost to feel the brightness of her own, now suddenly she felt her own again sharply, like clean linen in a breeze, and suddenly burstingly and sadly too, like something that had been yours and neglected and that sometime would die without notice that it was gone. And then she could not refuse safety for the youth in another.

The sailor stayed that night, in the loft. And the next day. And the next night. And then he made her promise that he might stay until his ship was surely gone.

"It was wrong," she'd say. "I should have told your grandfather ... but he had stayed one night, it was already a deception ... and what could I do?"

She brought food to him, secretly. At first she had refused to talk to him. And then I think someday he must have begun a story of some far place he had seen and her hand had lingered, in spite of herself, on the door-knob.

It was a strange thing to think of, my grandmother listening to those stories, maybe when she should have been at work in the fields, guiltily, in fear that my grandfather might find her out, not wanting to listen but the sun slipping down towards the trees while she sat there with her hands still on her apron and the words about those far places sounding in this little building of our own.

Her eyes would have a strange look when she'd repeat those stories to me, and I knew she forgot that I was there.

"The ship goes slower now, going into a place called Marseilles, only they don't spell it the way it sounds, because it is far-off and the words there are not the same as ours are, and the water there is blue and deep like the colour of a flower ..."

"... They call it China and the people there eat with little sticks, and the feet of the women are bound with wood, and in the market-places the fowls are hung with the feathers on until the head drops off ..."

"... and there all the people have flaxen hair and everyone knows how to play a tune and they dance in the streets and they seem to be always laughing ..."

"... and there their skins are all dark and everywhere there is the smell of spice and fruit, fruit everywhere in the streets, oranges, and limes, and grapes, and melons, and dark sweet fruits I have never seen, and the dark women have combs in their hair and lace, even in the smallest houses ..."

"... The wind is sharp on deck when you leave and sharp on your skin as knives and when it is night the waves break their dark tongues against the sides of the ship steadily, as if they were blind, but when you come there it is summer all the time ..."

And then I would scarcely be listening either, because I *was* that man, in all those places, listening to the story but moving along with it, in it now, like the way you watch the current of the brook so steadily that after a while you are floating along too ... and when I helped Michael to water the cows that night or carry in the wood my body would be slow and the place where my body was did not seem to be a real place at all. I had to go everywhere and do everything that man had ever done.

One night the sailor told her something I didn't believe he could have meant. He told her the sea was a lonely thing. He told her if she'd bring him some old clothes, he'd find work somewhere on the land, that's where he wanted to stay. She said she had thought he spoke the truth, because he spoke so earnestly.

The next morning he was gone. She took the clothes for him, but he was gone.

"WHAT DO YOU WANT me to tell them," she said, "the others ...?"

I don't remember the words I used then, they were probably not the same at all for any of it as these, but I remember what I was trying to say. I may not have talked that way then, but it was the way I thought.

"Tell them ..." I said. "Do you remember when you were young? Were there sometimes ... when you heard the whistle of a train ... did you stand still and it was like your own life was going by in the train and everything in the place where you stood was struck with a quiet, it was a quiet you couldn't call to, like the way the flowers lie on a grave after everyone has gone home ...?"

"I am an old woman," she said.

"But think," I said, "sometimes, when you were young ... in the fall when the hay was cut and the moonlight was on the fields and you stepped outside, was it lovely, but like a mocking, was there something like you couldn't wait, like it was all somewhere else ... or in the winter when the sun went down and the wind was sort of blue over the frozen fields ... or even in the summer, like now, even in the hot growing afternoons would there sometimes be a minute when you'd think of somewhere else or something or someone else somewhere and a fright and a shiver would go through you like the shiver of the grass in the sun ... or when you thought of the sea ...?"

"What do you say?" she said sharply.

"Or the sea. Did you ever see a picture of a ship sailing ... just a picture ... and all at once you were there in the picture, and life moved in you then, sharp and clean and not waiting, and the sea went everywhere, moving a little always, bright and blue and deep, going everywhere, touching everywhere ...?"

"David," she said, and her voice was funny, soft but sort of frightened, "come here by the window. Let me look at you."

I went to the head of her bed and she reached up and took my face between her hands.

"You have blue eyes," she said, "haven't you?" I suppose she must have heard someone speak of my eyes, because she'd never seen them with her own.

"And your hair is dark, isn't it … very dark … and thick at the temples?" I supposed she knew that because she was passing her hands over it.

"And somehow your face seems to move all the time even when it is still, like there was a breeze behind it, lightening and shadowing … and your eyes go away, they keep going away …"

She had certainly never heard anyone say anything like that. She said that as if suddenly her eyesight had come back and she was really seeing me for the first time. I thought, she is an old woman, wandering.

It gave me such a funny feeling that I moved away a little. I began to feel restless. It wasn't quite midnight, and there was a shortcut across the fields and over the marsh and down the cut to the station. But I wanted to be there in lots of time for the train. I kept one hand in my pocket to make sure my ticket was still there.

"I must go," I said.

"Will you kiss me," she said, "before you go?" Suddenly I felt foolish. I didn't want to do it at all. But I knelt over and kissed her cheek.

It was strange then. Her face didn't feel like the faces of other old women who had kissed me when I was a child. It seemed almost like a young woman's cheek. I don't know why, but it made me think of Helen.

I don't know why, but I thought of Helen then stronger than I had thought of her all that night. I had kissed Helen that afternoon, down by the river where the sweet smell of the clover and the clean moist river-smell had seemed to get into the kiss too. I didn't tell her I was going away, because it was light and I thought I will come back someday and nothing between us will be changed, the way nothing here changes, it did not seem like good-bye. But now in the darkness, suddenly I knew it was good-bye, that I would never kiss her again.

The thought of Helen was so strong then, the way the first girl you've kissed when you are young can seem to have in her all the places there are to go to too, that it was stronger almost than the voice of the places that were beyond the sea. I thought, I can't leave her.

And then, ever so faintly and from far-off, the whistle of the train crept like a cry across the still fields and into the room and I knew that if I did not run across the fields soon, soon the train would go by and then it would blow again, leaving the station, and the sound would come back to me and there would be a stillness after that more terrible than the stillness of the moonlight. I felt in my pocket for the ticket. It was still there.

"You *will* tell them?" I said quickly.

"Yes," she said. "I will try."

I must go now. I must. I said, "Goodbye." And yet I hesitated because it seemed as if there should be something more than that.

"It's all right," she said softly. "You have said goodbye."

I was almost at the door when suddenly she called me back.

"Look," she said. She pointed to a tiny drawer in the bureau. "Inside a book. Is there something there?"

I thought, she is wandering, but I opened the drawer quickly and took out the book. A tiny locket dropped from between the pages onto the floor.

"It's a locket," I said.

"Yes," she said, "take that. It's for you."

I looked at it. I had never seen her wear the locket herself. She was never a woman for things about her neck or her arms. I thought, she is wandering again. Did she think *I* could wear a locket?

Or maybe she thought it was valuable, that I might need money, that I could sell it. I could see it was not a valuable thing, the workmanship was poor and the metal was tarnished, but I didn't tell her that. I felt a lump in my throat.

"It's lovely, grandma," I said. "I will keep it."

"I am an old woman," she said so softly that I could scarcely hear her voice as I turned to go.

I ran across the fields, dark now because the moon had gone, and across the marsh where fog lifting from the river made a dew almost as cold as the first fall frost, and through the long dark cut where the train ran, not thinking at all now because the time was so short and the great body of the train was already humming in the rails where my feet touched them. I didn't have time to think at all until I was on the train, until I was really there, and I could feel in my pocket and know there was nowhere I could lose it now.

I had time to think then. But somehow there was something funny about the whistle of the train. It sounded the same as ever, leaving the station. It sounded as if I were not close to it even yet. It was still ahead of me and the lonesome sound was still there, as if it did not know I had heard, really heard this time, as if no one would ever really hear, as if I were not following behind at all.

The faces of the people were all strange, and the easy way they talked and laughed about things that had no body in them was all strange, but I was still alone. These faces were strange, but somehow they were not real, because they were here and now, like the faces were real in the places you could think of, the places where the faces would be strange but you would be with them. The places that were not yet.

My ticket was gone and I was moving, moving now through the dark against the pane, and then I thought of home. I thought of them sleeping at home.

I thought of them at home, and I had never before seen as sharply as I did then the way the shadows of the maples latticed the ground where they met over the mountain road that was cool even in the summer, or how the field sloped up behind the barn so you could lie in the grass and narrow your eyelids and make the dark mountains come as small and close as you liked, or the faces of my mother and father tired and quiet when the lamp was first lit at the supper table in the fall ... or felt so plainly the curling of my bare toes on the hay stubble when the hay was first cut ... or heard so clearly Michael's good voice that night I was lost in the swamp ...

I thought of my grandmother and I wondered if she was sleeping too. I wondered if she would be able really to tell them.

I thought of the locket, and I went out between the cars where there would be no one to see me. I took it from my pocket and turned it over in my hand. The wheels were racing beneath me and the darkness was running by and I opened it and looked inside.

I held it up closer in the dim light then, because there was an old-fashioned picture beneath the oval glass. The face was the face of a sailor in a middy, a face about the age of mine. It was one of those pictures where the eyes always follow you.

I knew then who it was and where it had come from. He must have given the locket to her, as a keepsake, or left it for her, that morning he went away. I closed the locket and put it back into my pocket.

But the eyes still seemed to follow me. Something about the face made me look again. The face was familiar, that was it. It was like someone. It was like someone I knew very well. I thought. It wasn't like my father, or my brother, or any of the neighbours, but I had seen that face before.

And then suddenly I knew where I had seen a face like that, beyond any mistaking. I had seen it in the mirror. It was my own.

I knew then how my grandmother had seen my face. "But what could I do ...? I shouldn't have listened, but what could I do?" I knew too what she had meant when she said that. There was no guilt anywhere. I knew she had loved her husband all the time, deeper than anything else, but I understood now what it was like to love a thing the way I myself loved home, and yet when the sun is still on the fields and something like the whistle of a train calls, what can you do?

I knew too why the train whistle would always be ahead for me and have the lonesome sound, but I having to follow. I knew whose blood my own was echoing, although my father's had not heard it.

And Helen, or Annette, or Maria, or any of you, if you should see this, will you understand? Will you understand that it was not ever you that was lacking, that your part of it was enough, that I meant to stay but ...? Will you understand that I can believe it now, that the sea is a lonely thing ... that I have been to all the places now and I know now that every place you come to, as soon as it is here and now the faces are not quite real, like the ones ahead? The places are all alike when you get there. I know there is no one place where I will be really among them.

That you may understand. This you will not. But will you *try* to understand about the whistle of a boat? How you forget all you *know* then. Maybe this time.

Maybe this place. Will you try to understand what it is like to hear the lonesome sound in the whistle of a boat and know it's lonesome always for you alone?

Will you try to understand what it's like when no matter where you hear the whistle of a boat, what can you do?

The Blizzard

MERNA SUMMERS

"THEY WERE AT IT again last night," Fred says to Philip as Algertha and I, puffy from lack of sleep, drag ourselves into the day. It's their regular Sunday breakfast joke, a joke that's as much a part of our weekend visits to the farm as the Saturday nights that precede it, evenings that only begin when Fred and Philip go to bed some time after midnight, leaving Algertha and me in the kitchen for one more cup of coffee.

Algertha's well is alkaline, and I don't care for her brand of instant coffee. Yet we drink cup after cup, talking.

Years ago, we were the Heartwell sisters, Algertha and Winona, daughters of Morgan Heartwell and his wife, Ruby, of the Fidelity district near Willow Bunch, Alberta. It's about this that we talk.

When other people, people like Uncle Emery and Aunt Elizabeth, talk about the past, there is "the Depression" and "during the War," and "after the War," layers of life gone by that peel off neatly and separately, like layers of an onion. But for people like Algertha and me, those divisions are too broad. They take in both too much and too little. I was ten in 1939 and sixteen in 1945. Algertha, two years older, was twelve in 1939 and eighteen in 1945. Of what use was "the War" to us? Too much happened in those years. We need our time set between closer boundaries.

By ourselves, on the nights when we are "at it again," we speak of "before the blizzard" and "after the blizzard." The blizzard is something not to be mentioned to outsiders, of course, but both Algertha and I can be remarkably accurate in dating anything that happened in the mid-war years. If someone mentions a particular salvage drive, for instance, or the Blackburns' two-headed calf being born, neither Algertha nor I ever needs to wonder if it happened in 1941 or whether it was 1942. We know.

We've got the *when* of those years down straight. Now if we could only get the *what* as well, maybe we could work ourselves past the need for these early-morning probings, or exorcisms, or whatever they are.

Even to each other, we never say, "Let's talk about what happened. Let's see if we can't understand it." Instead, we sidle into our memories, using excuses. A cake plate that was Mother's, heaped with softening Nanaimo bars, sits on Algertha's kitchen table, and I use the sight of it as a stepping-stone by which to re-enter the past. Or Algertha, scenting my Yardley's English Lavender, the toilet-water that Mother used, says—shyly for her—"Do you remember, Nonie...."

Many of the memories are trivial, unimportant. Yet how can we know? To Algertha and me, scavenging the past, anything could be the clue we seek, the beam that would serve as a bridge from where we are now to where we were before the blizzard. Since we don't know what we are looking for, we save splinters and painstakingly fit them together.

Last week I remembered the magazines from which Mother encouraged us to fill our scrapbooks with pictures of the corgi-toting little princesses, Elizabeth and Margaret Rose.

"Why were all our magazines English, do you suppose?" I ask Algertha.

Neither Mother nor Daddy was English. Daddy was born in the Fidelity district, the son of homesteaders from Pennsylvania. Mother came out from Nova Scotia as a young woman to teach at Fidelity School. Where her people had come to Nova Scotia from wasn't known to us, any more than we knew where she had heard of the many English magazines she subscribed to, never mind why she wanted them.

As often happens, a memory of mine triggers a memory in Algertha, though Algertha remembers much more than I do anyway. Algertha's kitchen tonight smells of glue. She's making a lampshade, gluing together polystyrene cups to form a large globe. Algertha has Mother's quick competence around the house, her busyness and her determination. But in being able to look at things straight and still bear them, she is our father's child. Of course she doesn't have his gentleness, his way of discerning where you were really *at* before he began to talk to you. And her irreverence, her way of putting distance between herself and anyone who comes too close, is both reminiscent of Mother and something that is all Algertha's own.

"Do you remember how Mother liked to call a run in a stocking a ladder?" she asks now. There's a harsh sound to her laugh, but she's quietly excited just the same. It's as if this clue, slight as it is, might fit together with some other to provide the piece we need to complete our puzzle.

As children, Algertha and I knew, in the way that children always know things but can't remember how they learned them, that Mother was not well liked around Fidelity. Admired, yes. Perhaps even envied, for we suffered less than most of our neighbours during the Depression, and Mother was acknowledged to be a good worker, and smart at anything she put her hand to.

But liked? No. Where she was concerned, there was never that easy give-and-take, the clumsy joking with which other women expressed their desire for friendship with each other. Something of the schoolteacher always clung to Mother.

In some ways, our memories of childhood seem like one long memory of being taken out of things. Algertha remembers when the new minister gave Ethelene Prill the Easter service solo to sing, an office heretofore performed by Algertha herself.

"That minister is taking a lot of latitude," Mother said. Mother liked a colourful phrase, wherever it came from, and her talk was as much salted with western expressions as it was uplifted by British ones. "He told me Ethelene had a sweet voice and ought to be encouraged," she said. "As well encourage a frog to croak when you could be listening to a meadowlark." And so Algertha and I were taken out of the junior choir.

In those years, Algertha and I shared Mother's reputation for being "clever with her hands." When a girls' sewing club was formed in our district the summer before the blizzard, we had a head start on the other members, for we had been assembling aprons and potholders since our legs got long enough to reach the sewing-machine treadle. That first year, club projects were chosen by age groups. Mrs. Grady, our leader, promised that a prize would be given for the best work in each group.

Looking back on it now, it seems to me that whatever her faults, Mrs. Grady could never be accused of not challenging her pupils. The project for the thirteen-year-olds, my age group, was to make a pair of cotton pyjamas. Each week Mrs. Grady showed us on a demonstration model how to perform one operation, from laying out pattern pieces to setting in sleeves, and we went home and struggled with our own cotton print. Only in my case it wasn't cotton. Mother had a piece of rayon print in the house, and she would pay no attention to my wails that "Mrs. Grady said it had to be cotton."

"Don't be silly," Mother said briskly. "If you do as good a job in rayon as the other girls do in cotton, you'll have to get the prize. Rayon is harder to sew."

But it didn't turn out that way. "I said cotton and I meant cotton," Mrs. Grady said, holding her ground when Mother tackled her on Achievement Day. And so Algertha and I were taken out of the Clothing Club.

Once Mother felt it necessary to take the whole family out of something—in this case the district in which we lived. Yet curiously that particular retreat—for that is what it was—provided Algertha and me with our happiest memory of the years before the blizzard. It's a memory we return to again and again on those nights in Algertha's kitchen when we are "at it again." We've gone over it so often that sometimes I think we no longer really remember our holiday, but only remember ourselves remembering it.

We don't talk often of how it began, and how we heard it beginning. It was a July afternoon when Mother's brother, Ernest, an uncle we had heard of in a vague sort of way, telephoned from Edmonton. Sitting at the kitchen table working on our scrapbooks, Algertha and I, of course, heard only Mother's half of the conversation. From that side it was evident that Uncle Ernest intended to visit us.

We were excited by this news, for, while our piano was covered with pictures of the Heartwells, Daddy's side of the family, we had never seen a photograph of any of Mother's brothers and sisters. We weren't even sure exactly how many of them there were.

But almost before we knew Uncle Ernest proposed coming, we knew that Mother had no notion of letting him. I realize now that, intimidated by the thought of listening ears along the telephone line, Mother said the first thing that came into her head.

"Morgan and I have promised to take the children on a little holiday," she told Uncle Ernest. "As a matter of fact, we're already packed. We couldn't disappoint the children."

It was the first we had heard of a holiday. As Mother turned away from the telephone, I saw that her neck was strangely splotched. When she spoke, it was as if there wasn't enough air in her chest to hold her voice up. "I'm going to my room," she told us. "I want to lie down for a few minutes."

If she had told us that she wanted to roost on the warming oven or lay eggs in the attic, we wouldn't have been more dumbfounded. Mother, lying down in the middle of the day?

When she emerged half an hour later, she looked more like herself: strong, in command, determined. "Hitch Nell up to the buggy, Algertha," she ordered. "We're going to your Uncle Emery's."

Our drive to Uncle Emery and Aunt Elizabeth's, a mile and a half from our place, was made in silence. Algertha and I were not in the habit of putting questions to Mother that she might not want to answer.

At Uncle Emery's, Algertha and I were sent out to the lawn swing. By the time Aunt Elizabeth called us in for the jam-on-bread that Mother called open-faced sandwiches, everything was settled. Uncle Emery was to do our chores while we went away for a few days' holiday—the word "camping" wasn't part of our vocabulary then—at Henderson's Lake.

"Henderson's Lake!" Algertha said the words scornfully when we got home and she and I were alone again. "Resurrection Slough, she means."

Mother, being Mother, had called the large pond twelve miles north of our farm by its more dignified name. Most people, like Algertha, had been calling it Resurrection Slough ever since the Seventh Day Adventists first began to hold camp meetings and mass baptisms there. Resurrection Slough was a place you might go to for a picnic on a Sunday. But for a holiday? As well make up a bed in the potato patch and call that holidaying. And yet today, when Algertha refers to "the holiday," I never mistake which one she means.

I'm uncomfortably aware that the portrait I have been painting of Mother so far does her an injustice. It has far too many dark strokes. I have been showing her only at those times when she was at odds with her neighbours or her daughters. And yet

Algertha and I have many memories of happy times, of gentle times, times of great warmth and enthusiastic living. Our three days at Resurrection Slough were such a time. But before we went we didn't know they were going to be. We only knew that we wanted to know why they were coming.

In our house, there were holes cut in the floors of the upstairs bedrooms, to let heat from downstairs rise in winter and do what it could to combat an enduring chill. Algertha's and my bedroom was above the living room. The guest room was above the kitchen, and it was to this room that we repaired when there was something we wanted to know. When we saw Daddy coming in from the fields for supper that day we stationed ourselves back from the hole in the floor. From there we listened to Mother tell Daddy what we already knew: that Uncle Ernest had phoned, that he wanted to visit us, and that she had put him off by telling him that we were going for a holiday. That holiday, she said, was to be at Henderson's Lake.

"You told him on the phone that we were going on a holiday?"

"Yes."

"I don't like it, Ruby," our father said. "If you've announced it on the phone, then we'll have to go. But I don't think anybody's going to be fooled into thinking this was planned and couldn't be put off."

"What else could I do?" Mother demanded. "Better the talk this will cause than the talk there would have been if he'd come."

"We could have faced talk," Daddy said,

"You don't know what it's like," Mother said. "The neighbours would never have been the same again. And the girls would have suffered for it."

Mother had made two objections. Daddy dealt with one of them. "The neighbours could like it or lump it," he said.

After a minute, "What are we going to do about the chores?" he asked.

"Emery will do them," Mother said. "I had to tell him and Elizabeth what we were up against. But being family, they're not likely to trumpet it around."

"Well, what's done is done," Daddy said wearily. "I never thought they'd bother you way out here."

When we had tiptoed back to our room, "What's the matter with Uncle Ernest?" I asked Algertha. She glared at me, and I knew at that moment she hated me because she didn't know either.

"Ask me an easy one," she said.

One thing about Mother. She had the ability, after each one of her set-tos with the world, to put it completely out of her mind, to go on as if the things or people who had disturbed the smooth course of her life no longer existed, had, in fact, never existed at all. Now, at Resurrection Slough, Uncle Ernest and the neighbours were forgotten. A holiday was a time for joy, and Mother became like an animated illustration of the joys of camping.

On the last afternoon, after we had polished off a loaf of crumpled egg sandwiches, some warm dill pickles, and a two-quart sealer of orangeade made from Veribest Drink Powders, we lolled on the beach waiting for the obligatory two hours to be up so we could go into the water. Mother began to sing, leading us in "There'll Always Be an England" and "Rosie, the Riveter." And then she taught us an action song she may have learned in her own childhood, a song that she called "Down Among the Dead Men." Do you know that song? The chorus goes:

We are the red men, feathers in our head men,
   Down among the dead men
      Pow wow.

First Daddy joined in. Mother became the very personification of the happy camper, her hands first bristling from her head as feathers and then, at the line, "Down among the dead men," swooping down toward the earth. Today I am glad that Algertha and I were able to overcome our feeling that we were getting too old for such monkeyshines, and that we joined in too.

We can fight with sticks and stones,
Bows and arrows, bricks and bones.
   Pow wow. Pow wow.
We're the men of the Old Dun Cow.
We are the red men, feathers in our head men,
   Down among the dead men
      Pow wow.

We come home from hunt and war
Greeted by a long-nosed squaw,
   Pow wow. Pow wow.
We're the men of the Old Dun Cow.
We are the red men, feathers in our head men,
   Down among the dead men
      Pow wow.

Singing, it was as if we all had one voice. I felt as if we were discovering for the first time that we were us. If somebody had given us a new name, I wouldn't have been surprised. "The Heartwells" seemed inadequate for what we were, for what we were becoming.

I suppose there was talk. But summer gave way to fall and fall to winter. There were moments, brief openings, when we would feel again the wonderful together-gladness that we had felt at Resurrection Slough. But for the most part, the dailyness of life took over.

THE AFTERNOON before the blizzard started, there were sundogs in the west.

"I don't like the look of it," Daddy said. "We could be in for quite a blow."

"Maybe they'll call off the dance," Mother said.

"They can't," Daddy said. "Billy leaves tomorrow."

In those early days of the war, every month or two saw another boy reach his eighteenth birthday, join up and be given a send-off by an approving community. Tonight it was to be Billy Baird's turn and, blizzard shaping up or no blizzard shaping up, we couldn't let him leave us, perhaps forever, without his whist drive and dance.

It was cold but the wind was mild when we left for the schoolhouse, the skirts of our "good dresses" hanging out over our ski pants so they wouldn't wrinkle. We sat on a blanket spread over a cushion of straw in the bottom of the sleigh-box and spread the horse-blankets over us. The runners groaned on the wind-packed snow, the harness jangled in rhythm with the trotting feet of the horses and we—Mother, Algertha and I—from under our covering of horse-blankets, added our voices to these comfortable sounds. We sang whatever came into our heads, both to help pass the time it took a team and sleigh to cover three miles, and—in Algertha's and my case—to let out some of the excitement building within us.

At the school, while Daddy took the horses to the barn and blanketed them, Mother, Algertha and I headed through the schoolhouse, a room that looked like the demesne of strangers with its desks removed and piled up in the kitchen. While our mothers bustled around setting up card tables and distributing pencils and score pads, Algertha and I joined the other young girls of the district around the stove in the kitchen.

Do you remember how patriotic our clothes were during the war? Little boys wore miniature army uniforms complete with wedge caps. The girls in the Fidelity kitchen that night wore dresses of rayon crêpe, printed for the most part, but trimmed with V-for-Victory breast pockets outlined in braid or lace. For jewellery, there were brooches in which a large V of red brilliants was followed by three dots and a dash. There were Union Jack brooches and bulldog brooches and necklaces made of pink celluloid maple leaves.

As we stood around the stove, Bernice Perkins told us of an encounter she had had in the Red and White store with a boy from south of town. It hadn't been much of an encounter, but she made the most of it.

"God knows what we'll do if any boy ever looks at us," Algertha said suddenly. "Mother will kill us."

I looked at my sister with admiration. First for the "God knows." Second, for mentioning boys, and the possibility of their admiring us. We scarcely ever thought of anything else, any of us, and other girls might report on things that actual boys had actually said to them. But only Algertha would have been bold enough to mention admirers that were only future and possible.

For a minute, nobody said anything. Then, "But surely your mother wants you to get married someday," Bernice said.

"Oh, I suppose so," Algertha said carelessly. "But I can't imagine how it's ever going to get started."

I knew what she meant. It was a long jump from Elizabeth and Margaret Rose to rides in some boy's rumbleseat. And suitors in rough tweed jackets of the variety favoured by our English magazines were a little hard to come by in either Fidelity or Willow Bunch.

That night I was wearing a blue crêpe dress with a pattern of red leaves. My shoes, unhappily, were still oxfords, but they were laced with what we called gilly ties, and they did have cuban heels. The dress was pretty, or at least, pretty according to my tastes at that time. But I had never been happy wearing it.

Mother had made it, from material bought at Bothwell's in Willow Bunch. I remember Mother finding the bolt, and my delight in the fact that it looked like the kind of goods that only a grownup-looking dress could come out of. I could see it made up, and myself wearing it, leaning on the arm of some faceless boy and dancing to "The West, a Nest and You."

In the store, "Miss," Mother called imperiously. She beckoned to Josie Symington. "Miss."

My picture dissolved. Josie, who had been helping a farmer find his fit in felt socks, turned slowly. A wave of red appeared over her collar and slowly advanced, like mercury rising, up her neck and face.

"I'll be right with you," she said. There was resentment in her voice. Josie Symington wasn't used to being called "Miss."

Our mothers had no more than got the card tables set up and the benches spread at right angles around the room than they decided to clear the floor again. It hadn't started to blow in earnest yet, but the air had had the taste of blizzard in it all day. It would be best to skip the cards and get on with the dancing.

"Where's the cornmeal?" Toady Bennett's voice rose over all others, self-important. The floor of Fidelity School was not only rough and slivery; it was uneven. Sprinkling cornmeal over it gave one the feeling of dancing on ball bearings, but it did make it possible to slide your feet, at least some of the time. And where you couldn't slide, you could step. We had a lot of high-steppers in Fidelity.

The music started, and the dance was like any other dance any other young girl has ever attended. Our floor might be rough, our feet might slide only by the grace of cornmeal, but details like these are mere stage dressing. What dances are really about—talking animatedly to the younger sisters of boys one would like a dance with, praying that the particularly ugly and freakish boy will not single oneself out for attention—these are surely the same everywhere.

In Fidelity, the boy one wished to avoid was Toady Bennett. Toady, of an age to have joined up, had failed his physical because of what I later learned were called undescended testicles. He was a great blob of a boy, massively fat and puffy even though he was over six feet tall. Even in August, Toady's complexion had the pallor of February. Now, when it really was February, he had a pale green, underwater look.

I read somewhere once that it is a psychological impossibility for an only child to have an inferiority complex. Remembering Toady, who was an only child, I am inclined to believe that must be so. Far from slinking back in corners, Toady bounced, slug-coloured, slug-fat, self-important, through all our dances. It was his continuing ambition to be able to boast that he had danced every dance. We all knew that we would be danced with once. But for Toady to fulfil his boast, it was necessary for some of us to be afflicted twice, or even three times. I used to wish that, like Invisible Scarlet O'Neill, I could press a nerve in my left wrist and disappear when Toady approached the door leading to the kitchen, an area that was the special preserve of the young girls.

But this night, something was to happen that would rivet all eyes, including those of the nervous young girls, on the unspeakable Toady.

Leaving the school building about ten o'clock with the intention of relieving himself in a snowbank, Toady galloped back, burst in through the cloakroom and shouted loudly.

"Attention. Attention, please." Not until the music had stilled and every dancer stopped in his tracks did Toady make his announcement.

"The chimney is on fire," he said. "Evacuate the school. Women and children first."

Because Toady had discovered it, no one wanted to take it seriously. Chimney fires weren't uncommon in country schools. We did head for our coats in the kitchen, but there was no panic.

"Toady's been watching too many RAF movies," someone said.

But this time, before Toady had discovered it, the fire had dropped sparks onto the shingles of the roof, and a crescent around the chimney was burning hungrily.

"This old shack will go up like tinder," I heard Cumberland Prill say. "We'd better carry out what we can and let her go."

There was a pause. Then I heard my father's voice. "I'm not going to just stand around and watch it burn," he said. "We can at least try to beat it out."

"I'm with you, Morgan," Uncle Emery said, and then everybody else was too. There was an old ladder in the barn, laid away in the days when people had supposed that the school would be painted every few years, and someone ran to fetch it. There were no gunny sacks around, but my father pulled out the heavy green curtains that we used for Christmas concerts, and ripped off a couple of lengths. He and Uncle Emery dipped these into the boiler of coffee on the kitchen stove and climbed up onto the roof. The other men set themselves to the task of supplying as much water as they could with the two buckets and the single copper boiler they had to work with.

For a time it seemed as if the fire would take the school. "They're wasting their time," I heard Alva Baird say. "They'll get themselves soaked and catch their death of cold." But he went right on hauling water.

Presently we could see that Dad and Uncle Emery were winning. The big flames vanished. There were moments of blackness before little flames licked up and were beaten out.

At last, "I think we've got her," Uncle Emery said.

They came down the ladder. The school was saved, relatively undamaged. But the dance didn't go on. Once the fire was out, we had to give heed to something we'd been too busy to deal with. The blizzard had started.

"The way she's blowing," Dutch Haidner said, "the roads'll be closed in an hour. We've got to get out of here."

So we hastily assembled in the school to present Billy Baird with his going-away present. Then horses were hitched up and their blankets, warm now and smelling enormously of horse, were dumped over women and children scrambling into the bottom of sleigh-boxes.

"Kill a Jerry for me, Billy," I heard someone yell. Then sleigh runners groaned and there was the retreating sound of harness rattling.

We didn't dare to wait for Dad and Uncle Emery's clothes to dry. Mother and Aunt Elizabeth took the reins to drive our sleighs home through the stinging wind, taking turns for the last miles at breaking trail along the fast filling road allowance. Daddy, wet and tired, shivered beside Algertha and me under our horse blankets.

Finally we made it home. Mother, when she came in from stabling the horses, had a frozen cheek. But it was our father we were worried about.

"Look at you." Mother's voice was accusing. "You're chilled to the bone. I'd better get you into dry clothes before you come down with something."

Dad sat by the cook stove, banked with coal against our absence, and Mother brought dry clothes and blankets. When Mother sent Algertha and me to our room, he looked as if he would never get warm again.

Upstairs, the blizzard seemed nearer.

In the morning, it was still blowing. Daddy, in bed now, was running a fever. His face was red and his eyes were glassy.

"Can't we call the doctor?" Algertha asked, but she knew the answer.

"The phones are out," Mother said. "Anyway the doctor could no more get over these roads than we can."

Mother would stay in the house with him, and Algertha and I would have to cope with the chores as best we could.

As we walked to the barn, a feeling of strangeness came over us. We knew it was our own farmyard, but everything in it—the granaries, the seed drills, the wagon boxes—was lost in a moving curtain of white. It was as if our familiar world had never been, as if it had been blotted out and would never return. When we reached the safety of the barn, with its warmth and the reassuring smell of cattle and horses, I turned to Algertha.

"Is Daddy going to be all right?" I asked.

"How the hell should I know?" Algertha spoke roughly. I knew then that she was afraid too.

"You start the milking and I'll go for the chop," she said.

"Let's both go together," I said.

We took the feed buckets and headed across the yard to the granary where the chopping was done. In the intense cold, all smells seemed fainter. Even the smell of chopped grain, which was perhaps more dust than scent anyway, seemed muted.

Ordinarily when Algertha and I helped Daddy with the chores, we took time to trace our names, or the initials of our latest "boyfriends" in the fur-thick dust on the fanning mill. Today we had no inclination for that. We just wanted to get on with the job. I leaned on the mill to brace myself as I stooped for a bucket of chop, and a small grey mouse, alarmed, scurried out from underneath it.

We milked the cows as best we could, and we slopped the pigs. Then we fed the pail-bunters, not bothering to separate the milk first. By the time the morning chores were done, it was time to start the evening ones.

Mother came down the stairs as Algertha and I entered from the back porch that evening, tired out, but with our jobs done.

"How's Daddy?" Algertha asked.

Mother's face was haggard. "His temperature's gone up to 106," she said. "I don't like the look of him at all."

We went upstairs. "I wish your mother would stop taking on," Daddy told us, "I'm not ready to peg out just yet."

We went downstairs and ate some jam sandwiches. Then we went back up to Daddy's room. He was sleeping now, but not resting. About nine o'clock he stopped tossing, opened his eyes and, as if continuing a conversation started earlier, suddenly demanded, "Come on. Let's sing it again."

"Sing what, Daddy?" one of us asked.

"Why, the Pow Wow song," he said. His voice sounded as if he were asking, "what else?"

"*We'll* sing it, Daddy," Algertha said. "You just rest."

So we tried to sing. We looked up. Mother had come to the door and she didn't care that we saw tears streaming down her cheeks. Over Algertha and me together there passed a chill of the skin surface, together with a paralysis of our thinking powers, the kind of paralysis that comes when the only things that can be thought are too bad for thinking.

Algertha got up and went to Mother. "Let me ride over to Uncle Emery's," I heard her beg.

Mother shook her head. "There's no way Emery can get the doctor, any more than we can," she said. "We're on our own, we three. We'll just have to do our best."

Soon she sent Algertha and me to bed.

"I'll never go to sleep," I told Algertha. But I did, and so did she.

Some time after midnight Mother came in and woke us. "Your father's died," she said, and her voice broke.

We got up and went down to the kitchen with her, and we sat together there until morning.

"I don't want you girls to worry about anything," I remember Mother saying. "We'll make out all right. Emery will see to it that we get a good man to help us with the farm."

In the morning she took us up to their bedroom to see Daddy. His skin now was a sort of furry blue colour, and I was surprised to see that his eyes were open.

"Shouldn't we close them?" Algertha asked.

"The undertaker will do that." Mother's voice was short. "We'll have all we can manage just to move him."

Move him?

"He'll have to be moved out of the house," Mother said. "There's no telling when the roads will be opened so's we can arrange to have him buried. We'll have to put him in a granary."

I started to cry again. Mother took me in her arms and began to pat my head. "There, there, honey," she said. "I know how you feel. But it doesn't make any difference now to Daddy where we put him." The sound of her voice made my own throat ache. "And we can't keep him in the house, Nonie," she said. "It's too warm."

We understood then. After a while we took the mattress off the Winnipeg couch in the kitchen and doubled it over to make a kind of stretcher. Mother took Daddy by the shoulders and Algertha took his feet, and they rolled him onto it. Then we all put on our coats and boots and mittens and carried him out to the nearest granary. It was empty, except for one bin in the corner where Daddy had dumped a few bushels of seed oats.

"I'll sit with him for a while," Algertha said.

"You'll do nothing of the kind," Mother said. "I won't have people saying we carried on like Catholics."

Then she softened and put one mittened hand on Algertha's shoulder. "Nothing can help him now," she said. "Or hurt him either."

It blew all that day and it blew all the next. The third day was quiet and cold, and Mother decided to send me on Nell to Uncle Emery's. Algertha would stay home to help her with the chores.

"Emery will find a way of getting Daddy to town," Mother said.

Uncle Emery hitched up his team while Aunt Elizabeth rubbed my hands and made me hot cocoa. Then, with Nell tied to the back of the sleigh-box and Aunt Elizabeth and me crouched in its depths under horse-blankets, Uncle Emery set out for our place. Several times he had to leave the road allowance, and to go ahead with the shovel to make trail for the team.

"The neighbours will be out clearing road too," Aunt Elizabeth said. "I hope Emery doesn't have too far to go before he hits some of their trails."

After we got home and Uncle Emery had warmed himself, he got up to go out to the granary.

"You'll want help," Mother said, ready to get her coat.

"I'll see," Uncle Emery said. "You wait here, Ruby. Maybe I can handle things myself."

Somehow Uncle Emery managed to get that stiff body into the sleigh-box alone, without help, and to cover it with a horse-blanket. His face, when he returned, was older than when he went out.

"There's something you'll want to know, Ruby," he said to Mother. "I wish I didn't have to be the one to tell you."

For a moment it seemed as if Uncle Emery had changed his mind, as if he wasn't going to speak after all. Then, "The mice have been at him," he said.

We heard the words, and they were all words that we knew. But put together, they brought us no message. "The mice have been at him."

I felt the meaning coming toward me from a long way off, and the dread was there even before I knew what it was for. Then it was as if a picture had been drawn.

"Oh, my God," Mother whispered. "Oh, my God."

I don't know what happened, what was said, what was felt, in the next few minutes. Later, when talk had turned to practical details, I remember Mother announcing that we would have a private funeral.

"A private funeral." Aunt Elizabeth's voice, echoing Mother's words, indicated that, to her mind at least, the words private and funeral were mutually contradictory. Such a thing had never been heard of in Willow Bunch.

"Are you sure that's what you want, Ruby?" Aunt Elizabeth asked. "It would cause a lot of talk."

"There's going to be talk whatever we do," Mother said. Then it was as if the truth of her own statement suddenly caught up with her.

"The whole country will be lapping this up," she said. "The story they've got … they'll be telling this on me for the next twenty years."

"We don't have to open the casket," Aunt Elizabeth said. "Evelyn Sellers tells me closed caskets are getting to be real common in the city. Nobody thinks anything of it."

But it wasn't eyes on Daddy's body that were worrying Mother. She hadn't even thought of that. It was eyes on *her*.

"Anyway," Aunt Elizabeth went on, "people will understand and make allowances."

"I'll not have anyone making allowances for me," Mother said.

Then it seemed that she didn't want a private funeral after all. What she wanted was to go to town with Uncle Emery and take the train to the city and leave Willow Bunch altogether.

"Would you and Emery keep the girls for a little while?" she asked. There was pleading in her voice. "You can have whatever kind of funeral you want. But I can't stay here."

"Your life is here, Ruby," Aunt Elizabeth said. "You can't move away, leave everything, just because…."

"I can't stay here," Mother said. "Even in Nova Scotia I never had to hang my head this low."

"You did the best you could, Ruby," Uncle Emery said.

But Mother wouldn't be changed. She threatened to walk behind the sleigh, in the tracks of Uncle Emery's runners, if he wouldn't take her.

Almost before we knew it, she was gone.

I can't remember what she said by way of farewell to Algertha and me. Everything before that moment seems real. Afterwards, when we went to live with Aunt Elizabeth and Uncle Emery, is real too. But it was as if the nature of reality had changed.

Aunt Elizabeth put as good a face on things as she could. "Ruby just broke down completely," I heard her explain over and over. "She was just overcome by grief."

Mother got a teaching job in the city. She sent cheques and notes as impersonal as bank reports to Uncle Emery. That was all.

People talked; of course they did. It wouldn't have been human not to. Algertha and I had to learn to deal with feelers like, "I guess your mother felt real bad about what happened," and direct questions like, "The mice didn't get very *much* did they?" But many people were kind. In any case, sooner or later everyone had said everything there was to say about the subject.

Uncle Emery and Aunt Elizabeth did what they could to cushion our shock and pain. Algertha and I wrote to Mother. There was no answer. "You've got to remember what a terrible shock your mother had," Aunt Elizabeth said. "A person doesn't get over something like that all at once."

There never came a day when Algertha and I said to each other, "Mother isn't going to send for us." I remember talking about what it would be like going to high school in the city instead of in Willow Bunch. But when August came and Mother hadn't been heard from, Aunt Elizabeth made arrangements for us to board in town with Mrs. Barlow.

The year I took my grade twelve, Algertha, who by then was working at the drugstore, got engaged to Fred Mills. In a flurry of excitement, she decided to go to the city to buy her wedding dress and going-away suit.

"But how will I know what to buy?" she cried. In the late forties that was a real problem. The New Look had appeared, even in Willow Bunch. But would it last? Algertha would be spending a lot of money—nearly a hundred dollars, probably—and she didn't want to have to throw it all out in a couple of years' time.

"Your mother will know the right thing to buy," Aunt Elizabeth said.

Aunt Elizabeth had arranged for cousins of hers in the city to put us up, but we were writing Mother that we were coming and we would telephone when we got there. By now she had become a person we couldn't just land in on.

We had a special mission to perform in seeing Mother. Aunt Elizabeth wanted to know which of Mother's things she ought to send her. "Ruby always prized her china and silver," she said, "so I expect she'll want those. But how much she'll have room for, I have no idea."

Mother's address when we found it was in a large red brick edifice overlooking the river valley, a building with narrow windows and stately porticoes that looked as if it might have been designed for legislative purposes. As a residence it was a place that spoke not of comfort but of respectability, of safeness.

We walked through silent hallways to the door of number seventeen and knocked. The door was opened by a woman we recognized as our mother. Her hair, Algertha remembers, was done in a style new to us, and she was wearing a dress we had never seen before.

She led us into a high-ceilinged parlour in which needlepoint-covered chairs were arranged at precise angles from the wall, and invited Algertha and me to seat ourselves on a cream-coloured brocade settee. It faced a window that I felt must overlook the river valley, but I couldn't be sure. Though it was only mid-afternoon, pale grey damask draperies were tightly drawn across the view.

Mother poured tea from a pot we had never warmed, and passed it to us in cups our lips had never touched. We told her that Aunt Elizabeth wanted to know which of her things she could send on.

"None, I think," Mother said. Her voice now was very even, with fewer inflections than I remembered in it. "As you can see, I'm quite comfortable here."

She'll give them to Algertha, I thought, for we had written her about Algertha's engagement. But: "Please ask Elizabeth to dispose of them any way she sees fit," she said.

Then she began to speak of city topics. She told us of her school in a new district near the university, where there were "some very nice families." She chatted of books she had been reading, "live theatre" she had been seeing. She rejoiced that the city was beginning to have a cultural life. Listening, it came to me that Mother's speech had lost its vivid turn of phrase, that it had become as grey as her damask draperies. She didn't ask about Aunt Elizabeth or Uncle Emery or Fidelity. She didn't even ask Algertha and me about *us*. It was as if we were behind a door she had closed, and this afternoon, for her, was something to be got through.

I am sure that the subject of Algertha's trousseau would never have come up, so impossible would it have been for us to have conceived of blurting out our concerns to this stranger, if Mother hadn't herself mentioned the word "fashion." Mother, it seemed, had joined the IODE, and she was "convening" a fashion show for her chapter. Possibly afraid we might linger over our tea, she told us that she would be leaving soon to make final arrangements for the fashion show, which was to be that evening.

"Why, that's swell," I said, before Algertha could stop me. "Algertha's up here to buy her trousseau, and we don't really know much about the new styles."

There was a brief pause. Then, "I'm sure you'll have no difficulty finding any number of suitable frocks," Mother said. "The shops are filled with enchanting things."

She motioned vaguely to a plate on the table. "You're sure you won't have another scone?" she asked.

"DO YOU REMEMBER Mother's napkins ... linen with cutwork bits in the corners?" Algertha asked last night. But I couldn't. We were there for nearly an hour, but I really seem able to summon up very little by way of images of Mother in that genteel apartment. I remember some of the things she said, but I can no longer remember how she looked. It seems odd, for I have no trouble seeing Algertha and me, perched on that unyielding settee, holding our teacups carefully forward and gazing at the grey draperies that shut out the view of the river.

Her goodbye to us is gone from my memory too. But I can remember Algertha and me, plain as plain, tiptoeing down the narrow halls that would take us back into the sunshine. Algertha stopped me before we reached the door. "Can you believe that she ever sang 'Down Among the Dead Men'?" Algertha asked, motioning back toward the woman we had just left. My sister's eyes glittered with malice.

I shook my head.

It was beyond imagining.

Voices Lost in Snow

MAVIS GALLANT

HALFWAY BETWEEN OUR TWO GREAT WARS, parents whose own early years had been shaped with Edwardian firmness were apt to lend a tone of finality to quite simple remarks: "Because I say so" was the answer to "Why?" and a child's response to "What did I just tell you?" could seldom be anything but "Not to"—not to say, do, touch, remove, go out, argue, reject, eat, pick up, open, shout, appear to sulk, appear to be cross. Dark riddles filled the corners of life because no enlightenment was thought required. Asking questions was "being tiresome," while persistent curiosity got one nowhere, at least nowhere of interest. How much has changed? Observe the drift of words descending from adult to child—the fall of personal questions, observations, unnecessary instructions. Before long the listener seems blanketed. He must hear the voice as authority muffled, a hum through snow. The tone has changed—it may be coaxing, even plaintive—but the words have barely altered. They still claim the ancient right-of-way through a young life.

"Well, old cock," said my father's friend Archie McEwen, meeting him one Saturday in Montreal. "How's Charlotte taking life in the country?" Apparently no one had expected my mother to accept the country in winter.

"Well, old cock," I repeated to a country neighbour, Mr. Bainwood, "How's life?" What do you suppose it meant to me, other than a kind of weather vane? Mr. Bainwood thought it over, then came round to our house and complained to my mother.

"It isn't blasphemy," she said, not letting him have much satisfaction from the complaint. Still, I had to apologize. "I'm sorry" was a ritual habit with even less meaning than "old cock." "Never say that again," my mother said after he had gone.

"Why not?"

"Because I've just told you not to."

"What does it mean?"

"Nothing."

It must have been after yet another "Nothing" that one summer's day I ran screaming around a garden, tore the heads off tulips, and—no, let another voice finish it; the only authentic voices I have belong to the dead: "… then she *ate* them."

IT WAS MY FATHER'S CUSTOM if he took me with him to visit a friend on Saturdays not to say where we were going. He was more taciturn than any man I have known since, but that wasn't all of it; being young, I was the last person to whom anyone owed an explanation. These Saturdays have turned into one whitish afternoon, a windless snowfall, a steep street. Two persons descend the street, stepping carefully. The child, reminded every day to keep her hands still, gesticulates wildly—there is the flash of a red mitten. I will never overtake this pair. Their voices are lost in snow.

We were living in what used to be called the country and is now a suburb of Montreal. On Saturdays my father and I came in together by train. I went to the doctor, the dentist, to my German lesson. After that I had to get back to Windsor station by myself and on time. My father gave me a boy's watch so that the dial would be good and large. I remember the No. 83 streetcar trundling downhill and myself, wondering if the watch was slow, asking strangers to tell me the hour. Inevitably—how could it have been otherwise?—after his death, which would not be long in coming, I would dream that someone important had taken a train without me. My route to the meeting place—deviated, betrayed by stopped clocks—was always downhill. As soon as I was old enough to understand from my reading of myths and legends that this journey was a pursuit of darkness, its terminal point a sunless underworld, the dream vanished.

Sometimes I would be taken along to lunch with one or another of my father's friends. He would meet the friend at Pauzé's for oysters or at Drury's or the Windsor Grill. The friend would more often than not be Scottish- or English-sounding, and they would talk as if I were invisible, as Archie McEwen had done, and eat what I thought of as English food—grilled kidneys, sweetbreads—which I was too finicky to touch. Both my parents had been made wretched as children by having food forced on them and so that particular torture was never inflicted on me. However, the manner in which I ate was subject to precise attention. My father disapproved of the North American custom that he called "spearing" (knife laid on the plate, fork in the right hand). My mother's eye was out for a straight back, invisible chewing, small mouthfuls, immobile silence during the interminable adult loafing over dessert. My mother did not care for food. If we were alone together, she would sit smoking and reading, sipping black coffee, her elbows used as props—a posture that would have called for instant banishment had I so much as tried it. Being constantly observed and corrected was like having a fly buzzing around one's plate. At Pauzé's, the only child, perhaps the only female, I sat up to an oak counter and ate oysters quite neatly, not knowing exactly what they were and certainly not that they were alive. They were served as in "The Walrus and the Carpenter," with bread and butter, pepper and vinegar. Dessert was a chocolate biscuit—plates of them stood at intervals along the counter. When my father and I ate alone, I was not required to say much, nor could I expect a great deal in the way of response. After I had been addressing him for minutes, sometimes he would suddenly come to life and I would know he had been elsewhere. "Of course I've been listening," he would protest, and he would repeat by way of proof the last few words of whatever it was I'd been saying. He was seldom present. I don't know where my father spent his waking life: just elsewhere.

What was he doing alone with a child? Where was his wife? In the country, reading. She read one book after another without looking up, without scraping away the frost on the windows. "The Russians, you know, the Russians," she said to her mother and me, glancing around in the drugged way adolescent readers have. "They put salt on the windowsills in winter." Yes, so they did, in the nineteenth century, in the boyhood of Turgenev, of Tolstoy. The salt absorbed the moisture between two sets of windows sealed shut for half the year. She must have been in a Russian country house at that moment, surrounded by a large Russian family, living out vast Russian complications. The flat white fields beyond her imaginary windows were like the flat white fields she would have observed if only she had looked out. She was myopic, the pupil when she had been reading seemed to be the whole of the eye. What age was she then? Twenty-seven, twenty-eight. Her husband had removed her to the country; now that they were there he seldom spoke. How young she seems to me now—half twenty-eight in perception and feeling, but with a husband, a child, a house, a life, an illiterate maid from the village whose life she confidently interfered with and mismanaged, a small zoo of animals she alternately cherished and forgot; and she was the daughter of such a sensible, truthful, pessimistic woman— pessimistic in the way women become when they settle for what actually exists.

Our rooms were not Russian—they were aired every day and the salt became a great nuisance, blowing in on the floor.

"There, Charlotte, what did I tell you?" my grandmother said. This grandmother did not care for dreams or for children. If I sensed the first, I had no hint of the latter. Out of decency she kept it quiet, at least in a child's presence. She had the reputation, shared with a long-vanished nurse named Olivia, of being able to "do anything" with me, which merely meant an ability to provoke from a child behaviour convenient for adults. It was she who taught me to eat in the Continental way, with both hands in sight at all times upon the table, and who made me sit at meals with books under my arms so I would learn not to stick out my elbows. I remember having accepted this nonsense from her without a trace of resentment. Like Olivia, she could make the most pointless sort of training seem a natural way of life. (I think that as discipline goes this must be the most dangerous form of all.) She was one of three godparents I had—the important one. It is impossible for me to enter the mind of this agnostic who taught me prayers, who had already shed every remnant of belief when she committed me at the font. I know that she married late and reluctantly; she would have preferred a life of solitude and independence, next to impossible for a woman in her time. She had the positive voice of the born teacher, sharp manners, quick blue eyes, and the square, massive figure common to both lines of her ancestry—the west of France, the north of Germany. When she said "There, Charlotte, what did I tell you?" without obtaining an answer, it summed up mother and daughter both.

My father's friend Malcolm Whitmore was the second godparent. He quarrelled with my mother when she said something flippant about Mussolini, disappeared, died in Europe some years later, though perhaps not fighting for Franco, as my mother had it. She often rewrote other people's lives, providing them with suitable and harmonious endings. In her version of events you were supposed to die as you'd lived. He would write sometimes, asking me, "Have you been confirmed yet?" He had never really held a place and could not by dying leave a gap. The third godparent was a young woman named Georgie Henderson. She was my mother's choice, for a long time her confidante, partisan, and close sympathizer. Something happened, and they stopped seeing each other. Georgie was not her real name—it was Edna May. One of the reasons she had fallen out with my mother was that I had not been called Edna May too. Apparently, this had been promised.

WITHOUT SAYING where we were going, my father took me along to visit Georgie one Saturday afternoon.

"You didn't say you were bringing Linnet" was how she greeted him. We stood in the passage of a long, hot, high-ceilinged apartment, treading snow water into the rug.

He said, "Well, she is your godchild, and she has been ill."

My godmother shut the front door and leaned her back against it. It is in this surprisingly dramatic pose that I recall her. It would be unfair to repeat what I think I saw then, for she and I were to meet again once, only once, many years after this, and I might substitute a lined face for a smooth one and tough, large-knuckled hands for fingers that may have been delicate. One has to allow elbowroom in the account of a rival: "She must have had something" is how it generally goes, long after the initial "What can he see in her? He must be deaf and blind." Georgie, explained by my mother as being the natural daughter of Sarah Bernhardt and a stork, is only a shadow, a tracing, with long arms and legs and one of those slightly puggy faces with pulled-up eyes.

Her voice remains—the husky Virginia-tobacco whisper I associate with so many women of that generation, my parents' friends; it must have come of age in English Montreal around 1920, when girls began to cut their hair and to smoke. In middle life the voice would slide from low to harsh, and develop a chronic cough. For the moment it was fascinating to me—opposite in pitch and speed from my mother's, which was slightly too high and apt to break off, like that of a singer unable to sustain a long note.

It was true that I had been ill, but I don't think my godmother made much of it that afternoon, other than saying, "It's all very well to talk about that now, but I was certainly never told much, and as for that doctor, you ought to just hear what Ward thinks." Out of this whispered jumble my mother stood accused—of many transgressions, certainly, but chiefly of having discarded Dr. Ward Mackey, everyone's doctor and a family friend. At the time of my birth my mother had all at once decided she liked Ward Mackey better than anyone else and had asked him to choose a name for me. He could not think of one, or, rather, thought of too many, and finally consulted his own mother. She had always longed for a daughter, so that she could call her after the heroine of a novel by, I believe, Marie Corelli. The legend so often repeated to me goes on to tell that when I was seven weeks old my father suddenly asked, "What did you say her name was?"

"Votre fille a frôlé la phtisie," the new doctor had said, the one who had now replaced Dr. Mackey. The new doctor was known to me as Uncle Raoul, though we were not related. This manner of declaring my brush with consumption was worlds away from Ward Mackey's "subject to bilious attacks." Mackey's objections to Uncle Raoul were neither envious nor personal, for Mackey was the sort of bachelor who could console himself with golf. The Protestant in him truly believed those other doctors to be poorly trained and superstitious, capable of recommending the pulling of teeth to cure tonsillitis, and of letting their patients cough to death or perish from septicemia just through Catholic fatalism.

What parent could fail to gasp and marvel at Uncle Raoul's announcement? Any but either of mine. My mother could invent and produce better dramas any day; as for my father, his French wasn't all that good and he had to have it explained. Once he understood that I had grazed the edge of tuberculosis, he made his decision to remove us all to the country, which he had been wanting a reason to do for some time. He was, I think, attempting to isolate his wife, but by taking her out of the city he exposed her to a danger that, being English, he had never dreamed of: This was the heart-stopping cry of the steam train at night, sweeping across a frozen river, clattering on the ties of a wooden bridge. From our separate rooms my mother and I heard the unrivalled summons, the long, urgent, uniquely North American beckoning. She would follow and so would I, but separately, years and desires and destinations apart. I think that women once pledged in such a manner are more steadfast than men.

"Frôler" was the charmed word in that winter's story; it was a hand brushing the edge of folded silk, a leaf escaping a spiderweb. Being caught in the web would have meant staying in bed day and night in a place even worse than a convent school. Charlotte and Angus, whose lives had once seemed so enchanted, so fortunate and free that I could not imagine lesser persons so much as eating the same kind of toast for breakfast, had to share their lives with me, whether they wanted to or not—thanks to Uncle Raoul, who always supposed me to be their principal delight. I had been standing on one foot for months now, midway between *"frôler"* and "falling into," propped up by a psychosomatic guardian angel. Of course I could not stand that way forever; inevitably my health improved and before long I was declared out of danger and then restored—to the relief and pleasure of all except the patient.

"I'd like to see more of you than eyes and nose," said my godmother. "Take off your things." I offer this as an example of unnecessary instruction. Would anyone over the age of three prepare to spend the afternoon in a stifling room wrapped like a mummy in outdoor clothes? "She's smaller than she looks," Georgie remarked, as I began to emerge. This authentic godmother observation drives me to my only refuge, the insistence that she must have had something—he could not have been completely deaf and blind. Divested of hat, scarf, coat, overshoes, and leggings, grasping the handkerchief pressed in my hand so I would not interrupt later by asking for one, responding to my father's muttered "Fix your hair," struck by the command because it was he who had told me not to use "fix" in that sense, I was finally able to sit down next to him on a white sofa. My godmother occupied its twin. A low table stood between, bearing a decanter and glasses and a pile of magazines and, of course, Georgie's ashtrays; I think she smoked even more than my mother did.

On one of these sofas, during an earlier visit with my mother and father, the backs of my dangling feet had left a smudge of shoe polish. It may have been the last occasion when my mother and Georgie were ever together. Directed to stop humming and kicking; and perhaps bored with the conversation in which I was not expected to join, I had soon started up again.

"It doesn't matter," my godmother said, though you could tell she minded.

"Sit up," my father said to me.

"I am sitting up. What do you think I'm doing?" This was not answering but answering back; it is not an expression I ever heard from my father, but I am certain it stood like a stalled truck in Georgie's mind. She wore the look people put on when they are thinking, Now what are you spineless parents going to do about that?

"Oh, for God's sake, she's only a child," said my mother, as though that had ever been an excuse for anything.

Soon after the sofa-kicking incident she and Georgie moved into the hibernation known as "not speaking." This, the lingering condition of half my mother's friendships, usually followed her having said the very thing no one wanted to hear, such as "Who wants to be called Edna May, anyway?"

Once more in the hot pale room where there was nothing to do and nothing for children, I offended my godmother again, by pretending I had never seen her before. The spot I had kicked was pointed out to me, though, owing to new slipcovers, real evidence was missing. My father was proud of my quite surprising memory, of its long backward reach and the minutiae of detail I could describe. My failure now to shine in a domain where I was naturally gifted, that did not require lessons or create litter and noise, must have annoyed him. I also see that my guileless-seeming needling of my godmother was a close adaptation of how my mother could be, and I attribute it to a child's instinctive loyalty to the absent one. Giving me up, my godmother placed a silver dish of mint wafers where I could reach them—white, pink, and green, over-lapping—and suggested I look at a magazine. Whatever the magazine was, I had probably seen it, for my mother subscribed to everything then. I may have turned the pages anyway, in case at home something had been censored for children. I felt and am certain I have not invented Georgie's disappointment at not seeing Angus alone. She disliked Charlotte now, and so I supposed he came to call by himself, having no quarrel of his own; he was still close to the slighted Ward Mackey.

My father and Georgie talked for a while—she using people's initials instead of their names, which my mother would not have done—and they drank what must have been sherry, if I think of the shape of the decanter. Then we left and went down to the street in a wood-panelled elevator that had sconce lights, as in a room. The end of the afternoon had a particular shade of colour then, which is not tinted by distance or enhancement but has to do with how streets were lighted. Lamps were still gas, and their soft gradual blooming at dusk made the sky turn a peacock blue that slowly deepened to marine, then indigo. This uneven light falling in blurred pools gave the snow it touched a quality of phosphorescence, beyond which were night shadows in which no one lurked. There were few cars, little sound. A fresh snowfall would lie in the streets in a way that seemed natural. Sidewalks were danger-ous, casually sanded; even on busy streets you found traces of the icy slides children's feet had made. The reddish brown of the stone houses, the curve and slope of the streets, the constantly changing sky were satisfactory in a way that I now realize must have been aesthetically comfortable. This is what I saw when I read "city" in a book; I had no means of knowing that "city" one day would also mean drab, filthy, flat, or that city blocks could turn into dull squares without mystery.

We crossed Sherbrooke Street, starting down to catch our train. My father walked everywhere in all weathers. Already mined, colonized by an enemy prepared to destroy what it fed on, fighting it with every wrong weapon, squandering strength he should have been storing, stifling pain in silence rather than speaking up while there might have been time, he gave an impression of sternness that was a shield against suffering. One day we heard a mob roaring four syllables over and over, and we turned and went down a different street. That sound was starkly terrifying, some-thing a child might liken to the baying of wolves.

"What is it?"

"Howie Morenz."

"Who is it? Are they chasing him?"

"No, they like him," he said of the hockey player admired to the point of demen-tia. He seemed to stretch, as if trying to keep every bone in his body from touching a nerve; a look of helplessness such as I had never seen on a grown person gripped his face and he said this strange thing: "Crowds eat me. Noise eats me." The kind of physical pain that makes one seem rat's prey is summed up in my memory of this.

When we came abreast of the Ritz-Carlton after leaving Georgie's apartment, my father paused. The lights within at that time of day were golden and warm. If I barely knew what "hotel" meant, never having stayed in one, I connected the lights with other snowy afternoons, with stupefying adult conversation (Oh, those shut-in velvet-draped unaired low-voice problems!) compensated for by creamy bitter hot chocolate poured out of a pink-and-white china pot.

"You missed your gootay," he suddenly remembered. Established by my grandmother, *"goûter"* was the family word for tea. He often transformed French words, like putty, into shapes he could grasp. No, Georgie had not provided a *goûter*, other than the mint wafers, but it was not her fault—I had not been announced. Perhaps if I had not been so disagreeable with her, he might have proposed hot chocolate now, though I knew better than to ask. He merely pulled my scarf up over my nose and mouth, as if recalling something Uncle Raoul had advised. Breathing inside knitted wool was delicious—warm, moist, pungent when one had been sucking on mint candies, as now. He said, "You didn't enjoy your visit much."

"Not very," through red wool.

"No matter," he said. "You needn't see Georgie again unless you want to," and we walked on. He must have been smarting, for he liked me to be admired. When I was not being admired I was supposed to keep quiet. "You needn't see Georgie again" was also a private decision about himself. He was barely thirty-one and had a full winter to live after this one—little more. Why? "Because I say so." The answer seems to speak out of the lights, the stones, the snow; out of the crucial second when inner and outer forces join, and the environment becomes part of the enemy too.

Ward Mackey used to mention me as "Angus's precocious pain in the neck," which is better than nothing. Long after that afternoon, when I was about twenty, Mackey said to me, "Georgie didn't play her cards well where he was concerned. There was a point where if she had just made one smart move she could have had him. Not for long, of course, but none of us knew that."

What cards, I wonder. The cards have another meaning for me—they mean a trip, a death, a letter, tomorrow, next year. I saw only one move that Saturday: My father placed a card faceup on the table and watched to see what Georgie made of it. She shrugged, let it rest. There she sits, looking puggy but capable, Angus waiting, the precocious pain in the neck turning pages, hoping to find something in the *National Geographic* harmful for children. I brush in memory against the spiderweb: What if she had picked it up, remarking in her smoky voice, "Yes, I can use that"? It was a low card, the kind that only a born gambler would risk as part of a long-term strategy. She would never have weakened a hand that way; she was not gambling but building. He took the card back and dropped his hand, and their long intermittent game came to an end. The card must have been the eight of clubs—"a female child."

The Authors

Alice Munro (1931–) was born in Huron County, Ontario, the setting of many of the works in her eleven collections of short stories and one novel (*The Lives of Girls and Women* [1971]). Often referred to as Canada's Chekhov, Munro has garnered both national and international acclaim for her fiction. Throughout her career she has won numerous literary prizes, including two Giller Prizes, three Governor General's Awards, the PEN/Malamud Award for Excellence in Short Fiction, and the Trillium Book Award. Her stories appear regularly in *The New Yorker* and also in *The Atlantic* and *The Paris Review*. Munro divides her time between Clinton, Ontario, and Comox, British Columbia. Her most recent collection of short stories is *The View from Castle Rock* (2006).

Alistair MacLeod (1936–) won respect and recognition for his two short-story collections, *The Lost Salt Gift of Blood* (1976) and *As Birds Bring Forth the Sun* (1986), which were combined and republished with two new stories in *Island* (2000). He was a professor of English at the University of Windsor and published his first novel, *No Great Mischief* (1999), just before he retired in 2000. The book won a slew of literary prizes, including the Trillium Book Award and the International IMPAC Dublin Literary Award. It stayed on the national bestseller list for more than a year. MacLeod was born in North Battleford, Saskatchewan, and now divides his time between Windsor, Ontario, and Cape Breton, Nova Scotia, where most of his stories are based.

Sam Selvon (1923–1994) left his native Trinidad in 1950 for the U.K., where he established himself as a writer with numerous publications, including *A Brighter Sun* (1952), *An Island Is a World* (1955), *The Lonely Londoners* (1956), *Ways of Sunlight* (1957), *Turn Again Tiger* (1958), *I Hear Thunder* (1963), *The Housing Lark* (1965), *The Plains of Caroni* (1970), *Those Who Eat the Cascadura* (1972), and *Moses Ascending* (1975). In 1978 Selvon moved to Calgary, where he wrote *Moses Migrating* (1983), which won the Writers' Guild of Alberta Fiction Award in 1982. He lived in Canada until his death in 1994.

Claire Messud (1966–) was born in the United States and grew up in Canada and Australia. Her latest book, *The Emperor's Children* (2006), was longlisted for the Man Booker Prize. She has been awarded the Addison Metcalf Award and a Strauss Living Award by the American Academy of Arts and Letters for her previously published work, including her debut novel, *When the World Was Steady* (1995) and her subsequent works *The Last Life* (1999) and *The Hunters* (2001). She has taught in the MFA program at

Warren Wilson College in North Carolina and in the Graduate Writing program at Johns Hopkins University. She is a frequent contributor of book reviews to *L.A. Weekly* and *The Globe and Mail.*

Dennis Bock (1964–) won the inaugural Danuta Gleed Literary Award and the British Betty Trask Award for his first book of stories, *Olympia* (1998). His first novel, *The Ash Garden* (2001), was a national bestseller and was shortlisted for the International IMPAC Dublin Literary Award, the Amazon.com/Books in Canada First Novel Award, the Kiriyama Prize, and the Commonwealth Writers' Prize. It won the Japan-Canada Literary Award. His most recent novel is *The Communist's Daughter* (2006). Bock lives in Guelph, Ontario.

M.G. Vassanji (1950–) was born in Kenya and raised in Tanzania. He completed a Ph.D. in physics at M.I.T. before moving to Canada in 1978. While working as a lecturer at the University of Toronto he wrote his first novel, *The Gunny Sack* (1989), which won the Commonwealth Writers' Prize. His second novel, *The Book of Secrets,* won the inaugural Giller Prize, and he won the prize again for *The In-Between Worlds of Vikram Lall,* published in 2002. His other books include the acclaimed novels *No New Land* (1991) and *Amriika* (1999), and *Uhuru Street* (1992), a collection of stories. Vassanji is a Member of the Order of Canada.

Madeleine Thien (1974–) is a graduate of the University of British Columbia's MFA Creative Writing program. Her first book of fiction, *Simple Recipes,* won four awards in Canada, was a finalist for a regional Commonwealth Writers' Prize for Best First Book, and was named a notable book by the Kiriyama Prize. Her first novel, *Certainty,* was published in 2006. Thien grew up in Vancouver and now lives in Quebec City.

Austin Clarke (1934–) was born and raised in Barbados and came to Canada in 1955 to study at the University of Toronto. His ninth novel, *The Polished Hoe* (2002), won several national and international awards, including the Giller Prize and the Commonwealth Writers' Prize. He has also written two memoirs and several collections of short fiction, including *In This City* (1992) and *There Are No Elders* (1993). Along with his writing career, Clarke has worked as a journalist, a diplomat, and a professor. He is a Member of the Order of Canada and continues to live in Toronto.

W.D. Valgardson (1939–) is the author of numerous novels, short stories, plays, and children's books. His works have been translated into many languages, including Icelandic, Swedish, German, Russian, and Ukrainian. Valgardson has won several awards and accolades, including the Ethel Wilson Fiction Prize for *The Girl with the Botticelli Face* (1992), the Books in Canada First Novel Award for *Gentle Sinners* (1980), and the BC Book Prize. He was raised in Gimli, Manitoba, and eventually settled in British Columbia, where he taught creative writing at the University of Victoria. In 2002 Valgardson was elected to the Royal Society of Canada, the highest academic honour in the country.

David Bezmozgis (1973–) is a writer and filmmaker. He has published stories in *The New Yorker, The Walrus,* and *Harper's* magazines. He holds a BA in English from McGill University and an MFA from the University of Southern California's School of Cinema-Television. His first book, *Natasha and Other Stories* (2004), garnered critical acclaim both in Canada and internationally. For this work, he won the Commonwealth Writers' Prize, the Danuta Gleed Literary Award, and the City of Toronto Book Award. He was born in Riga, Latvia, and immigrated to Canada with his family when he was six. He lives in Toronto.

Vincent Lam (1974–) was born in London, Ontario. His family is from the expatriate Chinese community of Vietnam. He studied medicine at the University of Toronto and is an emergency physician who also does international air evacuation work and expedition medicine on Arctic and Antarctic ships. His non-fiction writing has appeared in *The Globe and Mail,* the *National Post,* and *Toronto Life* magazine, and he co-authored the medical book *The Flu Pandemic and You* (2006). He won the 2006 Giller Prize for his first collection of short stories, *Bloodletting and Miraculous Cures* (2006).

Janice Kulyk Keefer (1953–) is an accomplished and prolific writer of fiction, poetry, and criticism whose work often revolves around the experiences of mid-twentieth century, first-generation European immigrants in Canada. She received the Marian Engel Award for her body of work in 1999.

Rohinton Mistry (1952–) is the author of three novels, *Such a Long Journey* (1991), *A Fine Balance* (1995), and *Family Matters* (2002), and a collection of short stories, *Tales from Firozsha Baag* (1987). His fiction has won many prestigious awards internationally. Born in Bombay, Mistry has lived in Canada since 1975.

PART 2: THIS ALL HAPPENED

Michael Winter (1965–) was born in England and grew up in Newfoundland. His autobiographical novel, *This All Happened* (2000), won the 2001 Winterset Award and was a finalist for the 2000 Rogers Writers' Trust Fiction Prize. His subsequent novel, *The Big Why* (2004), won the Drummer General's Award for Fiction and was a finalist for the Thomas H. Raddall Prize and the Trillium Book Award as well as a *Globe and Mail* Top 100 Book for 2004. He is also the author of two collections of short fiction, *Creaking in Their Skins* (1994) and *One Last Good Look* (1999). Winter teaches part-time at the University of Toronto's Continuing Studies department and divides his time between Toronto and St. John's.

Lisa Moore (1964–) was nominated for the Giller Prize for *Open* (2003), a collection of short stories, and again for her novel *Alligator* (2005), which was also chosen by *The Globe and Mail* as one of the Top 100 Books in 2005 and won both the Commonwealth Writers' Prize and the ReLit Award. Moore studied fine art at the Nova Scotia College of Art and Design and creative writing at Memorial University. She published her first collection of short stories, *Degrees of Nakedness,* in 1995. She lives in St. John's, where she sets many of her fictional works. She has written radio plays for CBC and columns for *The Globe and Mail* and is the editor of *The Penguin Book of Contemporary Short Stories by Canadian Women.*

Isabel Huggan (1943–) wrote her first book, *The Elizabeth Stories,* in 1984. Based in small-town Ontario, where she grew up, this collection won many awards. Her husband's work took her family to Kenya, which provided the inspiration for her next book, *You Never Know* (1993). *Belonging* (2003), a travel memoir that also includes three short stories, won the Charles Taylor Prize for literary non-fiction in 2004. She has taught creative writing workshops in Canada as well as in the Philippines, Hong Kong, Australia, Switzerland, and France, where she currently resides.

Michael Redhill (1966–) is a poet, playwright, and novelist. He served on the editorial board of Coach House Press from 1993 to 1996 and is the current editor and publisher of *Brick,* a literary magazine. He is the author of two collections of poetry, *Asphodel* (1997) and *Light-Crossing* (2001), and a collection of short stories, *Fidelity* (2001). His novel *Martin Sloane* (2003) was nominated for the Giller Prize; a second novel, *Consolation,* was published in 2006. His most recent works for the theatre are *Goodness* and *Building Jerusalem,* winner of a Dora Award. He lives in Toronto.

Gayla Reid (1945–) was born in Australia and came to Canada to study at the University of British Columbia. She is the founder of the feminist literary quarterly *A Room of One's Own* and has taught women's studies at Vancouver Community College. She has won the Journey Prize, a National Magazine Award, the Ethel Wilson Fiction Prize, and the Marian Engel Award for her works of fiction, including *To Be There with You* (1994), *All the Seas of the World* (2001), and *Closer Apart* (2002). She divides her time between Vancouver and Sydney, Australia.

Dionne Brand (1953–) is the author of eighteen books, has contributed to seventeen anthologies, and has made four documentary films for the National Film Board of Canada. She was born in Trinidad and moved to Toronto in 1970. She won the Governor General's Award for Poetry and the Trillium Book Award in 1997 for *Land to Light On* (1997). Her novel *In Another Place, Not Here* (1996) was shortlisted for the Chapters/Books in Canada First Novel Award and the Trillium Book Award, and was published in the U.S. and the U.K. to great acclaim. Her latest book, *What We All Long For* (2005), won both the 2006 City of Toronto Book Award and the Harbourfront Prize. She has an MA in the philosophy of education. Brand is a professor of creative writing and holds a Research Chair at the University of Guelph.

Elizabeth Hay (1951–) was born in Owen Sound, Ontario. During her career as a writer and broadcaster she did documentary work for CBC radio in Yellowknife, Winnipeg, and Toronto and went on to work as a freelance broadcaster in Latin America from 1984 to 1986. Her novel *A Student of Weather* (2000) was nominated for the Giller Prize. She has twice been a nominee for the Governor General's Award, for *Small Change* in 1997 and for *Garbo Laughs* in 2003. In 2001 she received the Marian Engel Award.

Sharon Butala (1940–) was born and raised in Saskatchewan, a prairie landscape that she honours in her writing and also through her work in environmental conservation. Her novel *The Perfection of the Morning* was a number-one bestseller and a finalist for the Governor General's Award. *Fever* (1990), a short story collection, won the 1992 Authors' Award for Paperback Fiction. Some of her other works include *The Garden of Eden* (1998), *The Gates of the Sun* (1994), and *The Fourth Archangel* (1992). Butala is a recipient of the Marian Engel Award, an honorary doctorate from the University of Saskatchewan, and the Saskatchewan Writers Guild Achievement Award and is an Officer of the Order of Canada.

Michael Crummey (1965–) won the Winterset Award for his first and bestselling novel, *The River Thieves* (2001). It was also shortlisted for the Giller Prize and the Commonwealth Writers' Prize. He has published three works of poetry, a collection of short stories, and, along with photographer Greg Locke, *Newfoundland: Journey into a Lost Nation* (2004). His latest novel, *The Wreckage,* was a finalist for the Rogers Writers' Trust Fiction Prize and the International IMPAC Dublin Literary Award as well as a *Globe and Mail* Top 100 Book of 2005. He lives in St. John's.

Adrienne Poy (Clarkson) (1939–) served as Canada's twenty-sixth Governor General from 1999 to 2005. In 1942 her family escaped Japanese-occupied Hong Kong and immigrated to Canada. In her successful career in broadcasting and as a public servant Clarkson has received many awards and honorary degrees in Canada and abroad. She is a Privy Councillor and a Companion of the Order of Canada.

Caroline Adderson (1963–) was nominated for both the Governor General's Award and the Commonwealth Writers' Prize and won the Ethel Wilson Fiction Prize for her first book, *Bad Imaginings* (1993). Her first novel, *A History of Forgetting* (1999), was nominated for the Rogers Writers' Trust Fiction Prize and the Ethel Wilson Prize. Her second, *Sitting Practice,* won the 2004 Ethel Wilson Prize. Her most recent collection of short stories, *Pleased to Meet You,* was longlisted for the 2006 Scotiabank Giller Prize. In addition to fiction, she has written for film and CBC radio. She lives in Vancouver.

Nancy Lee (1970–) is a fiction writer and poet, and she teaches creative writing at Simon Fraser University's Writing and Publishing Program. She was born in Cardiff, Wales, and now lives in Vancouver. Her first story collection, *Dead Girls* (2003), was chosen as the number-one book of the year by *NOW* magazine. It was also chosen as a book of the year by *The Vancouver Sun, The Globe and Mail,* and the *Toronto Star* and was shortlisted for the Danuta Gleed Literary Award.

Guy Vanderhaeghe (1951–) was born in Esterhazy, Saskatchewan. He is the author of four novels, *My Present Age* (1984); *Homesick* (1989), co-winner of the City of Toronto Book Award; *The Englishman's Boy* (1996), winner of the Governor General's Award for

Fiction and the Saskatchewan Book Awards for Fiction and a finalist for the Giller Prize and the International IMPAC Dublin Literary Award; and, most recently, *The Last Crossing* (2002), winner of the Canadian Booksellers Association Libris Award for Fiction Book of the Year and a regional finalist for the Commonwealth Writers' Prize for Best Book. Vanderhaeghe is an Officer of the Order of Canada.

Carol Windley (1947–) was born on Vancouver Island and lives in Nanaimo. Her fiction has been published in literary magazines across Canada, including *The Malahat Review* and *Event*. *Visible Light* (1993), her debut collection of short stories, was nominated for the Ethel Wilson Fiction Prize and the Governor General's Award. Her most recent collection of short stories, *Home Schooling* (2006), was shortlisted for the Giller Prize. One of the stories in that collection won the Western Magazine Award for Fiction in 2002.

Anita Rau Badami (1961–) is the author of two bestselling novels, *Tamarind Mem* (1997) and *The Hero's Walk* (2001). Her second novel won the Commonwealth Writers' Prize and Italy's Premio Berto and was named a Washington Post Best Book of 2001. It was also longlisted for the International IMPAC Dublin Literary Award and the Orange Prize for Fiction and shortlisted for the Kiriyama Prize. Both novels have been published in many countries throughout the world. She is the recipient of the Marian Engel Award. Her third novel, *Can You Hear the Nightbird Call?*, will be published in 2007. Rau Badami lives in Montreal.

PART 3: LUNCH CONVERSATION

Michael Ondaatje (1943–) is the author of the novels *In the Skin of a Lion*, *The English Patient*, and *Anil's Ghost*. His other books include *Running in the Family*, *Coming Through Slaughter*, *The Cinnamon Peeler*, and *Handwriting*. His new novel, *Divisadero*, was published in 2007. Ondaatje was born in Sri Lanka and came to Canada in 1962. He lives in Toronto.

Ethel Wilson (1888–1980) was born in Port Elizabeth, South Africa. She was orphaned by the age of ten and came to Vancouver to live with her maternal grandmother. Wilson started publishing short stories in the 1930s and her first novel, *Hetty Dorval*, appeared in 1947. For her contribution to Canadian literature Wilson received the Lorne Pierce Medal and the Canada Council Medal; she was also a Member of the Order of Canada. Her best known work is *Swamp Angel*, published in 1954.

Lynn Coady (1970–) was born in Cape Breton. She is the author of three novels, *Strange Heaven* (1998), *Saints of Big Harbour* (2002), and *Mean Boy* (2006), and one collection of short fiction, *Play the Monster Blind* (2000). She has received many awards for her fiction, including the Dartmouth Book Award, the Atlantic Independent Award, the Booksellers' Choice Award, the Canadian Authors Association Air Canada Award for Most Promising Writer Under Thirty, and the Canadian Authors Association Jubilee Award for Short Stories.

Joseph Boyden (1966–) won the Rogers Writers' Trust Fiction Prize for his first novel, *Three Day Road* (2005). It was also shortlisted for the Governor General's Award. His collection of short stories, *Born with a Tooth* (2003), was shortlisted for the Upper Canada Writers' Craft Award. His non-fiction work has been published in *Maclean's* magazine. He divides his time between Northern Ontario and Louisiana, where he teaches writing at the University of New Orleans.

Sandra Birdsell (1942–) was born in Winnipeg. Her first novel, *The Missing Child* (1990), received the W.H. Smith/Books in Canada First Novel Award in 1989. Her second novel, *The Chrome Suite* (1992), won the McNally Robinson Book of the Year Award and was nominated for a Governor General's Award. A third short story collection, *The Two-Headed Calf* (1997), was also a Governor General's Award nominee. This book was followed by a children's novel, *The Town That Floated Away* (1997), which won both a Silver Birch Award and a Red Cedar Award. She received the Marian Engel Award in 1993. Her most recent novel is *Children of the Day* (2005).

Wayne Johnston (1958–) has set most of his fiction in his birthplace, Newfoundland, and one of his best known titles, *The Colony of Unrequited Dreams,* fictionalizes the life of Joey Smallwood, the flamboyant first premier of that province. Johnston's work has been translated into many languages and has twice been shortlisted for the Giller Prize.

Carol Shields (1935–2003) was born in Illinois. She moved to Ottawa to study English and remained in Canada for the rest of her life. Her novel *Unless* (2002) was a finalist for the Man Booker Prize, the Giller Prize, and the Governor General's Literary Award. Her previous novel, *The Stone Diaries* (1993), won the Pulitzer Prize, the National Book Critics Circle Award in the United States, and the Prix de Lire in France. Her novel *Larry's Party* (1997) won the Orange Prize for fiction and was a finalist for the Giller Prize. She received the Charles Taylor Prize for non-fiction for her biography of Jane Austen.

Timothy Taylor (1963–) is a recipient of a National Magazine Award, winner of the Journey Prize, and the only writer ever to have three stories published in a single edition of *The Journey Prize Anthology*. He is the co-author of *The Internet Handbook for Canadian Lawyers*. His works of fiction include *Story House* (2006), *Silent Cruise* (2002), and *Stanley Park* (2001), which was nominated for the Giller Prize the year it was published and was chosen for the Canada Reads competition in 2007. His travel, humour, arts, and business pieces have been published in various magazines and periodicals, including *Saturday Night*. He was born in Venezuela and now lives in Vancouver.

Joan Clark (1934–) was born and raised in the Maritimes. She lived for more than twenty years in western Canada before returning to the East and settling in Newfoundland. She is the author of a number of award-winning books for adults, including *An Audience of Chairs* (2006), which was longlisted for the International IMPAC Dublin Literary Award, *Latitudes of Melt* (2000), and *Eiriksdottir* (1993), as well as seven acclaimed children's books. Clark's honours include the Marian Engel Award and an honorary doctorate from Sir Wilfred Grenfell College. She lives in St. John's.

Timothy Findley (1930–2002) was a prolific writer whose novels include *Spadework* (2001), *Headhunter* (1993), *Not Wanted on the Voyage* (1984), *Famous Last Words* (1981), and *The Wars* (1977). Findley was a two-time winner of the Governor General's Award: *The Wars* won the 1977 award for fiction; *Elizabeth Rex*, a play, won the 2000 award for drama. The recipient of many accolades for his fiction, non-fiction, and drama, including the Chalmers Award and the Edgar Award, Findley was made an Officer of the Order of Canada and a Chevalier de l'Ordre des Arts et des Lettres in France.

Bronwen Wallace (1945–1989) was born in Kingston, Ontario. Her poetry and short stories have been anthologized and have appeared in periodicals across the country. She won a National Magazine Award, the Pat Lowther Award, the Du Maurier Award for Poetry, and in 1989 was named Regional Winner of the Commonwealth Poetry Prize in the U.K. Five volumes of her poetry have been published, as well as a book of essays, *Arguments with the World* (1992). Her first collection of short stories, *People You'd Trust Your Life To* (1990), was a national bestseller.

Margaret Atwood (1939–) is the author of more than forty works of award-winning fiction, poetry, critical essays, and books for children. Her work has been published in over thirty-five countries and includes the popular novels *Cat's Eye* (1988), *The Handmaid's Tale* (1985), and *The Blind Assassin*, which won the 2002 Booker Prize. Her most recent book is *Moral Disorder* (2006), a collection of stories. She recently invented a device called the LongPen machine that allows authors to sign books for fans anywhere in the world.

PART 4: PAPER SHADOWS

Wayson Choy (1939–) was brought up in Vancouver's Chinatown in the 1940s and has repeatedly and evocatively written about life in that community. His work has garnered him a Trillium Book Award and a City of Vancouver Book Award, as well as nominations for both the Giller Prize and the Governor General's Award.

Sean Virgo (1940–) has won the CBC literary competition twice and the BBC3 short story competition. He was born in Malta and grew up in South Africa, Malaya, Ireland, and the U.K. He immigrated to Canada in 1966 and became a citizen in 1972. Virgo has published a number of works of both poetry and fiction, including *Pieces for the Old Earth Man* (1974), *White Lies and Other Fictions* (1981), *Wormwood* (1989), and *A Traveller Came By: Stories About Dying* (2000).

Matt Cohen (1942–1999), who died in December 1999, is the bestselling and widely translated author of thirteen novels, as well as poetry, collections of short stories, books for children, and works of translation from French to English. His last novel, *Elizabeth and After*, won the 1999 Governor General's Award, and his previous novel, *Last Seen*, was a finalist for both the Governor General's Award and the Trillium Award, and was chosen by Margaret Atwood as Best Book of 1996 (*Maclean's*). In 1998 Matt Cohen received the Toronto Arts Award for Writing. His novel *Emotional Arithmetic* is now a feature film, starring Susan Sarandon, Roy Dupuis, Max von Sydow, and Christopher Plummer.

Sheila Heti (1976–) studied playwriting at the National Theatre School in Montreal and philosophy at the University of Toronto. Her first book, *The Middle Stories* (2001), was nominated for several literary prizes, including the ReLit Award and the Upper Canada Writers' Craft Award, and won the 2002 K.M. Hunter Artists Award. Her novel *Ticknor* (2006) was a finalist for the Trillium Book Award. She is the creator of Trampoline Hall, a popular monthly lecture series, and the musical *All Our Happy Days Are Stupid,* and writes regularly about the visual arts. She lives in Toronto.

Virgil Burnett (1928–) is an author and an artist. He has written for numerous publications, including *TriQuarterly, The Malahat Review, Poetry,* and *Harper's* magazine. His work includes *Towers at the Edge of the World* (1983) and the illustrated novel *A Comedy of Eros* (1984). A retrospective exhibit covering five decades of his illustrative works was shown at the library of the National Gallery of Canada in 2006. Burnett was born in Kansas and moved to Canada in the 1970s. He is a Professor Emeritus of Fine Arts at the University of Waterloo and lives in Stratford, Ontario.

Eric McCormack (1938–) was born in a small village in Scotland. He moved to Canada in 1966 and attended the University of Manitoba. Since 1970 he has taught English at St. Jerome's University in Waterloo, Ontario, specializing in seventeenth-century and contemporary literature. His book *The First Blast of the Trumpet Against the Monstrous Regiment of Women* (1997) was nominated for the Governor General's Award for Fiction. His most recent book, *The Dutch Wife* (2004), was nominated for the Toronto Book Award. McCormack also frequently reviews for *The Globe and Mail.*

Barbara Gowdy (1950–) received the Marian Engel Award in 1996 and has been a finalist for the Giller Prize, the Governor General's Award, the Commonwealth Writers' Prize, the Trillium Book Award, and the Rogers Writers' Trust Fiction Prize. Her novels, *The Romantic, The White Bone,* and *Mister Sandman,* and two collections of short stories, *We So Seldom Look on Love* and *Falling Angels,* have appeared on bestseller lists throughout the world. Her most recent work, *Helpless,* was published in 2007. Gowdy lives in Toronto.

Rudy Wiebe (1934–) was born in an isolated farm community of about 250 people in a region near Fairholme, Saskatchewan. He draws on his boyhood experiences in Canada's West in his recently published memoir *Of This Earth: A Mennonite Boyhood in the Boreal Forest* (2007). He won a Governor General's Award for his novel *The Temptations of Big Bear* (1973). He taught literature and creative writing at colleges and universities in Canada, the United States, and Germany until his retirement. His other works include *First and Vital Candle* (1979) and *Sweeter Than All the World* (2002), among others. Wiebe was awarded the Royal Society of Canada's Lorne Pierce Medal in 1986 and is an Officer of the Order of Canada.

Audrey Thomas (1935–) has three times received the Ethel Wilson Fiction Prize, for *Intertidal Life* (1984), *Wild Blue Yonder* (1990), and *Coming Down from Wu* (1995). She is the author of sixteen works of fiction and has been honoured for her body of work with several honorary doctorates as well as the Marian Engel Award and the W.O. Mitchell Literary Prize. Her works include *Isobel Gunn* (1999) and *Two in the Bush and Other Stories* (1981), a collection of her short fiction. In 2003 she received the Terasen Lifetime Achievement Award for an Outstanding Literary Career in British Columbia. More than twenty-five of her plays and stories have been broadcast on CBC. She lives in Victoria and on Galiano Island.

Leon Rooke (1934–) is the author of seven novels, including *The Fall of Gravity,* which was chosen by *The Globe and Mail* as one of the top books of 2000. His 1981 novel *Shakespeare's Dog* won the Governor General's Award and his novel *A Good Baby* was made into a feature film. Other major awards include the W.O. Mitchell Literary Prize, the Canada-Australia Literary Prize, and the CBC Fiction Prize. He has published over three hundred short stories as well as poetry and plays, and is the founder of the Eden Mills Writers' Festival. His most recent novel is *A Beautiful Wife* (2005). A native of North Carolina, Rooke has lived in Canada for many years.

Thomas King (1943–) is a novelist, editor, historian, advocate, children's book author, professor of English, and broadcaster. In each capacity his work focuses on Canada's First Nations people. He was born in California and worked as a photojournalist in Australia before moving to Canada in 1980. He is also the creator of the popular CBC Radio dramas *The Dead Dog Café*, followed by *Dead Dog in the City.* He was a finalist for the Governor General's Award for his book *A Coyote Columbus Story* (1992) and again for *Green Grass, Running Water* (1993), and won the Trillium Book Award in 2004 for *The Truth About Stories* and the McNally Robinson Book of the Year Award for *A Short History of Indians in Canada* (2006). King is a Member of the Order of Canada.

Annabel Lyon (1971–) has published her short fiction in *Toronto Life, The Journey Prize Anthology,* and *Write Turns: New Directions in Canadian Fiction.* She is the author of two collections of stories, *Oxygen* (2000) and *The Best Thing for You* (2004). Lyon is also a frequent contributor to *The Vancouver Sun, The Globe and Mail,* and *Geist* magazine. She lives in Vancouver.

Susan Swan (1945–) is a novelist and a humanities professor at York University. She is also the vice chair of the Writers' Union of Canada. She worked as a journalist in both magazines and newspaper. Her fictional work has been shortlisted for the Ontario Trillium Award and the W.H. Smith Best First Novel Award. One of her novels, *The Wives of Bath,* was made into a feature film, *Lost and Delirious,* which was shown in thirty-one countries after its debut at Sundance 2001 and the Berlin Film Festival. She lives in Toronto. Her latest novel is *What Casanova Told Me* (2005).

Stephen Leacock (1869–1944) was born in England in 1869. His family immigrated to Canada in 1876 and settled on a farm north of Toronto. He was an essayist, teacher, political economist, historian, and writer, and is best known for his collections of humorous stories, including *Sunshine Sketches of a Little Town* and *My Financial Career and Other Follies*. He received numerous awards and distinctions, among them the Governor General's Award and the Lorne Pierce Medal. The Leacock Medal for Humour was established in his name, and a postage stamp was issued in his honour.

PART 5: MY GRANDFATHER'S HOUSE

Charles Ritchie (1906–1995) was a career diplomat who played a major role in Canada's twentieth-century emergence as an important diplomatic power. He was also a celebrated diarist and memoirist, winning the Governor General's Award for his wartime diary, *The Siren Years*.

Charles G.D. Roberts (1860–1943) was known as the father of Canadian poetry. He was born in Douglas, New Brunswick, and raised in Westcock, near the Tantramar marshes, and this landscape was the inspiration for most of his prose and poetry. He published his first book of poems, *Orion, and Other Poems* (1880), at age twenty. Many more collections of poetry would follow, including *In Divers Tones* (1887) and *Songs of the Common Day and Ave! An Ode for the Shelley Centenary* (1893). Roberts was awarded the Lorne Pierce Medal for distinguished service to Canadian literature in 1926, and was knighted in 1935.

Sinclair Ross (1908–1996) was born on a homestead near Shelbrooke in northern Saskatchewan. In 1941 he published his first novel, *As for Me and My House*, an evocative look at prairie life during the Depression. The prairie is also the major setting for his two collections of short fiction, *The Lamp at Noon and Other Stories* (1968) and *The Race and Other Stories* (1982). In Ross's later novels, *The Well* (1958), *Whir of Gold* (1970), and *Sawbones Memorial* (1974), he continues his exploration of prairie life and its power to challenge as well as sustain its inhabitants. Upon his retirement Ross lived in Greece and then in Spain. He returned to Montreal in 1980 and two years later moved to Vancouver, where he remained until his death in 1996.

Margaret Laurence (1926–1987) was born in Neepawa, Manitoba. After working as a reporter in Winnipeg, Laurence lived in Africa, the first two years in Somalia, the next five in Ghana, where her husband, a civil engineer, was working. She translated Somali poetry and prose during this time, and began her career as a fiction writer. Her work set in Africa includes her first novel, *This Side Jordan*, and a collection of short fiction, *The Tomorrow-Tamer*, as well as her memoir, *The Prophet's Camel Bell*. Her five books set in the fictional town of Manawaka were patterned after her birthplace and its people: *The Stone Angel, A Jest of God, The Fire-Dwellers, A Bird in the House*, and *The Diviners* became Canadian classics. Laurence received many honours over her lifetime, including two Governor General's Awards for Fiction and more than a dozen honorary degrees.

Morley Callaghan (1903–1990) was born and raised in Toronto. He was educated at the University of Toronto and as a student worked part-time for the *Toronto Star Weekly*, where he came into contact with Ernest Hemingway. Although he would continue to work as a journalist when necessary, Callaghan is best known for his fictional work, in particular his short stories. The four-volume *The Complete Stories* (2003) collects ninety of his stories. His other work includes *The Loved and the Lost* (1951), which won the Governor General's Award, as well as *The Many Colored Coat* (1960), *A Passion in Rome* (1961), and *Our Lady of the Snows* (1985). His last novel was *A Wild Old Man Down the Road* (1988). Toward the end of his life Callaghan was named a Companion of the Order of Canada.

Gabrielle Roy (1909–1983) was born in St. Boniface, Manitoba. Her family was originally from Quebec. After working as a schoolteacher in isolated Manitoba villages and in St. Boniface, Roy travelled to Europe, where she lived for two years. During this time she began to write fiction. She received many honours for her work, including three Governor General's Awards, France's Prix Femina, and Quebec's Prix David.

Lucy Maud Montgomery (1874–1942) was born in Prince Edward Island, the setting for nineteen of her twenty novels. Her first book, *Anne of Green Gables* (1908), met with immediate critical success both in Canada and internationally, and Montgomery followed this work with seven sequels. The Anne series continues to thrive and is constantly being revived through television series, plays, and reprints of the novels. Her autobiographical trilogy focusing on a second Island orphan, Emily Starr, has also been adapted for film. A prolific writer, Montgomery also wrote about five hundred short stories and poems.

Hugh Garner (1913–1979) immigrated to Canada from England in 1919 when he was a child. Garner worked at the *Toronto Star*, joining the newspaper as a copy boy after leaving school at age sixteen. He rode freight trains and took up work across Canada and the U.S. during the Depression and fought in the Spanish Civil War and the Second World War. He is the author of a hundred short stories, seventeen books, and hundreds of articles and radio and TV scripts. His best-known book is *Cabbagetown* (1950), a novel of working-class realism. His collection entitled *Hugh Garner's Best Stories* won the 1993 Governor General's Award.

Sheila Watson (1909–1998) was born in New Westminster, British Columbia. She studied and later worked as an elementary teacher in her native province before pursuing further graduate studies in English at the University of Toronto, where she worked under the supervision of Marshall McLuhan. Watson published five works of fiction, including *The Double Hook* (1959) and *Deep Hollow Creek* (1992), a novel she'd written in the late 1930s. With her husband, poet Wilfred Watson, she founded the literary magazine *White Pelican* in Edmonton, where they both taught English at the University of Alberta.

Ernest Buckler (1908–1984) was raised in West Dalhousie, Nova Scotia. He spent most of his life writing and farming in the Annapolis Valley. He published his first short story in the respected American magazine *Esquire* in 1937. He is best known for his 1957 novel *The Mountain and the Valley*. His other works include the memoir *Ox Bells and Butterflies* (1968) and the novel *The Cruelest* Month (1963). He was an Officer of the Order of Canada.

Merna Summers (1933–) was born in Alberta, where she still resides. She worked as a reporter and freelance journalist before she began writing fiction. She has won literary awards for her work in Canada and internationally, including the Katherine Anne Porter Prize for short fiction, the Ohio State Award, the Writers' Guild of Alberta Award, and the Marian Engel Award. Her work includes the short story collections *North of the Battle* (1988), *Calling Home* (1982), and *The Skating Party* (1974).

Mavis Gallant (1922–) was born in Montreal and moved to Paris in 1950 to write fiction. Since then she has published over a hundred stories in *The New Yorker* and several collections of stories, including *From the Fifteenth District* (1976), *Paris Stories* (2002), and *Montreal Stories* (2004). She is a Companion of the Order of Canada and has received many honorary doctorates from Canadian universities. She has won many awards, including the Governor General's Literary Award for *Home Truths: Selected Canadian Stories* (1981), the Canada Council for the Arts Molson Prize, the Blue Metropolis International Literary Grand Prix, and the Rhea Award for the Short Story. Gallant continues to reside in Paris.

Acknowledgments

I would like to thank the many colleagues and friends who advised me during the difficult process of making the selections for this anthology.

In particular, I would like to thank the faculty and staff at my alma mater, the University of Guelph. During my 2006 writer-residency every effort was made to ensure that I had the time and the space to work.

Moreover, without the wonderful collection at that university's McLaughlin Library, many discoveries would not have occurred and many problems would have remained unsolved.

Jane Urquhart
Stratford, Ontario
Summer 2007